P9-CJW-059

Exit Betty

The Beloved Stranger

Maris

Tyndale House books by Grace Livingston Hill.
Check with your area bookstore for these best-sellers.

LIVING BOOKS ®

1 *Where Two Ways Met*
2 *Bright Arrows*
3 *A Girl To Come Home To*
4 *Amorelle*
5 *Kerry*
6 *All Through the Night*
7 *The Best Man*
8 *Ariel Custer*
9 *The Girl of the Woods*
10 *Crimson Roses*
11 *More Than Conqueror*
12 *Head of the House*
14 *Stranger within the Gates*
15 *Marigold*
16 *Rainbow Cottage*
17 *Maris*
18 *Brentwood*
19 *Daphne Deane*
20 *The Substitute Guest*
21 *The War Romance of the Salvation Army*
22 *Rose Galbraith*
23 *Time of the Singing of Birds*
24 *By Way of the Silverthorns*
25 *Sunrise*
26 *The Seventh Hour*
27 *April Gold*
28 *White Orchids*
29 *Homing*
30 *Matched Pearls*
32 *Coming Through the Rye*
33 *Happiness Hill*
34 *The Patch of Blue*
36 *Patricia*
37 *Silver Wings*
38 *Spice Box*
39 *The Search*
40 *The Tryst*
41 *Blue Ruin*
42 *A New Name*
43 *Dawn of the Morning*
44 *The Beloved Stranger*
45 *The Gold Shoe*
46 *Through These Fires*
47 *The Street of the City*
48 *Beauty for Ashes*
49 *The Enchanted Barn*
50 *The Finding of Jasper Holt*
51 *The Red Signal*
52 *Tomorrow About This Time*
53 *Job's Niece*
54 *The Obsession of Victoria Gracen*
55 *Ladybird*
56 *The Prodigal Girl*
57 *The Honor Girl*
58 *The Chance of a Lifetime*
59 *Astra*
60 *Miranda*
61 *Mystery Flowers*
63 *The Man of the Desert*
64 *Miss Lavinia's Call*
65 *An Unwilling Guest*
66 *The Girl from Montana*
67 *A Daily Rate*
68 *The Story of a Whim*
69 *According to the Pattern*
70 *In the Way*
71 *Exit Betty*
77 *The Ransom*
78 *Found Treasure*
79 *The Big Blue Soldier*
80 *The Challengers*
81 *Duskin*
82 *The White Flower*
83 *Marcia Schuyler*
84 *Cloudy Jewel*
85 *Crimson Mountain*
86 *The Mystery of Mary*
87 *Out of the Storm*
88 *Phoebe Deane*
89 *Re-Creations*
90 *Sound of the Trumpet*
91 *A Voice in the Wilderness*
92 *The Honeymoon House*
93 *Katharine's Yesterday*

EXIT BETTY

LIVING BOOKS®
Tyndale House Publishers, Inc.
Wheaton, Illinois

This Tyndale House book
by Grace Livingston Hill
contains the complete text
of the original hardcover edition.
NOT ONE WORD
HAS BEEN OMITTED.

Printing History
J.B. Lippincott edition published 1920
Tyndale House edition/1994

3 in 1 ISBN 1-56865-735-8

Printed in the United States of America

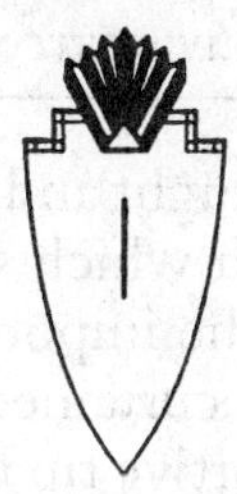

THE crowd gave way and the car glided smoothly up to the curb at the canopied entrance to the church. The blackness of the wet November night was upon the street. It had rained at intervals all day.

The pavements shone wetly like new paint in the glimmer of the street lights, and rude shadows gloomed in every cranny of the great stone building.

Betty, alone in the midst of her bridal finery, shrank back from the gaze of the curious onlookers, seeming very small, like a thing of the air caught in a mesh of the earth.

She had longed all day for this brief respite from everyone, but it had passed before she could concentrate her thoughts. She started forward, a flame of rose for an instant in her white cheeks, but gone as quickly. Her eyes reminded one of the stars among the far-away clouds on a night of fitful storm, with only glimpses of their beauty in breaks of the overcast sky. Her small hands gripped one another excitedly, and the sweet lips were quivering.

A white-gloved hand reached out to open the car

door, and other hands caught and cared for the billow of satin and costly lace with which she was surrounded, as if it, and not she, were the important one.

They led her up the curtained way, where envious eyes peeped through a furtive rip in the canvas, or craned around an opening to catch a better glimpse of her loveliness, one little dark-eyed foreigner even reached out a grimy, wondering finger to the silver whiteness of her train; but she, all unknowing, trod the carpeted path as in a dream.

The wedding march was just beginning. She caught the distant notes, felt the hush as she approached the audience, and wondered why the ordeal seemed so much greater now that she had actually come to the moment. If she had known it would be like this—! Oh, why had she given in!

The guests had risen and were stretching their necks for the first vision of her. The chaplet of costly blossoms sat upon her brow and bound her wedding veil floating mistily behind, but the lovely head was bowed, not lifted proudly as a bride's should be, and the little white glove that rested on the arm of the large florid cousin trembled visibly. The cousin was almost unknown until a few hours before. His importance overpowered her. She drooped her eyes and tried not to wish for the quiet, gray-haired cousin of her own mother. It was so strange for him to have failed her at the last moment, when he had promised long ago to let nothing hinder him from giving her away if she should ever be married. His telegram, "Unavoidably detained," had been received but an hour before. He seemed the only one of her kind, and now she was all alone. All the rest were like enemies, although they professed deep concern for her welfare; for they were leagued together against all her dearest wishes, until she had grown weary in the combat.

She gave a frightened glance behind as if some intangible thing were following her. Was it a hounding dread that after all she would not be free after marriage?

With measured tread she passed the long white-ribboned way, under arches that she never noticed, through a sea of faces that she never saw, to the altar smothered in flowers and tropical ferns. It seemed interminable. Would it never end? They paused at last, and she lifted frightened eyes to the florid cousin, and then to the face of her bridegroom!

It was a breathless moment, and but for the deep tones of the organ now hushing for the ceremony, one of almost audible silence. No lovelier bride had trod those aisles in many a long year; so exquisite, so small, so young—and so exceeding rich! The guests were entranced, and every eye was greedily upon her as the white-robed minister advanced with his open book.

"Beloved, we are met together tonight to join this man—"

At that word they saw the bride suddenly, softly sink before them, a little white heap at the altar, with the white face turned upward, the white eyelids closed, the long dark lashes sweeping the pretty cheek, the wedding veil trailing mistily about her down the aisle, and her big bouquet of white roses and maidenhair ferns clasped listlessly in the white-gloved hand.

For a moment no one stirred, so sudden, so unexpected it was. It all seemed an astonishing part of the charming spectacle. The gaping throng with startled faces stood and stared. Above the huddled little bride stood the bridegroom, tall and dark and frowning, an angry red surging through his handsome face. The white-haired minister, with two red spots on his fine scholarly cheeks, stood grave with troubled dignity, as though somehow he meant to hold the little still bride responsible for this unseemly break in his beautiful service. The organ died away with a soft crash of the keys and pedals as if they too leaped up to see; the scent of the lilies swept sickeningly up in a great wave on the top of the silence.

In a moment all was confusion. The minister stooped, the best man sprang into the aisle and lifted the flower-like head. Someone produced a fan, and one of the ushers hurried for a glass of water. A physician struggled from his pew across the laps of three stout dowagers, and knelt, with practiced finger on the little fluttering pulse. The bride's stepmother roused to solicitous and anxious attention. The organ came smartly up again in a hopeless tangle of chords and modulations. People climbed upon their seats to see, or crowded out in the aisle curiously and unwisely kind, and in the way. Then the minister asked the congregation to be seated; and amid the rustle of wedding finery into seats suddenly grown too narrow and too low, the ushers gathered up the little inert bride and carried her behind the palms across a hall and into the vestry room. The stepmother and a group of friends hurried after, and the minister requested the people to remain quietly seated for a few minutes. The organist by this time had recovered his poise and was playing soft tender melodies, but the excited audience was not listening.

"I thought she looked ghastly when she came in," declared the mother of three frowsy daughters. "It's strange she didn't put on some rouge."

"Um-mm! What a pity! I suppose she isn't strong! What did her own mother die of?" murmured another speculatively, preparing to put forth a theory before anyone else got ahead of her.

"Oh! The poor child!" sympathized a romantic friend. "They've been letting her do too much! Didn't they make a handsome couple? I'm crazy to see them come marching down the aisle. They surely wouldn't put off the wedding just for a faint, would they?"

And all over the church some woman began to tell how her sister's child, or her brother's niece, or her nephew's aunt had fainted just before her wedding or during it, till it began to seem quite a common performance, and one furnishing a unique and interesting part of the program for a wedding ceremony.

Meanwhile on a couch in the big gloomy vestry room lay Betty with a group of attendants about her. Her eyes were closed, and she made no move. She swallowed the aromatic ammonia that someone produced, and she drew her breath a little less feebly, but she did not open her eyes, nor respond when they spoke to her.

Her stepmother stooped over finally and spoke in her ear:

"Elizabeth Stanhope! Sit up and control yourself!" she said sharply in a low tone. "You are making a spectacle of yourself that you can never get over. Your father would be ashamed of you if he were here!"

It was the one argument that had been held a successful lash over her poor little quivering heart for the last five years, and Betty flashed open her sorrowful eyes and looked around on them with a troubled concentration as if she were just taking in what had happened.

"I'm so tired!" she said in a little weary voice. "Won't you just let me get my breath a minute?"

The physician nodded emphatically toward the door and motioned them out:

"She'll be all right in just a minute. Step outside and give her a chance to get calm. She's only worn out with excitement."

She opened her eyes and looked furtively about the room. There was no one there, and the door was closed.

She could hear them murmuring in low tones just beyond it. She looked wildly about her with a frantic thought of escape. The two windows were deeply curtained, giving a narrow glimpse of blank wall. She sprang softly to her feet and looked out. There was a stone pavement far below. She turned silently and tried a door. It opened into a closet overflowing with musty hymn books. She closed it quickly and slipped back to her couch just in time as the door opened and the doctor came back. She could catch a glimpse of the others through the hall open door, anxiously peering in. She gathered all her self-control and spoke:

"I'm all right now, Doctor," she said quite calmly. "Would you just ask them to send Bessemer here a minute?"

"Certainly." The doctor turned courteously and went back through the door, half closing it and making her request in a low tone. Then her stepmother's excited sibilant whisper:

"Bessemer! Why, he isn't here! He went down to the shore last night."

"Sh-h-h!" came another voice, and the door was shut smartly.

Betty's eyes grew wide with horror as she lay staring at the closed door, and a cold numbness seemed to envelop her, clutching at her throat, her heart, and threatening to overwhelm her.

Bessemer not here! What could it mean? Her mind seemed unable to grasp and analyze the nameless fear that awaited her outside that door. In a moment more they would all swarm in and surround her, and begin to clamor for her to go back into that awful church—and *she could not!*—EVER! She would far rather die!

She sprang to her feet again and glided noiselessly to the only remaining uninvestigated door in the room. If this was another closet she would shut herself inside and stay till she died. She had read tales of people dying in a small space from lack of air. At least, if she did not die she could stay here till she had time to think. There was a key in the lock. Her fingers closed around it and drew it stealthily from the keyhole, as she slid through the door, drawing her rich satin gown ruthlessly after. Her fingers were trembling so that she scarcely could fit the key in the lock again and turn it, and every click of the metal, every creak of the door, sounded like a gong in her ears. Her heart was fluttering wildly and the blood seemed to be pouring in torrents behind her eardrums. She could not be sure whether there were noises in the room she had just left or not. She put her hand over her heart, turned with a sickening dread to look about her prison, and behold, it was not a closet at all, but a dark landing to a narrow flight of stone steps that wound down out of sight into the shadows. With a shudder she gathered her white gown about her and crept down the murky way, frightened, yet glad to creep within the friendly darkness.

There were unmistakable sounds of footsteps overhead now, and sharp exclamations. A hand tried the door above and rattled it violently. For an instant her heart beat frightfully in her throat at the thought that perhaps after all she had not succeeded in quite locking it, but the door held, and she flew on blindly down the stairs, caring little where they led only so that she might hide quickly before they found the janitor and pried that door open.

The stairs ended in a little hall and a glass door. She fumbled wildly with the knob. It was locked, but there was a key! It was a large one and stuck, and gave a great deal of trouble in turning. Her fingers seemed so weak!

Above the noises grew louder. She fancied the door was open and the whole churchful of people were after her. She threw her full weight with fear in the balance, and the key turned. She wrenched it out of the rusty keyhole, slid out shutting the door after her, and stooping, fitted in the key again. With one more Herculean effort she locked it and stood up, trembling so that she could scarcely keep her balance. At least she was safe for a moment and could get her breath. But where could she go? She looked about her. High walls arose on either hand, with a murky sky above. A stone walk filled the space between and ran down the length of the church to a big iron gate. The lights of the street glistened fitfully on the puddles of wet in the depressions of the paving stones. The street looked quiet, and only one or two people were passing. Was that gate locked also, and if so could she ever climb it, or break through? Somehow she must! She shuddered at the thought of what would happen if she did not get away at once. She strained at the buttons on her soft white gloves and pulled the fingers off, slipping her hands out and letting the glove hands hang limp at her wrists. Then with a quick glance backward at a flicker of light that appeared wavering beyond the glass door, she gathered her skirts again and fled down the long stone walk. Silently, lightly as a ghost she passed, and crouched at the gate as she heard footsteps, her heart beating so loudly it seemed like a bell calling attention to her. An old man was shuffling past, and she shrank against the wall, yet mindful of the awful glass door back at the end of the narrow passage. If they should come now she could not hope to elude them!

She stooped and studied the gate latch. Yes, it was a spring lock, and had no key in it. Stealthily she tried it and found to her relief that it swung open. She stepped around it and peered out. The gateway was not more than a hundred feet from the brightly lighted corner of the main avenue where rows of automobiles were lined up waiting for the wedding ceremony to be over. She could see the chauffeurs walking back and forth and chatting together. She could hear the desultory wandering of the organ, too, from the partly open window near by. A faint sickening waft of lily sweetness swept out, mingled with a dash of drops from the maple tree on the sidewalk. In a panic she stepped forth and drew back again, suddenly realizing for the first time what it would be to go forth into the streets clad in her wedding garments. How could she do it and get away? It could not be done!

Down the street, with a backward, wistful glance at the church, hurried a large woman with a market basket. Her curious eyes shone in the evening light and darkness of the street. There was something about her face that made Betty know instantly that this woman would love to tell how she had seen her, would gather a crowd in no time and pursue her. She shrank farther back, and then waited in awful fear and tried to listen again. Was that a rattling at the glass door? She must get away no matter what happened! Where? Was there an alleyway or anything across the block? Could she hope to cross the street between the shadows unnoticed?

She looked out fearfully once more. A girl of her own age was approaching around the corner, paddling along in rubbers, and a long coat. She was chewing gum. Betty could see the outline of a strong good-natured jaw working contentedly as she was silhouetted against the light. She had her hands in her pockets, and a little dark hat worn boyishly on the back of her head, and she was humming a popular song. Betty had slipped behind the half open gate again and was watching her approach, her desperation driving her to thoughts that never would have entered her mind at another time. Suddenly, as the girl passed directly in front of the gate, Betty leaned forward and plucked at her sleeve:

"Wait!" she said sharply; and then, with a pitiful pleading in her voice, "Won't you help me just a minute, please?"

THE girl came to a standstill abruptly and faced about, drawing away just a hairbreadth from the detaining hand, and surveying her steadily, the boyish expression in her eyes changing to an amused calculation such as one would fancy a cowboy held up on his native plains by a stray lamb might have worn.

"What's the little old idea!" asked the girl coldly, her eyes narrowing as she studied the other girl in detail and attempted to classify her into the known and unknown quantities of her world. Her face was absolutely expressionless as far as any sign of interest or sympathy was concerned. It was like a house with the door still closed and a well-trained butler in attendance.

"I've got to get away from here at once before anybody sees me," whispered Betty excitedly, with a fearful glance behind her.

"Do you want me to call a cab for you?" sneered the girl on the sidewalk, with an envious glance at the white satin slippers.

"Oh, no! Never!" cried Betty, wringing her hands in desperation. "I want you to show me somewhere to go out of sight, and if you will I'd like you to walk a block or so with me so I won't be so—so conspicuous! I'm so frightened I don't know which way to go."

"What do you want to go at all for?" asked the girl bluntly, with the look of an inquisitor, and the intolerance of the young for its contemporary of another social class.

"Because I *must!*" said Betty with terror in her voice. "They're coming! Listen! Oh, help me quick! I can't wait to explain!"

Betty dashed out of the gate and would have started up the street but that a strong young arm came out like a flash and a firm young fist gripped her arm like a vise. The girl's keen ears had caught a sound of turning key and excited voices, and her quick eyes pierced the darkness of the narrow court and measured the distance back.

"Here! You can't go togged out like that!" she ordered in quite a different tone. She flung off her own long coat and threw it around the shrinking little white figure, then knelt and deftly turned up the long satin draperies out of sight and fixed them firmly with a pin extracted from somewhere about her person. Quickly she stood up and pulled off her rubbers, her eye on the long dark passageway whence came now the decided sound of a forcibly opened door and footsteps.

"Put these on, quick!" she whispered, lifting first one slippered foot and then the other and supporting the trembling Betty in her strong young arms, while she snapped on the rubbers.

Lastly, she jerked the rakish hat from her own head, crammed it down hard over the orange-wreathed brow and gave her strange protégée a hasty shove.

"Now beat it around that corner and wait till I come!" she whispered, and turning planted herself in an idle attitude just under the church window, craning her neck and apparently listening to the music. A second later an excited usher, preceded by the janitor, came clattering down the passageway.

"Have you seen anyone go out of this gate recently?" asked the usher.

The girl, hatless and coatless in the chill November night, turned nonchalantly at the question, surveyed the usher coolly from the point of his patent leather shoes to the white gardenia in his buttonhole, gave his features a cursory glance, and then shook her head.

"There might have been an old woman come out a while back. Dressed in black, was she? I wasn't paying much attention. I think she went down the avenue," she said, and stretched her neck again, standing on her tiptoes to view the wedding guests. Her interest suddenly became real, for she spied a young man standing in the church, in full view of the window, back against the wall with his arms folded, a fine handsome young man with pleasant eyes and a head like that of a young nobleman, and she wanted to make sure of his identity. He looked very much like the young lawyer whose office boy was her "gentleman friend." Just to make sure she gave a little spring from the sidewalk that brought her eyes almost on a level with the window and gave her a brief glimpse, enough to see his face quite clearly; then she turned with satisfaction to see that the janitor and the usher had gone back up the passageway, having slammed the gate shut. Without more ado the girl wheeled and hurried down the street toward the corner where Betty crouched behind a tree trunk, watching fearfully for her coming.

"Aw! You don't need to be that scared!" said the girl, coming up. "They've gone back. I threw 'em off the scent. Come on! We'll go to my room and see what to do. Don't talk! Somebody might recognize your voice. Here, we'll cut through this alley and get to the next block. It's further away and not so many folks passing."

Silently they hurried through the dark alley and down the next street, Betty holding the long cloak close that no gleam of her white satin might shine out and give away her secret, her heart beating like a trip-hammer in her breast, her eyes filled with unshed tears, the last words of her stepmother ringing in her ears. Was she making her father ashamed? Her dear dead father! Was she doing the wrong thing? So long that thought had held her! But she could not go back now. She had taken an irrevocable step.

Her guide turned another corner abruptly and led her up some stone steps to the door of a tall, dingy brick house, to which she applied a latchkey.

The air of the gloomy hall was not pleasant. The red wallpaper was soiled and torn, and weird shadows flickered from the small gas taper that blinked from the ceiling. There were suggestions of old dinners, stale fried potatoes, and pork in all the corners, and one movement toward the stairs seemed to stir them up and set them going again like old memories.

The stairs were bare and worn by many feet, and not particularly clean. Betty paused in dismay, then hurried on after her hostess, who was mounting up, one, two, three flights, to a tiny hall bedroom at the back. A fleeting fear that perhaps the place was not respectable shot through her heart, but her other troubles were so great that it found no lodgment. Panting and trembling she arrived at the top and stood looking about her in the dark, while the other girl found a match and lighted another wicked little flickering gas burner.

Then her hostess drew her into the room and closed

and locked the door. As a further precaution she climbed upon a chair and pushed the transom shut.

"Now," she said with a sigh of evident relief, "we're safe! No one can hear you here, and you can say what you please. But first we'll get this coat and hat off and see what's the damage."

As gently as if she were undressing a baby the girl removed the hat and coat from her guest, and shook out the wonderful shining folds of satin. It would have been a study for an artist to have watched her face as she worked, smoothing out wrinkles, shaking the lace down and uncrushing it, straightening a bruised orange blossom, and putting everything in place. It was as if she herself were an artist restoring a great masterpiece, so silently and absorbedly she worked, her eyes full of a glad wonder that it had come to her once to be near and handle anything so rare and costly. The very touch of the lace and satin evidently thrilled her; the breath of the exotic blossoms was nectar as she drew it in.

Betty was still panting from her climb, still trembling from her flight, and she stood obedient and meek while the other girl pulled and shook and brushed and patted her into shape again. When all was orderly and adjusted about the crumpled bride, the girl stood back as far as the limits of the tiny room allowed and surveyed the finished picture.

"There now! You certainly do look great! That there band of flowers round your forehead makes you look like some queen. 'Coronet'—ain't that what they call it? I read that once in a story at the Public Library. Say! Just to think I should pick that up in the street! Good night! I'm glad I came along just then instead o' somebody else! This certainly is some picnic! Well, now, give us your dope. It must've been pretty stiff to make you cut and run from a show like the one they got up for you! Come, tune up and let's hear the tale. I rather guess I'm entitled to know before the curtain goes up again on this little old stage!"

The two tears that had been struggling with Betty for a long time suddenly appeared in her eyes and drowned them out, and in dismay she brought out a faint little sorry giggle of apology and amusement and dropped on the tiny bed, which filled up a good two-thirds of the room.

"Good night!" exclaimed the hostess in alarm, springing to catch her. "Don't drop down that way in those glad rags! You'll finish 'em! Come, stand up and we'll get 'em off. You look all in. I'd oughta known you would be!" She lifted Betty tenderly and began to remove her veil and unfasten the wonderful gown. It seemed to her much like helping an angel remove her wings for a nap. Her eyes shone with genuine pleasure as she handled the hooks deftly.

"But I've nothing else to put on!" gurgled Betty helplessly.

"I have!" said the other girl.

"Oh!" said Betty with a sudden thought. "I wonder! Would you be willing to exchange clothes? Have you perhaps got some things you don't need that I could have, and I'll give you mine for them? I don't suppose perhaps a wedding dress would be very useful unless you're thinking of getting married soon, but you could make it over and use it for the foundation of an evening dress—"

The other girl was carefully folding the white satin skirt at the moment, but she stopped with it in her arms and sat down weakly on the foot of the bed with it all spread out in her lap and looked at her guest in wonder.

"You don't mean you *wantta give it up!*" she said in an

awed tone. "You don't mean you would be willing to take some of my old togs for it?"

"I certainly would!" cried Betty eagerly. "I never want to see these things again! *I hate* them! And besides, I want to get away somewhere. I can't go in white satin! You know that! But I don't like to take anything of yours that you might need. Do you think these things would be worth anything to you? You weren't thinking of getting married yourself sometime soon, were you?"

"Well, I might," said the other girl, looking self-conscious. "I got a gentleman friend. But I wasn't expectin' to get in on any trooso like this!" She let her finger move softly over the satin hem as if she had been offered a plume of the angel's wing. "Sure, I'll take it off you if I've got anything you're satisfied to have in exchange. I wouldn't mind havin' it to keep jest to look at now and then and know it's mine. It'd be somethin' to live for, jest to know you had that dress in the house!"

Suddenly Betty, without any warning even to herself, dropped upon her knees beside the diminutive bed and began to weep. It seemed somehow so touching that a thing like a mere dress could make a girl glad like that. All the troubles of the days that were past went over her in a great wave of agony, and overwhelmed her soul. In soft silk and lace petticoat and camisole with her pretty white arms and shoulders shaking with great sobs she buried her face in the old patchwork quilt that her hostess had brought from her village home, and gave way to a grief that had been long in growing. The other girl now thoroughly alarmed, laid the satin on a chair and went over to the little stranger, gathering her up in a strong embrace, and gradually lifting her to the bed.

"You poor little kid, you! I oughtta known better! You're just all in! You ben gettin' ready to be married, and something big's been troubling you, and I bet they never gave you any lunch—er else you wouldn't eat it—and you're just natcheraly all in. Now you lie right here an' I'll make you some supper. My name's Jane Carson, and I've got a good mother out to Ohio, and a nice home if I'd had sense enough to stay in it; only I got a chanct to make big money in a fact'ry. But I know what 'tis to be lonesome, an' I ain't hardhearted, if I do know how to take care of misself. There! There!"

She smoothed back the lovely hair that curled in golden tendrils where the tears had wet it.

"Say, now, you needn't be afraid! Nobody'll getcha here! I know how to bluff 'em. Even if a policeman should come after yeh, I'd get around him somehow, and I don't care what you've done or ain't done, I'll stand by yeh. I'm not one to turn against anybody in distress. My mother always taught me that. After you've et a bite and had a cup of my nice tea with cream and sugar in it you'll feel better, and we'll have a real gabfest and hear all about it. Now, you just shut your eyes and wait till I make that tea."

Jane Carson thumped up the pillow scientifically to make as many of the feathers as possible and shifted the little flower head upon it. Then she hurried to her small washstand and took a little iron contrivance from the drawer, fastening it on the sickly gas jet. She filled a tiny kettle with water from a faucet in the hall and set it to boil. From behind a curtain in a little box nailed to the wall she drew a loaf of bread, a paper of tea and a sugar bowl. A cup and saucer and other dishes appeared from a pasteboard box under the washstand. A small shelf outside the tiny window yielded a plate of butter, a pint bottle of milk, and two eggs. She drew a chair up to the bed, put a clean handkerchief on it, and spread forth her table. In a few minutes the fragrance of tea and toast pervaded the room, and water was bubbling happily for the eggs. As easily as if she had a chum to dine with her she sat down on the edge of the bed and invited her guest to supper. As she poured the tea she wondered what her colaborers at the factory would think if they knew she had a real society lady visiting her. It wasn't every working girl that had a white satin bride thrust upon her suddenly this way. It was like a fairy story, having a strange bride lying on her bed, and everything a perfect mystery about her. She eyed the white silk ankles and dainty slippers with satisfaction. Think of wearing underclothes made of silk and real lace!

It seemed to Betty as if never before in all her life had she tasted anything so delicious as that tea and toast and soft-boiled egg cooked by this wonderful girl on a gaslight and served on a chair. She wanted to cry again over her gladness at being here. It didn't seem real after all the trouble she had been through. It couldn't last! Oh, of course it couldn't last!

This thought came as she swallowed the last bite of toast, and she sat up suddenly!

"I ought to be doing something quick!" she said in sudden panic. "It is getting late and I must get away. They'll be watching the trains, perhaps. I ought to have gone at once. But I don't know where I can go. Give me some old things, please. I must get dressed at once."

"Lie down first and tell me who you are and what it's all about. I can't do a thing for you till I know. I've got to go into this with my eyes open or I won't stir one step," she declared stubbornly.

Betty looked at her with wide eyes of trouble and doubt. Then the doubt suddenly cleared away, and trust broke through.

"I can trust you, I'm sure! You've been so good to me! But it seems dreadful to tell things about my family, even to one who has been so kind. My father would be so hurt—"

"Your father? Where is your father? Why didn't he take care of you and keep you from getting into such big trouble, I'd like to know?"

The blue eyes clouded with tears again.

"My father died five years ago," she said, "but I've always tried to do as he would want to have me do. Only—this—I *couldn't.*"

"H'm!" said Jane Carson. "Then he prob'ly wouldn't of wanted you to. Suppose you take the rest of those togs off. I'll find you a warm nightgown and we'll get to bed. It's turning cold here. They take the heat off somewhere about six o'clock in the evening, and it gets like ice up here sometimes."

Jane shivered and went to her small trunk, from which she produced a coarse but clean flannelette nightgown, and Betty, who had never worn anything but a dainty lingerie one before in all her life, crept into it thankfully and cuddled down with a warm feeling that she had found a real friend. It was curious why she did not shrink from this poor girl, but she did not, and everything looked clean and nice. Besides, this was a wonderful haven of refuge in her dire necessity.

MEANWHILE, in the stately mansion that Betty had called home, a small regiment of servants hastened with the last tasks in preparation for the guests that were soon expected to arrive. The great rooms had become a dream of paradise, with silver rain and white lilies in a mist of soft green descending from the high ceilings. In the midst of all, a fairy bower of roses and tropical ferns created a nook of retirement where everyone might catch a glimpse of the bride and groom from any angle in any room. The spacious vistas stretched away from an equally spacious hallway, where a wide and graceful staircase curved up to a low gallery, smothered in flowers and palms and vines; and even so early the musicians were taking their places and tuning their instruments. On the floor above, where room after room shone in beauty, with costly furnishings, and perfect harmonies, white-capped maids flitted about, putting last touches to dressing tables and pausing to gossip as they passed one another:

"Well, 'twill all be over soon," sighed one, a wan-faced girl with discontented eyes. "Ain't it kind of a pity, all this fuss just for a few minutes?"

"Yes, an' glad I'll be!" declared another, a fresh young Irish girl with a faint, pretty brogue. "I don't like the look of my Lady Betty. A pretty fuss Candace her old nurse would be makin' if she was here the night! I guess the madam knew what she was about when she give her her walkin' ticket! Candace never could bear them two boys, and *him* was the worse of the two, she always said."

"Well, a sight of good it would do for old Candace to make a fuss!" said the discontented one. "Any anyhow, he's as handsome as the devil, and she's got money enough, so she oughtn't complain."

"Money ain't everything!" sniffed Aileen. "I wouldn't marry a king if I wasn't crazy about him!"

"Oh, you're young!" sneered Marie with disdain. "Wait till your looks go! You don't know what you'd take up with!"

"Well I'd never take up with the likes of *him!"* returned the Irish girl grandly, "and what's more he knows it!" She tossed her head meaningfully and was about to sail away on her own business when a stir below stairs attracted their attention. A stout, elderly woman, dressed in a stiff new black silk and an outrageous hat, came panting up the stairs looking furtively from side to side, as if she wished to escape before anyone recognized her.

"It's Candace!" exclaimed Aileen. "As I live! Now what d'ye wantta know about that! Poor soul! Poor soul! Candy! Oh!—Candy! What iver brought ye here the night? This is no place for the loikes of you. You better beat it while the beatin' is good if ye know which side yer bread's buttered!"

But the old nurse came puffing on, her face red and excited:

"Is she here? Has she come yet, my poor wee Betty?" she besought them eagerly.

"Miss Betty's at the church now gettin' married!" announced Marie uppishly, "and you'd best be gettin' out of here right away, for the wedding party's due to arrive any minute now and madam'll be very angry to have a servant as doesn't belong snoopin' round at such a time!"

"Be still, Marie! For shame!" cried Aileen. "You've no need to talk like that to a self-respectin' woman as has been in this house more years than you have been weeks! Come along, Candace, and I'll slip you in my room and tell you all about it when I can get away long enough. You see, Miss Betty's being married—"

"But she's *not!*" cried Candace wildly. "I was at the church myself. Miss Betty sent me the card to be sure and come, and where to sit and all, so she'd see me; and I went, and she come up the aisle as white as a lily and dropped right there before the poolpit, just like a little white lamb that couldn't move another step, all of a heap in her pretty things! And they stopped the ceremony and everybody got up, and they took her away, and we waited till pretty soon the minister said the bride wasn't well enough to proceed with the ceremony and would they all go home, and I just slipped out before the folks got their wraps on and took a side street with wings to my feet and got up here! Haven't they brought her home yet, the poor wee thing? I been thinkin' they might need me yet, for many's the time I've brought her round by my nursin'."

The two maids looked wildly at one another, their glances growing into incredulity, the eyebrows of Marie moving toward her well-dressed hair with a lofty disapproval.

"Well, you'd better come with me, Candy," said

Aileen drawing the excited old servant along the hall to the back corridor gently. "I guess there's some mistake somewheres; anyway, you better stay in my room till you see what happens. We haven't heard anything yet, and they'd likely send word pretty soon if there's to be a change in the program. You say she fell—?"

But just then sounds of excitement came distantly up to them and Aileen hastened back to the gallery to listen. It was the voice of Madam Stanhope angrily speaking to her youngest son.

"You must get Bessemer on the phone at once and order him home! I told you it was a great mistake sending him away. If he had been standing there, where she could see him, everything would have gone through just as we planned it—"

"Aw! Rot! Mother. Can't you shut up? I know what I'm about and I'm going to call up another detective. Bessemer may go to the devil for all I care! How do you know but he has, and taken her with him? The first thing to do is to get that girl back! You ought to have had more sense than to show your whole hand to my brother. You might have known he'd take advantage—"

Herbert Hutton slammed into the telephone booth under the stairs and Madam Stanhope was almost immediately aware of the staring servants who were trying not to seem to have listened.

Mrs. Stanhope stood in the midst of the beautiful empty rooms and suddenly realized her position. Her face froze into the haughty lines with which her ménage was familiar, and she was as coldly beautiful in her exquisite heliotrope gown of brocaded velvet and chiffon with the glitter of jewels about her smooth plump neck, and in her carefully waved black hair as if she were quietly awaiting the bridal party instead of facing defeat and mortification.

"Aileen, you may get Miss Betty's room ready to receive her. She has been taken ill and will be brought home as soon as she is able to be moved," she announced, without turning an eyelash. "Put away her things, and get the bed ready!" One could see that she was thinking rapidly. She was a woman who had all her life been equal to an emergency, but never had quite such a tragic emergency been thrust upon her to camouflage before.

"James!" catching the eye of the butler, "there will be no reception tonight, of course, and you will see that the hired people take their things away as soon as possible, and say that I will agree to whatever arrangements they see fit to make, within reason, of course. Just use your judgment, James, and by the way, there will be telephone calls, of course, from our friends. Say that Miss Betty is somewhat better, and the doctor hopes to avert a serious nervous breakdown, but that she needs entire rest and absolute quiet for a few days. Say that and nothing more, do you understand, James?"

The butler bowed his thorough understanding and Madam Stanhope sailed nobly up the flower-garlanded staircase, past the huddled musicians, to her own apartment. Aileen, with a frightened glance, scuttled past the door as she was closing it.

"Aileen, ask Mr. Herbert to come to my room at once when he has finished telephoning, and when Mr. Bessemer arrives send him to me at once!" Then the door closed and the woman was alone with her defeat, and the placid enameled features melted into an angry snarl like an animal at bay. In a moment more Herbert stormed in.

"It's all your fault, Mother!" he began, with an oath. "If you hadn't dragged Bessemer into this thing I'd have had her fixed. I had her just about where I wanted her, and another day would have broken her in. She's scared to death of mental hospitals, and I told her long ago that it would be dead easy to put a woman in one for life. If I had just hinted at such a thing she'd have married me as meek as a lamb!"

"Now look here, Bertie," flared his mother excitedly, "you've got to stop blaming me! Haven't I given in to you all your life, and now you say it's all my fault the least little thing that happens! It was for your sake that I stopped you; you know it was. You couldn't carry out any such crazy scheme. Betty's almost of age, and if those trustees should find out what you had threatened, you would be in jail for life, and goodness knows what would become of me."

"Trustees! How would the trustees find it out?"

"Betty might tell them."

"Betty might *not* tell them, not if she was *my wife!"* He bawled out the words in a way that revealed no blissful future to the one who should have the misfortune to become his wife. "I think I'd have her better trained than that. As for you, Mother, you're all off, as usual! What do you think could possibly happen to *you?* You're always saying you do everything for me, but when it comes right down to brass tacks I notice you're pretty much of a selfish coward on your own account."

For a moment the baffled woman faced her angry uncontrolled son in speechless rage, then gathered command of the situation once more, an inscrutable expression on her hard-lined face. Her voice took on an almost pitiful reproach as she spoke in a low, even tone that could hardly fail to bring the instant attention of her spoiled son.

"Bertie, you don't know what you're talking about!" she said, and there was a strained white look of fear about her mouth and eyes as she spoke. "I'm going to tell you, in this great crisis, what I did for you, what I risked that you might enjoy the luxury which you have had for the last five years. Listen! The day before Mr. Stanhope died he wrote a letter to the trustees of Betty's fortune giving very explicit directions about her money and her guardianship, tying things up so that not one cent belonging to her should pass through my hands, which would have left us with just my income as the will provided, and would have meant comparative poverty for us all except as Betty chose to be benevolent. I kept a strict watch on all his movements those last few days, of course, and when I found he had given Candace a letter to mail, I told her I would look after it, and I brought it up to my room and read it, for I suspected just some such thing as he had done. He was very fussy about Betty and her rights, you remember, and he had always insisted that this was Betty's house, her mother's wedding present from the grandfather, and therefore not ours at all, except through Betty's bounty. I was determined that we should not be turned out of here, and that you should not have to go without the things you wanted while that child had everything and far more than she needed. So I burned the letter! Now, do you see what the mother you have been blaming has done for you?"

But the son looked back with hard glittering eyes and a sneer on his handsome lustful lips:

"I guess you did it about as much for your own sake as mine, didn't you?" he snarled. "And I don't see what that's got to do with it, anyway. Those trustees don't know what they missed if they never got the letter, and you've always kept in with them, you say, and made them think you were crazy about the girl. They pay you Betty's allowance till she's of age, don't they? They can't lay a finger on you. You're a fool to waste my time talking about a little thing like that when we ought to be planning a way to get hold of that girl before the trustees find out about it. If we don't get her fixed before she's of age we shall be in the soup as far as the property is concerned. Isn't that so? Well, then, we've got to get her good and married—"

"If you only had let her marry Bessemer quietly," whimpered his mother, "and not have brought in all this deception. It will look so terrible if it ever comes out. I shall never be able to hold up my head in society again—!"

"There you are again! Thinking of yourself—!" sneered the dutiful son, getting up and stamping about her room like a wild man. "I tell you, Mother, that girl is *mine,* and I won't have Bessemer or anybody else interfering. *She's mine!* I told her so a long time ago, and she knows it! She can't get away from me, and it's going to go the harder with her because she's tried. I'm never going to forgive her making a fool out of me before all those people! I'll get her yet! Little fool!"

Herbert was well on his way into one of those fits of uncontrollable fury that had always held his mother in obedience to his slightest whim since the days when he used to lie on the floor and scream himself black in the face and hold his breath till she gave in; and the poor woman, wrought to the highest pitch of excitement already by the tragic events of the evening, which were only the climax of long weeks of agitation, anxiety, and plotting, dropped suddenly into her boudoir chair and began to weep.

But this new manifestation on the part of his usually pliable mother only seemed to infuriate the young man. He walked up to her, and seizing her by the shoulder, shook her roughly.

"Cut that out!" he said hoarsely. "This is no time to cry. We've got to make some kind of a plan. Don't you see we'll have the hounds of the press at our heels in a few hours? Don't you see we've got to make a plan and stick to it?"

His mother looked up, regardless for once of the devastation those few tears had made of her carefully groomed face, a new terror growing in her eyes.

"I've told James to answer all telephone calls and say that Betty is doing as well as could be expected, but that the doctor says she must have perfect quiet to save her from a nervous breakdown—" she answered him coldly. "I'm not quite a fool if you do think so—"

"Well, that's all right for tonight, but what'll we say tomorrow if we don't find her—"

"Oh! She'll come back," said the stepmother confidently. "She can't help it. Why, where would she go? She hasn't a place on earth since she's lost confidence in that cousin of her mother's because he didn't come to her wedding. She hasn't an idea that he never got her note asking him to give her away. Thank heaven I got hold of that before it reached the postman! If that old fussbudget had been here we should have had trouble indeed. I had an experience with him once just before I married Betty's father, and I never want to repeat it. But we must look out what gets in the papers!"

"It's rather late for that, I suspect. The bloodhounds'll be around before many minutes and you better think up what you want said. But I'm not so sure she wouldn't go there, and we better tell the detectives that. What's the old guy's address. I'll call him up long-distance and say she was on a motoring trip and intended to stop there if she had time. I'll ask if she's reached there yet."

"That's a good idea, although I'm sure she was too hurt about it to go to him. She cried all the afternoon. It's a wonder she didn't look frightful! But that's Betty! Cry all day and come out looking like a star without any paint either. It's a pity somebody that would have appreciated it couldn't have had her complexion."

"That's you all over, Mother, talking about frivolous things when everything's happening at once. You're the limit! I say, you'd better be getting down to business! I've thought of another thing. How about that old nurse, Candace? Betty used to be crazy about her. What became of her?"

Mrs. Stanhope's face hardened, and anxiety grew in her eyes.

"She might have gone to her, although I don't believe she knows where she is. I'm sure I don't. I sent her away just before we began to get ready for the wedding. I didn't dare have her here. She knows too much and takes too much upon herself. I wouldn't have kept her so long, only she knew I took the trustee's letter, and she was very imprudent about it once or twice, so that I didn't really dare to let her go until just a few days ago. I thought things would all be over here before she could do any harm and Betty would be of age and have her money in her own right, and being your wife, of course there wouldn't be any more trouble about it."

"Well, you better find out what's become of her!" said the young man with darkening face. "*She* ought to be locked up somewhere! She's liable to make no end of trouble! You can't tell what she's stirred up already! Ring for a servant and find out of they know where she is. Ten to one that's where Betty is."

Mrs. Stanhope, with startled face, stepped to the hall and summoned Aileen:

"Aileen, have you any idea where we could find Miss Betty's old nurse, Candace?" she asked in a scathing tone, studying the maid's countenance. "I think it might be well to send for her in case Miss Betty needs her. She was so much attached to her!"

Aileen lifted startled eyes to her mistress' face. There was reserve and suspicion in her glance.

"Why, she was here a few minutes ago," she said guardedly. "It seems Miss Betty sent her an invitation, and when Miss Betty took sick she was that scared she ran out of the church and come here to find out how she was. She might not have gone yet. I could go see."

"Here! Was she here?" Mrs. Stanhope turned her head to her son and her eyes said: "That's strange!" but she kept her face well under control.

"Yes, you might go and see if you can find her, Aileen, and if you do, tell her I would like to see her a moment."

Aileen went away on her errand and Mrs. Stanhope turned to her son.

"Betty can't have gone to her unless there was some collusion. But in any case I think we had better keep her here until we know something."

Quick trotting steps were heard hurrying along the hall and a little jerky knock announced unmistakably the presence of Candace.

Mrs. Stanhope surveyed the little red-faced creature coolly and sharply:

"Candace, you have broken one of my express commands in returning here without permission from me, but seeing it was done in kindness I will overlook it this time and let you stay. You may be useful if they bring my daughter home tonight and I presume she will be very glad to see you. Just now she is—umm—" she glanced furtively at her son, and lifting her voice a trifle, as if to make her statement more emphatic—"she is at a private hospital near the church where they took her till she should be able to come home. It will depend on her condition whether they bring her tonight or tomorrow or in a few days. Meantime, if you like you may go up to your old room and wait until I send for you. I shall have news soon and will let you know. Don't go down to the servants' quarters, I wish to have you where I can call you at a moment's notice."

Candace gave her ex-mistress a long, keen suspicious stare, pinned her with a glance as steely as her own for an instant, in search of a possible ulterior motive, and then turning on her little fat heel, vanished like a small fast racer in the direction of her old room.

"Now," said Mrs. Stanhope, turning with a sigh of relief, "she's safe! I'll set Marie to watch her and if there's anything going on between those two Marie will find out."

But Herbert Hutton was already sitting at his mother's desk with the telephone book and calling up long distance.

All the long hours when he had expected to have been standing under the rose bower downstairs in triumph with his bride, Herbert Hutton sat at that telephone in his mother's boudoir alternately raging at his mother and shouting futile messages over the phone. The ancient cousin of Betty's mother was discovered to be seriously ill in a hospital and unable to converse even through the medium of his nurse, so there was nothing to be gained there. Messages to the public functionaries in his town developed no news. Late into the night, or rather far toward the morning, Bessemer was discovered at a cabaret where his persistent mother and brother had traced him, too much befuddled with his evening's carouse to talk connectedly. He declared Betty was a good old girl, but she might go to thunder for all he cared; he knew a girl "worth twice of her."

His mother turned with disgust from his babbling voice, convinced that he knew nothing of Betty's whereabouts. Nevertheless, by means of a financial system of threats and rewards which she had used on him successfully for a number of years, she succeeded in impressing upon him the necessity of coming home at once, and just as the pink was beginning to dawn in the gray of the morning, Bessemer drove up in a hired car, and stumbled noisily into the house, demanding to know where the wedding was. He wanted to kiss the bride.

Candace, still in her stiff black silk, stood in the shadowy hall, as near as she dared venture, and listened, with her head thoughtfully on one side. Betty in her note about the wedding had said she was going to be married to Bessemer. But Bessemer didn't sound like a bridegroom. Had Bessemer run away then, or what? But some things looked strange. She remembered that Aileen had spoken as if Herbert was the bridegroom, but she had taken it for a rare slip of the tongue and thought nothing of it. When Aileen next came that way, she asked her if she happened to have got hold of one of the invitations, and Aileen, with her finger on her lips, nodded, and presently returned with something under her apron:

"I slipped it from the wastebasket," she said, "and Miss Betty got a holt of it, and there was a tremenjus fuss about something, I couldn't make out what; but I heard the missus say it was all a mistake as she gave the order over the phone, and she must have misspoke herself, but anyhow she thought she'd destroyed them all and given a rush order and they would be all right and sent out in plenty of time. So she sticks this back in the wastebasket and orders me to take the basket down and burn it, but I keeps this out and hides it well. I couldn't see nothin' the matter with it, can you?"

"There's *all* the matter with it!" declared the angry nurse as she glared at the name of Herbert Hutton thoughtfully, and read between the lines more than she cared to tell.

NOT two miles away, Betty lay safe and warm in the flannelette nightgown, and watched Jane Carson turn out the light and open the window. A light leaped up from the street and made a friendly spot of brightness on the opposite wall, and Betty had a sense of coziness that she had not felt since she was in boarding school with a roommate.

"Now," said Jane, climbing into bed and pulling up the covers carefully lest she should let the cold in on her guest, "let's hear!—You warm enough?"

There was a curious tenderness in her voice as if she had brought home a young princess and must guard her carefully.

"Oh, perfectly!" said Betty, giving a little nervous shiver. "And I'm so glad to be here safe away from them all! Oh, I've needed someone to advise me so much! I haven't had a soul since they sent my old nurse away because she dared to take my part sometimes."

Suddenly Betty buried her face in the pillow and began to sob and Jane reached out quick gentle arms and gathered her in a close comforting embrace. In a moment more Betty had gained control of herself and began to explain:

"You see," she said, catching her breath bravely, "they were determined I should marry a man I can't *endure,* and when I wouldn't they tried to *trick* me into it anyway. I never suspected until I got into the church and looked around and couldn't see Bessemer anywhere; only the other one with his evil eyes gloating over me, and then I knew! They thought they would get me there before all that church full of people and I wouldn't dare do anything. But when I realized it, I just dropped right down in the aisle. I couldn't stand up, I was so frightened."

"But I don't understand," said Jane. "Were there *two* men?"

"Oh, yes," sighed Betty, "there were two."

"Well, where was the other one, the one you *wanted* to marry?"

"I don't know—" said Betty with a half sob in her voice. "That's just what frightened me. You see they were my stepmother's two sons, and it was my father's dying wish that I should marry one of them. I didn't really *want* to marry Bessemer, but I simply *loathed* Herbert, the younger one, who was so determined to marry me. I was terribly afraid of him. He had been frightfully cruel to me when I was a child and when we grew up he was always tormenting me; and then when he tried to make love to me he was so repulsive that I couldn't bear to look at him. It really made me sick to think of ever marrying him. Oh—I wouldn't—no matter who asked me. So Bessemer and I decided to get married to stop the trouble. They were always nagging him, too, and I was kind of sorry for him."

"But why should you marry anybody you didn't want to, I'd like to know!" exclaimed Jane in horror. "This is a free country and nobody ever makes people marry anybody they don't like anymore. Why didn't you just beat it?"

"I thought about that a good many times," said Betty, pressing her tired eyes with her cold little fingers, "but I couldn't bring myself to do it. In the first place, I didn't know where to go, nor what to do. They never would let me learn to do anything useful, so I couldn't have got any work; and anyhow I had a feeling that it wouldn't be possible to get away where Herbert couldn't find me if he wanted to. He's that way. He always gets what he wants, no matter whom it hurts. He's *awful*—Jane—really!"

There was a pitiful note in her voice that appealed to the mother in Jane, and she stooped over her guest and patted her comfortingly on the shoulder:

"You poor little kid," she said tenderly, "you must have been worried something awful, but still I don't get you; what was the idea in sticking around and thinking you *had* to marry somebody you didn't like? You coulda gone to someone and claimed pertection. You could uv appealed to the p'lice if worst came to worse—!"

"Oh! But Jane I couldn't! That would have brought our family into disgrace, and Father would have felt so *dreadfully* about it if he had been alive! I couldn't quite bring myself, either, to go against his dying request. We had always been so much to each other, Daddy and I. Besides, I didn't mind *Bessemer so much*—he was always kind—though we never had much to do with each other—"

"Well, I don't think I'd have stopped around long to please a father that didn't care anymore for me than to want me to marry somebody I felt that way about!" said Jane, indignantly. "I haven't much use for a father like that!"

"Oh, but he wasn't like that!" said Betty, rising up in her eagerness and looking at Jane through her shining curls that were falling all about her eager, troubled young face, "and he did love me, Jane, he loved me better than anything else in the whole world! That was why I was willing to sacrifice almost anything to please him."

"Well, I'll be darned!" said Jane Carson, sitting up squarely in bed and staring at the spot of light on the wall. "That gets my goat! How could a man love you and yet want to torment you?"

"Well, you see, Jane, he hadn't been very fond of them when they were boys"—she spoke it with dignity and a little gasp as if she were committing a breach of loyalty to explain, but realized that it was necessary—"and he felt when he was dying that he wanted to make reparation, so he thought if I should marry one of them it would show them that he had forgiven them—"

"It—may—be—so," drawled Jane slowly, nodding her head deliberately with each word, "but—I don't see it that *way!* What kind of man was this father of yours, anyway?"

"Oh, a wonderful man, Jane!" Betty eagerly hastened to explain. "He was all the world to me, and he used to come up to school weekends and take me on beautiful trips and we had the best times together, and he would tell me about my own dear mother—"

Betty's hand grasped Jane's convulsively and her voice died out, in a sudden sob. Jane's hand went quickly to the bright head on the pillow:

"There! there!" she whispered tenderly, "don't take on so, I didn't mean anything, I was just trying to dope it out; get it through my bean what in thunder—! Say! Did *he* TELL *you* he wanted you to marry those guys?"

"Oh, no, he left word—it was his dying request."

"Who'd he request it to?"

"My stepmother."

"H'm! I thought so! How'd you know he did? How'd you know but she was lyin'?"

"No," said Betty sorrowfully, "she wasn't lying, she showed me the paper it was written on. There couldn't be any mistake. And his name was signed to it, his dear handwriting, just as he always wrote it with the little quirl to the S that wasn't like anybody else. It went through me just like a knife when I saw it, that my dear father should have asked me to do what was so very very hard for me to think of. It was so much harder to have it come that way. If he had only asked me himself and we could have talked it over, perhaps he would have helped me to be strong enough to do it, but to have *her* have to *tell me!* She felt that herself. She tried to be kind, I think. She said she wanted to have him wake me up and tell me himself, but she saw his strength was going and he was so anxious to have her write it down quick and let him sign it that she did as he asked—"

"Well, you may depend on it he never wrote it at all—or anyhow, never knew what he was signing. Like as not she dragged it out of him some way while he was out of his mind or so near dying he didn't know what he was about. Besides, they mightta some of 'em forged his name. It's easy to copy signatures. Lotsa people do it real good. If I was you I wouldn't think another mite about it. If he was a man like you say he is, he couldn'ta done a thing like that to his own little girl, not on his life! It ain't like real fathers and mothers to. I know, fer I've got a mother that's a peach and no mistake! No, you may depend on it, he never knew a thing about that, and marrying a guy like that is the last thing on earth he'd want you to do."

"Oh, do you really think so? Oh, are you *sure?*" cried Betty, clinging to Jane eagerly, the tears raining down her white cheeks. "I've thought so a thousand times, but I didn't dare trust myself to decide."

"Yes, I'm sure!" said Jane, gathering her in her arms and hugging her tight, just as she would have done with a little sister who had waked up in the night with a bad dream. "Now, look here, you stop crying and don't you worry another bit. Just tell me the rest if there's any rest, so I'll know what to bank on. Who is the other guy, the one you didn't mind marryin'? What became of him?"

"Why, that's the queer part," said Betty, troubled again. "He didn't seem to be anywhere, and when they carried me into the room back of the church and fanned me and got water to bathe my face, a doctor came and gave me some medicine and sent them all out, and I asked him to send Bessemer to me. I wanted to find out why he hadn't been standing up there by the minister the way I expected. I heard the doctor go out and ask for Bessemer and I heard my stepmother's voice say, 'Why, Bessemer isn't here! He's gone down to the shore!' and then somebody said, 'Hush,' and they shut the door, and I was so frightened that I got up and tried all the doors till I found one that led down some stairs, and I locked it behind me and ran and found you!"

"You poor little kid!" cried Jane, cuddling her again. "I sure am glad I was on the job! But now, tell me, what's your idea? Will they make a big noise and come huntin' you?"

"Oh, yes!" said Betty wearily. "I suppose they will. I *know* they will in fact. Herbert won't be balked in anything he wants—Bessemer won't count. He never counts. I'm sort of sorry for him, though I don't like him much. You see they had been making an awful fuss with him, too, about some actress down at the shore that he was sending flowers to, and I knew he didn't have a very easy time. So when he came in one day and asked me why I didn't marry *him* and settle the whole thing that way, I was horrified at first, but I finally thought perhaps that would be the best thing to do. He said he wouldn't bother me any, if I wouldn't bother him; and we thought perhaps the others would let us alone then. But I might have known Herbert wouldn't give in! Bessemer is easily led—Herbert could have hired him to go away tonight—or they may have *made* him ask me to marry him. He's like that," she said sadly. "You can't depend on him. I don't know. You see, it was kind of queer about the invitations. They came with Herbert's name in them first, and my stepmother tried to keep me from seeing them. She said they were late and she had them all sent off; but I found one, and when I went to my stepmother with it she said it was a mistake. She hadn't meant me to be annoyed by seeing it; and she didn't know how it happened; she must have misspoken herself—but it had been corrected and they would rush it through and send them right from the store this time so there wouldn't be any delay. I tried to think it was all right, but it troubled me, for I saw that Herbert hadn't given up at all—though he pretended to go away, and I hoped I wouldn't have any more trouble—but I might have known! Herbert never gave up anything in his life, not even when Father was living. He always managed to get his way, somehow—"

"Did he love you so much?" Jane asked awesomely.

Betty shuddered.

"Oh, I don't know whether it was love or hate! It was all the same. I hate to think about him—he is—*unbearable,* Jane! Why, Jane, once he told me if he ever got me in his power he'd break my will or kill me in the attempt!"

"Well, now, there, kid! Don't you think another bit about him, the old brute! You just lie down and sleep as easy as if you was miles away. They won't any of 'em ever find you here with me, and I've pulled the washstand in front of the door, so you needn't be dreaming of anybody coming in and finding you. Now go to sleep, and tomorrow I'll sneak you away to a place where they can't ever find you. Good night, kid!" and Jane leaned down and kissed the soft hair on the pillow beside her. Betty flung her arms about her newfound friend and kissed her tenderly:

"Oh, you've been so good to me! What should I ever have done if I hadn't found you. You were like an angel. I think surely God must have sent you to help me."

"I shouldn't wonder if He did!" said Jane thoughtfully. "An angel in a mackintosh! Some angel!"

Jane Carson with her eyes wide open lay staring into the darkness and thinking it all over. She did not waste much time marveling over the wonder that it had all happened to her. That would do for afterward when there was nothing else to be done about it. Now there must be some plans made and she was the one to make them. It was quite plain that the wonderful and beautiful Elizabeth Stanhope, the plans for whose wedding had been blazoned in the papers for days beforehand, was not at present capable of making or carrying out anything effective. Jane was. She knew it. She was a born leader and promoter. She liked nothing better than to work out a difficult situation. But this was the most difficult proposition that she had ever come up against. When her father died and her mother was left with the little house and the three younger children to support in a small country village, and only plain sewing and now and then a boarder to eke out a living for them all, she had sought and found, through a summer visitor who had taught her Sunday school class for a few weeks, a good position in this big eastern city. She had made good and been promoted until her wages not only kept herself with strict economy, but justified her in looking forward to the time when she might send for her next younger sister. Her deft fingers kept her meager wardrobe in neatness—and a tolerable deference to fashion, so that she had been able to annex the "gentleman friend" and take a little outing with him now and then at a moving picture theater or a Sunday evening service. She had met and vanquished the devil on more than one battlefield in the course of her experience with different department heads; and she was wise beyond her years in the ways of the world. But this situation was different. Here was a girl who had been brought up "by hand," as she would have said with a sneer a few hours before, and she would have despised her for it. She raised up on one elbow and leaned over once more to watch the delicate profile of this gentle maiden, in the dim fitful light of the city night that came through the one little window. There had been something appealing in the beauty and frankness of the girl-bride, something appalling in the situation she had found herself in. Jane Carson didn't know whether she was doing right or not to help this stray bride. It made her catch her breath to think how she might be bringing all the power of the law and of money upon her reckless young head, but she meant to do it, just the same.

Elizabeth Stanhope! What a beautiful name! It fitted right in with all the romance Jane had ever dreamed. If she only could write scenarios, what a thriller this would make!

Then she lay down and fell to planning.

THE morning dawned, and still no word from the missing bride. But the brief guarded sentences which Herbert Hutton had telephoned to the newspapers had been somehow sidetracked, and in their place a ghastly story had leaked out which some poor, hard pressed reporter had gleaned from the gossip in the church and hurried off to put into type before there was time for it to be denied. Hotfoot the story had run, and great headlines proclaimed the escape of Betty even while the family was carefully paving the way for the report of a protracted illness and absence, if need be, till they could find trace of her. The sun rose brightly and made weird gleaming of the silver wire on which the dying roses hung. The air was heavy with their breath, and the rooms in the early garish light looked out of place as if some fairy wand had failed to break the incantation at the right hour and left a piece of magicland behind. The parlor maid went about uncertainly, scarcely knowing what to do and what to leave undone, and the milk cars, and newsboys, and early laborers began to make a clatter of every day on the streets. The morning paper, flung across the steps with Betty's picture, where Betty's reluctant feet had gone a few hours before, seemed to mock at life, and upstairs the man that Betty thought she went out to marry, lay in a heavy stupor of sleep. Happy Betty, to be resting beneath the coarse sheet of the kindly working girl, sleeping the sleep of exhaustion and youth in safety, two miles from the rose-bowered rooms!

Long before day had really started in the great city Jane Carson was up and at work. She dressed swiftly and silently, then went to her little trunk, and from it selected a simple wardrobe of coarse clean garments. One needed mending and two buttons were off. She sat by the dingy window and strained her eyes in the dawn to make the necessary repairs. She hesitated long over the pasteboard suit box that she drew from under the bed. It contained a new dark blue serge dress for which she had saved a long time and in which she had intended to appear at church next Sabbath. She was divided between her desire to robe the exquisite little guest in its pristine folds and her longing to wear it herself. There was a sense of justice also which entered into the matter. If that elegant wedding dress was to be hers, and all those wonderful silk underclothes, which very likely she would never allow herself to wear, for they would be out of place on a poor working girl, it was not fair to repay their donor in old clothes. She decided to give the runaway bride her new blue serge. With just a regretful bit of a sigh she laid it out on the foot of the bed, and carefully spread out the tissue papers and folded the white satin garments away out of sight, finishing the bundle with a thick wrapping of old newspapers from a pile behind the door and tying it securely. She added a few pins to make the matter more sure, and got out a stub of a pencil and labeled it in large letters, "My summer dresses," then shoved it far back under the bed. If any seeking detective came he would not be likely to bother with that, and he might search her trunk in vain for white satin slippers and wedding veils.

Breakfast was next, and she put on her cloak and hurried out for supplies for the larder had been heavily depleted the night before to provide for her guest. With a tender glance toward the sleeper she slipped the key from the lock and placed it in the outside of the door, silently locking her guest within. Now there would be no danger of anyone spiriting her away while she was gone, and no danger that the girl might wake up and depart in her absence.

She stopped a newsboy on his way to the subway and bought a paper, thrilling at the thought that there might be something in it about the girl who lay asleep in her little hall bedroom.

While she waited for her bundles she stole a glance at her paper, and there on the front page in big letters ran the heading:

STANHOPE WEDDING HELD UP AT ALTAR BY UNCONSCIOUS BRIDE

Relatives Seek Runaway Girl Who Is Thought to Be Insane

She caught her breath and rolled the paper in a little wad, stuffing it carelessly into her pocket. She could not read any more of that in public. She hastened back to her room.

Betty was still sleeping. Jane stood watching her for a full minute with awe in her face. She could not but recognize the difference between herself and this fine sweet product of civilization and wealth. With the gold curls tossed back like a ripple of sunshine, and a pathetic little droop at the corners of her sweet mouth, nothing lovelier could be. Jane hurried to the window and turned her back on the bed while she perused the paper, her rage rising at the theories put forth. It was even hinted that her mother had been insane. Jane turned again and looked hard at the young sleeper, and the idea crossed her mind that even she might be deceived. Still, she was willing to trust her judgment that this girl was entirely sane, and anyhow she meant to help her! She stuffed the paper down behind the trunk and began to get breakfast. When it was almost ready she gently awoke the sleeper.

Betty started at the light touch on her shoulder and looked wildly around at the strange room and stranger face of the other girl. In the dim light of the evening she had scarcely got to know Jane's face. But in a moment all the happenings of the day before came back, and she sat up excitedly.

"I ought to have got away before it was light," she said gripping her hands together. "I wonder where I could go, Jane?" It was pleasant to call this girl by her first name. Betty felt that she was a tower of strength, and so kind.

"I have this ring," she said, slipping off an exquisite diamond and holding it out. "Do you suppose there would be any way I could get money enough to travel somewhere with this? If I can't I'll have to walk, and I can't get far in a day that way."

Betty was almost lighthearted, and smiling. The night had passed and no one had come. Perhaps after all she was going to get away without being stopped.

Jane's face set grimly.

"I guess there won't be any walking for you. You'll have to travel regular. It wouldn't be safe. And you don't want no rich jewelry along either. Was that your wedding ring?"

"Oh, no; Father gave it to me. It was Mother's, but I guess they'd want me to use it now. I haven't anything else."

"Of course," said Jane shortly to hide the emotion in her voice. "Now eat this while I talk," thrusting a plate of buttered toast and a glass of orange marmalade at her, and hastening to pour an inviting cup of coffee.

"Now, I been thinking," she said sitting down on the edge of the bed and eating bits of the piece of toast she had burned—Betty's was toasted beautifully—"I got a plan. I think you better go to Ma. She's got room enough for you for awhile, and I want my sister to come over and take a place I can get fer her. If you was there she could leave. Mebbe you could help Ma with the kids. Of course we're poor and you ain't used to common things like we have them, but I guess you ain't got much choice in your fix. I got a paper this morning. They're huntin' fer you hotfoot. They say you was temperary insane, an' 'f I was you I'd keep out o' their way awhile. You lay low an' I'll keep my eye out and let you know. I've got a little money under the mattress I can let you have till that ring gets sold. You can leave it with me an' I'll do the best I can if you think you can trust me. Of course I'm a stranger, but then, land! So are you! We just *gotta* trust each other. And I'm sending you to my mother if you'll go!"

"Oh!" said Betty, springing up and hugging her impulsively, "you're so good! To think I should find somebody just like that right in the street when I needed you so. I almost think God did it!"

"Well, mebbe!" said Jane, in her embarrassment turning to hang up a skirt that had fallen from its hook. "That's what they say sometimes in Chrishun Deavor meetin'. Ever go to Chrishun Deavor? Better go when you get out home. They have awful good socials an' ice cream, and you'll meet some real nice folks. We've got a peach of a minister, and his wife is perfec'ly dandy. I tell you I missed 'em when I came to the city! They was always doing something nice fer the young folks."

"How interesting!" said Betty, wondering if she might really be going to live like other girls. Then the shadow of her danger fell over her once more, and her cheek paled.

"If I can only get there safely." She shuddered. "Oh, Jane! You can't understand what it would be to have to go back!"

"Well, you're not going back. You're going to Tinsdale, and nobody's going to find you ever, unless you want 'em to! See? Now, listen! We haven't any time to waste. You oughtta get off on the ten o'clock train. I put out some clothes there for yeh. They ain't like yours, but it won't do fer you to go dressed like a millionairess. Folks out to Tinsdale would suspect yeh right off the bat. You gotta go plain like me, and it's this way: You're a friend I picked up in the city whose mother is dead and you need country air awhile, see? So I sent you home to stay with Ma till you got strong again. I'm wirin' Ma. She'll understand. She always does. I kinda run Ma anyhow. She thinks the sun rises an' sets in me, so she'll do just what I say."

"I'm afraid I oughtn't to intrude," said Betty soberly, taking up the coarse, elaborately trimmed lingerie with a curious look, and trying not to seem to notice that it was different from any she had ever worn before.

"Say! Looka here!" said Jane Carson facing round from her coffee cup on the washstand. "I'm sorry to criticize, but if you could just talk a little slang or something. Folks'll never think you belong to me. *'Intrude!'* Now, that sounds stuck up! You oughtta say 'be in the way,' or something natural like that. See?"

"I'm afraid I don't," said Betty dubiously, "but I'll try."

"You're all right, kid," said Jane with compunction in her voice. "Just let yourself down a little like I do, and remember you don't wear silk onderclothes now. I'm afraid those stockings won't feel very good after yours, but you gotta be careful. An' 'f I was you I'd cut my hair off, I really would. It's an awful pity, it's so pretty, but it'll grow again. How old are you?"

"Almost twenty-one," said Betty thoughtfully. "Just three months more and I'll be twenty-one."

"H'm! Of age!" said Jane with a sharp significant look at her, as if a new thought had occurred. "Well, you don't look it! You could pass for fifteen, especially if you had your hair bobbed. I can do it for you if you say so."

"All right," said Betty promptly without a qualm. "I always wanted it short. It's an awful nuisance to comb."

"That's the talk!" said Jane. "Say 'awful' a lot, and you'll kinda get into the hang of it. It sounds more—well, *natural,* you know; not like society talk. Here, sit down and I'll do it quick before you get cold feet. I sure do hate to drop them curls, but I guess it's best."

The scissors snipped, snipped, and the lovely strands of bright hair fell on the paper Jane had spread for them. Betty sat cropped like a sweet young boy. Jane stood back and surveyed the effect through her lashes approvingly. She knew the exact angle at which the hair should splash out on the cheek to be stylish. She had often contemplated cutting her own, only that her mother had begged her not to, and she realized that her hair was straight as a die and would never submit to being tortured into that alluring wave over the ear and out toward the cheekbone. But this sweet young thing was a darling! She felt that the daring deed had been a success.

"I got a bottle of stuff to make your hair dark," she

remarked. "I guess we better put it on. That hair of yours is kinda conspicuous, you know, even when it's cut off. It won't do you any harm. It washes off soon." And she dashed something on the yellow hair. Betty sat with closed eyes and submitted. Then her mentor burnt a cork and put a touch to the eyebrows that made a different Betty out of her. A soft smudge of dark under her eyes and a touch of talcum powder gave her a sickly complexion and when Betty stood up and looked in the glass she did not know herself. Jane finished the toilet by a smart though somewhat shabby black hat pulled well down over Betty's eyes, and a pair of gray cotton gloves, somewhat worn at the fingers. The high-laced boots she put upon the girl's feet were two sizes too large, and wobbled frightfully, but they did well enough, and there seemed nothing more to be desired.

"Now," said Jane as she pinned on her own hat, "you've gotta have a name to go by. I guess you better be Lizzie Hope. It kinda belongs to yeh, and yet nobody'd recognize it. You don't need to tell Ma anything you don't want to, and you can tell her I'll write a letter tonight all about it. Now come on! We gotta go on the trolley a piece. I don't see havin' you leave from the general station. We'll go up to the junction and get the train there."

With an odd feeling that she was bidding good-by to herself forever and was about to become somebody else, Betty gave one more glance at the slim boylike creature in the little mirror over the washstand and followed Jane out of the room, shuffling along in the big high-heeled boots, quite unlike the Betty that she was.

WARREN Reyburn laid down his pen and shoved back his office chair impatiently, stretching out his long muscular limbs nervously and rubbing his hands over his eyes as if to clear them from annoying visions.

James Ryan, his office boy and stenographer, watched him furtively from one corner of his eye, while his fingers whirled the typewriter on through the letter he was typing. James wanted to take his girl to the movies that evening and he hadn't had a chance to see her the day before. He was wondering if Mr. Reyburn would go out in time for him to call her up at her noon hour. He was a very temperamental stenographer and understood the moods and tenses of his most temperamental employer fully. It was all in knowing how to manage him. James was most deferential, and knew when to keep still and not ask questions. This was one of the mornings when he went to the dictionary himself when he wasn't sure of a word rather than break the ominous silence. Not that Mr. Reyburn was a hard master, quite the contrary, but this was James' first place straight from his brief course at business school, and he was making a big bluff of being an old experienced hand.

There was not much business to be done. This was Warren Reyburn's "first place" also in the world of business since finishing his law course, and he was making a big bluff at being very busy, to cover up a sore heart and an anxious mind. It was being borne in upon him gradually that he was not a shouting success in business so far. The rosy dreams that had floated near all through his days of hard study had one by one left him, until his path was now leading through a murky gray way with little hope ahead. Nothing but sheer grit kept him at it, and he began to wonder how long he could stick it out if nothing turned up.

True, he might have accepted an offer that even now lay open on his desk; a tempting offer, too, from a big corporation who recognized the influence of his old family upon their particular line of business; but it was a line that his father and his grandfather had scorned to touch, and he had grown up with an honest contempt for it. He just could not bring himself to wrest the living from the poor and needy, and plunder the unsuspecting, and he knew that was what it would be if he closed with this offer. Not yet had he been reduced to such depths, he told himself shutting his fine lips in a firm curve. No, not if he starved!

That was the legitimate worry that ruffled his handsome brow as he sat before his desk frowning at that letter. He meant to begin dictation on its answer in another five minutes or so, but meantime he was forcing himself to go over every point and make it strong and clear to himself, so that he should say, "No!" strongly and clearly to the corporation. It might do harm to make his reason for declining so plain, but he owed it to his self-respect to give it nevertheless, and he meant to do so. After all, he had no business so far to harm, so what did it matter? If nothing turned up pretty soon to give him a start he would have to change his whole plan of life and take up something else where one did not have to wait for a reputation before he could have a chance to show what was in him.

But underneath the legitimate reason for his annoyance this morning there ran a most foolish little fretting, a haunting discomfort.

He had taken his cousin to a wedding the night before because her husband had been called away on business, and she had no one to escort her. They had been late and the church was crowded. He had had to stand, and as he idly looked over the audience he suddenly looked full into the great sad eyes of the sweetest little bride he had ever seen. He had not been a young man to spend his time over pretty faces, although there were one or two nice girls in whom he was mildly interested. He had even gone so far as to wonder now and then which of them he would be willing to see sitting at his table day after day the rest of his life, and he had not yet come to a satisfactory conclusion. His cousin often rallied him about getting married, but he always told her it would be time enough to think about that when he had an income to offer her.

But when he saw that flower-face, his attention was held at once. Somehow he felt as if he had not known there was a face like that in all the world, so like a child's, with a frank yet modest droop to the head, and the simplicity of an angel, yet the sadness of a sacrificial offering. Unbidden, a great desire sprang up to lift for her whatever burden she was bearing, and bring light into those sad eyes. Of course it was a passing sensation, but his eyes had traveled involuntarily to the front of the church to inspect the handsome forbidding face of the bridegroom, and with instant dissatisfaction he looked back to the girl once more and watched her come up to the altar, speculating as those who love to study humanity are wont to do when they find an interesting subject. How had those two types ever happened to come together? The man's part in it was plain. He was the kind who go about seeking whom they may devour, thought Warren Reyburn. But the woman! How could a wise-eyed child like that have been deceived by a handsome face? Well, it was all speculation of course, and he had nothing to do with any of them. They were strangers to him and probably always would be. But he had no conception at that time what a small world he lived in, nor how near the big experiences of life lie all about us.

He watched the lovely bride as all the audience watched her until he saw her fall, and then he started forward without in the least realizing what he was doing. He found himself half way up the side aisle to the altar before he came to himself and forced his feet back to where his cousin was sitting. Of course he had no right up there, and what could he do when there were so many of her friends and relatives about her?

His position near the side door through which they carried her made it quite possible for him to look down into her still face as they took her to the vestry room, and he found a great satisfaction in seeing that she was even more beautiful at close hand than at a distance. He wondered afterward why his mind had laid so much stress upon the fact that her skin was lovely like a baby's without any sign of cosmetics. He told himself that it was merely his delight to learn that there was such a type, and that it ran true.

He was therefore not a little disappointed that the minister, after the congregation had waited an unconscionable time for the return of the bride, came out and announced that owing to her continued collapse the ceremony would have to be postponed. The clatter of polite wonder and gossip annoyed him beyond measure, and he was actually cross with his cousin on the way home when she ranted on about the way girls nowadays were brought up, coddled, so that a breath would blow them away. Somehow she had not looked like that kind of a girl.

But when the morning papers came out with sensational headlines proclaiming that the bride had run away, and suggesting all sorts of unpleasant things about her, he felt a secret exultation that she had been brave enough to do so. It was as if he had found that her spirit was as wise and beautiful as her face had been. His interest in the matter exceeded all common sense and he was annoyed and impatient with himself more than he cared to own. Never before had a face lured his thoughts like this one. He told himself that his business was getting on his nerves, and that as soon as he could be sure about one or two little matters that he hoped would fall into his hands to transact, he would take a few days off and run down to the shore.

Again and again the little white bride came across his vision and thoughts, and hindered the courteous but stinging phrases with which he had intended to illumine his letter. At last he gave it up and taking his hat went out in the keen November air for a walk to clear his brain.

This was James Ryan's opportunity. It was almost twelve o'clock and no harm in calling the "forelady" in the cotton blouse department of the big factory. He swung to the telephone with alacrity.

"I want to speak with Miss Carson, please. Yes, Miss J. Carson. Is that Miss Carson? Oh, hello, Jane, is that you?"

"Yes, it is *Mister* Ryan," answered Jane sweetly.

"Jane!"

"Well, didn't you 'Miss Carson' me?"

"Give it up, Jane. You win. Say, Jane!"

"Well, Jimmie?"

"That's my girl, say how about that wedding veil? Been thinking any more about it?"

There was silence for a moment, then a conscious giggle, the full significance of which James Ryan was not in a position to figure out.

"Say, Jimmie, quit your kiddin'! You mustn't say things like that over the phone."

"Why not?"

"'Cause. Folks might listen."

"I should worry! Well, since you say so. How about seein' a show together tonight?"

"Fine an' dandy, Jimmie! I'll be ready at the usual time. I gotta go now, the boss is comin'. So long, Jimmie!"

"So long, darling!"

But the receiver at the other end hung up with a click, while Jane with a smile on her lips thought of the pasteboard box under her bed and wondered what Jimmie would say if he could know. For Jane had fully made up her mind that Jimmie was not to know. Not at present, anyhow. Sometime she might tell him if things turned out all right, but she knew just what lordly masculine advice and criticism would lie upon James Ryan's lips if she attempted to tell him about her strange and wonderful guest of the night before. Maybe she was a fool to have trusted a stranger that way. Maybe the girl would turn out to be insane or wrong somehow, and trouble come, but she didn't believe it; and anyhow, she was going to wait, until she saw what happened next before she got Jimmie mixed up in it. Besides, the secret wasn't hers to tell. She had promised Betty, and she always kept her promises. That was one reason why she was so slow in promising to think about a wedding veil in response to James Ryan's oft repeated question.

That evening on the way to the movies Jane instituted an investigation.

"Jimmie, what kind of a man is your boss?"

"White man!" said Jimmie promptly.

"Aw! Cut it out, James Ryan! I don't mean how'd 'e look, or what color is he; I mean what kind of a *man* is he?"

"Well, that's the answer. White man! What's the matter of that? I said it and I meant it. He's white if there ever was one!"

"Oh, that," said Miss Carson in scorn. "Of course I know he's a peach. If he wasn't you wouldn't be workin' for him. What I mean, is he a *snob?"*

"No chance!"

"Well, I saw him *with* 'em last night. I was passin' that big church up Spruce Street and I saw him standin' with his arms folded so—" she paused on the sidewalk and indicated his pose. "It was a swell weddin' and the place was full up. He had a big white front an' a clawhammer coat. I know it was him 'cause I took a good look at him that time you pointed him out at church that evenin'. I wondered was he *in with* them swells?"

Her tone expressed scorn and not a little anxiety, as if she had asked whether he frequented places of low reputation.

"Oh, if you mean, *could* he be, why that's a diffrunt thing!" said James the wise. *"Sure,* he could be if he wanted, I guess. He's got a good family. His uncle's some high muckymuck, and you often see his aunts' and cousins' names in the paper giving teas and receptions and going places. But he don't seem to go much. I often hear folks ask him why he wasn't some place last night, or phone to know if he won't come, and he always says he can't spare the time, or he can't affort it, or something likc that."

"Ain't he rich, Jimmie?"

"Well, no, not exactly. He may have some money put away, or left him by someone. If he don't have I can't fer the life of me see how he lives. But he certainly don't get it in fees. I often wonder where my salary comes from, but it always does, regular as the clock."

"Jimmie, doesn't he have *any* business at all?"

"Oh, yes he has business, but it ain't the paying kind. Fer instance, there was a man in today trying to get his house back that another man took away from him, and my boss *took the case!* He took it *right off the bat* without waiting to see whether the man could pay him anything or not! He can't! He's only a poor laboring man, and a rich man stole his house. Just out an' out stole it, you know. It's how he got rich. Like as not we'll lose it, too, those rich men have so many ways of crawling out of a thing and making it look nice to the world. Oh, he'll get a fee, of course—twenty-five dollars, perhaps—but what's twenty-five dollars, and like as not never get even the whole of that, or have to wait for it? Why, it wouldn't keep *me* in his office long! Then there was a girl trying to get hold of the money her own father left her, and her uncle frittered away and pertends it cost him all that, and *he's* been supporting *her!* Well, we took that, too, and we won't get much out of that even if we do win. Then there come along one of these here rich guys with a pocket full of money and a nice slick tongue wanting to be protected from the law in some devilment, and *him* we *turned down flat!* That's how it goes in our office. I can't just figger out how it's coming out! But he's a good guy if there ever was one!"

"I should say!" responded Jane with shining eyes.

"Say, Jimmie, what's the matter of us throwin' a little business in his way—real, payin' business, I mean?"

"Fat chance!" said Jimmie dryly.

"You never can tell!" answered Jane dreamily. "I'm goin' to think about it. Our fact'ry has lawyers sometimes. I might speak to the boss."

"Do!" said Jimmie sarcastically. "And have yer labor for yer pains! We'll prob'ly turn *them* down. Fact'ries are *always* doing things they hadn't ought to."

But Jane was silent and thoughtful, and they were presently lost in the charms of Mary Pickford.

The evening papers came out with pictures of Elizabeth Stanhope and her bridegroom that was to have been. Jane cut away the bridegroom and pasted the bride's picture in the flyleaf of her Bible, then hid it away in the bottom of her trunk.

WHEN Betty found herself seated on the day coach of a way train, jogging along toward a town she had never seen and away from the scenes and people of her childhood, she found herself trembling violently. It was as if she had suddenly been placed in an airplane all by herself and started off to the moon without any knowledge of her motor power or destination. It both frightened and exhilarated her. She wanted to cry and she wanted to laugh, but she did neither. Instead she sat demurely for the first hour and a half looking out of a window like any traveler, scarcely turning her head nor looking at anything in the car. It seemed to her that there might be a detective in every seat just waiting for her to lift her eyes that he might recognize her. But gradually as the time dragged by and the landscape grew monotonous she began to feel a little more at her ease. Furtively she studied her neighbors. She had seldom traveled in a common car, and it was new to her to study all types as she could see them here. She smiled at a dirty baby and wished she had something to give it. She studied the careworn man and the woman in black who wept behind her veil and would not smile no matter how hard the man tried to make her. It was a revelation to her that any man would try as hard as that to make a woman smile. She watched the family with five children and nine bundles, and counted the colors on a smart young woman who got in at a way station. Every minute of the day was interesting. Every mile of dreary November landscape that whirled by gave her more freedom.

She opened the little shabby handbag that Jane had given her and got out the bit of mirror one inch by an inch and half backed with pasteboard on which lingered particles of the original green taffeta lining and studied her own strange face, trying to get used to her new self and her new name. Jane had written it, Lizzie Hope, on the back of the envelope containing the address of Mrs. Carson. It seemed somehow an identification card. She studied it curiously and wondered if Lizzie Hope was going to be any happier than Betty Stanhope had been. And then she fell to thinking over the strange experiences of the last twenty-four hours and wondering whether she had done right or not, and whether her father would have been disappointed in her, "ashamed of her," as her stepmother had said. Somehow Jane had made her feel that he would not, and she was more lighthearted than she had been for many a day.

Late in the afternoon she began to wonder what Tinsdale would be like. In the shabby handbag was her ticket to Tinsdale and eight dollars and a half in change. It made her feel richer than she had ever felt in her life, although she had never been stinted as to pocket money. But this was her very own, for her needs, and nobody but herself to say how she should spend either it or her time.

Little towns came in sight and passed, each one with one or two churches, a schoolhouse, a lot of tiny houses.

Would Tinsdale look this way? How safe these places seemed, yet lonely, too! Still, no one would ever think of looking for her in a lonely little village.

They passed a big brick institution and she made out the words, "State Hospital," and shuddered inwardly as she thought of what Jane had told her about the morning paper. Suppose they should hunt her up and *put her in a mental hospital,* just to show the world that it had not been their fault that she had run away from her wedding! The thought was appalling. She dropped her head on her hand with her face toward the window and tried to pretend she was asleep and hide the tears that would come, but presently a boy came in at the station with a big basket and she bought a ham sandwich and an apple. It tasted good. She had not expected that it would. She decided that she must have been pretty hungry and then fell to counting her money, aghast that the meager supper had made such a hole in her capital. She must be very careful. This might be all the money she would have for a very long time, and there was no telling what kind of an impossible place she was going to. She might have to get away as eagerly as she had come. Jane was all right, but that was not saying that her mother and sisters would be.

It was growing dark, and the lights were lit in the car. All the little babies had been given drinks of water, and strange things to eat, and tumbled to sleep across laps, on seats, anywhere they would stick. They looked so funny and dirty and pitiful with their faces all streaked with soot and molasses candy that somebody had given them. The mother looked tired and greasy and the father was fat and dark, with unpleasant black eyes that seemed to roll a great deal. Yet he was kind to the babies and his wife seemed to like him. She wondered what kind of a home they had, and what relation the young fellow with the shiny dark curls bore to them. He seemed to take as much care of the babies as did their father and mother.

The lights were flickering out in the villages now and gave a friendly inhabited look to the houses. Sometimes when the train paused at stations Betty could see people moving back and forth at what seemed to be kitchen tables and little children bringing dishes out, all working together. It looked pleasant and she wondered if it would be like that where she was going. A big lump of loneliness was growing in her throat. It was one thing to run away from something that you hated, but it was another to jump into a new life where one neither knew nor was known. Betty began to shrink inexpressibly from it all. Not that she wanted to go back! Oh, no; far from it! But once when they passed a little white cemetery with tall dark fir trees waving guardingly above the white stones she looked out almost wistfully. If she were lying in one of those beside her father and mother how safe and rested she would be. She wouldn't have to worry anymore. What was it like where Father and Mother had gone? Was it a real place? Or was that just the end when one died? Well, if she were sure it was all she would not care. She would be willing to just go out and not be. But somehow that didn't seem to be the commonly accepted belief. There was always a beyond in most people's minds, and a fear of just what Betty didn't know. She was a good deal of a heathen, though she did not know that either.

Then, just as she was floundering into a lot of theological mysteries of her own discovery the nasal voice of the conductor called out: "Tinsdale! Tinsdale!" and she hurried to her feet in something of a panic, conscious of her short hair and queer clothes.

Down on the platform she stood a minute trying to get used to her feet, they felt so numb and empty from long sitting. Her head swam just a little, too, and the lights on the station and in the houses near by seemed to dance around her weirdly. She had a feeling that she would rather wait until the train was gone before she began to search for her new home, and then when the wheels ground and began to turn and the conductor shouted "All aboard!" and swung himself up the step as she had seen him do a hundred times that afternoon, a queer sinking feeling of loneliness possessed her, and she almost wanted to catch the rail and swing back on again as the next pair of car steps flung by her.

Then a voice that sounded a little like Jane's said pleasantly in her ear: "Is this Lizzie Hope?" and Betty turned with a thrill of actual fright to face Nellie Carson and her little sister Emily.

"Bobbie'll be here in a minute to carry your suitcase," said Nellie efficiently; "he just went over to see if he could borrow Jake Peter's wheelbarrow in case you had a trunk. You didn't bring your trunk? O, but you're going to stay, aren't you? I'm goin' up to the city to take a p'sition, and Mother'd be awful lonesome. Sometime of course we'll send fer them to come, but now the children's little an' the country's better fer them. They gotta go to school awhile. You'll stay, won't you?"

"How do you know you'll want me?" laughed Betty, at her ease in this unexpected air of welcome.

"Why, of course we'd want you. Jane sent you. Jane wouldn't of sent you if you hadn't been a good scout. Jane knows. Besides, I've got two eyes, haven't I? I guess I can tell right off."

Emily's shy little hand stole into Betty's and the little girl looked up:

"I'm awful glad you come! I think you're awful pretty!"

"Thank you," said Betty, warmly squeezing the little

confiding hand. It was the first time in her life that a little child had come close to her in this confiding way. Her life had not been among children.

Then Bob whirled up, bareheaded, freckled, whistling, efficient, and about twelve years old. He grabbed the suitcase, eyed the stranger with a pleasant grin, and stamped off into the darkness ahead of them.

It was a new experience to Betty to be walking down a village street with little houses on each side and lights and warmth and heads bobbing through the windows. It stirred some memory of long ago, before she could scarcely remember. She wondered, had her own mother ever lived in a small village?

"That's our church," confided Emily, as they passed a large frame building with pointed steeple and belfry. "They're goin' to have a entertainment t'morra night, an' we're all goin' and Ma said you cud go too."

"Isn't that lovely!" said Betty, feeling a sudden lump like tears in her throat. It was just like living out a fairy story. She hadn't expected to be taken right into family life this way.

"But how did you know I was coming on that train?" she asked the older girl suddenly. "Jane said she was going to telegraph, but I expected to have to hunt around to find the house."

"Oh, we just came down to every train after the telegram came. This is the last train tonight, and we were awful scared for fear you wouldn't come till morning, an' have to stay on the train all night. Ma says it isn't nice for a girl to have to travel alone at night. Ma always makes Jane and me go daytimes."

"It was just lovely of you," said Betty, wondering if she was talking "natural" enough to please Jane.

"Did you bob your hair 'cause you had a fever?" asked Nellie enviously.

"No," said Betty, "that is, I haven't been very well, and I thought it might be good for me," she finished, wondering how many questions like that it was going to be hard for her to answer without telling a lie. A lie was something that her father had made her feel would hurt him more deeply than anything else she could do.

"I just love it," said Nellie enthusiastically. "I wanted to cut mine, an' so did Jane, but Ma wouldn't let us. She says God gave us our hair, an' we oughtta take care of it."

"That's true, too," said Betty. "I never thought about that. But I guess mine will grow again after awhile. I think it will be less trouble this way. But it's very dirty with traveling. I think I'll have to wash it before I put it on a pillow."

That had troubled Betty greatly. She didn't know how to get rid of that hair dye before Jane's family got used to having it dark.

"Sure, you can wash it, if you ain't 'fraid of takin' cold. There's lots of hot water. Ma thought you'd maybe want to take a bath. We've got a big tin bathtub out in the back shed. Ma bought it off the Joneses when they got their porcelain one put into their house. We don't have no runnin' water but we have an awful good well. Here's our house. I guess Bob's got there first. See, Ma's out on the steps waitin' fer us."

The house was a square wooden affair, long wanting paint, and trimmed with little scrollwork around the diminutive front porch. The color was indescribable, blending well into the surroundings either day or night. It had a cheerful, decent look, but was very tiny. There was a small yard about it with a picket fence, and a leafless lilac bush. A cheerful barberry bush flanked the gate on either side. The front door was open into a tiny hall and beyond the light streamed forth from a glass lamp set on a pleasant dining room table covered with a red cloth. Betty stepped inside the gate and found herself enveloped in two motherly arms, and then led into the light and warmth of the family dining room.

THERE was a kettle of stew on the stove in the kitchen, kept hot from supper, for Betty, with fresh dumplings just mixed before the train came in, and bread and butter with applesauce and cookies. They made her sit right down and eat, before she even took her hat off, and they all sat around her and talked while she ate. It made her feel very much at home as if somehow she was a real relative.

It came over her once how different all this was from the house which she had called home all her life. The fine napery, the cut glass and silver, the stately butler! And here was she eating off a stone china plate thick enough for a table top, with a steel knife and fork and a spoon with the silver worn off the bowl. She could not help wondering what her stepmother would have said to the red and white tablecloth, and the green shades at the windows. There was an old sofa covered with carpet in the room with a flannel patchwork pillow, and a cat cuddled up cosily beside it purring away like a teakettle boiling. Somehow, poor as it was, it seemed infinitely more attractive than any room she had ever seen before, and she was charmed with the whole family. Bobbie sat at the other end of the table with his elbows on the table and his round eyes on her. When she smiled at him he winked one eye and grinned and then wriggled down under the table out of sight.

The mother had tired kind eyes and a firm cheerful mouth like Jane's. She took Betty right in as if she had been her sister's child.

"Come, now, get back there, Emily. Don't hang on Lizzie. She'll be tired to death of you right at the start. Give her a little peace while she eats her supper. How long have you and Jane been friends, Lizzie?" she asked, eager for news of her own daughter.

Betty's cheeks flushed and her eyes grew troubled. She was very much afraid that being Lizzie was going to be hard work:

"Why, not so very long," she said hesitatingly.

"Are you one of the girls in her factory?"

"Oh, no!" said Betty wildly, wondering what would come next. "We—just met—that is—why—*out one evening!*" she finished desperately.

"Oh, I see!" said the mother. "Yes, she wrote about going out sometimes, mostly to the movies. And to church. My children always make it a point to go to church wherever they are. I brought 'em up that way. I hope you go to church."

"I shall love to," said Betty eagerly.

"Is your mother living?" was the next question.

"No," answered Betty. "Mother and Father are both dead and I've been having rather a hard time. Jane was kind to me when I was in trouble."

"I'll warrant you! That's Jane!" beamed her mother happily. "Jane always was a good girl, if I do say so. I knew Jane was at her tricks again when she sent me that telegram."

"Ma's got you a place already!" burst out Nellie eagerly.

"Now, Nellie, you said you'd let Ma tell that!" reproached Bob. "You never can keep your mouth shut."

"There! There! Bob, don't spoil the evening with anything unkind," warned the mother. "Yes, Lizzie, I got you a position. It just happened I had the chance, and I took it, though I don't really b'lieve that anythin' in this world just happens, of course. But it did seem providential. Mrs. Hathaway wanted somebody to look after her little girl. She's only three years old and she is possessed to run away every chance she gets. Course I s'pose she's spoiled. Most rich children are. Now, my children wouldn't have run away. They always thought too much of what I said to make me trouble. But that's neither here nor there. She does it, and besides her ma is an invalid. She had an operation, so she has to lie still a good bit, and can't be bothered. She wants somebody just to take the little girl out walking and keep her happy in the house, an' all."

"How lovely!" exclaimed Betty. "I shall enjoy it, I know."

"She's awful pretty!" declared Emily eagerly. "Got gold curls and blue eyes just like you, and she has ever an' ever so many little dresses, and wears pink shoes and blue shoes, an' rides a tricycle."

"How interesting!" said Betty.

"You'll get good wages," said the mother. "She said she'd give you six dollars a week, an' mebbe more, an' you'd get some of your meals."

"Then I can pay my board to you," cried Betty.

"Don't worry about that, child. We'll fix that up somehow. We're awful glad to have you come, and I guess we shall like each other real well. Now, children, it's awful late. Get to bed. Scat! Lizzie can have her bath an' get to bed, too. Come mornin's half way here already!"

The children said good-night and Betty was introduced to the tin bathtub and improvised bathroom—a neat little addition to the kitchen evidently intended originally for a laundry. She wanted to laugh when she saw the primitive makeshifts, but instead the tears came into her eyes to think how many luxuries she had taken all her life as a matter of course and never realized how hard it was for people who had none. In fact it had never really entered her head before that there were people who had no bathrooms.

Betty was not exactly accustomed to washing her own hair, and with the added problem of the dye it was quite a task; but she managed it at last, using all the hot water, to get it so that the rinsing water was clear, and her hair felt soft. Then, attired in the same warm nightgown she had worn the night before, which Jane had thoughtfully put in the suitcase—otherwise filled with old garments she wished to send home—Betty pattered upstairs to the little room with the sloping roof and the dormer window and crept into bed with Nellie. That young woman had purposely stayed awake, and kept Betty as long as she could talk, telling all the wonderful things she wanted to know about city life, and Betty found herself in deep water sometimes because the city life she knew about was so very different from the city life that Jane would know. But at last sleep won, and Nellie had to give up because her last question was answered with silence. The guest was deep in slumber.

The next morning the children took her over the house, out in the yard, showing her everything. Then they had to take her down to the village and explain all about the little town and its people. They were crazy about Betty's beautiful hair and much disappointed when she would insist on wearing her hat. It was a bright sunny morning, not very cold, and they told her that nobody wore a hat except to church or to go on the train, but Betty had a feeling that her hair might attract attention, and in her first waking hours a great shadow of horror had settled upon her when she realized that her people would leave no stone unturned to find her. It was most important that she should do or be nothing whereby she might be recognized. She even thought of getting a cap and apron to wear when attending her small charge, but Nellie told her they didn't do that in the country and she would be thought stuck-up, so she desisted. But she drew the blue serge skirt up as high above her waistband as possible when she dressed in the morning so that she might look like a little girl and no one would suspect her of being a runaway bride. Also she had a consultation with herself in the small hours of the morning while Nellie was still fast asleep, and settled with her conscience just what she would tell about her past and what she would keep to herself. There was a certain reserve that anyone might have, and if she was frank about a few facts no one would be likely to question further.

So next morning she told Mrs. Carson that since her parents' death she had lived with a woman who knew her father well, but lately things had been growing very unpleasant and she found she had to leave. She had left under such conditions that she could not bring away anything that belonged to her, so she would have to work and earn some more clothes.

Mrs. Carson looked into her sweet eyes and agreed that it was the best thing she could do; they might follow her up and make all sorts of trouble for her in her new home if she wrote for her things; and so the matter dropped. They were simple folks, who took things at their face value and were not over inquisitive.

On the third day there arrived a long letter from Jane in which she gave certain suggestions concerning the new member of the family, and ended: "Ma, she's got a story, but don't make her tell any more of it than she wants. She's awful sensitive about it, and trust me, she's all right! She's been through a lot. Just make her feel she's got some folks that loves and trusts her."

Ma, wise beyond her generation and experience, said no more, and took the little new daughter into her heart. She took the opportunity to inform the village gossips that a friend of Jane's had come to rest up and get a year's country air, boarding with them; and so the amalgamation of Betty Stanhope into the life of the little town began.

The "job" proved to be for only part of the day, so that Betty was free most of the mornings to help around the house and take almost a daughter's place. That she was a rare girl is proved by the way she entered into her new life. It was almost as if she had been born again, and entered into a new universe, so widely was her path diverging from everything which had been familiar in the old life. So deep had been her distress before she came into it that this new existence, despite its hard and unaccustomed work, seemed almost like heaven.

It is true there was much bad grammar and slang, but that did not trouble Betty. She had been brought up to speak correctly, and it was second nature to her, but no one had ever drummed it into her what a crime against culture an illiterate way of speaking could be. She never got into the way of speaking that way herself, but it seemed a part of these people she had come to know and admire so thoroughly, as much as for a rose to have thorns, and so she did not mind it. Her other world had been so all wrong for years that the hardships of this one were nothing. She watched them patch and sacrifice cheerfully to buy their few little plain coarse new things. She marveled at their sweetness and content, where those of her world would have thought they could not exist under the circumstances.

She learned to make that good stew with carrots and celery and parsley and potatoes and the smallest possible amount of meat, that had tasted so delicious the night she arrived. She learned the charms of the common little bean, and was proud indeed the day she set upon the table a luscious pan of beans of her own baking, rich and sweet and brown with their coating of molasses well baked through them. She even learned to make bread and never let anyone guess that she had always supposed it something mysterious.

During the week that Nellie was preparing to go to the city, Betty had lessons in sewing. Nellie would bring down an old garment, so faded and worn that it would seem only fit for the ragbag. She would rip and wash, dye with a mysterious little package of stuff, press, and behold, there would come forth pretty breadths of cloth, blue or brown or green, or whatever color was desired. It seemed like magic. And then a box of paper patterns would be brought out, and the whole evening would be spent in contriving how to get out a dress, with the help of trimmings or sleeves of another material. Betty would watch and gradually try to help, but she found there were so many strange things to be considered. There, for instance, was the up and down of a thing and the right and wrong of it. It was exactly like life. And one had to plan not to have both sleeves for one arm, and to have the nap of the goods running down always. It was as complicated as learning a new language. But at the end of the week there came forth two pretty dresses and a blouse. Betty, as she sat sewing plain seams and trying to help all she could, kept thinking of the many beautiful frocks she had thrown aside in the years gone by, and of the rich store of pretty things that she had left when she fled. If only Nellie and Jane and little Emily could have them! Ah, and if only she herself might have them now! How she needed them! For a girl who had always had all she wanted it was a great change to get along with this one coarse serge and aprons.

But the sewing and other work had not occupied them so fully that they had not had time to introduce Betty into their little world. The very next evening after she arrived she had been taken to that wonderful church entertainment that the girls had told her about on the way from the station, and there she had met the minister's wife and been invited to her Sabbath school class.

Betty would not have thought of going if Nellie and her mother had not insisted. In fact, she shrank unspeakably from going out into the little village world. But it was plain that this was expected of her, and if she remained here she must do as they wanted her to do. It was the least return she could make to these kind people.

The question of whether or not she should remain began to come to her insistently now. The children clamored every day for her to bind herself for the winter, and Jane's mother had made her most welcome. She saw that they really wanted her; why should she not stay? And yet it did seem queer to arrange deliberately to spend a whole year in a poor uncultured family. Still, where could she go and hope to remain unknown if she attempted to get back into her own class? It was impossible. Her mother had just the one elderly cousin whom she had always secretly looked to to help her in any time of need, but his failing her and sending that telegram without even a good wish in it, just at the last minute, too, made her feel it was of no use to appeal to him. Besides, that was the first place her stepmother would seek for her. She had many good society friends, but none who would stand by her in trouble. No one with whom she had ever been intimate enough to confide in. She had been kept strangely alone in her little world after all, hedged in by servants everywhere. And now that she was suddenly on her own responsibility, she felt a great timidity in taking any step alone. Sometimes at night when she thought what she had done she was so frightened that her heart would beat wildly as if she were running away from them all yet. It was like a nightmare that pursued her.

Mrs. Hathaway had sent for her and made arrangements for her to begin her work with the little Elise the following week when the present governess should leave, and Betty felt that this might prove a very pleasant way to earn her living. The Hathaways lived in a great brick house away back from the street in grounds that occupied what in the city would have been a whole block. There was a high hedge about the place so that one could not see the road, and there were flower beds, a great fountain, and a rustic summerhouse. Betty did not see why days passed in such a pleasant place would not be delightful in summertime. She was not altogether sure whether she would like to have to be a sort of servant in the house—and of course these cold fall days she would have to be much in the house—but the nursery had a big fireplace in it, a long chest under the window where toys were kept, and many comfortable chairs. That ought to be pleasant, too. Besides, she was not just out looking for pleasant things on this trip. She was trying to get away from unbearable ones, and she ought to be very thankful indeed to have fallen on such comfort as she had.

There was another element in the Carson home that drew her strongly, although she was shy about even thinking of it, and that was the frank, outspoken Christianity. "Ma" tempered all her talk with it, adjusted all her life to God and what He would think about her actions, spoke constantly of what was right and wrong. Betty had never lived in an atmosphere where right and wrong mattered. Something sweet and pure like an instinct in her own soul had held her always from many of the ways of those about her, perhaps the spirit of her sweet mother allowed to be one of those who "bear them up, lest at any time they dash their feet against a stone." Or it might have been some memory of the teachings of her father, whom she adored, and who in his last days often talked with her alone about how he and her own mother would want her to live. But now, safe and quiet in this shelter of a real home, poor though it was, the God-instinct stirred within her, caused her to wonder what He was, why she was alive, and if He cared? One could not live with Mrs. Carson without thinking something about her God, for He was an ever-present help in all her times of need, and she never hesitated to give God the glory for all she had achieved, and for all the blessings she had received.

The very first Sabbath in the little white church stirred still deeper her awakening interest in spiritual things. The minister's wife was a sweet-faced woman who called her "my dear" and invited her to come and see her, and when she began to teach the lesson Betty found to her amazement that it was interesting. She spoke of God in much the same familiar way that "Ma" had done, only with a gentler refinement, and made the girls very sure that whatever anybody else believed, Mrs. Thornley was a very intimate friend of Jesus Christ. Betty loved her at once, but so shy was she that the minister's wife never dreamed it, and remarked to her husband Sunday night after church, when they were having their little quiet Sabbath talk together, that she was afraid she was going to have a hard time winning that little new girl that had come to live with Mrs. Carson.

"Somehow I can't get away from the thought that she comes from aristocracy somewhere," she added. "It's the way she turns her head, or lifts her eyes or the quiet assurance with which she answers. And she smiles, Charles, never grins like the rest. She is delicious, but somehow I find myself wondering if I have remembered to black my shoes and whether my hat is on straight, when she looks at me."

"Well, maybe she's the daughter of some black sheep who has gone down a peg, and our Father has sent her here for you to help her back again," said her husband with an adorable look at his helper. "If anyone can do it you can."

"I'm not so sure," she said, shaking her head. "She maybe doesn't need me. She has Mrs. Carson, remember, and she is a host in herself. If anybody can lead her to Christ she can, plain as she is."

"Undoubtedly you were meant to help, too, dear, or she would not have been sent to you."

His wife smiled brilliantly a look of thorough understanding: "Oh, I know. I'm not going to shirk any but I wish I knew more about her. She is so sad and quiet, I can't seem to get at her."

Even at that moment Betty lay in her little cot bed under the roof thinking about the minister's wife and what she had said about Christ being always near, ready to show what to do, if one had the listening heart and the ready spirit. Would Christ tell her what to do, she wondered, now right here, if she were to ask Him? Would He show her whether to stay in this place or seek further to hide herself from the world? Would He show her how to earn her living and make her life right and sweet as it ought to be?

Then she closed her eyes and whispered softly under the sheltering bedclothes. "O Christ, if You are here, please show me somehow and teach me to understand."

WHEN Betty had been in Tinsdale about a month it was discovered that she could play the piano. It happened on a rainy Sunday in Sunday school, and the regular pianist was late. The superintendent looked about helplessly and asked if there was anybody present who could play, although he knew the musical ability of everybody in the village. The minister's wife had already pleaded a cut finger which was well wrapped up in a bandage, and he was about to ask someone to start the tune without the piano when Mrs. Thornton leaned over with a sudden inspiration to Betty and asked:

"My dear, you couldn't play for us, could you?"

Betty smiled assent, and without any ado went to the instrument, not realizing until after she had done so that it would have been better policy for her to have remained as much in the background as possible, and not to have shown any accomplishments lest people should suspect her position. However, she was too new at acting a part to always think of these little things, and she played the hymns so well that they gathered about her after the hour was over and openly rejoiced that there was another pianist in town. The leader of Christian Endeavor asked her to play in their meeting sometimes, and Betty found herself quite popular. The tallest girl in their class, who had not noticed her before, smiled at her and patronized her after she came back from playing the first hymn, and asked her where she learned to play so well.

"Oh, I used to take lessons before my father died," she said, realizing that she must be careful.

Emily and Bob came home in high feather and told their mother, who had not been able to get out that morning, and she beamed on Betty with as warm a smile as if she had been her own daughter.

"Now, ain't that great!" she said, and her voice sounded boyish just like Jane's. "Why, we'll have to get a pianna. I heard you could get 'em cheap in the cities sometimes—old-fashioned ones, you know. I heard they have so many old-fashioned ones that they have to burn 'em to get rid of 'em, and they even give 'em away sometimes. I wonder, could we find out and get hold of one?"

"I guess 'twould cost too much to get it here," said Bob practically. "My! I wisht we had one. Say, Lizzie, 'f we had a pianna would you show me how to read notes?"

"Of course," said Betty.

"Well, we'll get one somehow! We always do when we need anything awfully. Look at the bathtub! Good-night! I'm goin' to earn one myself!" declared Bob.

"Mrs. Crosby's gotta get a new one. P'raps she'll sell us her old one cheap."

That was the way the music idea started, and nothing else was talked of at the table for days but how to get a piano. Then one day Emily came rushing home from school all out of breath, her eyes as bright as stars, and her cheeks like roses. "Mrs. Barlow came to our school today and talked to the teacher, and I heard her say she was going away for the winter. She's going to store her goods in the service company barn, but she wants to get somebody to take care of her piano. I stepped right up and told her my mother was looking for a piano, and we'd be real careful of it, and she's just delighted; and—it's coming tomorrow morning at nine o'clock! The man's going to bring it!"

She gasped it out so incoherently that they had to make her tell it over twice to get any sense out of it; but when Bob finally understood he caught his little sister in his arms and hugged her with a big smacking kiss.

"You sure are a little peach, Em'ly!" he shouted. "You're a pippin of the pippins! I didn't know you had that much nerve, you kid, you! I sure am proud of you! My! Think of havin' a pianna! Say, Lizzie, I can play the base of chopsticks now!"

The next evening when Betty got home from the Hathaways there was the piano standing in the big space opposite the windows in the dining room. Ma had elected to have it there rather than in the front room, because it might often be too cold in the front room for the children to practice, and besides it wouldn't be good for the piano. So the piano became a beloved member of the family, and Betty began to give instructions in music, wondering at herself that she knew how, for her own music had been most desultory, and nobody had ever cared whether she practiced or not. She had been allowed to ramble among the great masters for the most part unconducted, with the meagerest technique, and her own interpretation. She could read well and her sense of time and rhythm were natural, else she would have made worse work of it than she did. But she forthwith set herself to practicing, realizing that it might yet stand her in good stead since she had to earn her living.

Little Emily and Bob stood one on either side and watched her as she played, with wondering admiration, and when Betty went to help their mother Bob would sit down and try to imitate what she had done. Failing, he would fall headlong into the inevitable chopsticks, beating it out with the air of a master.

It was the piano that brought to Betty's realization the first real meaning of the Sabbath day. Bob came down early and went at the piano as usual, banging out chop-sticks, and a one-fingered arrangement of "The Long, Long Trail," while his mother was getting breakfast. Betty was making the coffee, proud of the fact that she had learned how. But Bob had accomplished only a brief hint of his regular program when the music stopped suddenly and Betty glanced through the kitchen door to see Ma standing with her hand on her son's shoulder and a look on her face she had not seen before: It was quite gentle, but it was decided.

"No, Bob! We won't have that kinda music on Sunday," she said. "This is God's day, an' we'll have all we can rightly do to keep it holy without luggin' in weekday music to make us forget it. You just get t' work an' learn 'Safely Through Another Week,' and if you can't play it right you get Lizzie to teach you."

Bob pouted:

"There ain't nothin' wrong with chopsticks, Ma. 'Tain't got words to it."

"Don't make any difference. It b'longs to weekdays an' fun, an' anyhow it makes you think of other things, an' you can't keep your mind on God. That's what Sunday was made fer, to kinda tone us up to God, so's we won't get so far away in the week that we won't be any kind of ready for heaven sometime. An' anyhow, 'tisn't seemly. You better go learn your Golden Text, Bob. The minister'll be disappointed if you don't have it fine."

Betty stood by the window thoughtfully looking out. Was that what Sunday was made for, or was it only a quaint idea of this original woman? She wished she knew. Perhaps sometime she would know the minister's wife well enough to ask. She would have liked to ask Ma more about it, but somehow felt shy. But Ma herself was started now, and when she came back to the kitchen, as if she felt some explanation was due the new inmate of the family, she said:

"I don't know how you feel about it. I know city folks don't always hold to the old ways. But it always seemed to me God meant us to stick to Sunday, and make it diff'rent from other days. I never would let my children go visitin', nor play ball, an' we always tried to have something good for supper fixed the night before. I heard somebody say a long time ago that it says somewhere in the Bible that Sunday was meant to be a sign forever between God and folks. The ones that keeps it are His'n, an' them as don't aren't. Anyhow, that's the only day we have got to kinda find out what's wanted of us. You wouldn't mind just playin' hymns and Sunday things t'day, would you?"

"Oh, no," said Betty interested. "I like it. It sounds so kind of safe, and as if God cared. I never thought much about it before. You think God really thinks about us and knows what we're doing then, don't you?"

"Why, sure, child. I don't just think, I *know* He does. Hadn't you never got onto that? Why, you poor little ducky, you! O' course He does."

"I'd like to feel sure that He was looking out for me," breathed Betty wistfully.

"Well, you can!" said Ma, hurrying back to see that her bacon didn't burn. "It's easy as rollin' off a log."

"What would I have to do?"

"Why, just b'lieve."

"Believe?" asked Betty utterly puzzled. "Believe what?"

"Why, believe that He'll do it. He said 'Come unto me, an' I will give you rest,' an' He said, 'Cast your burden on the Lord,' an' He said 'Castin' all yer care 'pon Him, fer He careth fer you,' an' a whole lot more such things, an' you just got to take it fer straight, an' act to it."

"But how could I?" asked Betty.

"Just run right up to your room now, while you're feelin' that way, an' kneel down by your bed an' tell Him what you just told me," said Mrs. Carson, stirring the fried potatoes with her knife to keep them from burning. "It won't take you long, an' I'll tend the coffee. Just you tell Him you want Him to take care of you, an' you'll believe what I told you He said. It's all in the Bible, an' you can read it for yourself, but I wouldn't take the time now. Just run along an' speak it out with Him, and then come down to breakfast."

Betty was standing by the kitchen door, her hand on her heart, as if about to do some great wonderful thing that frightened her:

"But, Mrs. Carson, suppose, maybe, He might not be pleased with me. Suppose I've done something that He doesn't like, something that makes Him ashamed of me."

"Oh, why, didn't you know He fixed for all that when He sent His Son to be the Saviour of the world? We all do wrong things, an' everybody has sinned. But ef we're rightly sorry, he'll forgive us, and make us His children."

Betty suddenly sat down in a chair near the door:

"But, Mrs. Carson, I'm not sure I *am* sorry—at least I know I'm *not*. I'm afraid I'd do it all over again if I got in the same situation."

Mrs. Carson stood back from the stove and surveyed her thoughtfully a moment:

"Well, then, like's not it wasn't wrong at all, and if it wasn't He ain't displeased. You can bank on that. You better go talk it out to Him. Just get it off your mind. I'll hold up breakfast a minute while you roll it on Him and, depend on it, He'll show you in plenty of time for the next move."

Betty with her cheeks very red and her eyes shining went up to her little cot, and with locked door knelt and tried to talk to God for the first time in her life. It seemed queer to her, but when she arose and hurried back to her duties she had a sense of having a real Friend who knew all about her and could look after things a great deal better than she could.

That night she went with Bob and Emily to the young people's meeting and heard them talk about Christ familiarly as if they knew Him. It was all strange and new and wonderful to Betty, and she sat listening and wondering. The old question of whether she was pleasing her earthly father was merging itself into the desire to please her heavenly Father.

There were of course many hard and unpleasant things about her new life. There were so many things to learn, and she was so awkward at work of all kinds! Her hands seemed so small and inadequate when she tried to wring clothes or scrub a dirty step. Then, too, her young charge, Elise Hathaway, was spoiled and hard to please, and she was daily tried by the necessity of inventing ways of discipline for the poor little neglected girl which yet would not bring down a protest from her even more undisciplined mother. If she had been independent she would not have remained with Mrs. Hathaway, for sometimes the child was unbearable in her naughty tantrums, and it took all her nerve and strength to control her. She would come back to the little gray house too weary even to smile, and the keen eye of Ma would look at her wisely and wonder if something ought not to be done about it.

Betty felt that she must keep this place, of course, because it was necessary for her to be able to pay some board. She could not be beholden to the Carsons. And they had been so kind, and were teaching her so many things, that it seemed the best and safest place she could be in. So the days settled down into weeks, and a pleasant life grew up about her, so different from the old one that more and more the hallucination was with her that she had become another creature, and the old life had gone out forever.

Of course as striking looking a girl as Betty could not enter into the life of a little town even as humbly as through the Carson home, without causing some comment and speculation. People began to notice her. The church ladies looked after her and remarked on her hair, her complexion, and her graceful carriage, and some shook their heads and said they should think Mrs. Hathaway would want to know a little more about her before she put her only child in her entire charge; and they told weird stories about girls they had known or heard of.

Down at the firehouse, which was the real clearing-house of Tinsdale for all the gossip that came along and went the rounds, they took up the matter in full session several evenings in succession. Some of the younger members made crude remarks about Betty's looks, and some of the older ones allowed that she was entirely too pretty to be without a history. They took great liberties with their surmises. The only two, the youngest of them all, who might have defended her, had been unconsciously snubbed by her when they tried to be what Bobbie called "fresh" with her, and so she was at their mercy. But if she had known it she probably would have been little disturbed. They seemed so far removed from her two worlds, so utterly apart from herself. It would not have occurred to her that they could do her any harm.

One night the firehouse gang had all assembled save one, a little shrimp of a good-for-nothing, nearly hairless, toothless, cunning-eyed, and given to drink when he could lay lips on any. He had a wide loose mouth with a tendency to droop crookedly, and his hands were always clammy and limp. He ordinarily sat tilted back against the wall to the right of the engine, sucking an old clay pipe. He had a way of often turning the conversation to imply some deep mystery known only to himself behind the life of almost anyone discussed. He often added choice embellishments to whatever tale went forth as authentic to go the rounds of the village, and he acted the part of a collector of themes and details for the evening conversations.

His name was Abijah Gage.

"Bi not come yet?" asked the fire chief settling a straw comfortably between his teeth and looking around on the group. "Must be somepin' doin'. Don't know when Bi's been away."

"He went up to town this mornin' early," volunteered Dunc Withers. "Reckon he was thirsty. Guess he'll be back on the evenin' train. That's her comin' in now."

"Bars all closed in the city," chuckled the chief. "Won't get much comfort there."

"You bet Bi knows some place to get it. He won't come home thirsty, that's sure."

"I dunno, they say the lid's down pretty tight."

"Aw, shucks!" sneered Dunc. "Bet I could get all I wanted."

Just then the door opened and Abijah Gage walked in, with a toothless grin all around.

"Hello, Bi, get tanked up, did yeh?" greeted the chief.

"Well, naow, an' ef I did, what's that to you?" responded Bi, slapping the chief's broad shoulder with a folded newspaper he carried. "You don't 'spose I'm goin' to tell, an' get my frien's in trouble?"

"Le's see yer paper, Bi," said Dunc, snatching at it as Bi passed to his regular seat.

Bi surrendered his paper with the air of one granting a high favor and sank to his chair and his pipe.

"How's crops in the city?" asked Hank Fielder, and Bi's tale was set a-going. Bi could talk; that was one thing that always made him welcome.

Dunc was deep in the paper. Presently he turned it over:

"Whew!" he said speculatively. "If that don't look like that little lollypop over to Carson's I'll eat my hat! What's her name?"

They all drew around the paper and leaned over Dunc's shoulder squinting at the picture, all but Bi, who was lighting his pipe:

"They're as like as two peas!" said one.

"It sure must be her sister!" declared another.

"Don't see no resemblance 'tall," declared the chief, flinging back to his comfortable chair. "She's got short hair, an' she's only a kid. This one's growed up!"

"She might a cut her hair," suggested one.

Bi pricked up his ears, narrowed his cunning eyes, and slouched over to the paper, looking at the picture keenly:

"Read it out, Dunc!" he commanded.

"Five thousand dollars reward for information concerning Elizabeth Stanhope!"

There followed a description in detail of her size, height, coloring, and so forth.

An inscrutable look overspread Bi's face and hid the cunning in his eyes. He slouched to his seat during the reading and tilted back comfortably smoking, but he narrowed his eyes to a slit and spoke little during the remainder of the evening. They discussed the picture and the possibility of the girl in the paper being a relative of the girl at Carson's, but as Bi did not come forward with information the subject languished. Someone said he had heard the Carson kid call her Lizzie, he thought, but he wasn't sure. Ordinarily Bi would have known the full name, but Bi seemed to be dozing, and so the matter was finally dropped. But the hounds were out and on the scent, and it was well for Betty sleeping quietly in her little cot beneath the roof of the humble Carson home, that she had committed her all to her heavenly Father before she slept.

"WELL, he gave me notice t'day," said James Ryan sadly as Jane and he rounded the corner from her boarding-house and turned toward their favorite movie theater. "I been expectin' it, an' now it's come!"

Jane stopped short on the sidewalk appalled:

"He gave you notice!" she exclaimed, as if she could not believe it was true. "Now, Jimmie! You don't mean it? Did he find any fault? He'd better not! B'leeve me, if he did he gets a piece of *my* mind, even if I am a poor workin' girl!"

"Oh, no, he didn't find any fault," said Jimmie cheerfully. "He was awful nice! He said he'd recommend me away up high. He's gonta give me time everyday to hunt a new place, an' he's gonta recommend me to some of his rich friends."

"But what's the matter of him keepin' you? Did you ast him that?"

"Oh, he told me right out that things wasn't working the way he hoped when he started; the war and all had upset his prospects, and he couldn't afford to keep me. He's gonta take an office way downtown and do his own letters. He says if he ever succeeds in business and I'm free to come to him he'll take me back. Oh, he's pleased with me all right! He's a peach! He certainly is."

"Jimmie, what'd you tell him?"

"Tell him? There wasn't much for me to tell him, only I was sorry, and I thanked him, and I told him I was gonta stick by him as long as I didn't have a place. Oh course I can't live on air, but seeing he's willing I should go out and hunt a place every day, why I ain't that mean that I can't write a few letters for him now and then. He don't have that many, and it keeps me in practice. I s'pose I've got to get another place but I haven't tried yet. I can't somehow bring myself to give him up. I kind of wanted to stick in my first place a long time. It doesn't look well to be changing."

"Well, if it ain't your fault, you know, why you can't help it," advised Jane.

They were seated in the theater by this time, and the screen claimed their attention. It was just at the end of the funny reel, and both forgot more serious matters in following the adventures of a dog and a bear who were chasing each other through endless halls and rooms, to say nothing of bathtubs, and wash boilers, and dining tables, and anything that came in their way, with a shock to the people who happened to be around when they passed. But suddenly the film ended and the announcements for the next week began to flash on the screen.

"We must go to that, sure!" said Jimmie, nudging Jane, as the Mary Pickford announcement was put on.

Then immediately afterward came the photograph of a beautiful girl, and underneath in great letters:

FIVE THOUSAND DOLLARS' REWARD FOR ACCURATE INFORMATION AS TO THE PRESENT WHEREABOUTS OF ELIZABETH STANHOPE

There followed further particulars and an address and the showing stayed on the screen for a full minute.

Jane sat gripping the arms of the seat and trying to still the wild excitement that possessed her, while her eyes looked straight into the eyes of the little bride whom she had helped to escape on the night of her wedding.

Jimmie took out his pencil and wrote down the address in shorthand, but Jane did not notice. She was busy thinking what she ought to do.

"What do you s'pose they want her for?" she asked in a breathless whisper, as a new feature film began to dawn on the screen.

"Oh, she's mebbe eloped," said the wise young man, "or there might be some trouble about property. There mostly is."

Jane said no more, and the pictures began again, but her mind was not following them. She was very quiet on the way home, and when Jimmie asked her if she had a grouch on she shivered and said, no, she guessed she was tired. Then she suddenly asked him what time he was going out to hunt for another job. He told her he couldn't be sure. He would call her up about noon and let her know. Could she manage to get out awhile and meet him? She wasn't sure either, but would see when he called her up. And so they parted for the night.

The next morning when Reyburn entered his office Jimmie was already seated at his typewriter. On Reyburn's desk lay a neatly typed copy of the announcement that had been put on the screen the night before.

"What's this, Ryan?" he questioned as he took his seat and drew the paper toward him.

"Something I saw last night on the screen at the movies, sir. I thought it might be of interest."

"Were you thinking of trying for the reward?" asked

Reyburn with a comical smile. "What is it, anyway?" And he began to read.

"Oh, no sir!" said Jimmie. "*I* couldn't, of course, but I thought mebbe *you'd* be able to find out something about her and get all that money. That would help you through until you got started in your own business."

"H'm! That's kind of you, Ryan," said the young lawyer, reading the paper with a troubled frown. "I'm afraid it's hardly in my line, however. I'm not a detective, you know." He laid the paper down and looked thoughtfully out of the window.

"Oh, of course not, sir!" Jimmie hastened to apologize. "Only you know a lot of society folks in the city, and I thought you might think of some way of finding out where she is. I know it isn't up to what you ought to be doing, sir, but it wouldn't do any harm. You could work it through me, you know, and nobody need ever know 'twas you got the reward. I'd be glad to help you out doing all I could, but of course it would take your brains to get the information, sir. You see, it would be to my interest, because then you could afford to keep me, and—I like you, Mr. Reyburn, I certainly do. I would hate to leave you."

"Well, now, I appreciate that, Ryan. It's very thoughtful of you. I scarcely think there would be any possibility of my finding out anything about this girl, but I certainly appreciate your thoughtfulness. I'll make a note of it, and if anything turns up I'll let you know. I don't believe, however, that I would care to go after a reward even through someone else. You know, I was at that wedding, Ryan!" His eyes were dreamily watching the smoke from a distant funnel over the rooftops in line with his desk.

"You were!" said Jimmie, watching his employer with

rapt admiration. He had no higher ambition than to look like Warren Reyburn and have an office of his own.

"Yes, I was there," said Reyburn again, but his tone was so far off that Jimmie dared approach no nearer, and resumed the letter he was typing.

About noon Jimmie called up the factory while Reyburn was out to lunch and told Jane that he expected to go out at two o'clock. Could she meet him and walk a little way with him? Jane said no, she couldn't, but she would try and see him the next day, then he could tell her how he had made out.

At exactly five minutes after two, Jane, having watched from a telephone booth in a drugstore—until Jimmie went by, hurried up to Reyburn's office and tapped on the door, her heart in her mouth lest he should be occupied with someone else and not able to see her before her few minutes of leave which she had obtained from the factory should have expired.

Reyburn himself opened the door to her, and treated her as if she had been a lady every inch, handing her a chair and speaking quite as if she were attired in sealskin and diamonds.

She looked him over with bright eyes of approval. Jane was a born sentimentalist, fed on the movies. Not for anything would she have had a knight rescue her lady fair who did not look the part. She was entirely satisfied with this one. In fact, she was almost tongue-tied with admiration for the moment.

Then she rallied to the speech she had prepared.

"Mr. Reyburn," she said, "I came to see you about a matter of very great importance. I heard you was a great lawyer, and I've got a friend that's in trouble. I thought mebbe you could do something about it. But first, I want to ast you a question, an' I want you to consider it perfectly confidential!"

Jane took great credit to herself that she had assembled all these words and memorized them so perfectly.

"Certainly!" said Reyburn gravely, wondering what kind of a customer he had now.

"I don't want you to think I can't pay for it," said Jane, laying down a five-dollar bill grandly. "I know you can't afford to waste your valuable time even to answer a question."

"Oh, that's all right," said Reyburn heartily. "Let me hear what the question is first. There may be no charge."

"No," said Jane hastily, laying the bill firmly on the desk before him. "I shan't feel right astin' unless I know it's to be paid for."

"Oh, very well," said Reyburn, taking the bill and laying it to one side. "Now, what is the question?"

"Well, Mr. Reyburn, will you please tell me what would anybody want to offer a reward, a big reward, like a thousand dollars—or several of them—for information about anyone? Could you think of any reason?"

Reyburn started. Reward again! This was uncanny. Probably this girl had been to the movies and seen the same picture that Ryan had told him about. But he smiled gravely and answered, watching her quizzically the while:

"Well, they might love the person that had disappeared," he suggested at random.

"Oh, no!" said Jane decidedly. "They didn't! I know that fer a fac'! What else could it be?"

"Well, they might have a responsibility!" he said thoughtfully.

"No chance!" said Jane scornfully.

"Couldn't they be anxious, don't you think?"

"Not so's you'd notice it."

"Well, there might be some property to be divided, perhaps."

"I'd thought of that," said Jane, her face growing practical. "It would have to be a good deal of property to make them offer a big reward, wouldn't it?"

"I should think so," answered Reyburn politely, watching her plain eager face amusedly. He could not quite get at her idea in coming to him.

"Would her coming of age have anything to do with it?" put Jane, referring to a much folded paper she carried in her hand, as if she had a written catechism which she must go through.

"It might." Reyburn was growing interested. This queer visitor evidently had thought something out, and was being very cautious.

"I really can't answer very definitely without knowing more of the circumstances," he said with sudden alarm lest the girl might take some random answer and let serious matters hinge on his word.

"Well, there's just one more," she said, looking down at her paper. "If a man was trying to make a girl marry him when she just hated him, could anybody make her do it, and would anybody have a right to put her in an insane 'sylum or anythin' ef she wouldn't?"

"Why, no, of course not! Where did you ever get such a ridiculous idea?" He sat up suddenly, annoyed beyond expression over disturbing suggestions that seemed to rise like a bevy of black bats all around the borders of his mind.

"See here," he said, sitting up very straight. "I really can't answer any more blind questions. I've got to know what I'm talking about. Why, I may be saying the most impossible things without knowing it."

"I know," said Jane, looking at him gravely. "I've thought of that, but you've said just the things I thought you would. Well, say, if I tell you about it can you promise on yer honor you won't ever breathe a word of it? Not to nobody? Whether you take the case or not?"

"Why, certainly, you can trust me to look out for any confidence you may put in me. If you can't I should prefer that you say nothing more."

"Oh, I c'n trust you all right," said Jane smiling. "I just mean, would you be 'lowed to keep it under yer hat?"

"Would I be allowed? What do you mean?"

"I mean would the law let you? You wouldn't *have* to go an' tell where she was or nothin' an' give her away? You'd be 'lowed to keep it on the q.t. an' take care of her?"

"You mean would it be right and honorable for me to protect my client? Why, certainly."

"Well, I mean you wouldn't get into no trouble if you did."

"Of course not."

"Well, then I'll tell you."

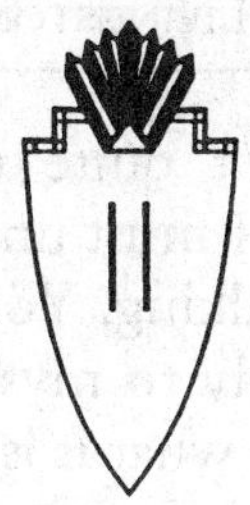

JANE opened a small shabby handbag, and took out a folded newspaper, opening it up and spreading it on the desk before him. "There!" she said, and then watched his face critically.

Reyburn looked, and found himself looking into Betty's eyes. Only a newspaper cut, and poor at that, but wonderfully real and mournful, as they had struck him when she lifted them for that swift glance before she sank in the church aisle.

"Where did you get this?" he asked, his voice suddenly husky.

"Out o' the mornin' paper." Her tone was low and excited. "Were you wanting to try for the reward?" Reyburn asked.

There was a covert sneer in the question from which the girl shrank perceptibly. She sprang to her feet, her eyes flashing:

"If that's what you take me for, I better be goin'!" she snapped and reached out her hand for the paper. But Reyburn's hand covered the paper, and his tone was respectful and apologetic as he said:

"Excuse me, I didn't quite understand, I see. Sit down, please. You and I must understand each other or there is no use in our talking. You can trust me to keep this conversation entirely to myself, whatever the outcome. Will you tell me what it is you want of me?"

Jane subsided into a chair, tears of excitement springing into her eyes.

"Well, you see, it's pretty serious business," she said, making a dab at the corner of one eye. "I thought I could trust you, or I wouldn't a come. But you gotta take me on trust, too."

"Of course," said Reyburn. "Now, what have you to do with this girl? Do you know where she is?"

"I certainly do!" said Jane, "but I ain't a-goin' ta tell until you say if there's anything you can do fer her. 'Cause you see, if you can't find a way to help her, I've gotta do it myself, an' it might get you into trouble somehow fer you to know what you ain't supposed to know."

"I see," said Reyburn, meekly. "Well, what are you going to tell me? Am I allowed to ask that?"

Jane grinned.

"Say, you're kiddin' me! I guess you are all right. Well, I'll just tell you about it. One night last November—you can see the date there in the paper, I was goin' home to my boardin' house in Camac Street, an' I was passin' the side of that church on Eighteenth an' Spruce, where the weddin' was—you know, fer you was there!"

Reyburn looked at her astonished.

"How did you know I was there?"

"I saw you through the window, over against the wall to the street side of the altar," said Jane calmly.

"How did you know me?"

"Oh, somebody I know pointed you out once an' said

you was goin' to be one of the risin' lawyers of the day," she answered nonchalantly, her face quite serious.

A flicker of amusement passed like a ray of light through his eyes, but his face was entirely grave as he ignored the compliment.

"Go on!"

"I saw there was a weddin' an' I stopped to watch a minute, 'cause I expect to get married myself some day, an' I wanted to see how they did things. But I couldn't get near the door, an' the windows were all high up. I could only see folks who were standing up like you were. So I thought I'd go on. I turned the corner and went longside the church listenin' to the music, an' just as I passed a big iron gate at the back of the church somebody grabbed me an' begged me to help 'em. I looked round, an' there was the bride, all in her white togs, with the prettiest white satin slippers, in the wet an' mud! I tried to get her line, but she cried out somebody was comin' back in the passageway, so I slipped off my coat an' hat and whisked her into 'em an' clapped my rubbers over her satin shoes, and we beat it round the corner. I took her to my room, an' gave her some supper. She was all in. Then I put her to bed, an' she told me a little bit about it. She didn't tell me much. Only that they had been tryin' fer a long time back to make her marry a man she hated, an' now they'd almost tricked her into it, an' she'd die if she had to do it. She wanted to exchange clothes with me, 'cause, of course, she couldn't get anywhere togged out that way, so we changed things, an' I fixed her up. In the mornin' I ran out an' got a paper, an' found they was sayin' she was temporary insane, an' stuff like that, an' so I saw their game was tryin' to get her in a 'sylum till they could make her do what they wanted. I fixed her up an' got her off to a place I know where she'd be safe. An' she's got a job an' doin' real well. But now they've got this here reward business out everywhere in the papers an' the movies, she ain't safe nowhere. An' I want somebody that's wiser'n me to take a holt an' do somethin'. I can't pay much, but I'll pay a little every month as long's I live ef it takes that long to pay yer bill, an' I have a notion she may have some money herself, though she didn't say nothin' about it. But there's a ring she left with me to sell, to pay fer what I gave her. It oughtta be worth somethin'. It looks real. I ain't sold it. I couldn't. I thought she might want it sometime—"

But Reyburn interrupted her excitedly.

"Do you mean to say that Miss Stanhope is in the city and you know where she is?"

"Now, don't get excited," warned Jane coolly. "I didn't say she was in this city, did I? I didn't say where she was, did I? I said she was safe."

"But are you aware that you have told me a very strange story? What proof can you give me that it is true?"

Jane looked at him indignantly.

"Say, I thought you was goin' to trust me? I have to trust you, don't I? Course you don't know who I am, an' I haven't told you, but I've got a good p'sition myself, an' I don't go round tellin' privarications! An' there's the weddin' dress, an' veil and fixin's! I got them. You can see 'em if you like—that is pervided I know what you're up to! I ain't taking any chances till I see what you mean to do."

"I beg your pardon," said Reyburn, trying to smile assurance once more. "You certainly must own this whole thing is enough to make anybody doubt."

"Yes, it is," said Jane. "I was some upset myself, havin' a thing like that happen to me, a real millionairess bride drop herself down on my hands just like that, an' I s'pose it *is* hard to b'lieve. But I can't waste much more time now. I gotta get back to my job. Is there anything can be done to keep 'em from gettin' her again?"

"I should most certainly think so," said Reyburn, "but I would have to know her side of the story, the whole of it, before I could say just what!"

"Well, s'pose you found there wasn't anythin' you could do to help her, would you go an' tell on her?"

Reyburn leaned back in his chair and smiled at his unique client:

"I shall have to quote your own language. 'What do you take me for?'"

"A decent man!" said Jane suddenly, and showed all her fine teeth in an engaging smile. "Say, you're all right. Now, I gotta go. When will you tell me what you can do?" She glanced anxiously at her little leather-bound wrist watch. It was almost time for Jimmie to return. Jimmie mustn't find her here. He wouldn't understand, and what Jimmie didn't know wouldn't hurt him.

"Well, this ought to be attended to, at once, if anything is to be done," he said eagerly. "Let me see. I have an engagement at five. How would seven o'clock do? Could I call at your boardinghouse? Would there be any place where we could talk uninterrupted?"

"Sure," said Jane, rising. "I'll get my landlady to let me have her settin' room fer an hour."

"Meantime, I'll think it over and try to plan something."

Jane started down the long flights of stairs, not daring to trust to the elevator, lest she should come face to face with Jimmie and have to explain.

Reyburn stood with his back to the room, his hands in his pockets, frowning and looking out the window, when Jimmie entered a moment later.

"I hope I'm not late, sir?" he said anxiously, as he hung

up his hat and sat down at his typewriter. "I had to wait. The man was out."

"Oh, that's all right, Ryan," said his employer, obviously not listening to his explanation. "I'm going out now, Ryan. I may not be back this afternoon. Just see that everything is all right."

"Very well, sir."

Reyburn went out, then opened the door and put his head back in the room.

"I may have to go out of town tonight, Ryan. I'm not sure. Something has come up. If I'm not in tomorrow, could you—would you mind just staying here all day and looking after things? I may need you. Of course you'll lock up and leave the card out when you go to lunch."

"Very well, sir."

"I'll keep in touch with you in case I'm delayed," and Reyburn was off again. When the elevator had clanked down to the next floor Jimmie went to the window and looked dreamily out over the roofs of the city:

"Aw!" he breathed joyously. "Now I'll bet he's going to do something about that reward!"

Reyburn hurried down the street to the office of an old friend where he had a bit of business as an excuse, and asked a few casual questions when he was done. Then he went on to a telephone booth and called up a friend of his mother's, with whom he had a brief gossip, ostensibly to give a message from his mother, contained in her last letter to him. None of the questions that he asked were noticeable. He merely led the conversation into certain grooves. The lady was an old resident and well known in the higher social circles. She knew all there was to know about everybody and she loved to tell it. She never dreamed that he had any motive in leading her on.

He dropped into a bank and asked a few questions, called up an address they gave him and made another inquiry, then dropped around to his cousin's home for a few minutes, where he allowed her to tell all she knew about the Stanhope wedding they had attended together, and the different theories concerning the escaped bride. Quite casually he asked if she knew whether the bride had property of her own, if so who were her guardians. His cousin thought she knew a lot, but, sifting it down, he discovered that it was nearly all hearsay or surmise.

When he reached Jane Carson's boardinghouse he found that young woman ensconced in a tiny room, nine by twelve, a faded ingrain carpet on the floor, a depressed looking bed lounge against the bleary wallpaper, beneath crayon portraits of the landlady's dead husband and sons. There was a rocking chair, a trunk, a cane-seat chair, and an oil stove turned up to smoking point in honor of the caller, but there was little room left for the caller. On the top of the trunk reposed a large pasteboard box securely tied.

Jane, after a shy greeting, untied the strings and opened the cover, having first carefully slipped the bolt of the door.

"You can't be too careful," she said. "You never can tell."

Reyburn stood beside her and looked in a kind of awe at the glistening white, recognized the thick texture of the satin, the rare quality of the rosepoint lace with which it was adorned, caught the faint fragrance of faded orange blossoms wafting from the filmy mist of the veil as Jane lifted it tenderly; then leaned over and touched a finger to the pile of whiteness, reverently as though he were paying a tribute to a lovely shrine.

Jane even unwrapped the little slippers, one at a time, and folded them away again, and they said no word until it was all tied back in its papers, Reyburn assisting with the strings.

"Now, ef you don't mind waitin' a minute I guess it would be safer to put it away now," she said as she slipped the bolt and ran upstairs.

She was back in a minute and sat down opposite to him, drawing out from the neck of her blouse a ribbon with a heavy glittering circlet at its end.

"Here's the ring." She laid it in his palm. He took it, wondering, a kind of awe still upon him that he should be thus handling the intimate belongings of that little unknown bride whom he had seen lying unconscious in a strange church a few short months before. How strange that all this should have come to him when many wiser, more nearly related, were trying their best to get some clue to the mystery!

He lifted the ring toward the insufficient gas jet to make out the initials inside, and copied them down in his notebook.

"Take good care of that. It is valuable," he said as he handed it back to her.

"Mebbe I better give it to you," she half hesitated.

"You've taken pretty good care of it so far," he said. "I guess you've a better right to it than I. Only don't let anybody know you've got it. Now, I've been making inquiries, and I've found out a few things, but I've about come to the conclusion that I can't do much without seeing the lady. Do you suppose she would see me? Is she very far away?"

"When do you want to go?" asked Jane.

"At once," he answered decidedly. "There's no time to waste if she is really in danger, as you think."

Jane's eyes glittered with satisfaction.

"There's a train at ten-thirty. You'll get there in the morning. I've written it all down here on a paper so you can't make any mistakes. I've written her a letter so she'll understand and tell you everythin'. I'll wire Ma, too, so she'll let you see her. Ma might not size you up right."

Reyburn wondered at the way he accepted his orders from this coolly impudent girl, but he liked her in spite of himself.

In a few minutes more he was out in the street again, hurrying to his own apartment, where he put together a few necessities in a bag and went to the train.

IT was one of those little ironies of fate that are spoken about so much, that when Warren Reyburn alighted from the train in Tinsdale, Abijah Gage should be supporting one corner of the station, and contributing a quid now and then to the accumulations of the week scattered all about his feet.

He spotted the stranger at once and turned his cunning little eyes upon him, making it obvious that he was bulging with information. It was, therefore, quite natural, when Reyburn paused to take his bearings, that Bi should speak up and inquire if he was looking for someone. Reyburn shook his head and passed on, but Bi was not to be headed off so easily as that. He shuffled after him:

"Say!" he said, pointing to a shackley horse and buckboard that stood near, belonging to a pal over at the freight house. "Ef you want a lift I'll take you along."

"Thank you, no," said Reyburn, smiling; "I'm not going far."

"Say!" said Bi again as he saw his quarry about to disappear. "You name ain't Bains, is it?"

"No!" said Reyburn, quite annoyed by the persistent old fellow.

"From New York?" he hazarded cheerfully.

"No," answered Reyburn, turning to go. "You must excuse me. I'm in a hurry."

"That's all right," said Bi contentedly. "I'll walk a piece with you. I was lookin' fer a doctor to take down to see a sick child. A doctor from New York. You ain't by any chance a doctor, are you?" Bi eyed the big leather bag inquiringly.

"No," said Reyburn, laughing in spite of his annoyance. "I'm only a lawyer." And with a bound he cleared the curb and hurried off down the street, having now recognized the direction described in Jane's diagram of Tinsdale.

Abijah Gage looked after him with twinkling eyes of dry mirth, and slowly sauntered after him, watching him until he entered the little unpainted gate of the Carson house and tapped at the old gray door. Then Bi lunged across the street and entered a path that ran along the railroad track for a few rods, curving suddenly into a stretch of vacant lots. On a convenient fence rail with a good outlook toward the west end of the village he ensconced himself and set about whittling a whistle from some willow stalks. He waited until he saw Bobbie Carson hurry off toward Hathaway's house and return with Lizzie Hope; waited hopefully until the stranger finally came out of the house again, touched his hat gracefully to the girl as she stood at the open door. Then he hurried back to the station again, and was comfortably settled on a tub of butter just arrived by freight, when Reyburn reached there. He was much occupied with his whistle, and never seemed to notice, but not a movement of the stranger escaped him, and when the Philadelphia express came by, and the stranger got aboard the parlor car, old Bi Gage swung his lumbering length up on the back platform of the last car. The hounds were hot on the trail now.

It was several years since Bi Gage had been on so long a journey, but he managed to enjoy the trip, and kept in pretty good touch with the parlor car, although he was never in evidence. If anybody had told Warren Reyburn as he let himself into his apartment late that night that he was being followed, he would have laughed and told them it was an impossibility. When he came out to the street the next morning and swung himself into a car that would land him at his office, he did not see the lank flabby figure of the toothless Bi standing just across the block, and keeping tab on him from the back platform, nor notice that he slid into the office building behind him and took the same elevator up, crowding in behind two fat men and effacing himself against the wall of the cage. Reyburn was reading his paper, and did not look up. The figure slid out of the elevator after him and slithered into a shadow, watching him, slipping softly after, until sure which door he took, then waited silently until sure that the door was shut. No one heard the slouching footsteps come down the marble hall. Bi Gage always wore rubbers when he went anywhere in particular. He had them on that morning. He took careful note of the name on the door: *"Warren Reyburn,* Attorney-at-Law," and the number. Then he slid down the stairs as unobserved as he had come, and made his way to a name and number on a bit of paper from his pocket which he consulted in the shelter of a doorway.

When Warren Reyburn started on his first trip to Tinsdale his mind was filled with varying emotions. He had never been able to quite get away from the impression made upon him by that little white bride lying so still amid her bridal finery, and the glowering bridegroom above her. It epitomized for him all the unhappy marriages of the world, and he felt like starting out somehow in hot pursuit of that bridegroom and making him answer for the sadness of his bride. Whenever the matter had been brought to his memory he had always been conscious of the first gladness he had felt when he knew she had escaped. It could not seem to him anything but a happy escape, little as he knew about any of the people who played the principal parts in the little tragedy he had witnessed.

Hour after hour as he sat in the train and tried to sleep or tried to think he kept wondering at himself that he was going on this wild goose chase, as he called it in his innermost thoughts. Yet he knew he had to go. In fact, he had known it from the moment James Ryan had shown him the advertisement. Not that he had ever had any idea of trying for that horrible reward. Simply that his soul had been stirred to its most knightly depths to try somehow to protect her in her hiding. Of course, it had been a mere crazy thought then, with no way of fulfillment, but when the chance had offered of really finding her and asking if there was anything she would like done, he knew from the instant it was suggested that he was going to do it, even if he lost every other business chance he ever had or expected to have, even if it took all his time and every cent he could borrow. He knew he had to try to find that girl! The thought that the only shelter between her and the great awful world lay in the word of an untaught girl like Jane Carson filled him with terror for her. If that was true, the sooner someone of responsibility and sense got to her the better. The questions he had asked of various people that afternoon had revealed more than he had already guessed of the character of the bridegroom to whom he had taken such a strong dislike on first sight.

Thus he argued the long night through between the fitful naps he caught when he was not wondering if he should find her, and whether he would know her from that one brief sight of her in church. How did he know but this was some game put up on him to get him into a mix-up? He must go cautiously, and on no account do anything rash or make any promises until he had first found out all about her.

When morning dawned he was in a state of perturbation quite unusual for the son and grandson of renowned lawyers noted for their calmness and poise under all circumstances. This perhaps was why the little incident with Abijah Gage at the station annoyed him so extremely. He felt he was doing a questionable thing in taking this journey at all. He certainly did not intend to reveal his identity or business to this curious old man.

The little gray house looked exactly as Jane had described it, and as he opened the gate and heard the rusty chain that held it clank he had a sense of having been there before.

He was pleasantly surprised, however, when the door was opened by Emily, who smiled at him out of shy blue eyes, and stood waiting to see what he wanted. It was like expecting a viper and finding a flower. Somehow he had not anticipated anything flowerlike in Jane's family. The mother, too, was a surprise when she came from her ironing, and, pushing her wavy gray hair back from a furrowed brow, lifted intelligent eyes that reminded him of Jane, to search his face. Ma did not appear flustered. She seemed to be taking account of him and deciding whether or not she would be cordial to him.

"Yes, I had a telegram from Jane this morning." She was scanning his eyes once more to see whether there was a shadow of what she called shiftiness in them. "Come in," she added grudgingly.

He was not led into the dining room, but seated on one of the best varnished chairs in the parlor, as they called the little unused front room. He felt strangely ill at ease and began to be convinced that he was on the very wildest of goose chases. To think of expecting to find Elizabeth Stanhope in a place like this! If she ever had been here she certainly must have flown faster than she had from the church on her wedding night.

So, instead of beginning as he had planned, to put a list of logically prepared keen questions to a floundering and suspecting victim, he found the clear eyes of Ma looking into his unwaveringly and the wise tongue of Ma putting him through a regular orgy of catechism before she would so much as admit that she had ever heard of a girl named Lizzie Hope. Then he bethought him of her daughter's letter and handed it over for her to read.

"Well," she admitted at last, half satisfied, "she isn't here at present. I sent her away when I found you was comin'. I wasn't sure I'd let you see her at all if I didn't like your looks."

"That's right, Mrs. Carson," he said heartily, with real admiration in his voice. "I'm glad she has someone so careful to look out for her. Your daughter said she was in a good safe place, and I begin to see she knew what she was talking about."

Then the strong look around Ma's lips settled into the sweeter one, and she sent Bob after the girl.

"Are you a friend of hers?" she asked, watching him keenly.

"No," said Reyburn. "I've seen her but once. She doesn't know me at all."

"Are you a friend of her—family?"

"Oh, no!"

"Or any of her friends or relations?" Ma meant to be comprehensive.

"No. I'm sorry I am not. I am a rather recent comer to the city where she made her home, I understand."

Ma looked at him thoughtfully for a moment. It wouldn't have been called a stare, it was too kindly for that, but Reyburn thought to himself that he would not have liked to have borne her scrutiny if he had anything to conceal, for he felt as if she might read the truth in his eyes.

"Are you—please excuse me for askin'—but are you a member of any church?"

Reyburn flushed, and wanted to laugh, but was embarrassed in spite of himself:

"Why, yes—I'm a member," he said slowly, then with a frank lifting of his eyes to her troubled gaze, "I united with the church when I was a mere kid, but I'm afraid I'm not much of a member. I really am not what you'd call 'working' at it much nowadays. I go to morning service sometimes, but that's about all. I don't want to be a hypocrite."

He wondered as he spoke why he took the trouble to answer the woman so fully. Her question was in a way impertinent, much like the way her daughter talked. Yet she seemed wholly unconscious of it.

"I know," she assented sorrowfully. "There's lots of them in the church. We have 'em, too, even in our little village. But still, after all, you can't help havin' confidence more in them that has 'named the name' than in them that has not."

Reyburn looked at her curiously and felt a sudden infusion of respect for her. She was putting the test of her faith to him, and he knew by the little stifled sigh that he had been found wanting.

"I s'pose lawyers don't have much time to think about being Christians," she apologized for him.

He felt impelled to be frank with her:

"I'm afraid I can't urge that excuse. Unfortunately I have a good deal of time on my hands now. I've just opened my office and I'm waiting for clients."

"Where were you before that? You did not just get through studying?"

He saw she was wondering whether he was wise enough to help her protégé.

"No, I spent the last three years in France."

"Up at the front?" The pupils of her eyes dilated eagerly.

"Yes, in every drive," he answered, wondering that a woman of this sort should be so interested now that the war was over.

"And you came back safe!" she said slowly, looking at him with a kind of wistful sorrow in her eyes. "My boy was shot the first day he went over the top."

"Oh, I'm sorry," said Reyburn gently, a sudden tightness in his throat.

"But it was all right." She flashed a dazzling smile at him through the tears that came into her eyes. "It wasn't as if he wasn't ready. Johnny was always a good boy, an' he joined church when he was fourteen, an' always kep' his promises. He used to pray every night just as faithful, an' read his Bible. I've got the little Testament he carried all through. His chaplain sent it to me. It's got a bullet hole through it, and blood marks, but it's good to me to look at, 'cause I know Johnny's with his Saviour. He wasn't afraid to die. He said to me before he left, he says: 'Ma, if anythin' happens to me it's all right. You know, Ma, I ain't forgettin' what you taught me an' I ain't forgettin' Christ is with me.'"

Mrs. Carson wiped her eyes furtively, and tried to

look cheerful. Reyburn wished he knew how to comfort her.

"It makes a man feel mean," he said at last, trying to fit his toe into the pattern of the ingrain carpet, "to come home alive and whole when so many poor fellows had to give their lives. I've often wondered how I happened to get through."

She looked at him tenderly:

"Perhaps your heavenly Father brought you back to give you more chance to do things for Him, an' get ready to die when your time comes."

There was something startling to this self-composed city chap in hearing a thing like this from the lips of the mother whose beloved son was gone forever beyond her teaching but had "been ready." Reyburn looked at her steadily, soberly, and then with a queer constriction in his throat he looked down at the floor thoughtfully and said:

"Perhaps He did."

"Well, I can't help bein' glad you're a church member, anyhow," said Mrs. Carson, rising to look out the window. "She needs a Christian to help her, an' I'd sooner trust a Christian. If you really meant it when you joined church you've got somethin' to fall back on anyhow. Here she comes. I'll just go an' tell her you're in here."

BETTY, her eyes wide with fear, her face white as a lily, appeared like a wraith at the parlor door and looked at him. It gave Reyburn a queer sensation, as if a picture one had been looking at in a story book should suddenly become alive and move and stare at one. As he rose and came forward he still seemed to see like a dissolving view between them the little huddled bride on the floor of the church. Then he suddenly realized that she was trembling.

"Please don't be afraid of me, Miss Stanhope," he said gently. "I have only come to help you, and if after you have talked with me you feel that you would rather I should have nothing to do with your affairs I will go away and no one in the world shall be the wiser for it. I give you my word of honor."

"Oh!" said Betty, toppling into a chair near by. "I—guess—I'm not afraid of you. I just didn't know who you might be—!" She stopped, caught her breath and tried to laugh, but it ended sorrily, almost in a sob.

"Well, I don't wonder," said Reyburn, trying to find something reassuring to say. "The truth is, I was rather upset about you. I didn't quite know who you might turn out to be, you see!"

"Oh!" Betty's hand slipped up to her throat, and her lips quivered as she tried to smile.

"Please don't feel that way," he said, "or I'll go away at once." He was summoning all his courage and hoping she wasn't going to break down and cry. How little she was, and sweet! Her eyes pleaded, just as they did in that one look in the church. How could anybody be unkind to her?

"I'm quite all right," said Betty with a forced smile, sitting up very straight.

"Perhaps I'd better introduce myself," he said, trying to speak in a very commonplace tone. "I'm just a lawyer that your friend Miss Jane Carson sent out to see if I could be of any service to you. It may possibly make things a little easier for you if I explain that while I never had heard of you before, and have no possible connection with your family or friends, I happened to be at your wedding!"

"Oh!" said Betty with a little agonized breath.

"Do you know Mrs. Bryce Cochrane?" he asked.

Betty could not have got any whiter, but her eyes seemed to blanch a trifle.

"A little," she said in a very small voice.

"Well, she is my cousin."

"Oh!" said Betty again.

"Her husband was unable to accompany her to the wedding, and so I went in his place to escort Isabel. I knew nothing of your affairs either before or after the wedding, until this announcement was brought to my notice, and Miss Carson called on me."

Betty took the paper in her trembling fingers, and looked into her own pictured eyes. Then everything seemed to swim before her for a moment. She pressed her hand against her throat and set her white lips firmly, looking up at the stranger with a sudden terror and comprehension.

"You want to get that five thousand dollars!" she said, speaking the words in a daze of trouble. "Oh, I haven't got five thousand dollars! Not now! But perhaps I could manage to get it if you would be good enough to wait just a little, till I can find a way. Oh, if you knew what it means to me!"

Warren Reyburn sprang to his feet in horror, a flame of anger leaping into his eyes.

"Five thousand dollars be hanged!" he said fiercely. "Do I look like that kind of fellow? It may seem awfully queer to you for an utter stranger to be butting into your affairs like this unless I did have some ulterior motive, but I swear to you that I have none. I came out here solely because I saw that you were in great likelihood of being found by the people from whom you had evidently run away. Miss Stanhope, I stood where I could watch your face when you came up the aisle at your wedding, and something in your eyes just before you dropped made me wish I could knock that bridegroom down and take care of you somehow until you got that hurt look out of your face. I know it was rather ridiculous for an utter stranger to presume so far, but when I saw that the sleuths were out after you, and when the knowledge of your whereabouts was put into my hands without the seeking, I wouldn't have been a man if I hadn't come and offered my services. I'm not a very great lawyer, nor even a very rising one, as your Miss Carson seems to think, but I'm a man with a soul to protect a woman who is in danger, and if that's you, I'm at your service. If not, you've only to say so and I'll take the next train home and keep my mouth shut!"

He took his watch out and looked at it hastily, although he had not the slightest idea what it registered, nor what time the next train for home left. He looked very tall and strong and commanding as he stood in his dignity waiting for her answer, and Betty looked up like a little child and trusted him.

"Oh! Please forgive me!" she cried. "I've been so frightened ever since Bob came after me. I couldn't think you had come for any good, because I didn't know anyone in the world who would want to help me."

"Certainly!" said Warren Reyburn with a lump in his throat, sitting down quickly to hide his emotion. "Please consider me a friend, and command me."

"Thank you," said Betty taking a deep breath and trying to crowd back the tears. "I'm afraid there isn't any way to help me, but I'm glad to have a friend, and I'm sorry I was so rude."

"You weren't rude, and that was a perfectly natural conclusion from my blundering beginning," he protested, looking at the adorable waves of hair that framed her soft cheeks. "But there is always a way to help people when they are in trouble, and I'm here to find out what it is. Do you think you could trust me enough to tell me what it's all about? Miss Carson didn't seem to know much or else she didn't feel free to say."

"I didn't tell her much," said Betty, lifting her sea-blue eyes. "She was a stranger, too, you know."

"Well, she's a mighty good friend of yours, I'll say, and she's acted in a very wise manner. She took more precautions than an old detective would have done. She told me only that someone was trying to make you marry a man you did not wish to marry. Is that correct?"

Betty shivered involuntarily and a wave of color went over her white face.

"It sounds queer," she said, "as if I hadn't any character or force myself, but you don't understand. No one would understand unless they knew it all, and had been through it for years. At first I didn't quite understand it myself. I'd better tell you the story. I thought I never could tell anyone, because they were my father's family, and I know he would shrink so from having it known, but I'm sure he wouldn't blame me now."

"He certainly would not blame you, Miss Stanhope. I have heard that your father was a wonderful man, with high principles. I feel sure he would justify you in appealing to someone who was willing to advise you in a strait like this. You know no woman need ever marry any man against her will."

"Not if it were her father's dying wish?"

"Certainly not. Miss Stanhope, did your father love you?"

"Oh, I'm sure he did. He was the most wonderful father! I've often thought that he would never have asked it of me if he had realized—"

"Did he ever during his lifetime seem to wish you to be unhappy?"

"Never! That was the strange part of it. But you see he didn't know how I felt. I think I'd better tell you all about it."

"That would be the better way, if it won't be too hard for you."

Betty clasped her small hands together tightly and began:

"My own mother died when I was quite a little girl, so Father and I were a great deal to each other. He used to look after my lessons himself, and was always very careful what kind of teachers I had. He was mother and father both to me. When I was ten years old my governess died suddenly while Father was away on a business trip, and one of our neighbors was very kind to me, coming in and looking after the servants and everything and keeping me over at her house for a few days until Father got back. She had a widowed sister visiting her, a rather young woman who was very beautiful. At least I thought she was beautiful then, and she made a great pet of me, so that I grew fond of her, although I had not liked her at first.

"After Father came home she used to slip over every day to see me while he was at his business, and he was grateful to her for making me happy. Then he found out that she was in trouble, had lost her money or something, and wanted to get a position teaching. He arranged to have her teach me, and so she came to our house to stay.

"Somehow after that I never seemed to see so much of my father as I used to do, for she was always there, but at first I didn't care, because she was nice to me, and always getting up things to keep me busy and happy. She would make my father buy expensive toys and books and games for me, and fine clothes, and so of course I was pleased. In about a year my father married her, and at first it seemed very beautiful to me to have a real mother, but little by little I began to see that she preferred to be alone with my father and did not want me around so much. It was very hard to give up the companionship of my father, but my stepmother kept me busy with other things, so that I really didn't think much about it while it was first happening.

"But one day there came a letter. I remember it came while we were at breakfast, and my father got very white and stern when he read it, and handed it over to my stepmother and asked whether it was true, and then she began to cry and sent me from the table. I found out a few days after that that my stepmother had two sons, both older than myself, and that she had not told my father. It was through some trouble they had got into at school which required quite a large sum of money to cover damages that my father discovered it, and he was terribly hurt that she should have concealed it from him. I learned all this from the servants, who talked when they thought I was not within hearing. There were days and days when my father scarcely spoke at the table, and when he looked at me it made a pain go through my heart, he looked so stern and sad. My stepmother stayed a great deal in her room and looked as if she had been crying. But after a few weeks things settled down a good deal as they had been, only that my father never lost that sad troubled look. There was some trouble about my stepmother's sons, too, for there was a great deal of argument between her and my father, of which I only heard snatches, and then one day they came home to stay with us. Something had happened at the school where they were that they could not stay any longer. I can remember distinctly the first night they ate dinner with us. It seemed to me that it was like a terrific thunder-storm that never quite broke. Everybody was trying to be nice and polite, but underneath it all there was a kind of lightning of all kinds of feelings, hurt feelings and wrong ones and right ones all mixed up.

"Only the two boys didn't seem to feel it much. They sort of took things for granted, as if that had always been their home, and they didn't act very polite. It seemed to trouble my father, who looked at them so severely that it almost choked me, and I couldn't go on eating my dinner. He didn't seem like my dear father when he looked like that. I always used to watch my father, and he seemed to make the day for me. If he was sad, then I was sad; and if he was glad then I was happy all over, until one day my stepmother noticed me and said: 'See, dear little Elizabeth is trembling. You ought not to speak that way before her, Charles.' And then Father looked at me, and all suddenly I learned to smile when I didn't feel like it. I smiled back to him just to let him know it didn't matter what he did, I would love him anyhow!"

During the recital Reyburn had sat with courteous averted gaze as though he would not trouble her with more of his presence than was absolutely necessary, now he gave her a swift glance.

Betty's eyes were off on distance, and she was talking from the depths of her heart, great tears welling into her eyes. All at once she remembered the stranger:

"I beg your pardon," she said, and brushed her hand across her eyes. "I haven't gone over it to anyone ever, and I forgot you would not be interested in details."

"Please don't mind me. I am interested in every detail you are good enough to give me. It all makes the background of the truth, you know, and that is what I am after," said Reyburn, deeply touched. "I think you are wonderful to tell me all this. I shall regard it most sacredly."

Betty flashed a look of gratitude at him, and noticed the sympathy in his face. It almost unnerved her, but she went on:

"The oldest boy was named Bessemer, and he wasn't very good-looking. He was very tall and awkward, always falling over things. He had little pale eyes, and hardly any chin. His teeth projected, too, and his hair was light and very straight and thin. His mother didn't seem to love him very much, even when he was a little boy. She bullied him and found fault with him continually, and quite often I felt very sorry for him, although I wasn't naturally attracted to him. He wasn't really unpleasant to me. We got along very nicely, although I never had much to do with him. There wasn't much to him.

"The other brother, Herbert, was handsome like his

mother, only dark, with black curly hair, black wicked eyes, and a big, loose, cruel mouth. His mother just idolized him, and he knew it. He could make her do anything on earth. He used to force Bessemer into doing wrong things, too, things that he was afraid to do himself, because he knew Father would not be so hard on Bessemer as on him. For Father had taken a great dislike to Herbert, and it was no wonder. He seemed to have no idea at all that he was not owner of the house. He took anything he pleased for his own use, even Father's most sacred possessions, and broke them in a fit of anger, too, sometimes, without ever saying he was sorry. He talked very disrespectfully of Father and to him, and acted so to the servants that they gave notice and left. Every few days there would be a terrible time over something Herbert had done. Once I remember he went to the safe and got some money out that belonged to Father and went off and spent it in some dreadful way that made Father very angry. Of course I was still only a little girl, and I did not know all that went on. Father was very careful that I should not know. He guarded me more than ever, but he always looked sad when he came to kiss me good-night.

"Herbert took especial delight in tormenting me," she went on with a sad faraway look in her eyes as if she were recalling unpleasant memories. She did not see the set look on Reyburn's face nor notice his low exclamation of anger. She went steadily on: "He found out that I did not like june bugs, and once he caught hundreds of them and locked me into a room with them with all the lights turned on. I was almost frightened to death, but it cured me of being afraid of june bugs." A little smile trembled out on Betty's lips. "Just because I wouldn't give him the satisfaction of letting him hear me scream," she finished. "Then he caught a snake and put it in my room, and he put a lot of burdocks in my hat so they would get in my hair. Foolish things those were, of course, but he was a constant nightmare to me. Sometimes he would tie a wire across the passages in the upper hall where I had to pass to my room, and when I fell my hands went down against a lot of slimy toads in the dark, for he always somehow managed to have the light go out just as I fell. There were hundreds of things like that, but I needn't multiply them. That's the kind of boy he was. And because he discovered that my father loved me very much, and because he knew my father disliked him, he spent much time in trying to torment me in secret. I couldn't tell my father, because he always looked so sad whenever there was trouble, and there was sure to be trouble between him and my stepmother if my father found out that Herbert had done anything wrong. One day my father came upon us just as Herbert had caught me and was trying to cut my curls off. I didn't care about the curls, but I knew my father did. I began to scream. Herbert gripped me so I thought I would die with the pain, putting his big strong fingers around my throat and choking me so I could not make any noise."

Reyburn clenched his hands until the knuckles went white and uttered an exclamation, but Betty did not notice:

"There was a terrible time then, and I was sent away to a school, a good many miles from home, where I stayed for several years. Father always came up to see me every weekend, for a few hours at least, and we had wonderful times together. Sometimes on vacation he would bring my stepmother along and she would bring me beautiful presents and smile and pet me, and say she missed me so much and she wished I would ask my father to let me come back and go to school in the city. But I never did, because I was afraid of Herbert. As I grew older I used to have an awful horror of him. But finally one vacation Father and stepmother both came up and said they wanted me at home. My stepmother went to my room with me and told me I needn't be afraid of Herbert anymore, that he was quite grown-up and changed and would be good to me, and that it would please my father to have all his family together happily again. I believed her and I told Father I would like to go. He looked very happy, and so I went home. Herbert had been away at school himself most of the time, and so had Bessemer, although they had been in trouble a good many times, so the servants told me, and had to change to new schools. They were both away when I got home. I had a very happy time for three weeks, only that I never saw Father alone once. My stepmother was always there. But she was kind and I tried not to mind. Then all of a sudden one night I woke up and heard voices, and I knew that the boys were back from the camp to which they had been sent. I didn't sleep much the rest of the night, but in the morning I made up my mind that it was only a little while before I could go back to school, and I would be nice to the boys and maybe they wouldn't trouble me.

"I found that it was quite true that Herbert had grown up and changed. He didn't want to torment me anymore, he wanted to make love to me, and I was only a child yet. I wasn't quite fifteen. It filled me with horror, and after he had caught me in the dark—he always loved to get people in the dark—and tried to kiss me, I asked Father to let me go back to school at once. I can remember how sad he looked at me as if I had cut him in the heart when I asked him."

During this part of the tale Reyburn sat with stern countenance, his fingers clenched around the arms of the chair in which he sat, but he held himself quiet and listened with compressed lips, watching every expression that flitted across the sweet pale face.

"That was the last time I was at home with my father," she said, trying to control her quivering lips. "He took me back to school, and he came three times to see me, though not so often as before. The last time he said beautiful things to me about trying to live a right life and being kind to those about me, and he asked me to forgive him if he had ever done anything to hurt me in any way. Of course I said he hadn't. And then he said he hoped I wouldn't feel too hard at him for marrying again and bringing those boys into my life. I told him it was all right, that someday they would grow up and go away and he and I would live together again! And he said some awful words about them under his breath. But he asked me to forgive him again and kissed me and went away.

"He was taken very sick when he got home, and they never let me know until he was dead. Of course I went home to the funeral, but I didn't stay; I couldn't. I went back to school alone. My stepmother had been very kind, but she said she knew it was my father's wish that I should finish my school year. When vacation came she was traveling for her health. She wrote me a beautiful letter telling me how she missed me, and how much she needed me now in her bereavement, and how she hoped another summer would see us together; but she stayed abroad two years and the third year she went to California. I was sent to another school, and because I was not asked about it and there didn't seem anything else to do, I went. Every time I would suggest doing something else my stepmother would write and say how sorry she was she could not give her consent, but my father had left very explicit directions about me and she was only trying to carry out his wishes. She knew me well enough to be sure I would want to do anything he wished for me. And I did, of course."

Reyburn gave her a look of sympathy and getting up began to pace the little room.

"IT was not until last spring that she sent for me to come home," went on Betty, "and was very effusive about how much she needed me and how she was so much better, and meant to be a real mother to me now, helping me see the world and have a good time. She took me from one summer resort to another. Of course it was pleasant after having been shut up in school all those years, but she kept me close with her all the time, and I met only the people she chose to have me meet. All the time she kept talking about 'dear Herbert' and telling how wonderful he was and how he had grown to be 'such a dear boy.' Finally he arrived and began the very first evening he was with us to coax me to marry him. At first he was very courteous and waited upon me whenever I stirred, and I almost thought his mother was right about his being changed. But when I told him that I did not love him and could not ever marry him I caught a look on his face like an angry snarl, and I heard him tell his mother I was a crazy little fool, and that he would break my neck for me after he got me good and married. Then his mother began to come to me and cry and tell me how dear Herbert was almost heartbroken, that he would never lift up his head again, and that I would send him to ruin. It was simply awful, and I didn't know how to endure it. I began to wonder where I could go. Of course I had never been brought up to do anything, so I could not very well expect to go out into the world and make my living."

"Didn't you have any money at all?" interrupted Reyburn suddenly.

"Oh, yes," she said, looking up as if she had just remembered his presence. "I had always plenty of spending money, but if I went away where they couldn't find me, why, of course, I would have to give that up."

"Why, where did your money come from? Was it an allowance from your stepmother, or did your father leave it to you, or what?"

"I'm not just sure," said Betty, with troubled brow. "I never really knew much about the money affairs. When I asked, they always put me off and said that I was too young to be bothered with business yet, I would be told all about it when I came of age. My stepmother harped a great deal on keeping me young as long as possible. She said it was my father's wish that I should be relieved of all care until I came of age. But there were some trustees in Boston. I know that, because I had to write to them, about once or twice a year. My stepmother was most particular about that. I think they were old friends of my own mother, though I don't know when I learned that. Father told me once that Mother had left me enough to keep me comfortably even without what he would leave me, so I'm sure I shall have enough to repay you if I could once get it."

"Don't worry about me!" he exclaimed. "It seems so terrible for you to have been alone in a situation like that! Wasn't there anyone you could appeal to for help?"

"No, not anyone whom I thought it would be right to tell. You see, in a way it was my father's honor. She was his wife, and I'm sure he loved her—at least at first—and she really was very good to me, except when it was a question of her son."

"I'm afraid I can't agree with you there!" he said sternly. "I think she was a clever actress. But excuse me. Go on, please."

"At last, when things had got so bad that I thought I must run away somewhere, my stepmother came into my room one morning and locked the door. She had been weeping, and she looked very sweet and pitiful. She said she had something to tell me. She had tried not to have to do it, for she was afraid it would grieve me and might make me have hard feelings against my father. I told her that was impossible. Then she told me that my father on his deathbed had called her to him and told her that it was his wish that I should marry one of her sons, and he wanted her to tell me. He felt that he had wronged them by hating them for my sake and he felt that I could make it all right by marrying one of them. My stepmother said that when she saw how infatuated dear Herbert was with me she hoped that she would be spared having to tell me, but now that I was treating him so she felt bound to deliver the message. Then she handed me a paper which said virtually the same thing which she had told me, and was signed by my father in his own handwriting."

"Was the paper written or printed?" interrupted Reyburn.

"I think it was typewritten, but the signature was Papa's. There could be no mistake about that, and he wouldn't have signed something he didn't mean." Betty sighed as if it were a subject she had worn into her heart by much sorrowful thought.

"It might be quite possible for him to have done that under influence or delirium, or when he was too sick to realize."

"Oh, do you think so?" Betty caught at the hope. "It seems so awful to go against Papa's last request."

"There is nothing awful but the idea of your being tied to that—beast!" said Reyburn with unexpected fervor. Betty looked at him gratefully and went on:

"I was simply appalled. I couldn't think, and I made my stepmother go away and leave me for a little while, but things got blacker and blacker and I thought I was going crazy. I couldn't marry Herbert even to please my father. The next day Bessemer arrived. He had been worrying his mother a lot about money, and when he arrived I couldn't help hearing what they said to him. They charged him with all sorts of dreadful things. They called him a disgrace, and threatened to let him be arrested, and a great many more such things. Finally his mother ended up by telling him she never had loved him and that if he made any more trouble about money she would cut him off without a cent. I was sitting upstairs in my room with my windows open, and all their talk floated right up to me. It made me feel sick, and yet I felt sorry for Bessemer, for lately whenever he had been around he had been kind to me, and sometimes I had stayed near him to get rid of Herbert. We often talked over our troubles together and sympathized with one another. He felt sorry for me, but he was weak himself and couldn't see any way out for either of us.

"They had pretty stormy times all that day. Late in the afternoon Herbert and Bessemer went to their mother's room and were closeted with her for two hours, after which Herbert went away in the car with his suitcase and bags as if he were not coming back soon. I watched him from my window, and in great relief went down to take a little walk, for I had stayed closely in my room all day trying to plan what to do. One thing that held me from running away was that it would be such a disgrace to the family, and I knew my father would have felt it so keenly. That was always the great trouble when the boys got into scrapes at college, my father would groan and say he felt disgraced to be so conspicuous before the world. So I hesitated to do what would have been a sorrow to him had he been alive.

"Half an hour later I was sitting alone in the twilight on one of the porches, and Bessemer came out and sat down beside me.

"He looked so sort of homely and lonesome that I put my hand on his arm and told him I was awfully sorry for him, and suddenly he turned around and said:

"Say, Betty, why don't you marry *me?* Then they can't say a word to either of us. Your father's wishes will be carried out and Herb'll have to whistle."

"At first I was horrified, but we talked a long time about it, and he told me how lonely he had always been, and how nobody had ever loved him, and he knew he wasn't attractive, and all that; and then he said that if I married him we would go away and live by ourselves and he would let me do just as I wanted to. He wouldn't bother me about anything. If I didn't love him he would keep out of my sight, and things like that, till I got very sorry for him, and began to think that perhaps after all it was the best thing that would ever come for either of us. So I said I would.

"It surprised me a little that my stepmother took it so calmly when we told her. She cried a little, but did it very prettily, and kissed Bessemer, and told him he was fortunate. Then she kissed me and said I was a darling, and that she would be so happy if it only weren't for poor dear Herbert.

"But after that they began to rush things for a grand wedding, and I let them do it because I didn't see anything else in the world for me."

Betty raised her eyes and encountered the clear grave gaze of Reyburn fixed on her, and the color flew into her cheeks:

"I know you think I'm dreadful," she said, shrinking. "I've thought so myself a thousand times, but truly I didn't realize then what an awful thing it would be to marry a man I didn't love. I only wanted to hurry up and get it done before Herbert came home. They said he had been called away by important business and might be at home any day. I gave my consent to everything they wanted to do, and they fixed it all just as they pleased. One thing that happened upset me terribly. When the wedding invitations came home my stepmother carried them off to her room. I was too sad to pay much attention anyway. But the next morning I happened to be down in the kitchen looking over the papers that the maid had taken down from the waste baskets to search for a missing letter and there in the pile I found one of the invitations partly addressed and flung aside, and the invitation was still in the envelope. I pulled it out with a ghastly kind of curiosity to see how I looked on paper, and there it read, Mrs. Charles Garland Stanhope invites you to be present at the marriage of her daughter Elizabeth to *Mr. Herbert Hutton!*

"My heart just stood still. With the paper in my hand I rushed up to my stepmother's room and demanded to know what that meant. She smiled and said she was so sorry I had been annoyed that way, that that was a mistake, the invitations had come wrongly engraved and she had had to send them back and have them done over again. She was afraid I might be superstitious about it, so she hadn't told me. She was very gentle and sweet and tried to soothe me, and called me 'Betty,' the name my father always had for me, and at last I went back to my room feeling quite comfortable. She had said she always felt troubled for poor Bessemer, that nobody could love him right, he was so homely, and now I was going to make everything right by marrying him. She was going to try to forget what I had done to poor dear Herbert, and just be happy about Bessemer. She talked so nicely that I kissed her, a thing I hadn't done in years, not since she was first married to Father. But somehow the shock of seeing Herbert's name on the invitation stayed with me, and I began to feel gloomier about it all and to wonder if perhaps I had done right. The last day I was terribly depressed and when I got to the church that night it suddenly came to me that perhaps after all I was not going to be free at all as I had hoped, but was just tying myself up to them all for life. I was thinking that as I walked up the aisle, and my throat had a big lump in it the way it always does when I'm frightened, and then I looked up hoping a glimpse of poor Bessemer's face would steady me and he wasn't there at all! And right over me, waiting beside the minister, to marry me stood *Herbert!* My knees just gave way under me, and everything got black so I couldn't go on another step, nor even stand up. I had to drop. I wasn't unconscious as you all thought—I heard everything that went on, but I couldn't do anything about it.

"After they had carried me into the other room and given me things to drink, and I could get my breath again I saw it all clearly. Herbert hadn't given up at all. He meant to marry me anyway. He had had the invitations printed with his name on purpose and they probably hadn't been changed at all. Everybody in that great church out there was *expecting* me to marry Herbert Hutton, and I *was not going to do it!* I didn't quite know how I was going to stop it, but I knew I had to! You see I was brought up to think a great deal about what people would think of me if I did anything out of the usual, and it seemed to me I had disgraced myself forever by dropping down in the aisle. I knew Herbert well enough to be sure he would carry that wedding through now if he had to hold me up in his arms till the ceremony was over, and I was desperate. I would have given everything I had in the world if the floor had opened and swallowed me up then, but of course I knew wild thoughts like that wouldn't get me anywhere, so I just shut my eyes and tried to think of a way; and then I asked them all to go out a minute and let me be quiet. The doctor who had come out of the church told them to go. I shall always bless that man, whoever he was! Then when they were gone I opened a door that had a key in it, and I locked it behind me and ran away down some stairs and out a passage that led to the street. That girl, Jane Carson, was passing and she put her own coat on me and took me to her room and sent me here. Oh, it's been so good to get here! Do you think they can take me away against my will?"

"Certainly not!" said the young man. "Not without some foul play, but I don't intend to give them any chance for that. By the way, when do you come of age?"

"In three weeks," said Betty, looking troubled. "Why, would I be safe after I was of age?"

"You certainly would not be under their guardianship any longer," said the lawyer, "and they would have no right to control your actions, unless of course you were incapacitated somehow and unfit to manage your own affairs."

Betty looked troubled.

"I've thought sometimes, ever since I saw that paper in which they hinted that I was temporarily insane, that they might try to shut me up in a mental hospital. Herbert wouldn't stop at anything. Could he do that?"

"They would have to get a doctor to swear that you were mentally unsound," said Reyburn, looking troubled. "Does he really love you, do you think, or does he only want to get you in his power for some reason?"

"It is more like that," said Betty sorrowfully, "he couldn't really love anybody but himself."

"Well, don't you worry. I'm going at the case at once, and I'll put those people where they'll have to walk a chalk line before many hours are over. The first thing I must do is to see those trustees of yours. Can you give me the names and addresses?"

He got out his fountain pen, and Betty told him all he wanted to know, that is, all she knew herself, and then suddenly it was train time and he hurried away. On the steps he paused and said in a low tone:

"Are you perfectly comfortable with these people for a few days until I can get you better accommodations where you will be safe?"

"Entirely," said Betty eagerly. "I wouldn't want to go elsewhere."

"But it must be very hard for one like you to be thrown constantly with illiterate, uncultured people."

Betty smiled dreamily:

"I don't think they are exactly uncultured," she said slowly. "They—well, you see, they make a friend of God, and somehow I think that makes a difference. Don't you think it would?"

"I should think it would," said Warren Reyburn reverently with a light in his eyes. "I think, perhaps, if you don't mind my saying it, that you, too, have been making a friend of God."

"I've been trying to," said Betty softly, with a shy glow on her face that he remembered all the way back to the city.

CANDACE Cameron paced her little gabled room restively, with face growing redder and more excited at every step. For several weeks now she had been virtually a prisoner—albeit a willing enough one—in the house of Stanhope. But the time had come when she felt that she must do something.

She had gone quietly enough about a proscribed part of the house, doing little helpful things, making herself most useful to the madam, slipping here and there with incredible catlike tread for so plump a body, managing to overhear important conversations, and melting away like a wraith before her presence was discovered. She had made herself so unobtrusive as to be almost forgotten by all save the maid Marie, who had been set to watch her; and she had learned that if she went to bed quite early in the evening, Marie relaxed her watch and went down to the servants' quarters, or even sometimes went out with a lover for awhile, that is, if the madam herself happened to be out also. On several such occasions she had made valuable tours of investigation through the madam's desk and private papers.

That she was overstepping her privileges as a servant in the house went without saying, but she silenced her Scotch conscience, which until this period of her existence had always kept her strictly from meddling with other people's affairs, by declaring over and over again to herself that she was doing perfectly right because she was doing it for the sake of "that poor wee thing that was being cheated of her rights."

Several weeks had passed since her sudden reestablishment in the family, and the reports of Betty, so hastily readjusted and refurbished to harmonize with the newspaper reports, had not been any more satisfying. Mrs. Stanhope had explained to the servants the day after the excitement that Miss Betty had become temporarily deranged, and later that she had escaped from the private hospital where she had been taken, and they were doing all in their power to find her. In reply to Candace's gimletlike questions she had given the name of a hospital where she said Betty had been taken at first, and everything seemed altogether plausible. But as the days went by and the horror of her absence grew into the soul of the lonely woman whose care Betty had been years, Candace became more and more restive and suspicious. It was these suspicions which sent her on her investigations, and made her uncannily wise to pry open secret locks and cover all trace of her absence after she had gleaned what knowledge she sought.

On this particular evening her excitement was due to having come across some correspondence bearing the signature of a man to whom a certain letter had been addressed, which had been entrusted to her charge by Betty's dying father and taken from her by his wife. For years she had been worried about that, and yet she had no absolute reason to doubt that the madam had not sent it to its destination, except as she knew its contents and read Mrs. Stanhope's character beneath the excellent camouflage. But tonight, even the briefest glance through the handle of letters showed plainly that those men in Boston never knew the master's wishes, or at least, if they knew them, they were utterly disregarding them.

Aroused on one point, her suspicions began to extend further. Where was Betty? Did her stepmother know, and was she somewhere suffering, alone, perhaps being neglected because she had not done as they wanted her to do? If the stepmother was capable of destroying a letter, was she perhaps not also capable of putting Betty out of the way? There were points of detail which of course did not harmonize with any such theory as this. Candace was no logician, but she was keen enough to feel that something was wrong. As for that theory of Betty's insanity she scouted it with a harsh laugh whenever it was mentioned in her hearing. Betty—keen, sweet, trusting little Betty *insane!* Nonsense! It was unthinkable. If she was in a hospital anywhere she was there without warrant, and it behoved her faithful old nurse to find a way out for her. This she meant to do against all odds, for she was thoroughly aroused now.

She went to the window and looked down into the lighted street. Over there not four blocks away rose the steeple of the church where Betty had gone to be married! Around the corner was the great brick pile of the hospital where her stepmother said she had been taken from the church, and from which she was believed by the other servants to have escaped.

Standing thus looking out into the light-starred city, Candace began to form a plan, her plump tightly garmented chest rising and falling excitedly as she thought it all out. It was up to her to find out what had become of Betty. But how was she to get away without being suspected? Somehow she must do it. She knew perfectly the address that had been on that letter. She had written it down carefully from memory as soon as it had been taken away from her. She must go to Boston and find that man to whom it had been written, and discover whether he had ever received it. But she could not go until she found out certainly whether or not Betty had ever really escaped from the hospital. Who knew but that she was shut up there yet, and the madam telling this tale all about and advertising with a five-thousand-dollar reward! In the movies, too! Such a disgrace on the family! How the master would have writhed at the publicity of his beloved daughter—poor wee thing!

Candace turned from the window with her lips set, and tiptoeing to the door, listened. Yes, it was Aileen who was coming lightly up the stairs, singing in a low tone. It was Aileen's evening out. That meant that Marie would be more than usually active on the upper floor. She must manage it before Aileen left and Marie was called upstairs, or there would be no opportunity to get away without Marie seeing her.

Hastily she gathered her silk dress, her cloak, and her hat into a bundle with her purse and her gloves, and tied them into an old apron, with the strings hanging free. Then stealthily opening the window, she dropped them out into the kitchen area below, close to the region of the ash cans. It was a risk, of course, but one must take some chances, and the servants would all be in the kitchen just now, laughing and talking. They would scarcely have heard it fall.

She listened a tense instant, then closed the window, and possessing herself of few little things, gathered hastily about the room, which she could stuff in her pockets, she opened her door softly, closed it behind her, and trotted off down the stairs just as if she were going about her ordinary duty. Listening a minute outside the kitchen door she slipped stealthily down the cellar stairs, and tiptoed over to the area door where the ashman took out the ashes. Softly slipping the bolt she opened the door and drew in her bundle. Then standing within, she quickly slipped the black silk over her housemaid's gown, donned her coat and hat and gloves, and sallied forth. A moment more and she was in the next street with the consciousness that she might have done the like anytime sooner, if she'd wanted, in spite of that little spy-cat Marie.

"If I want to go back I'll just say I went after my insurance book," she chuckled to herself as she sped down the street in the direction of the hospital.

Arrived at the big building she asked to see the list of patients taken in on the day of Betty's wedding, and succeeded in getting a pretty accurate description of each one, sufficient at least to satisfy her that Betty was not among them. Then she asked a few more bold questions, and came away fully convinced that Betty had never been in that hospital.

By this time it was nine o'clock, and she meant to take the evening train for Boston, which left, she was sure, somewhere near midnight. She took a trolley to her old lodgings where she had been since Mrs. Stanhope had sent her away the first time, and hastily packed a small handbag with a few necessities, made a few changes in her garments, then went to see a fellow lodger whom she knew well, and where she felt sure she could easily get a check cashed, for she had a tidy little bank account of her own, and was well known to be reliable.

Having procured the necessary funds, she made her way to the station and found that she still had an hour to spare before the Boston train left.

Settled down at last in the back seat of a common car,

she made herself as comfortable as her surroundings would allow, and gave herself up to planning the campaign that was before her.

Canny Candace did not go at once to the office of the brothers, James and George McIntyre, though she looked them up in the telephone book the very first thing when the train arrived in Boston even before she had had a bite to eat, and her cup of tea which meant more to her than the bite. She reasoned that they would be busy in the early hours and not be able to give her their undivided attention. She had not lived out all her life for nothing. She knew the ways of the world, and she had very strict ideas about the best ways of doing everything. So it happened that when she was at last shown into the office of the McIntyres, Warren Reyburn who had traveled to Boston on the sleeper of the same train that she had taken the night before, was just arising from an earnest conference with the two men. With her first glance, as the three emerged from the inner office, Candace saw that the two elder gentlemen were much disturbed and it flitted through her mind that she had come at an inopportune moment. Then her quick eye took in the younger man and her little alert head cocked to one side with a questioning attitude. Where had she seen him before? Candace had the kind of mind that kept people and events card-indexed even to the minutest detail, and it didn't take many seconds for her to place Warren Reyburn back in the church at the wedding, standing against the wall with his arms folded. She had noticed him particularly because he was so courteous to a little old lady who came in too late to get a seat. She had studied him as he stood there, waiting for the wedding march, and she had thought how handsome he looked and how fine it would have been if her wee Betty had been getting a man like that in place of the weak-faced Bessemer Hutton. She had watched to see who he was with, and felt deep satisfaction when she noticed him lean over and speak to Mrs. Bryce Cochrane as if he belonged to her. He wasn't her husband, because she knew Mr. Cochrane, who had been a favorite with Mr. Stanhope and much at the house. This man might be Mrs. Cochrane's brother or the likes, and she had pleased herself watching him till Betty arrived and took all her thoughts. So now she stood with her little round head in its hectic hat tilted interestedly to one side, watching, ears on the keen to catch any word, for all the world like a bit brown sparrow saucily perched on another man's window, where it really had no right to be.

At last one of the McIntyre's shook hands gravely with the younger man, and the other one attended him to the door, talking in low tones. The McIntyre thus set at liberty, turned questioningly toward the stranger, who was not slow in getting to her feet and coming forward.

"You will maybe be Mr. James McIntyre?" she asked, lifting her sea-blue eyes set in her apple-red face, and fixing her firm little lips in dignity. Candace was a servant and knew her place, but she felt the importance of her mission, and meant to have no disrespect done to it.

"I am Mr. George McIntyre," the gentleman replied, and, indicating the man at the door, "Mr. James McIntyre will be at liberty in a moment, but perhaps I will do as well?"

Candace cocked a glance toward the elderly back at the door; and then returned her look to Mr. George:

"You'll maybe be knowing Mr. Charles Stanhope?" she propounded, as if she were giving him a riddle, and her blue eyes looked him through and through:

"Oh, surely, surely! He was a very close friend! You—knew him?"

"I was Miss Betty's nurse who cooked the griddle

cakes for you the morning after the funeral—" she said, and waited with breathless dignity to see how he would take it.

"Oh! Is that so!" He beamed on her kindly. "Yes, yes, I remember those cakes. They were delicious! And what can I do for you? Just sit down. Why, bless me, I don't know but that your coming may be very opportune! Can you tell me anything of Miss Betty?"

Candace pressed her lips together with a knowing smile as much as to say she might tell volumes if it were wise, and she cast a glance at the other brother who was shaking hands now with his visitor and promising to meet him a little later:

"Yon man'll be knowing a bit, too, I'll be thinking," she hazarded nodding toward Reyburn as he left. "He was at the wedding, I'm most sure—!"

The elder McIntyre gave her a quick glance and signaled to his brother to come near:

"This is Miss Stanhope's nurse, the one who cooked breakfast for us at the time of the funeral," he said, and to Candace, "This is Mr. James McIntyre."

Candace fixed him with another of her inquisitive little glances:

"I've some bit papers put by that I thought ye might like to see," she said with a cautious air. "I've kept them fer long because I thought they might be wanted sometime, yet I've never dared bring them to your notice before lest I would be considered meddlin', and indeed I wasn't sure but you had them already. Will you please to look over them papers and see if you've ever seen them before?" She drew forth an envelope from her bag and handed it to them. "It's a bit letter that Mr. Stanhope wrote the day he was dyin' an' then copied and give to me to mail, and his lady took it away, sayin' she would attend to it. What I want to know is, did ye ever get the letter? If ye did it's all right and none of my business further, an' I'll go on my way back home again and think no more about it; but if ye didn't then there it is, an' you ought to see it, that's sure!"

The two men drew eagerly together and studied the trembling lines:

"It's his writing all right," murmured one, under his breath, and the brother nodded gravely:

"You say that this was the original of a letter that was given to you to mail to us?"

Candace nodded.

"It's what he wrote first, and got ink on it, an' then wrote it over. I can't say what changes he made, as I didn't read it, but this he gave to me to burn, and before I gets it burned my lady comes in and takes the letter from me while he was sleepin'; and so I hid the bit papers, thinkin' they might be a help to wee Betty sometime. And oh, can ye tell me anything of my little Lady Betty? Is she safe? Did she come to you for refuge? You needn't be afraid to tell me. I'll never breathe a word—!"

The two brothers exchanged quick glances of warning and the elder man spoke:

"My good woman, we appreciate your coming, and these papers may prove very useful to us. We hope to be able to clear up this matter of Miss Stanhope's disappearance very soon. She did not come to us, however, and she is not here. But if you will step into the room just beyond and wait for a little while we may be able to talk this matter over with you."

Very courteously he ushered the plump, apprehensive little woman into the next room and established her in an easy leather chair with a quantity of magazines and newspapers about her, but she kept her little head cocked anxiously on one side, and watched the door like a dog whose master has gone in and shut the way behind him; and she never sat back in her chair nor relaxed one iota during the whole of the two hours that she had to wait before she was called at last to the inner office where she found the handsome young man whom she remembered seeing at the wedding.

She presently found that Reyburn was as keen as he was handsome, but if she hadn't remembered him at the wedding as a friend of that nice Mrs. Cochrane, she never would have made it as easy as she did for him to find out things from her, for she could be canny herself on occasion if she tried, and she did not trust everybody.

THE mysterious disappearance of Candace from the Stanhope house caused nothing short of a panic. Herbert and his mother held hourly wrangles, and frantically tried one thing and then another. Day after day the responses came in from the advertisements they had caused to be put forth. Everyone was hotfoot for the reward, but so far little of encouragement had been brought out. More and more the young man was fixing his mind on the idea that Candace had something to do with Betty's disappearance, so he was leaving no stone unturned to find the nurse as well as the girl. To this end he insisted on seeing personally and cross-examining every person who came claiming to have a clue to the lost girl.

That morning, at about the same hour when Candace walked into the office of the McIntyre brothers in Boston, James, the butler, much against his dignity, was ushering a curious person into the presence of the son of the house. James showed by every line of his noble figure that he considered this duty beneath his dignity, and that it was only because the occasion was unusual that he tolerated it for a moment, but the man who ambled observantly behind him, stretching his neck to see everything that was to be seen in this part of the great house, that he might tell about it at the firehouse, failed to get the effect. He was wondering why in thunder such rich people as these seemed to be, couldn't afford carpets big enough to cover their whole floors, instead of just having skimpy little bits of pieces dropped around here and there, that made you liable to skid all over the place if you stepped on one of them biasly.

Herbert Hutton lifted his head and watched Abijah Gage slouch into the room. He measured him keenly and remained silent while Abijah opened up. There had been many other applicants for that reward that day, with stories cunningly woven, and facts, substantiated by witnesses, in one case a whole family brought along to swear to the fabrication; but as yet Herbert had not found a promising clue to his missing bride, and the time was going by. In a few days it would be too late, and his undisciplined spirit raged within him. It was not only his bride he wanted, it was her fortune, which was worth any trouble he might take; and every day, every hour, every minute now, it was slipping, slipping, slipping from his eager grasp.

Abijah was a little overawed in the presence of this insolent man of the world, but he felt he had, for almost the first time in his life, truth on his side, and he was strong in the power of it. With a cunning equal to the one that matched him he dealt out his information bit by bit, giving only enough at a time to make his victim sure it was the real thing this time; and then he halted stubbornly and would say no more until that five thousand dollars was signed and sealed over to him. They had a long argument, but in the end Bi won, and was given certain documents which he was satisfied would stand in court. A little later the telephone in Reyburn's office rang sharply, and when Jimmie Ryan responded a voice that he had never heard before asked for Mr. Warren Reyburn.

"He's out of town," Jimmie replied.

"How soon will he be back?" The voice was like a snarl.

"I'm not quite sure. He's called to Boston on business," swelled Jimmie loyally.

An oath ripped over the wire, and Jimmie raged within, and quailed. Was his idol then losing a great case?

"He might be back in a few hours," insinuated Jimmie. "Who shall I say called up if he should have me over long distance?"

"You needn't say anybody! I'll call up again," growled the voice, and the man hung up.

Jimmie sat for a long time in blissful reverie. "He's getting there!" he whispered to himself. "He'll get the big cases yet, and I can keep my first place. I must see Jane tonight and tell her."

Meanwhile, back at Tinsdale improvements had been going on at the Carsons. Bob, always handy with tools, had been putting in a tank over the bathtub. They had one at the house on the hill, only it was run by a windmill. Bob had a friend who was a plumber's son, and from him had obtained some lengths of secondhand water pipe and an old faucet. He had conceived the idea of a tank on the roof, and his first plan had been only a rainwater tank, but gradually as his vision widened he included a force pump in the outfit of desires. He hung around the plumbers until they unearthed an old force pump somewhat out of repair, and for a few days' assisting the plumber Bob acquired it, together with after-hour help to put it into operation. The next object was a tank, which seemed at first to represent the impossible; but the grocer at last offered a suggestion in the shape of several large empty hogsheads which he readily accepted at the price of four Saturday's work in the store.

All Bob's extra time was put into these improvements, and he was as excited every night when it grew dark and he was forced to come to supper because he couldn't see any longer to work, as if he had been building an airship.

The day the hogsheads were marshaled and connected and the force pump sent its first stream into them was a great occasion. The family assembled in the yard, with Elise Hathaway, who had been allowed to come over for a few minutes with Betty. Bob and his plumber friend pumped, and Emily climbed to the attic window, which overlooked the row of hogsheads, ranged so that the water would flow from one to the other, and acted as pilot to the new enterprise. As the first stream from the force pump, which Bob had lavishly painted red, crept its way up the pipes and began to wet the bottom of the first and highest hogshead Emily gave a little squeal of delight and shouted "It's come! It's come! The water's come!" and the family below fairly held their breath with the wonder of it. Not that such a thing could be, but that their own freckled, grinning Bob should have been able to achieve it.

There was an elaborate system of tin conductors which conveyed the waste water from the bathtub out through a hole in the wall of the little laundry bathroom, and distributed it along the garden beds wherever its controller desired to irrigate. Thus the system became practical as well as a luxury. There was also an arrangement of gutter pipes for carrying off any surplus water from the hogsheads, so saving the Carson house from possible inundation at any time of heavy storms.

After the plumbing was finished Bob painted the laundry neatly inside with beautiful white paint and robin's-egg blue for the ceiling, and Betty told him it almost made one think of going swimming in the ocean. Next he began to talk about a shower bath. Betty told him what one was like and he began to spend more days down at the plumber's asking questions and picking up odd bits of pipe, making measurements, and doing queer things to an old colander for experiment's sake. The day that Warren Reyburn came for the first time Bob had the shower partly finished and ready to erect, and the next day saw it complete with a rod for the rubber curtain that Betty had promised to make for him. He and she were planning how they would make further improvements on the house before Jane and Nellie should come home for their summer vacation week. Betty had thoroughly entered into the life of the little household now, and was a part of it. She saved her own small wages, and grudged all she had to spend for necessary clothes, that she might contribute further to the comfort and beauty of the general home.

After Warren Reyburn's visit the last barrier between Betty and Ma seemed to be broken down. As soon as she had closed the door she flew into the other room and flung her arms around Ma's neck, bursting into soft weeping on her motherly shoulder. Ma had done a rapid turning act when she heard her coming, for in truth she had been peeping behind the green window shade to watch the handsome stranger go down the street, but she would have dropped the iron on her foot and pretended to be picking it up rather than let Betty suspect her interest in the visitor.

"Oh, Mother," she murmured in Mrs. Carson's willing ear, "I have been so frightened—"

"I know, dearie!" soothed the mother, quite as if she had been her own. "I know!"

"But he was very kind," she said lifting her head with

an April effect of tears. "He's going to try to fix things for me so that I don't need ever to be afraid of anyone making trouble for me anymore. You see, I sort of ran away. There was somebody I was afraid of who troubled me a great deal."

"Yes, dearie, I thought as much," said Ma. "Jane kind of gave me to understand there was something like that. I'm real glad there's somebody goin' to look into your affairs an' fix things right for you. I knew you was restless an' worried. Now it'll get all straightened out. He's got a nice face. I trusted him first off. He's a church member, an' that's somethin'. They ain't all spiritual, but they're mostly clean an' just an' kindly, when they're anythin' at all but just plain hypocrites, which, thank the Lord, there ain't so many as some would have us believe. Now wash your face, dearie, an' run back to your place so you can come home early, for we're goin' to have the old hen with dumplin's for supper to celebrate."

That was one charming thing about that household: They celebrated every blessed little trifle that came into their lives, so that living with them was like a procession of beautiful thanksgivings.

It was while Betty was eating the gala "hen," delicious in its festive gravy and dumplings, that she looked off across the little dining room to the dark window with its twinkling village lights in the distance and thought of the stranger. A dark fear flashed across her sweet face and sparkled in the depths of her eyes for just an instant. Was it perhaps the distant bay of the hounds on her trail, coming nearer every moment? Then she remembered the heavenly Father and her newfound faith, and turned back to the cheery little room and the children's pleasant clatter, resolved to forget the fear and to trust all to Him who cared for her. Perhaps He had sent the pleasant stranger, and the thought brought a quiet little smile to settle about her lips. She laughed with Bob and Emily at how they had got wet with a sudden unexpected shower from the new bath while they were arranging the curtain on the rod, and Emily had turned the faucet on without knowing it. The patient-eyed mother watched them all and was satisfied.

How good it is that we cannot hear all the noises of the earth at the same time, nor know of every danger that lurks near as we are passing by! We grumble a great deal that God does not send us as much as we think He might, but we give scarce a thought to our escape from the many perils, lying close as our very breath, of which we never even dream.

At that moment, as they sat quietly eating their happy meal, a deadly particular peril was headed straight for Tinsdale.

Abijah Gage and Herbert Hutton boarded the evening train for Tinsdale together and entered the sleeper. Abijah shuffled behind, carrying the bags, a most extraordinary and humiliating position for him. He had never been known to carry anything, not even himself if he could help it, since the day his mother died and ceased to force him to carry in wood and water for her at the end of a hickory switch. He glanced uneasily round with a slight cackle of dismay as he arrived in the unaccustomed plush surroundings and tried to find some place to dump his load. But the well-groomed Herbert strode down the long aisle unnoticing and took possession of the section he had secured as if he owned the road.

"You can sit there!" he ordered Bi with a condescending motion, dropping into his own seat and opening a newspaper.

Bi sat down on the edge of the seat, and held on to the arm in a gingerly way as if he were afraid to trust himself to anything so different. He looked furtively up and down the car, eyed the porter, who ignored him contemptuously and finally came back and demanded his sleeper ticked with a lordliness that Bi did not feel he could take. But somehow the ticket got tangled in his pocket, and Bi had a hard time finding it, which deepened his indignation at the porter.

"I ain't takin' no sass from no one. My seat's paid fer all right," he said distinctly for the enlightenment of the other passengers, and Herbert Hutton reached out a discreet arm and dropped something in the porter's hand which sent him on his way and left Bi snorting audibly after him.

"You'd better shut up!" growled the dictator to Bi. "We don't want to be conspicuous, you know. If you can't hold your tongue and act as if you had ever traveled before, I'll get off this train at the next station and you can whistle for your reward. Do you understand?"

Bi dropped his toothless lower jaw a trifle and his little eyes grew narrow. This was no way to manage affable Bi. He loved a good visit, and he had counted on one all the way to Tinsdale. He had no idea of sitting silent.

"I understand," he drawled, "an' I'll be gormed ef I'll agree. I ain't told you yet where we get off, an' I don't have to ef I don't wantta. Ef you can't treat me like a gen'l'man you know where you can get off, an' I ain't havin' to state it."

Herbert Hutton drew his arrogant brows in a frown of annoyance, and whirled around to placate his guide:

"Now see here, you old popinjay, what's got into you?"

"No, sir, I ain't nobody's papa," babbled Bi, seeing he had scored a point. "I have enough to do to support myself without any family."

"That's all right, have it your own way, only shut up

or we'll have somebody listening. Have a cigar. Take two. But you can't smoke 'em in here, you'll have to go to the smoking room. Wait! I'll see if we can get the drawing room."

The porter appeared and the change was effected, to the great disappointment of Bi, who kept continually poking his head out to get a glimpse of the fine ladies. He would much have preferred staying out in the main car and getting acquainted with people. His cunning had departed with the need. He had put things in the hands of this surly companion, and now he meant to have a good time and something to tell the gang about when he got home.

About midnight the train drew into a station and Herbert Hutton roused himself and looked out of the window. Bi, whose cunning had returned, followed his example. Suddenly he leaned forward excitedly and tapped the glass with a long finger:

"That's him! That's the guy," he whispered excitedly as another train drew in and passengers began to hurry down the platform and across to the waiting sleeper.

"Are you sure?"

"Sartin!"

"You mean the one with the coat over his arm, and the two men behind?" He stopped short with an exclamation.

Bi looked up cunningly. Now what was up? He saw a thundercloud on the face of his companion.

With embellishments Herbert Hutton asked if Bi had ever seen the two tall gray-haired men who were walking with their prey.

Bi narrowed his eyes and denied any knowledge, but perceived there were more sides than two to the enigma. Now, what could he figure out of those two guys? Were there more rewards to be offered? If so, he was a candidate. He wondered what chance there was of getting away from H. H. and sauntering through the train. He found, however, a sudden willingness on the part of his companion to vanish and let him do the scout work for the rest of the night.

With a sense of being on a vacation and a chance at catching big fish Bi swung out through the train. Bumping down among the now-curtained berths, adjusting his long form to the motion of the express, lurching to right and to left as they went round a curve, falling over an occasional pair of shoes and bringing down lofty reproaches from the sleepy porter, he penetrated to the day coaches and at last located his quarry.

They were sitting in a double seat, the younger man facing the two older ones, and had evidently been unable to get sleepers. Bi hung around the water cooler at the far end of the car until he had laid out his plans; then he sauntered up to the vacant seat behind the three men and dropped noiselessly into its depths, drawing his hat down well over his face, and apparently falling into instant slumber, with a fair sample of Tinsdale snoring brought in at moderate distances.

The conversation was earnest, in well-modulated voices, and hard to follow connectedly, for the men knew how to talk without seeming to the outside world to be saying anything intelligible. Occasionally a sentence would come out clear-cut in an interval of the rhythm of the train, but for the most part Bi could make little or nothing of it.

"In all the years we've been trustees of that estate we haven't seen her but twice," said one of the older men; "once at her father's second marriage, and again at his funeral. Then we only saw her at a distance. Her stepmother said she was too grief-stricken to speak with anyone, and it was by the utmost effort she could be present at the service."

"She looked very frail and young," said the other old man; "and her hair—I remember her hair!"

Bi changed his position cautiously and tried to peer over the back seat, but the voices were crowded together now, and the younger man was talking earnestly. He could not catch a syllable. "Trustees!" That word stayed with him. "Estate" was another promising one, and the fact that her hair had been remembered. He nodded his old head sagaciously, and later when the three men settled back in their seats more comfortably with their eyes closed he slid back to the water cooler and so on through the sleeper to the drawing room.

Hutton was sleeping the sleep of the unjust, which meant that he woke at the slightest breath, and Bi's breath was something to wake a heavier sleeper. So they sat and planned as the train rushed on through the night. Now and again Bi took a pilgrimage up to the day coach and back to report the three travelers still asleep.

About six o'clock in the morning the train slowed down, and finally came to a thrashing halt, waking the sleepers uncomfortably and making them conscious of crunching feet in the cinders outside, and consulting voices of trainmen busy with a hammer underneath the car somewhere. Then they drowsed off to sleep again and the voices and hammering blended comfortably into their dreams.

The passengers in the day coach roused, looked at their watches, stretched their cramped limbs, squinted out to see if anything serious was the matter, and settled into a new position to sleep once more.

Bi, stretched for the nonce upon the long couch of the drawing room while his superior occupied the more comfortable berth, roused to instant action, slipped out to the platform and took his bearings. He had lived in that part of the country all his life and he knew where they ought to be by that time. Yes, there was the old sawmill down by Hague's Crossing, and the steeple over by the soft maple grove just beyond Fox Glove. It would not be a long walk, and they had a garage at Fox Glove!

He sauntered along the cinder path; discovered that the trouble with the engine was somewhat serious, requiring to wait for help, took a glimpse into the day coach ahead to assure himself that the three men were still asleep, and sauntered back to the drawing room.

His entrance roused the sleeper, who was on the alert instantly.

"Say, we got a hot box an' a broken engyne!" Bi announced. "It'll take us some time. We ain't far from Fox Glove. We could santer over an' git a car an' beat 'em to it!"

"We could?" said Hutton. "You sure? No chances, mind you!"

"Do it easy. Those guys are asleep. They won't get to the junction 'fore ten o'clock, mebbe later, an' they can't possibly get to our place 'fore 'leven."

"Lead the way!" ordered Hutton, cramming himself into his coat and hat.

"Better slide down on the other side," whispered Bi as they reached the platform. "We kin go back round the train an' nobody'll notice."

As if they had only come out to see what was the matter they idled along the length of the train around out of sight, slid down the bank, took a short cut across a meadow to a road, and were soon well on their way to Fox Glove in the early cool of the spring morning, a strangely mated couple bent on mischief.

Back on the cinder track the express waited, dreamily indifferent, with a flagman ahead and behind to guard its safety, and while men slept the enemy took wings and flew down the white morning road to Tinsdale, but no one ran ahead with a little red flag to the gray cottage where slept Betty, to warn her, though perchance an angel with a flaming sword stood invisibly to guard the way.

BOB had just finished feeding the chickens when the automobile drew up at the door, and he hurried around the house to see who it might be. He was rather looking for the return of that nice lawyer again. He felt the family expected him sometime soon. Perhaps he would be to breakfast and Mother would want some fresh eggs.

They had dropped Bi at the edge of the village and there were only Hutton and the driver who had brought them. Bi had no mind to get mixed up in this affair too openly. He valued his standing in his hometown, and did not wish to lose it. He had an instinct that what he was doing might make him unpopular if it became known. Besides, he had another ax to grind.

Bob did not like the looks of the strange dark man who got out of the car and came into the yard with the air of a thrashing machine bolting into whatever came in his way. He stood sturdily and waited until he was asked who lived there, and admitted with a stingy "yes" that it was Mrs. Carson's house. A thundering knock on the front door followed, and the other man in the car got out and came into the yard behind the first.

"Well, you needn't take the door down," snapped Bob, and scuttled around the house to warn his mother, aware that he had been rude, and glad of it.

It was Betty who came to the door, for Ma was frying bacon and eggs for breakfast, and Bob hadn't been quite soon enough. She started back with a scream, and eluding the hand that reached for her arm, fairly flew back to the kitchen, taking refuge behind Mrs. Carson, with her eyes wild with fear and her hand on her heart, while Hutton strode after her.

Mrs. Carson wheeled around with her knife in her hand and faced him:

"What do you mean by coming into my house this way, I'd like to know?" she demanded angrily, putting her arm around Betty.

"I beg your pardon," said Hutton, a poor apology for courtesy slipping into his manner. "I don't suppose you know it, but that is my wife you are harboring there, and she ran away from home several months ago! I have just discovered her whereabouts and have come to take her away!"

Ma straightened up with the air of a queen and a judge, while Betty stifled a scream and in a small voice full of terror cried: "It isn't true, Mrs. Carson, it isn't true! Oh, *Mother,* don't let him take me!"

Mrs. Carson pushed Betty behind her, the knife still in her other hand, and answered with dignity:

"You've made a big mistake, Mr. Herbert Hutton; this isn't your wife at all. I know all about you."

Hutton put on a look of instant suavity.

"Oh, of course, madam, she has told you that, but I'm sorry to have to tell you that she is not in her right mind. She made her escape from the mental hospital."

"Oh, rats!" shouted Bob, and vanished out the kitchen door, slamming it behind him.

Emily, frightened and white, stood just outside, and he nearly knocked her over in his flight. He pulled her along with him, whispering in her ear excitedly:

"You beat it down to the fire gong and hit it for all you're worth! Quick!"

Emily gave him one frightened look and sprang to action. Her little feet sped down the path to the lot where hung the big fire gong, like two wild rabbits running for their lives, and in a moment more the loud whang of alarm rang through the little town, arousing the "gang" and greatly disconcerting Bi, who was craning his neck at the station and watching the fast-growing speck down the railroad track. That sure was the train coming already. How had they made it so soon?

But Bob was on his stomach in the road scuttling the ship that was to have carried away the princess. The chauffeur was fully occupied in the house, for he had been ordered to follow and be ready to assist in carrying away an insane person, and he had no thought for his car at present. It was an ugly job, and one that he didn't like, but he was getting big pay, and such things had to be done.

Bob's knife was sharp. He always kept it in good condition. It did many of the chores about the house, and was cunning in its skill. It cut beautiful long punctures in the four tires, until there was no chance at all of the car's going on its way for some time to come. Then he squirmed his way out on the opposite side from the house, slid along by the fence to the side door, around to the back like a flash and without an instant's hesitation hauled up his elaborate system of drainage. He stuck the longest conductor pipe through the open window of the old laundry, clutched at the sill and swung inside, drawing the pipe in after him.

The altercation in the kitchen had reached white heat.

Hutton's suavity was fast disappearing behind a loud angry tone. He had about sized up Ma and decided to use force.

It was a tense moment when Bob, his hasty arrangements made, silently swung open the laundry door in full range of the uninvited guests and waited for the psychological moment. Mrs. Carson had dropped her knife and seized the smoking hot frying pan of bacon as a weapon. She was cool and collected, but one could see in her eyes the little devil of battle that sometimes sat in Bob's eyes as she swung the frying pan back for a blow. Suddenly out flashed a cold steel eye, menacing, unanswerable, looking straight into her own.

At that instant, unannounced and unobserved, through the laundry door lumbered a long ugly tin conductor pipe, and the deluge began. Straight into the eyes of the would-be husband it gushed, battering swashingly down on the cocked revolver, sending it harmlessly to the floor, where it added to the confusion by going off with a loud report, and sending the chauffeur to the shelter of the parlor. Bob never knew how near he came to killing someone by his nasty service, and Ma never had the heart to suggest it. Instead she acted promptly and secured the weapon before the enemy had time to recover from the shock.

Bob, in the laundry, standing on a chair mounted on a board across the bathtub, sturdily held his wobbling conductor pipe and aimed it straight to the mark. Of course he knew that even a well-filled phalanx of hogsheads could not hold the enemy forever, but he was counting on the fire company to arrive in time to save the day.

Gasping, clawing the air, ducking, diving here and there to escape the stream, Herbert Hutton presented a spectacle most amusing and satisfying to Bob's boy mind.

"Beat it, Lizzie, beat it! Beat it!" he shouted above the noise of the pouring waters. But Betty, white with horror, seemed to have frozen to the spot. She could not have moved if she had tried, and her brain refused to order her to try. She felt as if the end of everything had come and she were paralyzed.

Down the street with dash and flourish, licking up excitement like a good meal, dashed the gang, the fire chief ostentatiously arraying himself in rubber coat and helmet as he stood on the side of the engine, while the hysterical little engine bell banged away, blending with the sound of the bell of the incoming train at the station. Bi, with his mouth stretched wide, and one foot holding him for the train while the other urged toward the fire and excitement, vibrated on the platform, a wild figure of uncertainty. Where duty and inclination both called, cupidity still had the upper hand.

For once Bi did not have to act a part as he stood watching the three travelers descend from the train. The excitement in his face was real and his gestures were quite natural, even the ones made by his one and only long waving toplock of gray hair that escaped all bounds as his hat blew off with the suction of the train. Bi rushed up to the three men wildly:

"Say, was you goin' down to Carson's house after that Hope girl?" he demanded loudly.

The three men surveyed him coldly, and the young one gave him a decided shove:

"That will do, my friend," he said firmly. "We don't need any of your assistance."

"But I got a line on this thing you'll want to know," he insisted, hurrying alongside. "There's a guy down there in a car goin' to take her away. He ain't been gone long, but you won't find her 'thout my help. He's goin' to take her to a insane institution. I let on I was helpin' him an' I found out all about it."

"What's all this?" said Reyburn, wheeling about and fixing the old fellow with a muscular young shake that made his toothless jaws chatter. "How long ago did he go? What kind of a looking man was he?"

"Lemme go!" whined Bi, playing to make time, one cunning eye down the road. "I ain't as young as I used to be, an' I can't stand gettin' excited. I got a rig here a purpose, an' I'll take you all right down, an' then ef he's gone, an I s'pose he must be, 'cause your train was late, why, we'll foller."

"Well, quick, then!" said Reyburn, climbing into the shackley spring wagon that Bi indicated, the only vehicle in view. The two trustees climbed stiffly and uncertainly into the backseat as if they felt they were risking their lives, and Bi lumbered rheumatically into the driver's place and took up the lines. It appeared that the only living thing in Tinsdale that wasn't awake and keen to go to the fire was that horse, and Bi had to do quite a little urging with the stump of an old whip. So, reluctantly, they joined the procession toward the Carson house.

As the stream from the hogshead gurgled smaller, and the victim writhed out of its reach and began to get his bearings, suddenly the outside kitchen door burst open and a crew of rubber-coated citizens sprang in, preceded by a generous stream of chemicals which an ardent young member of the company set free indiscriminately in his excitement. It struck the right man squarely in the middle and sent him sprawling on the floor.

Bob dropped the conductor pipe in exhausted relief and flew to the scene of action. It had been fearful to be held from more active service so long. Emily, outside, could be seen dancing up and down excitedly and directing the procession, with frightened shouts, "In there! In the kitchen! Quick!" as the neighbors and townsmen crowded in and filled the little kitchen demanding to know where the fire was.

Mrs. Carson with dignity stepped forward to explain:

"There ain't any fire, friends, an' I don't know how you all come to get here, but I reckon the Lord sent you. You couldn't a-come at a better moment. We certainly was in some trouble, an' I'll be obliged to you all if you'll just fasten that man up so't he can't do any more harm. He came walkin' in here tryin' to take away a member of my family by force, an' he pointed this at me!"

She lifted the incriminating weapon high where they could all see.

Herbert Hutton, struggling to his feet in the crowd, began to understand that this was no place for him, and looked about for an exit, but none presented itself. The chauffeur had vanished and was trying to make out what had happened to his car.

Hutton, brought to bay, turned on the crowd like a snarling animal, although the effect was slightly spoiled by his drabbled appearance, and roared out insolently:

"The woman doesn't know what she's talking about, men; she's only frightened. I came here after my wife, and I intend to take her away with me! She escaped from a hospital some time ago, and we've been looking for her ever since. This woman is doing a very foolish and useless thing in resisting me, for the law can take hold of her, of course."

The crowd wavered and looked uncertainly at Mrs. Carson and at Betty cowering horrified behind her, and Hutton saw his advantage:

"Men," he went on, "there is one of your own townsmen who knows me and can vouch for me. A Mr. Gage. Abijah Gage. If you will just look him up—he was down at the station a few minutes ago. He knows that all I am saying is true!"

A low sound like a rumble went over the little audience and they seemed to bunch together and look at one another while some kind of an understanding traveled from eye to eye. An articulate syllable, "Bi!" breathed in astonishment, and then again "Bi!" in contempt. Public opinion, like a panther crouching, was forming itself ready to spring, when suddenly a new presence was felt in the room. Three strangers had appeared and somehow quietly gotten into the doorway. Behind them, stretching his neck and unable to be cautious any longer, appeared Bi's slouching form. Crouching public opinion caught sight of him and showed its teeth, but was diverted by the strangers.

Then suddenly, from the corner behind Ma, slipped Betty with outstretched hands, like a lost thing flying to its refuge, straight to the side of the handsome young stranger.

He put out his hands and drew her to his side with a protecting motion, and she whispered:

"Tell them, please; oh, make them understand."

Then Reyburn, with her hand still protectingly in his, spoke:

"What that man has just said is a lie!"

Hutton looked up, went deadly white and reeled as he saw the two elderly men.

The crowd drew a united breath and stood straighter, looking relieved. Bi blanched, but did not budge. Whatever happened he was in with both crowds. Reyburn continued:

"I carry papers in my pocket which give authority to arrest him. If the sheriff is present will he please take charge of him. His name is Herbert Hutton, and he is charged with trying to make this lady marry him under false pretenses in order to get control of her property. She is not his wife, for she escaped before the ceremony was performed. I know, for I was present. These two gentlemen with me are the trustees of her estate."

Estate!

The neighbors looked at Betty respectfully.

Bi dropped his jaw perceptibly and tried to figure out how that would affect him. The sheriff stepped forward to magnify his office, and the silence was impressive, almost reverent. In the midst of it broke Bob's practical suggestion:

"Shut him in the coal shed. It's got a padlock an' is good an' strong. He can't kick it down."

Then the law began to take its course, the fire gang stepped out, and Mrs. Carson set to work to clean up. In the midst of it all Reyburn looked down at Betty, and Betty looked up at Reyburn, and they discovered in some happy confusion that they still had hold of hands. They tried to cover their embarrassment by laughing, but something had been established between them that neither could forget.

THE days that followed were full of bliss and peace to Betty. With Hutton safely confined in the distant city, and a comfortable sum of her accumulated allowance in the Tinsdale bank, with a thorough understanding between herself and her trustees and the knowledge that her estate was large enough to do almost anything in reason that she wished to do with it, and would be hers in three weeks, life began to take on a different look to the poor storm-tossed child. The days in the Carson home were all Thanksgivings now, and every member of the family was as excited and happy as every other member. There were arguments long and earnest between Betty and her benefactor as to how much she might in reason be allowed to do for the family now that she had plenty of money, but in the end Betty won out, declaring that she had wished herself on this family in her distress, and they took her as a man does when he marries, for better for worse. Now that the worse had passed by she was theirs for the better, and she intended to exercise the privilege of a daughter of the house for the rest of her natural life.

Bi Gage was worried. He was still trying to get something out of the estate for his part in the exercises, and he vibrated between Tinsdale and Warren Reyburn's office working up his case. The five-thousand-dollar reward was as yet unpaid, and the papers he held didn't seem to impress the functionaries nearly so much as he had expected. It began to look as though Bi had missed his chances in life once more, and when he took his old seat in the firehouse and smoked, he said very little. Popular opinion was still crouching with her eye in his direction and it behooved him to walk cautiously and do nothing to offend. So while he smoked he cogitated in his cunning little brain, and hatched out a plan by which he might get in with the heiress later, perhaps, when things had quieted down a little and she had her money.

Betty received a pitiful letter from her stepmother, trying to explain away her part in the affair and professing to be so relieved at the news that Betty was still alive and well that she cared nothing about anything else, not even the fact that poor dear Herbert was landed in jail, or that the fortune which she had schemed so long to keep in her own power was wrested from her so ignominiously. She begged Betty to come back to their home and "be happy again together."

But Betty was so happy where she was that she could afford to be generous and try to forget her wrongs. She wrote a decent little note gently but firmly declining to come "home" ever again, making it quite plain that she was no longer deceived by honeyed phrases, and closing with a request that if in future any communication might be necessary it should be made through her lawyer, Mr. Warren Reyburn.

This same Warren Reyburn had returned to his city office in a very much exalted state of mind. He could not get away from that little hand of Betty's that had been laid so tremblingly and confidingly in his; and yet how could he, a poverty-stricken lawyer with absolutely no prospects at all, ever dare to think of her, a lady of vast estates. Still, there was some comfort in the fact that he had still some business to transact for her, and would have to return to Tinsdale again. He might at least see her once more. So he solaced himself on his return trip, feeling that he had done some good work, and that he would have a pleasant report to give to Jane Carson when he called upon her, as he meant to do the next day.

He arrived at home to find James Ryan in a great state of excitement. A pile of mail had arrived, and he had memorized the return addresses on the outside of all the envelopes. One was from a big corporation, and another bore a name widely spoken of in the circles of the world of finance. Jimmie, in close council with Jane Carson, had decided that it must be from that person who called up twice on the phone and swore such terrible oaths when he found that Reyburn was away.

Jimmie hovered nervously about, putting things to rights, while Reyburn read his mail. He had come to the smallest envelope of all, a plain government envelope now, and nothing had developed. Jimmie saw his first place fast slipping away from him and his heart grew heavy with fear. Perhaps after all nothing good had turned up yet.

Suddenly Reyburn sprang up and came toward him with an open letter, holding out his hand in a joyous greeting:

"Read that, Ryan! We're made at last, and I shan't have to let you go after all!"

Ryan read, the letters dancing before his delighted eyes, every one wearing an orange blossom on its brow. It was from an old established and influential firm, asking

Reyburn to take full charge of all their law business, and saying they had been referred to him by two old friends in Boston, who by the way were Betty's two trustees.

"Come on, Ryan, come out to lunch with me! We've got to celebrate," said Reyburn. "I have a hunch somehow that you have been the one that brought me this good luck. You and a Miss Jane Carson. You both share alike, I guess, but you were the first with your five-thousand-dollar reward story."

"Jane Carson!" said Jimmie mystified. "Why, *she's* my *girl!*"

"Your girl?" said Reyburn, a queer look coming in his eyes. "You don't say! Well, you're in some luck, boy, with a girl like that! And, by the way, next time you see her, ask her to show you her wedding dress!"

And not another word would Reyburn tell him, though he recurred frequently to the subject during the very excellent lunch which they had together in friendly companionship.

They spent the afternoon composing the brief and comprehensive letter in response to the momentous one of the morning, and in the evening together they sought out Jane Carson, Reyburn staying only long enough to outline the ending of the Elizabeth Stanhope story, while Jimmie remained to hear the beginning, and get a glimpse of the wedding gown, which Reyburn assured Jane he was sure she need never return. He said he thought if the owner of it was married ever in the future she would be likely to want a gown that had no unpleasant associations.

Great excitement prevailed in Tinsdale as the weeks went by. Betty had bought the lots either side of the Carson house, and wonderful improvements were in progress. A windmill was being erected and water pipes laid scientifically. Workmen arrived, some of them from the village, some from the city. Extensive excavations went on about the old house, and stone arrived. It began to be whispered about that "Miss Stanhope," as Betty was now called, was going to build the house all over and all of stone.

The work went forward rapidly as work can go when there is money enough behind it, and the family, living in the little old part of the house, and still using the faithful tin bathtub and shower of Bob's manufacture, now looked forward to real bathrooms on the bedroom floor, with tiled floors and porcelain fittings. Large windows cropped out on the new walls that were going up, a wide stone chimney and porches. A charming little stone affair in the back yard that went up so quietly it was hardly noticed until it was done suddenly became the home of a big gray car that arrived in town one morning. Betty gave up her position at the Hathaways' so that she could have more time to superintend the work and see that it was just as she wanted it, and she and Bob spent hours going over the plans together, he making many wise suggestions. Mrs. Hathaway called her "Miss Stanhope" with elaborate ceremony, and made Elise kiss her whenever she met her.

Betty went to a nearby town and bought some pretty clothes, and a lot of things for Ma and Emily and Bob. A beautiful new piano came by express and took the place of Mrs. Barlow's tinpanny one.

Then Betty went up to the city and bought more things, furniture and silver and curtains and rugs, and brought Jane back with her to take a rest and see the little old house once more before it became the big new house, and stay until she was ready to be married; for Betty was determined to have the house ready for Jane's wedding.

When all the new beautiful things began to arrive

Betty told Ma that she had taken her in when she was poor and homeless and absolutely penniless, and now all these things were her reward, and Betty couldn't do enough ever to thank her for what she had done for her. They had offered a five-thousand-dollar reward for news of her, and Ma had done more than ten thousand and thousands of thousands of dollars' worth of holding back news about her, and she was never going to get done giving her her reward.

Of course Betty brought Nellie home, too, and established her in a lovely new room just fit for a young girl, and began to pet her and fix her up with pretty things as any loving sister might do if she had money of her own.

All this time Reyburn had much business to transact in Tinsdale, for Betty had asked him to look after all the little details about the building for her, and he had to come down every weekend and look things over to see that she was not being cheated. And once he brought Jimmie down with him for Ma to look over and approve and they had a wonderful time with the two best hens in the hencoop for dinner. Ryan incidentally gave his approval to Betty.

During these visits Reyburn was making great strides in the wisdom and the knowledge of the love of God. One could not be in that family over Sunday and not feel the atmosphere of a Christian home. Even Jimmie felt it and said he liked it; that he wanted his home to be that way when he had one. He went obediently to church with Jane, and marveled at the way social classes were getting all muddled up in his world.

The Christmas time was coming on when the house finally got itself completed and was ready for living, and with holly and mistletoe and laurel they made it gay for the wedding. Betty spent several days with Jane in New York picking out Jane's "trooso" things, and then a few more days doing some shopping of her own, and at last the wedding day arrived.

Nobody thought it queer, though Jimmie felt just the least bit shy when the two trustees of Betty's estate arrived the night before from Boston and incorporated themselves into the wedding party. Ma seemed to think it was all right, so nobody said anything about it.

But after the ceremony when Jane and Jimmie were happily married, Jane looking very young and pretty indeed in Betty's old wedding gown, veil and slippers and all, and standing under the holly bell in the laurel arch to be congratulated just as it had been arranged, there suddenly came a hush over everybody. Jane noticed for the first time that Betty was not anywhere in the room. Then everybody's eyes went to the wide staircase, and here came Betty trailing down the stairs on the arm of Reyburn, wearing still the little white organdie she had worn a few minutes before as a bridesmaid, only she had thrown aside the rose-colored sash and put over her brow a simple tulle veil, and her arms were full of little pink rosebuds and lilies of the valley.

Up they walked in front of the minister just where the others had stood, and were married with the same sweet simple service, and everybody was so surprised and delighted and excited and breathless that Bob simply couldn't stand it. He slipped into the little music room where the piano had been installed, turning a handspring on the floor, and then sat down and played chopsticks on the piano with all the pedals on, till Ma had to send Emily in to stop him.

About the Author

Grace Livingston Hill is well known as one of the most prolific writers of romantic fiction. Her personal life was fraught with joys and sorrows not unlike those experienced by many of her fictional heroines.

Born in Wellsville, New York, Grace nearly died during the first hours of life. But her loving parents and friends turned to God in prayer. She survived miraculously, thus her thankful father named her Grace.

Grace was always close to her father, a Presbyterian minister, and her mother, a published writer. It was from them that she learned the art of storytelling. When Grace was twelve, a close aunt surprised her with a hardbound, illustrated copy of one of Grace's stories. This was the beginning of Grace's journey into being a published author.

In 1892 Grace married Fred Hill, a young minister, and they soon had two lovely young daughters. Then came 1901, a difficult year for Grace—the year when, within months of each other, both her father and husband died. Suddenly Grace had to find a new place to live (her home was owned by the church where her husband had been pastor). It was a struggle for Grace to raise her young daughters alone, but through everything she kept writing. In 1902 she produced *The Angel of His Presence, The Story of a Whim,* and *An Unwilling Guest*. In 1903 her two books *According to the Pattern* and *Because of Stephen* were published.

It wasn't long before Grace was a well-known author, but she wanted to go beyond just entertaining her readers. She soon included the message of God's salvation through Jesus Christ in each of her books. For Grace, the most important thing she did was not write books but share the message of salvation, a message she felt God wanted her to share through the abilities he had given her.

In all, Grace Livingston Hill wrote more than one hundred books, all of which have sold thousands of copies and have touched the lives of readers around the world with their message of "enduring love" and the true way to lasting happiness: a relationship with God through his Son, Jesus Christ.

In an interview shortly before her death, Grace's devotion to her Lord still shone clear. She commented that whatever she had accomplished had been God's doing. She was only his servant, one who had tried to follow his teaching in all her thoughts and writing.

THE BELOVED STRANGER

Tyndale House books by Grace Livingston Hill.
Check with your area bookstore for these best-sellers.

COLLECTOR'S CHOICE SERIES

1 *The Christmas Bride*
2 *In Tune with Wedding Bells*
3 *Partners*
4 *The Strange Proposal*

LIVING BOOKS®

1 *Where Two Ways Met*
2 *Bright Arrows*
3 *A Girl To Come Home To*
4 *Amorelle*
5 *Kerry*
6 *All Through the Night*
7 *The Best Man*
8 *Ariel Custer*
9 *The Girl of the Woods*
10 *Crimson Roses*
11 *More Than Conqueror*
12 *Head of the House*
14 *Stranger within the Gates*
15 *Marigold*
16 *Rainbow Cottage*
17 *Maris*
18 *Brentwood*
19 *Daphne Deane*
20 *The Substitute Guest*
21 *The War Romance of the Salvation Army*
22 *Rose Galbraith*
23 *Time of the Singing of Birds*
24 *By Way of the Silverthorns*
25 *Sunrise*
26 *The Seventh Hour*
27 *April Gold*
28 *White Orchids*
29 *Homing*
30 *Matched Pearls*
32 *Coming Through the Rye*
33 *Happiness Hill*
34 *The Patch of Blue*
36 *Patricia*
37 *Silver Wings*
38 *Spice Box*
39 *The Search*
40 *The Tryst*
41 *Blue Ruin*
42 *A New Name*
43 *Dawn of the Morning*
44 *The Beloved Stranger*
60 *Miranda*
61 *Mystery Flowers*
63 *The Man of the Desert*
64 *Miss Lavinia's Call*
77 *The Ransom*
78 *Found Treasure*
79 *The Big Blue Soldier*
80 *The Challengers*
81 *Duskin*
82 *The White Flower*
83 *Marcia Schuyler*
84 *Cloudy Jewel*
85 *Crimson Mountain*
86 *The Mystery of Mary*
87 *Out of the Storm*
88 *Phoebe Deane*
89 *Re-Creations*
90 *Sound of the Trumpet*
91 *A Voice in the Wilderness*
92 *The Honeymoon House*
93 *Katharine's Yesterday*

CLASSICS SERIES

1 *Crimson Roses*
2 *The Enchanted Barn*
3 *Happiness Hill*
4 *Patricia*
5 *Silver Wings*

THE BELOVED STRANGER

LIVING BOOKS®
Tyndale House Publishers, Inc.
Wheaton, Illinois

This Tyndale House book
by Grace Livingston Hill
contains the complete text
of the original hardcover edition.
NOT ONE WORD
HAS BEEN OMITTED.

Printing History
J.B. Lippincott edition published 1933
Tyndale House edition/1992

3 in 1 ISBN 1-56865-735-8

Printed in the United States of America

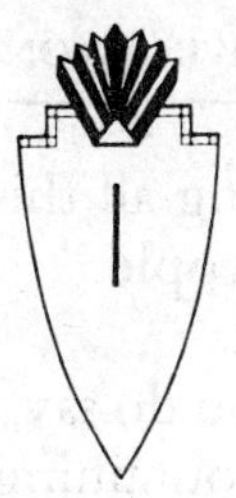

SHERRILL stood before the long mirror and surveyed herself critically in her bridal array.

Rich creamy satin shimmering, sheathing her slender self, drifting down in luscious waves across the old Chinese blue of the priceless rug on which she stood! Misty white veil like a cloud about her shoulders, caught by the frosty cap of rare lace about her sweet forehead, clasped by the wreath of orange blossoms in their thick green and white perfection, flowers born to nestle in soft mists of tulle and deepen the whiteness, the only flower utterly at home with rich old lace.

Sherrill stooped to the marble shelf beneath the tall mirror and picked up a hand glass turning herself this way and that to get a glimpse on every side. There seemed to be no possible fault to be found anywhere. The whole costume was a work of art.

"It's lovely, isn't it, Gemmie?" she said brightly to the elderly woman who had served her aunt for thirty years as maid. "Now, hand me the bouquet. I want to see how it all looks together. It isn't fair not to be able to get the effect one's self after taking all this trouble to make it a pleasant sight for other people."

The old servant smiled.

"What quaint things you do say, Miss Sherry!" she said as she untied the box containing the bridal bouquet. "But don't you think maybe you should leave the flowers in the box till you get to the church? They might get a bit crushed."

"No, Gemmie, I'll be very careful. I want to see how pretty they look with the dress and everything. Aren't they lovely?"

She took the great sheaf of roses gracefully on one arm and posed, laughing brightly into the mirror, the tip of one silver slipper advancing beneath the ivory satin, her eyes like two stars, her lips in the curves of a lovely mischievous child; then advancing the other silver shod foot she hummed a bar of the wedding march.

"Now, am I quite all right, Gemmie?" she asked again.

"You are the prettiest bride I ever set eyes on," said the woman looking at the sweet fair girl wistfully. "Ef I'd had a daughter I could have asked no better for her than that she should look like you in her wedding dress," and Gemmie wiped a furtive tear from one corner of her eye over the thought of the daughter she never had had.

"There, there, Gemmie, don't go to getting sentimental!" cried Sherrill with a quick little catch in her own breath, and a wistful sudden longing in her breast for the mother she never had known. "Now, I'm quite all right, Gemmie, and you're to run right down and get Stanley to take you over to the church. I want you to be sure and get the seat I picked out for you, where you can see everything every minute. I'm depending on you, you know, to tell me every detail afterward,—and, Gemmie, don't forget the funny things too. I wouldn't want to miss them you know. Be sure to describe how

Miss Hollister looks in her funny old bonnet with the ostrich plume."

"Oh, now Miss Sherrill, I couldn't be looking after things like that when you was getting married," rebuked the woman.

"Oh, yes, you could, Gemmie, you've got the loveliest sense of humor! And I want to know *everything*! Nobody else will understand, but you do, so now run away quick!"

"But I couldn't be leaving you alone," protested the woman with distress in her voice. "It'll be plenty of time for me to be going after you have left. Your Aunt Pat said for me to stay by you."

"You have, Gemmie, you've stayed as long as I had need of you, and just everything is done. You couldn't put another touch to me anywhere, and I'd rather know you are on your way to that nice seat I asked the tall dark usher to put you in. So please go, Gemmie, right away! The fact is, Gemmie, I'd really like just a few minutes alone all by myself before I go. I've been so busy I couldn't get calm, and I need to look into my own eyes and say good bye to myself before I stop being a girl and become a married woman. It really is a kind of scary thing you know Gemmie, now that I'm this close to it. I don't know how I ever had the courage to promise I'd do it!" and she laughed a gay little trill full of joyous anticipation.

"You poor lamb!" said the older woman with sudden yearning in her voice; the old, anticipating and pitying the trials of the young. "I do hope he'll be good to you."

"Be good to me!" exclaimed Sherrill gayly. "Who? Carter? Why of course, Gemmie. He's wonderful to me. He's almost ridiculous he's so careful of me. I'm just wondering how it's going to be to have someone always fussing over me when I've been on my own for so many years. Why, you know, Gemmie, these last six months I've been with Aunt Pat are the first time I've had anybody who really cared where I went or what I did since my mother died when I was ten years old. So you don't need to worry about me. There, now, you've spread that train out just as smooth as can be, please go at once. I'm getting very nervous about you, really Gemmie!"

"But I'll be needed, Miss Sherry, to help you down to the car when it comes for you."

"No, you won't, Gemmie. Just send that little new waitress up to the door to knock when the car is ready. I can catch up my own train and carry it perfectly well. I don't want to be preened and spread out like a peacock. It'll be bad enough when I get to the church and have to be in a parade. Truly, Gemmie, I want to be alone now."

The woman reluctantly went away at last, and Sherrill locked her door and went back to her mirror, watching herself as she advanced slowly, silver step after silver step, in time to the softly hummed Lohengrin. But when she was near to the glass Sherrill's eyes looked straight into their own depths long and earnestly.

"Am I really glad," she thought to herself, "that I'm going out of myself into a grown up married person? Am I perfectly sure that I'm not just a bit frightened at it all? Of course Carter McArthur is the handsomest man I ever met, the most brilliant talker, the most courteous gentleman, and I've been crazy about him ever since I first met him. Of course he treats me just like a queen, and I trust him absolutely. I know he'll always be just the same graceful lover all my life. And yet, somehow, I feel all of a sudden just the least bit scared. Does any girl *ever* know any man *perfectly?*"

She looked deep into her own eyes and wondered. If she only had a mother to talk to these last few minutes!

Of course there was Aunt Pat. But Aunt Pat had never been married. How could Aunt Pat know how a girl felt the last few minutes before the ceremony? And Aunt Pat was on her way to the church now. She was all crippled up with rheumatism and wanted to get there in a leisurely way and not have to get out of the car before a gaping crowd. She had planned to slip in the side door and wait in the vestry room till almost time for the ceremony and then have one of her numerous nephews, summoned to the old house for the occasion to be ushers, bring her in. Aunt Pat wouldn't have understood anyhow. She was a good sport with a great sense of humor, but she wouldn't have understood this queer feeling Sherrill was experiencing.

When one stopped to think of it, right on the brink of doing it, it was a rather awful thing to just give your life up to the keeping of another! She hadn't known Carter but six short months. Of course he was wonderful. Everybody said he was wonderful, and he had always been so to her. Her heart thrilled even now at the thought of him, the way he called her "Beautiful!" bending down and just touching her forehead with his lips, as though she were almost too sacred to touch lightly. The way his hair waved above his forehead. The slow way he smiled, and the light that came in his hazel eyes when he looked at her. They thrilled her tremendously. Oh, there wasn't any doubt in her mind whatever but that she was deeply in love with him. She didn't question that for an instant. It was just the thought of merging her life into his and always being a part of him. No, it wasn't that either, for that thrilled her too with an exquisite kind of joy, to think of never having to be separated from him any more. What was it that sent a quiver of fear through her heart just at this last minute alone? She couldn't tell.

She had tried to talk to Gemmie about it once the day before, and Gemmie had said all girls felt "queer" at the thought of being married. All nice girls that is. Sherrill couldn't see why that had anything to do with the matter. It wasn't a matter of nicety. Gemmie was talking about a shrinking shyness probably and it wasn't that at all. It was a great awesomeness at the thought of the miracle of two lives wrought into one, two souls putting aside all others and becoming one perfect life.

It made Sherrill feel suddenly so unworthy to have been chosen, so childish and immature for such a wonder. One must be so perfect to have a right to be a part of such a great union. And Carter was so wonderful! Such a super-man!

Suddenly she dropped upon one silken knee and bowed her lovely mist-veiled head.

"Dear God," she prayed softly, long lashes lying on velvet cheeks, gold tendrils of hair glinting out from under lacy cap, "O, dear God, make me good enough for him!" and then, hesitantly in a quick little frightened breath, "Keep me from making any awful mistakes!"

Then having shriven her ignorant young soul, she buried her face softly, gently, in the baby roses of her bouquet and drew a long happy breath; feeling her fright and burden roll away, her happy heart spring up to meet the great new change that was about to come upon her life.

She came softly to her feet, the great bouquet still in her clasp, and glanced hurriedly at the little turquoise enamel clock on her dressing table. There was plenty of time. She had promised to show herself to Mary the cook after she was dressed. Mary had broken her knee cap the week before and was confined to her couch. She had mourned distressedly that she could not see Miss Sherrill in her wedding dress. So Sherrill had promised her. It had been one of the reasons why she had got rid of Gemmie. She knew Gemmie would protest at her going about in her wedding veil for a mere servant!

But there was no reason in the world why she couldn't do it. Most of the people of the house were gone to the church. The bridesmaids left just before Gemmie, and Aunt Pat before them. Herself had watched the ushers leave while Gemmie was fixing her veil. Of course they had to be there ages before anyone else.

The bridesmaids and maid-of-honor had the next two rooms to her own, with only her deep closet between, and there were doors opening from room to room so that all the rooms were connected around the circle and back to Aunt Pat's room which was across the hall from her own. It had been one of the idiosyncrasies of the old lady that in case of burglars it would be nice to be able to go from room to room without going into the hall.

So the rooms were arranged in a wide horseshoe with the back hall behind the top of the loop, the middle room being a sitting room or library, with three bedrooms on either side. Nothing would be easier than for her to go swiftly, lightly, through the two rooms beyond her own, and through the door at the farther end of the second room into the back hall that led to the servants' quarters. That would save her going through the front hall and being seen by any prying servants set to keep track of her till she reached the church. It was a beautiful idea to let old Mary see how she looked, and why shouldn't she do it?

Stepping quickly over to the door that separated her room from the next she slid the bolt back, and turned the knob cautiously, listening; then swung the door noiselessly open.

Yes, it was as she supposed, the girls were gone. The room was dimly lit by the two wall sconces over the dressing table. She could see Linda's street shoes with the tan stockings stuffed into them standing across the room near the bureau. She knew them by the curious cross straps of the sandal-like fastening. Linda's hat was on the bed, with the jacket of her silk ensemble half covering it. Linda was always careless, and of course the maids were too busy to have been in here yet to clear up. The closet door was open and she saw Cassie's suitcase yawning wide open on the floor where Cassie had left it in her haste. The white initials, C.A.B. cried out a greeting as she crept stealthily by. Cassie had been late in arriving. She always was. And there was Carol's lovely imported fitted bag open on the dressing table, all speaking of the haste of their owners.

Betty and Doris and Jane had been put in the second room, with Rena, the maid of honor whom Aunt Pat had wanted her to ask because she was the daughter of an old friend. It was rather funny having a maid of honor whom one hadn't met, for she hadn't arrived yet when Sherrill had gone to her room to dress, but assurance had come over the telephone that she was on her way in spite of a flat tire, so there had been nothing to worry about. Who or what Rena was like did not matter. She would be wholly engaged in eying her dear bridegroom's face. What did it matter who maid-of-honored her, so Aunt Pat was pleased?

Sherrill paused as she stepped into this second room. It was absolutely dark, but strangely enough the door to the left, opening into the middle room had been left open. That was curious. Hadn't Carter been put in there to dress? Surely that was the arrangement, to save him coming garbed all the way from the city!

But of course he was gone long ago! She had heard

him arrange to be early at the church to meet the best man who had been making some last arrangements about their stateroom on the ship. That was it! Carter had gone, and the girls, probably not even knowing that he occupied that room, had gone out that way through what they supposed was the sitting room instead of using the other door into the hall.

So Sherrill, her soft train swung lightly over her arm, the mist of lace gathered into the billow that Gemmie had arranged for her convenience in going down stairs, and the great sheaf of roses and valley-lilies held gracefully over her other arm stepped confidently into the room. She looked furtively toward the open door where a brilliant overhead light was burning, sure that the room was empty, unless some servant was hovering about watching for her to appear.

She hesitated, stepping lightly, the soft satin making no sound of going more than if she had been a bit of thistle down. Then suddenly she stopped short and held her breath, for she had come in full sight of the great gilt-framed pier glass that was set between the two windows at the back of the room, and in it was mirrored the full length figure of her bridegroom arranging his tie with impatient fingers and staring critically into the glass, just as she had been doing but a moment before.

A great wave of tenderness swept over her for him, a kind of guilty joy that she could have this last vision of him as himself before their lives merged; a picture that she felt would live with her throughout the long years of life.

How dear he looked! How shining his dark hair, the wave over his forehead! There wasn't any man, not *any* man, *any*where as handsome—and *good,* she breathed softly to herself—as Carter, *her man!*

She held herself back into the shadow, held her very

breath lest he should turn and see her there, for—wasn't there a tradition that it was bad luck for the bride to show herself in her wedding garments to the groom before he saw her first in the church? Softly she withdrew one foot and swayed a little farther away from the patch of light in the doorway. He would be gone in just a minute of course and then she could go on and give Mary her glimpse and hurry back without being seen by anyone. She dared not retreat further lest he should hear her step and find out that she had been watching him. It was fun to be here and see him when he didn't know. But sometime, O sometime in the dear future that was ahead of them, she would tell him how she had watched him, and loved him, and how all the little fright that had clutched her heart a few minutes before had been melted away by this dear glimpse of him.

Sometime, when he was in one of those gentle moods, and they were all alone—they had had so little time actually alone of late! There had always been so many other things to be done!—But sometime, soon perhaps, when he was giving her soft kisses on her eyelids, and in the palm of her hand as he held her fingers back with his own strong ones, then she would draw him down with his face close to hers and tell him how she had watched him, and loved him—!

But—! What was happening? The door of the back hall, that was set next to the nearest window was opening slowly, without sound, and a face was appearing in the opening! Could it be a servant, mistaken her way? How blundering! How annoyed he would be to have his privacy broken in upon!

And then the face came into the light and she started. It was a face she had seen before, a really pretty face, if the make-up on it had not been so startling. There was something almost haggard about it too, and wistful, and the eyes were frightened, pleading eyes. They scanned the room hurriedly and rested upon the man, who still stood with his back to the room and his face to the mirror. Then the girl stepped stealthily within the room and closed the door as noiselessly as she had opened it.

Who was it? Sherrill held her breath and stared. Then swift memory brought the answer. Why, that was Miss Prentiss, Carter's stenographer! But surely, no one had invited her! Carter had said she was comparatively new in the office. He had not put her name on the list. How dared she follow him here? Had something come up at the last minute, some business matter that she felt he must know about before he left for his trip to Europe? But surely, no one could have directed her to follow him to the room where he was dressing!

This all went swiftly through Sherrill's mind as she stood that instant and watched the expression on the girl's face, that hungry desperate look, and something warned her with uncanny prescience. So Sherrill stood holding that foolish bouquet of baby roses and swinging lily-bells during what seemed an eon of time, till suddenly Carter McArthur saw something in the mirror and swung around, a frozen look of horror and anger on his handsome face, and faced the other girl.

"What are you doing here, Arla?" he rumbled in an angry whisper, and his bride, standing within the shadow trembled so that all the little lily-bells swayed in the dark and trembled with her. She had never heard him speak in a voice like that. She shivered a little, and a sudden thought like a dart swept through her. Was it conceivable that he would ever speak so to her? But—of course this intruder ought to be rebuked!

"I have come because I cannot let this thing go on!" said the girl in a desperate voice. "I have tried to do as you told me. O, I have tried with all my might—" and her voice broke in a helpless little sob, "but I can't do it. It isn't *right!*"

"Be still can't you? You will rouse the house. Do you want to bring disgrace upon us all?"

"If that is the only way," said the girl desperately, lifting lovely darkly circled eyes to his face, and suddenly putting her hands up with a caressing motion and stealing them around his neck; desperate clinging arms that held him fast.

"I can't give you up, Cart! I can't! I *can't!* You promised me so long ago you would marry me, and you've always been putting me off—and now—*this! I can't!*"

"Hush!" said the man sternly with a note of desperation in his voice. "You are making me hate you, don't you know that? Don't you know that no good whatever can come of this either for me or yourself? How did you get here anyway? Have you no shame? Who saw you? Tell me quick!"

"Nobody saw me—" breathed the girl between sobs, "I came up the fire escape and along the back hall. This was the room I came to that day to take dictation for you when you had a sprained ankle and had to stay out here. Don't you remember? Oh, Cart! You told me then that some day you and I would have a house just like this. Have you forgotten how you kissed my fingers, and the palm of my hand when they all had gone away and left us to work?"

"Hush!" said the man, his face stern with agony. "No, I haven't forgotten! You know I haven't forgotten! I've explained it all to you over and over again. I thought you were reasonable. I thought you understood that this was necessary in order to save all that I have worked so hard to gain."

"Oh, but Cart! I've tried to, but I can't! I cannot give you up!"

"You won't have to give me up," he soothed impatiently. "We'll see each other every day as soon as I get back from this trip. We'll really be closer together than if we were married, for there'll be nothing to hinder us having good times whenever we like. No household cares or anything. And really, a man's secretary is nearer—"

There came a sharp imperative tap on the door of the sitting room. McArthur started and pushed the weeping girl from him into a corner.

"Yes?" he said harshly going over to the door. "Has the car come for me? Well, say I'll be there in just a minute. There is plenty of time by my watch. But I'll be right down."

There was a painful silence. Sherrill could see the other girl shrinking behind a curtain, could hear the painful breathing as she struggled to keep back the sobs, could see the strained attitude of Carter McArthur as he stood stiffly in the middle of the room glaring toward the frail girl.

"Arla, if you love me you must go away at once," he said sternly coming toward the girl again, and now he was within the range of the next room and Sherrill had to shrink further back into the shadow again lest he should see her.

Suddenly she saw him stoop, put both arms about the other girl, draw her close to him, and put his lips down on hers, hungrily, passionately, kissing her and devouring her with his eyes, just as he had sometimes on rare and precious occasions done to Sherrill! Sherrill clutched her bridal flowers and shivered as she shrank into the shadow and tried to shut the sight out by closing her eyes, yet could not.

A great awful cold had come down upon her heart, caught it with an icy hand, and was slowly squeezing it to death. She wanted to cry out, as in a nightmare, and waken herself; prove that this was only a hideous dream, yet something was stopping her voice and holding her quiet. It must not be that he should hear her, or see her! It must never happen that she should be drawn into this dreadful scene. She must keep very still and it would pass. This awful delirium would pass, and her right mind would return! She was going pretty soon to the church to be married to this man, and all this would be forgotten, and she would be telling him sometime how she had watched him and loved him as he prepared to go forth and meet her, her dear bridegroom! He would be kissing *her* fingers, and *her* eyelids this way—But no! She was going crazy! That would never happen! A great wall had come down between them. She knew in her heart that now she would never, never tell him! He would never take her in his arms again, or kiss her lips or eyelids, or call her his! That was over forever. A dream that could not come true.

Then an impassioned voice broke the stillness and cut through to the depths of her being. It was his voice with that beloved quality she knew so well!

"O, my darling, my darling! I can't stand it to see you suffer so! There will never be any girl like you to me. Why can't you understand?"

"Then if that is so," broke out the weeping girl lifting her head with sudden hope, "come with me now! We can get out the way I came and no one will see us. Let us go away! Leave her and leave the business, and everything. No one will see us! Come!"

The man groaned.

"You *will* not understand!" he murmured impatiently. "It is not possible! Do you want to see me ruined? This girl is rich! Her fortune and the connection with her family will save me. Sometime later there may come a time when I could go with you, but not now!"

Then into the midst of the awfulness there swung a sweet-toned silver sound, a clock just outside the door striking the hour in unmistakable terms, and Carter McArthur started away from the girl, fairly flinging her in his haste, till she huddled down on her knees in the corner sobbing.

"Shut up, can't you!" said the man wildly as he rushed over to the mirror and began to brush the powder marks from his otherwise immaculate coat, "Can't you see you're goading me to desperation? I've *got* to go *instantly!* I'm going to be late!"

"And what about me?" wailed the girl. "Would you rather I took poison and lay down in this room to die? Wouldn't that be a nice thing to meet you when you came back from the church?"

But with a last desperate brush of his coat Carter snapped out the light, and swung out into the upper hall, slamming the door significantly behind him, and hurrying down the stairs with brisk steps that tried to sound gay for the benefit of the servants in the hall below.

The girl's voice died away into a helpless little frightened sob, and then all was still.

And Sherrill stood there in the utter darkness trying to think, trying to gather her scattered senses and realize what had happened; what might happen next. That something cataclysmic had just taken place that would change all her after life she knew; but just for that first instant or two after she heard her bridegroom's footsteps go down the stairs and out the front door she had not got her bearings. It was all that she could do just then to stand still and clutch her great bouquet while the earth reeled under her trembling feet.

The next instant she heard a sound, soft, scarcely perceptible to any but preternaturally quickened senses, that brought her back to the present, the necessity of the moment and the shortness of time.

The sound was the tiniest possible hint of stirring garments and a stealthy step from the corner where the weeping girl had been flung when the angry frightened bridegroom made his hasty exit.

Instantly Sherrill was in possession of herself and reaching forward accurately with accustomed fingers, touched the electric switch that sent a flood of light into the sitting room.

Then Sherrill in her white robes stepped to the doorway and confronted the frightened, cowering, blinking interloper, who fell back against the wall, her hands outspread and groping for the door, her eyes growing wide with horror as she caught the full version of her lover's bride.

FOR just an instant they faced one another, the bride in her beauty, and her woe-begone rival, and in spite of her Sherrill could not help thinking how pretty this other girl was. Even though she had been crying and there were tears on her lashes. She was not a girl whom crying made hideous. It rather gave her the sweet dewy look of a child in trouble.

She stood wide-eyed, horror and fear on her face, the soft gold of her hair just showing beneath a chic little hat. She was dressed in a stylish street suit of dark blue with slim correct shoes and long wristed wrinkled white doeskin gloves. Even as she stood, her arms outspread and groping for refuge against the unfriendly wall, she presented an interesting picture. Sherrill could not help feeling sorry for her. There was nothing arrogant about her now. Just the look of a frightened child at bay among enemies.

"How long have you known him?" asked Sherrill trying to keep her voice from trembling.

The other girl burst forth in an anguished tone, her

hands going quickly to her throat which moved convulsively:

"Ever since we were kids!" she said with a choking sob at the end of her words. "Always we've been crazy about each other, even in High School. Then after he got started up in the city he sent for me to be his secretary so we could be nearer to each other till we could afford to get married. It has never been any different till you came. It was you—*you* who took him away from me—!" and the girl buried her hands in the drabbled little handkerchief and gave a great sob that seemed to come from the depths of her being.

Sherrill felt a sudden impulse to put her face down in her lovely roses and sob too. It somehow seemed to be herself and not this other girl who was sobbing over there against the wall. Oh, how could this great disaster have befallen them both? Carter! Her matchless lover! This girl's lover too! How could this thing be?

"No," she said, very white and still, her voice almost toneless and unsteady, "I never took him away from you. I never knew there was such a person as you!"

"Well, you took him!" sobbed the other girl, "and there's nothing left for me but to kill myself!" and another great sob burst forth.

"Nonsense!" said Sherrill sharply. "Don't talk that way! That's terrible. You don't get anywhere talking like that! Hush! Somebody will hear you! We've got to be sensible and think what to do!"

"Do?" said Arla dropping her hands from her face and flashing a look of scorn at the girl in bridal array. "What is there to do? Oh, perhaps you mean how you can get rid of me the easiest way? I don't see why I should make it easy for you I'm sure, but I suppose I will. I'll go away and not make any more trouble of course. I suppose I knew that when I came, but I *had* to come! Oh!—" and she gave another deep sob and turned her head away for an instant, then back to finish her sentence, "and you will go out to the church to marry him. It is easy enough for you to say 'hush' when you are going to marry him!"

"Marry him!" said Sherrill, sudden horror in her voice, "I could never marry him after *this!* Could *you?"*

"Oh, yes," said the girl in a quivering, hopeless voice, "I'd marry him if I got the chance! You can't love him the way I do or you would too. I'd marry him if I had to go through hell to do it!"

Sherrill quivered at the words. She was watching this other girl, thinking fast, and sudden determination came into her face.

"Then you shall!" she said in a low clear voice of determination. "You may get taken at your word. You may have to go through hell for it. But I won't be responsible for that. If you feel that way about it you shall marry him!"

The other girl looked up with frightened eyes.

"What do you mean?"

"I mean you shall marry him! Now! To-night!"

"But how could I?" she asked dully. "That would be impossible."

"No, it is not impossible. Come! Quick. We have got to work fast! Hark! There comes somebody to the door. Come with me! Don't make a sound!"

Sherrill snapped the light off and grasping the gloved hand of the girl she pulled her after her through the dimly lighted middle rooms and inside her own door, which she swiftly closed behind her sliding the bolt.

"Now!" she said drawing a breath of relief, "We've got to work like lightning! Take off your gloves and hat and dress just as fast as you can!"

Sherrill's hands were busy with the fastening of her veil. Carefully she searched out the hairpins that held it and lifted it off, laying it in a great billow upon the bed, her hands at once searching for the fastening of her own bridal robe.

"But what are you going to do?" asked the other girl staring at her wildly though she began automatically to pull off her long gloves.

"I'm going to put these things on you," said Sherrill, pulling off her dress over her head frantically. *"Hurry,* won't you? The car is probably out there waiting now. They'll begin to get suspicious if we are a long time. Take off your hat quick! And your dress! Will it just pull over your head? Hurry I tell you! What kind of stockings have you got on? Tan ones? That won't do. Here, I've got another pair of silver ones in the drawer. I always have two pairs in case of a run. Sit down there and peel yours off quick! I wonder if my slippers will fit you. You'll have to try them anyway, for we couldn't get any others!"

Sherrill kicked her silver slippers off, and groped in the closet, bringing out an old pair of black satin ones, and stepping into them hurriedly. The jeweled buckles glinted wickedly.

Her mind was working rapidly now. She dashed to her suitcase and rooted out a certain green taffeta evening gown, a recent purchase, one that she had especially liked, and she had planned to take with her, in case anything should delay her trunk. She dropped it over her own head, pulling it down with hurried hands and a bitter thought of what pleasure she had taken in it when she bought it. If she had known—Ah, *if she had known!* But there was no time for sentiment.

The other girl was fitting on the silver stockings and shoes, her hands moving slowly, uncertainly.

"Here, let me fasten those garters!" said Sherrill almost compassionately. "You really must work faster than this!

Stand up. Can you manage to walk in those shoes? They're a bit long aren't they? My foot is long and slim. Stand up quick and take off that dark slip. Here, here's the white slip," and she slid it over the golden head of the other girl. Queer their hair was the same color! Sherrill's mind was so keyed up that she thought of little painful things that at another time would not have attracted her attention.

"But I can't do this!" said Arla Prentiss suddenly backing away from the lovely folds of ivory satin that Sherrill was holding for her to slip into. "I couldn't ever get away with it! Cart would kill me if I tried to do a thing like this!"

"Well, you were talking about killing yourself a few minutes ago," said Sherrill sharply, wondering at herself as she said it, "it would be only a choice of deaths in that case, wouldn't it? For mercy's sake stand still so I won't muss your hair! This dress has *got* to go on you, and mighty quick, too!"

"But I couldn't get away with a thing like this!" babbled Arla as she emerged from the sweeping folds of satin and found herself clothed in a wedding garment, drifting away in an awesome train such as her wildest dreams had never pictured.

"Oh, yes, you could," said Sherrill, snapping the fastenings firmly into place and smoothing down the skirt hurriedly. "All you've got to do is to walk up the aisle and say yes to things."

"Oh, I *couldn't!*" said Arla in sudden terror. "Why, they would know the minute I reached the church that it wasn't you! They would never let it get even as far as walking up the aisle. They would *mob* me! They would *drive me out—!*" she paused with a great sob and sank down to the chair again.

"Get up!" said Sherrill standing over her fiercely.

"You'll ruin that dress! Hark! There is someone coming to the door! Hush! Yes? Are you calling for me?" Sherrill spoke in a pleasant casual tone. "Is the car ready for me? You say it's been ready ten minutes? Oh, well," she laughed a high little unnatural trill, "that's all right! They always expect a bride to be late. Well, tell the man I'll be down in a minute or two now!"

The maid retreated down the stairs and Sherrill flew over to the bed and took up the wedding veil carefully.

"Now, stand there in front of the mirror and watch," she commanded as she held the lace cap high and brought it down accurately around the golden head. "Stand still please. I've got to do this in just a second. And now listen to me."

"But I can't! I can't really!" protested the substitute bride wildly. "I couldn't let you do this for me!"

"You've *got to!*" said Sherrill commandingly. "I didn't get up any of this mess, and it's up to you to put this wedding through. Now listen! The man who is to take me—*you* in—is a stranger to me. His name is Nathan Vane. He's a second cousin of my mother's family and he's never seen me. He hadn't arrived yet when I came up to dress. Neither had the maid-of-honor, and she's a stranger to me too. Her name is Rena Scott. They'll both be waiting at the door for you and will be the only ones who will have a chance to talk to you. All you'll have to do will be to smile and take his arm and go up the aisle. This is the step we're taking"—Sherrill stood away and went slowly forward. "You'll see how the others do it. You're clever, I can see. And when you get up there all you've got to do is answer the questions, and say things over after the minister, only using your *own* name instead of mine. Ten to one nobody will notice. You can speak in a low voice. The maid of honor will take your bouquet and you'll need to put out your left hand for the ring. Here! You must have the diamond too!" and Sherrill slipped her beautiful diamond engagement ring off her finger and put it on Arla's.

"Oh," gasped Arla, "you're wonderful! I *can't* let you do all this!"

"Hold your head still!" commanded Sherrill. "This orange wreath droops a little too much over that ear. There! Isn't that right? Really, you look a lot like me! I doubt if even the bridegroom will know the difference at first, wedding veils make such a change in one!"

"Oh, but"—gasped Arla, "Carter *will* know me. I'm *sure* he will! And suppose, suppose he should make a scene!"

"He won't!" said Sherrill sharply. "He hasn't the nerve!" she added cryptically, and suddenly knew that it was true and she had never known it before.

"But if he should!"

"He won't!" said Sherrill more surely, "And if he does we'll all be in it, so you won't be alone."

"Oh! Will you be there too?" Arla said it in a tone of wonder and relief.

"Why, of course," said Sherrill in the tone of a mother reproving a child. "I'll be there, perhaps before you are."

"Oh, why don't you go *with* me?"

"That would be a situation wouldn't it?" commented Sherrill sarcastically. "Former bride and substitute bride arrive together! For heaven's sake don't weep on that satin, it's bad luck! And don't talk about it any more or you'll have me crying too, and that would be just too bad! Here! Take your bouquet. No, hold it on this arm, and your veil and train over the other, now! All set? I'm turning off this light, and you must go out and walk right down the steps quickly. They are all caterer's people out there, they won't know the difference. You really look a lot like me. For mercy's sake don't look as if you were going to your own funeral. Put on a smile and *wear it all the evening*. And listen! You tell Mr. McArthur as soon as you get in the car on the way back with him, that if he plays any tricks or doesn't treat you right, or doesn't bring you back smiling to your reception, that I'll tell everybody here the whole truth! I'll tell it to everybody that knows him! And I mean what I say!"

"Oh!" gasped Arla, with a dubious lifting of the trouble in her eyes, and then, *"Oh!* Do we *have to come back* for the *reception!* Can't we just disappear?"

"If you disappear the whole story will come out in the papers to-morrow morning! I'll see to that!" threatened Sherrill ominously. "I'm not going to be made a fool of. But if you come back and act like sane people and go away in the usual manner, it will just be a good joke that we have put over for reasons of our own, see? Now go, quick! We mustn't get them all worked up because you are so late!"

Sherrill snapped out the light and threw open the door, stepping back into the shadow herself and watching breathlessly as Arla took the first few hesitating steps. Then as she grew more confident, stepping off down the hall, disappearing down the stairs, Sherrill closed the door and went over to the window which overlooked the front door.

The front steps were a blaze of light, and she could see quite plainly the caterer's man who was acting as footman, standing by and helping a vision in white into the car. The door slammed shut, and the car drove away with a flourish. Sherrill watched till it swept around the curve, and went toward the gateway. Then she snapped on a tiny bed light and gathered in haste a few things, her black velvet evening wrap, her pearl evening bag, a small sheet of note paper and her gold pencil. She would have to write a note to Aunt Pat. Her mind was racing on ahead! The keys to her own little car! Where had she put them? Oh, yes, in the drawer of her desk. Had she forgotten anything?

The bride's car had barely turned into the street ere Sherrill went with swift quiet steps back through those two rooms again, into the back hall, cautiously out through the window that Arla had left open, onto the fire escape, and down into the side yard.

It was but the work of a moment to unlock her door of the garage. Fortunately the chauffeur was not there. He had taken Aunt Pat of course, and everybody who would have known her was at the church. With trembling fingers she started her car, backed out the service drive and whirled away to the church.

She threaded her way between the big cars parked as far as she could see either way from the church. Could she manage to get hidden somewhere before the service really began?

Breathlessly she drove her car into a tiny place on the side street perilously near to a fire plug, and recklessly threw open her door. The police would be too busy out in the main avenue to notice perhaps, and anyway she could explain to them afterwards. Even if she did have to pay a fine she must get into that church.

A hatless young man in a trim blue serge suit was strolling by as she plunged forth from her car, and fortunately, for she caught the heel of her slipper in the billowy taffeta that was much too long for driving a car, and would have gone headlong if he had not caught her.

"I beg your pardon," he said pleasantly as he set her upon her feet again, "Are you hurt?"

"Oh, no!" said Sherrill, smiling agitatedly. "Thank you so much. You saved me from a bad fall. I was just in a terrible hurry," and she turned frantic eyes toward the looming side of the church across the street.

The young man continued to keep a protective arm about her and eye her anxiously.

"You're sure you're not hurt?" he asked again. "You didn't strike your head against the running board?"

"No!" she gasped breathlessly, trying to draw away, "I'm quite all right. But please, I must hurry. I am late now."

"Where do you want to go?" he asked, shifting his hand to her elbow and taking a forward step with her.

"Over there!" she motioned frantically, "to the church. I must get in before the ceremony begins."

"You ought to wait until you get your breath," he urged.

"I can't! I've *got* to get there!" and she tried to pull away from him and fly across the street. But he kept easy pace with her, helping her up to the curb.

"Don't you want to go around to the front door?" he said as she turned toward the side entrance.

"No!" she said, her heart beating so fast that it almost choked her. "This little side door. I want to get up to the choir loft."

"Well, I'm coming with you!" he announced fairly lifting her up the steps. "You're all shaken up from that fall. You're trembling! Can I take you to your friends? You're not fit to be alone."

"I'm—all—right!" panted Sherrill fetching a watery smile and finding the tears right at hand.

"Don't hurry!" he commanded, circling her waist impersonally with a strong arm and fairly lifting her up the narrow winding stair that led to the choir loft, "You've plenty of time. Don't you hear? Those are the preliminary chords to the wedding march. The bride must be just at the door! Take it slow and easy!"

They arrived at the top of the stair in an empty choir loft. It was a church of formal arrangement, with the organ console down out of sight somewhere and the choir high above the congregation, visible only when standing to sing, and then only to one who dared to look aloft.

The whole quiet place was fully screened by plumy palms, and great feathery tropical ferns, and not even a stray from the street had discovered this vantage point from which to watch the ceremony. They had it all to themselves. No curious eyes could watch the face of the agonized bride-that-was-to-have-been.

Sherrill nestled in wearily against the wall behind the thickest palm, where yet she could peer through and see everything. She thanked her unknown friend pantingly with a hasty fervor, and then forgot he was still beside her.

Breathlessly she leaned forward looking down, catching a glimpse of the bridegroom as he stood tall and handsome beside the best man, a smile of expectancy upon his face. Her bridegroom, watching for *her* to come! Her heart contracted and a spasm of pain passed over her face. She mustn't, O, she mustn't cry! This wasn't *her wedding!* This was something she must nerve herself to go through. This was something tragic that must move aright or all the future would be chaos.

Then she remembered and her eyes turned tragically, alertly down the aisle to the front door, her hand unconsciously pressed against her heart in a quick little frantic motion.

Yes, the bride had arrived! Of course she might have known that or the wedding march would not be ringing out its first stately measures! Yes, there was the huddle of rainbow-colored dresses that were the bridesmaids. How glad she was that none of them were really intimate friends. All of them new friends from Aunt Pat's circle of acquaintances. Her own girlhood friends were all too poor or too far away to be summoned. The first of them, the pink ones, were stepping forward now, slowly differentiating themselves from the mass of color, beginning the procession with measured, stilled thread; and back in the far dimness of the hall silhouetted against the darkness of the out-of-doors she could see the mist of whiteness that must be the bride, with the tall dark cousin beside her. Yes, the bride had come. Sherrill's secret fear that she might somehow lose her nerve and escape on the way to the church was unfounded. This girl really wanted Carter enough to go through this awful ordeal to get him! Besides, a girl couldn't very well run away and hope to escape detection in a bridal outfit. Sherrill felt a hysterical laugh coming to her lips that changed into a quiver of tears, and a little shiver that ran down her back. And then suddenly she felt that strong arm again just under her elbow, supporting her, just as her knees began to manifest a tendency to crumble under her.

"Oh, thank you!" she breathed softly letting her weight rest on his arm. "I'm—a little—nervous—I guess!"

"You aren't fit to stand!" he whispered. "I wonder if I couldn't find you a chair down there in the back room?"

She shook her head.

"It wouldn't be worth while," she answered, "the ceremony will soon be over. You are very kind, but I'll be all right."

He adjusted his arm so it would better support her, and somehow it helped and calmed her to feel him standing there. She had no idea how he looked or who he was. She hadn't really looked at him. She just knew he was kind, and that he was a stranger who didn't know a thing about her awful predicament. If he had been a friend who knew she couldn't have stood him there. But it was like being alone with herself to have him staying there so comfortingly. After it was over she would never likely see him again. She hoped he would never know who she was nor anything about it. She hadn't really thought anything about him as a personality. He was just something by the way to lean upon in her extremity.

The pink bridesmaids were half way up the middle aisle now, the green at the formal distance behind, the violet just entering past the first rank of seats with the blue waiting behind. Their faces wore the set smile of automatons endeavoring to do their best to keep the step. There was no evidence so far that either the wedding party or the audience had discovered anything unusual about this wedding or unexpected about the bride. She suddenly gasped at the thought of the gigantic fraud which she was about to perpetrate. Had she a right to do this? But it was too late to think about that now.

Sherrill's eyes went back to the bridegroom standing there waiting, his immaculate back as straight and conventional as if nothing out of the ordinary had occurred a half hour before. She remembered with a stab of pain the powder that he had brushed from his left lapel. Was there any trace of it left? She had a sudden sick faint feeling as if she would like to lay her head down and close her eyes. She reeled just a tiny bit, and the young man by her side shifted his arms, putting the right one unobtrusively about her so that he could the better steady her, and putting his left hand across to support her elbow. She cast him a brief little flicker of a smile of gratitude, but her eyes went swiftly back to the slow procession that was advancing up the aisle, so slow it seemed to her like the march of the centuries.

The bride was standing in the doorway now, just behind the yellow-clad maid-of-honor, her hand lying on the arm of the distant cousin, her train adjusted perfectly; no sign on the face of the maid-of-honor that she had noticed it was the wrong bride whom she had just prepared for her appearance. They didn't know it yet! Nobody knew what was about to happen except herself! The thought was overwhelming!

Suddenly her eyes were caught by the little figure in gray down in the front seat. Aunt Pat! Poor Aunt Pat! What would she think? And after all her kindness, and the money she had spent to make this wedding a perfect one of its kind! She must do something about Aunt Pat at once!

Her trembling fingers sought the catch of her hand bag and brought out pencil and paper. The young man by her side watched her curiously, sympathetically. Who was this lovely girl? What had stirred her so deeply? Had she perhaps cared for the bridegroom herself, and not felt able to face the audience during the ceremony? Or was the bride her sister, dearly beloved, whom she could not bear to part from? They truly resembled one another, gold hair, blue eyes, at least he was pretty sure this one's eyes were blue, as much as he could judge by the brief glimpse he had had of them here in the dimness of the gallery.

She was looking about for some place to lay her paper, and there was none, because the gallery rail was completely smothered in palms.

"Here!" he said softly, sensing her need, and drew out a broad smooth leather note book from his pocket, holding it firmly before her, his other arm still about her.

So Sherrill wrote rapidly, with tense trembling fingers:

"Dear Aunt Pat:

I'm not getting married to-night. Please be a good sport and don't let them suspect you didn't know. Please, dearest."

Sherrill.

The young man beside her had to hold the note book very firmly. He couldn't exactly help seeing the hastily scrawled words, though he tried not to, he really did. He was an honorable young man. But he was also by this time very much in sympathy with this unknown lovely girl. However, he treated the whole affair in the most matter of fact way.

"You want that delivered?" he whispered.

"Oh, would you be so good?"

"Which one? The little old lady in gray right down here?"

"Oh, how did you know?" Sherrill met his sympathetic gaze in passing wonder.

"I saw you looking down at her," he answered with a boyish grin. "You want her to read it before she leaves the church?"

"Oh, yes, please! Could you do it do you think?"

"Of course," he answered with confidence. "Do you happen to know if there is a door at the foot of these stairs opening into the church?"

"Yes, there is," said Sherrill.

"Well, there's no one else in the seat all across to the side aisle. I don't know why I couldn't slide in there without being noticed while the prayer is going on."

"Oh, could you do that?" said Sherrill with great relief in her eyes, and looking down quickly toward the front seat that stretched a vacant length across to the flower-garlanded aisle. "Would you mind? It would be wonderful! But, there's a ribbon across the seat."

He grinned again socially.

"It would take more than a ribbon to keep me out of a seat I wanted to get into. Are you all right if I leave you for a minute?"

"Of course!" said Sherrill drawing herself up and

trying to look self sufficient. "Oh, I can never thank you enough!"

"Forget it!" said the young man. "Well, I'd better hurry down and reconnoiter. *Sure* you're all right?"

"Sure," she smiled tremulously.

He was gone, and Sherrill realized that she felt utterly inadequate without him. But suddenly she knew that the procession had arrived at the altar and disposed itself in conventional array. Startled she looked down upon them. Did nobody know yet? She should have been watching Carter's face. But of course he would have had his back to her. She could not have told what he was feeling from just his back could she?

She moved a little farther and could see his face now between the next two palms, and it was white as death, white and frightened! Did she imagine it? No, she felt sure. He had swung half reluctantly around into his place beside Arla, but he lifted his hand to his mouth as if to steady his lips and she could see that his hand trembled. Didn't the audience see that? They would. They could not help it. But they would likely lay it to the traditional nervousness all bridegrooms were supposed to feel. Still, *Carter!* He was always so utterly confident, so at his ease anywhere. How could they credit him with ordinary nervousness?

But the ceremony was proceeding now, *her* bridegroom, Carter McArthur, getting married to *another* girl, and there she was above him, unseen, watching.

"Dearly beloved, we are gathered together in the sight of God and in the presence of this company to join together this man and this woman in the bonds of holy matrimony—"

A great wrench came to Sherrill's heart as she looked down and realized that but for a trifling accident she would even now be standing down there in that white dress and that veil getting married! If she had not tried to go through those two rooms without being seen, if she had not planned to go and show herself to Mary—poor Mary who was lying on her bed even now thinking she was forgotten—if just such a little trifle as that had not been, she would be down there with Carter now, blissfully happy, being bound to him forever on this earth as long as they both should live. So irrevocable!

For an instant as she thought of it her heart contracted. Why did she do this awful thing, this thing which would separate her forever from the man she loved so dearly? She could have slipped back into her room unseen, the other girl would have gone away, afraid to do anything else, she could have gone to the church and nobody would ever have been the wiser. She would have been Mrs. McArthur. Then what could Arla Prentiss do? Even if she had taken her life few would have ever heard of it.

But she Sherrill Cameron, even if she were Sherrill McArthur, would never have been happy. She knew that, even as she looked down into the white face of the staring, stony-eyed bridegroom. For between her and any possibility of joy there would always have come that look on his face when he had kissed the other girl, and told her he would always love her best. She never could have laughed down nor forgotten that look. How many other girls had he said that to, she wondered? Was Arla, too, deceived about it? She evidently thought, that she, Sherrill, was her only rival. But there might have been others too. Oh, if one couldn't trust a man what was the joy of marriage? If one were not the only one enthroned in a man's heart why bind oneself to his footsteps for life? Sherrill had old-fashioned simple ideas and standards of love and marriage. But Sherrill was wondering if she would ever be able to trust *any* living man again, since Carter who had always seemed such a paragon of perfection had proved himself so false and weak! No, she could never have married him, not after seeing him with Arla. Oh, were all men like that?

And there he was getting married to the other girl, and not doing a thing about it! She was sure he knew now, and he was making no protest.

And then suddenly she saw her own heart and knew that somewhere back in her mind she had been harboring the hope that he would do something. That he would somehow—she didn't know how for it wasn't reasonable—find a way to stop this marriage and explain all the wrong, and that joy would find its way through sorrow! But he wasn't doing a thing! He didn't dare do a thing! Fear, stark and ugly was written upon his face. He *knew* himself to be guilty. He was standing there before the assembled multitude, the "dearly beloved" of the service, and not one of them knew a thing about what was happening but himself, and he knew, and he *wasn't doing a thing!* He *didn't dare!*

And then, just down below her in the front seat a little motion attracted her eyes. A white ribbon lifted and a figure slid beneath. A young man in a blue serge suit with a pleasant face had glided so quietly into the seat beside the little gray lady with the white laces that nobody around her seemed to have even noticed. He was handing her a folded paper and whispering unobtrusively a word in her ear. Aunt Pat had her note now and in a moment she would know the truth! How would Aunt Pat take it? She was perfectly capable of rising in her delicate little might and putting a stop to the service. How awful it would be for everybody if she did that! Perhaps the note ought to have been held up until the service was over.

Then even with the thought came that frightful challenge. Was it only last night at the rehearsal that they had joked over it?

"Therefore if any man can show just cause why they may not lawfully be joined together, let him now declare it, or else hereafter forever hold his peace."

Her eyes were fastened on Aunt Pat in terror! What if Aunt Pat should arise and say she knew a just cause! Oh, why had she sent that note down so soon? If she could only recall it!

But Aunt Pat was sitting serenely with the note in her hand, reading it, and a look of satisfaction was on her lips, the kind a nice house cat might wear when she had just successfully evaded detection in licking the creamy frosting from a huge cake. Actually, Aunt Pat was looking up with a smile on her strong old face and a twinkle in her bright old eyes. It was almost as if she were *pleased!* The young man in the blue serge who had delivered the note was nowhere in sight, and yet she couldn't remember seeing him slip out again, though the white ribbon was swaying a little as if it had recently been stirred.

That deathly stillness settled down over the audience, an audible stillness, even above the voice of the organ undertone; and Sherrill, puzzling over Aunt Pat, turned fascinated eyes toward her erstwhile lover. How was he standing this challenge? Whichever girl he thought was standing beside him, surely he could not take this calmly. Oh, if she might only look in his face and see his innocence written there! Yet she knew that could never be!

But she was not prepared for the haggard look she saw on his face, a terror such as a criminal at bay might wear when about to face an angry mob who desired to hang him. The look in his eyes was awful! All their gay brilliancy gone! Only fear, uncertainty, a holding of the breath to listen! His hands were working nervously. She felt almost a contemptuous pity for him, and then a wrenching of the heart again. Her lover, to have come to such a place as that! Almost she groaned aloud, and looked toward the radiant bride, for radiant she really seemed to be, carrying out her part perfectly. Sherrill had felt she could do it. She was clever, and she had an overwhelming love!

And yet in spite of her horror over what was happening, somehow as she looked down there it seemed to be her own self that was standing there in that white satin garb and veil about to take sweet solemn vows upon her. What had she done to put her bright hopes out of her life forever! Oh, hadn't she been too hasty? Might there not have been some other explanation than the only obvious one? Ought she perhaps to have gone in and confronted those two in each other's arms?

Then suddenly the girl down there before the altar spoke, and her voice was clear and ringing. The great church full of people held their breath again to catch every syllable:

"I, Arla, take thee, Carter,—"

Sherrill felt her breath coming in slow gasps, felt as if someone were stifling her. She strained her ears to hear, on through that long paragraph that she had learned so carefully by heart, her lips moving unconsciously to form the words ere she heard them. And Arla was speaking them well, clearly, with a triumphant ring to them, like a call to the lover she had lost. Could he fail to understand and answer? Sherrill pressed her hands hard upon her aching heart and tried to take deep breaths to keep her senses from swimming off away from her.

Again she had a feeling as if that girl down there was herself; yet she was here looking on!

And now it was the bridegroom's turn!

Sherrill closed her eyes and focussed every sense upon the words. Would he respond? Would he do something or would he let it go on? For now he surely knew!

His voice was low, husky, she could scarcely hear the words above the tender music that she herself had planned to accompany the troth they were plighting. Afterwards she fancied it must have been by some fine inner sense rather than the hearing of her ears that she knew what he was saying, for he spoke like one who was afraid!

"I Carter, take thee, *Arla—!*"

A-h-h! He had said it. He knew now and he had accepted it! He was taking the words deliberately upon his lips. Shamedly, perhaps, like one driven to it, but he had taken them. Her lover was marrying another girl! He had not even tried to do anything about it!

With a little gasp like a deep driven sob she dropped upon her knees and hid her face in her hands, while the gallery in which she knelt reeled away into space, and she suddenly seemed to be hurled as from a parapet by the hands of her erstwhile bridegroom, down, down into infinite space with darkness growing all about her. Ah! She had been foolish! Why had she not known that this would happen to her? Love like hers could not be broken, torn from its roots ruthlessly, without awful consequences. How had she thought she could go through this and live through it? Was this the end? Was she about to die, shamelessly, and all the world know that she had a broken heart?

Ahh!

A breath of fresh air came sharply into her face from an opening door just as she was about to touch an awful depth, a strong arm lifted her upon her feet, and a glass of cool water was pressed to her lips.

"I thought this might be refreshing," a friendly casual voice said, not at all as if anything unusual were happening.

She drank the water gratefully, and afterward she wondered if it were only fancy that she seemed to remember clinging to a hand. But of course that could not have been.

He looked down at her smiling, as if he might have been a brother.

"Now, do you feel you have to stay up here till this performance is ended and all the people escorted out below?" he asked pleasantly, "or would you like to slip down now and get your car out of traffic before things get thick? You look awfully tired to me, but if you feel you should stay I'll bring up a chair."

"Oh," said Sherrill bewilderedly, "Is it,—Are they almost —?"

She leaned forward to look.

"Just about over I fancy," said the man who was steadying her so efficiently.

And as if to verify his words the voice of the clergyman came clearly:

"I pronounce you husband and wife. . . . Whom therefore God hath joined together, let no man put asunder."

She shuddered and shrank back. The man could feel her tremble as he supported her.

"This would be a good time if you are going to slip away," he whispered. "There is just the brief prayer and then the procession out is rather rapid. I fancy traffic will thicken up quickly after they are out. Or, would you rather wait until they are all gone?"

"Oh, no!" said Sherrill anxiously, "I must get back to the house if possible before they get there!"

"Then we should go at once!"

She cast one more glance down at the two who stood with clasped hands and bowed heads, and rapidly reviewed what was to come.

After this prayer there was the kiss!

She shivered! No, she did not want to see Arla lift her radiant head for that kiss. She had watched him kiss her once that night, she could not stand it again.

"Yes! Let us go quickly!" she whispered hurriedly with one last lingering glance, and then stumbled toward the stairs.

Out in the cool darkness with a little breeze blowing in her face and the bright kind stars looking down Sherrill came to herself fully again, her mind racing on to what was before her.

She was glad for the strong arm that still helped her across the street, but she felt the strength coming into her own feet again.

"I can't ever be grateful enough to you," she said as they reached the car, and she suddenly realized that she had treated him as if he were a mere letter carrier or a drink of water, "you have done a lot for me tonight. If I had more time I would try to make you understand how grateful I am."

"You needn't do that," he said gently. "You just needed a friend for a few minutes and I'm glad I happened by. I wonder if there isn't something more I could do? I'm going to drive you home of course if you'll let me, for you really shouldn't try yourself, believe me. Or is there some friend you would prefer whom I could summon?"

"Oh, no," she said looking frightened, "I don't want *any*one I know. I want to get back before they miss me—And really, I think I could drive. Still if you don't mind, it *would* be a great help. But I hate to take more of your time."

"I'd love to," he said heartily. "I haven't another thing to do this evening. In fact I'm a stranger in town and was wondering what I could do to pass the time until I could reasonably retire."

"You seem to have been just sent here to help in a time of need," she said simply as he put her into the car and then took the wheel himself.

"I certainly am glad," he said. "Now, which way? Couldn't we take a short cut somewhere and keep away from this mob of cars?"

"Yes," said Sherrill roused now fully to the moment. "Turn to the left here and go down that back street."

"I wonder," he said as they whirled away from the church with the triumphant notes of the wedding march breaking ruthlessly into their conversation, "if there wouldn't be some way I could serve you the rest of the evening? I'm wholeheartedly at your service if there is any way in which just a mere, may I say friend, can help out somewhere?"

"Oh," said Sherrill giving him a startled look in the

semi-darkness, "you're really wonderfully kind. But—I hate to suggest any more, and—it's such a silly thing!—"

"Please," said the young man earnestly, "just consider me an old friend for the evening, won't you, and ask what you would ask if I were."

Sherrill was still a second, giving him a troubled look.

"Well, then—would you consider it a great bore to go back with me to that reception and sort of hang around with me a while? Just as if you were an old friend who had been invited to the wedding? You see, I—Well, I'm afraid I'll have to explain."

"You needn't if you don't want to," said the young man promptly. "I'll be delighted to go without explanations. Just give me my cue and I'll take any part you assign me if I can help you in any way. Only, how the dickens am I going to a swell wedding reception in a blue serge suit?"

"Oh," said Sherrill blankly. "Of course, I hadn't thought of that. And I suppose there wouldn't be any place open near here where we could rent some evening things? Well, of course it was a foolish idea, and I oughtn't to have suggested it. I'll go through the thing all right alone I'm sure. I'm feeling better every minute."

"No," said the young man, "It *wasn't* and *you're not!* I've got a perfectly good dress suit and all the fixings in a suitcase up in my room in the hotel and it's just around that corner there. If you think it wouldn't make you too late I could just park you outside a minute and run up and get the suitcase. Then I could put it on in the garage or somewhere couldn't I? Or would it be better for me to get dressed in the conventional manner and take a taxi back?"

"Oh," laughed Sherrill nervously. "Why, we'll stop at the hotel of course. It won't take you long, and they can't have started home yet, can they?"

"They haven't got the bride and groom into their car yet, if you ask me," said the young man blithely. "I doubt if they're out at the front door to judge by that music. I've sort of been humming it inside since we started. You know there's always delay getting the cars started. Here's the hotel. Shall I really stop and get my things?"

While she waited before the hotel she put back her head and closed her eyes, her mind racing ahead to the things she had to do. The worst nightmare of the evening was yet to come, and for an instant as she faced it she almost had a wild thought of leaving the whole thing, kind young man and all and racing off into the world somewhere to hide. Only of course she knew she wouldn't do it. She couldn't leave Aunt Pat like that!

And then almost incredibly the young man was back with a suitcase in his hand.

"I had luck," he explained as he swung himself into the car, "I just caught the elevator going up with a man to the top floor. I had only to unlock my door, snatch up my suitcase and lock the door again, so I caught the elevator coming back. I call that service. How about it?"

"You certainly made record time," said Sherrill. "Now turn right at the next corner and go straight till I tell you to turn."

They were out in a quiet street and making good time when she spoke again.

"I've got to tell you the situation," she said gravely, "or you won't understand what it's all about and why I want you to help. You see, this was *my* wedding to-night."

"Your wedding?" He turned a startled face toward her.

"Yes, and I doubt whether very many have taken it in yet that I wasn't the bride."

"But,—why—how—when—?"

"Yes, of course," explained Sherrill. "It all happened less than an hour ago. I was all dressed to go to the church and I happened to find out about *her*. I—saw them together—saying good bye—"

She caught her breath trying to steady her voice and keep the tears back, and he said gently:

"Don't tell me if that makes it harder. I'll get the idea all right. You want me to hang around and be an old friend, is that the idea?"

"That's it," said Sherrill, "I thought if I just had *some*body—somebody they all *didn't know*—somebody they could think had been an old friend back in my home in the west before I came here, it wouldn't be so hard."

"I understand perfectly," he said, "I am your very special oldest friend, and I'll do my noblest to help you carry off the situation." His voice was gravely tender and respectful, and somehow it gave her great relief to know he would stand by her for the evening.

"You are wonderful," she said in a shaky little voice. "But, I never thought, is there,—have you a wife or, or—somebody who would mind you doing that for a stranger?"

He laughed blithely, as if he were glad about it.

"No, I haven't a wife. I haven't even somebody. Nothing to worry about in that direction. Though I wouldn't think much of them even if I had if they would mind lending me for such an occasion."

"Well, I guess I'm not worth much that I'm letting you do it, but things are almost getting me. I was pretty tired and excited when it happened, and then you know it was less than an hour ago, and kind of sudden."

"Less than an hour ago!" said the young man appalled.

"Why, how did you work it to get the other girl there all dressed up?"

"I waited till he had started to the church. I guess I was dazed at first and didn't know what to do. I just dragged her into my room and made her put on the wedding things, and sent her off in the car. You see the man who was to give me away was a distant cousin who didn't know me, had been late in arriving, and the maid-of-honor was a friend of my aunt's who had never seen me, either."

"But didn't the bridegroom know?"

"Not until he saw her coming up the aisle, or—I'm not sure *when* he knew, but—" there came that piteous catch in her voice again, "I don't know just *when* he knew, but he accepted it all right. He—used *her name* in the service, not mine. I haven't thought much yet about what I did. But I guess it was a rather dreadful thing to do. Still—I don't know what else I could have done. The wedding was all there, and *I* couldn't marry him, could I? Perhaps you think I am a very terrible girl. Perhaps you won't want to pose as my friend now you know."

He could hear that the tears were very near to the surface now and he hastened to say earnestly:

"I think you are a very brave and wonderful girl."

"Here's where we turn," she said breathlessly, "and I think that's their car down two blocks away. They have to go in the front drive, but we'll go on around here to the service entrance. Then we can get in before they see us."

"And by the way, oughtn't I know your name?" he said quietly. "Mine is Graham Copeland, and you can call me 'Gray' for short. It will sound more schoolmatish won't it? All my friends call me Gray."

"Thank you," said Sherrill gravely. "And I'm Sherrill

Cameron. That was my aunt Pat you took the note down to. She is Miss Catherwood. She didn't know either. I had to write and tell her."

"I couldn't help seeing some of the words," he admitted. "Will she stand by you?"

"I—don't know—!" Sherrill hesitated, "I thought I saw a twinkle in her eye, but it may have been indignation. She's rather severe in her judgments. She may turn me right out of the house after it's over. But if I can only get through the evening without shaming her, I won't care. She's been so very kind to me. I know this will be hard for her to bear. She stands very high in the community and is very proud. But she'll be nice to you. And then, there'll be the bridesmaids and ushers. I'll introduce the rest of them. You won't be expected to know everybody. Here we are, and that's the first car just coming into the drive now! Oh, we're in plenty of time! Just leave the car right here. This is out of the way. Yes, lock it. Now, come, we'll go up the fire escape if you don't mind, and then we won't have to explain ourselves."

Swiftly they stole up the iron stairs, Sherrill ahead, reaching down a guiding hand in the dark, giggling a little, nervously, as they stepped inside the window. Then she scuttled him down the back hall, opened a door to a small room that had been fixed up for the occasion as a dressing room, showed him how to find the front stairs, and directed him where to meet her as soon as he was ready.

Back through the two dim rooms where she had so recently come face to face with catastrophe, she hurried; only they were not in confusion now. The maids had been there straightening up. There were no traces of Cassie's suitcase nor Linda's street shoes. All was in immaculate order, the door thrown open to accommodate the expected crowds.

Sherrill slipped into her own room and fastened both doors.

Here too were signs of straightening. Her suitcase was closed, the closet doors and bureau drawers shut, everything put carefully away. But this room of course was not to be used for the guests. It was where the bride was expected to dress for going away.

Sherrill dashed to the dressing table and tried to obliterate as far as possible the traces of the past hour's experience from her face. She didn't care personally how she looked, but she did not want the assembled multitude to remark on her ghastly appearance. If she must go through this evening she would do it gallantly.

She waited long enough to possess herself of a great ostrich fan that just matched the green of her frock. It would be wonderful to hide behind if need came, and give her a brave outfit. Then she put on the gorgeous necklace of emeralds, with three long pendants of emeralds and diamonds, a family heirloom that Aunt Pat had given her just that day. She must have something to replace the bridal pearls that were hers no longer. There were some rings and bracelets too. She hadn't had much time to get acquainted with them. She fingered them over and chose one luscious square cut emerald for her finger. Her hands also should go bravely, not missing the diamond which she had worn for the past four months.

She slipped the magnificent ring on her finger, closed her eyes for a second taking a deep breath, then hurried down stairs.

There were sounds of approach at the front of the house, gay chatter of bridesmaids disembarking from their respective cars. Aunt Pat was just entering the front door leaning on Gemmie's arm. Off in the far corner of the great reception room to the right she could see Carter with his bride huddled under the bower of palms and flowers like a pair of frightened fowls between the clearing of two storms. The bride had her back toward the hall and was talking earnestly. Carter was half turned away too, casting furtive frantic glances behind him, an ungroomly scowl upon his handsome brow. Poor Arla! Her hell had probably begun!

Sherrill unfurled her green fan and went bravely forward to meet Aunt Pat.

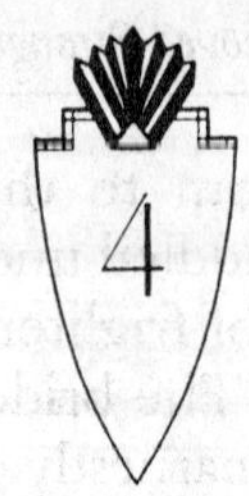

GEMMIE gave Sherrill a frightened scrutinizing glance, took the old lady's wrap and scarf and fled, casting another worried puzzled look behind her.

Sherrill took her aunt's arm. The old lady was smiling affably, but there was an inscrutable look about her. Sherrill couldn't tell whether it held disapproval or not. It was a mask, she could see that.

"What's her name? Who is she?" demanded the old lady out of the side of her mouth, without moving her lips or disturbing her smile. She was steering Sherrill straight toward the bridal bower. Sherrill had to speak quickly, keeping her own lips in a smile that she was far from feeling.

"She's his secretary, Arla Prentiss. He's known her for years."

"H'm! The puppy!" grunted the old lady under her smile, and then raising her voice a little. "Come, let's get this line in order! Where's this bride and groom? Mrs. McArthur, Mr. McArthur—" her voice was smooth, even, jovial and yet frigid, if such a combination can be imagined. Just as if she had not been calling the groom "Carter" for the past six weeks!

The bride and groom swung around to face her, the bride with a heightened color and a quick lifting of her chin as of one who expects a rebuff, the groom with every bit of color drained from his handsome face, and points of steel in his sulky eyes.

"I'm sure I hope you'll both be very happy," said Aunt Pat with a grimly humorous twist of her smile, implying perhaps that they didn't deserve to be, and then with just a tinge of the Catherwood haughtiness she took her place in the line as had been arranged.

Now had come the most trying moment for Sherrill, the one spot in the program that she hadn't been able to think out ahead. It was as if she had blindly shut her eyes to the necessity of speaking to these two, unable to prepare the right words of formal greeting, unable to school her expression. And here she was facing them with that silly smile upon her lips and nothing in her heart to say but horror at the situation, which such a brief time ago had been so different!

And then, just as a strange constriction came in her throat to stop any words she might try to form with her cold dumb lips, and her smile seemed to her to be fading out across the room and getting hopelessly away from her forever, she felt a touch upon her arm, and there miraculously was Copeland, meticulously arrayed in evening garb, a cheery grin upon his face, and gay words upon his lips:

"Is this where you want me to be, Sherrill?"

The ice melted from Sherrill's heart, her frightened throat relaxed, fear fled away and the smile danced back into her eyes. He had come in just the nick of time. A warm feeling of gratitude flowed around her heart and her voice returned with a delightful little lilt.

"Oh, is that you, Gray? How did you manage to get back so soon? Yes, this is just where I want you. Let me introduce you to the bride, Mrs. McArthur, my friend Mr. Copeland of Chicago. Mr. McArthur, Graham."

Arla eyed the two keenly.

"Were you old schoolmates?" she asked the stranger brightly, "Carter and I went to school together from kindergarten up through senior high."

"Well, not exactly schoolmates," answered Copeland with an amused glance at Sherrill, "but we're pretty good friends, aren't we, Sherrill?" He cast a look of deep admiration and understanding toward the girl in green and she answered with a glowing look.

"I should say!" she rippled a little laugh. "But come, Graham, they're all arriving in a bunch, and you've got to meet the bridesmaids and ushers. Here, come over to Aunt Pat first!" and they swung away from the astounded bridal couple with formal smiles.

"Aunt Pat, I want you to know Mr. Graham Copeland of Chicago. He's been a really wonderful friend to me. She's Miss Catherwood, Gray. I've told you about her."

"And why haven't I been told about *him* before?" asked Aunt Pat as she took the young man's hand and gave him a keen quick friendly look. Then, as her old eyes twinkled, "Oh, I have met him before, haven't I? You had a blue coat on when I saw you last!" and her lips twisted into what would have been called a grin if she had been a few years younger.

"You're one of the conspirators in this practical joke we're playing, I suppose?" And her eyes searched his again.

"I trust I'm a harmless one, at least," he said gracefully.

And then there came a sudden influx of bridesmaids,

preening their feathers and chattering like a lot of magpies.

They gushed into the room and seemed to fill it with their light and color and jubilant noise.

"Sherrill Cameron! Whatever did you put over on us?"

"Oh, Sherrill, you fraud! All these weeks and we thinking *you* were the bride!"

"What was the idea, Sherrill? Did you expect us to fall over in a faint when we saw another bride?"

"But we all thought it was you for the longest time!"

"I didn't!" said Linda, "I knew when she got out of her car that there was something different about her!"

"Sh!"

Into the midst of the bevy of voices, came Sherrill's clear controlled one, sweet, almost merry, though Aunt Pat turned a keen ear and a keen eye on her and knew she was under great strain:

"Girls! Girls! For pity's sake! Hush with your questions! Come and meet the bride, and then get into the receiving line quick! Don't you see the guests are beginning to arrive?"

The girls turned dizzily about, as Sherrill with a smile almost like her own natural one, approached the bride:

"Arla—" the name slipped off her tongue glibly, for somehow with Aunt Pat and Graham Copeland in the background she felt more at her ease, "Arla—" The bride turned in quick astonishment to hear herself addressed so familiarly, "let me introduce your bridesmaids. This is Linda Winters, and Doris Graeme—"

She went on down the row, speaking their names with more and more confidence, and suddenly the best man, who had been on some errand of his office, loomed frowning beside her.

"And oh, here's the best man! Carter, you'll have to

make the rest of the introductions. I simply must get these girls into place! Here come all the ushers too! I'll leave you to introduce them to your wife!" She said it crisply and moved away to make room for them, pushing the laughing bridesmaids before her and arranging them, with room for the ushers between, though every one knew as well as she did where they ought to stand, having rehearsed it only the night before.

Then Sherrill slid behind them back to her place by Aunt Pat and the stranger, a place that had *not* been rehearsed the night before.

It was a hard place, a trying place, the worst place she could have been. She knew that when she chose it. But she had to face the music, and knew it was better to do it merrily at the head of the line than skulking at the foot where there would be plenty of time for explanations and questions.

So as the crowd of guests surged into the big lovely room, filled with curiosity and excitement, and ready to pull any secret one might have from the air and waft it to the world, it was Sherrill who stood at the head of the line in her lettuce green taffeta, the little frock she had bought as a whimsie at the last minute, her second best silver slippers, and the gorgeous Catherwood emeralds blazing on her neck and arms and finger. She was wafting her great feather fan graciously, and by her side was a handsome stranger! Would wonders never cease? The guests stepped in, gave one eager avid glance and hastened to the fray.

Aunt Pat was next the stranger, smiling her cat-in-the-cream smile, with twinkles in her eyes and a grim look of satisfaction.

"You ought to be at the head of the line, Aunt Pat," demurred Sherrill. "I really don't belong in this line at all."

"Stay where you are!" commanded the old lady. "This is *your* wedding not mine. Run it the way you please. I'm only here to lend atmosphere." She said it from one corner of her mouth and she twinkled at the stranger. She was standing next to the bride and groom but she hadn't addressed two words to them since her congratulations. However, they were getting on fairly well with the best man and maid of honor on the other side, and the stage was set for the great oncoming crowd.

Mrs. Battersea with her ultra-modern daughter-in-law in the wake headed the procession, with the Reamers, the Hayworths and the Buells just behind. They represented the least intimate of the guests, the ones who would really be hard to satisfy. Sherrill with a furtive glance up at the tall stranger by her side, aware of his kindly reassuring grin, felt a sudden influx of power in herself to go through this ordeal. It helped too, to realize that several others were having an ordeal also. It probably wasn't just what this stranger would have chosen to do, to play his part in this strange pageant, and she was sure Aunt Pat hated it all, though she was entering into the scene with a zest as if she enjoyed it. Aunt Pat hated publicity like a serpent.

And there were the bride and groom. One could scarcely expect them to enjoy this performance. Sherrill cast them a furtive glance. The bride was a game little thing. She was holding her head high and conversing bravely with all those chattering bridesmaids, who kept surging out of line to get a word with her. And Carter, well, Carter had always been able to adjust himself to his surroundings pretty well, but there was a strained white look about him. Oh, whatever he might have felt for either of his prospective brides, it was scarcely likely that he was enjoying this reception. It was most probable that he would give all he possessed to have a nice hole open in the floor and let him and his Arla through out of sight.

So Sherrill drew a deep breath, summoned a smile, and greeted Mrs. Battersea, sweeping up in purple chiffon with orchids on her ample breast.

"Now, Sherrill, my dear," said the playful lady, "what does this all mean? You've got to give us a full explanation of everything."

"Why, it was just that we thought this would be a pleasant way to do things," smiled Sherrill, "Don't you think it was a real surprise? Mrs. Battersea, do let me introduce my friend Mr. Copeland of Chicago. Oh, Mrs. Reamer, I'm so glad you got well in time to come—!"

Suddenly Sherrill felt a thrill of triumph. She was getting away with it! Actually she was! Mrs. Battersea had been not only held at bay, but entirely sidetracked by this new young man introduced into the picture. She closed her mouth on the question that had been just ready to pop out and fixed her eyes on Copeland, a new fatuous smile quickly adjusted, as she passed with avidity to the inquisition of this stranger. Here was she, the first in the line, and it was obviously up to her to get accurate information concerning him and convey it as rapidly as possible to the gathering assembly. Sherrill could see out of the tail of her eye this typical Battersea attitude, even as the guest put up her lorgnette to inspect the young man. She felt a pang of pity for her new friend. Did he realize what he was letting himself in for when he promised to stand by her through this? Oh, but what a help he was! How his very presence had changed the attitude that might have been, the attitude of pity for a cast off bride! And, too, he had brought in an element of mystery, of speculation. She could see how avidly

Mrs. Battersea was drinking in the possibilities as she approached.

But Sherrill drew another breath of relief. The young man by her side would be equal to it. She need not worry.

And there too was Aunt Pat! She would not let the first comer linger too long with the new lion of the occasion.

Even with the thought, she heard the woman's first question, and saw Aunt Pat instantly, capably, if grimly, take over the Battersea woman. Whether Aunt Pat was going to forgive Sherrill afterward or not for making such a mess of a beautiful stately wedding which she had financed, she would be loyal now and defend her own whether right or wrong. That was Aunt Pat.

Yes, those two could be depended upon.

And then came Mrs. Reamer fairly bursting with curiosity, and Sherrill was able to smile and greet her with a gracious merriment that surprised herself, and then interrupt the second question with, "Oh, but you haven't met my friend Mr. Copeland of Chicago yet. Graham, this is Mrs. Reamer, one of our nearest neighbors."

The Haywards and Buells were mercifully pressing forward, eager to get in their questions, and Sherrill thankfully handed over Mrs. Reamer to Copeland who dealt with her merrily. So with a lighter heart and well turned phrases she met the next onslaught, marveling that this terrible ordeal was really going forward so gayly, and presently she began to feel the thrill that always comes sooner or later to one who is accomplishing a difficult task successfully.

She was on a strain of course, like one who pilots an airship through the unchartered skies for the first time perhaps, yet she knew that when she got back to earth and her nerves were less taut there was bound to be a reaction. Just now the main thing was to keep sailing and not let anyone suspect how frightened and sick at heart she really was; how utterly humiliated and cast out she felt, with another bride standing there beside the man who was to have been her husband. And he smiling and shaking hands, and withal deporting himself as if he were quite satisfied. She stole a glance at him now and again between hand shakes and introductions, and perceived that he did not appear greatly distraught. His assurance seemed to have returned to him, the whiteness was leaving his lips, his eyes were no longer deep moldering angry fires. He really seemed to be having a good time. Of course he too was playing a part, and there was no telling what his real feelings were. Equally of course he was caught in the tide of the hour and had to carry out his part or bolt and bear the consequences of publicity of which she had warned him. She remembered that he had always been a good actor.

But there was another actor in the line who utterly amazed her. Arla, the bride, filled her part graciously, with a little tilt triumphant to her pretty chin, a glint of pride in her big blue eyes, an air of being to the manor born that was wholly surprising. There she stood in borrowed bridal attire, beside a reluctant bridegroom, wearing another girl's engagement ring, and a wedding ring that was not purchased for her, bearing another girl's roses and lilies, standing under a bower that did not belong to her; and yet she was carrying it all off in the most delightfully natural way. To look at her one would never suspect that an hour ago she had been pleading with her lover to run away with her and leave another girl to wait in vain for him at the church. Well, perhaps she deserved to have her hour of triumph. She certainly was getting all she possibly could out of it. One would never suspect to look at her that she was a girl who had threatened just a little while before to kill herself. She looked the ideal radiant bride.

Sherrill's eyes went back to the face of her former lover for just an instant. It was lit with one of his most charming smiles as he greeted one of his old friends. How she had loved that smile! How like a knife twisting in her heart was the sight of it now! Every line of his face, every motion of his slim white hands, the pose of his fine athletic body, so familiar and so beloved, how the sight of them suddenly hurt her! He was not hers any more! He belonged to another girl! Her mind and soul writhed within her as the thought pierced home to her consciousness with more poignancy than it had yet done. He belonged to another!

But there was something worse than even that. It was that he never really had been what she thought him. There never had existed the Carter McArthur whom she had loved or all this could not have happened.

For an instant it all swept over her how terrible it was going to be to face the devastation in her own life after this evening was over.

Then more people swarmed in and she put aside her thoughts and faced them with a frozen smile upon her face, wondering why everybody did not see what agony she was suffering. She must not look at him again, not think about him, she told herself breathlessly as she faced her eager guests and tried to say more pleasant nothings.

At last there came a lull in the stream of guests and Copeland turned to her confidentially, the gay smile upon his lips, but a graver tone to his voice:

"I'm wondering what you've done about the license? Anything? It might make trouble for all concerned if that's not attended to to-night before they leave. I don't know what your law is in this state, but I'm sure it ought to be looked into right away. I'm a lawyer you know and I can't help thinking of those things."

Sherrill turned a startled face toward him.

"Mercy, no! I never thought of it. We had a license of course. Wouldn't that do?"

He shook his head slightly.

"I'm afraid not. Do you know where the license was got? If we could get hold of the man—"

"Yes, I went along. But the office would be closed to-night wouldn't it?"

"I suppose so. Still if we knew the man's name he might be willing, if there were sufficient inducement, to come over here at once and straighten things out for us."

"Oh, that would be wonderful! Perhaps he'd come for twenty-five dollars, or even fifty. I'd offer him fifty if necessary. It would be dreadful to have that kind of trouble."

Her eyes were full of distress.

"There, don't look so troubled," he said putting on his grin again. "Remember you're a good little sport. This can all be straightened out I'm sure. If you could just give me a clue to find that man. You don't know his name I suppose?"

"Yes, I do," said Sherrill eagerly. "His mail was brought in while we were there and I saw the name on the letters. Afterwards, too, somebody called him by it so I am sure it was he. The name was Asahel Becker. I remembered it because it was so queer. Maybe we could find it in the telephone book. But would he have his stamps and papers and seals and things? Could he get them do you think if we offered him enough?"

"It's worth trying. If you will tell me where I can telephone without being heard by this mob I'll see what I can do."

"There's a booth in the back of the hall under the stairs, but I'll go with you of course."

"No, please, if you are willing to trust me, I think I can handle this without you. You have been taking an awful beating and this is just one thing you don't need to do. Just give me the full names, all three. Here, write them on the card so I won't make a mistake, and then you stay right here and *don't worry!* If I need you I'll come for you."

He gave her a reassuring smile and was gone. Sherrill found she was trembling from head to foot, her lips trembling too. She put up an unsteady hand to cover them. Oh, she must not give way! She must snap out of this. She must not remember yesterday when she went joyously to get that license,—and how her beautiful romance was all turned to dust and ashes!

Just then the three elderly Markham sisters hove in sight moving in a body, fairly bristling with question marks and exclamation points, and she had plenty to do again baffling them, with no Copeland there beside her to help.

But blessed Aunt Pat turned in to help and soon had drawn the attention of all three.

"And this other bride," said the eldest sister, Matilda by name, leveling her gaze on Arla as if she were a museum piece, and then bringing it back to Aunt Pat's face again. "Did you say she was a relative too? A close relative?"

"Yes, in a way," said Aunt Pat grimly, "but not so close. Quite distant in fact. It's on the Adamses side of the family you know."

Sherrill gasped softly and almost gave a hysterical giggle, just catching herself in time.

"Indeed!" said Miss Markham giving the bride another appraising glance, "I wasn't aware there were Adamses in your family. Then she's not a Catherwood?"

"Oh, no!" said Aunt Pat with pursed lips, "In fact," and her voice sounded almost like a chuckle, "the relationship was several generations back."

"Ohh!" sighed the inquisitor lowering her lorgnette and losing interest. "Well, she seems to be quite attractive anyway."

"Yes, isn't she? Now let me introduce you—"

But suddenly Sherrill saw Copeland coming toward her and her eyes sought his anxiously.

"You must be desperately tired," he said in a low tone as he stepped into the line beside her, "couldn't we run away outside for just a minute and get you into the open air?"

"Oh, yes!" said Sherrill gratefully, "Come through here."

She led him to the long French window just behind the line, open to the garden terrace, and they stepped out and went down the walk where pale moonlight from a young moon was just beginning to make itself felt.

"It's all right," he assured her comfortably, drawing her arm within his own. "He'll be here shortly with all his papers and things. He didn't want to do it at first, but finally snapped at the bait I offered him and promised to be here within the hour. Now, had you thought where we can take him?"

"Yes," said Sherrill, "up in that little room where you dressed. That is quite out of the way of all guests and,—" she stopped short in the walk and looked up at her escort with troubled eyes, "we'll have to tell them—the bride and groom—won't we?" Her gaze turned back toward the house anxiously. He could see how she was dreading the ordeal.

"Not yet," he said quickly, "not till our man comes.

Then I'll just give the tip to the best man to ask them to come upstairs. You leave that to me. I'll attend to it all. You've had enough worry."

"You are so kind!" she murmured, beginning to walk along by his side again.

He laid his hand gently over hers that rested on his arm.

"I'm glad if I can help. And by the way I told this Mr. Becker to come to the side entrance and ask for me, and I took the liberty of asking the butler to keep an eye out for him and let me know at once."

"Oh, thank you," she said, "I don't know what I should have done without you!"

"I am honored to be allowed to help," he said, glad that she had not taken away her hand from his touch, although he was not quite sure she was aware of it, she seemed so distraught. "As far as I am concerned," he went on brightly, "if it weren't that you are taking such a beating I'd be having the time of my life!"

Sherrill gave him a quick convulsive laugh that seemed very near to tears.

"Oh, if it weren't all so very terrible," she responded wistfully, "I'd think it was almost fun, you're being so splendid!"

"You're a brave girl!" said Copeland almost reverently.

They had reached the end of the garden walk.

"I suppose we ought to go back in there," said Sherrill with a little shiver of dislike. "They'll be wondering where we are."

They turned and walked silently back a few steps, when suddenly a bevy of young people broke forth hilariously from the house swinging around the corner from the front piazza and evidently bound for the garden.

"Oh!" said Sherrill shrinking back, "We've got to meet them!"

"Isn't there some place we can hide for a minute until they have passed?" asked Copeland with a swift glance at their surroundings, "Here, how about this?" and he swung aside the tall branches of privet that bordered the path around the house and the hedge.

Sherrill stepped in and Copeland after her and the branches swung together behind them shutting them in together. There was not much space, for it happened that the opening in the hedge had been near the servants' entrance door, and the hedge curved about across the end, and at the other end it rose nearly twelve feet against the end of the side piazza where they had come out. It made a little room of fragrant green, scarcely large enough for them to stand together in, with the ivy-covered stone wall of the house behind them.

There in the sweet semi-darkness of the spring night, where even frail new moonlight could not enter except by reflection, and with only a few stars above, they stood, face to face, quietly, while the noisy throng of guests trooped by and rollicked down to the garden.

Sherrill's face was lifted slightly and seemed a pale picture made of moonlight, so sweet and sad and tired and almost desperate there in the little green haven. Copeland looking down suddenly put out his arms and drew her close to him, just as a mother might have drawn a little troubled child, it seemed to her. Drew her close and held her so for an instant. She let her head lie still against his shoulder, startled at the sweetness that enwrapt her. Then softly she began to cry, her slim body shaking with the stifled sobs, the tears coming in a torrent. It was so sweet to find sympathy even with a stranger.

Softly he stooped and kissed her drenched eyelids,

kissing the tears away, then paused and looked down at her reverently.

"Forgive me!" he said tenderly in a low whisper, "I had no right to do that—now! I'm only a stranger to you! But—I wanted to comfort you!"

She was very still in his arms for a moment and then she whispered so softly that he had to bend to hear her: "You *aren't* a stranger, and—you *do*—comfort me!"

Suddenly above their heads there arose a clatter inside the window of the butler's pantry.

"Quick, get those pattie shells! The people are coming out to the dining room. We must begin to serve!"

Dishes began to rattle, trays to clatter, a fork fell with a silvery resonance. The swinging door fell back and let in another clatter from the kitchen. Hard cold facts of life began to fall upon the two who had been so set apart for the moment.

"We must go back at once!" said Sherrill making hasty dabs at her eyes with her scrap of lace handkerchief.

"Of course," said Copeland offering a large cool square of immaculate linen.

Then he took her hand and led her gravely out into the moonlight, pulled her arm possessively through his and accommodated his step to hers.

When they came to the long window where they had escaped a few minutes before he looked down at her.

"Are you all right?" he asked softly.

"All right!" she answered with a brave little catch in her breath, and smiled up at him.

He still held her hand and he gave it a warm pressure before he let her go. Then they stepped inside the room and saw the end of the long line of guests progressing slowly down the hall and Aunt Pat hovering behind them looking this way and that, out the front door, and into the vacated library. It was evident she was looking for Sherrill for as they came forward her brow cleared, she smiled a relieved smile, and came to meet them.

Just an instant she lingered by Sherrill's side as Copeland stepped to the dining room door to look over the heads of the throng and reconnoitre for seats for them all.

"I don't know how you have planned," said the old lady in something that sounded like a low growl, "nor how long this ridiculous performance has been going on, but I thought I'd remind you that it will be necessary for that girl to have some baggage if you expect to carry this thing out. I don't want to interfere with your plans, but there's that second suitcase, the one that wasn't marked that we had sent up. It hasn't been returned yet you know. I suppose you'll have to see that she has things enough to be decent on ship board, unless she has time enough to get some of her own. But if you let that lace evening dress, or that shell-pink chiffon go I'll never forgive you. It's bad enough to lose the going-away outfit, but I suppose there isn't any way out of that. A couple of evening dresses and some sport things ought to see her through. Don't be a fool and give up everything!" and Miss Catherwood with her head in the air and a set smile on her aristocratic face swept on to the dining room.

Sherrill stood startled, looking after her doubtfully. Did that mean that Aunt Pat was angry? Angry yet going to stand by till it was all over to the last detail? Or did it mean that she understood the awful situation better than Sherrill knew? She was a canny old lady. How wonderfully she had stood and met that line of hungry gossip mongers! But yet, she might still be angry. Very angry! To be the talk of the town when she had done so much to make this wedding perfect in every way. To have people wondering and gossiping about them! It would be dreadful for Aunt Pat!

Sherrill had a sudden vision of what it might be to face an infuriated Aunt Pat and explain everything after it was all over, and she had that panicky impulse once more to flee away into the world and shirk it,—never come back any more. But of course she knew she never would do that!

Then Copeland touched her on the arm.

"Please, do we follow the rest, or what?" and she perceived that they two were left alone in the room, with only the end of the procession surging away from them toward the dining room.

Sherrill giggled nervously.

"I haven't much head, have I?" she said. "I've got to go upstairs a minute or two and put some things in a suitcase. It won't take long. Perhaps I'd better go now."

"Yes," said Copeland thoughtfully. "Now would be a good time. I'll wait here at the foot of the stairs for you."

She flew up the stairs with a quick smile back at her helper. He was marvelous! It could not be that he was an absolute stranger! It seemed as if she had known him always. Here she had almost laid bare her heart to him and he had taken it all so calmly and done everything needful, just as if he understood all the details. No brother could have been tenderer, more careful of her. She remembered his lips on her eyelids and her breath came quickly. How gentle he had been!

She hurried to her own room and miraculously found Gemmie there before her, the suitcase in her hand.

"Your Aunt Pat thought you might be wanting this," said the woman respectfully, no hint of her former surprise in her eyes, no suggestion that aught was different from what it had been when the old servant left her there in her wedding dress ready to go to the church.

"Oh, yes!" said Sherrill in relief. "You'll help me, won't you, Gemmie?"

With half frenzied fingers Sherrill went to work, laying out things from her suitcase and bags, separating them into two piles upon the bed. The black satin evening dress, the orchid, and the yellow, those ought to be enough. Aunt Pat wasn't especially crazy about any of those. She put aside the things that were marked with her own initials, not one of those should go. She shut her lips tight and drew in a sharp little breath of pain.

Gemmie seemed to understand. She gathered those things up quickly and put them away in the bureau drawers. Gemmie's powers of selection were even keener than Sherrill's.

It did not take long, three or four minutes, and Gemmie's skillful fingers did the rest.

"There, now, Miss Sherrill, I can manage," she said. "You run back. They'll be missing you."

It was as if Gemmie was also a conspirator.

"Thank you, Gemmie dear!" said Sherrill with a catch in her voice like a sob, and closed the door quickly behind her.

Copeland was waiting at the foot of the stairs and they found places saved for them close to the bride's table, a little table for two, and the eyes of all upon them as they sat down.

Sherrill saw the Markham sisters looking eagerly from Copeland to herself and back again, and nodding their heads violently to one another as they swept in large mouthfuls of creamed mushrooms and chicken salad. She had an impulse to put her head down on the table and laugh, or cry. She knew she was getting very near to the limit of her self control.

But Copeland knew it also, and managed to keep her busy telling him who the different people were.

After all the ordeal was soon over, even to the cutting of the wedding cake by a bride very much at her ease, and enjoying her privileges to the last degree. If Arla never was happy again she was to-night.

And then after all the matter of the license which loomed like a peril in Sherrill's thoughts was arranged so easily. Just a quiet word from the butler to Copeland, a quiet sign from Copeland to the best man. Sherrill had put money in her little pearl evening bag which she slipped to Copeland as they went upstairs together while the bride was throwing Sherrill's bouquet to the noisy clamoring bridesmaids down in the hall. Sherrill and Copeland were presumably escorting the bride and groom to their rooms to change into traveling garb, and no one noticed them enter the little room off the back hall where the representative of the law was waiting.

Just a few quiet questions from the grizzly old man who had come to make the legal part right, and who looked at them as only three more in the long procession that came to him day by day. They waited, those five, the best man doing his best not to seem too curious about it all, while those important seals were placed, and the proper signature affixed, and then Sherrill hurried the bride away to dress. A frightened almost tearful bride now, afraid of her, Sherrill was sure.

Almost the last lap of this terrible race she was running! There would be one more. She would have to face Aunt Pat, but that she dared not think about yet. This present session with the bride who had taken her place was going to be perhaps the hardest of all.

SHERRILL led her white bride through the two middle rooms again, hurriedly, silently, remembering with sharp thrills of pain all that had happened earlier in the evening. She dreaded intensely the moment when they two would be shut in together again. One would have to say something. One could not be absolutely silent, and somehow her tongue felt heavy and her brain refused to think.

But Gemmie was there! Dear Gemmie! Ah! She had forgotten Gemmie! What a relief! Gemmie with her most professional air of dignity.

The frightened little bride did not feel relief however at her presence. She faltered at the doorway and gave Sherrill a pitiful look of protest. Sherrill drew her inside and fastened the door, feeling suddenly an infinite pity for this girl among strangers in a role that belonged to another.

"Oh, here is Gemmie!" she said gently. "She will help you off with the veil and dress. Gemmie knows how to do it without mussing your hair."

Arla submitted herself to Gemmie's ministrations and

Sherrill hovered about looking over the neatly packed suitcase, and the great white box that Gemmie had set forth on the bed.

"Oh, you have the box ready for the wedding dress, haven't you, Gemmie?" said Sherrill feeling she must break this awful silence that seemed to pervade the room. "That's all right. Gemmie will fold it for you and get it all ready to be sent to whatever address you say."

"Oh," began Arla, with a hesitant glance toward Gemmie and then looking Sherrill almost haughtily in the eye, "I couldn't think of keeping it. I really couldn't!"

"Certainly you will take it," said Sherrill sternly. "It is your wedding dress! *You* were married in it. *I* wouldn't want it you know."

Arla answered with a quick-drawn startled "Oh!" of comprehension. Then she added, "And I'm afraid I wouldn't either!"

Over Sherrill's face there passed a swift look of sympathy.

"I see," she said quietly. "You wouldn't want it of course. I'm sorry. You are right. I'll keep it."

Arla was silent until she was freed from the white veil and sheathing satin, but when Gemmie brought forth the dark slip and lovely tailored going-away costume that Sherrill had prepared for herself she suddenly spoke with determination:

"No," she said with a little haughty lifting of her pretty chin, "I will wear my own things away. Where are they? Did somebody take them away?"

"They are here," said Sherrill, a certain new respect in her voice that had not been there before. "But—you are perfectly welcome to the other dress. I think it would fit you. We are about the same size."

"No," said Arla determinedly, "I prefer to wear my

own dress. It is new and quite all right. Wouldn't you prefer to wear your own things?" She asked the question almost fiercely.

"I suppose I would," said Sherrill meekly. "And I remember your dress. It was very pretty. But I just wanted you to feel you were perfectly welcome to wear the other."

"Thank you," said Arla in a choking voice, "but there is no need. You have done enough. You really have been rather wonderful, and I want you to know that I appreciate it all."

Gemmie, skillfully folding the rich satin, managed somehow to give the impression that she was not there, and presently took herself conveniently out of the room.

Sherrill looked up pleasantly.

"That's all right," she said with a wan smile, "and now listen! I've packed some things for you in this suitcase. I think there will be enough to carry you through the trip."

"That wouldn't be necessary either," said the other girl coldly, "I can get some things somewhere."

"I'm afraid not," said Sherrill. "You'll barely have time to make the boat train. The ship sails at midnight. You might be able to stop for a few personal things if you don't live too far out of the way, but you'd have to hurry awfully. You couldn't take more than five minutes to get them, and you couldn't possibly pack for a trip to Europe in that time."

"Then I can get along without things!" said the bride with a sob in her voice.

"Don't be silly!" said Sherrill in a friendly voice. "You can't make the trip into an endurance test. You've got to have the right things of course. You're on your wedding trip you know, and there may be people on board that Carter knows. You've got to look right."

She wondered at herself as she said all this coolly to this other girl who was taking the trip in her place. It was just like a terrible dream that she was going through. A wild thought that perhaps it was a dream passed through her weary mind. Perhaps she would presently wake up and find that none of all this nightmare was true. Perhaps there wasn't any Arla, and Carter had never been untrue!

Idle thoughts of course! She pushed them frantically from her and tried to talk practically.

"I haven't put much in, just some sports things and three little evening dresses. Necessary under things and accessories of course. Some slippers too, and there's a heavy coat for the deck. The bag is fitted with toilet articles. You won't need to stop for any of your own unless you feel you must."

"Oh, I feel like a criminal!" the bride said suddenly, and sank into a chair with her golden head bowed and her face in her hands, sobbing.

"Nonsense!" said Sherrill under the same impulse with which she might have dashed cold water in the girl's face if she had been fainting. "Brace up! You've got through the worst! For pity's sake don't get red eyes and spoil it all. Remember you've got to go down stairs and smile at everybody yet. Stop it! Quick!"

She offered a clean handkerchief.

"Now look here! Be sensible! Things aren't just as either you or I would have had them if we'd had our choice! But we've got this thing to go through with now, and we're not going to pass out just at the last minute. Be a good sport and finish your dressing. There isn't a whole lot of time you know. Say, that is a pretty frock! I hadn't noticed it closely before. It certainly is attractive. Come, get it fastened and I'll find your shoes and stockings."

Arla accepted the handkerchief and essayed to repair

the damages on her face, but her whole slender body was quivering.

"I've—taken your—hus—band—," she began with trembling lips.

"You have not!" said Sherrill with flashing eyes. "He's *not my* husband, thank goodness!"

"You'd—have—been—happpp-py—" sobbed Arla, "if—you—just—hadn't—found—out—! It would have been much bbbet-ter if I had kkkkilled myself!"

"Don't you suppose I'd have found out eventually that he was that sort? And what good would your killing yourself have been? Haven't you any sense at all? For pity's sake stop crying! *You're* not to blame." Sherrill was frantic. The girl seemed to be going all to pieces.

"Yes I am! I've taken your husband—!" went on Arla getting a fresh start on sobs, "and I've taken your wedding away from you, and now you want me to take your clothes—*And I can't do it!"*

"Fiddlesticks!" said Sherrill earnestly. "I tell you I don't *want* your husband, and if anybody wanted a frantic wedding such as this has been they are welcome to it. As for the clothes, they're all new and have never become a part of me. I'm glad to have you have them, and anyway you've *got* to, to carry out this thing right! Now stop being a baby and get your shoes on. I tell you the time is going fast. Listen! I *want* you to have those things. I really do! And I *want* you to have just as good a time as you can. Don't you believe it?"

"Oh, you're wonderful!" said Arla suddenly jumping up and flinging her slender young arms around Sherrill's neck, "I just love you! And to think I thought you were so different! Oh, if I'd known you were like this I wouldn't have come here! I really wouldn't!"

"Well, I'm glad you came!" said Sherrill fiercely. "I didn't know it but I guess I really am. Of course I'm not having a particularly heavenly time out of it, but I'm sure in my heart that you've probably done me a great favor, and some day when I get over the shock I'll thank you for it!"

"Oh, but I wouldn't have wanted to hurt you," sighed Arla, her red lips still quivering, "I really wouldn't. I've always been—well—decent—!"

"That's all right!" said Sherrill blinking her own tears back. "And I wouldn't have wanted to hurt you either. There! Let's let it go at that and be friendly. Now, please, powder your nose and brisk up. *Smile!* That's it!"

Just then Gemmie came back, a big warm coat over her arm, richly furred as to collar and sleeves.

"It's getting late, Mrs. McArthur!" she suggested officially, and presented Arla's chic little hat and doeskin gloves with a look of approbation toward them. Gemmie had decided that the substitute bride must be a lady. At least she knew how to buy the right clothes.

Arla paused at the door as Gemmie stepped off down the hall to direct the man who had come to take the suitcase, and whispered to Sherrill:

"I'll never forget what you've done for me! *Never!*" she said huskily.

"That's all right," said Sherrill almost tenderly as she looked at the pretty shrinking girl before her, "I'm just sorry you couldn't have had a regular wedding instead of one all messed up with other things like this."

"Oh, but I never could have afforded a wedding like this!" sighed Arla wistfully.

"Well, it might at least have been peaceful," said Sherrill with a tinge of bitterness in her voice, "But never mind. It's over now, and I hope a good happy life for you has begun. Try not to think much about the past. Try to make yours a happy marriage if it can be done."

They passed on together down the hall to the head of

the stairs where Carter McArthur and his best man stood waiting, and as she saw her bridegroom standing there so handsome and smiling and altogether just what a happy bridegroom ought to look like there came to Arla new strength. She lost her sorrowful humility and became the radiant bride again. That was her *husband* standing there waiting for her! *Her* husband, not another girl's! Only a short walk down the stairs now, a dash to the car, and she would be out and free from all this awfulness, and into a new life. She might be going into hell, but she was going with him, and it was what she had chosen.

Then suddenly, as Arla's hand was drawn within the arm of her bridegroom and they walked smilingly down the stairs with measured tread, Sherrill, falling in behind, felt greatly alone and lost. A sinking feeling came over her. Was she going to fall? That would be dreadful, now when it was almost over. Must she walk down those steps alone? Couldn't she just slip back to her room and stay there till they were all gone?

But just as she faltered at the top step she felt a hand under her arm and a pleasant voice said in her ear:

"Well, is it all over now but the shouting?" and she looked up to see the cheerful grin of Copeland.

She had forgotten his existence in the last few tense minutes, but he had been waiting, had seen her weakness, and was there just at the right moment.

"Did anybody ever before pick up a friend like you right out of the street in the dark night?" she asked suddenly, lifting grateful eyes to his face.

"Why, I thought it was *I* who picked *you* up!" he answered quickly with a warm smile.

"Well, anyway you have been wonderful!"

"I'm only too glad if I have been able to live up to the specifications," he said earnestly, and finished with his delightful grin again.

The people down in the hall looking up said to one another:

"Look at those two! They look as if it was *their* wedding, don't they? Who *is* he do you suppose, and where has he been all this time?"

Sherrill stood with the rest on the wide front veranda watching the bride and groom dash across to their beribboned car which awaited them. She even threw a few of the pink rose petals wherewith the guests were hilariously pelting the bridal couple. Even now at this last moment, when she was watching another girl go away with her bridegroom, she must smile and keep up appearances; although her knees felt weak and the tears were dangerously near.

Mrs. Battersea had stationed herself and her lorgnette in the forefront, and fixed her eagle eye especially on Sherrill. If there was still any more light on the peculiar happening of the evening to be gleaned from a view of the original bride off her guard, at this last minute, she meant to get it.

Sherrill suddenly visioned her and it had the effect of making her give a little hysterical giggle. Then Copeland's hand on her arm steadied her again, and she flashed a grateful smile up to meet his pleasant grin.

Mrs. Battersea dropped her lorgnette, deciding that of course this was the other lover appeared just at the last minute, only *how* did they get that other girl?

They were all gone at last. The last guest had joked Aunt Pat on her wonderful surprise wedding, the last bridesmaid had taken her little box of wedding cake to sleep on and stolen noisily away. Just Aunt Pat and Sherrill and Copeland left standing alone in the wide front hall as the last car whirled away.

Copeland had stayed to the end, as if he were a part of the household, stayed close by Sherrill, taken the burden of the last conversations upon himself as if he had the right, made every second of those last trying minutes just as easy for her as possible, kept up a light patter of brilliant conversation filling in all the spots that needed tiding over.

"And now," said he turning to the hostess as the last car whirled down the lighted driveway, "I have to thank you, Miss Catherwood, for a most delightful evening. Sherrill, it's been wonderful to have had this time with you. I must be getting on my way. I think your butler is bringing my things."

Just then the butler came toward them bearing Graham Copeland's suitcase and high hat. Sherrill looked up in surprise. With what ease he had arranged everything so that there would be no unpleasant pauses for explanation.

But Aunt Pat swung around upon him with a quick searching look at Sherrill.

"Why, where are you staying?" she asked cordially.

"I'm at the Wiltshire," he answered quickly, "I hadn't time to get into proper garb before the ceremony, so I brought my things up here and Sherrill very kindly gave me a place to dress."

"Well, then why don't you just stay here to-night? It's pretty late I guess. We've plenty of rooms now you know," and she gave him a little friendly smile that she gave only to an honored few whom she liked.

"Thank you," he said with an amused twinkle at Sherrill, "that would be delightful, but I've an appointment quite early in the morning, and my briefcase is at the hotel. I think I'd better go back to my room. But I certainly appreciate the invitation."

"Well, then, you'll be with us to dinner to-morrow night surely. That is, unless you and Sherry have made other plans."

"I certainly wish I could," said the young man wistfully, "but unfortunately I am obliged to take the noon train for Washington to meet another appointment which is quite important."

Aunt Pat looked disappointed.

"I wonder," said the young man hesitantly, "I'm not sure how long I shall be obliged to stay in Washington, several days likely as I have some important records to look up at the Patent Office, but I shall be passing through the city on my way to New York some time next week probably. Would I be presuming if I stopped off and called on you both?"

"Presuming?" said Aunt Pat with a keen look at Sherrill. "Well, not so far as I know," and she gave one of her quaint little chuckles.

"I do hope you can," said Sherrill earnestly with a look that left no doubt of her wish in the matter.

His eyes searched hers gravely for an instant and then he said as though he had received a royal command:

"Then I shall surely be here if it is at all possible. I'll call up and find out if it is convenient."

"Of course it'll be convenient!" said the old lady, *"I'm* always at home whether anybody else is or not, and *I'll* be glad to see you."

He bowed a gracious thanks, then turned to Sherrill as if reluctant to relinquish his office of assistant.

"I'll hope you'll be—" he hesitated, then finished earnestly, "all right."

There was something in his eyes that brought a warm little comforted feeling around her heart.

"Oh, yes!" she answered fervently. "Thank you! You were—It was wonderful having you here!" she finished with heightened color.

"Oh, but you're not going that way!" said the old

lady. "Gemmie, tell Stanley to bring the car around and take Mr. Copeland—"

A moment more and he was gone and Sherrill had a sudden feeling of being left alone in a troublous world.

Now she must have it out with Aunt Pat!

Slowly she turned away from the door and faced the old lady, all her lovely buoyant spirits gone, just a weary troubled little girl who looked as if she wanted to cry.

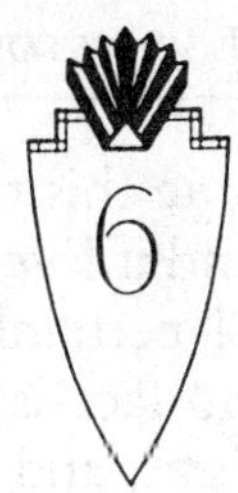

"WELL," said Aunt Pat with grim satisfaction in her voice, "you never did anything in your life that pleased me so much!"

"Oh, you darling Aunt Pat!" said Sherrill her face glowing with sudden relief, and quick tears brimming unbidden into her eyes.

"Why certainly!" said the old lady crisply. "You know I never did like that Carter McArthur. Now, come upstairs to my room and tell me all about it!"

"Oh, but aren't you too tired to-night, Aunt Pat?" asked Sherrill, struggling under the shock of relief.

"Bosh!" said Aunt Pat. "You know neither you nor I will sleep a wink till we've had it out. Run get your kimono on. I suppose you gave the grand new one to that little washed-out piece. Of course she had to have it. But put on your old one with the blue butterflies. I like that one best anyway. Gemmie,—" raising her voice to the faithful maid who was never far away, "Send up two plates of *every*thing to my room. *Every*thing, I said. We're hungry as bears. Neither of us ate as much as a bird while that mob was here. No, you needn't worry,

Gemmie, it won't hurt me this time of night at all. I'm as chipper as a squirrel, and if I've stood this evening and all the weeks before it I certainly can stand one good meal before I sleep. The fact is Gemmie, things have come out my way to-night, and I don't think anything could very well hurt me just now."

"Yes, Ma'am!" said Gemmie with a happy glance toward Sherrill.

A general air of good cheer pervaded Aunt Pat's room when Sherrill, in her old kimono of shell pink satin with blue butterflies fluttering over it, and her comfortable old slippers with the lamb's wool lining and pink feather edges, arrived and was established in a big stuffed chair at one side of the open fire. Aunt Pat with her silver hair in soft ringlets around her shoulders, sat on the other side of the fire robed in dove gray quilted silk.

Gemmie brought two little tables and two heaping trays of food, and left them with the lights turned low. The firelight flickered over the two, the young face and the old one.

"Now," said Aunt Pat, "Who *is* he?"

Sherrill looked up puzzled.

"The other one, I mean. You certainly picked a winner this time if I may be permitted a little slang. He seems to be the key to the whole situation. Begin with him! Where have you been keeping him all this time? And why haven't I been told about him before? Is he an old schoolmate, to quote Mrs. Battersea, and how long have you known him?"

"I haven't!" said Sherrill with a sound of panic in her voice.

"You *haven't?"* asked her aunt with a forkful of chicken salad paused half way to her mouth. "What do you mean, you haven't? You certainly seemed to know him pretty well, and he you."

"But I don't, Aunt Pat. I don't really know him at all."

"But—where did you meet him?"

"On the street."

"On the street! When?"

"To-night."

"Mercy!" said Aunt Pat with a half grin. "Explain yourself. You're not the kind of girl that goes around picking up men on the street."

"No!" said Sherrill with a choke of tears in her voice. "But I did this time. I really did. At least—he says he picked me up. You see, I fell into his arms!"

"Mmmm!" said Aunt Pat enjoying her supper and scenting romance. "Go on. That sounds interesting."

"Why, you see it was this way. I parked my car in a hurry to get up into the gallery and when I went to get out I caught my toe in one of those long ruffles, or else I stepped on it, anyway, I fell headlong out on the pavement. Or at least I would have if this man hadn't been there and caught me. I guess I was so excited I didn't really realize that I was pretty well shaken up. Perhaps I struck my head, I'm not sure. It felt dizzy and queer afterward. But he stood me up and brushed me off and insisted on going across the road with me. I guess I must have been unsteady on my feet for when he found I wanted to go upstairs to the gallery he almost carried me up, and he was very nice and helpful. He took that note down to you and then got me a drink of water."

"H'm!" said Aunt Pat with satisfaction. "He's what I call a real man. Nice face! Makes me think of your father when he was young. I couldn't make out how you'd take up with that little pretty-face McArthur nincompoop after seeing a man like this one."

"Why, Aunt Pat!" said Sherrill in astonishment, "I never knew you felt that way about Carter! You never said you did!"

"What was the use of saying? You were determined to have him. But go on. How did this Graham fellow get up here, and how did he get to calling you by your first name, and you him?"

"Well, you see, I slipped out just before the ceremony was over. He said I wasn't fit to drive, he'd either drive himself or get some friend if I said so. But I was in a hurry so I let him drive. I wasn't thinking about formalities then. I knew I ought to get back home quickly. Anyhow he was so respectful I knew he was all right."

"H'm! There are respectful crooks sometimes! But never mind, go on."

"But really Aunt Pat, I don't know what you'll think of me! I haven't had time before this to think what a dreadful thing it was I did, a total stranger, but it didn't seem so then. It seemed just a desperate spot in life. You'd let a stranger pull you out of the street when a mad dog was coming or something like that. I'm afraid you'll be horrified at me. But he was really very kind. He offered to do anything in the world, said he was a stranger in town with the evening to pass, before he met a business appointment in the morning, and if there was any way at all he could help—"

"For mercy's sake, child, stop apologizing and tell things as they happened. I'm not arraigning you."

"Well, I let him come home with me. I knew it would be easier if there was someone that everybody didn't know, and I let him come."

"H'm!" said the old lady with a thoughtful smile that the firelight showed off to perfection. "Well, he certainly was clever enough. But how did he get a dinner coat?"

"Oh, we stopped at the hotel and got his suitcase. He'd been to a dinner the night before in Cleveland. I let him dress in the little room at the end of the back hall.

We came in up the fire escape just before the first car arrived."

"H'm! Clever pair!" commented the old lady as she took delicate bites of her creamed mushrooms. "Well, now get back to your story. How long have you known about this other girl, Artie, was that her name?"

"Arla."

"Silly name! But go on. How long has this double business been going on?"

"I don't know," said Sherrill wearily, "always I guess."

"I mean when did you find it out?"

"Just after you left the house for the church," answered the girl with downcast eyes. Now she was at the beginning of the real story, and it suddenly seemed to her as if she could not possibly tell that part.

The old lady gave her a startled look. She knew that they were now come to the crux of the matter. Sherrill had been so brave up to this point and had carried matters off with such a spirit that she had somehow hoped that Sherrill was not so hard hit. Hoped against hope perhaps, that the final discovery was but the culmination of long suspicions.

"You don't say!" said the old lady, her usual seriocomic manner quite shaken. "But how? I don't see what—How—!"

Sherrill shut her eyes and drew a quick deep breath, then began.

"I was all ready. So I made Gemmie hurry on to the church. I wanted her to be there to see it all, and I wanted to go and see Mary the cook. I'd promised her to come after I got dressed. I knew Gemmie would try to stop me so I wouldn't let her wait as she wanted to. As soon as she was gone I unlocked my door into the next room, and went softly through toward the back hall."

Sherrill had to stop for another deep breath. It seemed as though she was about to go through the whole terrible experience again.

"Well?" said the old lady sharply laying down her fork with a click on the china plate.

"As I stepped into the end room which was dark," she began again trying to steady her voice, "I saw that the door into the middle room was open and the light streaming across the floor. I listened for an instant but heard nothing. I was afraid some of those strange servants would be snooping about. Then I stepped softly forward and saw Carter standing before the long mirror arranging his tie."

"Yes?" said the old lady breathlessly.

"I watched him just a second. I didn't want to stir lest he would hear me, and I wanted him to see me first as I came up the aisle—"

Sherrill's voice trailed away sorrowfully. Then she gathered strength again.

"But while I watched him I saw the door beside the mirror open noiselessly, and that girl came in!"

"H'm!" said Aunt Pat allowing herself another bite of oyster pattie, but keeping her eyes speculatively on her niece. "She must have come up the fire escape or somebody would have seen her."

"She did," said Sherrill wearily, putting her head back and closing her eyes for an instant. Somehow the whole thing suddenly overwhelmed and sickened her again. It seemed she could not go on.

"Well?" said the old lady impatiently. "Did she see you?"

"No." Sherrill's voice was almost toneless. "No, but—"

"There! there! child! I know it's hard, but it's got to

be told once, and then we'll close it over forever if you say so."

"Oh, I know," said Sherrill, sitting up and taking up her tale with a little shudder that seemed to shake her whole slender self.

"No, she didn't see me. She was looking at him. She went straight to him and began to talk, and I could see by his whole attitude that they were old friends. He was shocked when he saw her, and very angry. He ordered her out and scolded her, but she pled with him. It was really heart breaking. Just as if he had been nothing to me. I couldn't help feeling sorry for her, though I thought her—Oh, at first I thought her the lowest of the low. Then I recognized her as his secretary, and of course I guess I thought still less of her, because she would have known that he was engaged."

"Yes, of course!" said Aunt Pat in a spritely tone. "Well, what else?"

"Well, she began pleading with him to go away with her. She reminded him that he had promised to marry her, and in his answer he acknowledged that he had, but oh, Aunt Pat! It is too dreadful to tell!"

"That's all right, Sherrill, get it out of your system. No way to do that like telling it all, making a clean sweep of it! Besides, sometime you'll want to look back on it and remember that you had the assent of someone else that you did the right thing. Even though you're sure you're right there will come times when you will question yourself perhaps."

"I know!" said Sherrill quickly with that sharp intake of breath that shows some thought has hurt, "I have already!" Her aunt gave her a sharp keen look.

"Poor kiddie!" she said gently.

"Oh, I know I never could have married him," went on Sherrill heart-brokenly. "Only it is so dreadful to have my life all upset in one awful minute that way! To know in a flash that everything you've ever counted on and trusted in a person had no foundation whatever! That he simply wasn't in the least what I had thought him. Why, Aunt Pat, he had the nerve to tell her that it didn't matter if he was marrying someone else, that wouldn't hinder their relation. He reminded her that after he got home from the wedding trip he would spend far more time with her than with me, and that whenever he wanted to get away for a few days it would be entirely possible! Oh, Aunt Pat—it was too dreadful—! And I standing there not daring to breathe! Oh!" Sherrill put her face down in her hands and shook with suppressed sobs.

"The dirty little puppy!" said Aunt Pat setting down her plate with a ring on the table. Then she got up from her big chair and came across to Sherrill laying a frail roseleaf hand on her bowed head.

"You poor dear little girl!" she said tenderly, more tenderly than Sherrill had ever heard her speak before.

For a moment then the tears had full sway, let loose by the unusual gentleness of the old lady's voice, till they threatened to engulf her. Then suddenly Sherrill lifted her face all wet with tears, and drew Aunt Pat's hand to her lips kissing it again and again.

"Oh, Aunt Pat! It's so wonderful of you to take it this way! You've done so much to make this a wonderful wedding, spent all this money, and then had it finish in a terrible scandal like this!"

"It's not a scandal!" protested the old lady. "You carried it off like a thoroughbred and nobody will ever know what happened. You were the bravest girl I ever knew. You are like your father, Sherrill." Her tone was very gentle now, and soft. It hardly sounded like herself, and her sharp old eyes were misted with sweet tears.

"And why wouldn't I take it this way, I should like to know when I was pleased to pieces at what had happened?"

Then suddenly she straightened up, marched back to her seat and took up her plate again. Her eyes were snapping now, and her tone was far from gentle as she said:

"But it was far too good a thing to happen to Carter McArthur. He ought to have been tarred and feathered! He deserves the scorn of the community! Go on. Tell me the rest! What excuse did he offer?"

"Oh, he said things about his business. He said he couldn't marry her, he had to marry influence and money! Aunt Pat, he seemed to think I had money, though I've told him I was poor, and that you were giving me my wedding. Or else, maybe he was just lying to her, I don't know—"

"Well," said Aunt Pat setting her lips wryly, "I suppose I'm to blame for that. I thought the thing was inevitable and I told him myself that you would be pretty well fixed after I was gone. He likely was figuring to borrow money or something."

Sherrill's head dropped again and she gave a sound like a groan.

"There! There! Stop that, child!" said the old lady briskly. "He isn't worth it."

"I know it," moaned Sherrill, "but I'm so ashamed that I loved a man like that!"

"You didn't!" said her aunt. "You loved a man you'd made up in your own imagination. Come, tell me the rest and then eat your supper or you'll be sick and then what'll Mrs. Battersea say?"

Sherrill gave a hysterical little giggle and lifting her head wiped away the tears.

"Well, then someone came to the door and told him

the car was waiting and it was late, and he got frantic. He told her to go away and then she threatened to kill herself, and suddenly he took her in his arms and kissed her—just the way he used to kiss me Aunt Pat—! Oh, it was awful. His arms went around her as if he was hungry for her! Oh, there was no doubt about how he felt toward her, not a bit! And then he kissed her again and suddenly threw her from him into the corner, turned out the light in the room, and went away slamming the door hard behind him."

"The poor fool!" commented Aunt Pat under her breath.

"I stood quite still holding my breath," went on Sherrill, "till suddenly I heard her move, and then I reached out and flashed on both lights in both rooms and she saw me."

"What happened?" The old lady's eyes were large with interest.

"I believe I asked her how long she had known him," said Sherrill wearily, "and she said *always,* that they had grown up and gone to school together, and then he had sent for her to come here and be his secretary till he could afford to marry her—"

"A beast! That's what he is!" murmured Aunt Pat. "A sleek little beast!"

"She said it was not until I came that he turned away from her. She said awful things to me. She said it was all my fault, that I had everything and she had nothing but him, and I had ruined her life and there was nothing for her to do but kill herself! And when I told her to hush, that there wasn't much time and we had to do something, she thought I meant that she was to get away quietly so no one would know. She raved, Aunt Pat! She said it was all right for me, that I was going to marry him. And when I told her that of course I couldn't marry him now, and asked her if she would marry a man like that she said she'd marry him if she had to go through hell with him!"

Aunt Pat's face hardened, though there was a mist across her eyes which she brushed impatiently away.

"Poor little fool!" she commented.

"So I dragged her into my room and made her put on my dress and veil. I guess that is all. She couldn't believe me at first. She said she couldn't do that, that he would kill her, but I told her to tell him that if he didn't treat her right, if he didn't go through the evening in the conventional way, or if he tried to throw it up to her afterward, that I would tell the whole world what he had done."

"Great work!" breathed Aunt Pat. "Sherry, you certainly had your head about you! And you certainly seemed to know your man better than I thought you did."

"Oh, Aunt Pat, it seems so awful for me to be sitting here talking about Carter when just a few hours before I thought he was so wonderful!"

"Yes, I know!" mused Aunt Pat with a faraway look. "I had that experience too once, ages ago before you were born."

"You did?" Sherrill looked up with wonder in her eyes.

"Yes," said Aunt Pat with a strangely tender look in her face, "I did. I was engaged to a young hypocrite once, and thought he was the angel Gabriel till I got my eyes open. Sometime I'll tell you all about it. There isn't anybody living now that knows the story but myself. I thought I was heartbroken forever, and when my grandmother told me that he just wasn't the man God had meant for me, and that He probably had somebody a great deal better waiting somewhere I got very angry at her. But that turned out to be true too, and I did have another lover who was a real man later. It wasn't his fault that we never married. Nor mine either. He died saving a little child's life. But the memory of him has been better for me all my life than if I'd married that first little selfish whiffet. So don't let yourself think that the end of the world has come, Sherrill."

Sherrill sat looking at the old lady and trying to reconstruct her ideas of her, wondering at the mellowing and sharpness that were combined in her dear whimsical old face.

"There, now, child, you've told enough!" said the old lady briskly. "Eat your supper and go to bed. Tomorrow you may tell me about everything else. We've had enough for to-night. I'll talk while you eat now. What do you want to do next? Go to Europe?"

"Oh, not Europe!" Sherrill shrank visibly.

"Of course not!" snapped the old lady with triumph in her eyes. "We'll go some place a great deal more interesting."

"I don't think I want to go anywhere," said Sherrill sadly. "I guess I had better just stay here and let people see I'm not moping. That is if I can get away with it."

"Of course you can!" lilted the old lady. "We'll have the time of our lives. They'll see!"

"The only place I'd want to go anyway would be out west by and by, back to my teaching. I'd like to earn money enough to pay you for this awful wedding, Aunt Pat!"

"Stuff and nonsense!" fumed the old lady. "If you mention that again I'll disinherit you! You hurt me, Sherrill!"

"Oh, forgive me, Aunt Pat! But you've been so wonderful!"

"Well, that's no way to reward me. Go away when

I'm just congratulating myself that I've got you all to myself for a while. Of course I don't fool myself into thinking I can keep you always. You're too good looking for that. And there are a few real men left in the world even in this age. They are not all Carter McArthurs. But at least let me have the comfort of your companionship until one comes along!"

"You dear Aunt Pat!"

"There's another thing we've got to consider tomorrow," said the old lady meditatively. "What are you going to do with those wedding presents?"

Sherrill lifted her face aghast at the thought.

"Oh, mercy! I never thought about them. How terrible! What could one do?"

"Oh, send most of them back. Send Carter those *his* friends sent. Don't bother about it to-night. We'll work it out. You run along to bed now, and don't think another thing about it."

Ten minutes later Sherrill was back in her own room.

Gemmie had been there and removed every trace and suggestion of wedding from the place. Sherrill's best old dresses hung in the closet, Sherrill's old dependable brushes and things were on the bureau. It might have been the night before she ever met Carter McArthur as far as her surroundings suggested.

She cast a quick look of relief about her, and went forward to the mirror and stood there, looking into her own eyes, just as she had done when she was ready for her marriage. Looked at her real self and tried to make it seem true that this awful thing had happened to her, Sherrill Cameron! And then suddenly her eyes wandered away from the deep sorrowful thoughts that she found in her mirrored eyes, with an unthinking glance at her slim white neck, and she started. Why! Where was her emerald necklace? She hadn't taken it off when she put on her kimono. She was sure she had not. She would have remembered undoing the intricate old clasp!

Frantically she searched her bureau drawers. Had Gemmie taken it away? Surely not. She went to the little secret drawer where she usually kept her valuable trinkets. Ah! There was the box it had come in! And yes, the ring and bracelets were there! She remembered taking them off. But not the necklace! Where could the necklace be? Perhaps it had come unfastened and dropped in the big chair while she was eating her supper!

She stepped across the hall quickly and tapped at the door of her aunt's room.

"Aunt Pat, may I come in a minute?" she called, and upon receiving permission she burst into the room excitedly:

"Aunt Pat! I've lost my emerald necklace! Could I have dropped it in your room?"

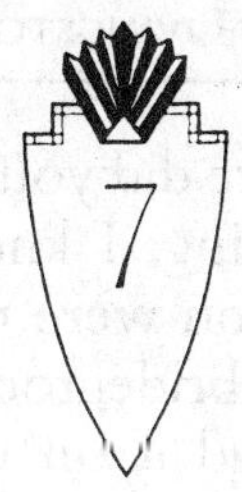

FOR a moment Sherrill and Aunt Pat stood facing one another, taking in the full significance of the loss from every side. Sherrill knew just how much that necklace was prized in the family. Aunt Pat had told her the story of its purchase at a fabulous price by an ancestor who had bought it from royalty for his girl bride. It had come down to Aunt Pat and been treasured by her and kept most preciously. Rare emeralds, of master workmanship in their cutting and exquisite setting! Sherrill stood appalled, aghast, facing the possibility that it was hopelessly gone.

"Oh, Aunt Pat!" she moaned. "You oughtn't to have given it to me! I—I'm—not fit—to have anything rare!—Either man or treasure—!" she added with a great sob, her lips trembling. "It—seems—I—can't—keep—*any*thing!"

Aunt Pat broke into a roguish grin.

"I hope you didn't call that man rare, Sherrill Cameron!" she chuckled, "and for sweet pity's sake, if you ever do find a real man don't put him on a level with mere jewels! Now, take that look off your face and use your head a little. Where did you have that necklace last? You wore it this evening, I know, for I noticed with great satisfaction that you were not wearing that ornate trinket your would-be bridegroom gave you."

"Oh, I thought I had it on when I came in here!" groaned Sherrill. "I just can't remember! I'm sure I didn't take it off anywhere! At least I can't remember doing it."

She rushed suddenly to the big chair where she had been sitting for the last hour and pulled out the cushions frantically, running her hands down in the folds of the upholstery, but discovering nothing but a lost pair of scissors.

She turned on the overhead lights and got down on her knees searching earnestly, but there was no green translucent gleam of emeralds.

Meanwhile Aunt Pat stood thinking, a canny look in her old eyes.

"Now look here, Sherrill," she said suddenly, whirling round upon the frantic girl, "you haven't lost your soul you know and we are still alive and well. Emeralds are just emeralds after all. Get some poise! Get up off that floor and go quietly down stairs! Look just casually wherever you remember to have been. Just walk over the same places. Don't do any wild pawing around, just merely look in the obvious places. Don't make a noise and don't say anything to the servants if any of them are up. I don't think they are. Gemmie thought they were gone to bed. I just sent Gemmie away. Then if you don't find it come up to me."

Sherrill made a little dismal moan.

"Oh, for mercy's sake!" said Aunt Pat impatiently. "It isn't as if you hadn't had a chance to wear them once anyway, and one doesn't wear emeralds, such emeralds, around every day. You won't miss them much in the long run even if you never find them. Now stop your hysterics and run down stairs, but don't make any noise!"

Sherrill cast a tearful look at her aunt and hurried away, stopping at her own room to get a little flashlight she kept in her desk.

Step by step she retraced the evening in an agony of memory. It wasn't just her losing the emeralds forever, it was Aunt Pat losing the pleasure of her having them. It was—well, something else, a horrible haunting fear that appeared and disappeared on the horizon of her mind and gripped her heart like a clutching hand.

When she came in her search to the long French window out which she and Copeland had passed to the garden such a little while before she paused and hesitated, catching her breath at a new memory. If it came to that *there* would be something she couldn't tell Aunt Pat! She couldn't hope to make her understand about that kiss! Oh! A long shudder went through her weary body and every taut nerve hurt like the toothache. How was she to explain it to herself? And yet—!

She unfastened the window with a shaking hand and touching the spring of her flash went carefully over the piazza, and inch by inch down the walk where they had passed, not forgetting the grassy edges on either side. On her way back she stopped and her cheeks grew hot in the dark as she held back the branches of privet and stepped within that cool green quiet hiding place. Oh, if she could but find it here! If only it had fallen under the shrubs. It would have been very easy for it to come unfastened while he held her in his arms. If only she might find it and be set free from that haunting fear. Just to know that he was all right. Just to be *sure—!* She felt again the pressure of his arms about her, so gentle, the touch of his lips upon her eyelids. It had rested and comforted her so. It hadn't seemed wrong. Yet of course he was an utter stranger!

But she searched the quiet hiding place in vain. There was no answering gleam to the little light that went searching so infallibly and at last she had to come in and give it up. There was utter dejection in her attitude when she came back to Aunt Pat, her lip trembling, her eyes filled with large unshed tears, that haunting fear in their depths. For of course she could not help but realize that that moment when he held her in his arms would have been a most opportune time for a crook to get the emeralds.

"There isn't a sign of them anywhere!" she said.

"Well," said Aunt Pat, "You can't do anything more to-night. Get to bed. You look worn to a thread. I declare, for anybody who went through the evening like a soldier you certainly have collapsed in a hurry. Lose a bridegroom, and take it calmly. Lost a bauble and go all to pieces! Well go to bed and forget it child! Perhaps we'll find it in the morning."

"But Aunt Pat!" said Sherrill, standing tragically with clasped hands under the soft light from the old alabaster chandelier, with her gold hair like a halo crowning her, "Oh, Aunt Pat! You *don't* suppose—*he*—took it, do you?"

"He?" said the old lady sharply whirling on her niece. "Whom do you mean? Your precious renegade bridegroom? No, I hadn't thought of him. I doubt if he had the nerve to do it. Still, it's not out of the thinking."

"Oh, Aunt Pat! Not Carter! I didn't mean Carter." She said astonished, "Of course he wouldn't do a thing like that!"

"Why of course?" snapped Aunt Pat grimly. "He knew the value of those stones, didn't he? And according to his own confession he needed money didn't he? If he would steal a girl's love and fling it away why not steal another girl's necklace? Deception is deception in whatever form you find it, little girl! However, I suppose Carter McArthur had enough on his hands this evening for one occasion and he likely wouldn't have had the time to stage another trick. But I hope you are not trying to suspect that poor innocent bystander that you dragged into your service this evening!"

"He was a *stranger!"* said Sherrill with white anxious lips and frightened eyes.

"H'm! Did he act to you like a crook, Sherrill Cameron?"

"No, Aunt Pat! He was wonderful! But—"

"Well, no more buts about it. Of course he had nothing to do with it. I know a true man when I see him if I am an old maid, and I won't have a man like that suspected in my house! You don't really mean to say you haven't any more discernment than that, do you?"

"No," said Sherrill managing a shaky smile, "I'm sure he is all right, but I was afraid *you* would think—"

"There! I thought as much! You thought *I* had no sense. Well go to bed. We're both dead for sleep. And don't think another thing about this to-night! Mind me!"

"But—oughtn't I to call the police?"

"What for? And have them demand a list of our guests and insult every one of them? No emeralds are worth the losing of friends! Besides, nobody can do anything about it to-night anyway. Now get to bed. Scat!"

Sherrill broke into a little hysterical laugh and rushing up to her aunt threw her arms around her neck and gave her a tender kiss.

"You are just wonderful!" she whispered into her ear, and then hurried back to her room.

Before her mirror she stood again looking sternly into

her own eyes. Such sorrowful tired eyes as looked back at her; such a chastened little face, utterly humble.

Somehow as she stood facing her present situation it seemed weeks, almost years, since she had stood there in wedding satin facing married life like an unknown country through which she had to travel. If she had known when she stood there smiling with her wedding bouquet in her arms, and her wedding veil, blossom-wreathed, on her head, that all this was to be, how would the laughter have died on her lips! How trivial would have seemed her faint fears! Had those fears been a sort of premonition of what was to happen in a few minutes, she wondered? She had read of such things, and perhaps they were in the air like radio sounds waiting to be picked up!

Oh, what a night! What an ending to all that lovely preparation! The tears welled suddenly into her eyes and a great feeling of being overwhelmed came over her anew. Dust and ashes! How had all the beauty of her life faded in a few short minutes! And how was she to face the long desert of the future?

Ah! To have lifted the goblet of Life to her lips, and suddenly to have had it snatched from her without even a single sip! How was she going to bear it all?

It was like coming up to a great stone wall and not being able to scale it, a stone wall on every side, and not even a desire left to try and get over it. All that she really wanted just now was to drop down and sleep and forget.

Well, that was just what she had promised Aunt Pat she would do, but even the effort seemed too much.

She turned from the mirror, too tired even to cry, and saw that Gemmie had laid out one of her plain simple night robes, nothing new and smart, just an old soft well worn gown out of her pleasant thoughtless past. Gratefully she crept into it and got into her bed.

She was too tired to think, too burdened to toss and weep. All she wanted was to sink down into oblivion; and that was just what happened. Tired Nature pulled a curtain about her and she drifted away into deep sleep.

But it was not a peaceful sleep. There were troublous times and buffetings. She was having to drive her car very fast over a rough wild road in a storm, and her wedding veil kept blowing over her eyes and getting tangled in her steering wheel. Carter seemed to be standing somewhere ahead in the darkness waiting for her with a terrible frown on his handsome face, the frown he had worn when he first saw Arla enter that door. She was late for her wedding and out of breath. She seemed to be lost on a wild prairie, and was afraid, terribly afraid!

Over and over she dreamed this with variations. Sometimes it was snowing and the sleet stung her cheeks, and shriveled the lilies of the bouquet in her lap, but she had to go on until she finally arrived at a strange dark rendezvous in an unknown country, and plunged out of her car letting it run away into the darkness without her. She groped about in the night to find her wedding, but there was only a closed and darkened church. She was filled with despair till a stranger, whom yet she seemed to have known all her life, came out of the shadows and helped her home. A stranger who kissed her gently when he left her at her door.

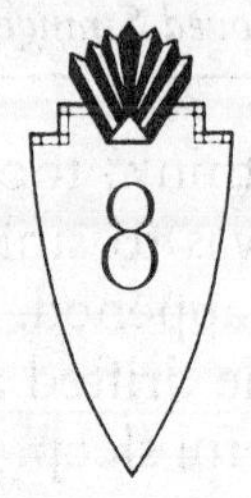

A great gust of perfume from many flowers was wafted out into the passageway as the steward threw open the door and ushered in Arla and Carter McArthur. Flowers everywhere! Sherrill's flowers!

Arla stepped back and closed her eyes quickly as if she had been struck in the face. Carter frowned angrily. He stepped inside and looked at the array. Flowers, fruit, confectionery! A hunted look passed over his face. This all represented what he had lost in the other bride. Popularity, wealth, influence! He began to examine the cards of the friends who had sent them. Sherrill's friends. All Sherrill's friends. None of his represented except the big basket of fruit from his underpaid office. He looked at it contemptuously. Smelton with his six children and sick wife, Johnny Farr the errand boy with a widowed mother, Miss Gaye the assistant secretary who wore bargain counter clothes and chewed incessant gum. Arla! Arla? Had Arla contributed to that basket of fruit too? He cast a quick look at her, his wife, swaying there in the doorway looking white and miserable. Could it be possible that those poor wretches had asked Arla to contribute to a voyage gift for her rival? He had a passing sense of what it might have meant to her to be asked. The whiteness of her face showed she was not enjoying the festive array. Just for an instant he forgot his own annoyance and realized sharply what all this might have been to her. And yet how well she had gone through with it! So confidently, almost radiantly. It had been maddening to have her so confident, when she had dared to interfere, yet somehow it had also stirred his pride in her. After all she was beautiful. No one could deny that! But she had gone beyond all limits in coming there to the house and precipitating this disaster. Yes, disaster! It meant destruction to his well laid financial plans. And no matter how lovely this unsought bride might be, how well she might carry off her position as his wife, that could not offset the fact that he had in himself no position for her to carry off. It had all been a big bluff dependent on Miss Patricia Catherwood's fortune. And what he was to do now remained to be seen. However crazy he might always have been about Arla, that did not alter the fact that he cared for money and position more than he cared for any living woman. And he had in his mind the comfortable realization that he could always get the adoration of another girl if one failed him, or became for the time unwise.

Arla rallied her self-control and quietly entered in the wake of the bags, drifting unobserved into a corner until the steward had left and they were alone.

Carter readjusted the baggage, placing his own suitcase on top impatiently. He was one who always expected those serving to anticipate his slightest unexpressed wishes. He swung savagely around to Arla stranded pitifully by the door, her arrogance and initiative all gone now, nothing but a frightened look in her eyes. She knew his moods. She understood that her time had come to pay for what she had done.

"Well, if that's what you wanted, there you have plenty of it!" he said waving his hand toward the gifts. "Enjoy it while you can. It'll probably be the last you'll see of this sort of thing. If you could only have made up your mind to wait awhile we might have had all this and more!"

The frightened look faded from Arla's eyes and lightning came instead. Her lips grew thin and hard. She turned away from him haughtily and busied herself removing her gloves. She looked very handsome and angry as she stood there not listening to him. He could not but see how smart she looked, how becoming her costume. She knew how to dress. If only he could weather this crisis somehow things might not be so bad after all. She really knew how to wear her clothes just as well as Sherrill, could perhaps make an appearance to suit his pride. And of course she was beautiful, of much the same type as Sherrill. That was what had attracted him to Sherrill in the first place that she had reminded him of Arla. And perhaps Arla could learn. She could get rid of her provincialism. She had learned a lot already. But the money! If he only could be sure—!

He swung around and began to fumble with the baggage, stowing one big suitcase that contained his wedding garments, back under the bed. Swinging another down and shoving it after. Of course the steward would attend to all that presently, but it suited him to be stirring, throwing things around. This was an awkward moment, various emotions were striving within him.

Arla stood where she had first entered, pulling off her long gloves deliberately, finger by finger, smoothing them carefully, thoughtfully. She was struggling to keep from bursting into tears.

The steward tapped at the door and Arla made no

move to answer it, but moved away and stood staring out of the porthole at the panorama of harbor lights. Already they were moving out into the stream and she had a strange dreadful feeling that she was heading out into the midstream of life, leaving behind all that she knew, all that she had hoped, going into a wild lonely sea of problems and perplexities and going utterly unprepared and unloved.

Carter had gone to the door. She heard the conversation vaguely, as if it had nothing to do with her. It was something about a radio message. The operator wished to speak to Mr. McArthur. Carter went out and Arla wondered idly why he was sending a radio message now, on his wedding night, but she was filled with indifference concerning it.

Carter had left the door unlatched as he went out and the draft from the open porthole cooled her hot cheeks. She turned to fasten the door, realizing that she was alone, a brief breathing space, and looked about her again.

Those flowers! How wonderful it would have been if they had been hers! If she had been a girl with friends who could send farewell greetings in such a costly style! Why all these gifts, the wedding that had preceded them, had been but the fulfillment of her childish fairy dreamings, all the things she had most wished for in life, and now they had come and how empty they were! How one's heart could starve in the midst of plenty!

She went about the room stealthily examining the cards, removing them with frightened hasty fingers. She would put them out of sight before Carter returned.

Some of the names she recognized as belonging to people who had been down the line and been introduced to her such a little time ago. They had gone through the motion of friendship with her but that would be all. She would likely never see them again. For a brief moment she had walked with the elite and been recognized by them, but she was not a part of them, never would be. They were not of her world! Her highest dreams had been realized and yet had brought her no joy. Emptiness and sawdust! How she hated it all! How she wished for the old sweet simple days when she went to high school in pretty gingham dresses and Carter carried her books for her, looked down adoringly into her eyes, told her how lovely she was!

Oh, what had she done, how had things gone wrong, that they had come to this night? She remembered the look he had given her as he waved his hand toward the flowers and told her to enjoy them while she could, that it was probably the last of that sort of thing she would see. She shivered with anguish as she felt his contempt all over again, and realized that he was not the Carter of her happy school days, not even the whimsical lover who had sent for her to be his secretary. She must face that fact and not give way to sorrow. Then her lips set with determination, and she stepped calmly to the bell and rang for the stewardess.

When the woman presented herself Arla waved toward the flowers.

"I would like you to take all those away," she said coldly. "They sicken me. Take them down to the steerage, please, and give them to the old women and the little children."

When Carter came back the flowers were all gone. The boxes of expensive confectionery were gone. There was left only the basket of fruit from the office standing alone on the dresser.

"Why,—where—what—?" asked Carter looking about and sensing the emptiness.

"I told the stewardess to take them down to the

steerage and give them to people who could enjoy them," she said in a cold steady voice.

Carter looked at her half startled. He had had so many startling things flung at him already this long terrible evening that one more or less made little impression. Then his eyes swept about the room again and he noticed the fruit.

"Why not that one too?" he asked his lips settling into their habitual sneering curve.

"Because that one is yours!" she answered steadily. "Because *I* paid for that myself!"

"You paid for it yourself?" he exclaimed looking at her in astonishment.

"Yes, I paid for it myself!" she answered, folding her gloves smoothly together again, and laying them out on the table.

"But—*why—?* Why should you pay for them? Why not the others? Who got up the idea?"

"It wasn't gotten up. I did it all. They don't even know about it. They hadn't any money to put into gifts. They have all they can do to keep from starving. Johnny's mother is likely dying to-night. He won't be able to get any flowers for her funeral! Smelton's wife has had a relapse and one of his children has a broken leg, the only child who had any job at all. Miss Gaye needs all her salary for gum. Who would you think would send you fruit from the office if I didn't?"

"But why *you?"* he asked again a strange incredulous look in his eyes.

"Why I?" answered the girl with a flash of her tear drowned eyes, and a sudden quiver of her lovely lip, "Why *I?* Because I was a *fool!* Because I'll always be a fool I suppose where you are concerned! Because I *thought* I loved you, and wanted you to have all the honor there was, even from an office like ours! It was just after you told me that I had always been—Oh, what's the use! I won't say those empty words over. I had a spirit of self-sacrifice. I thought I loved you enough to sacrifice myself! That was before I found out I couldn't stand it! It was before I told your other bride that I'd go through hell to marry you. It was even before I understood what hell was like!"

"Did you tell her that?" His face was white with anger and a strange wild remorse.

"Yes, I told her that when she said she wouldn't marry you after what she'd seen, and asked me if I would, and I said I'd go through hell to marry you! But, I didn't know what hell could be like then, even at the beginning. I thought I was in it then, but I *wasn't.*"

A wave of shamed color swept over his face leaving it white as death. He almost staggered and put out his hand to steady himself against the wall.

"You don't care that you're putting me through hell, do you?" he whined impressively.

She gave him a withering glance.

"You deserve it," she said fiercely, "I don't! I've always tried to be as decent as you would let me. I never played fast and loose with you. I've loved you always,—and—I love you—now! God help me! Why do I love you? Oh, why? You are despicable! You know you are! How could anybody love a little handsome selfish beast like you? And yet I do! Oh, what a wedding night!"

She threw herself suddenly down upon the bed and wept bitterly. And he, trembling, almost ashamed, filled with passionate remorse and angry retaliation, turned the light off and crept humbly to her side kneeling, groping for her hand. Her words had lashed him through fury into a sudden brief fleeting vision of himself.

"Arla!" he said, reaching after her in the dark, "Arla! Don't cry that way! I do love you!"

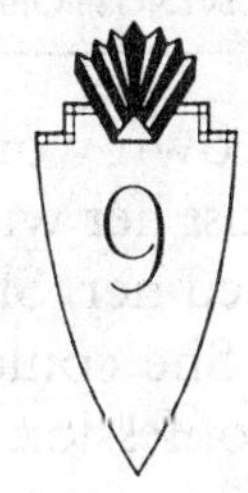

SHERRILL awoke in the morning with a gorgeous sunlight streaming across the lovely old blue rug, lighting her familiar room cheerfully.

Then instantly, as if someone had struck her across the heart with a club, there came to her a remembrance of all that had happened since she awoke in that room so joyously yesterday morning. The future, drab and desolate, stretched itself away before her, a dreary prospect.

Sherrill's soul turned sick at her own desolation, and all the horror of her situation rushed over her with a realization of details which she had not had time for last night in the sudden stress and need for immediate action.

And now of course the first thought that occurred was, had she done right? Was her action too hasty? Had there been any other way? What would other girls have done? *Could* she have married him knowing the truth about him?

Of course if there had been the least doubt about it, if there had been any chance at all that she was misjudging him, she would have been wrong not to have given him an opportunity to explain, to clear himself if he could.

But she had heard his own words. She had seen him clasp that other girl and kiss her with the same passionate fervency that he had kissed her. She had seen his face as he took her in his arms. She could never forget it. Yes, she had heard his own confession that he still loved the other girl, and that after his marriage and wedding trip they would be freer than ever—! *Ah!* She caught her lips between her teeth with a trembling breath. How that sight, those words had stabbed her! Oh, no, there was no possibility of doubt. He was false-hearted. He had *meant* to be false!

If he had just been weak and fallen into this situation one could forgive. Forgive, but not marry. She could never marry a man whom she could not trust.

But he had been deliberately false, and she could scarcely be sorry for him. No, she could only be sorry for that poor desperate girl who had been willing to go through hell to have him.

Well, there was such a thing as hell on earth of course. Her own present outlook seemed not far situated from such a location, and yet she knew if she had to go through even a mild kind of hell for the rest of her life she would rather take it alone than tied up to a man whom just a few short hours before she had been joyously preparing to marry. No, she must be thankful that a kind Providence had even in such a tragic moment prevented her from marrying Carter McArthur.

And yet though all that was true, Sherrill Cameron lay with wide desperate eyes staring out at a sunlit desolation.

She closed her eyes again and tried to wish herself back to sleep, but the eyes flew open like a doll's that had lost their weights. She knew that she was definitely awake for the day, and could not drop back into merciful oblivion again even for a brief space. She must face what was before her.

So she lay staring about her room that had sheltered so much of her joy and happy anticipation, and suddenly from every wall and corner things started out at her that had been connected with her courtship. A great bunch of dried grasses that she and Carter had gathered the day they took their first walk together. It filled a thin crystal vase on the mantel and made a thing ethereally lovely. Gemmie never would have known that it was a reminder of dear dead days.

High over her white marble mantel was fastened a pennant. It spoke of the first football game she had attended with Carter, less than a year ago! Gemmie wouldn't have realized that the pennant spoke eloquently of a lost past.

Knotted carelessly on the corner of a signed etching on the opposite wall, for no apparent reason at all, was a bow of scarlet ribbon, a memento of last Christmas, kept because Carter had tied it about her hair the morning they were skating together, and then had drawn her face back and kissed her, behind a sheltering hemlock tree that hid them from the view of the other skaters on the creek. And that was another memory that she must cut out and throw away. It did not belong to her and never had belonged it seemed! Gemmie had no idea what that red ribbon meant.

Over on her desk that bronze paper weight! Gemmie never had known that it had been on his desk the day she first went with Carter to his office. She had admired it and he had given it to her. That was before Arla came to be his secretary! Ah, but he had known and loved Arla first! He loved her enough *afterwards* to have sent for Arla. And yet he had gone right on with his intimacy with Sherrill! The bronze too must go into the discard!

And over on the bureau, that little ivory figurine! Gemmie had always admired that. But she did not know that Carter had bought it for her in a curio shop the day they went together to New York.

Oh! She could not bear these memories! She must not! She would give way and weep. And weeping was not for her to-day! She must keep a mask of happiness on her face. She must not let anyone suspect that her life was shattered by that wedding as it had come out last night. They must think it was all planned, or at least that a definite and friendly change was made before the ceremony. She could not go around and explain the whole thing as it had happened. Even if she were willing on her own part, she could not explain what involved others' secrets. No, she must play her part through to the end and keep a brave, cheerful, even merry face. How was she to do it?

Then suddenly she could not bear the sight of those things on her wall and she sprang up and dashed the bunch of grasses down, sweeping them into the fireplace where Gemmie had carefully laid a fire.

The vase was only a plain little thing from the five-and-ten-cent store, but it seemed to understand what was expected of it, and as Sherrill lifted the grasses swiftly from it, it toppled, and rolled slowly, deliberately down upon the hearth and smashed into a thousand pieces.

Sherrill stood for an instant looking at it regretfully, almost as if it had a personality. Poor fragile thing! Too bad for it to lose its existence through no fault of its own. It had been part of a lovely bit of beauty, but at least now she would not have it around to remind her of the grasses and the day that they were picked!

She stooped and swept the pieces quickly with her little hearth broom into a newspaper, and wrapped them carefully, putting them into the wastebasket. Now they were gone. Even Gemmie wouldn't be reminded to ask where the grasses were.

Then she touched a match to the fire and it swept up and licked the grasses out of existence in one flash.

Sherrill turned to the room again. She mounted a chair and pulled down the pennant, stuffing it fiercely into the wastebasket. She snatched the bow of ribbon from the picture frame and dropped it into the fire. She caught up the bronze paper weight. That wouldn't burn! Nor the ivory figurine! What could she do with them? Give them away? They might somehow come back to face her some day, and she wanted to be utterly rid of them. Ah! There was one place where she would never be likely to see them again. She might send them to Carter's office. But no, that would be only to bring back to his mind the days they had had together and that she did not want. She wanted only to sever all connection with him, to wipe out from both his memory and hers, in so far as was possible, all thought of one another. Then only would she be able to lift up her head and breathe freely again.

She unlocked a little secret drawer in her desk to put the bronze and ivory out of sight, and came on a packet of notes and brief letters from Carter. There hadn't been many because he had been right there to see her every day. She had almost forgotten these letters and some programs and clippings. She seized them now and flung them into the middle of the fire, closing her eyes quickly that she might not see the flames licking around her name in that handwriting that had been so beloved, turning her back lest she should repent and snatch them out to read them over again. She must not! No, it would unnerve her! It would make her heart turn back and lash her for what she had done in giving her bridegroom over to another girl. She must not because he never had been hers! He was not worth the great love she had given him.

And now she remembered how unworthy she herself had felt to marry him, and how she had prayed, and wondered. Was this awful thing that had happened in some mysterious way an answer to her prayer? Oh, it was all a mystery! Life itself was a mystery. Joy one minute and awful sorrow and desolation the next! Sorrow! Sorrow! Sorrow!

Suddenly from the next room through the closed door there came a burst of wild sweet song:

"When I have sorrow in my heart,
What can take it away?
Only Jesus in-ah my heart
Can take that sorrow away."

It was Lutie, the fresh-cheeked young girl who came in certain days in the week to help with the cleaning. Lutie had the windows of the guest room open and was beginning her weekly cleaning. Sherrill's windows were open too and that was why the words came so distinctly. But how strange that such words should come to her just now when she was so filled with sorrow!

Lutie was banging things around, drawing the bed out, and the bureau, setting chairs out of the way and running the vacuum cleaner over the floor. Sherrill could hear the thump as the cleaner hit the baseboards now and then. And Lutie's voice rang out clear again in the next verse:

"When I have fear in-ah my heart,
What can take it away?

Only Jesus in-ah my heart
Can take that fear away."

Sherrill began slowly, languidly to dress, listening to the song. Fear in the heart. She considered herself. Did she have fear in her heart? Yes, she recognized a kind of dread of the days that were before her. Not fear of anything tangible perhaps, but fear of gossip, criticism, prying eyes. Fear of having to face all that would come in the wake of that wedding that was hers and yet was not. Fear of a drab future, a long lonely way ahead, no home of her own. She could never have a home of her own now, nor anyone to care for her and enjoy life with her. For she would never dare trust a man again, even if she ever found one whom she could love.

"When I have sin in-ah my heart—"

piped up Lutie joyously,

"What can take it away?
Only Jesus in-ah my heart
Can take that sin away."

Sherrill was not especially interested in sin. She had never considered herself to be much of a sinner, and her thoughts wandered idly considering her own case more than the song as she listened to the lilt of Lutie's voice in the closing verse:

"When I have Jesus in-ah my heart,
What can take Him away?
Once take Jesus into my heart
And He has come to stay!"

There was a pause in the singing and the sound of voices in the hall. Thomas the house man had come up to get the rugs to give them a good cleaning in the back yard. Lutie was demurring, but finally tapped hesitantly at Sherrill's door.

Sherrill in her negligee opened the door.

"Miss Sherrill, Thomas was wanting to get your rug for cleaning but I guess you aren't ready yet, are you? I wasn't sure whether you were in your room or not."

"That's all right Lutie," said Sherrill, stepping through into the next room where the girl was at work, "tell him to go in and take it. I can finish without a rug."

Sherrill went to the guest room bureau and began to arrange her hair and Lutie came back after helping the man roll up the rug.

"That's a curious song you were singing, Lutie," said Sherrill pleasantly. "Where in the world did you get it? It sounds like a negro spiritual."

"I don't guess it is, Miss Sherrill," said the girl pausing in her dusting, "I got it down to our Bible class. It is pretty words, isn't it? I like that part about Jesus taking your sorrow away. I sing it a lot."

"But you've never had any sorrow, Lutie," said Sherrill wistfully, eyeing the girl's round rosy cheeks and happy eyes.

"Oh, Miss Sherrill, you don't know," said Lutie sobering suddenly. "I've had just a lot! First my mother got awful sick for two whole years, and then when she got better my sister just older'n I died. And my little brother has hurt his hip and they don't think he'll ever walk again."

"Oh, Lutie," cried Sherrill in dismay, "that is a lot of trouble!"

"Oh, but that's not all," said the girl drawing a deep sigh. "My dad got some steel filings in his eye about nine months ago, and they think he's going blind, and now they've laid him off the job so my brother Sam and I are the only ones working, except Mother now and then when she can get a washing to do. And our house is all mortgaged up and the bank closed last week where we had our money saved to pay the interest and now we'll maybe lose the house; and Mother needs an operation only she can't stop working to go to the hospital. And—" the girl caught her lip between her little white teeth to hold it from trembling, and Sherrill could see that there were tears in her eyes, "and—then—my boy friend got mad and started going with another girl because I wouldn't run off and get married and leave the family in all that mess!"

The big tears rolled out now, and down the round cheek, and Lutie caught a corner of her apron and brushed them hastily away.

"Excuse me, Miss Sherrill," she said huskily. "It just sometimes gets me—"

"You poor dear child!" said Sherrill putting down her hairbrush and coming over toward her. "Why, you poor kid you! I never dreamed you could have all that to bear! And *yet* you could sing a song like that!" She regarded the girl earnestly. "You certainly are brave! But Lutie, you know a boy friend that would do a thing like that isn't worth crying after." Sherrill said it, and suddenly knew she was speaking out of her own experience.

"I know it!" gulped Lutie, "I know he ain't, but sometimes it all just comes over me. You see I was right fond of him."

Then she flashed a smile like a rainbow through her tears and brightened.

"But I don't feel like that much now since I got Jesus in my heart like the song says. He really drives the sorrow away, and I'm mostly glad just to let Him have

His way with me. If it wasn't fer Him I couldn't stand it. He really does take the sorrow away you know. I guess you likely know that yourself, Miss Sherrill, don't you? But you see I haven't known Jesus so long so I just have to talk about Him and sing about Him most all the time to keep myself reminded what a wonderful Saviour I've got."

Sherrill turned a searching, hungry look upon the little serving maid.

"Where did you get all that, Lutie?"

"Down at our Bible class, Miss Sherrill. I been going there about a year now. We got a wonderful teacher down there. We study the Bible, and it's just wonderful what he makes us see in it. I just wish you'd come down sometime and visit, Miss Sherrill, and see what it's like."

"Maybe I will,—sometime," said Sherrill slowly still studying the girl as if there were some strange mystery about her.

"It ain't a very grand place," said Lutie apologetically. "Maybe you might not like it. It's just a plain board floor, and the walls are cracked and the seats are hard. It ain't like your church. The windows are painted white because they look into an alley. Maybe you wouldn't think it was good enough for you. But I'd like you to come once and see. The singing's just heavenly, and the teacher's grand! Everybody loves it so they just can't bear to go home."

"Why, I wouldn't mind things like that!" said Sherrill earnestly. "Indeed I wouldn't. I'll come sometime, I really will. I'd like to see what it's like. When do you meet?"

"Monday evenings!" said Lutie with dancing eyes. "Oh, Miss Sherrill, if you'd come I'd be that proud!"

"Why of course I'll come!" said Sherrill heartily, relieved that she could do anything to make Lutie's eyes shine like that, half curious too to see what it was that had made this simple girl happy in the face of such terrible troubles.

Sherrill carried the memory of the girl's face with her as she went back to her room to finish her dressing. What a light had come into her eyes when she said what a wonderful Saviour she had! Saviour! Saviour from what? Her sorrow? Her fear? Her sin? Lutie couldn't be such a great sinner. It was probably just a lot of phrases she had picked up in some evangelistic meeting, poor thing, but if she thought she was comforted by it there must be some good in it. Anyway Sherrill decided she would go and find out. If there was any cure for sorrow surely she herself needed it. And she drew a heavy sigh and went downstairs to face the morning after her own wedding day without a bridegroom.

She tried as she walked down the broad front stairs to forget how that other bride had looked, smiling and proud, holding her head high. And how Carter had looked, haughty, handsome, carrying it all off just as if it had been planned that way.

Carter! What had he thought? How had he taken it? Strange that he had not shown a sign, nor spoken a word to her. Did she fancy it or had there been a furtive look of fear in his eyes? Anyhow it was plain enough that he had avoided looking straight at her. Not once had he looked her in the eyes. Not once attempted to draw her aside and speak to her. She did not know from his looks whether he was very angry or only relieved to have had things work out this way.

Her heart was very heavy as she thought of this. It seemed to blot out the happy days of the past, to make Carter into an utter stranger. Yet, of course it was better so. That was what she wanted only somehow the awfulness of his attitude overcame her anew as she came down to the setting of the last act of that tragedy that had ended her high hopes. How was she going to bear the future?

And then, suddenly, just at the foot of the stairs she remembered the emeralds! The emeralds and the stranger! And down upon her like some gigantic bird of prey swept her fear of the night before!

MISS Catherwood was already at the breakfast table looking as fresh and chipper as if she had gone to bed at nine o'clock the night before. She was opening her mail and there was a smile of satisfaction on her face. She gave Sherrill a keen look as she came into the room.

"Well, I'm glad to see you're still a good sport!" she said with her funny twisted grin. "But you didn't sleep very well, did you? There are dark circles under your eyes. Sit down and eat a good breakfast. Oh, I know you think you don't want a thing but a cup of coffee, but that's not the way to act. You've got a few hard days before you and you've got to keep your looks through them or people will say you are mourning after that sap-head, and you don't want that. Come, set to work. We've got to get at sending back those presents. You'll feel better when they are out of the house."

Sherrill gave a little moan and dropped her face into her hands.

"Oh!" she groaned, "How impossible it all seems! But if I could only find the necklace I wouldn't mind any of the rest!"

Aunt Pat flung a wise glance at the bowed head.

"That'll turn up all right," she said, "Come, child, chirk up. I've been wondering. Can you think back and be sure when you last had it?"

Sherrill shook her head.

"No. I've been trying, but I can't be sure. If I only could it would take a big load from my mind."

"Well *I* can!" said Aunt Pat. "You had the necklace on when you sat in the dining room eating your supper after you came in from outside. I know for I sat and watched the lights in those stones and I remember thinking how well they became you, and how they brought out the color in your cheeks and the gold in your hair."

Sherrill's head came up suddenly with a light of hope in her eyes and a soft flush on her cheeks.

"Are you *sure* you saw them on me at the table, Aunt Pat? Perfectly sure?"

"Perfectly sure," said Aunt Pat steadily, studying the girl quietly.

"Well, that's something!" said Sherrill with a sigh of relief. "At least I didn't lose it—in the garden!"

"No, you didn't lose it in the garden," said Aunt Pat with a wicked little grin. "Now don't think anything more about it. Let's get at those presents. First you sit down and work out a little model note sweet and gracious that will fit all the presents and not tell a thing you don't want known."

Sherrill presently brought it to her aunt for her approval.

"My dear—

The sudden change in our plans for the wedding has left me in an embarrassing situation, having in my possession a lot of lovely gifts which do not by right belong either to me or to Mrs. McArthur. I am therefore of course returning all the gifts and apologizing for having been the unintentional cause of so much trouble to the donors.

But I do want to add just a little word of my appreciation for your beautiful gift, and to thank you for your delightful intention for my pleasure. It is so wonderful to see such gracious evidence of friendship.

Very sincerely,
Sherrill Cameron."

"I think that is quite a nice bit of English!" said Aunt Pat with satisfaction when she had read it. "It says all that needs to be said and tells nothing. It ought to be published. It would be so helpful to other girls caught in like predicaments."

Sherrill broke into hysterical laughter.

"Oh, Aunt Pat! You're a scream! As if there was ever another girl caught in such a predicament!" she said.

"I don't know," said the old lady dryly, "You can't tell how many girls have had a situation like yours, only most of them likely didn't have the nerve to handle it the way you did yours. There must have been some girls who were too great cowards to back down from a church full of wedding guests, and the wedding march just on the tiptoe to begin. They probably paid afterwards, and paid double too. Surely Sherrill you aren't the only one who ever found at the last minute that her lover was made of coarse clay. Don't ever fancy, no matter how hard a thing you have to go through, that your experience is unique. This old world has been going on a good many hundred years and there are precious few situations that haven't happened over and over again. Cheer up, child, that's a model letter and you're a good little sport!"

Miss Catherwood handled the return of the presents in a masterly manner. Her secretary and Sherrill wrote the notes while Gemmie and the butler under her supervision repacked the gifts. It was amazing how quickly the things were marshaled from the tables into their neat original packages each with its dainty note attached. Sherrill grew so interested in seeing how much she could accomplish that she almost forgot her anxiety about the emeralds.

It comforted her greatly that the necklace had not been lost while she was out with Copeland. But later in the day something occurred which brought back her uneasiness and that nameless fear again. Oh, to know certainly, who, if anyone, was connected with the disappearance of the jewels!

It was late in the afternoon and Miss Catherwood had just said they had done enough for to-day and must stop and rest. Just then the hall door opened timidly and Lutie showed a deprecating face.

"Please, Miss Catherwood, might I come in and speak to you a moment?" she asked shyly.

"Why of course, Lutie. Come right in," said the old maid cheerily. "What is it?"

"Why, Miss Catherwood, I found something," she said earnestly, holding her two hands cupped, the one in the other. "Maybe it isn't much account, but it looked to me as if it might be something real. It's only a little thing, and I thought if I gave it to any of the other servants they might laugh, but I knew you would know whether it was valuable or not."

Lutie dropped a delicate bit of brightness into the old lady's hand and stood back waiting shyly.

Aunt Pat held the bit of jewelry in her delicate old hand for an instant and examined it carefully. Then she looked up at the girl.

"Where did you find this, Lutie, and when?"

"Just now, ma'am, in the little back room off the servants' hall. It was on the floor just under the edge of the little writing table, and I most swept it up, but then I saw it glittering, and it first looked like a bit of Christmas-tree tinsel, but when I looked closer it seemed like something real."

"H'm!" said Aunt Pat significantly, and looking up at Sherrill added: "It's from the emerald necklace, Sherry, a whole inch of the chain and part of the clasp!"

Sherrill gave a startled exclamation, and the old lady turned to Lutie again.

"Thank you, Lutie, for bringing it straight to me. Did you speak to any of the other servants about it?"

"No," said Lutie. "I was afraid they'd laugh at me. They tell me I'm fussy about little things."

"Well, that's a good trait sometimes," said the old lady. "I'm glad you brought it straight to me. Yes, it's valuable. It's part of something we had lost. You might keep your eye out while you're cleaning to see if you find any more of it. Now, suppose you come and show us just where you found this." They followed Lutie to the little room in the servants' hall.

"Thank you, Lutie," said Miss Catherwood when she had showed them the exact spot, "I shan't forget this!"

"Oh, that's all right, ma'am. I'm glad you weren't angry at my bothering you."

Lutie withdrew with a shy flame blazing in her cheeks.

Aunt Pat turned to Sherrill who was searching the room over, vainly hoping to find more of the necklace.

"Now, Sherrill," said Aunt Pat, "tell me just who was in this room and where each one stood. What were they here for anyway, in this back room?"

"They came to get the license fixed up with the right names," said Sherrill half shivering at the memory, "We sent for the clerk and he sat right there in that chair all the time he was here."

"And where did you stand?"

"Most of the time over there by the door. Once I stepped over to the table while I was explaining to him that I had changed my mind about marrying Carter."

The old lady gave her a swift look.

"Where was Carter at the time?"

"He stood just back of me."

"H'mm! How did he look when you explained that you had changed your mind about marrying him?"

"I didn't look at him. I was trying to keep my voice from trembling."

"Did he say anything or make any motion that seemed like a protest?"

"He cleared his throat in a nervous kind of way. I had a fancy that he was afraid I was going to tell more than I did. He stirred uneasily."

"And didn't he speak at all?"

"Only to answer the questions that were put to him by the clerk. Of course Mr. Copeland had explained the situation to the clerk in a general way and the questions that were put were mere form. He just assented to everything. Mr. Copeland had really made it very easy for us all."

"H'mm!" said Aunt Pat thoughtfully, and then reverted to the bridegroom.

"And Carter assented to all the questions did he? He made it very plain that he was marrying that other girl by intention? He didn't make any protests nor attempt any explanations?"

"Not a word." Sherrill's voice told how deeply that fact weighed upon her.

"Little whippersnapper!" ejaculated the old lady indignantly. "Well, it's just what I would have expected of him! He hasn't the backbone of a jellyfish. He was born a coward! Perhaps you can't blame him so much. He probably had ancestors like that. Well, now, tell me, how long did you stand there?"

"I stepped away immediately after he had answered his questions and made a place for her,—for the bride—to stand."

"And did you watch Carter's face while she was being questioned?"

"I wanted to, but just then he dropped his handkerchief. He acted very nervous and he stooped over to pick it up. It seemed to take him a long time. He didn't seem to want to look at me. I tried to make him. It seemed as if I must make him look at me just once so that we could get adjusted to things. Just a look from him that he was ashamed, or that he felt I had done the right thing, would have made it so much easier. I felt so unhappy and frightened!"

"I know you did, dear child. Of course! But don't have any question but that you did the right thing. Well, who else was there? Carter and that girl and the clerk and you? Was Mr. Copeland in the room?"

"Not at all," said Sherrill quickly. "He stood outside in the hall every minute. I'm sure of that."

"He didn't even step back into the room when you all came away?"

"No," said Sherrill with assurance. "I'm positive of that for he waited for me at the door and walked across to the middle room with me, and Carter and Arla were behind us. The clerk went ahead, down the back hall and to the back stairs the way he had come. He went out of the room before any of us left it."

"Who was in the room last?"

"Why, Carter—and his—that is—the—bride!" she finished with a quick sharp breath.

"You're sure?"

"Yes, I looked back and called to her to follow me and I would help her get ready. Carter was just behind her. He had apparently dropped his handkerchief again and was stooping to pick it up."

"H'm! What did he do with it?"

"Why, I think he put it in his pocket."

"And he didn't look up even then?"

"No." Her voice was grave and very sad. "He seemed as if he was ashamed. He almost looked—well,—frightened!"

"Probably was," said Aunt Pat dryly, "ashamed and baffled. He had been hoping to get a lot besides a bride in marrying you. I didn't tell you, but I came on him looking at the emeralds the morning I gave them to you. He seemed tremendously impressed with them. In fact he looked as if he were just gloating over them. He didn't know I saw him. He thought he was alone. But I can't help thinking if he'd got them he'd have pawned them before the night was over."

"Oh, Aunt Pat!" exclaimed Sherrill in dismay. "Why,—he—really spoke very beautifully about them. He said he was so proud that I should have regal jewels. He said he only wished that he were able to give me such things, but he hoped some day he could."

"Oh yes, he could talk!" sniffed Aunt Pat. "He was mealy-mouthed. But don't try to defend him Sherrill. I know it hurts to have him turn out that way but you might as well understand the truth at once and not go to getting him up on a pedestal again. Now, I've got to think what to do for Lutie. I like to encourage the sort of thing she did, bringing that bit of chain straight to me. She's a good girl, and probably needs help. I wonder if I should give her money?"

"Did you know that she has a little lame brother, Aunt

Pat?" asked Sherrill, "And her father is going blind and her mother needs an operation?"

"Mercy no!" said Aunt Pat looking up from the bit of chain she was examining. "Why, how did you find that out? We must do something for them right away."

"Yes, they are afraid they are going to lose their house too. They can't pay the interest on their mortgage. The bank closed where they kept their savings, and she and her brother are the only ones working."

"Well, for mercy's sake!" said Aunt Pat greatly disturbed, "And to think they never said a word! Why wasn't I told of this sooner? When did you find it out, Sherrill?"

"Just this morning," said the girl thinking back through the day, "I heard Lutie singing in the next room to mine where she was cleaning. She was singing about what to do when you had sorrow in your heart, or something like that. I asked her where she got the song and said I guessed she never had a sorrow and then she told me all about it."

"H'm!" said Aunt Pat thoughtfully.

Then she opened the door and called to Gemmie who was never very far away from her mistress' call.

"Gemmie, go see if Lutie has gone home yet. If she hasn't tell her I want her a minute."

Then she turned back to her niece.

"Sherrill, this is the setting of one of the tiny emeralds from that chain, see, one of the wee ones up near the clasp. Now, where do you suppose the rest of it is? You know the clasp used to be weak, but I had it fixed, at least I supposed I had. I sent it to the jeweler's before I gave it to you. See! This evidently has been stepped on, or else yanked from the chain! How the links are crushed! Now, the question is, where did the necklace drop, and who was there when it happened?"

Sherrill looked up with troubled eyes, the haunting fear coming back to her soul, but Lutie came in just then and she had no opportunity to answer her aunt.

"I sent for you, Lutie," said Miss Catherwood pleasantly, "because I want to tell you that there is a reward for finding this chain and for bringing it straight to me."

Lutie had been a bit troubled at being sent for, but now her face showed great relief and swift protest.

"Oh, no ma'am," she said breathlessly, "I couldn't think of taking anything for just doing my duty."

"Well, you're not, I'm giving it! That's different! I'm giving it because I'm grateful, and you've done me a big favor, one that no money can pay for. You've given me one little clue to something valuable and cherished that I've lost. And now, listen. I've just found out that you've got a lame brother, and your father has trouble with his eyes and your mother needs an operation. In that case I want to help. Yes, it's my right! You don't suppose we were put into this world to be pigs with what God gave us, do you? I want to see your mother on her feet again, and if there's anything that can be done for your father and brother I want to help do it. Sometimes operations will do wonders with eyes you know. Another doctor might put your father where he could go to work again."

"Oh, Miss Catherwood! You're too good!" began Lutie, tears of gratitude rolling down her cheeks and her lip trembling into a big smile like a rainbow upside down. "I don't know as my mother would think it was right to take help from anyone, but it's wonderful of you to suggest it."

"She'd think it right to take it from God, wouldn't she?" snapped the old lady crisply. "Well, this is just God's money and He told me to give you what you needed. There's no further use in discussing it. I'm coming to see your mother in a very few days."

"Well, maybe—" hesitated Lutie, her eyes shining with the great possibility, "if you'd let us work afterwards and pay it off when we can."

"Pay it back to somebody else then, not me," chuckled Aunt Pat in full form now. "I don't want you to have that on your mind. If you ever get able just help somebody else out of trouble. I tell you God told me to give you what you need, without any strings to it! And, oh yes, Lutie, if you should find any more of this just bring it to me at once no matter how busy I may be. It was a necklace and it had green stones in it. Big ones and little ones."

Lutie's eyes grew wide.

"I wonder if that green bead I picked up was one!" she exclaimed. "It was just a tiny little bit, looked like glass. At first I thought it was a bead, but then I thought it was glass, and I swept it up with the dust. It hadn't any hole like a bead in it."

"Where did you find it, Lutie? What did you do with it?"

"Why I found it in the big crack between the floor boards over under the bureau. I had to pry it out with a hairpin. I gathered it up with the dust when I thought it wasn't anything but glass and put it in the waste for Thomas to burn. Wait, I'll run down and see if I can find it. Thomas went down to the grocery for cook. I don't think he's burned the trash yet!"

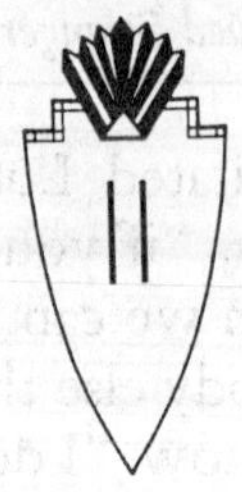

LUTIE sped on swift feet and was presently back again, her eyes shining, a tiny green particle held in the palm of her hand.

Miss Catherwood examined it carefully and Sherrill drew close.

"It is, *it is!*" cried Sherrill. "It's one of the wee little stones by the clasp, Aunt Pat!"

"Yes," said Aunt Pat grimly, "Whoever got away with the rest of the stones missed this one anyway."

Then the old lady turned to Lutie.

"Well, you've done me another favor, Lutie. Here's a bit of money I happen to have in hand. Take it and run home now and get something extra nice for supper just for my thanks offering. Tell your mother I'll be over soon."

When Lutie had finished her happy and incoherent thanks and gone Sherrill came and put her arms around the old lady's neck.

"You are wonderful, Aunt Pat!" she said and kissed her tenderly.

"Nonsense!" said the old lady with an embarrassed

grin. "Nothing wonderful about it! What's money for if it isn't to help along your fellow men and women? And besides you don't know but I may have my own selfish reasons for doing it."

"A lot of people don't feel that way about it, Aunt Pat!"

"Well, that's their lookout!" she answered. "All I've got to say is they miss a lot then."

"But Aunt Pat, aren't you going to do anything more about this now? Aren't you going to call the police and report the loss, or—ask anybody, or anything? Aren't you even going to tell the servants?"

"I've already told the servants that someone who was here last night lost a valuable necklace, and offered a good-sized reward for finding it, but only Gemmie knows it was your necklace. Gemmie would miss it of course when she came to put your things away. She was always very fond of those jewels and was pleased that I was giving them to you. She would have to know. But Gemmie won't say anything."

"But dear Aunt Pat! I do want everything possible done to find it even if it makes a lot of unpleasantness for me. I'd rather have it found. To think that you should have had the keeping of it all these years and then I should lose it the very first time I wore it! Oh, Aunt Pat, I must get it back to you!"

"Back to *me!*" snorted the old lady quite incensed. "It's not mine any more. It's yours, child, and I mean to have it back to you if possible of course, but if not there's nothing to break your heart about. Stop those highstrikes and smile. You are just as well off as you were last week. Better I think, for you are rid of that selfish pig of a lover of yours!"

Sherrill suddenly giggled and then buried her face on her aunt's shoulder.

"Aunt Pat," she said mournfully, "Why do you suppose this had to happen to me? Why did I have to be punished like this?"

"I wouldn't call it punishment, child," said the old lady patting Sherrill's shoulder. "I'd say it was a blessing the Lord sent to save you from a miserable life with a man who would have broken your heart."

"But if that is so," wailed Sherrill, "why didn't He stop me before it went so far? Before it would hurt so much?"

The old lady was still a minute and then she said:

"Perhaps He did, and you wouldn't listen. Perhaps you had some warnings that you wouldn't heed. I don't know. You'll have to look into your own life for that."

Sherrill looked at her aunt thoughtfully, remembering little happenings that had made her uneasy. The time Carter had gone away so hurriedly back to his former home without explanation. The letter addressed to him in a girl's handwriting that had fallen from his pocket one day which seemed to embarrass him but which he put back without a word. The telegram he sent her to say he was called to New York when afterward she discovered he had been West again, and when she innocently asked about it he gave but a lame excuse. The conversation she had overheard about him on the trolley calling in question his business principles. The queer way he had acted about not wanting to purchase her necklace at a certain store where she had admired a string of pearls, but had insisted on choosing one from another place. Oh, little things in themselves, but they had made her vaguely uneasy when they happened. Had they been warnings? Perhaps she should have sifted them. But she had been so reluctant to believe anything against him, so determined to shut her eyes to any fault of his!

There was that day, too, when she had come to the

office unannounced and found Arla sitting very close to Carter, her hand in his, her head on the desk, crying. They had jumped apart and Arla had gone quickly out of the room with her handkerchief to her eyes. Carter had been angry at her for coming in without knocking, and had explained that Arla's mother had just died and he had been comforting her, there was nothing else to it. That incident had troubled her greatly and they had had more than one discussion about it, until her own love and trust had conquered and she had put it away from her mind. What a fool she had been!

She had argued afterwards that of course he was not perfect and that when they were married she would help him to overcome his faults. He seemed so devoted! Then there would surge over her that feeling of his greatness, his ability and good looks, his many attractions, and she would fall once more under the spell of wonder that one so talented as he should love her.

Sharply, too, there came to memory the night before when she had stood looking into her own mirrored eyes wondering and shrinking back. Was that shrinking the result of those other fears and warnings? Oh, what a fool she had been! Yes, there had been plenty of warning. She was glad of course that she was mercifully delivered from being married to him, but oh, the desolate dreariness of her present situation! A drab life of loneliness to be looking forward to. To have thought herself beloved, and then to find her belief was built on a rotten foundation!

They had come out now, crossed the servants' hall, and the back sitting room where Carter had dressed for his wedding, and paused at the head of the stairs for a moment. Sherrill slipped her arm lovingly about the old lady's shoulders, and Aunt Pat patted her hand cheerfully. Then as they stood there they heard the doorbell ring and some packages were handed in, two great boxes.

"More presents!" gasped Sherrill aghast, "Oh, if there was only something we could do to stop them!"

"Well," said the old lady with a grin, "we might send out announcements that you were not married and 'please omit presents' at the bottom of the card."

Once again Sherrill's tragedy was turned into ridicule and she gathered up her courage and laughed.

"You're simply wonderful, Aunt Patricia! You brace me up every time I go to pieces. That's just what—!" Sherrill stopped suddenly, and her cheeks got red.

"That's just what what?" asked the old lady eyeing her interestedly.

"Oh, nothing! You'll laugh at me of course. But I was only going to say that's just what that stranger did last night. He seemed to know exactly how I was feeling and met me at every point with a pleasant saneness that kept me going. I shall always be grateful to him."

"H'm!" said Aunt Patricia approvingly, "Well, I thought he had a lot of sense myself."

Then Gemmie came forward with more boxes.

"We're not going to open them to-night, Gemmie, no matter what it is," said Miss Catherwood decidedly. "We're just too tired to stand the sight of another lamp or pitcher or trumpet whichever it is. We'll let it go till morning."

"But it's flowers, ma'am," protested Gemmie. "It says 'Perishable' on them, Miss Catherwood!"

"Flowers?" said the old lady sharply, giving a quick glance at Sherrill as if she would like to protect her. "Who would be sending flowers now? It must be a mistake!"

"It's no mistake, ma'am, there's one for each of you.

This small one is yours, and the big one is Miss Sherrill's."

She held the two boxes up to view.

Sherrill took her box wonderingly. It seemed as if this must be a ghost out of her dead happy past. For who would be sending her flowers to-day?

She untied the cord with trembling fingers, threw back the satiny folds of paper, and disclosed a great mass of the most gorgeous pansies she had ever seen. Pansies of every hue and mixture that a pansy could take on, from velvety black with a yellow eye down through the blues and yellows and purples and browns to clear unsullied white. There were masses of the white ones arranged in rows down at the foot of the box, with a few sprays of exquisite blue forget-me-nots here and there, and the whole resting on a bed of delicate maiden hair fern.

The fragrance that came up from the flowers was like the woods in spring, a warm fresh mossy smell. Had pansies an odor like that? She had always thought of them as sturdy things, merry and cheery, that came up under the snow and popped out brightly all summer. But these great creatures in their velvet robes belonged to Pansy royalty surely, and brought a breath of wildness and sweetness that rested her tired eyes and heart. She bent her face to touch their loveliness and drew a deep breath of their perfume.

The card was half hidden under a great brilliant yellow fellow touched with orange with a white plush eye. She pulled it out and read the writing with a catch in her breath and a sudden quick throb of joy in her heart. Why should she care so much? But it was so good to have flowers and a friend when she had thought all such things were over for her.

"I hope you are getting rested," was written on the card just above his engraved name, Graham Copeland.

A sudden chuckle brought Sherrill back to the world again, the warm glow from her heart still showed in her cheeks, and a light of pleasure in her weary eyes.

"The old fox!" chuckled Aunt Pat.

"What is the matter?" asked Sherrill in quick alarm.

"Why, he's sent me sweetheart roses! What do you know about that? Sweetheart roses for an old woman like me!" and she chuckled again.

"Oh, Aunt Pat! How lovely!" said Sherrill coming near and sniffing the bouquet. "And there are forget-me-nots in yours too! Isn't it a darling bouquet?"

"Yes, and the fun of it is," said Aunt Pat with a twinkle of sweet reminiscence in her eyes, "that I had a bouquet almost exactly like this when I went to my first party years ago with my best young man. Yes, identical, even to the lacepaper frill around it, and the silver ribbon streamers!"

Aunt Pat held it close and took deep breaths with half closed eyes, and a sweet faraway look on her face.

In due time Patricia Catherwood came out of her brief trance and admired the box of pansies.

"Aunt Pat," said Sherrill suddenly, her great box of sweetness still in her arms, as she looked down at them a little fearfully, very wistfully, "he wouldn't have sent these if he had—"

"No, of course not!" snapped the old lady. "I declare I'm ashamed of you, Sherrill Cameron. Can't you ever trust anybody any more just because one slim pretty man disappointed you? Just get on the job and learn how to judge real men and you won't have any more of that nonsense. Take those flowers to your room and study them, and see what you think about the man that sent them."

"Oh, I trust him perfectly, Aunt Pat. I'm quite sure he is all right. I *know* he is! But I was afraid you would think—!"

"Now, look here, if you are going to keep charging me with all the vagaries that come into your head 'you and I will be two people!' as an old nurse of my mother's used to say. For pity's sake, forget those emeralds and go and put your flowers in water. Unless perhaps you'd rather Gemmie did it for you!" she added with an acrid chuckle.

"Oh, no!" said Sherrill, quickly hugging her box in her arms, her cheeks flaming crimson. "Look, Auntie Pat. Aren't they dear? And yours are dear too. Almost as dear as yourself."

There was a tremble in her voice as she stooped and kissed the old lady on the sweet silver waves of hair just above her brow, and then she hurried away laughing, a dewy look about her eyes.

It was so nice not to feel utterly forgotten and out of things, she told herself as she went to her room with her flowers. It was just like him and his thoughtfulness to do this to-night! This first night after that awful wedding that was not hers! Somehow as she took the pansies out one by one and breathed their sweetness, laid them against her cheek with their cool velvety touch the weariness went out of her. It seemed to her as if by sending these blossoms he had made her understand that he knew this was a hard night and he was still standing by, although he could not be here, helping her through. She thought the joy that bubbled up in her heart was wholly gratitude.

"Pansies for thoughts!" she said to herself and smiled with heightened color, "Is that why he sent them? Forget-me-nots! Oh—!"

She rang for a great crystal bowl and arranged the

flowers one at a time, resting on their bed of ferns, and she was not tired any longer. She had lost that sense of being something that was flung aside, unwanted.

She got herself quickly into a little blue frilly frock for dinner, and fastened a few pansies at her breast, pale blue and white and black among the fluffy frills. She came down to find the old lady in gray chiffon with a sweetheart rose at her throat, and the bouquet otherwise intact in a crystal vase before her.

It was after all a gay little meal. The two had lost their sense of burden. They were just having a happy time together, getting nearer to each other than they ever had been before, and the hazy forms of a youth of the past dressed in the fashion of another day, and a youth of the present very much up to date standing in the shadows behind their chairs.

"I've been thinking of that question you asked me, why all this had to come to you," said the old lady, "I wonder—! You know it might have been that God has something very much better He was saving for you, and this was the only way He could make you wait for it!"

"I shall never marry anybody now, Aunt Pat, if that's what you mean!" said Sherrill primly though there was a smile on her lips.

"H'm!" said Aunt Pat smiling also.

"I could really never again trust a man enough to marry him!" reiterated Sherrill firmly, nestling her chin against the blue velvet cheek of the top pansy.

Aunt Pat replied in much the same tone that modern youth impudently use for saying "Oh yeah?", still with a smile, and a rising inflection, "Ye-*es?*"

"This man is just a friend. A stranger sent to help in time of need," explained Sherrill to the tone in Aunt Pat's voice.

"H'mmm!" said Aunt Pat. "It may be so!"

ARLA'S triumph was brief. She found Carter anything but a lover the next morning. He was surly and crabbed to her at breakfast, found fault with her attire and her make-up, told her her lips were too red for good taste, even went so far as to say that Miss Cameron never stained her fingernails. Arla felt as if she had been stabbed. She could scarcely finish her breakfast.

But because she had determined to make this marriage a success she bore his criticism, even ignoring his reference to his other bride though the tears were not far away, and a smouldering fire burned in her eyes. Was this other girl to be held up to her as a paragon the rest of her days? Oh, he was cruel!

She studied his sullen face, his selfish lips and saw these traits in him for the first time!

And she, by marrying him in that underhanded way, had forfeited a right to protest against such words. She could not flare out at him and tell him he had loved her enough to marry her and therefore he need not compare her with another. He had not married her by his own initiative, she had married him, and taken him as it were unaware, where he could not help himself.

The cold flamed into her face and then receded leaving it deathly white and making the redness of her lips but the more startling!

Then when they went on deck almost the first person he sighted was a man from whom he had borrowed largely but a few days before on the strength of his marriage into the Catherwood fortune.

Without explanation he dashed around a group of deck chairs, upsetting one in his haste, colliding with a man and swinging around to the other side of the ship without any seeming reason at all.

Arla followed him breathlessly, trying not to appear to be running a race. She was nonplussed. What was the matter with Carter? She had never seen him act in such a crazy way.

When she at last brought up panting at the secluded hiding place that he had selected she watched him in dismay. His face was actually lowering.

"What in the world is the matter with you, Carter?" she asked, almost tenderly. She began to think perhaps all that had happened yesterday had unsettled his mind.

"Everything in the world is the matter with me!" he said in a harsh tone. "Everything terrible that could happen to a man in any position!"

Arla studied him, still with that troubled look in her eyes, knowing that he would presently explain himself. She had not been his secretary for some months without knowing his habits.

"That was Mr. Sheldon that we passed as we came up the companionway. Didn't you recognize him?" He turned and glared at her as if she were responsible for Mr. Sheldon being on board.

"Sheldon? What Sheldon?" asked Arla in a pleasant tone, "I don't know any Mr. Sheldon, do I?"

"No!" said Carter, "You don't *know* him, socially of course, but it's not many hours since you witnessed his signature on some papers in the office!"

He paused impressively.

Arla looked puzzled and waited again, but Carter was still trying to impress her. At such time he could take on a fairly ponderous look, though he was not a large man, by merely swelling up proudly and looking down at her.

"Well, what of it?" asked Arla half impatiently after she had waited a reasonable time for explanation.

"What of it? And *you* can say what of it! You who wrote out those papers for him to sign, you who heard the whole conversation, and know that it was on the strength of my expectation of being able to raise a large sum in the near future that he loaned me the money I needed to finance—" he stopped abruptly, conscious that this very wedding trip was a part of the business he had to finance, the ring that sparkled on her finger, the pearls she had worn to the altar. He couldn't quite tell her that! Even in his present state of mind he couldn't be as raw as that.

"Well—?" she said again almost haughtily, watching him narrowly. His whole attitude toward her, his very tone had become offensive.

"*Well?* No, there is nothing well about it!" he snapped. "That man is a friend of the Catherwoods. He knows the Catherwood lawyer intimately. And he knows Sher—he knows Miss Cameron by sight. I have been with her when we met him. Don't you realize—? You can't be so blind as not to know that it would be nothing short of disastrous for him to know what has happened! Why, it's even conceivable that he might stop payment on that check now. He could radio a message to his bank you know. And then I'd be in a worse hole than I'm in already. You know as well as I do."

"Well, but he couldn't possibly know what had happened from merely meeting us together on deck!" said Arla haughtily.

"Couldn't he? You don't think he's sharp enough? Well, let me tell you he's keen. How long do you think it would take him to cancel his agreement if he discovers that instead of marrying an heiress I am tied to a penniless secretary?"

The words cut to the quick! Arla caught her breath and set her lovely teeth sharply in her red under lip, trembling with humiliation and anger.

He cast a furtive glance at her and grew only the more hateful, realizing perhaps to what depths he had descended.

"Well, you needn't cry-baby about that!" he said sharply, "You might as well understand what kind of a hole you've put me in!"

"I've put you in—!" said Arla fiercely. *"I!"*

"Yes you!" said the man, now beyond all bounds of self-control. *"I* didn't do it, did I? It was *you* who came to the Catherwood house fifteen minutes before the hour set for the wedding and got hysterics all over the place and drove me crazy so that I didn't know what I was doing! It was *you* that staged a scene with Sherrill and got yourself married to me wasn't it? I didn't know anything about it, did I? What could *I* do?"

There was an ominous silence while Arla struggled to control her voice. Presently she spoke in a tone of utter sadness as if she were removed from him by eons of time.

"Then all you told me last night was untrue!" she said. "Then you lied to me about your great love that you said you had for me!"

Suddenly the man grew red and shamed looking.

"I didn't say it was a lie!" he said. "This has nothing to do with that!"

"No, but I did!" said Arla. "And it has everything to do with that! I went through agony and humiliation to save you from marrying a girl you did not love because I believed you still loved me, and had only fallen for her because you needed her money. I was trying to save you from yourself, to save our love that in the past has been so sweet and true. And this is what I get! You tell me I have put you in a hole! Well, I'm in the same hole! What do you think it is for me to be married to a man that talks that way? Do you think I'm enjoying a wedding trip like this?"

"Well, it was none of my doings!" said the man shrugging his shoulders angrily. "I told you what kind of a fix I was in. I explained the whole matter to you didn't I?"

"Not until you had failed to get me to go out west on a vacation where I couldn't find out about it until afterwards! Not until your wedding invitations were about to come out," said Arla steadily.

"Well, I *tried* to tell you before. I tried to let you know by my actions—!"

"Yes, you tried to be disagreeable to me!" said Arla. "I suppose I ought to have understood you were trying to cast me off like a wornout garment. But I didn't! I thought you were worried about your business. I forgave everything because—I—loved you!"

The man gave an angry exclamation.

"There you are bawling again! Oh, women! They do nothing but make trouble and then they weep about it. A man is a fool to have anything to do with women!"

Arla lifted angry eyes.

"You would have talked that way to your paragon of

a Sherrill Cameron, I suppose?" she said, dashing away her tears.

He gave her a furious look.

"Can anything be more tantalizing than a jealous woman?" he sneered. "Well, I think we've gone far enough. I didn't come up here to listen to the kind of talk you've been giving me. I wanted to make you understand that we're in a very critical situation and we've got to do something about it! We've simply got to avoid meeting people, at least together."

"Just what do you mean by that?"

"Just what I said! We can't afford to have Sheldon get onto this. And he isn't the only one on board that knows us. I met Bixby this morning in the smoking room. He asked after Sh—, he asked after the bride of course and made some silly joke about having admired her first, and I had to tell him you were seasick, that you were a bad sailor and might not be able to appear at meals during the voyage. He knows Sheldon you know, is a sort of a henchman of his, and it won't do to have him talking. I think that's our best bet anyhow to save complications, just you stay close in your cabin, except late at night we can slip out and take a walk on deck where the rest don't usually come."

A wave of indignation passed over Arla's beautiful face.

"So that is the way you intend to treat me on my wedding trip!" she said bitterly, "keep me shut up in my room! Your bride! Well, I'll know how much to believe the next time you tell me you love me! How about you staying in and letting me do the talking?"

"But don't you see that wouldn't do? They all know Sh—, that is they all knew Miss Cameron."

"I see that you are perfectly crazy about money. You love money better than honor or decency or me."

"Now, you're being unreasonable!" said the man irritably, "I've told you our fortune hangs upon what happens in the next few days. I can't help it, can I, that my investments failed? Everybody else is having the same trouble. If the wedding had gone through as planned there wouldn't have been any trouble about money. I could have got around the old lady and got a loan of a hundred thousand or two to tide me over. But now—"

"But now, since she found you out, and the fortune isn't available you mean to take it out on me! who really is the wronged one from the beginning. Well, I won't stand for it, that's all! I'm not going to stay shut in and have you roaming around perhaps with some handsome brunette who has another fortune lying around!"

Her eyes were blazing wrathfully. Her tone was low but very angry. He watched her furtively. It wouldn't do to let her get started on that line. She could mess things up a lot more if she chose to.

"Look here, Arla!" he swung around upon her. "Be sensible! Haven't I told you that my business will go under completely and leave me utterly bankrupt if I can't tide over the next six months and pay my indebtedness. And now, just when I think I'm going to be able to swing it you get childish and balk at helping me."

"I'm not childish and I don't balk at helping you when it's right and reasonable. But I won't be lied about, and I don't intend to allow anybody to mix me up with the girl you didn't marry, not to save twenty businesses. Besides, I don't see what a mere fifty thousand matters. Even if Mr. Sheldon does refuse to pay the twenty-five thousand now, and the other twenty-five thousand in two or three months you still have a lot more thousands that you can't do anything about. You can't save your business anyhow you try, and it's better to realize that and give it up. Just let them take over what you have and don't try to launch out. Begin again in a small way and I'll help you!"

"Ah, but there's where you are mistaken, Arla! I've found a way. I'm sure I've found a way to swing the rest of that. Just last night a way came. I can't tell you about it yet, but it's sure! And we shall be on easy street yet, my girl! Just have a little patience. A day or two after we've landed on the other side I shall have everything all fixed up."

His eyes narrowed and he looked at her cunningly.

She gave him a quick furtive glance.

"And suppose you didn't? Suppose you are mistaken?" Her breath came sharply. "Don't you know you are throwing away something sweeter and finer than any money or any business that you could ever have?"

Perhaps because her words went deeper than she understood they angered him the more.

"Get out of my way!" he roared, forgetting he was on an ocean liner. "If you're my wife take my orders then! Don't you dare to stir out of the cabin again in daylight unless I say you may. Go! I don't want to see you any more, you make me tired! Talk about wedding trips? *I'm* having a glorious one!"

"Hush!" said Arla imperatively in a low controlled voice, "There's your Mr. Sheldon just below you coming up the stairs!"

Carter turned and saw the puffy red face of the financier advancing pompously up to where he stood, but when he turned back to give Arla a warning scowl she was not there. There seemed no way that she could have gone, but she was gone. Carter was left embarrassed and awkward to meet the dignified scrutiny of the man he wished to placate. He wished frantically that he knew how much of his conversation had been overheard.

BY a way that her need had discovered to her in the sudden crisis Arla had fled to her stateroom. Having locked her door she stood for an instant with clenched fists down at her sides, her teeth set in her trembling underlip, fighting back the tears that filled her eyes, fighting down the anger, the remorse, the dismay that threatened to overwhelm her. Then she began to walk up and down the small room like a young lion in a cage.

Suddenly her mood changed. She grew calmer. She took a book and a warm coat, went out on the deck and found an out-of-the-way nook where Carter would have to hunt to find her, and sat down, pretending to read, but really thinking out the way before her step by step. If she had to go back twenty-four hours would she have been willing to marry Carter? She refused to answer that question. It was too late. She must go forward!

She stayed in her hiding place until long past the lunch hour, subsisting on the cup of broth that was brought around on deck in midmorning. Still Carter had not found her, or perhaps had not chosen to seek her. Then soon after lunch time a young man came breezily by her chair, paused, hesitated, and then cried out:

"Great Caesar's ghost! If this isn't Arla Prentiss! Say, now, what do you know about that? I'm in luck, aren't I?"

Arla looked up, dismay in her soul, for there before her stood the soda clerk from her home town drug store, crude and breezy and familiar as ever. He had known her all her life, had bestowed various boxes of candy upon her, had attempted to pay her attention sometimes, though she had always been able to laugh him off. Still, he was genuine and somehow the real hearty admiration in his eyes now warmed her heart, even while she was wondering what Carter would say when he found that Hurley Kirkwood was on board.

But there was no dismay in Hurley Kirkwood's heart. He was joyously glad to see her. He had been somewhat like a stray cat till he sighted her, having no acquaintances on board, and being adrift in the world for the first time in his life.

"Say, now, this is great!" said Hurley, quickly drawing up a camp stool and settling down to enjoy himself. "Say, now, Arla, are you alone? Taking a trip to Europe alone? Say, now, if I can be of any service!"

Arla gave a little shiver.

"No, I'm not alone," she smiled, "my husband is around here somewhere! I'm on my wedding trip, Hurley!"

"Boom! Just like that!" said Hurley slapping his hands together noisily. "Hopes busted at the first word! Well, I congratulate you, Arla. But say now, when did it happen? You kept it mighty still, didn't you? Didn't any of the home folks come to the wedding? Your Aunt Tilly wouldn't have missed it I'm sure if she'd known."

Arla suddenly realized that there was another part of her world yet to be dealt with.

"Yes, it was rather sudden," said Arla, "You see Carter found he had to go abroad and of course it made a splendid wedding trip. I had practically no warning whatever. We just got married and rushed off to catch this boat."

"Well, you certainly put one over on the home town," said Hurley. "Sorry I didn't know about it. You might have wired. There's about a dozen I know would have come on to see you off. And me, why I could have made it easy. I been in New York three days just bumming!"

Arla tried not to shudder again at the thought. It seemed to her that nothing could have been more perfectly the last straw at that terrible wedding of hers than to have had Hurley Kirkwood appear on the scene. She registered a distinct thanksgiving that she had been saved so much at least.

And yet, as he talked on, giving her homely items of domestic interest about her Aunt Tilly's rheumatism, old Mrs. Pike's having lost all her money when the bank closed and going to the poor house, Lila Ginn's latest escapade of running away with a drummer, and the party the high school kids had at a road house that made all the school board sit up and take notice, somehow Arla felt the tension in her taut nerves relax. After all it was comforting just to hear of home folks and home town and things that happened in the years before Carter had loved and tried to marry another woman. It was good to forget if only for a few minutes the problems and perplexities of her own present situation.

Hurley Kirkwood made a good soda clerk. He knew how to kid everybody in town with a special brand of kidding for each individual. There was something vivid and interesting about Hurley in spite of his crudeness, and presently Arla forgot herself so far as to be laughing heartily at some of the stories Hurley told.

Hurley had saved up his money, and he was just explaining to Arla how he had always wanted this trip to Europe and mapping out the course of travel he had planned for himself, when suddenly a stern and forbidding Carter arrived on the scene. He fairly glared at the poor soda clerk whom he had never liked, mainly because he presumed to be friendly with Arla. Carter had never approved of Arla's being friendly with Hurley. Just because she had gone to school with him did not give a mere soda clerk the right to take the girl of a man like himself to *anything!* Not even a ball game in the early evening played in his own neighborhood! Not even if he started out alone and just *met* Arla and sauntered with her to the grandstand and bought her peanuts, which is what had happened one summer evening when Carter's interest in Arla was in its initial stages.

Therefore Carter glared at Hurley and gave him a passing:

"Oh, Hurl, you here! Not serving in your official capacity as drink slinger on board are you?"

There was utter contempt in Carter's tone. All the venom and fury that he had been holding in his heart for Arla during the morning because she had not obeyed him, and had been evading him, he vented in that one contemptuous sentence.

And Hurley, gay, crude, a bit obtuse, not easily hurt, could not but recognize the unfriendliness and grew red and embarrassed. He attempted to rise to the occasion by slapping the dignified Carter on the shoulder and offering congratulations in his native style.

"My sympathy, Cart!" he said with a guffaw, "I hear you been getting tied! Only wish I'd been there to be best man. I'd have given you a great send off! But say now, isn't it great we both got on the same little old boat together! My word! I got something to write home to the little old home town now! Mebbe that won't make 'em all sit up and take notice! Cart and Arla got tied at last! We been looking for news and an invite this long while and then you went and done it on the sly! But say now, I certainly do wish you a lotta happiness!"

Carter's face had grown more and more stern during this harangue and now his tone was like a slap in the face as he made another attempt to put this boo from home in his place.

"I am sure Mrs. McArthur and I are greatly obliged to you for your interest," he said disagreeably, and then turned to Arla sternly.

"My dear, I shall have to ask you to come down to the stateroom at once. There is a matter I must discuss with you."

But Arla was resenting her husband's attitude. A sudden loyalty for the home town and the people and things that used to be dear to her surged over her. Carter had no call to insult this well meaning but ignorant youth who stood there red and hurt and wondering over the unnecessary coolness in Carter's tone. She knew that Carter was venting upon him all the injury and indignation he felt for her, and she turned lightly away from the command and answered:

"All right, Carter, I'll be down presently. I want to finish my talk with Hurley first. He's been telling me all about the people at home."

Carter could scarcely believe his senses. Arla was standing out against him. He stared at her in consternation a moment with an icy look, then turned on his heel and marched away.

She did not look after him as he went. She did not

dare to think what effect her attitude would have upon him. It was the first time in her acquaintance with him,—which had dated from her very young childhood,—that she had ever defied him. She had pled with him, she had wept, she had been sweet and submissive, but she had never openly defied him before and she was trembling over it. She found herself almost panic stricken. Perhaps hc would never speak to her again. Perhaps he would divorce her. Yet it was what she had resolved in those morning hours of meditation that she would do, defy him, show him that he could not order her about. Would she be able to carry it out?

For another half hour she asked questions about the people at home, questions in which she had not the slightest interest, but which she knew would bring forth voluble answers, long enough to protect her from having to say much back. Hurley was delighted. In all his acquaintance with her taken altogether he had never had this much speech of her. He admired her greatly, and was tremendously flattered that she had stayed to talk with him. He was so flattered that he forgot Carter's insulting tone.

When Arla had finally ceased to tremble and felt that she had sufficient control of herself to carry out the program she had planned for herself she arose sweetly.

"Well, now, I really must go to that longsuffering husband of mine," she said smiling, "It's been so nice to meet you again, to hear all the news from home, and to know you're going to have such a lovely trip." And then she was gone and Hurley knew that he was dropped as definitely as she had always dropped him in the old days when he brought her candy and she accepted it graciously, but always had a reason why she couldn't go to the movies with him.

Hurley went and stood by himself staring off at the sea

and wondering why it was. Here he had been having as nice a time with her as anyone would need to ask to have, and all of a sudden he was out of it, just out! That was all! He knew as well as if she had told him that he wouldn't likely come in contact with either of them the rest of the voyage. Oh, maybe meet and bow or something like that, but nothing more. And here he had been fool enough to fancy that now that he had money enough to take a trip abroad they would be friendly and he would have somebody to talk to now and then, just be friendly with any time he liked! Well, maybe it was just his imagination. He decided he'd forget it. Probably they'd be all right the next time he met them. Maybe he'd try to get at their table and then they'd have to be friendly.

When Arla reached the stateroom Carter was not there. She was likely being punished. So she put on one of Sherrill's prettiest negligees and lay down to rest. That is her body was resting but her mind was madly working. She was looking life in the face, realizing all sorts of possibilities. Well, that other girl had been right. It was no enviable path she had chosen for herself, but having chosen it, being married, the thing she had so much desired, she must make it a success if that were a possible thing to do. She had not attained her wish unless she was able to hold him. And she saw keenly enough that this was the crucial time. What she did now would count through the years. Oh, for wisdom to know what was the best thing to do!

Carter did not return to the stateroom until it was nearly time for dinner. He found Arla attired in black lace and looking fairly regal, putting the last touches to her facial expression. She turned an indifferent glance at him and in spite of his smouldering anger he was startled at her beauty. Sherrill had never been more beautiful!

Arla certainly was a stunning looking woman. There was some satisfaction in that for the future. If he ever pulled through this hard time he could be proud of her. There was an air about her that he had never seen before, a certain smartness that he had always admired in Sherrill. He did not realize that Arla was wearing one of Sherrill's costumes which was the work of an artist and had cost a fabulous sum. He simply saw that Arla was looking more wonderful than he had ever seen her look before. For a moment he was almost ready to forgive her and take her into his arms. Then she turned and gave him a haughty indifferent glance and his anger boiled again.

"What are you all rigged up like that for?" he snarled, even while his eyes gloated over the lovely curves of her throat and white shoulders. "You're not planning to do what I forbade you to do?"

"Forbade?" said Arla with slightly uplifted eyebrows. "Really! I shouldn't recognize any such word as that between us! That isn't what marriage means. Not in this age and generation! If you mean am I going down to dinner, I certainly am. If you don't want to go with me that's entirely up to you. I am sure Hurley Kirkwood will be delighted to take me in to dinner. I can tell people you are seasick you know. But as this is the first ocean voyage I've ever had, and may be the last one I'll ever get, I intend to enjoy every minute of it in spite of your disagreeableness."

"You don't care what happens to me and my business then? I thought you professed to love me!" he said after a long silence during which he went and stared out the porthole.

"Why, I supposed I did too," said Arla lightly, "but as for caring what happens to you and your business at such a price as you demand, I'm not so sure that I do."

He was still a much longer time now, staring out at the endless waves of the ocean.

"Then do I understand that you refuse to comply with my request and stay out of sight during the voyage."

"Yes, I do!" said Arla coolly, taking up her hand mirror and examining her profile carefully and the wave of her lovely gold hair.

"But why, Arla? You have always wanted me to get on. You know I want it for you as much as for myself—!"

"Oh!" interrupted Arla in a surprised voice, "no, I didn't know that!" Her tone was sweet and innocent. "Did you want it for me as much as for yourself when you were going to marry Sherrill Cameron?"

He gave a quick angry exclamation.

"Can't you leave her out of the question now we're definitely done with her?" he asked desperately.

"I'm sorry," said Arla, "I'd like to, but the trouble is she somehow won't be left out. You see she was there, and I'm not so sure she's definitely out of it either."

"Well, then, if you must bring her in, yes, I did do it for your sake as much as my own. I thought an alliance with her would bring the needed funds and position, and later, well,—there are such things as divorces you know!"

She turned a steely eye to him.

"Carter, if you had been brought up in the social world of to-day there might be some excuse for your daring to say a thing like that to me, but both you and I had decent mothers who didn't believe in such things, and when you say that you are insulting both Miss Cameron and myself. You said something of that sort last night I remember, just before you flung me off in the corner and went out to marry your other bride. I don't know how I ever forgave it in you enough to be willing to marry you except that I thought you were beside yourself and didn't realize what you were saying. It was preposterous you know! And if I didn't think you were still rather beside yourself I certainly wouldn't stay here with you now and listen to such talk."

"Very well, now, if you are so interested in me and my business," he said at last, "what would you suggest that we do? You know the facts, that I need a large sum of money to tide me over and if I can get it I can keep my business floating till this depression is past. If I don't I either have to give up and lose everything or else probably go to jail!"

"I would *not* go to jail!" said Arla. He gave her a sudden quick startled look. But Arla went steadily on talking, not looking at him. "I would take the next boat back as soon as I landed and arrange to give over my business interests in such a way that while it might be a total loss of all that has been gained through the last three years, your name would be cleared and you could go honorably into some more modest business and have a chance of making good. You will remember I happen to have been present in the office when an offer was made to you which would have made that possible!"

"Oh!" exclaimed the man angrily, "I'm not an utter fool!"

"Are you sure?" asked the woman. "Sometimes I wonder!"

After a long silence the man spoke again in a voice of smouldering wrath:

"Well, come on, I suppose you've got to have it your way and go down to dinner even if it wrecks everything! It was bad enough before, but now that the situation is further complicated by the appearance of that country bunkum from home I don't see how we can possibly get by without trouble. How in the world are you going to explain him to people if he chooses to barge in on us?"

"I don't expect to explain him or anybody else we may happen to meet. This is not a private boat and anybody has a right on board who pays his fare. Please remember that I had nothing whatever to do with his being here. As far as I am concerned I see no reason why we shouldn't go about our business as anybody else does. If your business was on an honest basis we could go about freely and enjoy ourselves without watching out for what people think."

"Women know nothing about business!" glowered Carter. "Well, come on, let's get this over."

So Arla in Sherrill's costly lace gown from an exclusive Paris house walked regally beside her husband and never showed by the flicker of an eyelash that she had recognized across the saloon another two people from home, a young man and his wife who had been in the same class in high school with Carter and Arla. It would be time enough for Carter to know they were on board when he had to meet them. They would be another element in this problem she was trying to solve.

THERE was a sense of peace in Sherrill's room next morning. The fragrance of the pansies pervaded the place. The delicate perfume spoke to her at once even before she opened her eyes. It brought the memory of the pleasant stranger, as if his presence were still lingering not far away to help.

Then she opened her eyes to see the pansies on the low bedside table where she had placed them. She reveled in their soft brightness, and was glad they were just pansies, not any of the more conventional flowers. They seemed to emphasize the simple frank friendship that had begun on the street, just plain honest friends helping one another. Pansies might grow in anybody's garden, only these of course were sort of glorified pansies. But it was a comfort that they did not recall the bridal bouquet nor any of the flowers in the church. Just simple pansies that she might love and lay her face against.

She reached out for the card that lay beside them on the table. Somehow that hastily penned line seemed to have a deeper meaning than just a wish that she was rested physically. It seemed to carry a desire that she might be healed in spirit from the deep hurt to her life that he could not help knowing that wedding must have been to her.

Little memories of the kindness in his eyes, merry eyes that yet held tenderness, came back to her; the turn of a sentence that made her laugh when he must have seen the tears were very near to coming; his pleasant grin. They all filled her with a warmth and comfort that was restful and almost happy.

She lay there thinking about him. How kind he had been! She was rejoicing in the presence of the pansies in their lovely fern setting when Gemmie tapped at the door and entered with a breakfast tray.

"Miss Patricia said you better eat before you get up," she announced, setting her tray down on a low table and drawing back the silk curtains.

Gemmie brought her negligee and put it about her, adjusted her pillows. Then she bustled over to the hearth and lighted a fire that was ready, though it was scarcely needed that bright spring morning. Sherrill began to perceive that Gemmie had something on her mind. She never bustled unless she was ill at ease. But Sherrill was too comfortable just at that moment to try and find out what it was, so she let Gemmie go on setting things straight on the dressing table and then setting them crooked again. At last she spoke.

"It's right awful about that necklace being gone, Miss Sherrill!"

Boom! A great burden of stone seemed suddenly to land back again in Sherrill's heart, just where it had been the day before, only a trifle heavier if possible.

"Yes," quavered Sherrill pausing in her first comforting swallow of coffee.

"Seems like we ought to do something about it right

away," went on Gemmie. "Seems like we oughtn't to let the time get away with us."

"Yes, Gemmie," said Sherrill distressedly, "but Aunt Pat wants to work it out in her own way. I think she has some idea about it, though she doesn't want to tell it yet. We are not to tell anybody about it you know."

"Yes, I know," said Gemmie severely as if she disapproved greatly. "But Miss Sherrill, it doesn't seem reasonable, does it? That necklace didn't have legs. It couldn't run away of itself, could it?"

"Not very well, Gemmie." Sherrill lay back against her pillows with distress in her eyes.

"There was only one stranger there, wasn't there, Miss Sherrill? I was wondering if you knew him real well. Was you right sure about him?"

"Stranger?" said Sherrill coldly. "Did you mean the clerk who came in to witness the license papers signed?"

"Oh, laws! No! Not him. I've known him for years. He used to live next door to my best friend, and he wouldn't steal a pin. He's too honest, if you know what I mean? But wasn't there a stranger there, Miss Sherrill? I came across him in the back hall just after I got back from the church. I went up to leave my hat and coat and I found him wandering around trying doors all along the hall."

"Oh, you mean my friend Mr. Copeland," said Sherrill with elaborate coolness. "No, I brought him there, Gemmie. He'd just come from the train and brought his suitcase to change here. I met him at the church. He's from out near my old home in the west you know, Gemmie. I put him in that little end room where we afterwards signed the papers. He's quite all right!"

Sherrill explained it all out slowly, her voice growing more assured as she went on, and ending with a ripple of laughter, though she felt that awful haunting doubt creeping into her mind again with the accompanying heaviness of heart.

"You know him right well do you? You're sure he wouldn't yield to temptation, are you? You know those stones are wonderful costly, Miss Sherrill!"

"Oh, for pity's sake, Gemmie! What an awful suggestion to make about a friend and guest of ours! You'd better not say that to Aunt Pat. She certainly would not be pleased. Of course he is entirely above suspicion. Why he is a friend, Gemmie!"

"Well! I didn't know how well you knew him," said Gemmie offendedly, "I never heard you speak of him before and I didn't know but what he might be somebody you hadn't seen in a long time, and didn't know how he'd turned out now he's growed up."

Sherrill managed a real laugh now and answered:

"No, Gemmie, nothing like that! Now, if you'll take this tray I'll get up. I want to get at those presents again. We got a lot done yesterday, didn't we?"

"Yes, Miss Sherrill, but you've not eaten your breakfast, and Miss Patricia will be all upset."

"All right, Gemmie, I'll eat a little more if you'll run and see if the morning mail has come yet. I'm expecting a letter. Aren't my flowers lovely, Gemmie? Mr. Copeland's the one that sent them to me."

Gemmie eyed the flowers half suspiciously.

"Yes," admitted Gemmie reluctantly, "for flowers that aren't roses, they're above most."

Then Gemmie, leaving a mist of insidious doubt in her wake, swept firmly out of the room, and Sherrill had a silly feeling that she wanted to throw the whole breakfast after her and burst into tears. How outrageous of the stupid old thing to get such a notion and try to rub it in! Of course her kind stranger friend was all right! She would not let such sickening doubts creep into her mind. Aunt Pat didn't think any such thing. She didn't herself. As she remembered the fine merry countenance and wide frank eyes she felt that it was utterly ridiculous to suspect such a man even though he was a stranger. Yet there was that heaviness planted for the day again, planted in the very pit of her stomach just like yesterday. Then she suddenly put her face down into her pillows and cried a few hot tempestuous worried tears till she remembered Gemmie would soon return with the mail and she mustn't have red eyes. So she stopped the tears and before Gemmie could come into the room again she sprang up and buried her face in the dewy sweetness of the pansies, touching her lips to their coolness hungrily. Oh, why did evil and suspicion and sin have to come in and spoil a world that would otherwise be bright? She would not, *would not* believe or entertain the slightest suspicion against Graham Copeland. They had made a compact of trust and friendship, and she would abide by her own intuition. Yes, and by Aunt Pat's judgment also.

And so when Gemmie entered Sherrill was bending over her flowers touching them delicately with her finger tips, lifting a pansy's chin lightly to look better into its face, and smiling into their gay little faces with a whimsical fancy that some of them were grinning just as their donor had done.

But Gemmie wore an offended air all that day, and went about poking into corners everywhere trying to find that necklace.

"I don't see why Miss Patricia won't have the police up here!" she declared. "I shan't be happy till that necklace is found! Who was that girl anyway, that bride? Did you ever see her before? Seems to me this is the queerest doings that ever was had about this house. I don't understand it myself. We never had doings around here that was out of the ordinary before. I mus' say I don't like it myself. Did you know that girl, Miss Sherrill?"

"Oh, yes, Gemmie," said Sherrill summoning a brave tone. "She was an old friend of Mr. McArthur's. In fact they had been sort of engaged for several years, and—then—well, they got separated—"

Sherrill's voice trailed off vaguely. She knew she was treading on very thin ice. How was she to make this all quite plausible to this sharp-eyed, jealous servant who loved her because she belonged to her beloved Miss Patricia, and yet not tell all the startling facts?

"You see, Gemmie," she went on bravely, taking up the tale and thinking fast, "she came just after you left with a message for Mr. McArthur and I happened to find out about it, so we had a little talk and fixed it up this way. It was rather quick work getting us dressed all over again, but I think we got by pretty well, don't you?" Sherrill finished with a little light laugh that sounded very natural, and Gemmie eyed her suspiciously.

"I ought to have stayed here!" she declared firmly. "I knew I oughtn't to've gone when I went. That was *your* wedding dress, not hers, and she had no business with it!"

"Oh, that!" laughed Sherrill gayly, "what did that matter? You see she didn't happen to have her own things with her, so we fixed it up that way, and I thought everything came off very well. She looked sweet, didn't she?"

"I didn't take notice to her," said Gemmie sourly. "When I saw it wasn't you I was that put out I could hardly keep my seat. I didn't think you'd be up to any tricks like that, Miss Sherrill, or I wouldn't have left you. If I hada been here I'd not have let her by having your wedding dress, not if she never got married. And your wedding, too. It was a shame!"

"Oh, no, Gemmie, it was lovely! Because you see when I found out a few things I didn't want to get married myself just then, so it turned out quite all right. I wouldn't want to marry a man who loved another woman, would you, Gemmie?"

"I wouldn't want to marry any man that lives!" sniffed Gemmie. "They're all a selfish deceiving lot. Not one good enough for a good girl like you."

"There you are, Gemmie! You think that and yet you are angry that I let another girl marry him!"

"Well, he was yours by rights after he'd went that far!" sniffed Gemmie getting out her primly folded handkerchief and dabbing at her eyes.

"Well, I didn't happen to want him when I found he really belonged to another girl," said Sherrill soberly, and wished that her heart didn't give such a sick plunge when she said the words. They were true of course, and yet her soul was crying out for the lover she had thought she had, though she didn't intend that this sharp-eyed woman should find it out. "And now, Gemmie, keep it all to yourself and let's forget about it. I'm back here to stay awhile, and I'm going to have the best time a girl can have. Do you happen to know where that little pale green knit dress of mine is, with the white blouse? I think I'd feel at home in that. Hasn't it got back from the cleaner's yet?"

"Yes, it came back three days ago but I put it away in the third floor closet. I didn't think you'd be needing it yet awhile."

"Oh, get it for me, Gemmie, will you? That's a dear! It's just the thing for this morning."

Sherrill hurried with her dressing and when Gemmie came back with the dress she slipped into it and with a gay little wave of her hand hurried down stairs, looking much brighter than she felt.

The next two days were full of hard work. It seemed that Miss Catherwood was in a great rush to get those presents out of the way.

But there does come an end to all things, even unpleasant ones, and Sherrill finally came to her aunt and laid a neatly written envelope in her lap.

"There, Aunt Pat, that's the last one of those awful notes I have to write. The very last one! And I'm glad! glad! glad! Now, what next?" and she looked drearily out of the window across the wide sweep of lawn and garden.

"Next we're going to get rested," said the old lady leaning back in her chair with a gray look about her lips. "I believe I'm tired, and I know you are. I've watched you getting thinner and thinner hour by hour. You've been a good sport, but now we've got to rest a little."

Sherrill sprang into alarm at once.

"You dear precious Aunt Pattie!" she cried, and was down on her knees beside her aunt's chair with her arm about her, looking earnestly into the tired old face.

"Oh, it's nothing," said Aunt Pat crisply, trying to rouse herself. "I just want a nap. I guess I've caught a bit of a cold perhaps. You need a nap too, and then afterwards we'll plan what we'll do next. How would you like to take a trip somewhere? You can be thinking about it while you're going to sleep."

THE next day was Sunday. Sherrill had been dreading it. Aunt Pat always went to church. Sherrill would be expected to go also, and she shrank inexpressibly from entering that church again, the church that had been decorated for her wedding, the church in which she had gone through that horrible experience, watching her bridegroom given to another woman. She almost decided to beg off, say she had a headache or something, only she knew a headache would bring alarm to the dear old lady and perhaps bring on a lot more complications that might be even worse than going to church. But oh, how she dreaded the soft lights from the stained glass, the exquisite music that would stir her soul to the depths and make her remember all the lovely things she had dreamed of and lost.

A dozen times during the early morning she thought of new excuses to stay at home, and even after she had her hat and gloves on and was on her way down stairs she had half an idea of telling Aunt Pat plainly how she longed to escape this experience, just this one Sunday anyway.

But when she got down stairs she found that the old lady was already in the car waiting for her and there was such a pleasant light of expectancy in her eyes that Sherrill had not the heart to suggest that she would not go.

"I got to thinking," said the old lady almost shyly, "I'd like to go to an old church where I went once with my best young man. Would you mind, Sherry?"

"Oh, I'd love it of course," said Sherrill deep relief in her voice. It would be so good to go to a new place where she would not have to go through that awful wedding again all during service. So good not to have to face the battery of eyes that would be watching to see just how she was taking life without her bridegroom. It would be such a relief not to have to sit and feel them wondering about her, thinking up things to say about her when they got home to their various dinner tables. Oh, many of the people in the home church were friends, nice pleasant people that she liked, but it was good not to have to be watched this first Sunday after her world had been turned upside down.

Dear Aunt Pat! She had known of course that she would feel like that, and had planned this to have something different.

"You see," said Aunt Pat suddenly, right into the midst of her thoughts, "James and I went out to this church a great many years ago. We started quite early Sunday morning for a walk to get away from everybody else for a while. We didn't plan where we were going,—or at least, maybe James did—he was like that, he thought of nice things and planned them out ahead—but we just started along the road."

Sherrill turned bright interested eyes on her sweet old aunt.

"We took hold of hands," confessed Miss Patricia with

a little pink tinge stealing into her soft roseleaf cheek. "It was very early when we started and there were no people about, not even a carryall on the road. We had a wonderful time. I had some caraway cookies in my silk bag that hung from my arm by little velvet ribbons. Soon there was dust on my best slippers, but I didn't care. We stopped before we went into church and James dusted them off. There were narrow velvet ribbon laces to my slippers, crossed at the ankle and tied in a little tassel bow."

Aunt Pat's eyes were sweet and dreamy.

"We talked about what we would do when we were married," went on the sweet old voice. "We planned a house with pillars and a great window on the stairs. I was going to do my own work. I had written down a list of things James liked to eat and I was learning to cook them."

"Oh," said Sherrill, bright-eyed, "it's just like a story book."

"Yes, it was," said Aunt Pat. "I was very happy. We walked a good many miles, but I wasn't tired. I didn't get tired in those days of course, but James slipped my hand through his arm, and that made it like walking on clouds!"

"Dear Aunt Pat!" breathed Sherrill.

"When we came to that little white church we knew we had come to the place we had been looking for, though we hadn't known what it was or where it was. But it was our church. We both exclaimed over it at once."

Sherrill nestled her hand in her aunt's hand.

"It was still early when we got there. The old sexton was just ringing the first bell, and it sounded out over the hills like music. The bell may have been out of tune but it sounded sweeter than any orchestra has ever seemed to me. We went and sat on a flat grave stone in the little cemetery under a tall elm tree and ate our seed cakes, and James put his arm around me and kissed me right there in the graveyard. It made me glad with a deep sweet gladness I had never felt before. It seemed just like heaven. And a bird high up sang a wonderful song that went through my heart with a sweet pain."

The little old lady had forgotten for the moment that Sherrill was there. Her eyes were dreamy and faraway.

"People ought never to get married unless they feel like that about each other, Sherry."

"No?" said Sherrill as if it were something she had just found out and were considering.

"You didn't feel like that about Carter McArthur, Sherrill."

"No," said Sherrill still gravely, "I don't think I did. I was just happy. Having a good time!"

There was a long minute of stillness, then Sherrill said shyly:

"Tell the rest, please, Aunt Patricia."

"Well," said the old lady, her eyes still on the faraway, "after a while the people began to come. They drove up in buggies and carryalls and phaetons, and a few in old farm wagons with boards across the sides for seats, and carpet on the boards. Then we got up and walked around among the white stones and read the names and dates until the sexton rang the second bell, and then we went in. A young girl with a pink ribbon and daisies on her hat played an old cabinet organ and I remember they sang 'Nearer my God to Thee,' and God seemed very near to us and we to Him."

"Yes?" said Sherrill nestling closer in a pause.

"We sat in the very last seat back by the door," went on the sweet old voice, "and James held my hand under the folds of my ruffles. I had on a very wide biadere striped silk skirt with three deep flounces, and they flowed over the seat beautifully. I can remember the strong warm feel of his hand now."

The tears began suddenly to come into Sherrill's eyes.

"We sat all through that service hand in hand and nobody the wiser," said Aunt Pat with a bit of her old chuckle, and then a softened light came into her eyes.

"We planned to go back there some day and be married in that church when James had got a good job. We loved that church! But, Sherry, we never went back there again! The next day they brought my James home with the mark of a horse's hoof on his temple."

She paused an instant, looking far away and added:

"Lutie's mother was the little child whose life he saved!"

"Oh, Aunt Patricia!" said Sherrill in a low awed voice. She understood now why helping Lutie's family was so important to Aunt Pat.

"I've never been back till to-day."

"My dear!" said Sherrill softly.

They were at the church now, a little white building set among the trees, with a quaint old graveyard surrounding it. A young sexton was tolling the bell. He would be perhaps the grandson of the old sexton who was there when the young Patricia walked up those steps with her James.

There were smart cars parked in the old sheds where farm wagons drawn by plow horses, and buggies and carryalls drawn by the family horses, used to be hitched so long ago. People were coming along the road dressed in stylish modern clothes. But as Sherrill looked at the pleasant white church she seemed to see the young Patricia in her wide hooped skirts with silken flounces and a broad flat hat with streamers, walking with her James up the steps of the house of God, and she had much ado to brush the tears away before she got out of the car, for people were hurrying by them in happy groups eyeing them curiously, as the shining limousine drew up before the flagstone path.

Sherrill watched her aunt furtively as they walked together up that path to the church. Her bright eyes had suddenly grown old and tired looking, and the soft cheeks and lips seemed to sag a little wearily. She walked without her usual spring, and when Sherrill drew her hand within her arm she leaned down heavily upon her as if she were grateful for the support. Her eyes were searching over to the right among the old mossy headstones. Sherrill felt she was looking for the place where she and her young lover had sat so long ago.

They went into the church and found a seat half way up. People stared in a kindly way and whispered about them, pondering who they were. There were quaint windows about the walls made of long panes of clear colored glass put together in geometrical forms like a kaleidoscope. The sun was casting long bright rays through them making quaint color effects of green and blue and yellow on people's chins and noses, and stabbing the old red ingrain carpet in the aisles with a sickly purple and red that did not match. But there was one window, back of the pulpit, high above the head of the minister, a gorgeous window, that was the work of a real master. It pictured an open tomb and an angel in a garden of lilies, with a wondrous blue light in a leaden sky where morning broke the gloom and shed a veil of loveliness over the lilies. Underneath in small clear letters were the words "Sacred to the memory of James and Patricia," and, "Joy cometh in the morning." Then a long ago date in characters so small they were hardly discernible.

Sherrill stared at it startled. So that was what Aunt

Patricia had done! Given this little stranger church a window! A window with a story that nobody understood! Aunt Pat had likely done it through her lawyer, or someone who did not even know her except as a client.

Sitting there in the weird light of stark mingled colors, studying that one lovely window, Sherrill worked it all out; the tragedy, and the sweetness of Aunt Patricia's long lonely life; the patience and utter cheerfulness that characterized her. What a lesson to a whining world! She wondered if Aunt Pat had anything besides her own strong self to rely upon? Did she know Lutie's secret? She was never one to talk religion, or to preach. She went regularly to church at least once a Sunday, and there was a little worn old-fashioned Bible on her bedside stand, but Sherrill had never seen her reading it, had never thought of her as being a strong religionist. Could it be that in her quiet way she too, like Lutie, had something in her heart, some great mysterious power beyond the earthly, that sustained her?

There was a little old wheezy cabinet organ played by a young girl with jingling silver bangles on her arms. The choir sat on a raised platform behind the organ and whispered a good deal among themselves. When they sang it was rousing. Not all the voices were cultured. When they sat down the green and purple from one of the windows played across their features grotesquely. An old man in the pulpit with the young minister prayed plaintively, yet there was something exceedingly sweet and uplifting in it, and Sherrill stole a look at the old lady by her side. There was a look of utter peace upon her face, as if a prayer of her own were winging upward to heaven beside the old man's petition.

The minister was a young seminary student, a bit crude, a bit conceited and greatly self-conscious. His words did not seem to mean much in relation to life. Sherrill was thinking of her aunt, and strangely too of Lutie's mother, the girl who had been rescued from death at such a cost. Now why was that? In all human reason it would seem that the young James with such a bright prospect of life, with such a partner as his Patricia, would have been worth infinitely more to the world than just Lutie's mother, a quiet humble mother of a servant girl. If there was a God supreme above all, surely He would manage His universe wisely, economically. And it seemed such an economic waste to kill a man with great possibilities that humble serving people might live. It did not seem reasonable.

And yet, in the great economy of life was it possible that the servant had some duty to perform, some place in the plan of things, that was important?

It was a baffling question to think upon, and Sherrill had not solved it when she rose to sing the last hymn. She only knew that her soul had been stirred to the depths, but more by Aunt Pat's story than the sermon, more by the great window with its resurrection story than by the service.

Kindly hands were put out shyly in welcome when the service was over as they passed down the aisle and out the door. The stately old lady walked sweetly among them, nodding here and there, smiling with that faraway look in her eyes, loving the gracious country folk collectively, because of one Sunday morning long years ago, and a lad that was long gone Home. You could see that they regarded her almost as if it had been an angel visiting their ancient place of worship. And Sherrill walked humbly in the shadow of that sweet soul's humble greatness.

The people stood back and hushed their chatter to watch the old lady away, but when she was out on the flagged path again she did not go down the walk but turned aside to the graveyard.

"This way," she breathed softly, and stepped on the young spring grass.

She led the way around to the side of the church, far back from the road, under a great elm tree.

"It was there we sat." She said it more as if talking to herself, and indicated with a little wave of her hand a great flat stone with an ancient date almost obliterated by lichens.

Then she turned about but a yard or two to the right, and stood, looking down at a small white stone with a single name "James" cut deep in its side, and a date of a generation ago.

Sherrill stood still startled, looking down at that name, realizing all it meant to her aunt to be standing there this morning, the first time she had come there since that beloved lost lover was laid there.

Just a moment they stood silently, Sherrill feeling the awe of the presence of a funeral pall. Yet there was nothing gloomy about the place. Clear spring sunshine flooding the spot, flicked with shadows of elm branches tossing in the light spring breeze. Birds caroling joyously overhead. The sound of friendly voices of the worshiper was just a few paces away, young laughter, the whirr of a motor starting from the church.

Unquestionably the young lover had not lain there all these years, his body crumbling to dust. He must be somewhere, doing something. Love and bravery and courage did not just blink out. That conviction came to Sherrill as a fixed fact, though she had never thought of such things before. Where was he, this James, and what faith had Aunt Pat that one day joy would come in the morning?

She thought of her own life, blighted right at the start.

Would there be joy, too, in some morning, for a life like hers that had found a lover false-hearted?

The old lady spoke.

"I'd like to have what's left of me put here when I am gone!" she said laying a hand on Sherrill's arm. "There's plenty of room. It doesn't matter of course, only it is pleasanter to think of being here than up under that great Catherwood monument at Laurel Hill. They can put my name there if they like, but I'll lie here. It'll be nice to think of getting up together in the morning."

"Dear Aunt Patty!" said Sherrill struggling with a constriction in her throat.

"I've put it all in my will of course, and the stone's been made ready, just Patricia and the date. But I thought I'd like somebody that belonged to me to understand."

"Of course!" said Sherrill tenderly, catching her breath and trying to steady her voice. "But—you're not going yet, dear—not for a long time. You wouldn't leave me—alone!"

"Why certainly not!" snapped the old lady with one of her quiet grins. "I've got to look after you for a spell yet. Come on, let's walk around. We don't want a lot of people staring at us. There's no need for them to know we're interested in just one grave. Let's walk around the church. There are some curious stones there, very old. James and I found them that day and talked about them. And there's a view,—look! away off to the hills! I think it's a lovely spot!"

"It is indeed," answered Sherrill, and almost envied her aunt for the joyous look on her face. How she had taken her sorrow and glorified it! Sherrill wondered if she, in like situation, could have risen to such heights, and felt how impossible it would have been for her. Felt how crushed she was by this her own sorrow which she recognized at once was so much less than what the old lady had borne for years unmurmuring, and said again to herself that there must have been some sustaining Power greater than herself or human weakness,—even human strength never could have borne it.

There was something glorified in the rest of that day. Sherrill felt that she had been allowed a glimpse into an inner sanctuary of a soul, and life could never again be the trivial, superficial thing that it had seemed to her before.

Aunt Pat was very tired and slept a great part of the afternoon, but in the evening she came down to the living room and sat before a lovely fire that Gemmie had kindled for them. She made Sherrill play all the old hymns she used to love. It brought the tears to hear the quavering voice that still had a note of sweetness in it, wavering through a verse here and there, and Sherrill trying to sing with her felt her own voice breaking.

Yet there was nothing gloomy about the old lady that night, and presently she was joking again in her snappy bright way, for all the world like a young thing, and Sherrill's heart was less heavy. Aunt Pat wasn't going away to leave her. Not now anyway.

SHERRILL needn't have worried about her aunt, for the old lady was up the next morning chipper as a bird, eating her breakfast with a relish.

"We're going to see Lutie's mother right away," she said. "We've got to get that family straightened out before we plan to do anything for ourselves."

"Oh, that will be wonderful!" said Sherrill who had arisen this morning with a great pall over life. Since there was no immediate action necessary she could not get hold of anything in which she was interested. But to help another household who were all in trouble intrigued her. It didn't occur to her either to realize that the canny old lady was wisely arranging to fill her days too full to brood over the past.

So they went to the neat little house where Lutie lived. Sherrill was amazed to see how attractive the little weatherbeaten house had been made. There was lack of paint on its ugly clapboards, lack of grace in all its lines, lack of beauty in its surroundings, for there were slovenly neighbors all about and a great hideous dump not far away to mar what otherwise might have been a bit of landscape.

But the ugly house had been smothered in quick growing vines. The ugly picket fence that also needed painting had been covered with rambler roses now beginning to bud, the yard had a neat patch of well cut lawn, with trim borders where young plants were beginning to give a good showing, and a row of pansy plants showed bright faces along the neat brick walk. The pansies winked brightly up at her like old acquaintances.

An ugly narrow court between houses had been concealed by tall privet hedge trained into an arched gateway, and there were nice white starched curtains at the windows upstairs and down. They might be only cheese cloth, but they made the house stand out like a thing of beauty in the midst of squalor.

"H'm!" said Aunt Pat appreciatively. "Pretty, isn't it? I don't know why I never thought to come here before."

The mother opened the door, wiping her hands on her apron which was an old towel girt about her waist. There was a fleck of soapsuds on her arm, and her face, though the morning was only half gone looked weary and worn.

"Oh, Miss Catherwood!" she said to Aunt Pat, her tone a bit awed.

She opened the door wide and welcomed them in casting a troubled eye over the room behind her to see if it was surely all in order.

"But you oughtn't to be washing!" objected Aunt Pat as she reached the top step and looked into the neat front room. "I thought you were sick. I heard you ought to go to the hospital."

The woman gave a helpless amused little laugh, not discourteous.

"No, I'm not sick," she said rather hopelessly, "I'm not near as bad off as some. I'll be all right when Father gets well. Come in won't you?"

Aunt Pat marched in gayly.

"Now, I'm not going to take up any more of your time than is necessary," she said as she sat down in the big old stuffed chair. "You go and shut off your dampers or gas or whatever it is that's worrying you, and I'll talk to you just five minutes and then you can get back and finish up what you've started. I suppose that's got to be done in spite of everything, but I've got something to say that's even more important."

The woman cast a sort of despairing look at her caller and with a half deprecatory glance toward Sherrill who had settled down on the old haircloth sofa she vanished into the back room where they could hear her turning on water, lifting dripping clothes from one tub to another, pulling a tin boiler across the top of an old fashioned iron range, and slamming the dampers back and forth.

She returned, pulling down her neat print sleeves, and fastening a clean apron over her wet dress.

Sherrill meanwhile had been looking around the little room, noting carefully the pretty trifles that Lutie had used to make the place homelike. There was even a little snap shot of herself that Sherrill recognized as one she had thrown in the waste basket. It was framed in glass with a black paper binding, and stood under the lamp on the small center table. Poor Lutie! Sherrill was deeply touched.

"Well," said Aunt Pat, "I'll get right to the point. My niece found out from Lutie that your husband is sick. How is he? Getting well fast?"

"No," said the woman sadly, "he doesn't improve at all now. He's pretty well discouraged. He said last night he guessed he had got to the end, and the sooner it came the better off we'd all be."

The woman was blinking the tears back, and swallowing hard. Her lips quivered as she spoke.

"Fiddlesticks!" said Aunt Pat briskly. "We'll see if something can't be done about that. Have you got a good doctor? Who is your doctor?"

"We haven't any doctor now," said the woman with a hopeless note in her voice. "We've tried three and he only got worse. He would not hear to having any more bills run up that we never can pay."

"H'm!" said Aunt Pat, "What doctors did you have?"

"Oh, we had the company doctor where he worked first, and he went on for two months and didn't make a mite of difference. And then we got Dr. Green. He was the doctor that examined him for his insurance several years ago, but he said just out plain he couldn't do him any good. And then we tried a specialist somebody recommended at the office where my son works, but he charged ten dollars every time he saw him, and ordered things that cost so much we couldn't get them, and said he ought to go to a private sanitarium for observation where they charge fifty dollars a week, and we had to give that up. Now we owe them all, and Lutie is paying them fifty cents a week, and Sam pays sometimes a dollar when he can spare it, dear knows when we'll get them all paid off."

"Well," said Aunt Pat with satisfaction, "then the coast is clear. That's good. Now, I'm going to send my doctor up to see him. How soon would it be convenient for him to come?"

The woman flushed.

"Oh, we couldn't really afford another doctor," she said in a worried tone. "It's very kind for you to take an interest in us but you see we just couldn't pay him now, and it only worries Father and makes him so he can't sleep."

"Yes, but you see my doctor won't cost you anything," said Aunt Pat. "He does these things as a favor for me. He's an old friend of mine, and he's been our family physician for years. He's very skillful too, and he'll tell me the truth. If anything can be done for your husband we'll find out what it is. And as for money, dear woman, aren't you and I both God's children? I've got some money that is just crying out to be spent somehow. They're after me to build an Art School with it, but if it could make your husband better I'd a lot rather have it used that way. And I take it God would be a great deal better pleased."

"Oh, but Miss Catherwood, I couldn't—! You're awfully good and I'll never forget it—but we couldn't! Oh, we never could!" The woman was crying openly now, into her nice clean blue and white checked apron. Sherrill had a sudden feeling that she would like to go over and put her arms around Lutie's mother and kiss her on her tired seamed forehead. Suppose it had been her mother? Sherrill's mother seemed so very many years away!

But Miss Catherwood was sitting up very straight now.

"Fiddlesticks end!" she said crisply. "As if you'd put pride between when it comes to getting your husband well! Listen! The Lord told me to come over here this morning and see what needed doing and do it. See? And you're not going to block the way. You're just going to be a dear sweet woman and do what you're told. How soon can you be ready for the doctor?"

"Oh!" sobbed the woman, "You're too good to us! Lutie said you were the salt of the earth—"

"Now, look here," fumed Aunt Pat, "Stop that kind

of talk. We don't need any salt around here just now. Wipe your eyes and tell me how soon I can have the doctor stop. Can you be ready for him by two o'clock? I think it likely he could be here about then. And while he's here I'm going to tell him to take a look at the little boy. Lutie said he had trouble with his hip."

"Oh, yes," wailed the mother as if the admission stabbed her to the heart. "They tell me he'll never walk again. He doesn't know it yet, poor kid. He keeps talking about when he's going to get well enough to play baseball with the other boys."

"Well, we'll see what can be done," said Aunt Pat with satisfaction. "And now, is there any way we can help you with this washing? Because you see we want you to be ready to have the doctor give you an examination too, and then we'll know where we stand."

"Oh, but I'm all right!" beamed the mother eagerly. "I don't need the doctor now. If my husband and boy could just get cured I'd be all right. It's just been the worry—"

"Well, that's all right too, but you're going to have the examination and then we'll find out what the doctor says about it. If he says you're all right why then no harm is done, but if he says you need an operation you're going to have it right away."

"Oh, but I couldn't be spared while my two men are sick," said the woman in alarm.

"Oh, yes, you could my dear!" said the old lady determinedly, "and it's a great deal better for you to be spared now than to wait until it's too late to help you. Don't be silly! Here comes Lutie. She'll look after the house and her brother while the three of you are in the hospital."

"Hospital?" said the woman frantically. "But we couldn't afford—!"

"Oh yes you could. It's all fixed I tell you. Here comes Lutie. How about that wash out there, Lutie? Can't you finish that up while your mother gets your father and brother ready to go to the hospital?"

"Oh, Miss Catherwood! Wouldn't that be too wonderful!" cried Lutie her cheeks growing red as a winter apple, and her eyes starry. "Of course I can finish up the wash. Only—" and she paused in consternation, "I'm supposed to go up to your house to help with the ironing at eleven o'clock."

"Well, that's off for to-day. I'll explain to the housekeeper. We've plenty of people there to finish the ironing for this once, and if we haven't it can go unironed. Now go to work quickly and don't let your mother get all fussed up about things."

When they got up to go Lutie looked at Sherrill wistfully.

"I been wondering if you really was going with me to the Bible class to-night," she said in a low tone. "I've been telling the other girls about you and they're so anxious for you to come. But now, I don't know as I can go this week. Maybe I'll be too busy here."

"Bible class?" said Aunt Pat scenting something interesting. "What's that? Where were you going with her, Sherrill?"

"She's been telling me about a class she attends," explained Sherrill. "Why, yes, I guess I can go tonight if you can find you can. I'd be interested to see what it's like."

"Of course you mustn't miss your Bible class, Lutie," said her mother with a wan smile. Then turning to Miss Catherwood she explained, "Lutie's been that taken up with her Bible study, and I'm glad she's got something since things have been so awful bad. But perhaps Lutie you'll be too tired."

"Oh, I'm never tired," said Lutie eagerly, "I'll go. Shall I come round to the house for you, Miss Sherrill?"

"No, I'll call for you with the little car," said Sherrill with sudden inspiration. "Then you won't have to walk when you are tired."

"Oh, that would be wonderful!" said Lutie as if Sherrill were offering her a ride in a chariot of state.

"Here Lutie, help me down these steps. I want to ask you some questions," said Aunt Pat imperatively.

Lutie helped the old lady carefully down the steps and as they walked out to the car Miss Patricia snapped out the questions.

"My niece said you lost some money. What bank?"

Lutie told her.

"H'm!" commented Miss Patricia. "Who owns your mortgage?"

Lutie gave the necessary information.

"H'm!" said the old lady, "I know them. I'll see what can be done. Don't you worry about losing your house. Just get your mother comfortable. And by the way, if your folks all have to go to the hospital you won't have time to work at the house till they get on their feet again, will you? It'll take about all your time to keep house here, won't it?"

"Oh, no! Miss Catherwood!" said Lutie in consternation, "I just couldn't afford not to work. There won't be anything for me to do but get Sam's breakfast and dinner and put up his lunch. I can give you just as much time as you want."

"That's all right then, Lutie. Don't you worry. But if you need to take a vacation for a few weeks why you just come to me and we'll fix it up so you won't lose anything by it. Now, Sherrill, are we all ready to go?"

They drove away amid exclamations of blessing from Lutie and her mother, and Sherrill felt a big lump rise in her throat as she looked back and saw them standing in the doorway, the mother waving her apron.

"That was wonderful of you, Aunt Pat!" said Sherrill eagerly. "That was dear of you! But it's going to cost you a lot of money."

"Well, you see, child, I figured if James gave his life to save Lutie's mother it was maybe my job to look after the rest of the family. And what's money in a case like that? If God thought saving her life was worth a man's life, then surely the least that I can do is to look after her, or somebody else's family if there hadn't been this one. I've you to thank for finding this out for me. I never thought to ask anything about them before, and Lutie never opened her lips. If I thought anything about them at all, I supposed they were all well and hearty and every one with a good job and thrifty. Lutie looks that way. What's this thing you're going to to-night?"

"Why, when she was singing that happy little song the other day I asked her where she got it. She told me about a class where they study the Bible and learn to be glad even when there's trouble. I said I would go with her some time."

"So, she's that kind, is she? Well, I'm glad. Now, here's the doctor's and I'll just run in and give him his orders. I'm hoping he isn't full up every hour today with operations or something. I'd hate to go back on my word."

A few minutes later she was back.

"He's going to see them at three o'clock. It's the best he can do. He's very busy. But I told him all about them and he promised me he'd do his best to put them all back in normal health again. Now, Sherrill, what did I do with the card Lutie wrote that mortgage company's address on? I want to stop and see my lawyer a minute and get him to fix that up and then we can go home and rest awhile. We've done a big piece of work."

"A wonderful piece of work," mused Sherrill. "Oh, Aunt Pat! You've done more with your life than any woman I know!"

"Fiddlesticks end!" said Aunt Pat scornfully, "I've not done the half that I should. Now Sherrill, while I'm seeing my lawyer I'd like you to do a little shopping for those people if you will. They'll need things to go to the hospital with, dressing gowns and kimonos and things, and decent suitcases to carry them in. I want them to be comfortable while they are there. That poor woman doesn't look as if she'd had a day's rest since she was born, and I mean she shall have. Get her a real pretty kimono, and brushes and things. Nice pretty ones. She likes pretty things I'm sure. Look at the way they've fixed up that old ramshackle house with just plants and vines. Not even paint! I'll give you the money and you get the necessary things. And I'm glad you're going to that Bible class. There are a lot of things in the Bible I don't understand, but I believe it from cover to cover, and I'd like to know more about it. I'm too old to study now, but you're not, and you can tell me all about it."

When they got home they found a stack of mail awaiting them. Notes of commiseration and protest from the people who had received their wedding gifts back again. Some letters, intended to cheer up Sherrill in her lonely estate of maidenhood, which made her very angry. A few giving her loving wishes from far off friends who hadn't yet heard of the change in the wedding arrangements.

She looked up listlessly from her lap full of letters and gave a deep sigh. How much more worth while was the world of helpfulness to which she had just been with her aunt, than this social world built around such an unstable foundation. She could sense through all these elaborate phrases that some of her old friends and playmates actually thought less of her because she had allowed herself to be washed up on the shore of maidenhood again, after she had once landed a man and got so far as wedding invitations.

Aunt Pat looked up sharply at the second sigh and handed over a letter.

"Well," she said triumphantly, "they haven't put your emeralds on the market yet, whoever it was that took them. Of course there has hardly been time for anybody to get them across the water. But if they attempt it it won't be long before we know who did it."

"Aunt Pat!" said Sherrill in astonishment. "Then you have done something about it after all!"

"Why of course, child! You didn't think I was a fool, did you? I called up the private detective who was here at the wedding and had a talk with him. He's been quietly watching all the places where they would be likely to be put on the market. They're all registered stones you know. Any jewel dealer of repute will be on the watch for them. Sooner or later they would have to turn up at the right place to get a reasonable price for them. I talked to my lawyer about them too, told him I didn't want publicity, and he's working quietly. So that's that and don't worry! They'll turn up if you were meant to get them back, and if you weren't all the worry in the world won't help you."

After lunch Sherrill went to lie down and had a long restful sleep. She had a sort of feeling when she woke up of being stranded on a desert island, and now that she was coming near to that Bible class that she had promised to attend she found a keen aversion to going. Why had she promised Lutie? Lutie was well enough herself, but Lutie had spoken of other girls who wanted to see her.

They would be common girls without education of course. They would have heard a lot of gossip about her wedding and how she didn't get married after all, and would be watching every move she made.

She half started to the telephone to tell Lutie that she was tired and would go another time, and then the eager look in Lutie's eyes came back to mind and she couldn't quite get the courage to call off the engagement. So she dressed herself in a plain quiet little knit dress of blue wool, and a small felt hat to match. It was one of her oldest sport dresses, and quite shabby now she thought. But she did not want to make Lutie feel that there was too much difference between them.

Miss Catherwood looked at her approvingly as she came into the room at dinner time.

"Some people wouldn't have known any better than to put on evening dress," she remarked irrelevantly, and smiled her queer twisted grin. "Well, I hope you have a good time, and be sure to listen for me."

DUBIOUSLY Sherrill parked her car and followed Lutie into the plain wooden building. If she hadn't promised Lutie she never would have gone to-night. She had lost her first curiosity about Lutie's source of peace, and if she had not seen how eager and pleased Lutie was about taking her she would have invented some excuse.

The building was not inviting. It was old and grimy. There had not been much money for fresh paint, and the floor was bare boards. A large blackboard and a battered old piano were the only attempts at furnishings beside the hard wooden benches, and the only decorations were startling Bible verses in plain print on white cards here and there about the walls.

"All have sinned and come short of the glory of God" was announced on the right; and Sherrill, entering, felt a shade of resentment at being classed with sinners. She had a feeling that her family had never been in that class.

There were other verses but she had not time to read them, for several young girls came up and Lutie introduced them.

One put a hand on Sherrill's arm intimately and with a sweet little smile said:

"We're so glad you have come. Lutie has been telling us about you, and we hope you will like it here. We just love it."

Again there was just the least bit of resentment in Sherrill's aristocratic soul that these girls should think her of their class, and expect her to be coming more than once. Yet there was something so winning about her smile, and so gentle in her manner that Sherrill began to wonder if perhaps she had been wrong. Perhaps these girls were not all in Lutie's class. It was difficult to tell. They wore nice clothes, one had a pretty little pink crepe, and a white beret, like any girl who had been out to play golf or tennis. There was an earnest air about them that made Sherrill like them in spite of herself. Could it be possible that she, Sherrill Cameron, was a snob? She must get out of this state of mind. She would not come here again likely, but while she was here she would be one of them, and do her best to enter into the things. She would be a good sport. She would be in their class, even if they were not in hers. After all, what was her class anyway? She was just a girl by herself who would have had to earn her own living somehow if Aunt Pat had not invited her to live with her. The fact that she had earned it hitherto teaching school instead of cleaning rooms and ironing as Lutie did, really made no difference of course. It was all silly anyway.

So Sherrill put out a friendly hand and greeted all the girls with her own warm smile, and they loved her at once. The strangest part about it was that somehow she couldn't help liking them. They were all so friendly and eager, what was the use of trying to act exclusive?

There was one thing she couldn't understand. She heard one of those girls just behind her speaking to Lutie.

The words came out between the clamor of the people who were gathering. "She's lovely, isn't she? Is she *saved,* Lutie?" And Lutie murmured something very low that Sherrill couldn't catch. Somehow she knew they were talking about her. And then the other girl said, "Well, we'll be praying for her tonight," and slipped away up front with a group of others, and whispered to them. They nodded, gave quick glances back, and a moment later Sherrill could see them off at one side bunched together with their heads bowed. A quick intuition told her they were praying for *her,* and the color mounted into her cheeks. Her chin went up a trifle haughtily. Why should she, Sherrill Cameron, need to be prayed for? And why should they *presume* to do it unasked?

But the room was filling up rapidly now. Lutie led her to a seat half way up and gave her a hymn book. The little group of praying ones had scattered, one to play the old piano, two others to distribute hymn books and Bibles, and suddenly the room burst into song, but she noticed that two or three of them still kept their heads bent, their eyes closed as if they were yet praying.

Sherrill looked around her in amazement. Here was a crowd of people, almost all young people, and they were singing joyously as if it made them glad to do so. They were singing with that same lilt that Lutie had had while she was working, and their faces all looked glad; although some of them obviously must be very poor, if one might judge from their garments and the weary look on their young faces, while others again were well dressed, and prosperous looking.

Presently they began to sing Lutie's song:

> *"If I have sorrow in my heart*
> *What can take it away?"*

and Sherrill, without realizing she was doing so, began to sing it herself, and felt a little of the thrill that seemed to be in the air.

She fell to thinking of her own interrupted life and wondering why it all had to be. Why couldn't Carter have been all right, the perfect man she had thought him? Why did it all have to turn out that way, in that sudden mortifying manner? If it only could have happened quietly! Not in the face of her whole invited world as it were.

But suddenly she felt the audience bowing in prayer, and was amazed to hear different voices taking up petitions, so many young people willing to pray in public! And so simply, so free from all self-consciousness apparently. It was extraordinary. Even little Lutie beside her prayed a simple sentence.

"Please, dear Father, don't let anything in us hinder Thy light from shining through us, so that others may see and find Thee."

Dear little soul! How had Lutie learned all this sweet simplicity? Just a little serving maid, yet she seemed to have something really worth while. What was this mysterious power? Just an idea? A conviction?

One of the prayers impressed her deeply. It came from a girl's voice up toward the front, perhaps one of those who had been introduced to her. It was "Dear Father, if any have come in here to-night not knowing Thee as Saviour, may they find Thee and not go out unsaved." Sherrill had a strange feeling that the prayer was for her although she couldn't exactly understand why she needed saving.

Then the prayers changed into song again, a rousing one:

"I've found a friend who is all to me,
His love is ever true;"

Ah! That was what she wanted Sherrill thought, a friend whose love was ever true. It was almost uncanny as if someone here knew just what she needed.

"I love to tell how He lifted me,
And what His grace can do for you,"

sang the audience, and then burst into that tremendous chorus that thrilled her, though she only half understood its meaning:

"Saved by His power divine,
Saved to new life sublime!
Life now is sweet and my joy is complete
For I'm saved, saved, saved."

Sherrill ran her eye through the rest of the verses and lingered on those lines,

"I'm leaning strong on His mighty arm;
I know He'll guide me all the way."

and experienced a sudden longing. If there was only someone who could guide her! Someone who could take away this utterly humiliated, lost feeling, and make her sure and strong and happy again the way she used to be before all this happened to her!

Then another hymn was called for and the eager young voices took on a more tender note as they sang, just as earnestly, only with deeper meaning to the words than any of the other songs had carried. Sherrill followed the words, and to her amazement found a great longing in her soul that she might be able to sing these words and mean them, every one.

"Fade, fade each earthly joy,"

That was what had been happening to her. The life that she had planned and that seemed all rosy before her had suddenly in a moment faded out.

"Jesus is mine!"

How she wished she might truly say that!

"Break every tender tie,"—

Ah! Her case exactly.

"Jesus is mine!"

rang the triumphant words. She glanced about at the eager young faces, so grave and certain. How could they be certain that Jesus was theirs? What did it mean anyway to have Jesus? Was it just a phrase? A state of mind? She studied several of them intently.

"Dark is the wilderness,
Earth has no resting-place,
Jesus alone can bless,
Jesus is mine!"

The tears suddenly welled into her eyes and she blinked them back angrily. She certainly did not want these stranger girls to think she was soft and sentimental.

The leader arose after the hymn was ended and prayed, just a few words, but it seemed to bring them all to the threshold of another world, an open heaven. Sherrill had never had such a feeling in a meeting before, not even in the solemn beautiful church where Aunt Patricia worshiped. And this was all so simple, and without any emotion except gladness!

There was a little stir all over the room. Everybody was opening Bibles. Lutie found the place and gave Sherrill one, and they all began to read together.

At first Sherrill did not pay much attention to what she was reading because she was so busy watching the others and feeling astonished. But gradually the words began to make themselves felt in her mind. She looked up at the speaker, startled to see if he were looking at her. She almost thought he must have known of her trouble and selected the passage because he knew she was to be here.

"Beloved, think it not strange concerning the fiery trial which is to try you, as though some strange thing happened unto you:—"

It was strange, though, thought Sherrill; how could she pretend it wasn't?

"But rejoice," the voices went on in unison, "inasmuch as ye are partakers of Christ's sufferings; that, when his glory shall be revealed, ye may be glad also with exceeding joy."

Christ's sufferings! How could her trouble have anything to do with what Christ had suffered on earth? He had never had any one go back on Him as she had; He had never been made a public laughing stock by anyone who was supposed to be His special friend—or stay, perhaps she was wrong! Had not His own disciple been the one who turned against Him, betrayed Him, laid the plot that led to His being nailed to the cross before the mocking multitudes?

These thoughts flashed through Sherrill's mind as she looked up from her Bible to give a grudging attention to the speaker.

"Let us see," he was saying, "to whom these words are addressed. Peter was writing a letter to Christians who had fled from their homes because of persecution. At the beginning of the letter he says that they, and himself with them, are 'begotten again' unto a living hope,—" Sherrill winced, her hopes were all dead.

"These words describe those to whom the letter is written. No one else has a right to the promises in the letter except those who are 'begotten again,'—born again. We must understand that clearly before we go on with the letter. If you want the joy that Christ can give even in the midst of suffering, remember that it is for you only if you are a child of God, born into His family by believing that Jesus Christ the Son of God was nailed to the cross because of your sins. He rose from the dead and He can give you life, but your new birth comes from more than just believing this *about* Him! Believing about Christ never saved anyone. It must be believing *in* Him. Believe that He took your condemnation upon Himself, and accept Him as your own personal Saviour."

Sherrill's eyes were fixed on the teacher's face now, utterly absorbed. She had never heard anyone talk like this before. It was quite possible she had sat in church often under sermons which included such doctrines, but they had never been able to reach her heart before, perhaps because her mind was too full of her own plans and thoughts. In fact it was probably the first time in her life that she had even read a portion of scripture with her mind on it. Her mind had always been politely aloof when she entered God's house, or found it necessary to take up a Bible.

A living hope. How she wished she might get one.

This teacher was talking just as Lutie had talked only more convincingly. And these people in the room looked at their teacher eagerly, earnestly, as if they understood from experience what he meant. She looked about on them wistfully. Could she get what they had? The teacher had said it came by believing in Christ, but how could one believe in someone who died so many years ago? How could one believe unless one knew and was convinced?

As if the man had read her thoughts and were answering them he went on.

"Belief is not an intellectual conviction. Belief is an act of the will, whereby you throw yourself on the promise of God and let Him prove Himself true. If someone asked you to take a ride in a new kind of airplane, you might not be able to go over every bit of its machinery and be sure that it was in perfect order, you might not understand the principle by which it worked, not be sure it could carry you safely; you might not even know the man who made it, nor have the wisdom to judge the principle under which it operated, but you could get into the plane and take a ride and let it prove to you what it claimed to be able to do. If you were in need of getting somewhere in a desperate hurry you might not even stop to think very carefully about it. You would say: 'This plane has taken others. I believe it will take me. At least I am going to trust myself to it.' And so you would get into the plane and fly away. Afterward when you have safely reached your destination then you are convinced that the plane can fly, for it has safely carried you. You have experience, but faith comes first. Now turn to Hebrews the twelfth chapter."

The room was filled with the rustling of Bible leaves as heads were bent, and the place was found. Sherrill blundered around among the books of the Bible like a person in a strange city trying to find a street. She was beginning back somewhere near Genesis, and her cheeks were a bit red with confusion. All these young people were turning straight to the right page with confidence. She tried to see over Lutie's shoulder without seeming to do so, to get the number of the page. Surely Bibles had pages didn't they? Why didn't he tell the page? Again that feeling of resentment at being caught in a humiliating position welled up in her. Why did she let herself come here to be made a fool of? All she could remember was Matthew, Mark, Luke, and John and that in connection with some old nursery rhyme.

But Lutie came to her rescue now and made short work of finding the place,—Lutie the little maid who did the cleaning and ironing! Wise in the scriptures!

Then every voice in the room began to read, and Sherrill read too, startled at how the words seemed meant just for her:

"My son, despise not thou the chastening of the Lord, nor faint when thou art rebuked of Him: for whom the Lord loveth He chasteneth, and scourgeth every son whom He receiveth. If ye endure chastening, God dealeth with you as with sons; for what son is he whom the Father chasteneth not?"

The teacher stopped them for a moment.

"The literal meaning of the word 'to chasten' here is 'to train a child.' Although you may be born again, a son of God, you are not to forget your subjection to the will of the Father. I wonder how many of you have been wondering why you have had to pass through some peculiar trial or testing? Have you found out yet that God was giving you that hard thing just to teach you to know Him better? Sometimes we are so taken up with the world, or with our own plans and selves that we haven't given a thought to God and He just had to take away the thing in which we were interested to make us give our attention to Him, that we might know His will, and get the full blessing He has prepared for us.

"I have sometimes seen a mother take away a toy from a little child in order to make him listen to her teaching and God often has to do that for His dearest sons. Go back to First Corinthians eleven thirty-one:

"'If we would judge ourselves, we should not be judged. But when we are judged, we are child-trained of the Lord, that we should not be condemned with the world.' The sons of God, that is believers, cannot be condemned with the world, and if they do not judge their careless and unworthy ways, then the Lord must deal with them and make them experience His chastening."

Sherrill wondered in passing if Aunt Pat had ever studied the Bible in this way. Did she know how the Bible fitted people's daily lives, and that a verse in one book explained a verse in another book?

And then the teacher whirled them back to the Old Testament for an illustration, and Sherrill had to have Lutie's help once more in finding the place. By this time she had determined that before another week—if she decided to come to that class again,—she would learn the books of the Bible.

The teacher was making plain now how God yearned for the love and fellowship of His children. He showed how disappointed God must be in them because they are so filled with themselves, so forgetful of the fact that they are on this earth only temporarily, getting ready for an eternal life.

It was a new view of God. Sherrill had never thought of herself as having any relationship to God at all, and now it seemed one either had to be a son or a deliberate rejector of the wonderful love and grace of God toward sinners. Sinners! As the teacher went on bringing more and more verses to their attention, Sherrill had a view of the Lord Jesus and began to get the realization that everybody was a sinner. She was appalled to think of herself under such a classification.

When the meeting finally closed with another wonderful prayer Sherrill was in a maze of bewilderment. She wanted to get away alone and think. There were so many questions that had come to her mind that, as she watched the young people gather around the teacher eagerly asking questions, she wished she had the courage to join them.

Lutie had excused herself to take a message to a girl across the room, and Sherrill left alone for the moment turned to the book table at the back of the room. What an array of little paper covered books with startling titles! They were all on topics she was in the dark about. A sign above them said they were only fifteen cents apiece. Sherrill picked out half a dozen and got out her purse, paying the pleasant faced boy who had charge of the table.

"Got a Scofield Bible?" asked the youth, waving his hand toward a collection of Bibles in various bindings.

"Why, no, what is a Scofield Bible?" asked Sherrill shyly, and realized at once as the youth stared at her, that she had shown great ignorance.

"Oh, it's the regular text of course," he explained politely, "only it has a lot of helpful notes that make it pretty plain about the dispensations and symbolism and covenants and things. It helps a lot to have them right there on the page with the text, that's all."

"How much are they?" asked Sherrill reaching for a small limp covered one in real leather.

"Well, that's about the most expensive one we have,"

said the boy looking at her with a new respect. "We have cheaper ones."

"But I like this one," said Sherrill, and paid for it feeling as if she had bought a gold mine. Now, perhaps she had something that would answer some of her questions!

When Lutie came back apologetic for being so long Sherrill had a package all done up ready to take home.

"They are wonderful books!" said Lutie casting wistful eyes at the book table. "I've got two or three for my own. We girls get different ones and lend them around among ourselves."

When Sherrill got home she went straight to her aunt's room.

Aunt Pat had gone to bed, but was lying bolstered up with pillows reading, and Sherrill noticed that her little Bible lay on the bed beside her.

"I've been buying some books," said Sherrill half shame-faced. "See what you think of them."

She undid her package and displayed them.

Miss Catherwood took up the Scofield Bible first and examined it curiously.

"I've heard about this," she said thoughtfully, "I'd like to look it over sometime. Maybe I'll get one too. They say it's very enlightening."

Then she went over the other books one by one.

"Yes, I know this one. It's by a president of a theological college, a wonderful man they say. I came across a notice of this book in a magazine. And this I know and love. I used to have a copy but someone borrowed it and never brought it back. But these others I never heard of. You'll have to read some of them aloud to me. I'd like to know what they are. The titles look wonderfully interesting. Well, how did you like the meeting? Was it a meeting?"

"Why no," said Sherrill thoughtfully, "It wasn't exactly a meeting, nor exactly like a school. I don't just know what to call it, but it was wonderfully interesting."

"Begin at the beginning and tell me all about it," said the old lady studying the vivid face before her. Sherrill hadn't worn that look of interest since the wedding night. The desolate haunted expression was almost gone.

After that first night Sherrill began to be fascinated with the study of the Bible. She realized of course that she had only as yet touched the outer fringes of the great truths it contained, but she really longed to know more, and she found that this, more than anything else, was able to help her forget her changed estate.

It was the second Monday night that she lingered till most of the others were gone, and asked a few questions that perplexed her about salvation. For she had come already to see her own need, and she finally in great simplicity said she would accept the Saviour.

When at last the teacher was free and turned to her, she shyly asked:

"Mr. Mackenzie, how can one tell,—does anybody really know—that is," she hesitated—"how would *I* know whether I am all right with God or not?"

She finished in a blaze of embarrassment. She had never spoken to anyone before about the thoughts of her own heart concerning God. She had a feeling it was almost immodest, for the people she knew never did it.

But with Spirit-taught gentleness and understanding the man of God answered her, putting her instantly at her ease, and treating the question as most natural and supremely important.

"Indeed you can know, most positively, Miss Cameron. Let me ask you first, have you ever realized that you—that we all of us—are sinners in God's sight, utterly unfit for His presence?"

"Yes, I have," said Sherrill earnestly. "I never did before, but last week I saw that."

"Then do you realize that you need to have the sin taken away that separates you from God?"

"Yes, oh, yes!" The tears sprang to her eyes.

"Then 'Behold the Lamb of God, who taketh away the sin of the world!' Just look to the Lord Jesus Christ as the One who bore on the cross all the guilt penalty for your sins. God poured out on His own Son all His righteousness wrath against us. 'For all have sinned and come short of the glory of God: being justified freely by His grace through the redemption that is in Christ Jesus.' Do you believe that?"

"I do," said Sherrill solemnly.

"Then read this aloud."

Mr. Mackenzie opened his Bible and pointed to a verse. Sherrill read:

"'Therefore being justified by faith we have peace with God through our Lord Jesus Christ.'"

"Read it again, very slowly please."

Sherrill read it again, very slowly, letting the truth sink deep. Suddenly a radiance broke through the puzzled earnestness of her face.

"I see it now," she said, "It's all right!"

"Then let's thank Him for so great salvation," said Mr. Mackenzie.

The rest had all gone but Lutie, and the three knelt together as Mr. Mackenzie poured out a thanksgiving for the new-born child of God.

So Sherrill went home that night with real news for Aunt Pat that kept that old saint awake half the night praising her Heavenly Father.

PRESENTLY the days settled down into regular normal living again, the lovely pansies had faded, and nothing more had been heard from the stranger.

Sherrill tried to put him out of her mind, tried not to start and look interested whenever the doorbell rang, or a package arrived. She tried to curb the feeling of disappointment each night when she went up to her room, that he had not come that day.

"He has forgotten us long ago," she told herself. "It was a mere incident in his life. He was just a passing stranger. He probably felt that he had done his entire duty toward us by sending those flowers. They were only sort of a bread-and-butter letter, and saved him the trouble of writing one. He has likely gone back to Chicago by this time and got immersed in business again. If he ever thinks of us again it will be to laugh sometime with his friends and tell about the queer wedding he once attended. Why should I be so silly as to keep on watching for him?"

But still she could not forget the stranger. And still there came no word of the lost jewels.

Aunt Pat kept a watchful eye upon Sherrill. She sent for maps and guide books. They studied routes of travel, they considered various cruises, planned motor trips, and betweenwhiles watched over Lutie's family, agreeing that they must not go away anywhere till the operations were all over and the invalids back at home doing well.

When the third Monday night came Lutie was up at the hospital waiting to hear the result of her mother's operation. Lutie's mother was in a very serious condition. Sherrill was restless and finally decided to go to the Bible class alone.

To her surprise the whole loving group of people at the mission knew about Lutie's anxiety and spoke tenderly of her. When the time of prayer came Sherrill listened in wonder to the prayers of faith that went up from many hearts for the life of Lutie's mother. Sherrill was amazed that they dared pray so confidently, and yet always with that submissive "Nevertheless, Thy will, not ours be done."

She had a feeling as she listened that she had been sitting in a dark place all her life, and that during the last three weeks light had slowly begun to break. It seemed that to-night the light was like glory all around her.

These people actually lived with God, referred everything to Him, wanted nothing that He did not send. They were in a distinct and startling sense a separated people, and she was beginning to long with all her heart that she might truly be one with them.

The meeting was more than half over, and the lesson for the evening was well under way when the woman who sat next to Sherrill on the end seat next the aisle, with a whispered word about catching her train, got up silently and slipped out. A moment later Sherrill became aware that someone else had taken her place, someone who had possibly been standing back by the door.

He came so silently, so unobtrusively, that Sherrill did not look up or notice him till he sat down, and then suddenly she seemed to feel rather than see that he was looking earnestly at her.

Startled she glanced up to find herself looking straight into Graham Copeland's smiling eyes!

Then Sherrill's face lighted with a great gladness, and something flashed from eye to eye. He reached quietly over and clasped her hand, just a quick clinging pressure that no one would have noticed, and her fingers returned it. Then something flashed again from hand to hand, some understanding and knowledge of mutual joy.

It was like finding a dear old friend after having lost him. It was the knowledge that everything precious in the world had not been lost after all.

She lifted another shy glance and caught that look in his eyes again, and was thrilled to think he was here. What a wonderful thing was this! Never in all her acquaintance with Carter McArthur had there been anything like this, but she did not think of that now. She was just glad, glad, glad!

He took hold of one side of her Bible when another reference was announced, their hands touched again, and joy ran trembling in the touch. Shoulder to shoulder, their heads bowed over the sacred Book they read the holy words together, and new strength and hope and sunshine seemed suddenly to come to Sherrill. This her friend had come back. He was all right. Her strange unwelcomed fears had been unfounded. Now she knew it. She had looked into his eyes and all was right. She was even gladder for that than that he was here.

This meeting with him might last only a few minutes more, it might never come again; but she was glad that he was this kind of man.

The class was crowded that night, and the chairs were

very close together. The aisles were narrow. Yet the nearness was pleasant, and the fellowship with God's people. She stole a glance at her new friend's face and saw that he was watching the speaker, listening interestedly. He was not bored. He had not come here just to take her away home and make a fashionable call upon her. He seemed to be as glad to be here as she was to have him, and to have entered into the spirit of the hour like any of them. Was that just an outstanding characteristic of his that he could adjust himself to any surroundings and seem to be at home?

But no, she felt he was truly in sympathy here, more even than he had been at that wedding reception. To a certain extent he had been an outsider there, entering in only so far as would help her, but it really seemed as if he belonged here. Or was that just her imagination?

She wondered if she ought to suggest going home. Perhaps he had only a short time. But he settled that by suddenly turning and smiling into her eyes and whispering,

"He's very fine, isn't he?" and suddenly her joy seemed running over so that she could hardly keep glad tears from her eyes. To have a friend like this, and to have him feel as she did about this sacred hour. Why that was greatest of all!

Then it came to her that just the other day she had felt that all the troubles in the world were crowded into her small life, and now all at once they had lifted. What did it mean? Was God showing her that He had infinitely greater joys in store for her somewhere than any she had lost?

These thoughts raced swiftly through her mind while her companion fluttered the leaves of the Bible finding the next reference as if his fingers knew their way well about the greatest book in the world, and then their hands settled together holding it again.

"Well," thought Sherrill, "I seem to be losing my head a little, but I'm just going to be glad while gladness is here." And then somehow their spirits seemed to go along together during the rest of the meeting, flashing a look of appreciation when something unusual was said.

The rest of the hour seemed all too short. It was like a bit of heaven to Sherrill. When it was over Copeland spoke graciously to the friends about her, and greeted the teacher when he came down to speak to them.

"You know we have a great Bible school out in my city too," he said with a smile as he shook hands with the teacher. "I don't get as much of it as I would like. I'm pretty busy. But sometimes I run in there for a bit of refreshment."

Out into the sweet darkness of the summer evening he guided her, his hand slipped within her arm in a pleasant possessive way. He seemed to have already located her car, and as they went toward it he said in vibrant tones:

"I didn't know you were interested in this sort of thing. I'm so glad. It gives us one more tie for our—friendship. I'm sure now that you must know the Lord Jesus."

"And oh, *do you?*" Sherrill's voice was vibrant too. "I've only known Him a very short time and I'm very ignorant, but—I want to learn."

Sherrill's hand was clasped in his now, but she did not realize it till he put her in the car.

"Shall I drive?" he asked, as if he had been taking care of her all his life.

"Yes, please," she said eagerly, "and, tell me, how did you happen to be there? How did you know I—?"

"Your aunt told me the way," he said, anticipating her

question. "I got to the house just after you had left. She told me how to find you and I came at once."

"Then—you had been there some time?"

"Yes. I came in during the singing just before the lesson. They certainly can sing there, can't they?"

"Oh, yes. But I'm sorry I didn't see you. I could have come out—" she hesitated.

"Wasn't it better to stay?" he asked smiling, looking down into her face, "It was a sweet and blessed fellowship and I needed something like that. I've been in a feverish sordid atmosphere ever since I left here and I was glad to get the world out of my lungs for a little while. Besides, I enjoyed watching your face. I got a double blessing out of the meeting from enjoying your interest."

"My face?" said Sherrill in sudden confusion. "Oh!" and she put up a hand to her flushed cheek. "Were you where you could see me? I didn't know there was anything in my face but ignorance and amazement. I can't get used to the wonders of the Bible."

"It was very—" he hesitated, then added, "very precious to watch," and his voice was almost reverent as he spoke.

"Oh!" said Sherrill at a loss for a reply. But he helped her by going on to speak in a matter-of-fact voice.

"I'm glad to get here at last," he said. "I've been going through a strenuous siege of work, in Washington and New York, back and forth, sometimes in such haste that I had to fly. No time to call my soul my own, and then an unexpected business trip to the south which kept me working night and day. I thought I would be able to stop off for a few hours before this, but I couldn't make it. I was afraid you would have forgotten me by this time."

"No," said Sherrill quickly. "I could not forget you. You came to me in a time of great trouble and I shall never forget how you helped me. I'm so glad to have another opportunity to really thank you. I didn't half know what I was doing that night."

"Well, I'm glad to be back at last," he said, "I didn't want to lose this friendship. It seemed to be something very rare sent to me right out of the blue you know."

He gave her a wonderful smile that set her heart thrilling.

"I'm surely losing my head," she told herself. "I mustn't be a fool. But I can't help being glad he is like this even if I never see him again."

Sherrill was sorry when the short ride was over and they had to go into the house and be conventional. She treasured the little quiet talk in the darkness. It was easier somehow in the dark to get acquainted and not be embarrassed at all they had been through together.

Aunt Pat was waiting for them eagerly and Sherrill felt her kind keen glance searching her face as she sat down.

"Now," said Aunt Pat, "before we begin to talk, how much time have we got to get acquainted? What time did you say you had to leave?"

"I think your local train leaves about ten after eleven," answered Copeland. "I have a taxi coming for me in plenty of time so I do not have to keep thinking about that. But perhaps I shall be keeping you up too late?"

He looked eagerly at the old lady.

"Late?" said the old lady laughing. "We're regular night hawks, Sherry and I. We often sit up till after midnight reading. I'm only sorry you have to go so soon."

All too rapidly the brief time fled. He seemed so like an old acquaintance that he fitted right into their pleasant cosy evening. Aunt Pat discovered that they had mutual acquaintances in Chicago and Sherrill sat listening to their talk and wondering how she could ever have entertained that haunting fear about this wonderful stranger. It was such a relief to have the fear gone forever. Not that she ever really suspected him herself, she still loyally maintained to her own heart, but she had been so afraid that others would if it ever came to an investigation.

Then he would turn and look at her suddenly and smile and something would happen to her heart, something wild and sweet that never had happened before. She did not understand it. Never in all her acquaintance with Carter McArthur had there been anything like this. It was like finding an old friend after having lost him. It was knowing that she had not lost every precious thing in the world after all. It was rest and peace and joy just to know she had a friend like that.

The lovely color flooded into her face and joy was in her starry eyes. That pinched look of suffering that Copeland had seen in her face the first night was gone. He looked again and again to make sure. It was not there any more. The glance in his eyes when he turned toward her always with that wonderful smile thrilled her as nothing had ever done before.

In vain she chided herself for feeling so utterly glad just because of his presence. He was only making a call, she told herself. But that gladness would keep surging over her like a healing tide that was washing away the pain and anguish she had received the night she found out that Carter was false to her. He might go away in a few minutes and she never see him again perhaps, but still she would be glad, glad that he had come to-night and reassured her that he was just what she had thought him at first. New strength and life and hope seemed to come to her as the moments flew by.

Aunt Pat took herself off upstairs for a few minutes to

hunt for a book they had been talking about and Sherrill had a little time alone with him.

"You are feeling better?" he said in a low tone, coming over to sit beside her on the couch, scanning her face searchingly.

"Oh yes," she said deeply touched at the tenderness of his tone. "I'm beginning to see some reasons why it all had to be. I'm beginning to understand what I was saved from!"

He reached out and laid his hand quietly over hers for an instant with a soft pressure.

"That is good to know!" he said gently. "You were very brave!"

"Oh, no!" she said, her eyelids drooping, "As I look back I'm so ashamed at the way I played out. It was dreadful the way I let you stand by and go through all that awful reception! But I'm so glad to have this opportunity to really thank you for what you did for me that night. As long as I live I will always feel that that was the greatest thing any man ever did for any woman in trouble. An utter stranger! You were wonderful! If you had been preparing all your life for that one evening you could not have done everything more perfectly."

"Perhaps I had!" he said very softly, his fingers closing about hers warmly again, his eyes catching hers as they lifted to look wonderingly at him, and holding her gaze with a deep sweet look.

Then suddenly Gemmie appeared at the door with her rubber-silent tread bearing a small table and placed it, covering it with a festive cloth. Gemmie, seeming to see nothing, but knowing perfectly, Sherrill understood, about those two clasped hands between them there on the sofa.

Gemmie brought coffee in a silver pot with delicate cups and saucers, tiny sandwiches, cinnamon toast, little frosted cakes and then an ice. Gemmie managed to keep in evidence until Aunt Pat returned with her book. Gemmie watching like a cat!

And the two talked, pleasant nothings, conscious of that touch that had been between them, conscious of the light in each other's eyes, glad in each other's presence, getting past the years of their early youth into a time and place where there was only their two selves in the universe. Wondering that anything had been worth while before, thinking, each, perhaps, that the other did not understand.

Aunt Pat came back with her book and ate with them, a happy little meal. She watched her girl contentedly, watched the young man approvingly, and remembered days of long ago and the light in a boy-lover's eyes. That was the same light or else she was mightily mistaken.

Then all at once Copeland looked at his watch with an exclamation of dismay, and sprang to his feet.

"It is almost time for my train!" he said, "I wonder what has become of my taxi! The man promised to be here in plenty of time."

"Gemmie! Look out and see if the taxi is there!" called Aunt Pat.

"No ma'am, there's no taxi come. I been watching out the window!" said the woman primly with a baleful look at Copeland as if his word was to be doubted. Gemmie thought he likely hadn't told the taxi man to come at all. She thought he likely wanted to stay all night.

"It isn't far, I'll try to make it!" said Copeland. "I'm sorry to leave in such a rush. You'll forgive me won't you? I've had such a wonderful time!"

"Why I'll take you of course," said Sherrill suddenly rousing to her privilege. "My car is right outside. Come, out this side door. We've time enough."

"But you'll have to come back alone!" he protested.

"I often do!" she laughed. "Come, we can make it if we go at once—although I wish you could stay."

"But I mustn't!" said Copeland. "I must get back at once. It's important!"

He took Aunt Pat's hand in a quick grasp.

"You have been good to let me come!" he said fervently. "May I come soon again?"

"You certainly may!" said Aunt Pat, "I like you young man! There! Go! Sherrill's blowing her horn. You haven't any time to waste!"

With an appreciative smile he sprang to the door and was gone. Aunt Pat watched them away and then turned back with a smile of satisfaction to see Gemmie standing at the back of the hall like Nemesis looking very severe.

"That's what I call a real man, Gemmie!" said Aunt Pat with a note of emphasis in her tone.

"Well, you can't most always sometimes tell, Miss Patricia," said Gemmie primly with an offended uplift of her chin.

"And then again you *can!*" said Aunt Pat gayly. "Now, Gemmie, you can wait till Miss Sherry comes back and then lock up. I'm going to bed."

Out in the night together Sherrill kept the wheel.

"I'd better drive this time," she explained as she put her foot on the starter. "It will save time because you don't know the way. You be ready to spring out as soon as I stop, if the train is coming."

Sherrill flashed around corners in the dark and brought up at the station a full two minutes before the train was due.

"I have my ticket, and my baggage is checked in the city," said Copeland smiling, "so this two minutes is all to the good."

He drew her hand within his arm and they walked

slowly up the platform, both conscious of the sweetness of companionship.

"I'm coming back soon," said Copeland, laying his free hand softly over hers again. "Your aunt said I might."

"That will be wonderful!" said Sherrill, feeling that it was hard to find words to express her delight. "How soon?"

"Just as soon as I can get a chance!" he said holding her hand a little closer in his own.

Then they heard the distant sound of the train approaching and had to turn and retrace their steps down the platform.

"I'll let you know!" he said.

Somehow it took very few words to complete the sweetness of the moment. The train thundered up and they stood there waiting, her arm within his.

"I wish you were going along," he said suddenly looking down at her with a smile. "It's going to be a long lonely journey, and there is a great deal I would like to talk to you about, but we'll save it for next time."

Then the train slowed down to a stop and the few passengers from up the road came straggling out.

Copeland and Sherrill stood back just a little out of the way till the steps should be passable, and as they looked up Mrs. Battersea hove in sight through the car door, coming back from an evening of bridge with some friends in the next suburb.

"Isn't that your Battledore-and-shuttlecock lady of the reception?" murmured Copeland with a grin.

Sherrill giggled.

"Mrs. Battersea," she prompted.

"Yes, I thought it was something like that."

The lady brought her heavy body down the car steps and arrived on the platform a few feet from them.

Copeland stooped a little closer and spoke softly:

"What do you say if we give her something to talk about? Do you mind if I kiss you good bye?"

For answer Sherrill gave him a lovely mischievous smile and lifted her lips to meet his.

Then Mrs. Battersea, the conductor just swinging to the step of the car and waving his signal to the engineer, the platform and all the surroundings, melted away, and heaven and earth touched. The preciousness of that moment Sherrill never would forget. Afterwards she remembered that kiss in comparison with some of the passionate half fierce caresses that Carter used to give, kisses that almost frightened her sometimes with their intensity, and made her unsure of herself, and she knew this reverent kiss was not in the same world with those others.

With that sweet tender kiss, and a pressure of the hand he still held, he left her and swung to the lower step which the conductor had vacated for a higher one as the train rolled out of the station.

He stood there as long as he could see her, and she watched him, drank in the look in his eyes, and suddenly said to her frightened happy heart, "He is dear! *Dear!* Oh, I love him! I *love* him! He is no longer a stranger! He is beloved! The Beloved Stranger!"

Then as the train swept past the platform lights into the darkness beyond, with her heart in her happy eyes she turned, and there stood Mrs. Battersea, her lorgnette up, drinking it all in! Even that last wave of the hand that wafted another caress toward her before he vanished into the darkness!

Sherrill faced her in dismay, coming down to earth again with a thump. Then with a smile she said in a cool little tone:

"Oh, Mrs. Battersea! You haven't your car here. May I take you home?"

And Mrs. Battersea bursting with curiosity gushed eagerly, "Oh, Sherrill Cameron, is that really you? Why how fortunate I am to have met you. I've just twisted my ankle badly and my chauffeur is sick to-night. I expected to take a taxi but there doesn't seem to be any."

Then as she stuffed her corporosity into Sherrill's little roadster she asked eagerly: "And who was that attractive man you were seeing off on the train? That couldn't have been the charming stranger who was at the wedding could it? Oh—Sherrill! Naughty, naughty! I thought there was a reason for the changes in the wedding plans!"

Sherrill was glad when at last she reached her own room and could shut the door on the world and shut herself in with her own thoughts and memories. But a moment later Gemmie knocked at the door and brought a message from her aunt that she would like to see her for a minute.

Gemmie looked at Sherrill's lovely red cheeks and smiling lips coldly, distantly. Sherrill felt as if she would like to shake her. But she gave her a brilliant smile and went swiftly to her aunt's room.

"Well," said the old lady from among the pillows of her old-fashioned four-poster, "I hope you see now that he never stole that necklace!"

"Aunt Pat!" said Sherrill in an indignant horrified tone, "I never thought he did! I *knew* he didn't! But I wanted him to come back to prove to *you* that he hadn't! He was *my* stranger. *I* knew he wasn't that kind, but I couldn't expect other people to realize what he was. I was afraid you would always suspect him if he didn't come back."

"H'm!" said the old lady contemptuously. "I know.

You didn't give me much credit for discernment. Thought you had it all. Now, run along to your bed, child. You've had enough for one evening. I just wanted you to know I think he's all right. Good night!"

SHERRILL awoke the next morning with a song in her heart, but while she was dressing she talked seriously with herself. It was utterly impossible, she told herself, that a splendid man like Graham Copeland could care about a girl he had seen only a few hours, and especially under such circumstances. There was that precious kiss, but it had been given half in fun, to carry out the joke on Mrs. Battersea. Men didn't think much of just a good-bye kiss, most men, that is. But her heart told her that this man was different. She knew that it had meant much to him.

Then she told herself to be sensible, that it was wonderful enough just to have a real friend when she was feeling so lonely and left out of everything.

Of course he was very far away. He might even forget her soon, but at least he was a friend, a young friend, to tide her over this lost humiliating spot in her life.

And he had said he would come soon again! Well, she mustn't count too much on that, but her heart leaped at the thought and she went about her room singing softly:

"When I have Jesus in my heart,
What can take Him away?
Once take Jesus into my heart,
And He has come to stay."

The trill of her voice reached across the hall to Aunt Pat's room and the old lady smiled to herself and murmured. "The dear child!" and then gave a little wistful sigh.

It was raining hard all day that day, but Sherrill was like a bright ray of sunshine. It was not raining rain to her, it was raining pansies and forget-me-nots in her heart, and she did not at all understand what meant this great light-heartedness that had come to her. She had never felt toward anyone before as she felt toward this stranger. She had utterly forgotten her lost bridegroom. She chided herself again and again and tried to be sober and staid, but still there was that happy little thrill in her heart, and her lips bubbled over into song now and then when she hardly knew it.

Aunt Pat sat with a dreamy smile on her lips and watched her, going back over the years to an old country graveyard and a boy with grave sweet eyes.

Three days this went on, three happy days for both Sherrill and Aunt Pat, and on the morning of the fourth day there came a great box of golden hearted roses for Sherrill, and no card whatever in them. An hour later the telephone rang. A long distance call for Sherrill.

With cheeks aflame and heart beating like a trip-hammer she hurried to the telephone, not even noticing the cold disapproval of Gemmie who had brought the message.

"Is that you Sherrill?" came leaping over the wire in a voice that had suddenly grown precious.

"Oh, yes, Graham!" answered Sherrill in a voice that sounded like a caress, "Where are you?"

"I'm in Chicago," said a strong glad voice, "I want to come and see you this afternoon about something very important. Are you going to be at home?"

"Oh, surely, yes, all day," lilted Sherrill, "but how could you possibly come and see me to-day if you are in Chicago?"

"I'm flying! I'll be there just as soon as I can. I'm starting right away!"

"Oh, how wonderful!" breathed Sherrill, starry eyes looking into the darkness of the telephone booth almost lighting up the place, smiling lips beaming into the instrument. "I—I'm—*glad!"*

"That's *grand!"* said the deep big voice at the other end of the wire, "I'm gladder than ever that you are glad! Are you all right?"

"Oh, quite all right!" chirruped Sherrill. "I'm righter than all right—*now!"*

"Well, then, I'll be seeing you—shortly. I'm at the flying field now, and I'm starting *immediately!* Good bye—*darling!"*

The last word was so soft, so indefinite that it gave the impression of having been whispered after the lips had been turned away from the instrument, and Sherrill was left in doubt whether she had not just imagined it after all.

She came out of the telephone booth with her eyes still starrier and her cheeks more rosy than they had been when she went in. She brushed by the still disapproving Gemmie who was doing some very unnecessary dusting in the hall, and rushed up to her aunt's room.

"Oh, Aunt Pat!" she said breathlessly, "He's coming! He's flying! He's coming this afternoon. Do you mind if we don't go to ride as we'd planned?"

"Who's coming, child?" snapped Aunt Pat with her wry grin and a wicked little twinkle in her eye, "Be more explicit."

"Why Graham is coming," said Sherrill eagerly, her face wreathed in smiles.

"Graham indeed! And who might Graham be? Graham Smith or Graham Jones? And when did we get so intimate as to be calling each other by our first names?"

For answer Sherrill went laughing and hid her hot cheeks in the roseleaf coolness of the old lady's neck. The old lady patted her shoulder and smoothed her soft hair as if she had been a baby.

"Well," said Aunt Pat with her twisted smile, "it begins to look as if that young man had a great deal of business in the east, doesn't it? It must be expensive to travel around in airplanes the way he does, but it's certainly interesting to have a man drop right down out of the skies that way. Now, let me see, what are you going to wear, child? How about that little blue organdy? You look like a sweet child in that. I like it. Wear that. Those cute little white scallops around the neck and sleeves remind me of a dress I had when I was sixteen. My mother knew how to make scallops like that."

"I'll wear it of course," said Sherrill eagerly. "How lovely it must have been to have a mother to make scallops for you. But I don't know as that is any better than having a dear precious aunt to buy them for you. You just spoil me, Auntie Pat! Aren't you afraid I'll 'spoil on you' as Lutie's mother says?"

"Well, I've tried hard enough," said the old lady smiling, "But I can't seem to accomplish anything in that line. I guess you are the kind that doesn't spoil."

All the morning Gemmie came and went with grim set lips and disapproving air, going about her duties scrupulously, doing all that was required of her, yet saying as plainly as words could have said that they were all under a blind delusion and she was the only one that saw through things and knew how they were being deceived by this flying youth who was about to appear on the scene again. She sniffed at the gorgeous yellow roses when she passed by them and wiped her eyes surreptitiously. She didn't like to see her beloved family deceived.

But time got away at last and Sherrill went to dress for the guest, for they had been consulting flying fields, and had found out the probable hour of his arrival.

Sherrill was just putting the last touches to her hair when Aunt Pat tapped at the door and walked in with a tiny string of pearls in her hand, real pearls they were, and very small and lovely.

"I want you to wear these, dearie," she said in a sweet old voice that seemed made of tears and smiles and reminded one of lavender and rose leaves.

Sherrill whirled about quickly, but when she saw the little string of pearls her face went white and her eyes took on a frightened look. She drew back and caught hold of the dressing table.

"Oh, not another necklace!" she said in distress. "Dear Aunt Patricia. I really couldn't wear it! I'd lose it! I'm afraid of necklaces!"

"Nonsense, child!" said the old lady smiling. "That other necklace is going to turn up sometime I'm sure. Remember I told you those stones were registered, and eventually if someone stole them, they will be sold, will ultimately arrive at some of the large dealers, and be traced. You're not to fret about them, even if it is some time before we hear of them. And as for this necklace, it's one I had when I was a little girl, and it is charmed. I always had a happy time when I wore it, and I want you to wear this for me this afternoon. I like to see you in it, and I like to think of you with it on. You'll do it for me, little girl. I never had a little girl of my own, and so you'll have to have them. I'm quite too old now to wear such a childish trinket."

So Sherrill half fearfully, let her clasp the quaint chain about her neck, and stooped and kissed the dear old lady on the parting of her silvery curls.

Sooner than Sherrill had dared to hope he came. She watched him from behind her window curtain while he paid the taxi driver and then gave a quick upward look at the windows of the house. No, she had not been mistaken in her memory of him. That firm clean, lean look about the chin, that merry twinkle in his eyes. The late afternoon sun lit up his well-knit form. There was a covert strength behind him that filled her with satisfaction and comfort. He was a man one could trust utterly. She couldn't be deceived in him!

Then Gemmie's cold voice broke stiffly on her absorption:

"The young man is here, Miss Sherrill!"

"Oh, Gemmie," caroled Sherrill as she hurried laughing from her window. "Do take that solemn look off your face. You look like the old meeting house down at the corner of Graff Street. Do look happy, Gemmie!"

"I always look as happy as I feel, Miss Sherrill," said Gemmie frigidly.

But Sherrill suddenly whirled on her, gave her a resounding kiss on her thin astonished lips, and went gayly past her down the stairs, looking like a sweet child, in her little blue organdy with the white scallops and pearls, and her gold hair like a halo around her eager face. The small blue slippers laced with black velvet ribbons about her ankles fairly twinkled as she ran down the steps, and the young man who stood at the foot of the stairs, his eyes alight with an old old story, thought her the loveliest thing he had ever seen.

Aunt Pat had managed to absorb every single servant about the place, suddenly and intensively, and there wasn't a soul around to witness their meeting, though perhaps it would not have made the least difference to them, for they were aware of nobody but their own two selves.

She went to his arms as to a haven she had always known she possessed, and his arms went round her and drew her close, with her gold head right over his heart, her cheek rubbing deliciously against the fine serge of his dark blue coat. Dark blue serge, how she loved it! He had worn a coat like that when she first found him!

He laid his lips against her forehead, her soft hair, brushing his face, and held her close for a moment, breathing:

"Oh, my darling!"

Then, suddenly they drew apart, almost embarrassed, each afraid of having been too eager, and then drew together again, his arm about her waist, drawing her into the small reception room, and down to the small sofa just inside the portiere.

The man laughed softly, triumphantly.

"I was afraid to come," he said. "I was afraid it would be too soon, after—after—that other man!"

"You mean Carter?" said Sherrill, and then with a sudden inner enlightenment, "Why, there never was any other man, but you." She said it with a burst of joy. "I thought there was, but now I know there *never* was! At least I thought he was what you are! There has *always* been you—in my thoughts I guess!" and she dropped her eyes shyly, afraid to have too quickly revealed her heart.

"How could I have been so mistaken!" she added with

quick anger at herself. "Oh, I should have had to suffer longer for being so stupid!"

But he drew her within his arms again and laid his lips on hers, then on her sweet eyelids, and then, his cheek against hers, he whispered, "Oh, my precious little love!"

Suddenly he brought something from his pocket, something bright and flashing, and slipped it on her finger. Startled she looked down and saw a great blue diamond, the loveliest she had ever seen, set in delicate platinum handiwork.

"That marks you as mine," he said with a wonderful look into her eyes. "And now, darling, we've got to work fast, for I haven't much time."

"Oh!" said Sherrill in instant alarm, "Have you got to go back again right away?"

"Not back again," he laughed, "but off somewhere else. And I don't know what you'll think of what I've come to propose. Maybe you'll think it is all wrong, rushing things this way when we've scarcely known each other yet, and you don't really know a thing about me or my family."

"That wouldn't matter," said Sherrill emphatically, without even a thought of the emerald necklace, though Gemmie at that moment was stalking noisily through the hall beyond the curtain.

"You precious one!" said Copeland drawing her close again and lifting one of her hands, the one with the ring on the third finger, to his lips.

"Well, now, you see, it's this way. I'm being sent quite unexpectedly to South America on a matter of very special business. It's a great opportunity for me, and if I succeed in my mission it means that I'll be on Easy Street of course. But I may have to stay down there anywhere from six weeks to six months to accomplish my purpose,—"

"Ohhh!" breathed Sherrill with a sound like pain.

He smiled, pressed her fingers close and went on speaking.

"I feel that way too, dearest. I can't bear to be away from you so long when I've only just found you. And I've been audacious enough to want to take you with me! Do you suppose you could ever bring yourself to see it that way too? Or have I asked too much? I've brought all sorts of credentials and things with me."

"I don't need credentials," said Sherrill nestling close to him, "I love you." And suddenly she felt she understood that other poor girl who had said she would marry Carter McArthur if she knew she had to go through hell with him. That was what love was, utter self-abnegation, utter devotion. That was why love was so dangerous perhaps to some. But this love was different. This man knew her Christ, belonged to him. Oh, what had God done for her! Taken away a man who was not worthy, and given her one of His own children!

His arms were about her again, drawing her close, his words of endearment murmured in her ear.

"You will go?" he asked gently. "You mean *you will go?"* There was an awed delight in his voice.

"Of course!" said Sherrill softly. "When would we have to go?"

"That's it," he said with a bit of trouble in his eyes as he looked down on her anxiously. "I have to go *to-night!* Would that be rushing you too much? I'd make it longer if I could, but there is need for great haste in my business. In fact if it could have waited until the next boat I wouldn't have been sent at all, a senior member of the firm would have gone in my place. But just now neither of them could get away so it fell to my lot, and I had no chance to protest."

Sherrill sat up and looked startled.

"To-night!" she echoed. "Why, I could go of course,—but—I'm not sure how Aunt Patricia would take it. She's been wonderful to me I wouldn't like to hurt her. I ought to ask her—!"

"Of course!" said Copeland. "Where is she? Let's go to her at once! I'll try to make her see it. And—well—if this thing succeeds I'll be able perhaps to make it up to her about losing you so suddenly. It might just happen that I would be put in the east to look after a new branch of the business. We could live around here if that would make it pleasanter for her."

"How wonderful!" said Sherrill, "Let's go up to her room! I know she'll be kind of expecting us."

So they went up the stairs with arms about one another, utterly unaware of Gemmie, peering out stolidly from behind the living room portieres.

They appeared that way in Aunt Pat's doorway when she had bidden them enter, for all the world like two children come to confess some prank.

"I see how it is with you," said Aunt Pat with a pleased grin as they stood a second, at a loss how to begin. "I expected it of course."

"I know you don't know a thing about me," began the lover searching around in his legal mind for the things he had prepared to say, "but I've brought some credentials."

"Don't bother!" said Aunt Pat indifferently. "I wasn't quite a fool! You didn't suppose I was going to put my child in danger of a second heart-break did you? I looked you up the day the first flowers came."

"Why, Aunt Pat!" said Sherrill aghast. "You said you

trusted him utterly! You said you knew a man when you saw one!"

"Of course I did!" said Aunt Pat not in the least disturbed, "I knew he was all right. But when it was a matter of you, Sherrill, I knew I had to have something more than my own intuition to go on. I wasn't going to go and give you away to every stranger that came along with a nice face and a pleasant manner. Some day I expect to go to heaven and meet your father and mother again, and I don't want them to blame me, so I called up my old friend Judge Porter in Chicago and asked him to tell me all he knew about this young man. Don't worry, young man, I made him think it was some business I wanted to place in your hands. But I found out a lot more than your business standing, and I knew I would, thanks to my old friend George Porter. I went to school with him and he always was very thorough in all he did. So, it's all right, young man. You have my blessing!"

Copeland's face fairly blazed with joy, but before he had time to thank the old lady Sherrill spoke.

"But there's more, Aunt Pat! He wants us to be married right away!"

"That's natural," said Aunt Pat dryly, with her wry smile.

"Yes, but Aunt Pat, he's being sent to South America and he has to go to-night!"

"To-night!" said the old lady alertly. "H'm! Well it's fortunate you have a wedding dress all ready, Sherrill."

"Oh," said Sherrill with a quick look of astonishment, "I hadn't thought about it. Could I wear that? I could just wear my going-away dress of course."

"No," said Aunt Pat. "Wear your own wedding dress! Don't let yourself be cheated out of that just because you had to lend it to another poor girl for a few minutes. Get your mind rid of that poor fool who would have married you and then made you suffer the rest of your life. Don't be foolish. It was *your* wedding dress and not hers. And she couldn't have hurt it much in that short time. Don't you think she ought to wear a real wedding dress, Graham?" asked the old lady briskly, turning to the young man as if she had known him since his first long trousers.

Copeland's eyes lighted.

"I'd love to see you in it!" he said, looking at Sherrill with adoring eyes.

"Oh, then I'll wear it of course," said Sherrill with starry eyes. "It was really awfully hard to give up wearing it, it was so pretty."

"Of course!" said Aunt Pat bruskly, "and why should you? Forget that other girl, and the whole silly muddle. Now, young man, what is there to do besides getting her suitcase packed? Have you got the license yet?"

"No, but I know where to get it and I'm going for it right away."

"Very well," said Aunt Pat, "I'll have the chauffeur take you. Sherrill, what about bridesmaids? Yours are all scattered."

"Do I have to have them?" asked Sherrill aghast.

"I don't see why," said her aunt. "I suppose we'll have to ask in a few friends, a dozen perhaps, just Cousin Phyllis, and her family and maybe the Grants, they're such old friends. I'll think it over."

"And I wouldn't have to be given away or any of that fuss either, would I? It all seems so silly," pleaded Sherrill. "I thought before that if I had to do it over again I'd never want all that. Couldn't Graham and I just walk down stairs together and be married without any elaborate extras?"

"You certainly could," said Aunt Pat. "If your Graham doesn't feel that he is being cheated out of his rights to a formal wedding."

"Not on your life!" grinned Graham Copeland. "I'd hate it all! But of course I'd go through a good many times that and worse to get her if it was necessary. All I want is a simple ceremony and your blessing."

"Blest be!" said Aunt Pat. "Now, get you gone and come back as soon as possible. Sherrill, send Gemmie to me and tell her to send up the cook. We'll scratch together a few green peas and a piece of bread and butter for a simple little wedding supper. No, don't worry, I won't do anything elaborate. What time do you have to leave, Graham? All right. She'll be ready!"

Sherrill stayed behind after her lover had gone, to throw her arms around her aunt's neck and kiss her many times.

"Oh, Aunt Pat! You are the greatest woman in the world!" she said excitedly.

"Well, you're getting a real man this time, and no mistake!" said the old lady with satisfaction. "When you have time I'll show you the letter my friend Judge Porter wrote about him, but that'll keep. You had better go and get your things together. I'll send Gemmie to help you as soon as I'm done with her."

So Sherrill hurried to her room on glad feet and began to get her things together. She went to the trunk room and found her own new suitcase with its handsome fittings, still partly packed as it had been on that fateful wedding night. She went to the drawers and closets and got out the piles of pretty lingerie, the lovely negligees, dumped them on the bed and looked at them with a dreamy smile, as if they were long lost friends come back to their own, but when Gemmie arrived stern and disapproving still, she had not got far in her packing.

"Miss Patricia says you're to lie down for half an hour

right away!" she announced grimly, "and I'm to do your packing. She says you're tired to death and won't be fit to travel if you don't."

"All right!" said Sherrill with a lilt in her voice, kicking her little blue slippers off and submitting to be tucked into her bed, blue organdy and all.

Gemmie with a baleful glance at her shut her lips tight and went silently about her packing, laying in things with skillful hand, folding them precisely, thinking of things that Sherrill in her excited state never would have remembered. And Sherrill with a happy sigh closed her eyes and tried to realize that it was really herself and not some other girl who was lying here, going to be married within the next few hours.

But there are limits to the length of time even an excited girl like Sherrill can lie still, and before the half hour was over she was up, her voice fresh and rested, chattering away to the silent woman who only sniffed and wiped a furtive eye with a careful handkerchief. It was all too evident that Gemmie did not approve of the marriage. But what could one do with such a woman who had been perfectly satisfied with a man like Carter? She was beyond all reason.

Sherrill went over to see her aunt for a few minutes and have a last little talk.

Aunt Pat invited just a very few of their most intimate friends, and some of those couldn't come on such short notice. "Just to make it plain that we're not trying to hide something," she said to Sherrill with her twinkly grin. "People are so apt to rake up some reason to gossip. But anyway what do we care? The Grants are coming and they are the pick of the lot, and Cousin Phyllis. She would never have forgiven us if she hadn't been asked. She did complain about the shortness of the time and want it put off till tomorrow, but I told her that was impossible."

Then Sherrill told her what Copeland had said about the possibility of his being located in the east when he returned, and Aunt Pat gave her first little mite of a sigh and said with a wistful look like a child:

"Well, if he could see his way clear to coming here to this house and living it would be the best I'd ask of earth any longer. It'll be your house anyway when I'm gone, and I'd like you to just take it over now and run it any time you will. I could sort of board or visit with you. I'm getting old, you know. You speak of it sometime to him when it seems wise, but don't be hampered by it of course," and Aunt Pat sighed again.

"You dear!" said Sherrill bending over her and kissing her tenderly, "I'd love it, and I'm sure he would too. Now don't you worry, and don't you feel lonesome, or we'll just tuck you in the suitcase and take you along with us to South America."

Aunt Pat grinned and patted Sherrill's cheek smartly. "You silly little girl! Now run along and get your wedding frills on. It's almost time for the guests to be here, and you are not ready."

So Sherrill ran away laughing, and had to tell Gemmie to please bring the big box containing the wedding dress.

"You're not going to wear *that!*" said Gemmie aghast.

"Certainly I am, Gemmie," said Sherrill firmly. "It's my dress isn't it? Hurry please. It's getting late!"

Gemmie gave her a wild look.

"I should have been told," she said coldly. "The dress should have been pressed."

"Nonsense, Gemmie, it doesn't matter whether there is a wrinkle or two, but there won't be. You put tissue in every fold. Anyway, you can't press it. It's too late!"

Gemmie brought the great pasteboard box, thumped

it down on the bed unopened and stalked into the bathroom, pretending to have urgent work there picking up damp towels for the laundry.

Sherrill, feeling annoyed at the stubborn faithful old woman, went over to the bed and lifted the cover of the big box.

There lay the soft white folds of the veil like a lovely mist, and above them like blossoms among the snow the beautiful wreath of orange blossoms, not a petal out of place. Gemmie had done her work perfectly when she put them away. And beneath the veil Sherrill could see the gleam of the satin wedding gown. Oh, it was lovely, and Sherrill's heart leaped with pleasure to think she might wear it again, wear it this time without a doubt or pang or shrinking!

She turned away humming a soft little tune and went about her dressing.

Gemmie had laid out all the lovely silken garments and it was like playing a game to put them on, leisurely, happily.

When she was ready for the dress she called Gemmie, and then Aunt Pat came in, ready attired in her soft gray robes, looking herself as lovely as any wedding could desire.

"I'm glad I can have a little leisure this time," she said settling into a big chair and smoothing her silks about her, "last time I had to be hustled off to the church when there were a hundred and one things I wanted to attend to at home. I don't know that I care much for church weddings anyway unless you *have* to have a mob."

Gemmie's eyes were red as if she had been weeping and she came forward to officiate at the donning of the dress with a long sorrowful look on her face.

It was just at that moment that there came a tap at the door and the waitress handed in a package.

"It was special delivery," she explained. "I thought maybe you'd want it right away."

"You might a known she'd no time to bother with the like of that now," said Gemmie ungraciously, taking the package from the girl.

"Oh, but I want to see it, Gemmie," cried Sherrill. "Thank you, Emily, for bringing it up. I want to see everything. You don't suppose anybody is sending a wedding present, do you, Aunt Pat? Don't tell me I've got to go through all that again!"

"Open it up, Gemmie!" ordered Aunt Pat. "It might be something Graham has had sent you, you know, Sherrill."

With something like a sniff Gemmie reached for the scissors and snipped the cords.

"It'll not be from him!" she said tartly, "It's from across the water!"

"Across the water?" said Sherrill and reached for the package.

"H'm! across the water!" said Aunt Pat sitting up eagerly. "Open it quick, Sherry. It might be interesting!"

IF Carter McArthur had been told on the first day out from New York that before the end of the voyage he would be almost reconciled to his fate as husband of a penniless bride, he would have been astonished. But it was nevertheless true.

Arla Prentiss had always been a clever girl, and Arla McArthur driven by necessity became almost brilliant in managing her difficult affairs. She had taken the material at hand and used it. Even Hurley Kirkwood and the two old high school classmates became assets in the affair. Before the voyage was over she had even won out with the man Sheldon and used him to her own ends.

How they came to be seated at a table in a pleasant but obscure corner of the dining room with Hurley Kirkwood, Helen and Bob Shannon and a very deaf old man who paid no attention to any of them, was never known to Carter McArthur. He was very angry when he discovered it, and put Arla through the third degree, but in the end he saw it was a good thing. There was nobody at the table they needed to be nervous about. The three old acquaintances had never heard of Sherrill Cameron and her gorgeous wedding at which she was not the bride, and would be very unlikely to hear now, at least before the voyage was over. Moreover they were good company and there was a certain pleasant intimacy that it could not be denied relieved the strain under which both Arla and Carter had been. There was no danger of some embarrassing question coming up.

Carter grew quite genial and like his old youthful self in their company, accepted the stale jokes about his fondness for Arla with the same complacency that he used to do in the old days when they first began to go together, and actually treated Arla with a degree of his former devotion. If he realized that Hurley Kirkwood was sending home daily bulletins of the honeymoon to a devoted group of fellow-citizens, it only filled him with a vague satisfaction. It comforted his self-esteem to feel that his home town still honored him even though Sherrill Cameron had found out that he was a scoundrel.

Besides all this there was a certain amount of protection in having one's own private little clique. It was almost as good as if Arla had been willing to stay in her stateroom and pretend to be seasick.

Then one evening, near the end of the voyage, Carter, coming out on deck to seek Arla where she usually sat, found her walking the deck arm in arm with the great financier, conversing with him vivaciously and seeming to be entirely at her ease.

She was wearing the loveliest of Sherrill Cameron's evening dresses, the orchid chiffon, and with the moonlight gleaming on her gold hair she looked like a dream. Evidently the financier thought she did also, for he was bending graciously to her and smiling.

Carter withdrew to a distance and watched them from afar, his eyes narrowing, his admiration growing for his lovely wife. Either she was going to be his utter undoing, or else somehow she had managed to wrap Sheldon around her little finger.

They had it out that night in the stateroom, very late, in a brief session. Carter poured invectives upon her, to which she listened absently, and then laughed.

"Oh, Carter, excuse me," she said condescendingly, "all that excitement is so unnecessary. You see Mr. Sheldon thinks I am Sherrill Cameron. He told me how much he had always admired my lovely hair and eyes, and said my aunt Miss Catherwood was a marvelous old lady!"

It was some minutes before Carter recovered from the shock of that and asked for details, but before they were finished he actually came to telling Arla that she was a wonderful woman, and that he loved her beyond anything on earth.

"If I had only realized how really clever you are, Arla, I would never have looked at Sherrill Cameron!" he said, and Arla drew a sharp breath and wished he had not said that. Wished that somehow she might get back her illusions about him. Sherrill Cameron had been right of course. One could not be happy with a man who had been torn from his pedestal. And yet, wasn't there some way to put him back there? To keep him from doing the things that made her despise him?

Several times after that Arla walked and talked with the great man, and Carter's temper was improving daily.

It was about three hours before they were expecting to land.

Arla had scribbled a letter to her Aunt Tilly in the home town telling briefly of her hasty marriage, because she knew that Hurley would spread the news widely and her aunt would be hurt if she did not receive some personal word. She had just returned from posting it and found Carter pulling out the suitcases from under the bed. He stacked them up in two piles, the ones that were to be left with the shipping company for the return voyage, the ones they were to take to the hotel with them. His own suitcase was on the top of one of the piles.

Suddenly he remembered some letters he had written which he wished to post on shipboard. He rushed out slamming the stateroom door behind him, and an avalanche of suitcases careened over to the floor. The top one burst open—perhaps it had not been securely latched—and some of the contents flowed out upon the floor.

Arla sprang forward to pick up the things before Carter's return. She had begun to realize that that was to be her perpetual attitude, always being ready to smooth the way before her husband if she wished to live peaceably with him. That was his wedding suit lying sprawled upon the floor. It would not be a wise note to introduce just at this stage, a reminder of that awful wedding.

Arla stooped and picked it up and as she lifted it she felt something slip out from between the loosened folds—or was it out of a pocket, the trouser pocket perhaps?—and slither along the floor.

She looked down quickly. Was it money? No, something bright and sparkling with green lights in it! Something gorgeous and beautiful lying there on the floor before her startled eyes!

She stopped and stared. What was it? Where had she seen that rarely wrought chain before and those wonderful green stones? Emeralds! They were Sherrill Cameron's emeralds. The necklace she had worn the night of the wedding! The necklace that everybody in the room had been talking about and admiring!

For an instant Arla stood there almost paralyzed facing the possibilities of how that necklace got into her husband's pocket. Over her face the whole gamut of emotions played in quick succession. Astonishment, horror, disgust, scorn, fear, and then a great determination.

Frantically she dropped the garments she held and grasped the glittering necklace, cradled it in her hand for an instant, caught the gorgeous lights in the beautiful gems. Was Carter planning to sell these rare jewels to get the fortune that was to have come from the alliance that her coming to the Catherwood house that night had foiled? Was that what he had meant, that he had found a way to get the rest of the money he needed to save his business schemes?

And was he excusing himself by saying that the jewels were a part of the wedding presents and therefore he had a right to take them? She knew that Carter was capable of such quibbling. Her heart sank. Was she also to have a thief as well as a trifler for a husband?

Outside the door she could hear footsteps coming along the passageway. He might return at any moment! A great panic came upon her. He *should not* be a thief! She would foil that as well as his attempt to marry the other girl!

Her first impulse was to hurl those stones from the porthole and destroy the evidence against him, but as she swayed to take a step in that direction she realized what she was doing. Those were Sherrill Cameron's jewels. Hurling them into the sea would not make Carter any less a thief, even though no one ever found it out. And Sherrill Cameron had been wonderful to her, generous in the extreme. She could not do that to her, throw her costly jewels in the sea! That other girl had already suffered greatly through herself, she should not also lose her property. No, the only possible way to undo the wrong that Carter had done was to return them to their owner. Somehow she *must* return them and yet shield Carter! Shield him from going to the penitentiary!

Hastily she wrapped the jewels in a clean handkerchief, tied the corners securely, and hid it in her own suitcase beneath the lingerie. Then she hurried back to pick up Carter's things. If she could only restore them to their place before he returned!

She schooled herself to go carefully, folding each garment without a wrinkle, laying everything smoothly back in its place. It seemed to her that it was hours before that suitcase was fastened and back on the top of the pile where he had left it.

Then she went to her own suitcase and began frantically hunting through it among the various fittings for a suitable container for the jewels. If she could only get them in the mail before it closed! She glanced at her wrist watch. There was a little over half an hour. She must not fail to get them in. She *must* get them wrapped in time! He should not be *allowed* to be a thief! He might have done many crooked things in business, doubtless had, she could not help the past, but in so far as she was able he should not be allowed to steal a lady's jewels! She never could endure life with that over her, that she had helped him to take the necklace of the girl who had given him up to her. It was too low and contemptible! He wouldn't be thinking himself of doing it if he weren't so utterly frantic about money! He had been decently brought up, just as decently as she was. He wasn't naturally a crook. She must protect him against his worst self.

And she must protect the necklace from her own weakness, too, she realized. If he should discover she had it, should look at her with his beautiful eyes, kiss her the way he did last night, ask her to surrender it, could she resist? She doubted her own strength. She must put that necklace where neither he nor she could ever get it again.

She found in the suitcase a little leather case containing lovely crystal bottles of perfume and lotions. She took out the bottles and packed the jewels carefully, swiftly, among soft folds of Sherrill's own fine handkerchiefs. Then scribbled a hasty note.

You must have dropped this when you were packing. I found it in the suitcase. I hope it has not caused you any anxiety.

Arla McArthur.

With the leather case wrapped in a bit of silk lingerie and then in paper she went hurriedly out and procured a mailing carton from the stewardess, addressed her package at a desk and was not satisfied until it was safe in the keeping of the ship's mail service.

When she went back Carter was directing the steward about the baggage. She was silent and abstracted putting a few last things in her suitcase. The baggage was all going up on deck at once. The whole ship was in a state of getting ready to land.

Carter too seemed absorbed in his own thoughts. Just before they left their stateroom he remarked briskly that they would go directly to the hotel and he would leave her there for the morning. He had some business to be transacted that must be attended to the first thing. Then he would be free to go about with her if all went well.

All during the slow process of arrival and landing and on the way to the hotel Arla was thinking what to do when her husband should discover his loss. Now that she was safe on land and the package in the return mail was presumably safe on its way to America she felt more sure of herself.

Nevertheless when they arrived and were at last left alone in their room, even before Carter began fumbling with the latch of his suitcase she found she was trembling. She could hardly take off her hat, she was afraid Carter would see that she was shaking.

She busied herself hanging up their garments, putting away her hat, washing her hands. Anything not to seem to be noticing Carter who was frantically flinging his things about on chairs, on the bed, the floor, anywhere, and finally turning his suitcase upside down and shaking out its corners.

"I've lost something!" he said when she came out from the closet where she had been arranging her dresses on hangers, and found him standing amid confusion. "It's something very important," he said, beginning again to pick up things and fling them about, to feel in pockets, poke into the fittings of his bag.

"Can I help you?" asked Arla, trying to steady her voice.

"No! No one can help me!" he said flinging a house coat across to the bed. "I can't find—Oh, it's here somewhere of course! It couldn't have got away! I *know* it's here! I'm *wild!* That's all. It couldn't have got away!" He seemed to be talking more to himself than to her. He seemed almost to have forgotten her existence.

"Oh, to think I had to be forced into such a situation!" he groaned at last flinging himself down in a chair and covering his face with his hands. "Was ever any man tormented as I have been?"

Arla came over and stood beside his chair, laying an icy hand on his bowed head. She was shaking from head to foot, but she tried to make her voice calm.

"I'd like to help you, Carter!"

"Well, you can't help me!" he said flinging rudely away from her. "It's all your fault anyway that I'm in such a situation. You put me here, how could you help me? It's too late! If you had wanted to help me you'd have done what I told you sooner and then everything would have come right—. No, you can't help me. You don't even know what it is I'm hunting for, and if you did you wouldn't understand!"

Arla stood still for a minute and then she went and sat down across from him.

"Listen, Carter!" she said in a cold clear voice, "I understand perfectly what you are looking for and what you meant to do. You are looking for Sherrill Cameron's emeralds and you won't find them because they are on their way back to her!"

He sat like one stunned for an instant and she thought he had not understood her. Then suddenly he sprang to his feet and glared at her. His hair was awry, his face was distraught, his eyes glittered like a mad man's. For an instant she thought he was going to strike her. He looked as if he might even have killed her for that minute, if he had had the means at hand. He was beside himself.

"You—! You—! You *dared!"* he screamed, and poured out upon her a stream of invectives that made her shudder with their cruelty.

But she must not cry. She must not show that she was afraid of him. This was the time she had to be strong. She had saved him from the penitentiary and now she must make him understand what danger he was in. Her courage rose to the necessity.

"Yes," she said steadily, "I dared! For *your* sake I dared!"

"For my sake!" he sneered. "You say you did it for *my sake?"*

"Yes, I did it for your sake. Remember you tried to marry another woman once for my sake. Well, I didn't do a thing like that, but I took away the knife that would have cut your throat. You didn't know what you were doing perhaps, you had been through so much. But afterward you would have realized and been ashamed. And I didn't intend to have a common thief for a husband!"

"Thief?" he cried furiously, "I had a perfect right after all that had been done to me. An underhanded—!"

"Stop!" said Arla coldly, "You are not the one to talk about anything underhanded. And you would not have found your argument would have stood before a court of law."

"It would never have come to a court of law. They wouldn't dream who had them. Besides, I had arranged to sell them at once!"

"You poor fool," said Arla, "didn't you know that that necklace was registered? Those stones were well known stones. I heard them talking about it at the reception. You couldn't have got away with it even if I hadn't interfered. You would have been in the penitentiary before three months were passed."

The man was white to the lips now, and sank back in his chair groaning. It was a piteous sight! Tears filled Arla's eyes in spite of her resolution.

Then he suddenly raised his head and glared at her again with his bloodshot eyes.

"And I suppose you don't think they'll trace your package and come after me to every country in Europe?" he snarled, terror in his face.

"No," said Arla coolly, "I wrote a note inside the box and told her she must have dropped the necklace into the suitcase when she was packing."

He was still, staring at her, the strained muscles of his face gradually relaxing. Then he dropped his head into his hands again and groaned aloud, groan after groan until Arla felt she could not stand another one.

At last he spoke again.

"Everything is lost!" he moaned. "I might as well be in the penitentiary. I can't meet my obligations! I can't ever get on my feet again! I am disgraced before the world!"

"Listen, Carter!" said Arla in a tone that demanded attention. "You are only disgraced if you have done something wrong. I saved you from doing one wrong thing. I'm glad I could. I never could respect you again if you had done that! But it's undone now. The necklace is on its way back, and no harm will come to you but losing your business. I'm glad you're losing that. I hate it! It is what made you forget your love for me and go after another woman. Oh, she may be a great deal more attractive than I am, and all that, but you belonged *to me*. By all that had gone before you were mine and I was yours. You knew that! By your own confession these past few days you know it now. Now stop acting like a baby and be a man! How do you think I feel having a husband like you?"

"What can I do?" he groaned.

"Sit up and stop acting like a madman," said his wife, turning away to hide the sorrow and contempt in her eyes. "If you'll get calm and listen I'll tell you what you can do, and I'll stand by and help you! What you should do is take the next boat back and hand over your business to your creditors. Then let's go Home and start anew. You can do it, and I can help you. Won't you listen to reason Carter, and let us be honest respectable people as our parents were?"

Carter slumped in his chair made no reply for a long long time. Arla sat tense, every nerve strained, waiting. She knew that her words had been like blows to him. She felt weak and helpless now that she had spoken. It was like waiting to see whether someone beloved was going to die or live.

But at last he lifted his head and looked at her. She was shocked at his face. It had grown old and haggard in that short time. He had the terrible baffled look of one who had walked the heights and been flung to the depths. She had never seen him before with the self-confidence stripped from him utterly.

"I could never get back to that!" he said and his voice was hoarse and hopeless.

"Yes, you could!" said Arla eagerly. "If you'd just be willing to give it all up and start over again!"

"Oh, you don't know!" he said still with that hopeless look in his eyes. "You don't know it all!"

"You'd be surprised!" said Arla springing up and going over to kneel beside him with her arm about him. "I know a lot more than you think I know. You left your books out one day and I thought they were the books you told me to look up that old metropolitan account in. I hadn't an idea what I was coming on until it was too late."

He looked at her startled, blanching.

"And you knew all that and yet you married me?"

"Yes," said Arla her voice trembling.

He suddenly dropped his head upon her shoulder.

"I'm not worthy of you," he groaned. "I guess I never was!"

"That has nothing to do with it, Carter!" she said almost fiercely, "I love you and *you shall* be worthy! Say you will, Carter, oh, say you will!"

Her tone fairly wrung the promise from him.

"I'm a rotten low down beast!" he said between his clenched teeth. "I can say I will, Arla, but I don't even know if I can do what I say I will."

"Yes, you can!" said Arla in the tone of a mother

determined to save her young. "You *shall!* I'll help you! I'll make you. When you're weak then I'll be strong for you! I've got to! I'll die if you can't be brought back to be a decent man again!"

For a long time his face was hidden on her shoulder, and his whole frame shook with emotion, but her arms were about him and she held him close, her tears raining down unheeded upon his bowed head.

At last he said in a low tone husky with emotion:

"If you can love me like that after all I've done to you, then perhaps I can! I'll try!"

Then eagerly she lifted his face to hers and their lips met, their tears mingling.

It was sometime after that that Arla spoke, gently, quietly.

"Now, oughtn't we to be doing something about a boat to go back on?"

Carter looked up and his capable business expression came upon him.

"I think first, perhaps, I'd better cable to that man that made the offer about the business. He'll maybe go back on it, or have done something else already you know."

"You're right!" said Arla. "Let's go together. I can't be separated from you now till it's all fixed."

"Yes, come!" he said catching her fingers. "Oh, Arla, there's may be something for us somewhere, when you can love me like this!"

Thus Arla entered on her life undertaking of making a man.

"This diamond," she said thoughtfully looking at the gorgeous ring on her finger, "and those pearls. Are they paid for, Carter?"

She watched him keenly as the slow color mounted to his forehead again and his eyes took on a shamed look.

"Because if they're not," she hastened to say, "Let's

send them back, I mean take them back or something. They're not really mine you know. They never were. You got them for her and I think of it every time I look at them. Some day when we can afford it you can get me some of my own, and I'd like that much better."

Carter went and stood by the window looking out with unseeing eyes. His perceptions were turned inside to himself. He was seeing just what kind of a contemptible failure he had been. Seeing it as nothing else but utter failure could have made him see.

"There's no end to it!" he moaned hoarsely.

"Yes, we'll get to the end of it, only let's make a clean sweep now once and forever. Suppose we sit down while we're waiting for the answer to that cable and write down a list of things that have to go back or be sold or something, and debts that have to be paid. Don't forget anything. Let's just look it all in the face and know where we stand."

"We don't *have* a place to stand!" said the disheartened man. "Every foot of ground under us is mortgaged. That's what you've—what we've—what *I've* brought you to, Arla!"

Arla's eyes had a strange light of hope in them as she looked at him. He hadn't said she had brought him to that. He had started to, but he hadn't said it. He had acknowledged that he had done it himself! There was some hope.

They had about a week to wait for the boat they had decided to take, and they went to cheap lodgings and made little excursions here and there on foot, seeing what they could of the old world in a humble way. Perhaps nothing could have better prepared Carter to go from a life of extravagance into plain homely economy like taking their pleasure without cost. For Arla wouldn't let them spend an unnecessary cent. She had everything down to the last penny now, and was determined that they should get free from debt.

"Some day," said Carter watching a young couple, obviously on their wedding trip, as they entered a handsome automobile and drove happily away, "Some day I'll bring you over here and we'll see Europe in the right way."

"Perhaps not," said Arla, her lips set with determination. "We've got to get over expecting things like that. If we ever get rich it might happen, and then of course it would be great, but it isn't likely, not for a long time anyway, and we're not going to expect it nor fret that we haven't got it. It's wanting things we hadn't got that has nearly wrecked our lives, and we're going to stop it! We're going to have a good time on nothing if we have to, and just be glad."

There was disillusionment in her voice and eyes, but there was cheer and good comradeship. Carter looked at her in wonder, and was strangely comforted.

But Arla turned away her disillusioned eyes and struggled to keep back sudden tears. She was getting on very well it was true. Carter had been far more tractable than she had hoped, and that gleam of self-abasement had been hopeful, yet she knew it was but transient. He was weak. He was full of faults. He would fall again and again. He would lapse back into his old self. The world was too full of temptations and ambitions for her to hope for a Utopian life with him. Hell was there with its wide open doors, and her strength was so small! She suddenly felt like sinking under it all. Just courage, her own courage, just determination, couldn't pull him out of this and make him into a decent man again, a man in whom she could trust, upon whom she could lean. Oh, for some strength greater than her own! Oh, for some power to right their lives! Happiness in such circumstances? She knew it was impossible. A good time on nothing? Yes, if they loved and trusted each other perfectly perhaps, but not when one had constantly to bear the other up.

Oh, she would go on as she had promised, stand by him through everything. She loved him. Yes, she loved him. But there was a desolate desperateness about it all. She knew it. She knew it even while she set her beautiful strong red lips in determination to go on and succeed. She knew intuitively that there was something lacking! Some great need that would come, some need for help outside of themselves. Just human effort couldn't accomplish it.

Would Carter ever come to see that he was radically wrong, not just unfortunate? Would his remorse over his failure ever turn to actual repentance?

Oh for something strong and true to rest down upon! And vaguely even while she tried to set her courage once more for higher attainment she knew that what she was trying to do was just another of the world's delusions. She never by her own mere efforts could save Carter from himself. She might help perhaps, better things in great degree, make life more bearable, more liveable, but still in the end there would be failure! What was it they needed? Oh, there must be something, some way!

So with desperation in her eyes, a vision of a future full of useless efforts, she turned back to her heavy task.

SHERRILL filled with a startled premonition that clouded her eagerness over the package, tore off the wrappings and pulled out the little bundle in its cover of silk, shook out the bit of lingerie, a sort of consternation beginning to dawn in her face. This was her own, one of the things that had been in Arla's suitcase!

Then she recognized the little leather case and snapped open the catch, dropping out the note that Arla had written. It fell unheeded to the floor.

But there were no lovely little bottles in the case! What was this, just handkerchiefs? She pulled them out, just catching the heavy little lump knotted in the handkerchief, before it fell.

With hands that trembled now with excitement she unknotted the corners of linen that Arla had tied so hastily, and stood staring as the gleam of the great green stones flashed out to her astonished gaze.

"Oh, Aunt Pat! It's *come!* My emerald necklace has *come back!* Look! The stones are all here! Gemmie! Oh Gemmie! Where are you? The emerald necklace has come back! It's *found!* It's found! Oh, isn't it wonderful that I should find it just now?"

Gemmie hurried in from the bathroom where she had been pretending to pick up the towels and place clean ones. Her eyes were still suspiciously red, and she came and stood there looking at the jewels, the most amazed, embarrassed, mortified woman that one could find, heartily ashamed at all she had been thinking and doing, almost half suspicious yet.

"Where did they come from?" she asked sharply. "Who took them?"

"What does it matter now?" sang Sherrill, "They're here and I don't have to worry any more! Oh, I'm so glad, so glad!"

"What this on the floor?" said Aunt Pat whose sharp eyes had sighted the twisted note.

Gemmie stooped down and handed the note to Sherrill and Sherrill read it aloud. Read the name too, Arla McArthur, and never thought how that last part was once to have been her own.

"Oh, Miss Sherrill!" Her voice was shaking with emotion. "It certainly is wonderful. And I'm that ashamed! And me thinking all this time—!"

But nobody was listening to Gemmie. Aunt Pat asked to see the note and Sherrill handed it happily over to her. She read it carefully and then with her little wry smile and a twinkle in her eye she remarked, "So, you dropped it in the suitcase when you were packing! Well, it may be so, Sherrill! Of course it may be so!"

Then when Gemmie had gone out of the room on some errand she said:

"Well, Sherrill, I'm glad you learned to trust him before it turned up!" and met with a wicked little grin and another twinkle of her bright eyes, her niece's indignant denial that she had ever done anything but trust him.

An hour later, dressed once more in her wedding satin, with the long silvery folds flowing out behind her, and the soft veil blossom-wreathed upon her head, Sherrill stood before her mirror. The faithful Gemmie knelt beside her arranging the folds of her train.

Someone tapped at the door and handed in a big box.

"It'll be your flowers," said Gemmie in an awe-struck voice. She brought in the box and opened it, carefully taking out the lovely bridal bouquet of wedding roses and lilies.

"It's much, much nicer than the other one, Miss Sherrill," she said in deep satisfaction, as her eyes gloated over the flowers. "They're a better quality of flower, they are indeed! And I like the white ribbons much better than the silver. It comes from the most expensive place in the city, too, it really does. They have all the quality orders—they! They really do!"

"Oh, you dear old silly," said Sherrill affectionately. "But it is lovely, isn't it? I like it better too!"

"Well, I like yer man, Miss Sherrill, I'll say that!" added Gemmie shamefacedly. "And now, I'll just be running over to see if Miss Pat wants anything. And mind you don't go to playing any more pranks on us, slipping in another woman on me fer a bride," she added anxiously.

"No, Gemmie, I'll stay right here this time," laughed Sherrill. "I won't give this man up to any other girl!"

So Sherrill stood before her mirror in her bridal array once more and looked into her own mirrored eyes. Happy eyes this time, without a shade of fear or hesitation in them. Eyes full of trust and hope. And suddenly as she faced herself she closed her eyes and lifted her head and spoke into the silent room: "Dear God, I thank you that you took away what I thought I wanted, even though it hurt, and gave me what you had kept for me. Oh, make me worthy of such joy, and make me always ready to yield to your will."

Silently she stood with bowed head for a moment more, and then with a lovely light in her face she lifted her head and went to meet her bridegroom at the head of the stairs.

The little assembly of congenial guests were waiting for them as the two walked down the stairs. An old musician friend of Aunt Pat's was playing the wedding march on the piano, and the minister stood waiting before a hastily assembled background of palms and ferns. Sherrill walked into the room on the arm of her bridegroom and took her place to be married, her heart swelling with joy and peace.

It was a simple ceremony, few words, solemn pledges, another ring to go with her diamond, and dear people coming up to congratulate her. There was one fine old gentleman among them, a friend of Graham's father, who told her what a wonderful man she was getting, and wished her the simple earnest wishes of a bygone day.

And there were amazing presents. Some of them had been sent her before and returned, and returned again now, laughingly, because their donors had had no time to get something new. And there was a gay happy little time with a few tears at the end. Then Sherrill kissed Aunt Pat and Gemmie too and in her pretty dark blue going-away dress that she had never worn until now, was whisked off in Aunt Pat's car to the airport, and taken in an airplane to New York. An hour later the ship weighed anchor and set sail for South America. It didn't seem possible that all this had happened since the golden hearted roses arrived that morning.

Sherrill and her beloved stranger husband stood at last

on deck in a quiet place alone. They watched the lights of their native land disappear into the distance, looked at the great moonlit ocean all about them, and clung closer together.

"To think that God saw all this ahead for me, and saved me for making such a terrible mistake!" said Sherrill softly.

"He knoweth the end from the beginning," quoted Graham, holding her hand close in his own, and looking down into her sweet eyes.

"Yes, but the best of all is," said Sherrill after a little pause, "that He brought me to know Himself. Graham, if I hadn't been stopped in what I thought I wanted most of all in the world, I would never likely have known the Lord Jesus, nor have found out what a wonderful book the Bible is."

"And I perhaps would never have found a girl who knew my Heavenly Father!" said Graham. "His will is always best."

Then softly he began to sing and her voice blended with his tenderly:

"Have thine own way, Lord! Have Thine own way!
Hold o'er my being absolute sway!
Fill with Thy Spirit till all shall see
Christ only, always, living in me!"

About the Author

Grace Livingston Hill is well known as one of the most prolific writers of romantic fiction. Her personal life was fraught with joys and sorrows not unlike those experienced by many of her fictional heroines.

Born in Wellsville, New York, Grace nearly died during the first hours of life. But her loving parents and friends turned to God in prayer. She survived miraculously, thus her thankful father named her Grace.

Grace was always close to her father, a Presbyterian minister, and her mother, a published writer. It was from them that she learned the art of storytelling. When Grace was twelve, a close aunt surprised her with a hardbound, illustrated copy of one of Grace's stories. This was the beginning of Grace's journey into being a published author.

In 1892 Grace married Fred Hill, a young minister, and they soon had two lovely young daughters. Then came 1901, a difficult year for Grace—the year when, within months of each other, both her father and husband died. Suddenly Grace had to find a new place to live (her home was owned by the church where her husband had been pastor). It was a struggle for Grace to raise her young daughters alone, but through everything she kept writing. In 1902 she produced *The Angel of His Presence, The Story of a Whim,* and *An Unwilling Guest.* In 1903 her two books *According to the Pattern* and *Because of Stephen* were published.

It wasn't long before Grace was a well-known author, but she wanted to go beyond just entertaining her readers. She soon included the message of God's salvation through Jesus Christ in each of her books. For Grace, the most important thing she did was not write books but share the message of salvation, a message she felt God wanted her to share through the abilities he had given her.

In all, Grace Livingston Hill wrote more than one hundred books, all of which have sold thousands of copies and have touched the lives of readers around the world with their message of "enduring love" and the true way to lasting happiness: a relationship with God through his Son, Jesus Christ.

In an interview shortly before her death, Grace's devotion to her Lord still shone clear. She commented that whatever she had accomplished had been God's doing. She was only his servant, one who had tried to follow his teaching in all her thoughts and writing.

MARIS

MARIS

LIVING BOOKS®
Tyndale House Publishers, Inc.
Wheaton, Illinois

This Tyndale House book
by Grace Livingston Hill
contains the complete text
of the original hardcover edition.
NOT ONE WORD
HAS BEEN OMITTED.

Living Books is a registered trademark of Tyndale House Publishers, Inc.

3 in 1 ISBN 1-56865-735-8

Printed in the United States of America

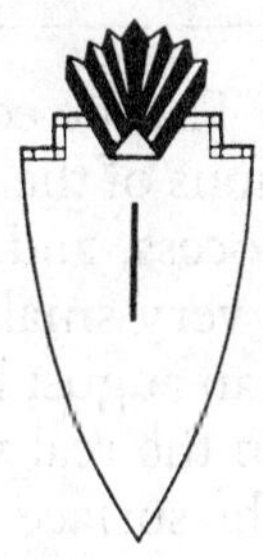

MARIS Mayberry awoke slowly that Wednesday morning and even before her eyes were open she had a heavy consciousness upon her of something being wrong, just a faint uneasiness, like a small dully-tinted cloud on the horizon, that seemed to carry a sense of menace. What was it? She groped for it in her thoughts and tried to bring it to life again, that she might dispel it from her new day and prove by morning's light that it had been nothing real, and it need no longer burden her soul.

But the uneasiness continued, and she roused herself to search for it. What had she been doing last night? Where had she been? She had been out late, for even with closed eyelids she sensed that it was mid-morning, and mother must be letting her sleep late.

Oh, now she knew! She had been out with Tilford. She had been to a grand family dinner. All the Thorpes had been there, and it had been very formal. The dinner had not been served till half past eight and they had sat at the table over two hours. And then there had been a long time afterward when she had been carefully taken over by each separate member of the Thorpe connection and instructed in the history and traditions of the clan.

It had been a long process, and most depressing. When it was over she had felt very small and unworthy to enter even the fringes of such an august body.

But that had not been the real weight of her burden. It had not quite come to the surface of her mind yet, but she felt intuitively that it was going to be fully as disturbing this morning, when she did remember it, as it had been the night before.

It had been rather late when they left the Thorpe mansion, for at the last minute after some of the cousins had left they had taken her up to the gallery and shown her the old family portraits, great oil paintings by famous artists, set in huge hideous gold frames. She had realized that this was a sort of final rite that was being performed upon her before she should be considered eligible to go on with her preparations for the nuptials.

But even the great gallery with the ancestors set in gold had not depressed her. She had known about them, and been told before by Tilford of the high points in each one's biography. She had been duly impressed by the ladies in high ruffs and puffs and chignons, and the gentlemen in knee breeches and lace ruffles and wigs. She had even found some crisp original comments to make upon each, that showed she appreciated their nobility, and stood to admire in their august presence. No, it was not the picture gallery that lay heavily on her mind. They were only painted ghosts of the dead. They could not disturb her future.

They had come away at last. She had received chilly kisses from her future mother-in-law and two aunts-in-law, and formal handclasps from the men of the family. Then Tilford had brought her away in his luxurious car, and she had tried to realize that in a few days now, three brief weeks to be exact, she was going to belong in that car. She would be a part of a life of luxury. It didn't seem real yet, but the glamour of it all had carried her so far, and some day of course she would realize it, and take it as a matter of course. Still such thoughts had not disturbed her. Now she was coming to it. She could see its shadow just a few steps ahead. Ah! Here it was!

They had turned into her home street, the moonlight shining very brightly on the house. Just the plain old white house where she had been born, big and roomy and comfortable and shabby. She hadn't thought of its shabbiness before. It had just been home to her, and always very dear. But now, in sudden contrast to the luxury where she had been all the evening, it stood out sharply, there in the moonlight. *Shabby!* That was what it really was! And it was too late to do anything about it now before the wedding!

Suddenly she had spoken out her thought, interrupting Tilford's eulogy of one of the ancestors whose portrait they had seen.

"This home needs *painting!"* she said. "It ought to have been done before. It must be looked after just as soon as we get back!"

Tilford had stopped abruptly and given her a strange questioning look, as if he were seeing something in her he had never seen before, and then a quick caution came into his eyes, an amused curve about his lips.

"That will scarcely need to trouble you by that time," he said almost curtly. "You will not be there any more, you know. It will no longer be your interest what the house looks like. You will seldom see it, of course. You will belong in another world."

And she had given him a quick startled look, seeing suddenly things she had never realized before, possibilities that loomed with sharp premonition, and now, overnight, had become a burden, a heavy menacing cloud on her horizon.

As if it had been a little bundle the contents of which she suspected but had never seen, she deliberately took the fear and undid its wrappings, searching what was to be found herein.

What had that look of Tilford's meant? Had he intended to let her see it, or was it something he was concealing till afterwards? Oh, that could not be. Surely he was but trying to remind her of the beautiful house where she had been all the evening, and the beautiful life that was to be hers!

Yet she must face this thing out and get rid of it. She could not have an uneasiness hovering even on the edge of her mind through these strenuous days. What was it that had caused that sudden startled pain in her heart? A pain that she had refused to recognize that night? She had commandeered sleep to drown it away last night. Better face it now once for all.

Was it the sudden knowledge that when she was married she would be leaving forever everything else that was dear to her?

Nonsense! What a foolish idea! Her people would still be her people, and as dear as ever. They would rejoice in her good fortune. They would be pleased and proud of her, and would enjoy many things that they had not been able to enjoy before.

But stay! Would they? Would her dear quiet father, and her sweet-faced mother ever come to know and like and fit in with all those Thorpes? Even, just casually? Ever feel like holding their own along that gallery of ancestors?

She was not ashamed of her family. They were grand. They were real people, and she wouldn't have them changed a whit in any way. But would those Thorpes ever recognize that? With no great fortune behind them, and no painted ancestors, could they understand how people could be noblemen and women without possessions?

And how would some of their opinions and standards harmonize? Would they have any thoughts in common? Politically, socially, religiously, intellectually? Even morally? Their standards were all so very different.

And how about herself? Was *she* going to be able to fit in with the Thorpes? But that was another question. She could think that through afterwards. She had first to ferret out the truth about that burden on her heart.

Had it really been that Tilford's words and tone, and the very glint in his eye, had seemed to expect that of course after they were married she would be utterly separated from her dear people? That their interests and concerns and affairs would be no more hers? That she would be henceforth apart from them so utterly that she was practically leaving all she loved behind her, and coming to him and his people and his interests? As if he had bought her body and soul!

That was it! That completely desolating thought!

Not once had it entered her head that she would be cut off from her people and her home after she was married.

Of course she was expecting to live in a home of her own, she and Tilford, and she had up to this time looked upon it as a delightful adventure, something like playing house when she was a child, only on a larger scale. She had looked upon Tilford as the gilded fairy who was going to make this lovely play possible. But not once before had it entered her head that the dear people and places and things would be cut out of her life forever after. In her family marriage meant that all concerned only acquired more dear relatives, and wider realms of things and places to love. They did not give up what they already had.

Did Tilford feel that way, that he wanted to cut her off from her people? That *he* had no interest in them for themselves? She hadn't thought about it before, but now she recalled that he had seldom seemed to care to linger in the house and talk to her father and mother, or be brightly interested in her sisters and brothers. He had always some excuse to call late for her, and leave at once.

Now she recalled also that her father had asked some puzzled questions now and then about the Thorpes, had tried to be friendly in the few minutes Tilford allowed him. Was it her fault too that she and Tilford had had so many engagements that there hadn't seemed to be time for her parents and family to get really acquainted with her fiancé?

She had taken it all so for granted. She had thought all those matters would settle themselves. And now that horrid cold feeling at the bottom of her heart, in the memory of Tilford's look last night! That feeling that she was about to leave everything that had been dear.

That wasn't as it should be, was it? All girls didn't feel that way, did they? They were in a sense leaving home, but they were going to be with the man they had chosen for life. Did she love Tilford enough to make up for leaving everyone and everything?

It suddenly became clear to her that she hadn't ever faced that question. She had just gone on through the brief weeks since he had asked her to marry him, in a daze of wonder that one so rich and influential and handsome and sought after had chosen her. It had seemed almost too good fortune to be true, and his way had carried everything before it.

Rides in his gorgeous car, admiration and flattery, social affairs that had heretofore not been in her sphere, the wonder and envy of all her old friends. And then Tilford's eagerness to bring everything to a consummation, to rush her through functions and ceremonies; prepare her for requirements that had not been before in her scheme of things, and plan for a wedding far beyond her highest ambitions. There hadn't been time to think. Had there been something missing, something not quite in accordance with her dreams? Something tender and shy and precious, almost too precious to dare expect? Words? Looks? The first touch of hands, the first reverent touch of lips?

Tilford's way had not been like that. He had carried everything with a high hand, stated what he wanted, and expected her to concede. His kisses had been almost formal, like taking a bite of fruit he had just purchased. She had tried to ignore a vague disappointment. There had been no dreamed-of thrill of joy. Was that all that love meant? Perhaps there was no such thing as romance in this age of the world. Somehow, in spite of Tilford's haste to possess her, there was a coldness, a matter-of-factness about him that left no room for the ecstasy that she had always expected to feel if she ever fell in love.

Was she in love? Perhaps she was only taking love for granted and it wasn't love at all.

Suddenly she sprang up sharply.

"Oh, snap out of it!" she said angrily aloud to herself.

What were all these foolish thoughts anyway that she was allowing to wander through her mind? It was too late to consider such questions, even if there were any truth in them which of course there wasn't. She was engaged to Tilford Thorpe, and wearing the most gorgeous diamond on her engagement finger that any girl in their town ever owned. And downstairs in the library there were neat white boxes of already addressed wedding invitations, awaiting only their stamps before they were taken to the postoffice. Perhaps her sister Gwyneth was even now putting on hundreds of stamps, and she ought to hurry down and help.

And over across the hall in the guest room closet there were many lovely garments hanging that she would never have thought she could afford if she were not marrying Tilford Thorpe. Also, down on her mother's desk was a thick envelope containing estimates from the expensive caterer that Tilford had said was the only caterer in town who was fitted to handle an affair like their wedding supper in a satisfactory way. She had gasped when she caught a glimpse of the figures that were written on those heavy expensive sheets. She had cringed as her brother Merrick leaned over her shoulder and read them aloud, fairly shouted them in an indignant tone so that the whole family could not help but hear. She recalled now with a sharp breath of pain the look of almost despair in her mother's eyes as she listened. She ought to get down as quickly as possible and straighten that out. Surely they could plan some way that would not cost so much! Poor father! All this was going to be so hard on him. She hoped that when she was married she would be able to lift the financial burden from his shoulders a little.

But all these things going on, the whole machinery set in relentless order for her wedding, and she daring to spend an idle thought on whether this was really romance or not!

Those invitations had to be mailed tomorrow, the exact number of days before the wedding that fashion decreed there should be, though the heavens should fall. It was much too late to alter anything even if she found out that she was not in love with her bridegroom. Even if she found out it was all a terrible mistake, she could not turn back now. Nothing short of a miracle could undo those inexorable plans. There was no time now to check things over. It was too late for that.

Well, forget it! She had enough to occupy her mind without letting it bring up questions like that, that ought to have been settled beyond a question long ago. But *when?* It had all been so sudden! If she had made a mistake she would doubtless have plenty of time to regret it.

But of course this was all nonsense. Everything was all right. She was making a brilliant marriage, and everybody thought so. Simply *every*body. Even her mother hadn't demurred. Even her father had only said: "Are you perfectly sure he is what you want, little girl?" and then had given her his blessing. Although as she thought of it now it seemed as if it had been almost a sad-eyed blessing.

Oh, what gloomy thoughts! And she had been so gay and happy before last night! It was just the effect of that awful family party with all the eulogies and injunctions that had depressed her. She simply must snap out of it.

She arose and began to dress rapidly, dashing cold water in her face, putting on a gay little rose-colored print dress that she knew was becoming. Likely Tilford would telephone her after lunch to go out for a few holes of golf, but she must be firm about it. She must stay at home and get those invitations stamped, and do a lot of other things that she had put off from day to day.

She began to hum a gay little tune, just to keep up the illusion that she had no misgivings, and she gave a final pat to her pretty hair, trying to make her eyes sparkle as she gave herself a brief glance in the mirror. Yes, she was all right, and everything was going to be lovely of course. She would do wonderful things for mother and dad and the others when she was a married woman, with time, and plenty of money to spend! That nonsense about being separated from them all was a ghost of the nighttime. Tilford had no such idea as that. Tilford was a splendid dependable young man. He would be a good son, and would always be wanting to make her happy. And after all, what was romance? Just a figment of a silly girl's imagining. When one grew up one got to be sane and sensible, and didn't yearn to be a Cinderella. After all, wasn't she marrying a fortune, and wasn't she going to Europe for her honeymoon?

Maris had finished her dressing and had almost regained her ecstasy of yesterday over her happy lot in life, when another memory of last night that she had almost forgotten suddenly came to the surface and cast a sinister shadow in her path. The wedding dress! How could she have forgotten so important a matter! And now, what was she to do about it?

She dropped down in a chair by the door and stared at the wall with troubled eyes.

Her mother had wanted white organdy for her from the first. She had thought it so suitable for a girl with a quiet background, and no great fortune.

"I know you are going to be a grand lady, dear," she had said wistfully, "but it seems so much better taste for you to dress simply, and not try to appear that you are one before you really are."

And Maris had agreed quite happily. She had always liked white organdy herself.

So her mother had made the dress most exquisitely, for she could do wonderful work with her needle. And the beautiful Carrick-macross lace, which had been in the family for years, had seemed just perfect, as if it were made for the simple dress pattern they had selected. The dress was almost finished, and even now was hanging under a white shroud from a long hook on the inside of the guest room closet door. Maris had taken a parting look at it last night before she went out with Tilford, noting with proudly happy eyes the exquisite finish, so workmanlike, so perfect! No Paris import could possibly excel this charming dress! And it was all done but a few stitches! Just a few more inches of lace to appliqué and it would be done! Dear mother! How she had worked over it. Sometimes when she must have been very tired. That last glimpse of her wedding gown had sent Maris on her way, starry-eyed to the family gathering.

And then, one of the first things that happened after she got there was that Mrs. Thorpe took her aside, before she had fairly got her wrap laid on the bed, and asked rather imperiously:

"And now, my dear, about your wedding gown. I was going to speak to you before, but I haven't really had the opportunity. What had you planned? Because I have a suggestion."

The color flew into Maris' cheeks and she held her head proudly, "with the Mayberry tilt" as mischievous young Gwyneth would have said.

"My wedding dress is all ready, thank you. It was the first thing I planned." She said it very quietly but firmly. Her future mother-in-law eyed her thoughtfully.

"Well, you are forehanded," said Mrs. Thorpe, pleasantly. "Most girls leave that until near the end. But, my dear, I'm wondering if you quite appreciate what a formal gown would be required for this wedding? Of course whatever you pick out would be *charming,* but it could easily be used for some less formal affair. You see, I've found just the right garment for you, at a very exclusive little shop where I frequently deal, and I'm quite sure you'll like it. It is perfect for the occasion, and one that you would always be proud to remember having worn on the greatest occasion of your life. Of course it was a bit expensive, and so I secured a special price on it. If you feel it is still too high I shall be glad to pay the extra expense, for I do feel that for the honor of the family you should have it."

Maris' color had drained away at this, and her eyes had become a deeper blue as she lifted her chin a bit haughtily. She could imagine the steel in her father's eyes if he should hear of this offer to help pay for his daughter's wedding dress. She could imagine the hurt in her mother's eyes at the interference.

"I think you will be pleased with my dress," she said a bit haughtily.

"Perhaps," said the older woman, "but nevertheless I would like you to see this dress of which I speak. I'm sure after you once see it nothing else will seem the proper thing."

"Then I wouldn't want to see it," laughed Maris with a tinge of asperity beneath the laughter.

"Oh, now, my dear, you certainly are not as narrow as that! But I must insist that you see it. I really feel very strongly about the matter, and of course I'll be glad to finance it."

Maris drew the Mayberry dignity about her.

"My father would not permit that of course," she said quietly.

"Well, of course, if he feels that way. But I didn't like to make suggestions without offering to pay for them. Then you'll see it tomorrow, won't you, Maris? I told the woman to hold it, that you would likely be in sometime in the morning. Of course if you have to delay till afternoon, just phone her and say when you will be there. Here's the address, and the phone number."

She handed Maris a card.

Maris took it reluctantly, looked at it a minute, struggled with her annoyance, and then lifted a face on which she tried to hold a winning smile:

"I could *look* at it," she said pleasantly, "but it really wouldn't be worth while for the woman to take the time to show it to me, because I simply couldn't do anything about it. I have my wedding dress, and I like it very much."

"But you will see it because I ask you to," said the older woman with an underlying tone of authority in her voice. "I have spoken to Tilford about it, and he feels that you should see it. I ask it as a special favor."

More family arrivals just then prevented further talk, and left Maris, bending the little troublesome card back and forth in her fingers. She finally slipped the card into her small evening bag and the thought of it was submerged in the dull monotony of the evening. But now it rose with all the imperiousness of the Thorpe family and seemed as binding upon her as if she had signed a contract to go and look at that dress. Tilford was in it too. Really, that wasn't fair! The bridegroom was not supposed to know anything about the bridal robe till he saw her in it for the first time as she came up the aisle. But perhaps Tilford's mother didn't realize that.

Well, what should she do? Just forget it? Could she get by? She had a feeling that perhaps it might be hard to explain to Tilford why she had ignored his mother's request. And over and above all she had a little shivery feeling that this matter of marriage was assuming a grave and sinister appearance. That word "formal affair" that Mrs. Thorpe had used last night had made it seem that it wasn't just a matter between herself and Tilford, but as if she were about to marry the whole Thorpe connection and come under their authority. Was that so?

And what should she do? She didn't want to make a useless fuss about what might after all prove to be a trifling matter. Perhaps she had better go and look at the dress and say she had seen it but she still felt that her own would be more suitable. And yet, even to compromise so much seemed almost disloyal to the mother who had worked so hard, and wrought love into every stitch of that exquisite fairy dress.

She had been so sure until last night that all the Thorpes would admire and praise it. And now she had a feeling that they would look on it with scorn. And perhaps if she went to look at this other sophisticated dress it might make her dissatisfied with her own lovely dress. Oh, how she hated the thought of all this interference!

Well, what should she do? Was it thinkable that she should tell her mother, and that they should go down and look at that dress? Was it at all possible that the lovely organdy was not formal and stately enough for this wedding that the Thorpes seemed to think was their wedding and not hers?

Suddenly she sprang to her feet, opened her door and listened a minute. She could hear a distant sound of dishes in the kitchen. A pang of conscience shot through her.

Mother was washing dishes, and she ought to be downstairs helping. By this time of course Gwyneth should have gone to school. And mother had dismissed the maid yesterday! She had pretended it was because Sally was inefficient, but Maris knew in her heart that her mother was trying to save money, just now when this wedding was going to be such an expense! And here was she lingering upstairs considering whether she wouldn't add more expense by buying another wedding dress at the most exclusive shop in the city! What utter nonsense! What ingratitude! Of course her lovely organdy was the right thing. It was beautiful as a dream, and nobody, not even Mrs. Thorpe, could say it wasn't. And anyway, Tilford would have to take her as she was. If he didn't like her in her own wedding dress he needn't marry her!

With her head held high she tiptoed across the hall to lift the white cheesecloth covering and reassure herself by another glimpse of the dress which had seemed so wonderful to her just last night.

And there hung the dress in all its white cloudiness. Nothing could have been lovelier! Formal? Yes, its very simplicity gave it an air of distinction! There was something about it that even formality might not question.

Then suddenly she saw that the lace which had been hanging from the sleeve last night, hung no longer. It was all delicately in place with tiny invisible stitches, exquisite and perfect. It was done!

Then mother must have sat up till all hours last night finishing it! For she knew by having watched the rest of the lace put on what a time it took, and what infinite care her mother used. It was all wrought together so perfectly that the sewing was only a part of the artistry.

Sudden tears sprang to her eyes! *Dear* mother!

Then it *had* been a crack of light beneath the sewing room door that she had thought she saw last night down the hall as she came softly up the stairs not to disturb anybody! When she looked again it was gone and she had thought it imagination. But mother must have heard her and turned the light off quickly so that she wouldn't know what she was doing, and then turned it on again when she was sure her child was asleep. Dear mother! Precious wedding dress! Not for any new formal relatives would she hurt her mother now, by even suggesting that they look at that other formal attire that had been urged upon her!

But there would be Tilford. If he should speak of it how would she answer? Well, perhaps she could run down sometime this morning and just look at the dress and then tell him she liked her own better.

Suddenly as she stood at the head of the stairs trying to think it out there came a frightened cry. Gwyneth from the distant kitchen suddenly flung the door open.

"Maris! Maris! Come quick! Something's happened to mother!"

AS Maris flew down the stairs on panic-stricken feet the telephone set up a wild ringing, and on top of that the doorbell shrilled out through the house, but Maris sped on to the kitchen where her intuition told her her mother would be. And there on the floor beside the sink with the dish towel still in her grasp, and her soft brown hair that was graying at the temples, fallen down around her shoulders, lay the mother. Her face was still and white, and Maris' frightened eyes could see no sign of breathing as she stooped down with a low cry. "Oh, mother! Mother! Mother! You dear little mother!"

"Yes, *very* dear to *you!*" said the sarcastic voice of her brother Merrick as he came angrily into the room. "What's the matter here?"

He caught a glimpse of his mother prone upon the floor and his young face hardened.

"If anything's the matter with mother you've yourself to thank for it. That doggone fool wedding is at the bottom of it all. I've seen it killing her day by day! Get out of the way and let me lift her up! Get some water, can't you?

Send for the doctor! Somebody answer that telephone and tell 'em to shut up and get out!"

He gathered up his mother in his strong young arms. Such a frail little limp white mother with the dish towel still in her hand!

He strode toward the couch in the dining room.

"Gwyn, can't you stop that telephone! It's fierce! Maris, can't you bring some water? Isn't there any aromatic ammonia around?"

Merrick was standing over his mother, frantically peering down at her white silent face.

A young man who had come in with Merrick and had up to this time stood in the doorway silently, answered the appeal in his friend's eyes and came over to the couch. He stooped over, listening, and laid his hand on the wrist.

Merrick looked at him with fear in his eyes.

"Is she—*gone?"* he murmured hoarsely.

"No, I think not," said the other. "Let's have that ammonia. Dip that towel in some water and wet her face."

Maris with white face and frightened eyes brought the bottle, and then got a wet cloth and began to bathe her mother's face. She knelt down beside the couch, and found she was trembling so that her knees would hardly support her.

The telephone had ceased and presently Gwyneth came to her brother.

"It's Tilford," she said. "He says he's got to speak to Maris."

"Well, he can't speak to Maris now. I'll tell his highness where to get off!" and Merrick strode out in the hall to the telephone.

If Maris heard at all she was too frightened to take it in. She knelt there tenderly bathing her mother's still white face, and trying to stop the trembling in her limbs, trying to keep her lips from quivering.

She was aware that somebody else, an outsider, was

kneeling beside her listening for a heartbeat, feeling for a slender evasive pulse in her mother's frail wrist, but she did not turn her head to look at him. It didn't occur to her to wonder who he was, or if she knew him. She was intent upon her mother's face. Was it too late? Was she gone from them forever? Would she never be able to tell her how she loved her? How sorry and ashamed she was that she had let her do so many hard things alone, while she had gone on her gay way having a good time and never noticing how hard she was making it for her precious mother.

She thought of many things while she knelt there so quietly bathing that white face, helping the man beside her to lift the head of the sick woman and hold the glass of restorative to her lips. She was examining herself, seeing herself as she had never seen herself before in all her happy carefree days.

Maris did not hear Merrick at the telephone, though he was shouting angrily:

"Well, you *can't* see my sister. She's busy. Our mother has been taken very ill. We aren't sure but she's dying. Get off this wire. I want to telephone for the doctor! Get off quick, I say!" Bang! Merrick hung up.

Then in a second he lifted the receiver again.

"Merrick, you must be crazy to speak to me this way. Do you realize what you are doing?" babbled forth the indignant voice of his future brother-in-law. "Tell Maris to come here at once. I must speak to her right away. I won't keep her but a moment, but I must tell her something right away!"

"Will you get out of my way?" yelled Merrick. "If my mother dies for want of a doctor we'll have you arrested for murder. Get off, I tell you! *Thunder,* have I got to go next door to get a message through to the doctor? Operator! Operator!"

"But Merrick, listen to me—"

"Oh, go to *thunder!"* roared Merrick. "No, I won't listen

to you. I'll go to the neighbor's phone and you can keep right on talking to yourself—" and Merrick banged the receiver down on the table and left Tilford protesting in dignified indignant tones. But Merrick had gone next door to telephone, and presently Tilford took it in that nobody was listening to him. A vast silence seemed to have dropped down upon the wire, and nobody was getting the benefit of his high-sounding words. Tilford was a handsome man, and usually depended a good deal on the effect of his personal appearance when he was talking, but he found himself at a great disadvantage just now, for his physical beauty had no effect whatever on the telephone wires. There didn't seem to be even an operator around to hear him. So at last he hung up in disgust. Somebody should suffer for this! Merrick of course was the greatest offender, but if Merrick were not available his sister should certainly take it. Perhaps it would be as well for him to go right around to the house now and see Maris personally, make her understand what an unforgivable thing her brother had done. He never had liked that fellow anyway. When he and Maris were married he would forbid Merrick the house! One didn't have to marry all one's wife's relatives of course. He would make her understand that thoroughly when the time came.

So Tilford Thorpe started on his way to see Maris.

Maris on her knees beside the dining room couch was holding a cloth wet in aromatic ammonia in front of her mother's face and crying in her heart: "Oh, God. Don't let her die! Oh, God, don't let my mother die!" and was coming out rapidly from the coma of gaiety into which the orgy of festivities connected with her engagement had plunged her.

As the agonized minutes passed and still that white face did not change, save for a quick catching of breath, faintly, so faintly that they weren't quite sure it had been a breath, it seemed as if the atmosphere rapidly became clear of a lot of things that had filled it for Maris in the past weeks. True values of things and people began to adjust themselves to her sharply awakened mind. Such things as special hours for wedding invitations to be mailed, and the importance of pleasing Tilford's relatives sank into insignificance. Years of tender care and sacrifice and precious love stood out in clear relief and importance. Strange sharp memories came and stood around like witnesses against her. The time when she had cut the vein in her wrist with the bread knife and mother had held it together till the doctor got there. The time when the bull had dashed into the garden from a herd that was going by on the street, and mother had sheltered her behind her own body. That was when she was only two and a half years old, yet she remembered how safe she had felt. The time when she had the whooping cough and almost died, with an unbelievable temperature, and mother had stayed up for two whole nights and days, most of the time on her knees bathing the hot little body under a blanket, trying to bring down the temperature. The time when there had had to be a blood transfusion and mother had offered her own. Such a precious mother who had guarded and served them all. Her deeds stood crowding about the couch hand in hand, silent witnesses of the past. And last of all her lovely wedding dress seemed to her troubled mind to come floating down the stairs and stand with the rest about that couch where the little gray-faced mother lay.

"Oh, mother, mother!" Maris suddenly cried, softly, and her hand paused with the wet cloth she was holding, and her head suddenly went down on her mother's breast for an instant of despair. Then up again instantly, just as strong hands lifted her and Merrick's voice, grown suddenly tender and more worried, said, "Take her in the other room. I'll look out for mother."

That roused her. She straightened up.

"No! No! I'm all right!" she whispered. "I must stay here!"

"There's the doctor!" announced Gwyneth, hurrying to open the door. And then they all made way for the doctor, and Maris felt those strong arms lifting her again and leading her to a chair.

She did not look up to see who it was. Her eyes were upon her mother's face there on the couch.

Someone brought her a glass of water and she drank it, and then went back to stand at the head of the couch and watch the doctor's face.

The strange young man was sent on an errand for the doctor, and Merrick went to telephone his father. Maris stayed to wait on the doctor and answer his questions, though she found it was fourteen-year-old Gwyneth who did most of the answering.

"I wasn't here," was all Maris could say in answer to some question about whether her mother had felt badly the day before, and what she had been doing.

"She had an awful headache yesterday," said Gwyneth sadly. "I guess she worked too hard. She would do so many things. I tried to help her but she sent me to do my home work and said she could do it all herself. But once I saw her put her hand over her heart and I asked her what was the matter, and she said, 'Oh, just a sharp pain.'"

"Had she been having pains in her heart?"

"She never complained," said Maris sadly. "I'm afraid we were all so busy with our own affairs that we didn't notice."

"She sewed a lot last night," volunteered Gwyneth. "She told me this morning she'd got it all done, what she was working on."

Tears sprang to Maris' eyes, and she turned away to hide them, and then turned back again as she heard her mother give a soft little breath of a sigh. Oh, was she coming back to them, or was she gone? She watched the grave face of the doctor anxiously, but he worked on quietly and gave no sign. Only asked for water, and a spoon, and handed the glass back to Maris.

A car drew up at the door. The young man came back and brought whatever it was that he had been sent for, but Maris took no notice of him. Some friend of Merrick's, she thought. Then a few minutes later a nurse arrived, and Maris caught her breath in hope and fear. But there was no time to ask questions. She must go upstairs and get the bed ready for the patient to be moved. There were sheets to hunt out, the good sheets. Where *were* the good sheets? Every one she unfolded seemed to be torn or badly frayed at the hems. Oh, the house was in perfect order for a wedding, but not for illness. And they had not been expecting to have any of the wedding party stay overnight with them, for they all lived in the town.

"There aren't any good sheets left, Maris," whispered Gwyneth. "Mother had me help her gather up the laundry for the man this morning, and we put the last good ones in the bag. She said she must run up some of the torn ones till the laundry got back."

Suddenly Maris took it in. Mother and Father had been scrimping on everything that there might be more to pay her wedding bills. There were beautiful garments hanging in her closet, costly garments, for her parents were sending her proudly away from their care; and her generous hope chest was full to overflowing with linen and percale sheets and pillow cases, smooth as silk, and fine of quality; and towels in abundance, rich and sumptuous as any bride might desire. But the mother of the bride must be put to bed in torn sheets!

Suddenly Maris' face went white and her lips set in a thin line of determination. She put back the torn sheets she had been unfolding hopelessly, and marched into her own room to her hope chest. She delved deep and brought out a wealth of lovely smooth sheets and pillow covers and brought them into her mother's room where Gwyneth was taking off the worn sheets that had been on the bed.

Gwyneth looked at her in startled dismay.

"But, Maris, those are your wedding things! You mustn't use those!"

"Why not?" said Maris grimly. "They're mine, aren't they? Mother bought them for me, didn't she? I have a right to use them the way I want to, don't I?"

"Yes, but mother wouldn't want you to use them up now. Not on her bed."

"I'm sure she would," said Maris, "if she knew how I feel about it. I'd rather use these now on mother's bed, Gwynnie, than on any grandest occasion that could ever come in my life. Wouldn't you feel that way, Gwyn, if they were yours?"

"Oh, yes, *I* would," said Gwyneth, "but then I wouldn't have the Thorpes to think about."

She said it so quaintly and so gravely that Maris would have broken down and laughed if she hadn't felt too frightened and too sad to laugh. But somehow it opened her eyes to the way her young sister felt about her future relatives.

And just then the doorbell pealed through the house.

"We must muffle that bell," said Maris. "The doctor said there mustn't be any noise. Mother starts every time she hears a sharp sound."

"I'll go," said Gwyneth.

"No, you stay here and help me. Tuck the sheets in over that side. The doctor wants to get mother in bed as soon as possible. They are going to bring her right up. Someone will go to the door, Merrick, or that young man he brought in with him. He's been very kind."

"Young man!" said Gwyneth. "Didn't you know who that was? That's Lane Maitland, the boy that used to live next door to us five years ago. Don't you remember him?"

"Lane Maitland? Why, yes, I remember him. But I

didn't know him. I guess I didn't even look at him. Gwyn, you run down and tell them we're ready. I'll wait here and put out some more towels. Maybe they'll need me to help get mother settled."

Gwyneth started, but as she passed the window she exclaimed:

"Oh, Maris! That must have been Tilford that rang the bell! There's his car out there now."

Maris looked up in dismay.

"Well, I can't see him now. You run down and tell him what's happened. Quick! Before Merrick gets there! Merrick hasn't any sense."

Gwyneth vanished, and Maris turned back the covers carefully. She could hear that they were bringing her mother up the stairs. The nurse was ahead, eyeing the arrangements with a quick keen glance. Maris had no more time to think of Tilford now. But surely he would understand.

Then there was so much to be done that Maris forgot Tilford entirely. She helped the nurse to undress her mother. There were things to be hunted for. A night dress and bed jacket. Mother just didn't seem to have anything. All her garments were worn. Maris was ashamed to hand them out. She dashed into her own room and opened the drawer where her own pretty lingerie was waiting to be packed for her trip abroad, selected a pretty gown and a little pink jacket with sprigs of embroidery scattered over it. The tears blinded her eyes as she hurried back with them to the nurse.

"Oh, haven't you something plainer, something old and worn?" said the nurse. "Keep these till she is able to sit up."

Maris felt as if her eager gift had been rejected but she hurried away and hunted again among her mother's things.

"That will do," said the nurse reaching for an old faded

gown with a tear half way up the back. "I shall want to cut it up the back anyway. It's easier to put it on without disturbing her."

Dear mother, so inert, lying there limp, while others arrayed her in her old garments. Mother who never let anyone do anything for her, and was always waiting on others! Oh, if she had only seen all this before. If mother didn't get well, would she ever be able to forgive herself and go on with life?

"Can you get me some ice?" asked the doctor crisply, breaking in on her frantic thoughts.

Maris dashed downstairs for the ice, and almost knocked over Tilford who was standing at the foot of the stairs, his handsome face snarled into an ugly frown.

"What on earth is the matter with you, Maris?" he said vexedly, reaching out his arms to prevent a collision. "You seem to be all wrought up. Can't you have a little self-control? And why have you had to keep me waiting so long when you know how busy I am this morning? I've been waiting here exactly fifteen minutes!" He glanced at his watch to be accurate. He was always accurate about details. "I sent you word that I was in a great hurry and would keep you only a moment, and yet you didn't come. I can't understand it."

He gave her a severe look as if she were a naughty child, and Maris burst into tears. Her lips quivered, but she controlled herself at once.

"Oh, hush, please," she said in a whisper. "We mustn't talk here. Mother is very sick indeed. The doctor said there must be absolute quiet. Come into the kitchen with me. I can't stop even a minute. The doctor wants some ice."

"Well, why doesn't he send the nurse after it? I saw a nurse go upstairs. Does he expect to make a pack horse of you?"

Maris flew to the refrigerator and began to work away at the ice with an ice pick and mallet. She was suddenly very angry. She had hoped for a little sympathy from Tilford, and he had only sharp words.

"Mercy! Don't you have a modern refrigerator?" ne said as he followed her annoyedly and stood watching her knocking off the chunks of ice. "I thought everybody had ice cubes now."

Maris shut her lips tight. At another time she might have explained that her father had had the money saved for an electric refrigerator and was just about to get one when she announced her intention of getting married soon, and everything else had to give way to get money for that. But now she was too angry to explain anything. Tilford was being disagreeable. He knew her father wasn't wealthy.

"Well, come and sit down somewhere," he went on haughtily. "I've got to tell you one or two things before you vanish again. Are these chairs all right to sit on? Kitchen chairs are apt to have flour and grease on them," and he inspected one with a disdainful finger.

"Anything in my mother's kitchen is perfectly clean," said Maris with uplifted chin.

"Oh, certainly, of course," said Tilford perfunctorily, "but servants aren't so careful."

"We have no servant," said Maris briefly.

"You have no servant? Why, what has become of Sally?"

"She is not here any more," said Maris. "And now, Tilford, you can sit down anywhere you like but I have no time to sit down. If you have anything to say, say it quickly. I'm taking this ice right upstairs. My mother is too precious to run any risks of delay."

"Nonsense!" said Tilford. "You probably are exaggerating the whole thing. Your mother is just tired, and will be all right in a few hours. You should get a good servant at once. Two of them, in fact, while you have a nurse in the house. Would you like me to stop at an employment agency and send a couple out?"

"Certainly *not!*" said Maris firmly. "We will look after our own household. Tell me quickly what you want for I've got to go, and I may not be able to come down again for some time."

"Well, really, Maris, I never saw you in a mood like this. I'm sure I hope your mother won't be ill often."

Maris didn't answer. She was working swiftly, gathering up the pieces of ice in a bowl and closing the refrigerator door softly, still sick-room conscious, he perceived. It was evident she meant what she said and would not be there long.

"Well, Maris," he said, more pleasantly, "what about this dress mother wants you to see?"

"Well, what about it?" said Maris still haughtily.

"Why, mother said you promised her to go and see it and try it on."

"No, I didn't promise her, Tilford. She told me about the dress and I told her that I had no need for a wedding dress, that I already had one, and then some people came in and we didn't talk any more. That's all. I have no need for another dress, and if I did I would pick it out myself."

"That's not a nice spirit, Maris. You certainly don't act like yourself this morning. I don't know what has come over you. Whatever was actually said, you are perfectly aware that my mother expressed a wish for you to have that dress and asked that you go and see it at once because she had had it reserved for you. I came this morning to take you down in my car to the shop, because I wanted to save you the trip, and you act this way. Come, get your hat and we will go at once. Slip on another dress, can't you? That one looks a bit like a kitchen rig."

Maris flashed a look at her bridegroom and spoke in low decided tones.

"I cannot possibly go anywhere today, Tilford, even if I wanted to go, which I certainly do not! I have no wish for another wedding dress. When I am married I shall wear the dress my mother made for me, and no other. If people do not like it they can look the other way. But at least until I am married I am the one to say what I shall wear. My mother sewed half the night last night to finish the lovely dress she has made for me, and I certainly shall not wear any other no matter whether it pleases anybody else or not."

Maris was very angry now. She was washing the pieces of ice and lifting them into a clean bowl.

Tilford's face was a study, if she had only had time to see it. Amazement and scorn struggled for the mastery.

"Your mother *made* your wedding dress!" he exclaimed in a tone of horror. "You were going to wear a *homemade* dress to *my wedding!* You were going to do a thing like that to *our family?"*

Maris wheeled and stared at him for a half second in amazement. She had never seen Tilford like this before. His handsome face was almost disfigured with scorn. Then she said crisply:

"Why, yes, I was. You see, I thought it was my wedding, not entirely yours. At least I thought it was *ours,* not your family's. And you have always seemed to rather like my homemade clothes. It didn't occur to me that you or anybody would have anything to say about my wedding dress."

"Well, I am amazed," said the haughty youth. "It seems my mother was entirely right in feeling she ought to do something about this. A homemade dress at a Thorpe wedding!" he repeated. "Really, Maris, you and I will have to have a plain talk. Suppose you take that ice upstairs and come right down and we will settle a few things, here and now. I know of course that you are very much wrought up. You have evidently been working too hard. Your people have no right to let you get so tired when you are to be married so soon. The strain of the festivities is enough without difficulties in your home. But it is time I made a few things quite plain to you that I have been taking for granted you understood."

"You have certainly made a good many things plain to me already," said Maris cryptically, as she rescued the last lump of ice from sliding off the table and plumped it into the bowl with the rest, "but I have no time nor desire to discuss anything more with you this morning. I'm going now."

She opened the back stair door and darted away.

He arose hastily and strode after her calling up the stairs.

"Listen, Maris. Have you sent off those wedding invitations yet? Because this is the last day they should go. If they aren't done suppose you give them to me and I'll take them home. Mother will have her secretary finish them."

But Maris closed the upper stair door quietly and firmly, and when he sought the front stairs and went half way up calling her name cautiously, the white clad nurse came silently out with her finger across her lips and shook her head at him. And though he waited for some minutes Maris did not appear again.

For Maris had other things to think about. Her mother was gasping for breath, and it was apparent that it was going to take swift work to save her life.

Two hours later the worst seemed over, for the present at least. The tired heart had taken up a slow, but dependable beat again, and the mother was sleeping. She had taken a few sips of nourishment, and her hand was lying in her husband's who sat beside her, gray and worn and anxious.

The nurse was putting her domain into immaculate order, report card and pencil, thermometer and medicine on the bedside stand; starched white uniforms hanging in the guest closet in place of the hastily removed wedding garments. The house had assumed a new atmosphere. Merrick had gone to get Sally to return to the kitchen. Gwyneth had gone to the store for the list of necessities her mother had made out before she suddenly dropped out of the day. The strange young man whom her sister had said was their old neighbor Lane Maitland, had disappeared along with the doctor. The nurse was with the patient, the house was very quiet. Maris had just returned from the attic where she had hidden the addressed wedding invitations, boxes and all, wrapped carefully in many thicknesses of tissue paper and stuffed under the eaves behind an old trunk, when the doorbell pealed through the house. She must go and muffle that bell before she did anything else, she thought to herself, as she hastened to answer the ring.

There stood the Thorpe chauffeur with a letter in his hand, addressed in Tilford's handwriting.

She frowned as she looked at it. There was something so assured and almost smug about even his writing. The thought darted through her mind unbidden, and she shut it out again. She must not think things like that about the man she was going to marry, even if he had been disagreeable when she needed sympathy and help. Everybody had faults, and of course Tilford had some little things—. She looked at the chauffeur questioningly.

"Were you to wait for an answer?"

"Yes ma'am I was to wait and see if you had any message."

Maris stepped into the living room and read the letter. It was not long.

> Dear Maris:
>
> Of course I realize that you were overwrought just now and I shall not hold it against you. I would not trouble you again today but that the time is getting short and this matter of the wedding dress is somewhat insistent. My mother feels as I do that we should not let this most suitable garment go, now that we have found it. So I have taken the liberty of having it sent up to your house. I will take care of the

bill myself. Call it a wedding gift if you like. I am told that it is the custom in some oriental lands for the groom to provide the wedding garment. And I am sure when you have seen it you will agree with us that it is most suitable for a formal occasion such as our wedding is to be, and that any mere homemade dress would be entirely out of place.

Let me know if I can help with the invitations. You know they should be mailed not later than this evening. The man will wait to see if you have any message.

Hoping that your mother is now feeling much better and that by tomorrow she will have fully recovered.

Yours as ever,

Affectionately,
Tilford

Maris had just reached the end of the letter when she heard the nurse calling softly, insistently:

"Miss Mayberry, could you come here a minute *quick!* I don't like the way your mother breathes and I want to telephone the doctor at the hospital."

LANE Maitland, as he rode away with the doctor who was going to drop him at a garage where he had left his own car for a slight repair, studied the doctor's grave face awhile before he spoke.

"Is Mrs. Mayberry going to get well, Doctor MacPherson?" he asked quietly.

The doctor gave him a keen glance.

"I'm not sure," he said thoughtfully. "If she pulls through the next day or two she may pick up. But it depends on several things even then. How well do you know the Mayberrys? You used to live next door, didn't you?"

"Yes, five years ago before we went to the west coast. I knew them pretty well. Maris was in my class in high school."

"Yes, I thought so. You and Maris used to play tennis over at the old court by the women's club, didn't you? I thought I remembered. Well, I suppose you've kept in touch with them from time to time, haven't you?"

"Well, not very closely," said Lane. "You know kids don't spend much time writing letters. But they were the first people I wanted to see when I got back. They were real people. Mrs. Mayberry was like a mother to me after my own mother died. She took care of me when I was sick once. I think a lot of her. I went around to the house with Merrick this morning, the first place I've been since I struck the town, just to see Mrs. Mayberry, and we found her lying on the floor in the kitchen. I haven't had a chance to ask any questions yet. I don't know whether she's been ill before, or this is a first attack, or what?"

"I guess it's what," said the doctor speculatively. "The whole trouble is the woman's worn out I think. She's worked too hard, and hasn't stopped to consider herself. To tell you the truth when I came in I thought she was gone. There didn't seem to be any heartbeat at all. But she was coming up wonderfully when I left. Unless there's another set-back she may pull out this time without any serious harm. And then again, the least little thing might blow her out like a candle. I'm not just sure how far her heart is involved. She's been a wonderfully wiry little woman with a lot of nerve and courage. You see, Mr. Mayberry was pretty hard struck by the depression, almost lost his business and his house, but managed to keep on his feet, and now I believe he is weathering it pretty well. But she's stood by him through thick and thin, and done more work than she should, and been up late nights. You knew the daughter, Maris, was making a grand marriage, didn't you?"

"Merrick said something about a wedding as we came in but I didn't quite catch the drift. He seemed to think it had something to do with his mother's condition."

"Yes, I shouldn't wonder. Maris is marrying into swelldom. A big snob, if you ask me. But don't say I said so. Of course he's rich, and painfully good-looking, but she's too nice a little girl to let that count for everything. Oh, I guess he's all right, decent and all that, but acts like he was frozen in the making. Wait till you meet him. However, I wouldn't wonder if it has been rather hard to keep up to the social standards of his set. Not but that the Mayberrys are every bit as good socially, and better, than the Thorpes, only they're not so afraid people won't know it. But I imagine there's been a lot of hard work and worry connected with trying to get ready all the fuss and feathers the Thorpes would expect. That's all. That good little mother is just worn out."

"But you think she could get well?"

"Yes, I think—I *hope* she could. That is, if she pulls through the next few days, she'd have a chance. But—there's more to it than that. She needs a quiet place away from everything that could possibly worry her. A place where she wouldn't hear anything but the clouds going by, and the flowers growing, and a bird or two now and then. If she could have about six months to a year in a place like that, yes, I'd say there was a good chance she might be her old self again and live out a healthy life. But I don't know how they ever could afford a thing like that."

Lane Maitland was still for a whole block, and then he said thoughtfully:

"I know a place like that, and it's standing idle. Let me know if it's needed, will you, Doctor?"

"I certainly will, son. And maybe I'll let you know soon. And then again—I might not get the chance. You can't tell. But I'll not forget."

Lane stopped at his garage and picked up his car. He drove thoughtfully back to the Mayberrys to get Merrick and take him after Sally. But he said nothing to Merrick about his talk with the doctor. He was remembering Maris when she was fourteen with her gold hair like a halo and her eyes shining. He used to carry her books home for her every day from school, that last year before he went away. He wondered why he had never kept up the correspondence with Maris. Only a Christmas card or two, and then they had lost sight of each other!

But something had to be done to help Mother Mayberry get well.

Then suddenly Merrick spoke:

"It's that doggone wedding that's got mother's goat!" he broke forth. "I don't see why Maris doesn't see it."

"What could she do about it if she did?" asked Lane gravely.

"Well, that's just it. It seems that when a girl lets herself think she's in love with a man that's the end of her. She's mesmerized, or something. She has to do just exactly what he tells her to, no matter if the whole family is going to the dogs on account of it."

Lane considered this and then he asked:

"Is Maris in love with this man? Really in love?"

"Oh, Gosh! How should I know? What is love, anyway? Thank goodness I've never been in love yet, but when I see any signs of it in myself I hope I'll have sense enough to consider whether my family that have loved me and slaved for me all my life are going to be alienated by it. It isn't right. It isn't reason."

"No," said Maitland, "it isn't right, but what are you going to do about it? The world has been going on that way pretty much ever since it was made, I guess. Of course people ought to consider, but they don't. It's just a glamour, I suppose, and you can't help yourself. But what's the matter with Maris' man? Isn't he all right?"

"All right? Well, I suppose most folks think he is. I guess he has pretty much that opinion himself, but not me! Oh, how we *don't* love one another! I tell you when this wedding is consummated he and I are going to be the most unloving brothers-in-law that ever were mismated. And I don't mean maybe. And as for my mother and his mother they're about as much alike as a wood thrush and a turkey."

"Not a very pleasant outlook," said Maitland, "but how does your sister reconcile all this?"

"My sister? Oh, she's *crazy!* That's what I say, love makes you crazy. You don't know what you're doing when you get in love. I hope I never get that way. Why, he rushed her, see? Took her out in his limousine. All the girls thinking he's grand just because he has curly eyelashes and a natural permanent wave. He got her a great hog of a diamond, and he's taking her on a trip to Europe for the honeymoon, and she's completely etherized. She doesn't know what it's all about yet. She'll wake up sometime when it's too late, and see what she's done to all of us, and to herself! I only hope our mother doesn't have to die to make her see!"

"She mustn't!" said Lane Maitland. "We mustn't let her! You know I had a kind of a share in her too. She nursed me through typhoid and I'll never forget it."

"So she did, brother. You're one of us. Mother thought a lot of you."

"Well, look here, Merrick, I want you to promise me something. I want you to give me your word of honor that you will let me help just as if I were a real son and brother, will you?"

Merrick gave him a look of appreciation, that held almost a hint of surprise.

"Why, sure, Lane, but I don't see how you could help, just now. Oh, errands, and things like that. Sure, we'll count on you, and love to do it. But—you sort of speak as if you had some inside dope. The doctor didn't say anything leery about mother, did he?"

"He said she was tired out. He said she needed a long rest. And if it comes to that I've got just the place. I want you to promise if she has to go away you'll call on me."

"Sure I will, and don't you be afraid I'll forget it, either. That's great! But here's Sally's house and I imagine we'd better get her back as soon as possible to the kitchen, for there's plenty for her to do there, I guess. Let's hope she's at home."

But just then Sally appeared at her door, curiously peering out to see what car was stopping before her place.

"Oh, there you are, Sally. Can you come along with us right away?" called Merrick. "Mother's been taken very sick, and we need you all kinds."

"Sure I'll come, Mister Merrick! Your ma sick! Now I jes' thought 'twould end up that way. I was so sure I didn't unpack my things much. I'll get my workin' cloes and come right in a little minute."

And true to her word, Sally didn't take long. She was soon out lugging a neat suitcase, and climbing into the back seat of the car.

As they turned into the home street Merrick sighted the limousine standing before the door.

"What the dickens!" he began scowling. "Why does that boob have to barge in on us when he knows we don't want him around?"

And then as the doctor's car shot around the corner and drew up behind the limousine, "Great Scott! Is that the doctor again? I thought he had to be at the hospital all the rest of the morning. He didn't tell you he was coming back, did he? You don't suppose mother's worse, do you? You don't suppose they've sent for him again, do you?" And with a white face Merrick leaned over, opened the door, and was out on the sidewalk before the car had really stopped.

"Easy, boy!" warned Maitland in a low tone. "Remember it's important there be no noise!"

Merrick nodded and flung himself silently across the lawn and in at the door, his heart beating wildly, anxiously.

The doctor was there before him though, and bending over the bed. Maris made way for him and slipped out into the hall.

"Mother wasn't breathing right and the nurse sent for him," she whispered to her brother, her white anxious face showing him that there was still cause for alarm.

Solemnly the sister and brother stood together, breathless, watching what went on in the sick room, grasping one another's hands without realizing it, as their anxiety increased.

The doctor was very grave at first. They could tell by the way he touched the pulse, by his low-toned inquiries to the nurse, by the way he listened to the heart, that this was no light matter. It seemed a long time before the tenseness around the bedside decreased, and fear seemed to be vanquished, sliding out of the room once more. It was almost as if the room itself had drawn a sigh of relief at the respite. Glancing at their father on the other side of the bed, still holding his wife's hand, they could see that the grayness was breaking about his eyes and lips once more, and hope was dawning again on his face. They hardly dared be sure till they heard the doctor's voice in a low murmur to the nurse: "That was a close shave," and saw her nodded response. They welcomed her alert hopeful movements as they watched her putting the medicine glass on the table, and writing something on the report card.

Then, and not till then, they withdrew to the hall window.

"What's the idea of that chauffeur out there?" murmured Merrick resentfully. "Is he waiting for something?"

Then suddenly Maris remembered.

"Oh!" she said, the color coming into her white face, "I forgot! He's waiting for an answer to a note."

"Well, you'd better let me go down and tell him you haven't time to write any answers now, that your mother has been near death's door again. You look fit to go to bed yourself."

"No!" said Maris quickly, "I must write it. You wouldn't understand. It won't take but a minute! Lend me your pencil."

Maris took the pencil and wrote on the back of the crumpled letter.

> Please do not send the dress. I cannot accept it on any condition. If it comes here I shall call the shop and tell them it is a mistake. You do not understand how you have hurt me. Mother is worse. I have no time to write more.
>
> Maris

She slipped it into an envelope and went down to the waiting chauffeur. "I'm sorry to have kept you waiting," she said, "but my mother was taken very sick again. I have had no time to write but a line."

But even as the chauffeur took the note and turned to go, Maris, to her dismay, saw a handsome delivery truck drive up and stop. A man in plum-colored livery with silver buttons got out and came up the walk bearing a mammoth white box tenderly.

Maris with hardening countenance stood and watched him come. She mustn't let him ring that terrible bell again, and she must remember to muffle it as soon as he was gone.

"Are you from Leon Archer's shop?" she asked. "Well, this is a mistake. You'll have to take it back. I just found out that it had been ordered, and was about to call up and tell them not to send it."

"But I was told to leave it here, ma'am!" said the man.

"Yes, but I'm telling you to take it back. I cannot receive it. It was a misunderstanding. I will call the shop immediately and explain."

Reluctantly the man turned with his magnificent box and went back to the truck, and Maris hurried to the kitchen to see what she could do to suppress the bell.

But she found Lane Maitland there ahead of her, perched on the stepladder, working away at the bell, which already showed signs of submission.

"Oh," said Maris with relief, "how did you know what I wanted?"

"Well, you see, I remembered that bell of old. You won't recall it likely, but I was sick in this house once, and I know how that bell used to go through my head when my fever was the worst."

"You're Lane Maitland, aren't you? I haven't had time to recognize you before. Of course I remember. Didn't I play picture puzzles with you when you were getting well? You've been very kind. I don't know how you happen to be here after this long absence, but I'm really grateful."

She gave him a tired little smile, and he grinned back like an old chum.

"That's all right, I'm here, and you can just count on me for anything I can do to help. I'm only too glad to get the chance to pay back some of the kindness I received. Is your mother worse that the doctor came back?"

"She was," said Maris, the trouble starting in her eyes again. "I think she is easier now. The doctor and nurse seem more cheerful. Now I must go back and see if I'm needed."

"Better lie down a bit yourself," advised Maitland. "You look rather all in."

"Perhaps I will after a little."

Then Sally eased in from the maid's room off the kitchen.

"Oh, Sally! I'm so glad you've come!" said Maris, and almost choked with tears as she said it, her relief was so great.

"That's all right, Miss Maris. You just go lay down. I'll ten' to all this," she said with a wave of her hand that included the dishevelled kitchen. "I'll have a meal ready on time. Don't you worry."

"I'll wipe dishes and set the table for you, Sally," said Lane Maitland cheerfully. "It won't be the first time I've helped in this kitchen, will it?"

"Sure, you wiped dishes fer me many a time, an' set tables too. He's a good wukker, Miss Maris. You run along. We'll get along fine!"

So Maris turned and went away, feeling suddenly that she must sit down quickly, or lie down, or she would presently crumple up on the floor the way her mother had done that morning.

She flung herself down on her own bed for a minute, trying to get rid of that whirly feeling and as her head sank into her pillow it seemed that all her troubles rushed over her at once. Mother sick, dear mother! Of course that was the worst. And the possibility that even if she should get well she would be an invalid all her life. How could the family get on without her?

For the moment her own marriage had sunk out of sight. Never once in all her gay bright plans had she considered the possibility of mother out of the picture, and herself away across the water where she couldn't help. Now it suddenly rushed over her as an impossibility to consider any such thing.

Well, she mustn't go on so far in the future. She could dare to live but one day at a time just now, perhaps only one hour. There was no telling what an hour might bring forth.

But there was the question of those invitations, and that dress! She hoped she had settled the dress, but there was no telling. Mrs. Thorpe had a very firm chin and when she wanted a thing she was in the habit of getting it. Would there have to be more battling? For she was determined on one thing. She would wear no other dress for her marriage than the one her precious mother had made. Even if it were not lovely and suitable, she would wear it anyway!

Well, she had done all she could about the dress for the present at least. If the Thorpes didn't like it they could stand it. Of course Tilford would be angry and she would have him to deal with next. She had seen him in a towering rage with other people two or three times, and she did not anticipate the experience. But it didn't matter, did it? Not anything mattered till mother got well. Why did such trifling unimportant matters have to come in and torment her now, when her heart was wrung with anxiety? And there were those invitations. What should she do about them? That all important date which the postmark was supposed to bear was rapidly passing by and could not be recalled. There would be a terrible rumpus among the Thorpes if the day went by without their being mailed. But it was unthinkable that she should invite people to her wedding when her mother lay at death's door! They surely couldn't expect that of her!

Yet, on the other hand, if mother should suddenly get well and the wedding go on as planned—though in her heart she felt this was not in the least likely, hardly possible—if the day had to be changed to please the Thorpes' ideas about when the invitations should go out, that would mean that father would have another awful expense. All those costly invitations engraved over again! Oh, she couldn't do that to father.

Well, and suppose she simply mailed them as had been planned all along, and then they had all to be recalled? Oh, it was too much of a problem for her weary mind to work out. She turned her head on her pillow and let slow tears trickle down her cheeks.

"Oh, God," she suddenly cried in her heart, "show me what to do. Please make it very plain. I don't know how to go on. I know I haven't been living very close to You these last few months. I've done nothing to deserve help. But won't You please straighten things out and bring mother back to us again?"

In the midst of her prayer she became aware of voices, children's voices outside, the boys and little Alexa, coming home from school. Alexa wasn't quite five and was only in kindergarten. Eric and Alec were in grade school. But what were they doing home at this hour? They usually took their lunch and didn't return till two o'clock. Was it a half-holiday?

She sprang up quickly. They mustn't be allowed to make a noise and disturb mother. Would Gwyneth be back from the store yet?

She hurried down and met the children as they were about to enter the house.

"Sh h h!" she said softly. "Mother is sick. You must be very quiet! Come around this outside way to the kitchen and Sally will give you some lunch. Why are you home at this hour?"

"Lexie has a sore throat," said Eric, the ten-year-old. "The teacher sent us home. She said we'd havta have the doctor and see if Lexie has the measles. If she has we can't any of us come back till we see if we get it too."

Maris' heart sank. Measles! More trouble!

"My froat is sore an' I want my muvver!" wailed Alexa with a quivering lip.

"That's all right, darling, sister will take care of you," said Maris, putting her arm around the little girl and drawing her close. "Come on, we'll go up to sister's room. You can get into my nice bed, and have a pretty little nightie on, and some lovely orange juice to drink," coaxed Maris, trying to think how she was to manage this new complication.

"No, I don't want ta go ta your bed. I want ta go ta muvver. I want my muvver!" Her voice had increased to a shrill roar.

Maris gathered the child up in her arms and carried her out through the garden to the hammock under a big tree, and sat down with her in her arms.

"Listen, Lexie," she said soothingly, "muvver dear had a bad fall down on the kitchen floor, and she hurted herself, and we had to send for the doctor. He put her to bed until she gets all mended up. He said she must lie very still and sleep a lot, and we mustn't try to wake her up for anything for awhile, so she would get all well."

The child looked up for a minute with great eyes filled with horror, and her baby lip puckered pitifully. Then she wailed again and two tears rolled down her pink cheeks.

"I want my muvver. I'se got a sore froat!"

"But Lexie, you don't want muvver to be sick a long, long time, do you? You want her to get well quick, don't you? You wouldn't like muvver to be so sick she couldn't ever get up again, would you?"

The child shook her head.

"Well, then, you're going to be a good, good little girl, as brave as a soldier, and let sister take care of you and make you well, till mother can get up again, aren't you?"

A slow reluctant nod.

"But my froat is sore. *Awful!"*

"Well, we'll go right upstairs and get into bed and send for our good Doctor MacPherson. He gives you nice sweet sugar pills, you know, and he'll make you well quick. Come on! Let's see how softly we can get up the stairs so we won't wake muvver."

Little by little she coaxed the child, until she finally yielded with a weak smile and said "Wes" she would be a good girl and not make a noise when sister took her up the stairs. At last Maris landed Lexie in her bed and began to undress the hot little body.

There was no question but Alexa had a fever, and it looked to Maris' inexperienced eyes as if there were some kind of faint rash beginning to appear. Oh, was this also to be added to the burdens? Measles and a wedding! A wedding and a quarantine sign on the door. Oh, what a mess! And what would Tilford say to it all?

Suddenly she began to laugh.

Alexa turned and stared at her in wonder.

"Vat is funny, Maris?" She tried to focus her heavy eyes on her sister who was laughing almost hysterically, though very quietly. It had to be either crying or laughing, and she preferred to laugh.

Suddenly she sobered. She must not let herself go like this. Too much depended upon her just now.

"I was only thinking how funny it was to have measles and a wedding at the same time."

Alexa gave a faint little giggle.

"Can't I be a fower girl?"

"Not if you have the measles."

"Is I got measles, Maris?"

"Well, maybe. We'll have to ask mother's nurse to come and look."

"Has muvver got a nurse? I want ta see her."

"I'll get her in a minute. You lie still and be a good girl."

"Awwright! Myrtle Hayes has gotted measles. She had 'em two days. She wasn't in school. Now I got 'em, mebbe! Isn't that funny?"

"Yes, very funny!" said Maris with a bitter little grin.

"When you got measles you get fowers an' paper dollies sent to you by the class. We sent some to Myrtle Hayes yestidday! Do you 'spose I got measles fum her, makin' her a paper dollie?"

"Oh, no. You have to be with people who have them to get them."

"Well, I was wif her two more yestiddays ago."

"Yes, that was it, likely. Now you lie still till I call the nurse."

Mrs. Mayberry was sleeping nicely and the nurse sitting by with a book. Maris almost envied her. She had no perplexities to settle. She had only to sit there and do her duty as it came to her hour by hour. Oh, of course there were responsibilities, but she was trained to meet them. And there was always the doctor at the end of the telephone to call upon in necessity. While here was she suddenly plunged from having a good time, into every kind of a mix-up, things she knew nothing at all about. As if it wasn't enough to be on the eve of her marriage with all sorts of new problems to deal with, without having her mother, the mainstay of the family taken down so desperately ill, and the baby of the house sick besides! And she had no training for such things, and no one to call upon in her extremity. She was the oldest child. Her father mustn't be more troubled than he was already, or he would break too. And Merrick was so hot-headed he was no help at all. As for Tilford, he had made it all too evident that none of this was his problem. She couldn't consult him, though of course she would have to tell him pretty soon the latest developments. What would Tilford say to a contagious disease? Well, she would soon find out, for there he was coming up the walk, she saw as she passed the window. His car was parked out in front.

But Maris did not run down to meet him. She followed the nurse back to the sick room and let Sally deal with the front door. One burden at once was all she could carry. Tilford would have to wait till she was free.

The nurse came in and examined the little girl. She said it looked like measles to her, but the rash wasn't coming out well. She hinted that it might even be scarlet fever.

"You know there's quite a bit of it around," she said. "Just keep her asleep till the doctor gets here if you can."

But Alexa was restless and wanted her mother, and it was some time before even a story kept her still enough to drop off to sleep.

As soon as Maris was sure the child was sound enough not to cry out and disturb their mother, she hurried down to Tilford. He met her with an angry frown.

"It seems to me, Maris, that you are very inconsiderate," he said as he glanced at his watch vexedly. "I have waited exactly sixteen minutes for you this time. And how long was it this morning? My time is valuable, you know.

Especially so just now when I am planning to be out of the country for at least six months. Hereafter I do wish you would try to come down promptly."

Maris was very tired, and overwhelmingly worried. The tears were very near to the surface and she needed comfort.

"I came as soon as I possibly could," she said trying to keep the tremble out of her voice. "You don't realize what has been going on here."

"Well, I certainly realize enough," he said coldly, sitting on a straight chair opposite the couch where she had dropped down. "I can't quite see how your family can be so inconsiderate to you, at a time like this, with your marriage so close at hand."

"What do you mean?" said Maris sitting very straight and flashing her eyes at him. "Do you think it was inconsiderate of my mother to drop unconscious on the floor while she was preparing to iron some of my pretty things for me? Do you think it was inconsiderate of my little sister to come home very sick from school, with a sore throat and probably a bad case of measles, or perhaps scarlet fever?"

"You don't mean that that has happened too?" said Tilford looking at her accusingly as if somehow it was all her fault.

"The doctor hasn't seen her yet, but the nurse is sure that it is one or the other."

"Well, for heaven's sake, Maris, have you had both of those?"

"I'm sure I don't remember," said Maris wearily, "I guess so. But anyway that doesn't matter. The fact remains that Alexa is very sick, and I've got to go right back to her as soon as possible."

"Not at all, Maris. You must not go near her again. You know even if you did have them when you were a child it is quite possible to get them a second time. I've heard of cases. And it would be simply out of the question to run the risk of you being down with measles on your wedding day, you know. You must telephone for another nurse if the one you have isn't adequate for the situation. I shouldn't think measles was much anyway. She'll probably be running around in a day or two. But you must not run any risks for the wedding."

"Wedding!" said Maris tonelessly. "We can't have a wedding if everybody is sick!"

"Nonsense!" said Tilford with his magnificent air, as if he owned the earth and would brook nobody's interference. "Sickness must not be allowed to interfere! I'm sure your mother isn't selfish enough to want you to put off your wedding just because she might not be able to attend when the day comes. And as for the child, why I can telephone my sister in Chicago to get my little niece ready to be flower girl in Alexa's place."

Maris gave her bridegroom an incredulous look. Was it possible that he was in earnest?

"I wasn't thinking of the ceremony, or the flower girl," she said coldly. "I couldn't think of getting married while my mother was lying at death's door, and my sister was so sick she needed me. You don't realize how sick mother is, or you wouldn't talk that way. Twice today we thought she was dying. The doctor said it was a miracle that she didn't. Do you suppose I could get married and go away across the ocean with my mother sick like that?"

"Well, just what would you propose to do about it?" he asked in a cold haughty voice. "Our reservations are all made for a certain day. We have the finest suite on the ship. I would have to forfeit a good deal of money to give them up now. Also you know that my sailing date is obligatory, as I have business appointments to meet which cannot be delayed. There is no such thing as putting off the wedding, and you'd better understand that at once. And now I think what you had better do is to run up and put a few necessities in a bag and come on home with me. It would be far better for you to stay at our home till the wedding day and then your nerves won't be all upset. Mother will agree with me, I know, and it will give us a chance to get all the arrangements perfected at our leisure."

"Tilford!" gasped Maris horrified. "How could you possibly think I could be spared now? Don't you know I must care for my little sister?"

"That's ridiculous, I tell you. I can get you a child specialist nurse who will handle this case much better than you can. You are just spoiling that child anyway with so much coddling. And I positively must assert my authority and put a stop to this!"

"Authority?" said Maris, and burst into a sudden hysterical giggle. "What authority have you over me?"

"The authority that that ring on your hand gives me," said the young man loftily. "You are as good as my wife now, when you are wearing that!"

"Authority!" repeated Maris slowly again, a kind of scorn creeping into her voice. "I thought it was a pledge of love and tenderness."

"Well, that, too, of course. But it is all based on authority."

"And what love and tenderness do you show when you talk in this way about my beloved family? When you want me to come away from them when they are very sick and need me. When you can suggest that I could possibly plan for a wedding with my mother at death's door!"

"Now, look here, Maris, I thought you were a sensible girl. Suppose all this had happened three weeks later, after we had been married and were half way across the ocean? Would you have insisted that the ship turn back and take you to your precious family?"

Maris caught her breath and stared at the young man

who suddenly seemed an alien, not a lover. Her face was very white. Slowly she rose from the couch and looked at him.

"It *didn't* happen three or four weeks later," she said steadily, "and we are not married yet, remember! I don't know that I ever want to be married if that is the way you feel about it."

There was a gravity in her voice that Tilford had never heard her use to him before.

"Miss Maris, your little sister is crying for you and I can't seem to stop her. I'm afraid she'll waken your mother!" came the low authoritative voice of the nurse.

Maris turned and flew up the stairs.

Tilford gave an exasperated look after her and said to the nurse, "Will you kindly ask her what she did with the wedding invitations? I can't find them where we left them yesterday."

The nurse gave him a calm glance and went upstairs without answering. But no word came from above, and Tilford presently took himself away.

Upstairs Maris was having her hands full trying to quiet the little sufferer and wishing the doctor would hurry. She had no time just now to think about weddings. It seemed to her that all the troubles of the universe had suddenly fallen into her pleasant life, and there was just nothing that could be done to right things. Everything was jumbled up. She didn't even want to think about Tilford. Just the memory of his handsome face turned her sick at heart. What was love anyway? Just a thing for fair weather?

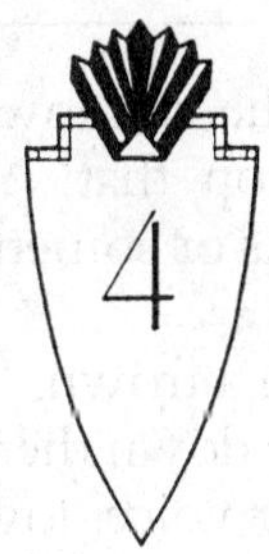

MARIS lay down on the bed beside her small sister, holding the hot little hand in her own, and her heart seemed just about as heavy as a heart could be.

But she talked on, making up a ridiculous story about a canary bird who wore rubber boots and got the measles and had nice orange juice to drink out of a silver spoon, and all the time her sub-conscious mind was aware of the little boys outside playing ball and yelling to each other at the top of their lungs. Oh, dear! She had tried to tell them their mother was sick, but they probably hadn't taken it in. It was good they were on this side of the house and not the other. Her mother perhaps could not hear them.

But then they drew nearer, close to the house, and began shouting some altercation about whether the ball had been out or not, and suddenly bang! bang! bang! came the ball against the wall of her room, close by the window.

The little girl started from her sleep.

"What's that, Maris?" she asked opening startled eyes.

"It's only Eric and Alec throwing their ball against the house." She tried to answer in a sleepy tone. "I'll tell them to stop it."

Then she called from the window:

"Boys! Eric! Alec! Stop that! You'll disturb mother! Can't you get some books or something and keep quiet for a little while?"

"Okay!" said Eric with a frown. "Can't we go down by the pond? All the kids are down there!"

Then she heard another voice, low-modulated, calling:

"Hey, boys! How about coming over and helping me mark the tennis court? Then we'll have a game or two before night."

The boys turned, entranced, and looking down Maris saw Lane Maitland standing on the other side of the hedge that separated the property next door, vacant just now. Why, did the Maitlands still own that place? How nice that was of Lane to help her out! He must have heard her call the boys.

As if he knew her thoughts he lifted his eyes to the window:

"How about that, Maris? Is that all right? I'll keep them the rest of the afternoon if you don't mind."

"Oh, that's kind of you!" she breathed with a relieved smile. "Gwyneth has gone on an errand for the nurse, and Sally has her hands full. I'm afraid I've got a case of measles up here."

"Say, that's tough luck. Have the boys had it?"

Maris shook her head.

"Well, you can count on me for anything you need. I'll handle the boys as long as you say. We might make a quarantine camp of our house if you find it really is measles. Go on back to your hospital and I'll start a detention camp."

He grinned pleasantly and walked off with the two delighted boys. Maris settled down to a few minutes' rest, her mind a tumult of troublesome questions.

But it was not for long. The doctor arrived and things

began to happen. Yes, decidedly, Alexa had the measles, and they were not behaving well either. He took Maris into the playroom at the end of the back hall and told her how serious measles might become if they were not looked after most carefully. He gave most detailed directions, and asked if she wanted him to get another nurse.

"No! Oh, no!" she said, appalled at the thought of the expense that would be to her already over-burdened father. "I want to take care of her myself. She is going to miss mother so. Mother always takes care of her."

The doctor grunted his approbation. This was a girl after his own heart. He had been afraid that she had been spoiled by her rich lover and his family, but she was running true to Mayberry tradition. She was loyal to her family.

"Well, we'd better get the playroom fixed up for her," he said, considering the possibilities. "It's a little farther from your mother's room, and that will give you a comfortable place for yourself. This door opening into the playroom from your room makes it just ideal. And of course you'll have the nurse to consult with in case you have any questions. You couldn't have a better one than Bonny. She's had a lot of experience. Now, don't you worry. We'll pull this little girl through in great shape. It won't be long before we get this rash out. Hard lines, Maris, but you always were a brave little soldier, even the time you had to have that cut on your chin sewed up when you were a kid!"

It was a relief of course to know that Alexa was not in such a serious condition as she had feared, but the immediate future loomed dismal and perplexing before her.

Maris summoned Merrick who had just come in, and stealthily they moved Alexa's little white bed into the playroom tiptoeing as silently up and down the hall as if they had been ghosts, till all was made comfortable for the little invalid. And then the nurse came and helped to get the child into the other bed, warming it carefully with hot blankets and water bottles, and little Alexa opened her heavy eyes and smiled at Maris.

"This is funny, Maris. Sleeping in the playroom!" she said in a weak little voice.

"Yes, isn't it, darling, and you can lie here and look right over to my bed in my room and wave at me in the morning. Won't that be nice?"

"Wes."

"Now, you're going to have some nice hot milk and then you're going to go to sleep again and get well as quickly as you can."

"Are you going to take care of mees, Maris?" she asked anxiously.

"Yes. Won't that be fun, dear? We'll have some lovely times together when you get all better. Paper dollies and stories."

"Wes. I wouldn't want a weal nurse. She's too gwowed-up and starchy. I want you for my nurse, Maris."

"All right, if you'll be a good girl. You must do just what I say, and you mustn't make a noise to make mother worse."

"Okay!" she said sleepily, meekly swallowing the spoonfuls of hot milk and closing her eyes.

Maris tiptoed into her own room to make up her bed afresh, and then dropped down to rest a moment. But Gwyneth opened the door softly and peeked in, and Maris went out to speak with her.

"What am I going to do about school, Maris?" asked the little girl. "Is it really measles?"

"Yes, but you've had them, dear."

"Doesn't make any difference," said Gwyneth sadly, "they won't let me keep on coming to school if I'm living in the house with it. I just telephoned over to Miss Price, and she said, no, I'd have to stay somewhere else if I wanted to keep on coming. And Maris, it's exams in three weeks now, and I'd hate awfully to get left behind and not make my grade."

Maris drew her brows in perplexity. How many problems there were that mother usually settled.

"But where could you stay, dear? You know mother would be terribly worried to have you away from home alone. If only we had a relative near by. But there isn't a soul."

"Couldn't I stay with Erminie Powers? She's only half a block away, and I could telephone every day. You know mother lets me stay all night with Erminie sometimes, and Mrs. Powers is just as particular as mother is."

"Well, but Gwyneth, that's a great deal to ask of anybody, to take in a boarder for two or three weeks."

"I won't have to ask her, she's already asked me," said Gwyneth. "She suggested it just as soon as she heard Lexie had the measles."

"You mean Erminie suggested it. But that's not her mother."

"Oh, but her mother came out to the door just now as I was passing by and said she would love to have me come. She said she counted our mother her very dearest friend, and she would so love to do something to help while mother is sick. She said to tell you she understood just how mother felt and she would take just as good care of me as she did of Erminie."

"Why, that is lovely, Gwynnie. Yes, I guess that would be the best thing for you. I didn't know but you might be needed to run errands here, but you'd be near enough for us to phone you if we needed you. Yes, I guess you'd better plan to do that. Go pack a suitcase, dear, the things you'll need for school, and church, and a couple of pretty dresses for dinner at night. Can you do it yourself, or do you want me to do it?"

"Oh, I'd love to do it," said Gwyneth. "But—Maris,

are you *sure* I wouldn't be needed? I wouldn't like to be away if mother got worse, not even if I failed in my exams."

"Of course not!" said Maris briskly. "We're not going to need you at all, I'm sure. Errands can be done after school, but there ought not to be many of those. And as for mother, of course if mother got worse I'd send for you at once. You don't need to worry about that, dear."

"You think mother is going to get well, don't you, sister?"

"Oh, I think so. I hope so. I'm sure the doctor feels she is getting along—that is, she hasn't had any more bad symptoms for the last three hours."

"Where is daddy?"

"He's in mother's room close by her bed, fast asleep in the big old rocking chair, with her hand in his," said Maris with a tender inflection in her tone, and a sweet look in her eyes.

"Isn't he *dear,* Maris?" said the younger sister. "If I ever get married I'm going to marry a man just like father! I like him a great deal better than these fancy handsome men that are selfish and think their wives have got to do as they say in everything. Daddy always acts as if mother were the most precious thing in the world to him. I never heard him cross with her, or fault-finding!"

There was a conscious little flush on Maris' cheeks, and her eyes were bright with unshed tears as she answered quickly:

"That's right, dear. Father and mother are wonderful with each other."

"Well, there aren't so many," said Gwyneth in a wise tone out of her fourteen years of experience. "I wish you'd see Elizabeth Randall's folks! My! Her father frightens me the way he talks to Elizabeth's mother. That's why I never like to go there when he's home. He always acts as if any of us girls were spiders, or thousand-leggers or something when he finds us there when he comes home. I never go there any more if I can help it, though I love Elizabeth. But she hasn't got a happy home like ours. Her mother always looks awfully sad. I think folks ought to be awfully careful who they marry for the sake of their children, don't you, Maris?"

"I certainly do!" said Maris, her cheeks flaming now, as she stooped and kissed her young sister to hide her own confusion. She wondered as Gwyneth tiptoed off happily to pack for her visit, whether Gwyneth had overheard any of Tilford's lofty rebukes and advice. And it came to her with a pang that there were some serious questions for herself to consider that she hadn't yet thought of in connection with this business of getting married. One couldn't just consider one's own part. There was the future and children to think of. It made life a very grave matter. As soon as mother was out of danger and Lexie on the way to recovery she must take time off and seriously consider her own future and whether she was absolutely *sure*—! But of course it was rather late for that! She glanced down at the blazing diamond on her finger and remembered what Tilford had said it represented.

Of course Tilford was a bit angry. He hadn't really meant that. But yet, there had been a note of seriousness in his voice as if back of all the love and tenderness he was supposed to have for her, the engagement did signify a sort of a business contract, in which he had all the rights, and she would have to submit. Every time she thought of it it troubled her. She must really have a plain tender talk with him and let him know how he had hurt her. He probably had no idea how he had made her feel, or even though he was disappointed and annoyed, he never could have gone quite so far.

Maris looked in on Lexie. She was sleeping nicely, and her head was not quite so hot, perhaps. It almost seemed as if the little hands were more moist. If only that rash would come out fully, and do its work instead of hanging back with that menacing reluctance what a relief it would be!

Maris slipped downstairs and found Sally in her element, preparing an appetizing supper, and making delicacies for the sick that the present state of the invalids would never allow them to eat. Sally would carry on below stairs and there was no need to worry about things there.

Merrick had gone to his father's office on an errand for him, and then to see a man whom he hoped would give him a job for the summer. Merrick would be through with his college freshman year in another two weeks. What a blessing he didn't have to go away anywhere to college, but had chosen one where he could live at home! What would she do without Merrick?

Somehow since morning it seemed as if the whole face of life had been changed for Maris. The family seemed brought back to their close relationships once more, and things were settling into their true values. Was that just since morning? It seemed several weeks as she reviewed the experiences through which she had passed, and today was as far removed from yesterday in all its plans and activities as it could possibly be. Yesterday seemed but a passing dream, and only today was real. Even Tilford and his self-important family did not loom so large. Why had she been so worried about what they thought? She would just go upstairs and lie down a few minutes and put them all out of her thoughts. Then her mind would be clear to know how to solve all her problems.

But just then the buzzer of the telephone, which had been substituted for the bell, burred out and startled her. She answered it, with sudden apprehension in her heart.

"Is that you, Maris?" The voice was a well-modulated one, smooth as butter and honey-sweet, with a neat little tang of authority beneath its honey-flow.

"Yes?" said Maris apprehensively.

"You poor child!" said the voice caressingly. "You certainly are having a terrific time! We have felt it for you all day, and have been talking over ways and means. By the way, I hope your mother is much better by this time, and your mind is relieved?"

"No, Mrs. Thorpe. She isn't any better," said Maris sorrowfully. "I'm afraid the doctor doesn't expect her to be really better very soon. She just isn't any worse this afternoon, and that is an encouragement, of course. It is very kind of you to inquire."

"Oh, not at all. Of course we were much disturbed by the news this morning, but I do trust that your doctor is wrong and she will soon be better. But you have a competent nurse, haven't you?"

"Yes, we have a good nurse," said Maris perfunctorily, wishing this homily would draw to a finish and she could go and rest.

"Well, that's half the battle, of course," said Mrs. Thorpe. "And your little sister? Is it really measles? What a pity! She will be so disappointed not to be in the wedding procession. But a child soon forgets, and I am sure my little granddaughter will be delighted to take her place, so you don't need to worry about that. And now, my dear, Tilford was obliged to go unexpectedly over to the clubhouse to meet a man on business and he asked me to call you up and remind you that you and he had an engagement this evening. I told him I didn't think it would be necessary, you are always so punctilious about your engagements, but I promised I would call. I suppose you remember Tilford's sister Irma is expecting you for dinner this evening at eight, don't you?"

Maris paused aghast! Did they actually expect her to attend another ghastly family dinner when she was in the midst of anxiety and sickness?

Maris took a deep breath and waited a second to steady her voice.

"Yes, I knew we had the engagement," she said slowly,

choosing her words, "but I supposed of course Tilford would make my apologies. I should have called up myself, but every minute has been filled with such anxiety and hard work that it hadn't occurred to me I should have let Irma know. I'm sorry. I hope she'll forgive me, and I'm sure she'll understand. I'll 'phone right away and ask her forgiveness. It was terrible, but of course if she knew the circumstances she wouldn't expect me to come."

"But my dear! You can't get out of a dinner engagement like that! You know that is one thing one has to do if one is alive, to keep a dinner engagement! No, Irma does not know anything about the series of upsets you have been having today. I purposely didn't tell her because I was sure you would see your duty and not cause her embarrassment. Besides, my dear, Tilford and I have arranged everything for you. We have secured a charming young nurse who is a specialist with children, and she will be at your house at five o'clock and take full charge of the little sister until she is well again. And at six o'clock Tilford will be there with the car to bring you and your suitcases, for my child, you are to stay with us until the wedding! We felt that it was imperative that you have your rest beforehand. We don't want a washed-out looking bride. Of course you can run down and see your mother every day or two if you feel that is necessary, and for the rest I shall take charge of you, and see that you live a normal unhurried care-free life. Besides, my dear, you must realize that there are a number of showers and parties that you are expected to attend during the next three weeks, affairs that are made for *you,* and are dependent on your presence for their success. Your friends and Tilford's have gone to a great deal of trouble and expense to show you their love and appreciation, and it would be the rudest thing possible for you to utterly spoil their parties now when it is too late to recall them. Besides, it can't possibly do your mother any good for you to mope in the house until she is well.

I'm sure that if she is not utterly selfish and were consulted she would say that I am entirely right.

"So we are arranging for you to be here during the next strenuous weeks until the wedding is over, and then your coming and going need not affect the patients in the house. So, my dear, run along and get packed, for the nurse will be there soon, and Tilford doesn't want to be kept waiting tonight, he says."

Maris was so still for a long moment that Mrs. Thorpe thought she must have hung up, or that something was wrong with the instrument. She began to jiggle the receiver up and down. Maris was so angry she could hardly trust herself to speak. She shut her eyes and leaned her head against the telephone. This was a crucial moment, and she dare not trust her overwrought feelings. Then she spoke:

"I suppose that you are trying to be kind to me, Mrs. Thorpe, and I should perhaps thank you for thinking of me, but what you have suggested is quite out of the question. We do not want another nurse, and if she comes I shall only have to send her away, so if she has not already started kindly tell her not to come. And as for your other suggestion, that I come to your house and stay, even for only the evening, it is quite impossible. Unfortunately for your plans I love my mother, and my little sister, and I would not be willing to be away from them in this time of trouble and anxiety. I could not, even for the sake of social etiquette, be willing to attend a party of any kind when my mother is lying at the point of death, and my whole family need me as they have never needed me before. I should think that anyone with any heart at all would know this and understand perfectly. My friends all would, and would not expect me to come. But if there are any who do not, I do not care. I shall go out no more till my mother is better, and I am not needed here. I will immediately call up the people who have invited me and inform them of the situation. And please do not trouble any further to make plans for me. You apparently do not understand my situation in the least."

"Oh, *really?*" said Mrs. Thorpe. "I should say you were an ungrateful girl. A headstrong little spitfire! Well, I have done my best to help you through a trying situation. I told Tilford he would better tell you himself, but he seemed to think I could handle the situation more delicately. I see he was wrong. Well, he will probably be around to explain himself how hard we have tried to fix things for you. Good afternoon!" and Mrs. Thorpe hung up.

When Maris turned away from the telephone she was trembling with indignation. The idea of expecting her to go out to dinner when her mother was so sick! Well, of course she should have remembered to telephone Irma. She would do it at once.

So she looked up the number and fortunately got her future haughty sister-in-law without trouble. She explained!

"I'm just as sorry as I can be that I didn't call you sooner, Irma, to let you know that I can't come to your dinner tonight," she said humbly, "but I supposed of course Tilford would tell you all about our trouble here. And to tell you the truth I have been so frightened all day, and so hurried and burdened that everything else was driven out of my head. I do hope you will forgive me for not sending you word at once. My mother is at the point of death and I cannot be away from the house."

"Oh, *really?*" said Irma coldly. "And what am *I* supposed to do? I invite my friends to meet my future sister-in-law and she stays away! Surely you won't put me in that position. You certainly can get away for a few hours, can't you? Aren't there enough in your family to look out for your mother? And there are such things as doctors and nurses. Surely her life is not dependent upon you. And nobody who will be here knows your mother, anyway."

"Oh, Irma!" said Maris aghast at such a cold-blooded attitude. "Would you go out to a dinner party when your mother might be dying?"

"I'm sure I hope I'd do my duty!"

It was very still on the line. If anybody was listening in they certainly didn't dare to breathe. Then Maris said quite calmly:

"Well, I'm doing my duty, and I'll *not* be at the dinner. I'm sorry!" And she hung up.

As Maris turned away again from the telephone there were angry tears in her eyes. She felt outraged that Tilford's relatives were insisting upon her attendance upon all festivities when she was in great anxiety. It seemed fairly inhuman. Just to save themselves embarrassment!

Suddenly she saw it all. They were ashamed of an alliance with plain people like the Mayberrys who didn't live on the Hill, nor own an estate, nor ride in a limousine. They didn't want to explain who was the mother of their son's fiancée. They wouldn't own that they felt that way of course, for they knew the Mayberrys were an old fine family, even if they hadn't much money. But it became just as plain as day to her that they intended, just as soon as the wedding was over, to separate her from her own people, and ignore those people entirely.They meant she should be absorbed into their family, and become a Thorpe!

All at once a great wave of hate for them all came over her so that she was quite startled and amazed at herself. She had never knowingly hated anybody in her life before. Tears of helpless rage poured into her eyes and down her face.

The telephone was in a little hall closet which Merrick had fitted up with a light overhead, a shelf for the instrument and a single pane of glass in the panel of the door.

As Maris came out she was aware of a shadow falling

across the hall floor from outside the door, and as she brushed the tears away from her eyes the shadow moved and became a man standing at the front door just outside the screen.

He was tapping gently on the door with the tips of his fingers. It was Lane Maitland.

"I didn't want to ring the bell lest I would disturb the invalids," he explained in a very low tone. "I just stepped over to say that the detention camp is in full action and the crew seem very well pleased with arrangements. They are scrubbing up for supper now, and sent me over to say that they will stay there till further orders from you. I'm detailed to tell Merrick to bring over a duffel bag with night things and tooth brushes and so on. Will the arrangement please your honor?"

He was smiling and utterly ignoring the tears on her face which she knew he could not help but see, and in spite of herself she smiled back.

"Don't tell me those boys thought of tooth brushes themselves!" she said with a hysterical giggle, openly digging her knuckles into her eyes to stop the flow of tears.

"Well, perhaps they didn't just go into the details," grinned Maitland, and suddenly became grave.

"The patients aren't any worse, are they?" he asked anxiously, taking obvious notice of her weeping now, which his kind tone only seemed to make uncontrollable.

"No," she said shaking her head and flipping away those unmanageable tears with the tips of her fingers, "not that I know of. It's not any worse than it was, I guess. But—well—I guess I'm just plain mad!" She gave a little hurt laugh. "I've been talking with some people who don't understand! Who *won't* understand! Who only think of themselves!"

"There are lots like that, aren't there?" he agreed. "And it's maddening. But when I get like that I like to remember what my mother used to say, that she was so glad God had said vengeance was *His* and *He* would repay where it was needed, and we didn't have to do a thing about it! *'Therefore,* if thine enemy hunger, feed him.'"

She looked at him for a minute and her face changed.

"I never thought of it like that," she said humbly. "I never realized that God would care about what people did to me. I thought I was all alone in it. But it would help a lot to realize He does, and He'll do the getting even if there's any getting even to be done."

A light came into Maitland's eyes, a light of satisfaction, as if she had measured up to what he had hoped.

"Yes, it takes the responsibility off us, doesn't it? I kind of hoped you'd feel that way. And now, is there anything I could do?"

"You've done a lot," she said earnestly. "You don't know how you've helped me. It's wonderful to know the boys are safe, and there's a chance they may not get the measles. But I'm afraid they'll be an awful nuisance to you."

"Not a bit of it. We're getting along fine. They're great kids and I like 'em. We're going to have the time of our lives. And now, I've had the telephone put in and you can call me any time you like, day or night. I've nothing else to do for the next few days but hang around here, and I'm glad to have such congenial company."

"I can't thank you enough!" said Maris earnestly, and impulsively she put out her hand. He took it in a quick hearty grasp, smiling, and was gone.

Maris started upstairs suddenly comforted. After all, if things went wrong, God could somehow set them right. She couldn't, not even with all the apologies in the universe. Then she bethought herself of several invitations for the near future that ought to be cancelled at once, and turning back went again to the telephone. She called up several numbers, telling her friends that her mother had been taken very ill and she would have to cancel all engagements for the present. Some of them were kindly and filled with dismay, and some of them were not at home and she had to leave a message with a servant,but she felt relieved when it was done.

Upstairs in her room at last she heard Lexie moaning and went to see if she could do anything to help her.

Then the clock downstairs struck six in soft silvery chimes, and almost on the dot Maris heard Tilford's car drive up and stop before the house. *Now what?* Her heart gave a frightened beat, and then she remembered.

"Oh, God, you're going to take charge!" she breathed as she heard Sally coming to her door.

AS Maris passed by her mirror she saw that her hair was all awry, and there were dark circles under her eyes in a white, white face. Tilford would tell her about it at once probably, but it didn't matter.

Out in the hall she met the nurse with a hot water bottle in her hand.

"Your father's feet are so cold," she explained in a whisper. "I'm afraid he's getting a nervous chill. You know he didn't eat anything at lunch time. I've tried to persuade him to go in another room and lie down, but he won't. I wonder if you could ask the maid to bring him up a cup of coffee. I want to get him warmed up. He oughtn't to be chilly this way."

"I will," said Maris. "Is mother all right?"

"Well, she's not all right by any means, but she hasn't had any more of those sinking spells since the doctor was here."

With a heavy heart Maris went on her way down the back stairs to give the order to Sally, and then into the living room where a frowning lover waited.

"You're not ready!" he announced in displeasure as she came in wearily trying to smile at him.

"Why, didn't your mother tell you I couldn't possibly come with you?"

"I haven't seen mother since I left the house just after lunch. I told her to remind you of our engagement and to say that you must be ready when I came for you. How long will it take you? Is your suitcase packed? I can wait exactly five minutes and no more. A man is calling me on long distance from Chicago and I must be at home when the call comes in."

"Well, you needn't wait, Tilford. I can't possibly come. I have called your sister and explained."

"That is unpardonable!" he said looking at her with a glitter of scorn in his eyes. "I'm afraid I shall have to insist. I shall have to exercise my authority. This isn't an ordinary dinner engagement. This is my sister's dinner to introduce you to our friends. It is very important. I cannot allow you to disregard it."

"Authority? Allow?" said Maris lifting puzzled eyes to his stony offended countenance.

"You are wearing my ring," he said significantly. "I told you this morning what I felt that means. Your mother has lasted all day. She will doubtless last a few hours longer without your help. I cannot allow you to confuse our wedding preparations this way for mere sentiment. I thought you had more strength of character than that!"

Maris stared at him for an instant longer and then she looked down at her ring as if she had never been acquainted with it before.

Slowly she put up her other hand and took the ring off holding it out to him.

"You had better take it back then. I could not wear a ring under those conditions." Her voice was very firm and very sad.

But he did not take the ring.

"You are beside yourself!" he said in tones like icicles. "You do not know what you are doing. I did not know you had such a temper. Put on that ring and stop acting like a child! You said you were never going to take it off when I put it on, and now look! Put it on quickly or you will drop it on the floor. It is too valuable a stone to be play-acting with. Don't for heaven's sake try to get your own way by being dramatic. It won't go down with me!"

Maris suddenly reached out and pushed the ring within his clasp and turning fairly flew up the stairs. Her face was ghastly white and her head was whirling, but she did not forget to go softly, and to the listening angry man below it seemed almost as if she had melted into mist, so silently she disappeared.

He stood for a minute looking down at the great lovely stone in its perfect setting, catching the evening sunlight that fell through the door, reflecting sharp bright lights in a prism of color. Then his anger rose still hotter. To think she would dare play with as costly a stone as that! To expect she could conquer him, Tilford Thorpe, when he had once given forth his mandate! And he had thought her so gentle! So pliable! So easy to mold!

Almost he started up the stairs after her! Then he thought better of that! That was doubtless what she wanted. She was likely in hysterics now, expecting him to find his way to her and yield to her wishes. But that was not the way to begin with her. Let her see what she had done! Let her go through the night without that wonderful ring! Let her know humiliation and shame and understand what a dreadful thing it was to stand out against him!

So he tucked the ring into his pocket and whirled on his heel, going out the screen door, which would have slammed if Maitland hadn't taken care that very noon to put a tiny pad of cotton in the spot where it would have slammed. He went out to his car and started it with far more noise than he needed. Let her hear that she had sent him away from her! Let her understand how final had been her act! Let her have time to fully realize what an awful, what an irreparable thing she had done in offending the whole mighty Thorpe connection! Let her think that it was all over forever between them. It would do her good. He wouldn't be in a hurry to make it up either. She would have to come crawling after him, and ask forgiveness, too. It wasn't for him to yield. He drove furiously away from her thinking his mad thoughts.

And up in her own room Maris knelt by the window over in the corner where Lexie couldn't see her from the bed, where no one would see her if they opened the door to call her; where only God could see her. And she said quietly in words that only God could hear: "Dear God, were You taking charge? Was that what You wanted me to do?"

And then quite simply she clasped her hands that were empty of her lovely ring and felt entirely naked and helpless, and was suddenly conscious of a great peace. God was taking charge, and it must have been what He willed, for there had been nothing else to do. She could not go away and make merry and leave her dear ones who needed her. And she could not wear Tilford's ring under those conditions!

Then she heard Merrick's hushed footsteps coming to her door and she arose quite calmly to meet him, stepping out in the hall and talking in low tones. Her brother's eyes searched her face.

"You all right, Maris?" he asked with an unwonted tenderness in his tone.

"All right, brother!"

"Where's Gwyn? I can't find her anywhere."

"I let her go over to Erminie's to stay a few days. You know they won't let her come back to school if she stays here, even though she has had the measles. Don't you think that was all right? She oughtn't to stay out of school. She'll only be worrying if she stays here."

"Sure that was all right. But what about the boys? They'll get it, I suppose."

"Maybe not. Lane Maitland has taken them over to his house to stay awhile. They're charmed. You're to take over a bag with some things for them. I was going to suggest that you stay there too, but I guess maybe we might need you here if anything happens in the night. Father isn't so well. The nurse said he was having a nervous chill."

"Say, that's awful!" said Merrick. "No, I'll stay here. Maybe I'd better go look at dad. Where is he?"

"Close by mother. The nurse says he won't leave her."

They went softly to the door, and looked in. It was very quiet in the shadowed room. The nurse was running the water in the bathroom. Their mother lay as quiet as she had been all day, and sometimes it seemed as if she were scarcely breathing. Her eyes were closed. The children's hearts contracted, and Maris could hardly keep from crying out in her agony as she recalled her brother's words that morning: "It's that fool wedding!" Was she the cause of her mother's sudden illness? Oh, she was, she knew she must be! Could she ever, ever forgive herself? If mother should die how could they ever go on living?

Merrick went softly over by his father and laid his hand on his head, startled to feel it hot and feverish.

His father looked up and tried to smile sadly.

Merrick stopped and whispered in his ear:

"It's all right, dad. Mr. Matthews says he'll extend the note. You needn't worry!"

A look of relief passed over the drawn worn features of the father and he drew a deep breath of a sigh.

Merrick slipped out softly and came back presently with a folding cot, and then again with a soft mattress.

The nurse came in with sheets and pillows.

"Now, Mr. Mayberry, you're going to lie down on this cot, close by your wife and then you'll be able to hear her if she stirs and wants anything," she whispered to him.

Maris saw Merrick bring their father's bathrobe and help him off with his coat, and then make him lie down, with another great sigh of relief. Then she hurried back to her own patient. Poor father! He had been worrying about something. A note that had to be extended? What was that? Had father been so hard put to it that he had had to borrow money to pay for her wedding? Oh, how had she been so blind? And she had been so thrilled and so involved in all the intriguing gaiety that Tilford had produced from day to day that she had not noticed! Was it possible that God had to send all these startling anxieties to bring her to her senses?

It was not quite time for Lexie's medicine yet. She seemed to be still sleeping. Maris dropped down on her bed for a moment and let these enlightening facts roll over her tired soul in a great condemning flood.

Then she began to go back and think it out. What a dear family she had always had! How they had always done everything together, and enjoyed it. Even being poor together! There was the year when father had thought that he was going to lose the house because he had had to let the interest on the mortgage lapse. How desperately they had all saved and planned, and tried to make a bit of money here and there to help. Even the children. She recalled Gwyneth at five years going into the woods with some children and bringing home quantities of spring beauties and hepaticas which she had tied in funny little bunches and taken out on the street and actually sold, for a penny a bunch! She could see their father's face now, when she had brought her entire fortune of eleven cents to him radiantly, and told him it was to pay the mortgage off. Such tears and tenderness and love! How their interests had all been one, and how the disasters and troubles had only served to make them love one another more! And now, somehow, she seemed to have drifted away from them all. It was as if she were an alien among them, going her own way, or rather Tilford's way, and having all her interests and pleasures in another world, a world they did not know. Why, she seldom had time to tell any of them any more what she was doing.

She recalled how she used always to come in no matter how late it was, when she had been out for the evening and tell her mother everything she had been doing. And always the whole family took such an interest in her comings and goings. But of late there had seemed to be almost a spirit of resentment whenever she spoke of where she had been or what she had been doing. Was it always like that when children got married? Did all the rest resent it? Did they lose each other forever and ever? A sudden great sob swelled in her throat and threatened to overwhelm her. Was this what being married to Tilford would mean? That she would no more belong to her precious family? That they would have no right to know of her affairs? Oh, she couldn't stand that! It wasn't right. It surely couldn't be the way God had planned life for a universe, to have those who married suddenly cut off entirely from everything that had always been precious. Why, her parents didn't know right now what she had been going through with the Thorpes. She didn't want them to know. It would hurt them terribly.

Or did they know? Was it possible that mother and father with their fine intuitions had sensed it? And could that be part of what had made mother sick? Dear sensitive mother! Oh, what was she going to do about it? And the wedding was only a few days off!

And then as if inanimate objects had become alive they trooped into her room and formed a procession in the darkness, stopping one after another for her consideration.

First came those wedding invitations, as if they had somehow escaped their wrapping in the attic and slid out of their white boxes and filed down two abreast to stand before her, condemning her. The very date of the wedding stood out in flaming letters across her vision, as if they would say: "We are now a day late! And tomorrow will be another day later! And the Thorpes are going to be horrified! What are you going to do about it? Are you going to let us be disgraced forever? Are we to be even more disgraced than we are already?"

Well, and what was she going to do? She had no one to ask. Her mother had passed beyond the consideration of any earthly trouble for the present. Her father was too worried and too much on the verge of illness himself to be consulted. If she dared to speak to Merrick about it his wrath would rise to unspeakable heights. There was no one but God to talk to about it. It must be decided tonight. She had to think it through somehow.

She drew a deep breath of protest and waved the invitations aside for the moment. She had to get Lexie settled for the night first before she took that up. But as she turned to meet the next perplexity in the procession she had the consciousness of those invitations standing just at her right hand sternly awaiting her first moment of leisure.

And next there floated softly up her lovely filmy wedding dress that mother had made, and looked at her with reproachful eyes, sadly, as if it had been set aside. As if it would say, "What are you going to do about me? Those Thorpes will despise me and scorn me if you insist on wearing me! Do you want to subject me to their criticism? You know they won't own I am lovely. They likely haven't the fineness to appreciate why I am better for your purpose."

And behind in the shadows, came a stiff white satin frock rustling arrogantly up beside the other. Though Maris had never seen it, nor even heard its description, she recognized it as the Thorpe dress from the exclusive shop, and it stood there beside her mother's charming creation of loveliness, and claimed precedence.

Just behind the two she sighted a host of dinners and showers and theater parties, and other affairs that she knew were booked for the coming days, and now were standing a-tiptoe for her attention.

And over it all she seemed to see her mother's troubled eyes looking at her. Oh, what was she to do, and however did she get involved in all this trouble?

And then she heard a tap at the door and rose to answer it, quick apprehension in her breast. Oh, was mother worse? Oh, mother mustn't die now, not before she had a chance to tell her how sorry she was that she had been so indifferent, and selfish. Oh, not before she had a chance to undo the hurts and get the troubles straightened out.

She opened the door and there stood Merrick, his eyes standing out in his white face startlingly, his lips quivering with angry excitement, and by his side Gwyneth, softly sobbing into the skirt of her little pink dimity that was all crumpled and pitiful and showed her brief petticoat, making her look such a child.

Merrick was grasping her shoulder furiously, clutching it as if he had a prisoner who must be put in chains at once, a gang leader at least.

"Where do you think I found this kid!" said Merrick excitedly. "Just guess where! This child not yet out of grammar school? Down at the drugstore, sitting at a little round table eating ice cream with one of the worst young bums this town affords!"

He gave Gwyneth's small shoulder another fierce shake, and she began to sob louder.

"Hush!" said Maris quickly. "You'll disturb mother! You'll wake Lexie. Come down in the living room where no one can hear you. You mustn't make a noise up here! You'll frighten mother. You might kill her!"

There came an instant's hush in the hostilities as the dire possibilities confronted the brother and sister, and the three of them trooped silently down the stairs to the far end of the living room, where Gwyneth curled herself into the corner of the big sofa with her head in a pillow and sobbed silently.

"Now," said Maris turning to her brother, "what do you mean, Merrick? Where did you find Gwynnie? I let her go over to Erminie's for the night, you know."

"Well, but she wasn't over at Erminie's. Erminie was there too, with another boy. They were out with the boys, if you please, as if they'd been grown up! And the worst young bums you can find anywhere. Rance Mosher! What do you think of that? His father had to bail him out of jail last week. He was arrested for running over a woman when he was drunk! Only seventeen, but he's got his name up in connection with several terrible affairs up at the 'Dark of the Moon' road house. And he was treating our sister to ice cream, sitting shoulder to shoulder with her down at the drugstore, trying to kiss her and hold her hand! My little sister, out in the public eye that way! The worst bum in the town!"

"He's just Erminie's cousin!" wailed Gwyneth, "and Erminie's mother said we might go with him and Harlan Wescott and get some ice cream! And he wasn't kissing me. He was only kidding!"

"I guess I can tell when a fella is trying to kiss a girl. I guess I could see what he had in his mind. Right out in a public place bringing my sister into disgrace! She's nothing but a child, Maris, and Harlan Wescott and Rance Mosher are a long way on in what our father and mother would call crime, and I'm not kidding! I know what I'm talking about! The nurse sent me after a prescription and while I was waiting for it, I turned around and saw my sister—!"

"Not so loud, Merrick, please," said Maris looking at him with troubled eyes.

"Well, it's a serious matter!" said the boy angrily.

"Yes, I know, but we mustn't let mother hear. Now, Gwyneth, tell me all about it. How did you happen to be there? You told me that Mrs. Howard never let Erminie go out evenings. That was why I was willing for you to stay over there. You knew mother wouldn't want you to be going out with big boys in the evening."

"Well, but Maris, it was just to the drugstore and it was only Erminie's cousin and his friend. And there wasn't any dessert for dinner, cause the maid was out, and we were hot and thirsty and—"

"Do you mean that Mrs. Howard *told* you to go? Did she say it to you, Gwyneth?"

"Why, no, it was Erminie who went upstairs and asked her."

"Did you hear her ask her?"

"No, I was downstairs talking to the boys, but she came down and said her mother said it was all right to go anywhere the boys wanted to take us, and they were going to take us afterwards to the movies. They said it was a swell picture, and we ought to see it!" Gwyneth burst into tears again at thought of her humiliation and loss.

"Well, I wouldn't be so sure Mrs. Howard knows anything about it, Gwyneth. I never did trust Erminie. But whether she said so or not, I'm sure mother wouldn't approve. And as for going to the movies with boys, you know she wouldn't like that. I think if Merrick will run over to Howards' and get your suitcase we'll just bring this visit to a close."

"Sure I will," said Merrick.

"Oh, *Maris!*" Gwyneth began to cry again, with heartrending sobs. "Then I can't go to school, and I'll not get promoted!"

Maris sat down beside her on the sofa and gathered her resisting young form into her arms.

"Listen, little sister, you mustn't cry so loud. You don't want to kill dear mother, do you? And we'll talk about the school afterwards. It is more important to take good care of you than to have you pass your examinations."

"But I was being taken perfectly good care of," she argued. "I wasn't really sure I was going to the movies, only they told me it would be something I ought to see. And Rance Mosher is a perfectly nice boy. He was awfully polite to me. He said I had nice eyes and he liked me, and he treated me just as if I'd been a lady. Merrick just doesn't like him, that's all. He was always fighting him when they were in school. Erminie says it's because Merrick stole Rance's girl once—"

"Look here, Gwynnie, you're talking about something you don't understand in the least," said Merrick severely. "I never stole Rance's girl. I didn't like her and didn't want her. But the girl came and asked me to take her home from the senior party because Rance was so drunk she was afraid of him, if you want to know the truth! And I know a lot of things about Rance that I'd be ashamed to tell you. If you knew all I know about him, all I've *seen,* myself, you would run from him worse than you would from a rattlesnake."

Gwyneth went into another fit of sobbing then, and Maris signed to Merrick to go after the suitcase and explain to Mrs. Howard that they needed Gwyneth at home.

"But I'm the head of my class, Maris! I'll l-l-lose my s-s-standing in s-s-school!" wailed the little girl.

"It's a great deal better to lose your standing in school than to lose your standing at home, and in the town, and—" she hesitated at the word that came to her lips, and then finished, almost in awe at herself—"and before *God!"*

The child lifted her wet eyes wonderingly.

"What do you mean, Maris? How could I lose my

standing at home or in the town, or even before God by eating ice cream in the drug store?"

"You could lose your standing at home by not keeping your word about staying in the house when you knew what mother and father would feel about your running around the streets at night after dark with older boys, even if they were Erminie's cousins! You could lose your standing in the town by letting yourself be associated even for a little while with boys who do not have a good reputation. You can lose a reputation very easily, but it's not so easy to get it back again. And then, Gwynnie, there are other things. I would rather mother told you about them, as she once told me when I was a little older than you, but it is never good for little girls to run around with boys much older than they are. It isn't natural, unless they belong to you. Lots of harmful things grow out of such friendships. I haven't time to tell you about them tonight. I'm very tired and so are you. But it's better for you to stay at home. I've been needing you ever since you went away."

"But—my s-school!" began Gwyneth again.

"We'll talk about the school tomorrow and see if anything can be done about it. In the meantime go to bed, and let's wait till another day."

But it was some time before she got the child quieted down and in bed, and even after she was asleep from sheer exhaustion, Maris found her catching her breath now and then in another sob.

The plot thickened. Problems on every hand. Gwyneth was another! And little Lexie, tossing and turning and crying out in delirium was the next one. Would the doctor never come?

Very late that night after the doctor's visit, when she had made the little girl as comfortable as possible, and stood watching the nurse and the doctor in a grave talk down the hall, of which she could make nothing, she crept to her bed, too weary to try to think. As she sank away into a restless sleep it seemed to her that all about her room were standing those problems. The wedding invitations slithering across the floor in a white heap as if they had done their best to attract her attention, the two dresses like ghosts of enemies in opposite corners, the shadowy parties grouped here and there about the room, and in the midst of them all, stalking in as she dropped from consciousness, stood Tilford and his mother watching her with angry questioning eyes.

OVER at the old Maitland place matters were moving along at a very satisfactory pace for the little boys who were temporarily parked there.

"Well, boys, we've received our orders from headquarters and now we've got to get to work," said Lane Maitland as he came back from his brief interview with Maris. "There are two more beds to be put in shape before dark, and the commissary department has got to rustle some food for supper. Tomorrow our old cook and her husband are arriving and we'll have more leisure then for amusement, but tonight we've got to get busy. How about jumping in the car and going down to the store with me? I need to lay in a supply of good things. What do you like best to eat?"

"Ice cream!" said Alec promptly.

"Aw, shucks! You can eat ice cream any time if you get a nickel. How about hot dogs and cook 'em out doors? That's more like camping."

"Well, how about both?" said Lane.

"Okay!" shouted both boys at once.

"Or how about strawberries? Does anybody like strawberries?"

"We sure do!" shouted Alec.

"Well, there used to be strawberries down in the garden. Let's go see if they have been choked out by weeds. There might be a few, you know, and then we could save the ice cream till tomorrow."

So they tramped down to the old overgrown garden and discovered a few late berries here and there, tasting more like wild ones than the old rare varieties that used to be cultivated in the years when the Maitlands were living there. The host went into the house and brought out a dish, and eager young fingers managed to fill a bowl in spite of the many surreptitious journeys they made to eager young mouths.

"Pretty nice work, old man," said Maitland when Alec brought him the bowl. "All right, now we have our dessert, we'll go down to the store and get our supplies. We'll need soap, and bread, and marshmallows to toast, and bacon for breakfast, and eggs. You like bacon and eggs, don't you, boys? And cream on your strawberries?"

"Oh, sure!"

"And toasted marshmallows?"

"I should say! Oh boy! This is going to be great!"

"Sure! We're going to have the time of our life!"

"We sure are!" said Eric.

"Oh, boy, don't I wish our new brother-in-law was going to be like you!" said Alec wistfully. "Then I wouldn't mind Maris getting married so much."

"Oh, do you mind her getting married?" asked the young man busying himself about putting the strawberries in the window where they would be cool.

"Why, sure we mind. Wouldn't you?" said Eric with a frown. "Wouldn't you mind having your best sister taken away from you entirely?"

"Oh, maybe it won't be like that," said Maitland, trying

to be matter-of-fact. "Maybe your new brother-in-law will be great. Perhaps you don't know him. Wait till you know him," he added hopefully.

"Who, Tilford? Not he!" sighed Eric hopelessly. "He's a snob. He's some swell! He can't take a joke, nor see one. He hates boys, and anyway we never would get to know him. He doesn't like us. He always acts as if we didn't exist."

"Well, let's forget it for tonight and have a good time, what do you say?"

"Okay!" said the boys, and they climbed eagerly into the car and were off to the store. And how they did enjoy going around the store picking out things they thought might be needed.

They made a fire out in the back yard, and cooked their sausages, made some cocoa there too, and when they had eaten their strawberries with plenty of cream and sugar they were really too full to hold another crumb of anything.

"And now," said Maitland cheerfully, "we'll wash up the dishes and go up and get our beds in order. After that it will be time to turn in."

"So soon?" said the boys who hated to lose a minute of this grand picnic.

"Oh, people always go to bed early when they are at camp. It's one of the rules, you know."

So they submitted and hurried back and forth to the house, bringing supplies and dishes and washing up.

Merrick came over with a suitcase of garments while they were making their beds, and grinned as they both tried to talk at once telling him about their supper out of doors.

"That's all right, kids, but if I hear of you making any trouble over here I'll come over and lam you one you won't forget, and I don't mean maybe."

They promised good behavior and dived into the suitcase arraying themselves for the night.

Merrick reported that there was little or no change in the sick ones, and looked gravely troubled as he said it, and when he was gone Maitland ordered lights out and everybody kneeling for prayers. He suggested that they pray for their mother and little sister. And the suddenly serious boys knelt and were very quiet for a long minute, beside their cots, till Maitland's voice broke in upon their devotions:

"Dear Lord, we want to thank You for being with us all day, and keeping guard over us and those we love. Keep guard over us during the night, both here and at the home house, and especially be with the sick ones. If it's Your will make them better in the morning. And help these boys to be strong and courageous, and to conquer themselves so that they will be ready to help in this time of stress. Teach them to trust themselves to Thee. We ask it in Christ's name."

Subdued and quiet they got into bed, and it was all still about them. They lay for awhile thinking of their mother, and the terrible possibilities that life held, life that had been so bright and engaging before this. They realized that God had bent down and was taking account of them, that they were, perhaps, in His eye more than they had thought. It was barely possible that He expected something of even them—just boys. They hadn't thought of that before.

But long after they fell asleep Lane Maitland lay across the room from them and thought of the girl in the next house who was bearing so many burdens just now. The girl he used to know so well, and who had grown even more lovely than she had been when they were in school together!

He thought of what the little boys had said about her fiancé. Was that just children's chatter? Was the man her equal? Was he worthy of so lovely a girl? He sighed as he thought about it. Well, it was not for him to think about. He would like to help her somehow, but that was not his job of course. Only it would be nice to know that someone was taking it over and doing it well. She needed comforting, he was sure, for she had looked terribly troubled that afternoon, and she had been grateful that he was looking after the boys. Well, he could at least do that. They were lively youngsters, and there was no place for such eager thoughtless vitality around sick people. Now, he must just stop thinking about that girl. She belonged to another man.

But it was not easy to turn his thoughts away from the affairs of these dear old friends of his boyhood days. The more perhaps because he had so recently lost his parents, and was practically alone in the world. For hours he lay thinking and finally got up to look out of the window toward the house next door and observe the lighted windows. They were not getting much rest over there, he was sure, for he could see shadows of moving forms now and again. He longed to know how the battle with death in one room, and with disease in another, was going. How would the others stand up under this hard time?

And while all this was going on, up in the Thorpe mansion on the side of the town always designated as "The Hill," the family were having a counsel of war.

Tilford had not gone to his sister's dinner. Since his fiancée for whom the dinner was given could not be there it would certainly look better for him to stay away too. So he stayed at home with his father and mother in a gloomy silence, and ate in an offended way through an excellent dinner.

"Well, really, Tilford, what happy circumstance has made you a guest in your home after your many and continued absences?" the father asked facetiously, as Tilford walked into the dining room and took his seat.

"Don't try to be funny, dad!" said Tilford heavily. "It's anything but a happy circumstance. I'm on the verge of insanity with all that has happened, and it seems impossible to work anything out that will better matters."

"Ah! Indeed! I hadn't heard of an impending disaster. Am I to be favored with a recital, or would you prefer to suffer in secret?"

"You're so trifling, dad, no wonder you don't hear the news. But of course you'll have to know," sighed Tilford heavily. "The whole trouble is with Maris' family. They have seen fit to throw a panic into the camp. I haven't been able as yet to ascertain whether it is something they planned in order to annoy us and assert their own importance, or whether it is just upset nerves, or what. But the long and the short of it is that Maris' mother had some sort of a nervous upset this morning, fainted away or something, and they are making a mountain out of it. Maris declares she can't go to Irma's dinner, given tonight wholly to introduce Maris to our friends. She has got hystericky and declares her mother is at the point of death and she can't leave her. I have tried my best to reason with her, but all to no avail, and then as if that wasn't enough, her baby sister comes home from kindergarten with the measles! Imagine it! Such a plebian common little childish ailment! And Maris insists she has to care for her. And she wouldn't be moved even when I secured a special child's nurse, and offered to pay her myself."

The father watched his son seriously.

"Well, now, that's too bad. Her mother sick! That's hard on a girl, I imagine. I don't see that that's anything to be so disturbed about, her not going to a dinner. Anybody would understand that. I thought she was a very nice sweet little girl myself when she was here last night. I thought you had made a very wise choice, and we are going to like her a lot. She'll fit right in with our family beautifully. Didn't you think so, mamma?"

"You don't understand, Mr. Thorpe," said his wife. She always called him Mr. Thorpe before the servants. "It's just her family trying to get in the public eye. They are very plain people and not in our class at all, and they're taking this opportunity, just at the most inconvenient time, to try to force themselves into the foreground. That mother has kept up all through the weeks perfectly well. She has seemed pleased enough at the way things were going, and she hasn't broken down. People don't break down all at once like that. If she has kept up so long and been perfectly healthy why should she suddenly start up and faint away? And what's a little faint anyway? I've had more than one myself, but I never let it interfere with my social duties, nor embarrass my family. But she, just the very day those invitations should have gone out, she chooses to collapse and scare the bride out of her wits. I say it's premeditated. She's just trying to force us to recognize her and show how important she is by putting a stop to all the festivities. Imagine daring to do that to Tilford's family, after all we've done for her."

"Why, now, mamma! What have we done for her?" Mr. Thorpe looked over his glasses and regarded his wife leniently.

"Done for her! Do you have to ask? Haven't we taken her up and made much of her, put her right on a pedestal, just as if she belonged in our set, and got her all these invitations among our social equals?"

"Social equals? Why mamma, what kind of an idea have you got of the Mayberrys? Don't you know I looked them up and they really belong to one of the fine old families?"

"Well, that may all be very well, Mr. Thorpe. Old families, yes. But old families without money degenerate. They live on the lower side of town, don't they? They live in an old rackabones of a house that needs painting terribly, and they go to a queer little church without a particle of style to it, and then insist on having the wedding, *our* wedding, in their own church, when I had gone to the trouble of asking our rector if they might have the use of our great beautiful church edifice, with its stately arches, and lovely chancel. It lends itself so gracefully to a formal wedding. I even offered to superintend the decorations myself. But no, they had to have their own ugly little church, and minister. I declare it's too vexing. And then, she insists she is going to wear some little frowsy dress that *her mother has made,* instead of a perfectly exquisite imported one that I suggested. She is certainly being too trying for anything. Do you know, Mr. Thorpe, that those wedding invitations haven't gone out yet? And this is the day they should have been mailed! Of course she is utterly ignorant of all social customs. But Tilford has exerted his utmost influence, and can't make her give them to him. She declares her mother is at the point of death and she can't send them out at present. And here are we all *disgraced* by having the invitations go out a day late."

"What difference does it make when the invitations go out?" asked Mr. Thorpe amusedly.

"There! That's just like you, Mr. Thorpe! As if you didn't know manners and customs, and understand that we'll be the laughing stock of all people who know what is the right thing to do."

"Well, I think you're all wrong, mamma. I think you ought to let that little girl manage her own affairs, at least until she's married to Tilford."

"Oh, you would, of course," sighed Tilford's mother. "I ought to have known better than to mention it before you. I wish you wouldn't say any more about it. My nerves are simply at the limit. I'm going down there tomorrow morning the first thing and have some words with that hystericky mother, and make her understand that she can't upset all our plans by a little gesture of illness! Tilford if you will come up to my room after you have finished your coffee, I'll be glad to discuss this matter with you and see what we can work out together about those invitations, but I simply can't stand your father's stupid remarks any longer. He knows better but he likes to annoy me. You'll have to excuse me!" and Mrs. Thorpe swept from the room.

Later Tilford went to his mother's boudoir and they continued their discussion.

"Listen, Tilford," said his mother as they settled down to talk, "has that child really got measles, or did it turn out to be scarlet fever?"

"I'm sure I don't remember," said Tilford gloomily. "What difference does it make?"

"Well, one is supposed to be a little more deadly than the other, that's all," said his mother frigidly. "And I've been thinking back. It wasn't real measles you had when you were a child, it was German measles, and it seems to me that I've heard that you can have all three. The other is French, isn't it? I can't remember. But if it's regular measles you'd better stay away from that house. *You* might get them, you know, and it seems to me I've heard it goes very hard with grown people when they get them. It's either measles or mumps. I'm not sure which. But you'd better be on the safe side and stay away. It would be simply dreadful if you should get the measles. It certainly would bring that family into the limelight with a vengeance. It would make you ridiculous, Tilford. People would never forget it that you couldn't get married because you had the measles!"

"For heaven's sake, mother! Haven't I trouble enough now without your bringing up an idea like that! You can't get measles unless you come into contact with the patient, and you can make sure I'll never do that."

"No, but seriously, Tilford, you'll just have to tell Maris that she can come here if she wants to see you, but that we don't approve of your running into danger! You'll simply have to make that girl give up her headstrong notions and let her precious family look out for themselves or *give you up!* I fancy that will bring her to her senses!" The mother finished with a triumphant gleam in her eyes, but

Tilford continued to march gloomily back and forth across the room.

"You don't know Maris," he said bitterly. "It wouldn't faze her in the least. When she gets started on something she has to finish it, no matter what she upsets."

"Well, but I thought you said she was so pliable, so easy to mold, so ready to yield to whatever you wanted. Those are your very words, my son."

"Yes, I know. I thought so. But I've found out it isn't so. She's got to have her own way if the heavens fall!"

"But can't you appeal to her love for you?"

"I don't know whether she has any. I thought she was crazy about me, but now she is simply blind. She's mad to have her own way and sacrifice herself for her poor ailing family."

"But Tilford! She must realize what a different station in life you are giving her. She must understand the enormous value of being your wife, and having everything that money can buy. She cannot look at that gorgeous diamond you gave her without realizing that. You can't tell me she'd give all that up just for sentiment."

"Wouldn't she? What would you say if I told you that she gave me back my ring tonight. Look at there!" and Tilford paused beside his mother and held out the flashing stone in the palm of his hand.

"Tilford!" His mother stared at the ring, hardly able to believe her eyes. "You don't mean you've quarrelled!"

"Call it what you please. There's the ring!" said the young man in a hard tone.

"The little ingrate!" said his mother indignantly. "And after all we've done for her! And just now at the last minute when the eyes of the whole town are upon us, and the wedding almost at the door! It would certainly serve her right if you were to take her at her word and let that end it. You know I always told you that you were in too great haste, especially when she was not in your social set. I told you no good would come of this engagement, and you would find it out after it was too late. But I certainly didn't expect it to end at this stage of the game. Have those invitations gone out yet? Perhaps it's just as well."

"Don't be a fool!" Tilford flung out at her. "You don't suppose I'm going to let her make a laughing stock of me after things have gone this far, do you? No! Certainly not. Rather than that I'll marry her and divorce her! Let her see that I'm her master! No girl can make a fool of me like that!"

"Well, that's true too, of course," sighed the mother. "Well, I suppose we've got to work out some plan. I think I'll appeal to the mother. That's a good line, you know. Tell the mother how she is spoiling her daughter's life and clouding it forever."

"I doubt if they'll let you see her," gloomed the son. "They've got her entirely surrounded by a nurse."

"You leave it to me!" said Mrs. Thorpe capably. "I'll soon quell the nurse. I never saw the nurse I couldn't command. Nor the mother I couldn't reach by some kind of an appeal. I wonder what time of day I'd better go? Doctors usually receive their patients in their offices in the morning, don't they? I'd better go before the doctor gets around. You'd better not appear in this at all. I'll speak as woman to woman, mother to mother, and all that, you know. It's probably the only way Maris can be managed, to get her mother roused up to the situation so that she'll tell her to snap out of this idea that she's got to be a sacrifice to them all. You leave it to me, Tillie dear. I'll bring it all out right. And about those invitations, if we can get them off in the morning I'm sure I can get the postmaster to fix the date on the postmark. That's a little thing to do, and nobody will be the wiser. People will just think their invitations were delayed on the way. Now Tilford, I'll tell you what you do! You run over to your sister's. They're about through with dinner now. You needn't stay long. Just look very serious and say that Maris is so disappointed, but you felt she ought to stay by her mother tonight, but that you're quite sure she will be all right in a day or two. Don't say anything about the measles. That's too grotesque. A bride having to stay away from a dinner especially made for her because her baby sister has the measles. Now, Tilford, cheer up, and take this thing sensibly. Don't give way to the idea that Maris is going to get away with a thing like this, or you'll have it to deal with all your life, and you'd better just take it in hand at the start and get it over with. You must be master of your own house, master of this situation. She's probably just trying to see how much she can get away with. But mother will stand by her boy, and we'll bring things into shape tomorrow all right. Only I do wish you had heeded my warnings and got to know Ethel Framer well. She is so smart, and so correct, and has so much money. You would never have caught her giving back a magnificent ring like that even in a joke."

"There, mother, don't begin on that. I'm fed up on that line. I may have made a mistake in choosing Maris but I don't intend to let anybody know it, and I certainly don't regret Ethel Framer. I had all I wanted of her the winter you tried to stuff her down my throat."

"Well, Tilford, I suppose you'll have to learn your lessons by experience just as we all do."

"Don't tell me *you* ever learned one that way, mother," sneered the spoiled youth. "If you had you wouldn't spend your time trying to force things upon me."

"Now, Tilford! What do you mean? Haven't I just offered to go and appeal to this girl's mother and straighten everything out for you, when you know she wasn't my choice in the first place?" The mother spoke in a high aggrieved tone.

"I wasn't referring to that, mother. I was thinking of that impossible Ethel person that you tried your best to make me marry. And you knew I never could bear a person with that kind of hay-colored hair and light lashes."

Mrs. Thorpe retired behind an expensive handkerchief and wiped a sketchy tear or two.

"Well, I'm sure I don't want to go and invade this impossible person's home and try to teach her her duty to her child," she complained pensively. "If you don't want me to do it, just say so."

"Oh, it won't do any harm to try it," said Tilford loftily. "Personally I don't think you'll get anywhere with it. She's a small woman but she's very much set in her way, and she doesn't like people to tell her what her duty is any better than you do, mother."

"Well, she shall hear it from me for once, anyway, whether she likes it or not," said Tilford's mother firmly. "Now, darling, go to Irma's first, and then why don't you run over to your club for a little while. You are looking awfully haggard and it really isn't good for you to dwell on your disappointments. You trust me! I'll work this thing all out for you. And Tilford, dear, just to be on the safe side, better talk to Maris over the phone instead of going to the house. I wouldn't run any risks at all of getting measles at your age!"

"Nonsense!" said Tilford sharply as he took himself out of his mother's room and shut the door firmly.

"Tilford," called his father, as he passed the library door on his way out, "how about a little game of chess with your old dad? We haven't played in a long time."

"Nothing doing!" drawled Tilford disrespectfully. "I'm going over to the club and play pool! I've got too much on my mind to play chess. Besides, that's an old man's game!" and Tilford went out the front door and gave it a decided slam.

The father sighed and went back to his paper. He did not really want to play chess. But it seemed to him that it was a very long time since Tilford had been a little boy.

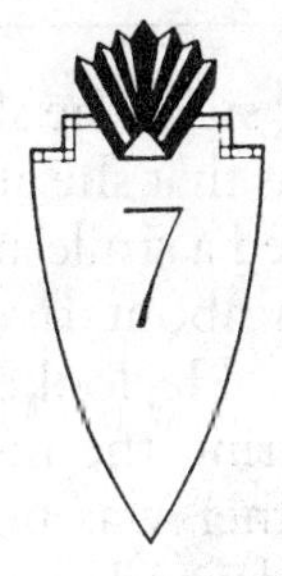

IT had been a very hard night at the Mayberry house. The mother had had another sinking spell. Not so terrifying as the others, but enough to make them send for the doctor, and look at each other with frightened eyes.

The spell had not lasted so long as the others, and she had responded more quickly to the medicine. But when it was all over and her tired heart was going steadily on again in almost a normal way, Father Mayberry had a shaking chill and had to be put to bed himself, though he protested most earnestly. Merrick had established himself as night nurse to watch over his father, and had come in once or twice when he heard Maris in Lexie's room. His eyes were large and worried, and he seemed to have matured during the night. He proved himself most efficient, administering his father's medicine on the hour, helping Maris to smooth the bedding and lift the little restless patient into a more comfortable position. Maris thought of it gratefully as she lay down again after the child was quieted. And then he came tapping at the door again with a glass of milk for Maris. His thoughtfulness was unprecedented.

"You've gotta keep your strength up, you know. What

would we do if you got sick?" he said earnestly. And Maris was so tired and anxious that she almost wept on his shoulder, though she managed a smile and a thank you.

The doctor came in about five o'clock and went the rounds of the patients. He looked relieved, but said he would run in again during the morning. He gave special directions that the mother was not on any account to be disturbed. Her hope depended upon utmost quiet and freedom from excitement. So far she had not seemed conscious of what was going on about her, but he warned them that she might come out of this state of utter collapse and even ask questions, and that they must maintain the utmost serenity and calm, and smile, and tell her to go to sleep, that all was well.

Then he went away and quiet settled down again. The nurse even caught a few winks of sleep, and hope seemed to have descended upon the house, with a certain degree of peace.

When Maris awoke from the longest nap she had had that night she found the bright sunshine streaming into her window, and the song of thrushes in the tall old tree around the house thrilling in the clear crystal air. A soft breeze was blowing the curtain. Oh, what would this day bring forth? Was the brightness of the morning a good omen?

As she washed her face, brushed her hair, and put on a fresh little cotton dress, she took up one by one the burdens that she knew would confront her, but somehow she couldn't seem to fit them on her back yet. She would have to go slowly. There was Gwyneth and her school to be dealt with the first thing. How good that the little boys were safe for a while at least. Of course they must not presume upon Lane Maitland's kindness, but he had seemed so genuine in his friendship that it was a relief to rely upon him for a few days anyway, till some other haven was offered.

Then she heard Lexie stirring and went to her at once. The problem would be more than ever how to keep noise from mother. Lexie must not be allowed to cry, poor little soul, miserable as she was. She must make her understand that mother had to be considered first. So, with a weary heart she marched into a new day.

Mrs. Thorpe usually took time by the forelock in anything she had to do, especially if it was something she did not anticipate with pleasure. It was a little after half past ten when her car drew up in front of the Mayberry residence, and she got out, pausing to lift her lorgnette to her eyes and take a long critical survey of the house before she walked up to the front door and applied for entrance.

She was smartly attired in a spring morning costume of black and white, designed to impress the family with her importance.

She was annoyed by the faint buzz of the doorbell after her vigorous attack upon it, and followed it up by a smart rapping with her immaculate white-gloved knuckles. But Sally came striding.

"Don't do that!" she whispered. "You'll wake the lady, and she's had a bad night!" She glared at the caller ominously.

"Oh, really? Well, I'll be the judge of what I'll do, and I'm in a hurry. Your bell didn't ring adequately. Where is Miss Mayberry? I want to see her at once."

"Ye can come and set. I'll tell her. She's gettin' her little sister ready for the doctor. She mebbee can't come right aways," said Sally grudgingly.

"Well, you can tell her I have no time to wait. I want to see her at once. Tell her it's Mr. Tilford Thorpe's mother."

"It wouldn't make no difference who it was," said Sally scathingly. "She can't come till she can," and Sally moved heavily away toward the stairs.

Mrs. Thorpe was not good at waiting. The house seemed deathly still to her. Nobody stirred to meet her.

She decided to take matters in her own hands. She arose and glanced about the room appraisingly, then she sailed into the hall and listened a moment. She heard a door open almost noiselessly, but no one was coming toward the stairs. With quick resolve she mounted the stairs, determination in her face. She had come to do something and it was best to get it over with as soon as possible. It was certainly fortunate that nobody was around to stop her. She didn't know the way to the sick room of course, but it would be easy to find. She would beard the lion in his den as it were before any keepers found out what she was going to do.

So with strong step she mounted the stairs, gave a swift glance about, decided on the door that probably opened into the master bedroom, and made for it with long easy steps.

She loomed in the doorway for an instant, a smart, well-upholstered figure, took in every detail with a glance, then marched over and stood at the foot of the bed, looking down on the white-faced woman who lay there with closed eyes, utterly limp.

The nurse had stepped across to the bathroom to fix fresh medicine, and had not seen her come. She was running the water, and had not heard her. No one else was about at the moment.

Mrs. Thorpe cleared her throat and began in a cheerful resonant voice.

"Good morning!" she said briskly. "I've come to have a little heart to heart talk with you, Mrs. Mayberry. I've come to beg you for the sake of your daughter and her future happiness, to rouse yourself and put off this desire to give in. Just rise up and conquer your natural feelings. You must know that every mother of a daughter has to face the matter of losing her some time or other, and it isn't worth while to make her and her bridegroom unhappy and spoil all their plans just for a little sentiment. Of course

I know how you feel. I'm having the same thing to bear, you remember. But I don't give way, and I felt sure if you realized how you are hurting Maris and Tilford you would just shake off this illness and let them go on with their plans. I—"

Suddenly a voice spoke in her ear, low but dominant.

"Stop! Get out of here!" and a large firm hand went over her mouth that was open to go on. It held there so firmly that the woman was almost choked. Then another hand went around her ample waist and gripped her arm in an iron clutch, the firm fingers digging into her flabby flesh painfully. And when she tried to cry out and struggle she only found herself more firmly held and unable to make a sound, as she was ignominiously propelled from the room and the door closed in her face.

She had caught a fleeting vision of great dark green eyes with fear in them, in the white face on the pillow, and a nurse hurrying in with a glass in her hand. Then the door closed and she was outside on the stair landing, suddenly confronting the doctor. And it wasn't any little cheap doctor as she had supposed, either. She recognized him as Doctor MacPherson, a man very high in his profession, and much sought after among her own social set.

She tried to speak but she found herself propelled at a breathless pace down the stairs, held by that vice-like grip, and actually a man's handkerchief stuffed in her mouth as any common gangster might have done. She had to clutch the stair rail with her own free hand lest she would fall headlong, but as soon as she arrived at the foot of the stairs and her feet felt solid floor beneath them, she wrenched the handkerchief angrily out of her mouth and flung it on the floor.

"Really!" she puffed. "What do you think you are doing, Doctor MacPherson?"

"I think I am getting you out of this house as rapidly as I know how!" said the eminent physician sternly. "Did you know what you were doing? Did you know you were talking to a woman at death's door, and you are very likely to have killed her? We've worked all night to keep her alive, and you come here and harangue her like that! Get out of this house as fast as you can, and don't you dare come here again until the family are able to look after themselves."

He opened the screen door and almost flung her—if one could be said to fling anything as substantial as Mrs. Thorpe—from the house.

"I guess you don't know who I am!" blustered Mrs. Thorpe breathlessly, as she drew herself up and tried to look dignified.

"I don't know who you are, and I don't want to know. I know you're a fool and a criminal. That's enough for me!"

"I am Mrs. Henry Watterson Thorpe of Heathcote on the Hill."

"I don't care a copper who you are! Get out quick!"

"You are most insulting! I shall certainly have you arrested!"

"If that woman upstairs dies I shall certainly have you indicted for murder! Now scram!" said the doctor.

Mrs. Thorpe scrammed with as much dignity as she could muster, and got into her car while her chauffeur held open the door for her and pretended not to see how upset she was. When they were started on their way toward home Mrs. Henry Watterson Thorpe of Heathcote on the Hill found that she was weeping. She hadn't been so shaken since she thought once during the depression that Henry had lost all his money. Somehow her ego was shaken. She was going home in disgrace, having failed in her mission. Like a warlord who instead of wearing a wreath of laurel in token of his victory, is brought home wounded lying on his shield.

But back in the old Mayberry house they were giving

little heed to how the intruder was feeling. They were doing all in their power to avert calamity.

They were all there, Maris her eyes wide with horror, and even her lips drained of every particle of color; Merrick just wakened from a bit of a morning nap he had snatched, trying to understand what had happened; even the father in a hastily donned dressing gown, his hand gripping the door frame, his lips trembling as he tottered over to the bed where his wife lay looking wildly from him to the nurse. For even though the doctor had been most miraculously quiet in his treatment of the intruder, the whole household was aroused. Gwyneth came rushing upstairs, with Sally just behind her trying to hush her, and from the farthest end of the back hall, where the playroom door had swung ajar, came Lexie's frightened wail; "Maris, vat's the matter? I vant my muvver!"

It was incredible how soon the doctor got back into the house and upstairs, after having expressed himself to the unwelcome visitor. And with what patience and tenderness he worked! Maris as she watched him turned away feeling that if any human doctor could save her mother he would.

He shut them all out of the room but the nurse and gave his orders in quick low tones.

The mother was still wide-eyed and apparently conscious for the first time of all that was going on about her, suffering acutely, too, for her hand would go to her heart feebly, and she would moan, and cry out sharply.

"There, there, sister! That was just a bad dream you had. Forget it! You're all right. We're going to have you all right in a little while."

The troubled eyes searched his face.

"That woman—?" she faltered.

"She's gone!"

"Why—did—she—come?"

"Oh, she just made a mistake and got the wrong house.

Don't think any more about her. Nurse, bring me those drops."

"Maris—?" the tired lips formed.

"Yes, Maris is right here," said the doctor, and at a sign Maris came in and stood by her mother.

"Show her how you can smile this morning," ordered the doctor as he carefully measured out the drops. "You're happy, aren't you, Maris?"

"Oh, yes, mother, I'm happy. You're—looking—so much—better!" The girl's voice faltered. She was wondering if she were saying the right thing, struggling with the tears that wanted to flow.

"Father—?" the word was so weak it could hardly be heard.

"Oh, he's right here too!" said the doctor breezily. "It's early though, Mrs. Mayberry. He isn't exactly dressed yet, but we don't mind. Now, you drink this and then take a little nap and you'll be all right."

The troubled eyes rested on Mr. Mayberry as he came in from across the hall where he had stood grayly by the door listening. He tried to smile as if there was nothing the matter. He took his wife's hand in his tenderly, and almost the flitting shadow of a smile came to her lips. Then the terror went out of her eyes, and she swallowed the medicine the doctor held and sighed gently like a tired child.

"The—children—?" The words were scarcely audible.

"All here and happy as clams, but you've had enough excitement for one morning. The children will come in later."

The doctor's voice was very low and gentle, but had that quality of authority that his patients always recognized. Mrs. Mayberry had another fleeting ghost of a smile in her eyes as she closed them. Suddenly Maris felt as if her mother was dying, and was trying to bid them all good-bye. Oh, was that it? She turned her head away to hide the quick tears that came. Oh, if mother died it would be herself who had killed her! Her wedding, just as Merrick had said! How could she ever go on living knowing that all her life?

"Now, all of you go away a little while, for mother wants to sleep," said the doctor in that cheerful tone of his that seemed to quell all fears and drive away fantastic shadows as if they were but smoke. "Mother's going to feel much better when she wakes up. Oh, much, *much* better!"

He waved them all out of the room, paused to give a direction to the nurse, then he came out to them where they were herded together, a frightened little group, around their father, Maris with slow tears running down her cheeks of which she was not aware.

"Well," said the doctor coming up to them with his grave tender smile, "that was a bolt out of a clear sky! But I think she has a chance even yet. She reacted better than I could have hoped. Who was that old horned toad, anyway, and how ever did she happen to barge in here?"

He looked from the one to the other of them, and suddenly Maris' white face flushed crimson, and then the color receded and left her whiter than before. It seemed almost as if she were swaying and about to fall.

"Oh, I see," said the doctor, "one of those things! Well, we won't say any more about it. But I certainly would like to get her up a tree and keep her there for awhile. I'd like to tell her a few more things that I didn't have time for at the moment."

The nurse came softly out of the room and caught the last few words. The semblance of a grin adorned her plain features for an instant.

"If you ask me," she said grimly, "I should say you said plenty. The last glimpse I had of the party as I passed the window showed her withering like Jonah's gourd."

"I'm not aware that I asked you, nurse," said the doctor with a twinkle. "Now, nurse, we want to keep that pulse going steadily without a lost beat. See what you can do, and telephone me at the slightest change. We're running no risks. Scatter, folks, and get some rest and some food. Wash your faces and comb your hairs. We aren't conquered yet. We may have to get another nurse for a night or two to relieve Miss Bonner till she takes a nap or two, but aside from that I believe we're going to win."

"You'll get no night nurse for me," said the nurse irately. "I'm good for another couple of nights if need be, and I want no other nurse messing in on my case, not when I've come this far."

"All right with me!" said the doctor with satisfaction. "I'd rather have you exclusively than any other two nurses I know. Now! Where's that little measle girl? How is she getting on?"

Maris led the way, brushing off the tears and trying to get a cheerful face before her little sister saw her. She paused in the hall with her hand on the doorknob.

"Doctor," she breathed softly, "please tell me! If—my mother dies—will you think—it was that woman's coming?"

The doctor looked her straight in the eye.

"Well, of course I wouldn't recommend performances like that as a general rule in treating a patient with a heart condition like your mother's, but, at the same time, I'm relying on your mother's rare sense of humor, Miss Maris. I think that was perhaps the best comedy ever put on in a sick room. It was so well enunciated that I heard every word of it as I was coming up the walk from my car. I didn't miss a thing. I thought at first it was some radio artist and the neighbors were indulging in an early morning broadcast. At the same time, of course you understand that I should leave no stone unturned to prevent a recurrence of the performance. Have you an idea that it is likely to happen again?"

Maris' eyes were darkly blue and inscrutable, and her lips trembled a little as she answered:

"I shall certainly do everything in my power to prevent it. No, I don't think anyone would dare do a thing like that twice. Not after what you said to her. Thank you, Doctor MacPherson."

Then they went into the room to see the little girl who was lying there crying softly into her pillow lest she would disturb her mother. The doctor called her "a brave boy" for being so thoughtful, and made her giggle in the midst of her tears.

She was a very miserable and uncomfortable little girl that morning for the measles were beginning to come out in flocks and she didn't like them. But the doctor was pleased with the way they were doing.

As he went out he looked sympathetically at Maris:

"You're having your hands full," he said, "but I'm not sure but it's just as well. You won't have so much time to worry about your mother. And you know it's going to be quite a time before she gets back to her former self. She'll need great care and rest, but I think she has a wonderful constitution, and there is good reason to hope she will get well. You can keep that in the back of your mind when you get discouraged. Of course I'm not promising anything, but that's what I really hope for. I'll do the best I can, and then it is all in God's hands."

A great relief flooded Maris' soul. She had been so sure that her mother was going, that she scarcely dared believe even now that the doctor still had hope.

"Oh, God!" she said in her heart, "I thank You! I thank You!"

Then she turned to her duties with a little lighter heart.

But when all was said it was not an easy day that was before her. A little girl who was not used to discomfort and pain, and not old enough to be philosophical about it, at least not for long periods at a time, who had to be entertained and kept from crying, both for her own physical good, and also for her mother's. Maris' strength and ability were to be taxed to the utmost. But the problems of yesterday had taken a back seat. The wedding invitations and twin wedding dresses might still be lurking in the shadows of her bedroom this morning, but she had no time to go there herself, and so she need not consider them. How trifling and unimportant any of them seemed in the light of this new day with its anxieties and duties.

Gwyneth came up to the door with a tray that Sally had sent. Orange juice for Lexie and a nice breakfast for Maris who hadn't eaten a mouthful yet since she got up.

Gwyneth's face was long and dreary.

"Sister, what am I going to do about school?" she asked in a desolate whisper, with a fearsome glance toward the far door of her mother's room.

"Oh, yes," said Maris cheerfully. "I've been thinking. You go to the telephone—perhaps you better wait til recess time, or noon, whichever you think is best—and call up your teacher. Or perhaps the principal would be better, whoever has the say about you. Tell her that mother is very sick and that your little sister has the measles. That you have had them and we do not think it likely you will take them again, but that you cannot be spared to go away from home at present as you are needed here to help. Ask if it is possible for you to have your lessons assigned each day, and you to take your examinations with the rest when you are able to return. If she doesn't seem willing call me and I will talk to her."

"But Maris, suppose I didn't understand something. Who would I ask?"

"I'm quite sure I would be able to help you. Or you could telephone to your teacher."

Slowly, reluctantly, the little girl went down to her task. She didn't like the thought of asking, and she would have felt so much more important and on-her-own to have stayed with Erminie. There was a lot more freedom of one kind and another at Erminie's house than either Gwyneth's mother or Erminie's knew about.

But a half hour later Gwyneth came back to Maris' door and announced happily that it was all fixed. The principal was to send her advance lessons each week, and she was to do her homework, and then when she went back there would be tests and all would be explained if she hadn't understood something. She seemed quite interested in apportioning her time for study, and keeping up with her classmates. It was a kind of game, and she was satisfied. After all there were only two more weeks to go.

Maris was downstairs later in the morning hunting a certain pair of scissors she needed for cutting out endless strings of paper dollies who could dance about upon Lexie's bed and be blown away with a breath to make a laugh for the restless little invalid. The telephone rang.

Maris started and looked troubled. This would likely be Tilford. There would be more discussion, and what could she say more than she had already said? Reluctantly she went to answer it. Would his mother have talked with him yet? If she had he would be very angry of course. It hadn't occurred to her before that *they* would be aggrieved at what the doctor had said, but of course they would.

But strangely the whole thing did not seem her burden any more. She was in a hard trying place, and it might be days before she got out of it, but God was going to lead her out some day, and she did not have to depend upon herself to get out. She had asked God to help and she believed He was going to do it. Anyway she hadn't any strength or wisdom of her own for this complicated situation. It was in the strength of this trust that she went to the telephone.

And then it wasn't Tilford at all. It was Lane Maitland. She almost laughed aloud with relief as she recognized his voice.

"This is Broadcasting Station Number Two," he said

solemnly, "reporting on Maitland Detention Camp. Twelve o'clock, noon, daylight saving time. The entire force of cadets slept well through the night, save for an hour when they were called out to engage in combat with a bat who had stolen into the barracks. Nevertheless, they arose on time, made their beds, took a swim in the creek, ate a hearty breakfast, had devotions, went through setting up exercises. Then an hour of study personally conducted by the scout master, played two sets of tennis, and now are about to indulge in a noonday repast. They will then put up a lunch and start on a hike to Conner's woods where they will hunt for wild flowers and lichens for tomorrow's natural science study, eat their lunch and return to camp about sundown. Communication may be had with them by telephoning to Conner's, Severn—1188, who will at once advise the scout master. In case cadets may be needed, they will return by bus which passes Conner's every fifteen minutes. If these arrangements are not agreeable, kindly advise at once. Lane Maitland speaking."

Maris gave a pleasant little giggle, and the heavy burden she had anticipated rolled away out of sight for the moment. It was like stooping to pick up a great iron weight and finding it only a bundle of feathers.

"Delightful!" she said. "Won't that be grand for the boys! I know they will love it. I approve most heartily. I only hope you won't be worn out. I don't see how I can ever thank you for what you are doing."

There came a tremble in her voice, and an answering sympathy in his as he replied:

"I'm having the time of my life, myself. But how about you? Did you have a hard night?"

"A busy one. Not so hard perhaps as it might have been. We were all up most of the night. Dad wasn't so well, and Lexie was restless, but we're all very thankful it was no worse. Mother seems to be resting all right just now."

Her voice trailed off sadly, and the listener thought he discerned anxiety returning to it.

"You are sure it's all right to take the boys away even as far as Conner's? I can keep them happy here at home if you prefer."

"No, I think it's all right. The doctor seems to think mother has a good chance, though of course he doesn't promise anything."

There was a catch in her voice, and the young man was quick to understand.

"Yes, I know," he said gently. "We've been praying, the boys and I," he added half shyly. "That helps!"

"Oh, thank you!" said Maris fervently. "That does help."

"Well, I won't keep you longer now. I'll report again this evening."

Maris turned from the telephone strangely comforted. What was there about that simple little conversation that had taken the tiredness away from her heart?

What a blessing that Lane Maitland had come home just at this time.

And then it suddenly came to her mind to wish vaguely that Tilford were something like Lane Maitland.

How Tilford would have loved that!

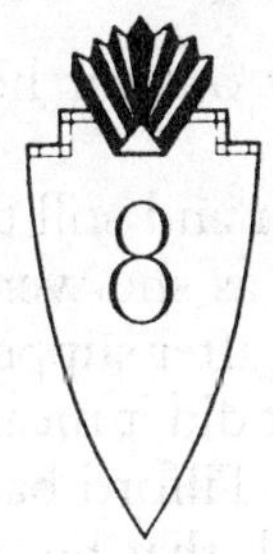

AS the day wore on toward sunset Maris had need of all the comfort there was to be had. It was not that any fresh calamity occurred, it was just that it was not easy to go on making endless strings of paper dollies, reading stories with eyes that were heavy for sleep, and a voice that lagged from very weariness. To be patient hour after hour with the poor petulant baby who couldn't understand why she felt so hot and miserable, who wanted things until they came and then snarled at them.

By this time, too, old friends and neighbors were getting to know that Mrs. Mayberry was very ill, and they kept coming to the door and asking for Maris, or calling up on the telephone and demanding to speak to her. Even the sign of quarantine on the door did not deter them. And every time she was called to the telephone or the front door she went with a tremor lest it would be some of the Thorpes. And yet she would not let herself think about that possibility. She could not prepare to deal with them, because it would surely be the unexpected with which she would have to deal. So she fell into the habit unconsciously of letting her heart cry out for help to God, as she went downstairs.

But the day wore on and still there was no word from the Thorpes, and now as she went to lie down and rest a little during an interval after supper, it began to seem ominous, this silence. What did it mean?

True, she had given Tilford back his ring and left him. But she could not think that he would take a repulse like that without an argument, or some kind of retaliation. A word was never final to him unless he were the one to speak it.

It suddenly came to her as she lay thinking this over, that she was falling more and more into the attitude of criticizing Tilford, comparing him with others, fearing his decisions. What was the matter with her? Didn't she love him the way a girl should love the man she was to marry?

It wasn't thinkable that Tilford was letting another day go by without making some move about those wedding invitations, either. And now it was definite in her mind that there was nothing she could do about them for the present. Her mother's condition all day had been unchanged. So far as she herself could judge her mother seemed to be sinking hour by hour. Each time she went to the room and cast a glance toward the bed, her mother's frail sweet face looked more delicate and ethereal, as if a great change was coming over her. And yet the doctor and the nurse did not seem to be particularly troubled. But to her inexperienced eyes there seemed no hope at all that she would rally. Obviously, under such conditions one could not send out wedding invitations.

And if mother should die?

Oh, she couldn't go into that thought, not so long as there was a breath of hope. But if mother should die what heart could she or anyone have for weddings?

And if mother didn't die, was the prospect of a wedding any more likely?

Even if she got well it would be a long time before she would be able to take up life again and look after her family!

The darkness had settled down about Maris and she had not turned on her light. Lexie was asleep, and there was no need to disturb her with a light. Besides it was pleasanter here on the bed looking out into the soft night. She could even see a few stars twinkling between the tree branches, and there was a soft radiance in the east where sometime soon the moon was about to rise. There was a soft little stir of a breeze that rustled the leaves of the big beech tree outside her window. She was so tired, that she longed to drift off and forget all her perplexities, yet her thoughts would not let go while those troublous questions were in her mind.

Suddenly she heard voices, just the other side of the hedge in the Maitland place, under the hemlock trees. It was Merrick and Lane. They had come to the old rustic seats to talk, in order not to disturb the boys, very likely. It was Merrick who was speaking. By the sound Maris judged he had stretched his length on the rickety old seat, and Lane was hanging up the hammock between the trees. She could hear the grating of the rings as they slipped into the hooks. The old hammock they used all to use so freely, the old hooks! Wouldn't they be rusty and unsafe?

But when Merrick spoke it seemed as if there must have been some thought-transference between him and herself, for he was voicing some of the very questions that had been in her mind.

"Well, I'm sure I don't know what's coming to us all," Merrick was saying in gloomy voice. "Even if mother gets well, it'll be a long time. The doctor owned that to me. A long time before she's able to be about among us again, looking after everything, you know."

Lane's voice was quiet but had a clear ring to it as he said: "Well, you know that nothing can come to you except with God's permission."

"You think that?" Merrick's voice was almost bitter as he asked the question.

"I know that."

"Doesn't look that way to me," said the younger fellow. "Looks more like some of them came from the devil."

"Well, the devil may have had something to do with them, but for some good wise reason of His own God permits them."

"I can't see that," said Merrick, and Maris, listening, could almost see the narrowing of Merrick's eyes and the wry twist of his lips. "I'm beginning to think God doesn't have anything to do with things. Look at marriage now. They say that marriages were made in Heaven. But most of 'em are a mess! I hope I never fall in love. If I do I'll go and drown myself or something. Marriage makes a lot of trouble for everybody."

"Look here now, brother! I object to a man that has as wonderful a father and mother as you have saying a thing like that!"

"Oh, yes, dad and mother, of course that's different. There aren't many like them. Why I believe if anything was to happen to mother, dad would just wilt away and die himself, he's so bound up in her."

"Well, I had a mother and father like that too, so I'm not listening to any tirades like that on marriage."

"Oh, well, I mean modern marriage. Of course, people used to be all right when dad and mother were young. But you take today. Take my sister. Here she's all wrapped up in that poor fish she's going to marry, and what's going to become of us when she's gone? Mother down sick for at least a year, dad hardly able to hold up his head till mother gets well, and there'll be only me to bring up the family. Nice hand I'll make bringing 'em up. I might make a stab at looking after the boys, but what am I going to do with

Gwyneth and Lexie? Where do you think I found Gwyn last night, after we'd sent her over to Howard's to stay all night and study? Down at the drugstore eating ice cream with Rance Mosher, the little rat! Maybe you don't know what he is, but I do, plenty!"

Merrick lowered his voice and talked earnestly. Maris couldn't hear what he said, but she knew he was telling Lane about something dreadful Rance had done, for Lane's low earnest tones showed that he fully agreed with Merrick in his judgment that Rance was no fit companion for Gwyneth.

"But look here, Merrick," said Lane, and now his voice was louder again so that she distinctly heard the words, "you don't need to worry about that. There'll be some way provided to take care of the family if such a situation arises. Maris and her husband would probably arrange to come and live with you, and she would take charge."

"Not she! She wouldn't be allowed to! You don't know Tilford. He's the most selfish brute that ever walked the earth!"

"Oh, but surely in circumstances like that! No decent man could refuse."

"Couldn't he? Well, maybe he isn't decent then. But even if he would we wouldn't want him. He thinks we're the scum of the earth and he's the top layer in paradise. Gosh! I couldn't ask any worse fate than to have to have him come and stay in the house awhile. He makes me so mad the way he bosses my sister around and makes her like it, that I can't see straight. It's partly what's killing mother, too. Maybe it's even that altogether. That and the fact that she's pretty sure that when Maris is married to him that's the end of her so far as we're concerned. And Gosh, mother's all bound up in Maris! That's what I mean. If God lets that thing happen to us all I can't see that He can care for any of us!"

"Well, even at that, God might have some great good wrapped up in it for you," said Lane Maitland's slow earnest voice, thoughtfully.

"I can't see it!"

"It might be there, even if you couldn't see it."

"Well, have it your own way, parson, but I tell you it's a pretty tough thing to swallow, having Maris marry that pill. He's all kinds of rich of course, and is taking her around the world or something like that for a honeymoon, but she might as well be going to Heaven as far as we are concerned, and I don't hope to ever see much of her again. Of course she doesn't see it. She thinks he's all right. But I'd rather see her marry a day laborer that was a good honest man than this poor fish, even though he did give her a diamond as big as a hen's egg."

It was all very still for a minute and then Maris heard Lane say slowly:

"She's a wonderful girl! It seems as though she ought to rate a man who was exceptionally fine!"

"Yes, that's what I'm saying," broke in Merrick. "She's a wonderful sister! She's always been wonderful, and fine and unselfish, and when I think of her tied to that bird, and having to put up with him all her life, and run around and pretend she likes it, it makes me see red! I don't see why God lets it happen. That's why I say marriage is a mess and I hope I never fall in love."

"Say, you know marriage wasn't meant to be a mess, and God planned the first marriage to be helpful to both the man and the woman. It wasn't till the man and woman tried to be independent of God that sin came into the world, and happiness was spoiled. It's somebody's fault when marriages go wrong."

"Oh, is it! And whose fault would it be?"

"Well, people ought to be careful who they pick to fall in love with in the first place. You don't *have* to fall in love with everybody you admire. You have to watch yourself.

You have to choose the right one. You have to get the one God planned for you."

"Oh, *yeah?* And how would you know who that was? Now I know a girl I like real well, but how do I know but she'd turn out to be some poor lily like all the ones that run down to Reno today to get disengaged? How you going to tell, I say?"

"Well, I don't know just whether my rule would apply to you or not, but in the first place, if I found I was getting really interested in a girl I'd find out whether she was a real sincere Christian or not. If she wasn't, and wouldn't take Christ as her Saviour and Lord, I'd quit right then and there. That would be my first step in deciding."

There was a sudden prolonged silence out under the trees. Merrick had been listening to a new idea. At last he said embarrassedly:

"Well, that's a new one on me. I'm afraid if I found a girl was all that I'd know I wouldn't qualify with her."

"Yes? Well, that would be something to think about, too," said Lane quietly. "In a true marriage both parties would have to qualify, wouldn't they? It's only as two people are dominated by the same Spirit, and are surrendered to the same Lord, that they can live together in harmony, isn't it?"

"I guess you're getting rather too deep for me, but you may be right," mused Merrick. "My sister is as good a Christian as there is, at least she was till she took to going around with this worldly guy, but I don't believe she's ever tried your system for I'm sure her precious Tilford is no Christian! She does a lot of things now that she didn't used to do, things she wasn't brought up to do. Oh, not bad things, you know, just worldly. She didn't used to think they were in her line. I don't believe she knows how she's changed."

"Yes, I feel sure your sister accepted Christ as her Saviour some years ago," said Lane almost reverently. "I remember when we were kids she told me about it. Her testimony was one of the things that made me want to know the Lord myself."

"I remember," said Merrick thoughtfully. "There was a Bible class started about that time, too. I went once or twice myself. It was real interesting. But the teacher got married and moved away. That's what I say, marrying is a mess. It's always breaking up things. I'm never going to fall in love."

"Well, at least wait till you find the right girl," said Lane, amusedly. "You know, really, Merrick, you're young yet! So am I for the matter of that, and we don't need to get so excited about it. For after all, the world has been going on this way for some time, marrying and giving in marriage, and where would we be if our parents had never married?"

"That's different," growled Merrick illogically.

"Just how?"

"Well, it's different from Maris marrying that poor fish, I tell you. I guess you never met him, did you? He's just too good-looking for any use, and he knows it, too."

"No, I never met him, but I sincerely hope your sister will be happy!" Lane's tone was suddenly very grave and sweet, and there was a tenderness in it that thrilled Maris and soothed her tired soul. There at least was one person who wasn't criticising her!

But Maris, as she lay there thinking for some time after the boys had said good night and gone away, felt as if somehow their conversation had thrown open a door which hitherto had been closed and locked. A number of things were disclosed to her startled view that she had never dreamed before.

There for instance was her family! She had not known that they felt unhappy about her marriage. Did they really, or was that just a figment of Merrick's imagination? Merrick, jealous that his sister should be going away with anybody else?

New insight seemed to come to her as she stared at the dark wall ahead of her and began to remember little things that had been said, little actions, withdrawings, that she had not noticed at the time, but that now stood out sharply. Her father, sighing heavily without explanation, only a sad smile when she questioned him. Her mother wiping away a tear and pretending it was only perspiration. Little things that in her hurry had passed without her taking much account of them. If she had stopped to consider she might have only laid them down to the natural premonition of the coming separation while she was on her wedding trip. But now she saw that it had been more than that. A stolid indifference on the part of her father and the children to anything that was said about Tilford. Mother always asked after him, and spoke brightly of him, but especially of late her father had been silent where he was concerned. Had they all taken a dislike to him? Did the rest feel as Merrick did? Of course she had known for some time that Merrick and Tilford did not hit it off very well, but she had laid it to the fact that Tilford was a little older. She had reasoned that when they were really related and got to know one another better, all that would pass away and they would all be fond of him and enjoy the good things of life together.

Now she suddenly saw what a fool she had been to imagine any such thing. And then once more came that shocking question, as it had the morning before when she awoke, was she *sure* that she was altogether satisfied with her choice of a life companion?

And was Tilford satisfied with her?

He had made it quite apparent that he was, until just recently, and perhaps his entire taking over of her affairs and ordering them had flattered her so that she did not see everything clearly. For certainly he had not been very comfortable to get along with the last day and a half. She had never imagined he could be as disagreeable as he had proved himself to be ever since her mother was taken sick. And that was just the time when one would have expected sympathy and devotion more than any other. It was the time when she had needed someone to lean upon. Her mother too ill to know what was going on, her father incapacitated by his love and anxiety, and Tilford only concerned about wedding invitations!

But towering head and shoulders above that thought there was another consideration, that made even the choice of a life companion take second place, and that was the dire straits of her beloved family, and their immediate need of herself.

It suddenly became very plain to her that the machinery of her pleasant days had been stopped short and utterly changed, and that she could not possibly go on with what she had planned. For even if her mother should rally soon and get back to a semblance of her former self, they could not get along without her. She was needed right here. Mother would not be fit for a long time to take over the reins of the household, and there was just nobody else in the world to do it. It was obviously her job.

Perhaps she hadn't recognized it before she heard Lane Maitland's clear-cut statement of what he seemed so sure she would do. Perhaps she hadn't even thought ahead so far. Her heart had just stood still and gasped at the great calamity that had come to pass. The future was nothing in her mind until she should know whether mother would live and be with them again, or would go away forever from this life. That was the one and only question in her mind. All the other matters, caring for the little sick sister, decisions about Gwyneth, ordering the household matters, and placating her angry lover, she had performed as in a dream, by a sort of automatic action of her brain. Her heart had been in attendance upon her mother, her dear, dear mother.

But now it was clear to her that even if mother got well sooner than she could possibly hope, that she would not feel free to get married and go away to the other side of the world seeking pleasure. Her place was here, at least for the present. And somehow she had to make that plain to her irate bridegroom.

Instinctively she knew it was going to be a battle, and while the contemplation of it wearied her inexpressibly, yet she was surprised to find that it was not the blasting disappointment that it might have been a few weeks before. The trip to Europe had lost its glamour in the light of immediate events. Being a grand lady in a new apartment of her own, furnished in the taste of her new mother-in-law, no longer loomed large on her horizon. All those things had faded and become unreal before the glaring light of real trouble. And somehow she was too tired to think what she ought to do about it. Had God sent all this distress down upon her to give her pause to think what she had been about to do?

Just what she would have thought if she could have known that Mrs. Thorpe, when she found out that the wedding dress had been rejected, had sent down her check to the Archer Shop and ordered the dress sent up to herself, it is hard to speculate. Fortunately she was spared that knowledge.

But Maris did not have a night of ease. Her rest was broken by a wailing voice:

"Sister I vant a dwink of vater!" and from that time on the night was disturbed. Lexie was restless and uncomfortable, and cried for this and that. Once at almost two o'clock the doctor came slipping in quietly, and Maris stole out to watch and listen at her mother's door, her hungry eyes searching his face as he went away, but his only answer to her unspoken appeal was a kindly smile.

As she stole back to Lexie again, Maris felt as if her heart would burst with the very uncertainty of it all.

For three days the strain went on, the doctor coming and going frequently, but saying little. And during those three days Lexie also was very sick indeed. Maris had little time to consider herself, nor even to realize that Tilford had not been near her in all that time, nor sent her any word. And when at last it did come to her mind, it was only with a sigh of relief that she had not had that to deal with also.

But the third night, during a respite, when Lexie seemed to be definitely better, and was sleeping quietly, and their mother was at least still with them, it did occur to her that perhaps Tilford had called and Sally had said she was busy. That would be like Sally. Sally was not given to graciousness. And after all, Tilford had his rights.

Or did he? Had he perhaps taken his ring with all it stood for and was counting himself free? Well, if he was like that she couldn't help it, and it was better to find it out now rather than when she was married to him. But she was too tired to think about it and dropped into a deep sleep.

The doctor came earlier than usual the next morning. He put them all out and stayed in their mother's room a long time. When he came out he called them into the living room and his manner was graver than usual.

"I want to tell you all the whole situation," he said looking straight into the anxious eyes of Mr. Mayberry. "I haven't told you much before because I wanted to be entirely sure and I didn't want to give you hope if there wasn't any. But I'm telling you now, Mrs. Mayberry has a clot of blood in one of the valves of the heart. It is a very serious condition, and one which may take her away in a moment's time. But at the same time if she can be kept alive, and kept absolutely still, I mean *still,* without moving hand or foot, for six weeks, it is possible that the condition may clear up and she may get well. I must tell you frankly that there isn't much hope for that, but there is a little hope, and you as a family can do a great deal to help this hope become a reality."

There was a tenseness in the room during this quiet speech that was fairly electric. Gwyneth in a frightened huddle by the piano gave a little gasp and put down her young head on her folded arms on the closed lid, but no one else stirred. Maris could not have got whiter than she already was, but her eyes seemed to grow wider and darker as she faced the doctor, and Merrick stood with folded arms just inside the door, his young face stern with purpose.

It was the father who lifted his bowed head with a sudden light in his eyes and spoke in a husky voice, but vibrant with a new hope:

"I need not tell you, Doctor," he said, "that we will everyone do all that is in our power to keep our dear one with us!"

Even in this darkest trouble there was something about their father's voice that the children would never forget. Gwyneth lifted her pretty little sorrowful face streaming with tears and looked at him, sighing as it were her own small name to his promise. Merrick murmured hoarsely:

"We sure will!" and turned away toward the window to hide his emotion. And Maris, wide-eyed, white-lipped, recognized that God had accepted her sacrifice and was putting her to the test, but her voice was clear and resolute as she said:

"Of course," without any reservations.

"Well, now, of course I knew you would feel that way, and I'm glad to have been able to give you even an atom of hope. But you'll have to know all that this entails. It will mean, first of all, a quiet house. It will probably mean another nurse so that the one you already have shall not give out before we are done, for Mrs. Mayberry must be watched every minute and run no risks of any interruption to her literally immovable condition. It is a state of things that could better be carried out to the letter in a hospital, but I do not dare risk transferring her to a hospital in her present state, therefore we'll have to bend conditions to meet the necessity, and make a hospital out of this house, and to that end *everything* else must have second place. She must have nothing to frighten or startle her, nothing *whatever* to worry her."

The eyes of the family assented to all he said and pledged their all to carry out his instructions.

"If, at the end of six weeks, I find Mrs. Mayberry's condition such as I hope, then as soon as she is able to be moved she should be taken to a quiet restful place that I have in mind where I am hoping she will in a few months regain her normal health."

He gave them a swift anxious glance and then went on:

"Now I realize that even with the slight hope I have been able to give you, these conditions will be hard for you all to bear, and will very much upset your life as a family, yet I am relying on you all. With your help much can be done!"

He finished with a grave sweet smile that endeared him to them all as they realized that he had at least taken away their utter hopelessness and given them a chance to do something for the beloved mother.

Then came the father's voice:

"Nothing will be too hard for us to bear if we may have our dear one back among us again!" and Maris and Merrick looked at the sudden new light that was growing in their father's eyes. Yes, their father was wonderful. They left the room with a kind of triumphal awe in their hearts that they had such a father and mother.

Half an hour later Tilford's car drew up in front of the house and Maris, looking out of the window just in time to see him coming up the walk, realized that her time of testing had arrived.

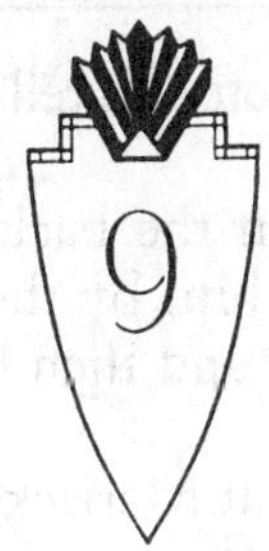

MERRICK had lingered in the hall until his father came out with the doctor, lingered as they stood at the door talking for a minute, and then, as the doctor left, he put his hand on his father's arm and spoke earnestly:

"Dad," he said, "You can count on me for every ounce that's in me. I got a job last night driving a bus on the Pike. I begin as soon as exams are over. The pay isn't great, but every cent of it's yours, and at least it'll help out for the extra nurse, and maybe a little over for what I eat. And when I get something better I'll lift all the burden I can from you!"

The father looked up and could not conquer the feeling in his voice;

"Son!" he said. "*Dear* son! Thank God for such a son!" and then he went upstairs wiping his eyes.

Merrick, his heart full of love and anxiety for the father who had seemed so stricken, and was struggling so bravely to have courage to go on, looked after him until he heard him go into the mother's room and softly close the door, and then Merrick went out the door and through the hedge to the Maitland house to tell his new friend what the doctor had said.

He found Lane out in the back yard superintending a painting job. He traced him by the sound of eager young voices, punctuated now and then by an older voice of instruction.

Lane gave one glance at Merrick's face and knew he had news.

"I've engaged some painters," he explained with a wink at the brother. "I'm glad you sent over those overalls. They just came in handy. This house has needed painting for some time, so the boys are going to try their hand at doing the back kitchen for a start. We have a good strong ladder, and it isn't far to the roof, even if they do take a drop now and then."

He grinned at Merrick.

"But they don't know how to paint," said Merrick. "They'll make a mess of it!"

The two little boys cast anxious eyes at their brother. Was he going to spoil everything for them now, just when they were having the time of their life? They looked fearsomely toward their host. But he only smiled and shook his head.

"You're mistaken," he said. "They are doing admirably. I gave them a lesson on painting just now. Not that I know so much myself about it, you know, but they are following my instructions to the letter. Let's you and I go over there under the trees and sit down a bit and talk. That's right, boys, long smooth strokes and not too much paint on the brush."

"Say, you're some friend!" said Merrick in admiration. "I don't think we're ever going to be able to thank you for what you're doing for these kids."

"Don't try," said Lane dryly. "I'm just having a chance to get a little back for what your mother did for me when I had typhoid fever. And incidentally these fellows are helping me through a very hard time. You know it hasn't been an easy thing for me to come back all alone to this house where I was so happy. I knew things here had to be looked after or they would go to wrack and ruin. So I came on to put the house in shape to sell. Then I was going to get away as quickly as I could. But these fellows have just helped me over the hard part and made me feel I love the old place almost too much to leave it. Here, get into that hammock, boy! You look as if you hadn't had a wink of sleep all night. Now, get on with your story. The boys won't hear, they're too intent on seeing how much paint they can slap on a single board. How are things over at the house? Any worse?"

"No! No worse than they have been, I guess, only the doc decided to tell us what was going on, that's all."

He told briefly what the doctor had said.

"Well, say, that's good, old fellow! I know it's serious, but it's good, too, to know there is *some* hope. I've been afraid all along there wasn't. But I knew a man who had that same trouble and he got over it. He was one of the professors at our college. Everybody thought he was going to die of course, but he came through in fine shape. But he had to lie absolutely still for several weeks. Now, what can we plan that will help things? Why couldn't you all come over here and live till the stress is over? There's plenty of room for everybody, and I could get out if that would make things any easier. Or couldn't you all be spared?"

"Say, you're great! But I don't think anybody could be spared just at present. Lexie's still in bed, and Gwynnie has to be watched over. She's like a ship without a rudder, that kid, without mother. But it's great of you to think about it. It's been enough for you to keep those noisy boys. I don't know what we would have done with them over there! They can't keep still a second. Oh, we'll have to talk it over. I don't just know what's coming. The doctor wants mother to go away when she's able, if she gets well enough, and then I don't know what'll become of everybody."

"What about that wedding? Will Maris really be going away?"

"Oh, I suppose so! I haven't asked. I don't know as she's even thought of it yet. But she'll have plenty of thinks coming pretty soon, I reckon. I thought I saw Tilford's car coming down the street as I started over here. He's the limit. It's lucky he's too refined to talk loud or we might have another catastrophe. If mother should happen to hear him talk she might not want to live."

"Well, look here, Merrick. You quit worrying! There'll be a way. Even if Maris goes off to Europe next week, or is it the week after?—we'll plan a way. You'll have to consider me a real brother and let me in on this thing. Maybe we can work something out. Anyway it isn't necessary to cross all the bridges on the highway before we come to them. We may find a detour or two and eliminate some of them. But you know I've got another house down in Virginia. Inherited it from an old aunt who just died, and that can come into the picture too, if it's necessary. There's a sweet old Scotch lady staying in it now. My aunt left provision in her will for her, and I just asked her to stay on for awhile. She used to be my aunt's companion, just an old friend of hers, but a real gentlewoman. We might work her in somehow if we need a woman to look out for the girls. Anyhow, don't you worry!"

"Thanks awfully, Lane! You're great! But whenever I think of the necessity I'm so mad I can't see. Any other decent man would be willing to put off his wedding awhile, or at least suggest they—well—we wouldn't *want* him to come here and live with us—that would be the limit. But he won't let Maris off, I know. I've overheard some of the things he's said to her, and he's impossible!"

Lane Maitland drew his brows down and set his lips

firmly for a minute as he stared at Merrick thoughtfully.

"Of course Maris ought to be strong enough to resist him," went on Merrick in a discouraged voice, "but I suppose that's a good deal to expect of a girl when her wedding invitations are all out and her man isn't willing."

"Are they out yet? I wondered."

"Why, I s'pose they're out. I haven't asked. I know they were all addressed, and I heard him roaring up the stairs at her about them. Everything has to toe the mark to live with him, but I s'pose she'll knuckle down and do just what he wants and then everything'll be lovely. My sister really has a nice disposition. That is, she did before that bird came around and spoiled everything."

Meantime Tilford Thorpe had arrived, and Maris answered Sally's tap on the door, lingered an instant to brush her disordered hair, and then with sudden impulse knelt beside her bed.

"Oh, Lord," she prayed earnestly, "help me, please. Show me just what to say. Show me definitely about this whole matter."

Then with a calmer heart than she had had since her mother had been taken sick she went quietly down the stairs.

It was like Tilford to act as if nothing had happened. To start right in on the thing in hand and ignore what had passed till he got ready to bring it up again and utterly demolish it.

He was standing out on the doorstep impatiently looking down the street, as if he had no part nor lot in this house and couldn't bear even to come into it. As if he resented that it had any right in Maris.

He turned, hat in hand, as she arrived in the hall like a shadow of her former self, so white and tired-looking, yet somehow more assured and at her ease.

"Good morning, Maris," he said formally. "Suppose you come outside in the sunshine. It isn't worth while for me to run any risks of contagion so near the wedding time now. Mother seems to think I may not have have had measles. I just ran down to ask if you had mailed those invitations yet. Because it really is necessary to do so at once. I cannot allow this foolishness to go on any longer. As it is we shall have to do a lot of explaining. If you will get them for me at once before there can be any further interruption, then my mind will be at ease and we can talk about several other important things that must be settled this morning. Bring the list, too, and I will take them right to my secretary down at the office and that will be off my mind—that is, if you haven't sent them. Have you?"

Maris looked at his cold handsome face and wondered how she had ever thought him lovable. He suddenly seemed so hard and self-centered. Why hadn't she felt this before? Why hadn't she known he would be like this in a time of stress? He hadn't even asked after the sick ones. Just plunged right into the one thing that he was so determined about. But perhaps it was as well. She could more easily say what she had to say if he was this way than if he had been gentle and kind. She studied him for a second before she answered, trying to imagine what it would be like if he should ask her pardon for the way he had talked to her the last time he came; trying to think how it would be if he should draw her into his arms and kiss her tenderly and say how sorry he was that she looked tired, and he wished there was some way he could help her.

But the imagining did not get very far with a screen door between them, and Maris somehow felt a repugnance toward going out on the front porch to talk. Tilford was holding the door open for her now however, and rather than make a scene she came out.

"Have you sent them?" he reiterated as she stepped out into the sunshine. He could not help but see the ravages of anxiety and loss of sleep now. "Heavens!" he added as he glanced at her. "What a sight you are! You had no right to do this so near to the wedding! You will look so old and worn I shall be ashamed of you. When did you send the invitations, Maris?"

"The invitations have not gone," said Maris quietly. "I did not send them because I am not going to be married on the thirtieth of June. There would be no point in sending invitations if there was to be no wedding."

"What do you mean, Maris? You can't possibly change the date! I have all my arrangements made, and have gone to a great deal of trouble to get those particular reservations. You can't do that to me."

"I'm sorry," said Maris calmly. "I did not plan this. I could not help it."

"Oh, really! Who did plan it? Your family? And just what date are they arranging for the wedding then? I should have supposed since they are so careful about expense they would have remembered that it would cost a lot more to get the invitations engraved all over again. But perhaps they are figuring to get the town crier to go out and publish the banns or something of that sort."

Tilford was very angry. There was a bright red spot on each cheek. His handsome eyes had sparks of wrath in them. He was forgetting himself and being unforgivably and quite plebeianly rude. He seldom allowed himself to overstep a formal address at least, no matter how angry he was.

Maris' face was desperately white, and her chin was lifted just the least bit.

"My family had nothing whatever to do with it," she said steadily. "They do not even know about it. They have not had time to think about weddings. We have been living in the midst of desperate sorrow here, Tilford. You do not seem to understand."

"Oh, pardon me! Did your mother die, Maris? Was it as bad as that? I should have supposed you would let me know if that happened. But I don't see why that should delay the wedding. I am sorry for you of course, but your mother is better off, and she wouldn't want you to change your plans. People don't stop for such things nowadays, you know, and since we are going abroad everybody will understand why we went ahead. Besides, if the funeral is soon, there will be really quite a decent interval between. Since it had to happen, I'm glad it happened now instead of next week. People will understand why we were late in sending invitations."

Maris looked at him aghast. Had he been drinking? He did drink sometimes at parties and big dinners, but not usually at other times. Not in the morning.

She was so still that he stopped talking and looked at her puzzled. There were tears in her eyes but she had that aloof look to which he was not accustomed in her.

"What's the matter? Why are you looking at me that way? I'm only being perfectly sensible. It's all out of date to be sentimental about the inevitable."

"Stop!" said Maris suddenly. "My mother is not dead!"

"Oh!" He looked at her as if she were somehow to blame. "Really, Maris, I don't see why you tried to give me that impression then. What is it you're trying to do? Just have an argument? Because I haven't time. Won't you get those invitations for me at once, and let us have done with this foolish argument!"

"Listen, Tilford," she said, trying to control her voice and speak quietly, although the thing she wanted to do most of all was to scream and burst into tears and run away from him. "Listen! I'm not going to get those invitations now or any other time because there can't be any wedding on June thirtieth! My mother is very sick. Far worse than we dreamed. She has a clot of blood in the heart, and while the doctor says there is a possibility that she may get well, it is just as possible that she may die at any minute. Under those circumstances you certainly know that I could not think of leaving home. Even if my mother should get well it would be at least a year before she would be able to take up her life again and look after her home and her children."

"A year!" said Tilford coldly. "Are you expecting me to put off my marriage for a year?"

"No," said Maris haughtily. "I did not suppose that you had anything to say about it. In fact I supposed that since I gave you back your ring you understood that that ended all between us. You made no protest and you did not come back to talk it over. But since you have insisted on having the invitations I am only making it plain to you that I cannot marry you. At least not for a very long time. And I'm not sure, since all this has happened, that I would want to, even then. I am just telling you that everything is over between us."

He looked at her with vexation and a kind of wonder in his eyes.

"Look here, Maris, of course I'm not going to allow you to carry out this ridiculous idea. In fact I'm sure you didn't expect me to. You think that you will gain a little time, and get me to coax you up and pet you and all that. I didn't come back with your ring because I thought you were in no mood to take care of it just then and I had better keep it until you came out of that silly mood. Just heroics, that's all it was when you thrust that ring into my hand. Of course I knew you were all worn out with the demands of your ridiculous family. But I knew if I gave in to you then you would only think you could go farther. I thought it would do you good just to go without your ring for a few days and see how it feels to have a ring like that and then have it gone. But you needn't think you can keep this up. I shall exercise my authority and demand that you come away from this house and take a good rest, and then we'll go on with the wedding as quietly as it can be done, and get away on the ocean to different scenes and get you all over this nonsense."

"Authority?" said Maris. "You have no authority over

me now. I gave you back your ring which you said was the sign of your authority. And I have no idea of leaving this house or family. They are my family and this is my home, and I would not go away from them now for all the rings in the universe. I love them, and they are in trouble, and that means that I am in trouble too. They belong to me, are a part of me. I owe them all the love and care I have."

"That's all nonsense, Maris. That's a fallacy of the dark ages. We don't owe our parents a thing in the world. That's an exploded theory invented by parents to keep their children cowed. We're done with all that now. Each one of us has to live his own life as he pleases. The modern generation has shifted all that nonsense and are proving that life is a free adventure each works out for himself. We—"

"Stop!" said Maris. "I don't want to hear another word of that kind of stuff. I thought you were a Christian—at least I supposed you thought you were."

"A Christian?" laughed Tilford disagreeably. "Well, why should you question that? I often go to church, don't I? I give to the Red Cross work, and the Welfare, I'm always generous! I was confirmed ten years ago. I've told you that, I'm sure—"

"None of those things make a Christian," said Maris. "I don't know much about it myself and I realize I haven't been a very wonderful Christian and have no right to criticize, but in these long nights of anxiety I've had time to think, and I've seen myself as God must see me, and I'm ashamed."

"Oh, for heaven's sake, Maris, don't go religious on me! I can't endure ranting women. Maris, think of all our plans! Think how much I've done to make you happy on this trip. Think of your love for me. You're angry now, but you do love me. You did love me when I gave you your ring, didn't you, Maris?"

Maris lifted clear honest eyes:

"I thought I did, but—I wonder—if I ever did? Perhaps I was carried away with the glamour of having you compliment me and take me around in a beautiful car."

"That is ridiculous, Maris. You are just overwrought. You loved me of course. I've seen it in your eyes. Here, let's go somewhere out of this awful glare of the sun and talk this thing out. I can't think what has got into you. Just because your mother is a little sick and you've sat up a few nights—You've made a mountain of a molehill. Come, get into the car and we'll take a little ride. It will freshen you up. No matter if you aren't dressed, we'll drive out into the country where nobody will see you."

"No!" said Maris firmly. "I can't go, and I can't stay to talk any more. There isn't anything to say, anyway. My mother is very low, and must be absolutely quiet for six weeks at least, not even moving her arms or hands. And if she lives to get better she will have to go away for several months for absolute rest. My sisters and brothers have no one but me to keep things together."

"Nonsense! Let your father get a housekeeper. Other men have to do things like that."

"A housekeeper could not look after the children. Lexie is only a baby yet, and the boys are very young."

"Oh, that's easy. The children can be sent away to good schools. They have schools for very young children conducted by the very newest methods, which would doubtless be far better for them than to be coddled the way your mother has been doing. For the matter of that if the children went away to school your father and brother could board. There are cheap boarding houses. They could let the house furnished and take a room somewhere near their business and take meals at a restaurant. I understand that is a cheap way to live."

They had been sitting down in the porch rockers as they talked, but suddenly Maris arose, drew herself up to her full height and spoke sharply:

"That is all I want to hear about that!" she said, her voice like icicles. "Even if I were sure that I loved you as I thought I did awhile ago, even if you had not done and said all the unpleasant, unloving things that you have done the past week when I was in trouble, I would never want to go away with you and leave my family in distress. I *know* I love my family, but I'm not at all sure that I *ever* loved you! Goodbye!"

And before Tilford's astonished eyes Maris turned and walked into the house and up the stairs.

Tilford sat there in the chair a long time expecting her to come back and ask to be forgiven, but she did not come. He was shocked at her stubbornness.

Now, what was his mother going to say? And after she had bought that wedding dress, too!

MARIS shut herself into her room and faced herself in her mirror. It was as if she felt the need of telling herself what had just happened. Lexie was comfortable for the moment and the mirror was out of her range. She stood and looked into her own eyes facing facts. She was not going to be married in a few days! She was not going to marry Tilford *ever!* That was as clear as if a voice had spoken and told her so. She realized now that she ought to have known that long ago. She was not going to Europe on her wedding trip! She was just a girl in her father's home, with a great many things to regret, and a great many to undo, and suddenly heavy burdens upon her unaccustomed shoulders.

So now, what was she going to do about it?

It was imperative for her soul's sake that she do something at once. She could not just stand and face this thing supinely. She had to go vigorously at something to right matters, now that she saw her mistakes. She must burn her bridges behind her.

Strange, she had no compunctions. No fears that perhaps she was going too fast. That perhaps Tilford would be back and change the whole thing, ask her to forgive him, show his real repentance for his hardness, tell her it was his mistake, that he truly loved her family and wanted to be a real son to them, that he loved her with all his heart and could not think of going on through life without her by his side. No possibility of that sort even crossed her imagination. If it had she would have known at once it could never happen. She had seen Tilford under the merciless light of testing and she could never again have illusions about him. Moreover she had seen her own heart in the light of this testing, and she knew that she too had been wanting in a number of things that a true heart union should have. She had looked upon her erstwhile engagement and forthcoming marriage as a beautiful gesture that would interfere not at all with the roots of her life, but would keep a continual round of pleasures always in the offing. And that wasn't what marriage should mean. That wasn't what it had meant to father and mother. For instance, she couldn't imagine herself lying on a sick bed as mother was at this moment and Tilford giving up everything to sit beside her and hold her hand. She couldn't even imagine herself getting much comfort out of it if he did.

Phrases of his with regard to her mother's possible death came floating sharply to her memory, and a wave of anger crimsoned her face, and receded leaving it deadly white again. If she had needed anything else to open her eyes after the way he had acted during the past few days that one thing was enough to have killed any love she might have had for him. No, it was better not to think of him at all. He was out of her life forever now, and it was best to be actively at work clearing away the debris from her little dead romance, if it could rightly be called a romance when it had not been built upon true love in the first place.

Well, what should she do first? Something decisive. Those wedding invitations! Those should be destroyed at once!

With a glance into Lexie's room to see that all was well

with her, she opened her own door softly and slipped out into the hall. As she did so she saw her father coming out of the room where he had been sleeping, dressed as if he were going to town. With troubled eyes she watched him go slowly downstairs, holding to the handrail like an old man, though he had never seemed old to her before. She followed him down, watching him wistfully. Wasn't there something she could do to relieve his worries? That note! She wondered if Merrick knew how much it was.

Her father had taken his hat from the rack in the hall closet and was going out the door! He ought not to go out! He wasn't strong enough. Where was Merrick? Perhaps he could go with him, or go for him.

Then Merrick appeared at the door and put out his hand to stop his father.

"Now, dad, where are you going?"

The father looked annoyed as if he had been caught playing hookey.

"Why, I just have to run out on an errand for a few minutes," he said apologetically. "I'll be right back."

"Now, dad, you're going down to the bank, you know you are, and you mustn't, see? We can't have you dropping down the way mother did. You've got to stay in and rest a bit. If somebody has to go down I'll go for you."

"You can't sign a note for me, son. I want to get that off my mind. If anything should happen to me I want that note signed."

"Look here, dad. Mr. Matthews said you needn't hurry. He said it was all right any time this week. He said for you not to come till mother was better. He said if you wanted him to he would send you up a note to sign."

"Well, I'd rather go myself. I want to talk it over with him. I may need a little more money than I had expected, with mother sick, you know. I've got to talk it over with him and get it off my mind. It will be better for me to go, son, and get this done."

"Not today, dad. You mustn't, really. If mother should have another turn like the other day you wouldn't want to be away. Suppose you just jot down on a paper how much more you want and I'll go down and talk to him myself. I'm a man and I think I can put it over. Mr. Matthews is a prince. He was great yesterday. You trust me, dad. If you don't I'll call up the doctor and raise the riot act, for you're not going out in this hot sun this morning!"

"Look here, son, it's only two blocks to the trolley, and it won't hurt me in the least. I tell you I've got to get this thing off my mind and it's a great deal worse for me to sit still and think about it than it is for me to go down town for a couple of hours and get things fixed up. And I must run down to the office, you know, for a few minutes. I haven't been there for three days."

"That's all right, dad. The office won't run away. You trust Mr. Temple, don't you?"

"Perfectly. But there are things that he can't decide. I must go and see about some orders that ought to have come in. They're important."

"Yes, dad, all right, you write down just what it is you want me to ask about and I'll bring the letters up. I'll talk it over with Mr. Temple and get him to send up any letters you ought to see."

"Son, you really can't interfere with me this way!" Mr. Mayberry tried to speak sternly, but his voice was shaken, and Merrick's heart was wrung. Poor dad! He was carrying a heavy burden! If he'd only had his eyes open before, and not let his father slave to keep him in college. He ought to be at work earning money to help in this time of need. But dad shouldn't go out today, weak as he was! Not if he had to tie him to keep him at home.

"See here, dad! Nothing doing!" Merrick put his strong young arms about his father, and turned him around by force. Loving force it was, else his father would have struggled with him and got free. But he walked with him the few steps back to the door, earnestly arguing.

"Son, it's very kind of you to take such care of me, but you don't quite understand. This note has got to be renewed today, and I must go down and attend to it myself. There are things that you wouldn't understand."

Suddenly Maris opened the screen door and stepped out beside them, laying her hand on her father's arm.

"Father," she said quietly, just as if she were going to ask him to buy her a dozen oranges at the store, "I heard you talking about a note. How much is it? Why don't we pay it off and get it out of the way?"

The father looked at her with a shamed, hurt look, as if she had discovered his inmost secret, and he had no more courage to face the world.

"My dear—!" he said and his voice trailed off uncertainly, "you wouldn't understand. It's just a little matter of business I must attend to at once."

"Why, of course I'll understand," said Maris smiling. "I know what a note is and I want to know how much it is."

"It's only a small matter," evaded her father, "but it's necessary to be businesslike even in small matters."

"Yes, I understand, father, but why don't we pay it off? You have to pay interest on notes, don't you, unless you pay them off? Isn't it better to get them paid and be done with it? Doesn't it save money to do that?"

"Yes, my dear," said her father with a sad little smile, "but you see I don't happen to have the money in hand just now, and there's likely to be more need very immediately. I must be prepared. I haven't the money—" he passed his hand over his forehead with a kind of desperate motion and sighed heavily.

"Yes, but I have it," said Maris briskly. "Have you forgotten that three thousand dollar legacy grandmother left me?"

"But that is yours, my dear! That is in the nature of a dowry. I have been so glad that you had a little something of your own, that you do not have to leave your father's house absolutely penniless. No, Maris, my dear, I couldn't possibly use your money."

"You certainly could, and you certainly will," said Maris briskly. "Come over here, father, out of the sun, and let me tell you about it. That's my money, you said, and I have a right to use it as I choose, don't I? And I choose to use it this way."

"Yes, but my dear, though I know and love you for your loving generous heart I could never use that money. What would your—what would Tilford say if he knew I took your money to pay my debts!"

"Tilford has nothing whatever to do with it!" said Tilford's erstwhile fiancée with a wave of her hand. "Tilford does not even know I have any money. I never told him and I never mean to. I'm going to use this money to lift the burdens off of us as a family. That is, as far as it will go. Perhaps it won't go very far. You haven't told me yet how much that note is. If I haven't got enough we'll raise the rest some other way, but we'll pay off as much as we can right now and have that out of the way. Is it more than three thousand dollars, father?"

"Oh, no," her father laughed. "It's only eight hundred and fifty. But you see I was going to get a couple of hundred more if I could, just to ease things up a little here, keep us going from day to day, you know, and pay a few of the smaller bills. I was hoping things would look up at the office in a month or so, and then everything would be all right again. You know there have been a number of necessary expenses—" He paused in dismay and Maris took up his words almost gaily, briskly, as if she had her hand on the helm of their little lifeboat now, and was steering straight for shore.

"Yes, I know, father, a lot of *un*necessary expenses, if you ask me, and all connected with getting me married off. But you see I've come to my senses at last, and I'm taking over as many bills as I can and helping you to get clear of all this that has rested so heavily on you. Now, Merrick, if you'll just get the data from father I'll run up and get a check. Merrick, don't dare let father go down town today, I'll be right back!" and Maris was off on light feet speeding up to her desk.

"Oh, but I can't let her do that!" said the father looking dazedly at his son. "It was to have been her dowry. Mother and I were so glad she had it. And Tilford! What will he think of me?"

"Tilford be hanged! What's he got to do with it? She'll never tell him. She *wants* to do it, dad. She's a peach, and you mustn't make her feel bad by refusing it. She's been worried about you, I could see. You've got to take it, dad. Haven't you been giving, giving, giving ever since we were born? And we've just taken and never helped a cent's worth!"

"It is the parent's place to give."

"Well, not forever. It's our place now. I only wish I had a legacy and I'd turn it all over to you. But I'll find a way to help too, you'll see."

Suddenly the father's head went down on his lifted hand, and Merrick could see that he was deeply stirred.

"Listen, dad," said Merrick trying to clear the huskiness from his throat, "that's no way to take it. It's no humiliation. Why can't we all be glad one of us has got it to clear the rest? Why aren't you pleased Maris isn't selfish? Why aren't you glad this note can be paid and you won't have to worry about it any longer?"

"I am. I will be!" said the father lifting his head with a sudden smile.

"That's the talk. Here comes Maris. Now, smile again. Turn on the works, quick!"

Mr. Mayberry met his daughter with a smile that was almost blinding, as she came down with a check in her hand.

"I'm just so happy I had it, father," she whispered as she put her arms around his neck and kissed him, and he held her close for a moment.

"You precious child!" he said. "It is wonderful of you to do this. Of course I didn't mean anybody to find out I was in a tight place, but this has lifted a great burden from me. Wait till I tell your mother about it. Just as soon as she is able to hear it."

"Don't be in too big a hurry, daddy," warned Maris. "Let her forget for a while that there are burdens. But we're going to make it our business to see that the burdens don't get heavy again, father. Now, if you want to do something for us you'll go in and drink that nice cold milk and egg that Sally has just made for you, and then you'll go and lie down and sleep a little while before lunch."

When father had obediently gone smiling in to follow her orders Maris turned to Merrick.

"Merrick, will you have time to step down to the stationer's and pay that bill before father sees it? Here's a blank check and you can fill it in. Here's what I think it is, but there may be something extra I've forgotten. I'd like to get that bill paid before father ever sees it."

Merrick flashed her a look.

"I certainly am proud of my sister!" he said. "It's the greatest thing I ever knew a girl to do, right on the edge of her wedding day, too!"

A startled look came over Maris' face and she almost opened her lips to explain, and then she closed them again. Somehow she felt as if she mustn't tell yet that there was to be no wedding. It seemed as if she must tell this first to her mother and father before she broadcasted it to the family. She struggled with a sudden desire to hug her brother who all at once seemed so grown up and dependable, but she knew it would embarrass him so she only smiled.

"It's only what you would have done yourself, you old fraud," she said tenderly.

"Never having been a girl before her wedding I don't know, but I'm sure I'd like to have the money to try," he said. "Wait till I get to working! You'll see!"

"Of course I will. Now, get away to the city and get that note paid. Have you got father's bank book and all the data? And say, Merrick, do you think there are any other notes or things?"

"No, I guess not, but I'll find out. He told me there would be a big caterer's bill and a florist bill, and cars for the wedding and—"

"Yes? Well, we won't worry about those just now," said Maris, "but if there's anything else he ought to pay please let me know."

"I should say it was my job if there's anything else."

"Well, you haven't got a legacy just now, Merrick."

"No, but I've got an expensive set of golf clubs, two tennis rackets and a canoe up at college I think I could sell. Watch me! I'll go my share, too. So long! I'll be back in time for dinner. Tell dad not to worry if I'm late," and Merrick hurried away in the sunshine.

Maris watched him a minute, her heart lighter than it had been for several days. What a dear boy he was anyway! What a precious family she had, and suddenly her heart thrilled with gladness that it was her right and privilege to watch over them and help them now without anyone to hinder nor say her nay.

She would have to explain Tilford's absence pretty soon of course, but not until she had got used to things herself and adjusted her life to its new order.

Then she turned and sped upstairs to her patient who about this time would be demanding some amusement.

But the wedding invitations were still hidden in the attic.

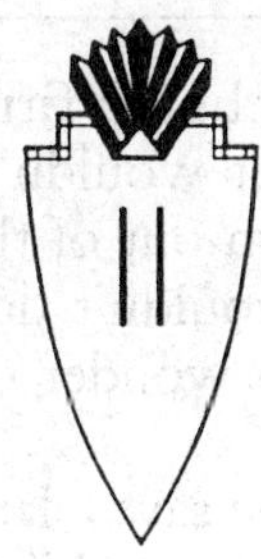

THE rest of that day was very full. It seemed there was no time to do the things she wanted very much to do at once. Lexie was hard to please. She was hot and restless and wanted her mother. She wanted to have the window shades up and be given a picture book, both of which were against the doctor's orders, for her eyes must be guarded carefully.

Maris did her best to make the child happy, meantime letting her own thoughts run ahead with plans. But it was not until almost eight o'clock in the evening that the little patient was finally asleep and Maris free to do what she would.

She slipped into her mother's room for a minute, and saw her father lying on the cot sleeping with a look of real rest on his face, and her heart was glad that she had been able to relieve him from at least one of his heavy burdens.

Quietly she slipped up to the attic and brought out the wedding invitations. She had a feeling somehow that she was committing burglary.

She had planned to burn them out in the incinerator, but when she touched their smooth thick surfaces, the double envelopes making such bulky firm white slabs, she realized that things like that wouldn't burn very easily. She would have to pull them out of their envelopes and burn them one by one. It wouldn't do to leave any traces of them about for Sally to wonder over and perhaps gossip about in the village.

Looking about her she saw a large box of excelsior that had come around the only wedding present she had as yet received. It was a great ugly old-fashioned lamp sent her by an old friend of the family, now in her nineties, who had moved out west some twenty years ago, when Maris was a baby. It was a hideous thing. The old lady had written that she had heard the Mayberry's oldest girl was going to be married pretty soon, so she thought she would send her a present. It was a lamp that had been given herself as a wedding present, and she thought Maris might like to have it because it was so old.

It was an oil lamp with a terrible glass shade on which a floral decoration had been poorly painted. Maris had looked at it in despair, and written a nice little note of thanks, and then hastily gathered up its parts and dumped the whole thing in the attic out of the way, for it came to her that it would never do to let Tilford see that lamp!

So here it was beside her as she turned to go down with her boxes of invitations, an ugly old lamp lying in a great lot of excelsior. Just the thing to start the thick envelopes burning.

Quickly she removed the lamp and took the box down with her. Soon those carefully addressed invitations were roaring up in smoke into the summer night, licked by crackling flames. The notable names of the town's four hundred stood out boldly in Maris' clear handwriting for an instant, and then were crumbled into black parchment.

Maris stood there and watched them burn, fascinated by the thought that her hopes of yesterday, and all she had built up for what she had thought would be happiness, were so quickly destroyed. An expensive little fire, but how much it meant! How quickly God had showed her when He got ready to act. It filled her with a kind of awe. Was God watching all her acts and plans that way? Did He watch everybody so, and take account of what was best for them? Was God as personal as that?

She lifted her eyes to the clear sky above, set with many stars. God taking account of her. God arranging things to make her see her mistakes before it was too late!

But yet, she had had her own free choice. Suppose she had yielded to Tilford and gone on? Would God have let her have her way and bear the consequences? That was something to think about when she had time. She gave a little shiver there in the darkness when she remembered Tilford's face as he talked to her that morning. What would it be to be under authority to a man who did not care for her dear ones? From whom even death could bring no sympathetic word?

She was poking among the ashes, lifting an envelope here and there that was sliding out of the way of the flame and keeping its identity in spite of the fire, when she heard Gwyneth coming through the kitchen. She had left Gwyneth studying hard in the library. Why didn't she stay there? She didn't want Gwyneth to see her holocaust. Gwyneth wouldn't understand, and might be horrified. She didn't want to have to explain, not yet. Not while trouble was in the house. Not while mother lay so ill.

She turned swiftly and met Gwyneth as she opened the kitchen door.

"Oh, here you are!" said the little girl. "Someone wants you on the phone. I think it's the doctor, but I'm not sure."

With sudden fear clutching at her heart Maris left her fire and hurried in, yet even as she went, reason returned. If it was the doctor it would only be some direction about her nursing. Nothing terrible could come from the doctor when he wasn't at the house. So, more composedly she went to answer the call. And then it was only an agent for a remedy for seasickness. He said he had heard she was going to take a sea trip for her honeymoon and he wanted to recommend this marvelous remedy. Might he call and tell her more about it. He had a list of notable people who had used it with great success.

Maris cut him off abruptly with the information that she had no need for any such remedy, and half vexed with a world that was continually meddling in other people's business, went back to her burning.

The fire had died down, and all the white corners seemed to be gone. Just to be sure, however, she put in the last of the excelsior with the box that had contained it, and the flames leaped up again in great shape and took every vestige of telltale white paper with them. Maris turned away with a sigh of relief. Those invitations could no more make trouble. They did not exist. It had all been a bad dream, those last days of frantically making out lists and addressing envelopes, of having Tilford telephone that some mistakes had been made in addresses, and he had another list, of having her father hover near worrying lest some old friend was being left out, or lest the plain little church they attended would not hold all these high and mighty guests. That was over. Purged by fire!

She turned a last look at the now dying fire, and cast upon it in her thoughts, the memory of that pretty wedding procession, the white trailing veil, the rainbow tinted bridesmaids, her two little sisters, Lexie as flower girl, and Gwyneth in her first long dress as maid of honor. All that pretty dream was gone now. She probably would never marry. Though if she did the dress that mother made would of course be used, no matter if she married a royal throne—which of course she wouldn't—having just turned down the nearest approach to anything like wealth and influence that would likely ever cross her path.

Nevertheless it was with a light heart that she locked the kitchen door and went upstairs. She felt easier in her mind than she had since she had caught that glimpse of the dear shabby old house and sensed the contemptuous scorn in Tilford's tone as he voiced the sentiment that he was not expecting her to have any further connection with it after she was married.

There was one more thing she meant to do tonight before she slept. She must make one more visit to the attic. She wanted to put that precious wedding dress away out of sight, where nothing could happen to it, and where no alien eyes could possibly search it out and bring it into criticism. If anything happened to mother—or if it didn't—that dress would always be her most prized possession.

There was a great white pasteboard box lined with satin paper. It had held a pair of lovely white pure wool blankets, the softest, finest blankets that could be found, with wide satin bindings. They were the last things that mother had bought for her, and she treasured them greatly. They were over mother now, tucked softly about her quiet form, covered scrupulously with an enshrouding sheet by the careful nurse so that no soil could possibly come to them. Maris was so glad that mother had them about her. It comforted her to have them there. The dear blankets that mother had bought. Precious mother who so seldom bought anything pretty or fine for herself.

And now that beautiful, strong box would be the very thing in which to put away her wedding dress.

She carried the dress to her own room and closing the door between it and the playroom where Lexie was, she folded the exquisite dress, breadth by breadth, with its perfect needlework and beautiful lace puffed out by tissue paper till not a fold nor crease was possible.

She looked at it there in the box as it lay, with a little spray of orange blossoms they had bought that last day of shopping together, nestled at the throat. It looked so like a lovely personality that had been sinned against, that dress. As if it were glad to be folded away and rest.

A bright tear sprang into Maris' eye and she closed the box quietly and tied it up. There must be no tears shed on that dress. Only smiles should greet it if it ever came out again.

She stood on a chair and put the box on the highest shelf of her roomy closet, far back where no one would ever be likely to notice it.

Then Maris went with swift soft tread back and forth a few times to bring the lovely dresses that had been prepared for her trousseau. There were not a great many of them, but each one was charming of its kind, and Maris had been pleased with them. But now they must go into seclusion. No one wanted to see the trousseau of a poor dead wedding hanging around. Besides, another nurse was coming now in a few minutes, a night nurse to relieve the first nurse, so that mother would not be alone a minute. She must hurry and make room for more stiff uniforms. There were a few things still hanging in the other guest room where father was sleeping at night now. She must get those out of the way before the nurse roused him and sent him to bed in earnest.

So, almost ruthlessly, those garments that had been bought so carefully, one at a time, and admired as each a prize in itself, were gathered into a heap on her arm and dumped unceremoniously on her bed to get the other closets empty before anyone discovered what she was doing. She locked her door while she was hurtling them into her own closet which suddenly seemed to lose its spaciousness as the grand garments were ushered in.

But at last they were all hung up, with a garment bag

guarding the entrance. In the morning she would find time to slip them into bags, or under covers, and then later if mother got well, and everything was all right and normal again she would bring them forth casually one by one as if she had always worn them, and nobody would remember that they had been wedding clothes.

Just then she heard Merrick drive up in Lane Maitland's car. The new nurse had arrived and she must go down and meet her.

But while Maris was showing the new nurse her way about, and helping to get her father settled for the night, Gwyneth had hopped into the car beside Merrick and was riding around to the Maitland garage with him.

"I gotta go with you because I gotta ask you something," she declared when he protested that she ought to be in bed.

"Listen, Merrick, isn't our Maris going to get married after all? Because the telephone rang and someone wanted her, and I smelled paper burning, so I went out into the kitchen and she was outside at the incinerator burning a whole lot of things, a big bonfire, and it flickered down and almost went out just as I got there. And so I went out to see if it was all safe while she went to the telephone, and I found down in the corner against the stone, just beginning to scorch around the edge, one of her wedding invitations! It was addressed to Tilford's aunt up at Coral Crest, so I knew it was an invitation, and anyway I pulled it out and took out the invitation and saw what it was."

"Oh, that was likely some that got spoiled in addressing," said the brother lightly. "You've just got one of your spells of romancing. You ought to be in bed."

"No, but truly, Merrick, it was. And there were a lot more little black squares down in the incinerator. I lighted a match and looked."

"All right, have it your own way. You'd better get a

detective and find out. I don't know anything about it," said Merrick crossly.

"Oh, but don't you wish it was true, Merrie? Don't you wish she wouldn't get married?"

"Oh, sure! Anything you want. I wish the sky would rain roses and the grass would grow gold dollars. Now, scram and get to bed before I spank you!"

TILFORD Thorpe went home to his mother and told her he was done with women. He didn't intend to marry ever, and he wanted it thoroughly understood that she needn't fling any of her stupid million-heiresses at him. He told her Maris was a liar, she had broken her word, and she had been stubborn and mulish about foolish things. And in the same breath he informed her that it was all her fault. That she had tried to force a silly dress on a girl who had too much pride to take advice, and she had broken his heart, and he would never be happy again. He prattled of suicide, and said it would serve his mother right, that she was always trying to manage his life for him and he hadn't a chance in the world to be himself, and a lot of like phrases, until she wept bitterly and wished she had never been born. And when he had exhausted his hurt pride upon her in invectives, and refused every kind of an offer to help she could think of, telling her if she had kept her everlasting tongue out of the whole matter he would still be happy, and soon married and off to Europe, he told her he was going off and get drunk, and she needn't try to find him either. He was his own master and he wouldn't be bound by her any longer.

When she suggested that he take the ring back to Maris and tell her he would let her put off the wedding till her mother was better, he raved and fairly bit the air, and slammed away to haunts known only to himself and his fellow club members. He remained away for three days, getting drunk. Thoroughly. Playing poker for high stakes and losing heavily.

He arrived home at last having run down an old woman carrying home a basket of groceries, got himself arrested and bailed out again, and came in looking like a wreck.

"Oh, Tillie dear! Where have you been?" wailed his mother as he entered her bedroom where she had been more or less in her bed, except for a social engagement or two, ever since her encounter with Doctor MacPherson.

"Now don't begin that song and dance!" said the youth insolently. "I've been where I've pleased to be. That's where you are too, isn't it? I came up here to see if you had any more light on the matter that concerns me most. Has Maris telephoned? I understood you to say that a little silent treatment might bring her around. Has she come?"

"I haven't seen her," said his mother sadly. "No, she hasn't telephoned. I'm afraid you're going to find that your girl is an utter failure in every way. It is as I told you in the first place, Tillie, it is never wise to go out of your own class when you really settle down seriously to get married. And really, my dear, even if she had come, I should not have received her. Not after the treatment I received in her home. They are an utterly worthless lot, my dear, and you are well rid of her!"

Tilford lit a cigarette and flung himself down in a white brocade chair, his hat slung to the back of his handsome head, his haggard eyes fixed angrily on his mother.

"Can that stuff!" he said fiercely. "You don't think I'm going to give her up after all this, do you? You don't think

I'm going to have the whole town see me trampled under foot and scorned, do you? Not if the whole generation of Mayberrys drive you out of their house. I'm in this thing to win, and I'm not going to be beaten off. After all, you had it coming to you. I told you you wouldn't get anywhere with that stubborn little woman. She's playing to win, but she's going to get the surprise of her life when she sees how things come out. I've got my plans all laid, and *I'm* going to win! Don't ask me anything about it. Just be ready to do whatever I tell you when the time comes. We may not have any wedding on June thirtieth in their little old dinky church, but we'll have a wedding all right, and don't you forget it. And we're sailing as per schedule, too. And when she's married and finds herself out on the ocean I guess she'll sing another tune."

"Now, Tillie!" said his mother with apprehension, "what are you going to do? You mustn't do anything scandalous! You mustn't get us in the papers."

"Oh, no! Don't you worry about that," bragged the young man. "I'll attend to what gets in the papers. I'll send in the write-up myself, just what I want printed. There won't be any scandal except in the eyes of her precious family. I'll fix it so there'll be plenty for them to contemplate."

"Oh, Tilford! You frighten me! You haven't been drinking, have you? You don't sound like yourself!"

"Well, if I have, is it your business?" he asked in a surly tone. "I can look out for myself, can't I? You brought me up to drink like a gentleman."

"Oh, Tilford!" wailed his mother. "You are being rude to me. If I brought you up to anything at all I brought you up to be courteous!"

"Courtesy be hanged! I'm done with the things you brought me up to. I'm going to get my wife the way I please and you can take the consequences."

"Oh, Tillie! You have been drinking. You never spoke

to me like that before! You certainly must be drunk!" wailed his mother looking at his wild eyes in horror.

Suddenly the father's substantial form loomed large and impressive in the doorway.

"Tilford!" his voice thundered. "You're forgetting yourself! Get out of your mother's room at once! Come with me!"

Tilford turned bewildered. His father's voice was reminiscent of his childhood's days when at rare intervals the usually loving indulgent father became a stern parent and administered a long needed chastisement most thoroughly, so that it was not soon forgotten.

Mr. Thorpe's large strong hand laid hold on his son's arm and propelled him out of the room and down the hall to his own room.

"Now!" he said, eyeing the young man with mingled sorrow and disgust. "See if you can get yourself sobered up. You're not fit to be around with decent people. And when you're sober, perfectly sober, I've something to say to you that will be to your advantage!"

"Now look here, dad, you've no right to treat me this way. I'm a man! I have rights!"

"Oh, are you? You don't look one! Look at your clothes. You appear to have been on a brawl for several days! You need a bath and some clean clothes. But even they wouldn't make a man of you, I'm afraid. Take off those clothes! Get under a cold shower and come to your senses. Get in there, I say!" and he took hold of his son's arm and literally shoved him into the luxurious bath room.

"Let me alone! You've no right—!" protested the angry son.

"Oh, haven't I? Well, we'll see!" and the father deliberately took the key out of the door and put it into the other side of the lock.

"Now, stay in here until you've had a bath and are fully sober!" he said. "I'll be back in half an hour and if you have come to yourself I'll let you out." The father shut the door and turned the key in the lock, then strode down the hall again to his own domain called by his wife a "den" and shut himself in.

A moment later, Mrs. Thorpe in an elaborate frilly negligee of grass green, her feet thrust into green satin mules that flapped as she waddled so that she had to change them for bed socks, because they made too much noise, stole cumbersomely down the hall, with furtive backward glances toward the den. She arrived breathlessly at her son's door, tried it, and entered, gave a frightened glance about and immediately located a sound in the bathroom. She hurried to the door and found it locked.

"Tilford!" she whispered softly. "Mother's precious boy!"

"Oh, *shut up!*" roared Tilford angrily. "Will you get out? Can't I take a bath without being trailed?"

Mrs. Thorpe heard the far sound of an opening door up the hall and beat a hasty retreat, making a dive into the sewing room and coming back with a pair of scissors and a thimble in her hand as if she had gone after them, in case she met her husband.

But the door of the den was closed again and she was unmolested. She retired to her bedroom to sob over the sorrows of the woman who had an ungrateful child and couldn't do anything about it.

Exactly half an hour afterward Tilford sat in a big comfortable chair in his own room, clothed, and to a degree in his right mind, sulking.

His father entered the room but he did not look up nor notice him.

His father sat down in a stiff straight chair, clasped his hands firmly together in front of him, leaned forward a little, and gazed steadily at the graceful form of the handsome youth attired in a costly silk dressing gown and expensive slippers. There was something unutterably wistful in the father's expression as he looked at his boy, and saw in retrospect the whole span of his life so far from babyhood. There was a depth of sadness in his eyes that told how much of a bitter disappointment that young life had been to him, the father.

When Mr. Thorpe broke the silence that was becoming painful to them both, his voice had a business-like crispness that belied his expression.

"Now, Tilford, have you recovered your sanity enough to understand what I am about to say, or shall I have to wait until you have had a sleep?"

"Don't be an ass!" was the boy's disrespectful reply.

"That will do. Don't add to your troubles by being insolent to your father. Are you sober yet?"

Tilford summoned all the dignity belonging to past generations:

"Certainly. I have been sober all the time."

"No, you were not sober. If you had been you should certainly suffer more than I am going to mete out to you at present. But I want you to understand that you cannot speak to your mother in the way I heard you speak. It is inexcusable, and I will not stand for it. If it is ever repeated you will discover that I have power to make you exceedingly sorry that you ever did it. Your fortune, you know, is all in my hands, and I shall certainly not leave a cent to a young man who does not treat his mother decently."

"Oh, dad! How tiresome you are ! Mother's such a fool! She won't let a fellow alone!"

"Exactly. According to you, your father's an ass and your mother's a fool. Then, may I ask, *what are you?* I think it might be well for you to reflect for awhile over that question, when you have a little leisure from your own important affairs."

The boy flung himself about in his chair, leaning over with his elbows on his knees, his face in his hands, and groaned aloud.

"Oh, why do I have to be tormented this way, when I already have enough trouble to drive a hundred men insane?"

The father's face softened and a tortured look came into his eyes.

"Son, I know you are unhappy, but this is something basic that must be maintained, no matter what you are suffering. You must never lower yourself, no matter what you are going through, to be insolent to your mother, and I demand that before you do anything else you go to your mother and apologize."

"What nonsense!" flung out Tilford. "I'm not a little kid!"

"No!" said the father with a sigh, "I would that you were! I would certainly try to whale some sense into you. But you are supposed to be a gentleman. At least you were born one, and I intend to try and keep you one if I have to fling every cent I might leave to you into the depths of the sea. I may not be very wise about training children and I may not know anything about philosophy or religion, but that is one thing you know I have always insisted upon, that you shall be respectful to your mother. Now, Tilford, before I say anything more to you I want you to go across the hall and beg your mother's pardon."

"Gosh, dad! Of all the silly baby ideas!"

"If you keep on you'll have a few more apologies to make before you get through. I intend to see this through to the end."

There was a long silence, and then Tilford arose haughtily, contemptuously:

"All right! Let's have it over with," he said. "Do I go alone or are you coming along to see whether I do it right?"

"I'm coming along!" said his father with dignity.

Silently they went across the hall, the door opened to the mother's astonished eyes, and the two entered.

Tilford stood like one himself aggrieved, and made a scornful apology.

"Mother, dad seems to think I was rude to you. I sincerely apologize. I have been so much upset the past few days that I scarcely knew what I was doing anyway."

"Yes, of course, my dear!" murmured the mother with a gush of tears. "Don't think any more about it, Tillie dear!"

Then the young man turned away with a look of disgust.

"Is that all, dad? Or is there more to this?"

The father answered sadly:

"If that is the best you can do we will let that go for the present, and you and I will return to my library."

"Heavens and earth!" ejaculated the irascible youth. But he followed his father across the hall and stood at the window scowling, awaiting the next act.

"Sit down, Tilford."

His father's voice was almost tender now.

"Tilford, perhaps you don't know how your father's heart has been yearning over you during these last few days. I couldn't help but see that something was wrong when I got back from Chicago. But your mother was so upset over you that I hardly liked to ask her for particulars. Suppose you try to tell me the details. Is Maris still in trouble? Is her mother no better?"

"Oh, Gosh! Dad! Have I got to go into all that? No, her mother isn't any better, at least they won't admit she is. And Maris hasn't sent out the invitations, and thinks she can't get married on June thirtieth, and that leaves me all up a tree. What am I to do? She's given me back my ring, and lets on it's all over between us."

"Well, but let's understand this, son. What did you do to get her into a state that she wanted to give back your ring? Were you kind and helpful to her in her distress when her mother was sick? Did you offer to do anything you could?"

"I? What could I do? I couldn't get a chance even to talk to her for more than a minute. She comes downstairs with a hot-water bottle, or to get a bowl of ice or something, and has to run right back upstairs before she hardly gets down. She won't send out the invitations, nor let me send them. Helpful? I? Certainly I tried to be. I offered to get those invitations off in plenty of time. But no, she wouldn't even tell me where they were. Said she couldn't send out invitations when her mother was at the point of death. Said her kid sister had measles and she couldn't do anything but hover over her family day and night. She looks like an old crow with black circles under her eyes! Pretty bride she'll be! Helpful and kind? Why, I even got a special child's nurse to go there and tend that hateful little spoiled brat so Maris could go out and keep her engagements with me. Would she go? Not she. Said she'd send the nurse away if I sent her. Said the kid wanted her or her mother."

"Of course. What could you expect?"

"Expect? I'd expect her to take the help I gave and do her duty toward me. Isn't that what being engaged means?"

"No, I wouldn't say so. She can't leave her duty at home when they are in trouble. You ought to have tried to enter into her troubles and sympathize with her. You ought to have tried to find out her burdens and help to lighten them."

"Well, I did. Certainly I did. There was the matter of a suitable wedding dress for the kind of wedding due our family. Mother found a peach of a dress and suggested she go and see it. Would she go? Not one step. I tried to explain that mother had had it reserved for her at a special price, but no, she said her mother had *made* a dress for her! Imagine a mother being able to make a good enough dress for our wedding! And when I tried to exercise my authority, and tell her that she had no right to carry things with such a high hand she gets mad and flings me back my ring."

"Son, look here! I don't know what is the matter with you. You have a wonderful little girl in that Mayberry child, and you don't seem to know it. You shouldn't try to order her ways, you shouldn't tell her what to wear, and you shouldn't expect her to leave a sick mother and sister. There are such things as right and wrong in this world, though the young people of today don't seem to recognize that any more. You've probably hurt that child more than she has hurt you. I don't know whether you've got it in you to love her the way she ought to be loved and guarded or not. And I don't know her well enough to know whether she loves you well enough to stand your doldrums and tantrums or not, but I should say there was just one thing that would set you two right, if you can be set right, and that is for you to get down on your knees and be a little humble. Take your ring back to her and tell her you have seen yourself, and you are ashamed of yourself. Tell her you've been a fool and an ass yourself, and ask her to forgive you. If you do that, and she really loves you, she's bound to forgive you, and you can start all over again. If she doesn't really love you then it's all wrong from the beginning and better broken up.

"But son, you'll have to make concessions! When you ask her to forgive you you've got to tell her that you're willing to put the wedding off till she's ready, and that you'll come and help her nurse her sick ones back to health, and comfort her and sympathize with her. You'll have to tell her that it's grand for her to have a mother who can make a wedding dress for her daughter, and that of course she must wear that dress and no other, whether our world or her world or anybody else's world considers it the latest thing or not. There is something rare in a dress that a mother's love prepares. But my son, I'll miss my guess if you don't find that dress quite the fit thing after all. The mother of that girl wouldn't want her to wear anything that wasn't all right. Don't you know enough to know that? Now go get your evening togs on and run over to her house and say you're sorry, and you'll see how quickly your troubles will smooth out."

The son whirled on his father with a great scorn in his face, a perfect fury of indignation in his voice:

"*Me* go and tell Maris I'm sorry? Not on your life I won't! Do you suppose I'm going to do the little whipped-dog act you've done all your life, giving in to every blessed thing mother has demanded? Not me. I know my way around better than that! I'll get her back, don't you fear, but it won't be that way! Not on my life it won't!" and the son angrily slammed out and down the hall to his own room, and locked himself in.

The father sat stricken in his chair, with his face buried in his hands, and let the whole disappointment of the years roll over him. That was what he was in his family! A little whipped dog! And his son, the hope of his failing years, had told him so! There was nothing he could think of that life had to offer so bitter as that.

THE second nurse who had come to relieve Miss Bonner was most kind and helpful. She didn't stay during the daytime usually. Her home was not far away and she went home to her own bed to sleep when her night's work was done. But now and then she would run in an hour or two earlier than she was due to begin work, and suggest that she look after Lexie while Maris ran out to get a breath of air, or do an errand. Lexie had become very fond of her. She was Scotch and had a store of quaint little stories about foxes and birds and "beasties" as she called them. She had a Scotch accent that fascinated the little girl, and a winning way with her, as well as a deep fund of humor. Lexie always hailed her coming with delight.

She came over thus one afternoon when Maris was particularly worn and discouraged, and with a sigh of relief Maris went downstairs, glad to get away for a few minutes from the scene of hard work and anxiety.

Maris went through the downstairs rooms. All was in order. There was nothing here that demanded her attention. She had already gathered all the bills out of mother's desk and attended to them; hunted up estimates from florists and caterers and let them know that the wedding was called off on account of illness in the family; written notes to her bridesmaids and a few intimate friends who knew about the wedding plans. There was absolutely nothing to demand her hands to work or her tired brain to think.

She went out into the kitchen, but Sally had it immaculate. Preparations for the family dinner were in progress as they should be at that hour. The specially prepared dishes and trays that would be needed for the invalids were in the ice box in order, and she could hear Sally stepping around in her own room just off the kitchen, getting into a clean dress to serve the evening meal. There was no reason why she should linger here.

She stepped out of the back door and looked up into the cherry tree, laden with its brilliant fruit, reached up idly and picked a cluster, eating them as she walked on around the back door and into the garden. She had a strangely desolate feeling that she was all alone in the world and there was no one to turn to for a comfort of which she felt in sudden terrible need. She told herself that this was what came of relaxing even for a minute in the midst of hard work and anxiety. It was better to keep right on and not take time off with a beautiful world in June, when all the things that belonged in such a June life were hanging in jeopardy. Here was she who was to have been married in lovely grandeur and off on a dream-trip to foreign lands in just a few days now, suddenly snatched from all this idyl of a luxurious life and plunged into heavy hard work and desperate anxiety, shot through here and there by stinging annoyances from people who ought to have been her strongest reliance, and finally separated entirely from them and left to go alone. It was strange! So strange!

And this desolate feeling.

It wasn't just anxiety now. One can get used in a way to

the monotony of a long drawn out anxiety. It wasn't just weariness nor yet a longing for the gaieties of the life she had been living for the last six months since she had been engaged to Tilford. It was this sense of having no one in heaven or earth to depend upon.

Everyone to whom she would naturally turn now to rest her soul had to be carefully guarded for their own sakes. Father, how frail he was! Not so stooped and tortured looking perhaps since he had that note paid, and some bills out of the way that had tormented him, but still it seemed as if a breath might blow him away. He would not get over that, of course, till mother got well.

Merrick mustn't have any more anxieties. He was only a boy anyway. He had finished his last examination and was to start driving his bus route tomorrow morning. She mustn't load her trials on him. He had a responsible job and must keep his mind free from worry. And of course Merrick wouldn't understand all her problems anyway.

But it wasn't just problems, either, this afternoon. It was just a hungry longing for something that satisfies. The feeling was strong that she had given up the life that had stretched out so enticingly before her, and while it was the right thing to do, of course, and she couldn't have done anything else, wouldn't have wanted to, would do over again all that she had done, yet now in the late afternoon waning of the sun, while the shrubbery made long shadows on the grass and the poppies and roses were still and lovely in the garden, and the sky so heavenly blue, the heart of her cried out for some part in the beauty of the world, some real joy that pain and sickness and peril could not take from her.

She paused to watch a big velvet bee roll and tumble and wallow around in the heart of a scarlet poppy with deep black center and ruffle of white. Then he bumbled up and buzzed across the bed, creeping deep into the heart of a purple iris, and dusting his coat with yellow pollen from its sleek purple walls. Was a bee happy, she wondered? Did God think of bees, or were they all just a part of a great creation that He had started and then left to go on its careless way? Oh, she knew better than that, of course. She knew the Bible said that not even a sparrow can fall without Him. But she couldn't get the sense today in her weary lonesome young heart, that God really cared about her and the uphill road she had started to walk.

It had been interesting to ease her father's financial difficulties, to see the furrows of his brow relax, and a look of relief come into his eyes. It had been good to feel that Merrick trusted her again. Although neither Merrick nor any of them knew yet that she had given up Tilford, it had been restful to have some of her troubled doubts settled by her definite stand for her family. But what was life going to be, as it went along, a long lonely stretch, bearing a mother's cares and anxieties, without the help of a strong love in her life?

Well, her heart was still too angry with Tilford to wish him back. He had been too appallingly indifferent to her desires for her to get over it so easily. Yet fragments of her broken dreams came often, floating tantalizingly just above her head, lovely things of gauze and rainbow, making her heart cry out to catch at them and draw them back again into her grasp.

She wandered on past the neat rows of the kitchen garden, where father with sometimes the help of Merrick, and the hindrance of the eager erratic labors of the little boys, had growing things in abundance for his household. Dear hard-working father! They must watch out that he didn't drop some day as mother had done. Working late at the office and then coming home to snatch the very last minute of the daylight to work in his garden!

As she walked around toward the side of the yard next to the Maitland place she thought she heard the echo of the boys' voices in the distance. Were they still painting the house? What a grand friend Lane was, to let them do things like this. The very importance of it, she knew, must greatly intrigue her small brothers.

A little path in the grass led over to the hedge that shut the Maitland property away from the Mayberry place. She followed it to the hedge, lured by the cool quiet under the hemlock trees, and as she paused and looked toward the Maitland house wondering if she could catch a glimpse of her young brothers painting, a voice spoke.

"Hello there, Maris, is that you, really out of doors for a few minutes? That's good. You've been shut in too long without a break. I asked Merrick last night if there wasn't some way we could get you out for a breath of air and a bit of sunshine. But the sun is hot yet, isn't it? How about stepping through the opening here and trying our new garden chairs. I ordered them by telephone and I think they're very comfortable. Come see if you don't think so."

Smiling she stepped through a thin place in the hedge and sat down in the long easy chair he offered her, finding surprising resilience and restfulness in the curious structure of steel that seemed to lend itself to every curve of her tired body.

"It's grand!" she said, putting her head back and relaxing. "Oh, isn't this a lovely place? What deep lovely shadows of almost blueness up there among the feathery hemlocks."

"Yes, I always loved this spot. Mother used to love it so. She used to talk about building an arbor out here so that she might come often and rest. But I'm not sure but I like just the trees above me rather than a roof."

"Oh, so do I!" said Maris taking a deep breath of the resinous pines about them. "How beautiful this is. Somehow I've never had time to stop and look at it. But you're making it look as it used to look when we were children. I remember I always thought your lawn was the loveliest stretch of greenness, with that great flower bed of your mother's, always bright with flowers."

He flashed an appreciative look at her.

"Do you remember mother?" he asked, after a brief moment.

"Oh, yes," she said, "I used to think she was the loveliest woman I knew, next to my own mother. You see in those days I used to think all mothers were like your mother and mine."

A floating shadow of disillusionment crossed her face.

"And you have found out differently?" he asked.

"And *how!*" she said with sudden emphasis.

He waited, but somehow knew that she would not go on. This was something that had to do with a part of her life in which he might not share.

"Your mother is precious!" he said. "My mother used to think she was wonderful."

"She—*is—!*" said Maris, struggling with a sudden unreasoning desire to cry. "You don't know how I miss her, just these few days since she's been sick."

"Don't I?" said Lane Maitland with a tender wistfulness in his voice.

"Oh, of course you do!" said Maris with sudden compunction.

"But it's not as if my mother was lost," went on Maitland. "I'm expecting to go to her some day. We've been wonderfully blest with parents, you and I. Not everybody has that. Both our mothers and fathers know the Lord."

"I suppose that does make a difference," said Maris half shyly. "I never thought of that before."

"Of course it does. It makes a difference to everybody. But I don't know what I should have done if I hadn't had the Lord Jesus Christ, and been conscious of His presence with me all the time. I couldn't have lived through that first loneliness when they were both gone."

There was a long silence and then Maris said wistfully:

"I wish I could realize God. I feel as if I were so alone just now. I've tried several times to pray, and read my Bible, but I don't seem to get anywhere. It's like saying empty words to a brass sky. And the Bible doesn't seem real when I read it."

She paused, half hoping, yet hardly daring to think that this young man, fine though he was, would have any definite help for her hungry heart. Her head was down in her hands and she could not see the gentle yearning look that he turned upon her.

"Perhaps you were asking things that you had no right to ask yet, and expecting light when you hadn't yet met the conditions. You know the condition of having understanding given by the Holy Spirit is that we shall come with a willing heart to believe what we find in the Book, and, too, God has never promised to answer the prayers of any but His own children. But you really did take Jesus Christ as your Saviour that time a few years ago when you united with the church, didn't you, Maris?"

"Oh, yes," she answered in a puzzled tone. "And I believe He is my Saviour of course. It's just that I can't seem to get any joy out of it. I can't seem to meet Him personally the way I'd like to, the way I believe my father and mother do. I used to be quite sure there was something very wonderful, a communion with Him that one could have in this life. I'm not so sure any more that that is for just ordinary people."

"God said 'whosoever *will*' didn't He? I'm quite sure the fellowship with Him is for anyone who wants it."

"Then why don't I have it? When I was saved that time, I thought that everything was going to be wonderful. Do you remember how the evangelist spoke of the joy of Christian living, and painted everything in bright colors? Yet I have never been conscious of that."

"Do you remember," he said, "how visiting speakers in school used to give us lectures on how wonderful it was to have good parents? Yet it was some time after I grew up that I became truly conscious of my father and mother, conscious of loving them and understanding them and wanting to be with them. In fact, it's only since I haven't them that I've learned to long for their companionship."

Maris looked up then as if she were startled.

"Why it's just the same with me," she said. "I think I never was conscious of how I loved my father and mother and wanted to be with them until lately. I've been going my own way. But these last few days I've been seeing how I have failed to appreciate them, and how I have hurt them so many times. Now a few minutes with father means so much. And a word from mother would mean everything, now that I don't have her."

"Yes, I know," he said sadly, "and the Christian life is often like that. Understand, I don't mean it's necessary for a person to live years after he's been saved before he learns to walk with the Lord. It's not normal or right. But if it has been so I think there comes a time when God brings us upstanding, perhaps through trouble, and we realize then that we don't have the fellowship we might have had. We see how we have grieved Him and how we have walked into the world, in ways that He would not go."

Maris nodded sadly. "Yes, I've done that!"

"It is then we wake up to how much we want Him," went on Lane. "And that's what He has been working toward all the time! To draw us after Him! Isn't it gracious of Him to want us?" Lane spoke tenderly, with awe in his voice.

"And then," he went on, "as soon as we find out how much we want Him, He delights to make Himself known to us. At least that is the way it has been with me."

"Does He? I wish I understood. He hasn't done it with me. What do you mean? Do you hear voices, or see visions, or what?"

"Oh, no," smiled Lane. "That is not His way of speaking to us now, because He doesn't need to any more. There is a far more intimate and wonderful relationship now than there ever was when He had to speak to man through the physical senses. Now," he sat up eagerly, "He is *in* us, you know."

Maris looked blank.

"I guess I don't understand," she said mournfully, "or else He isn't in me."

"Yes, He says He lives in everyone who has accepted Him as Saviour. That's why I asked you if you surely had. You see, when you accept Him, you're not just getting a ticket to heaven, you are receiving *His life*. You were dead in sin, now you are born from above. The third person of the Godhead comes into your heart to dwell. Don't ask me how. I only know it's so—because He says so, and also just as you know who is living in your house, even though you don't see them all the time. I found some years ago that the reason I wasn't having real fellowship with the Lord was because I was looking for Him *outside* somewhere. I wanted to talk to someone at a certain distance. I wanted to hear, or *feel* something. When all the time He was living *in* me, quietly waiting for me to recognize Him and yield to Him. It made all the difference in the world.

"And when you get to counting on the fact of His presence within you," went on Lane, as Maris sat listening wide-eyed, "you find that you get to depending on that 'Other' all the time. You are conscious of His personal, intimate love as never before, you're conscious that He is speaking to your inmost soul more clearly than ever you heard a voice, and you are conscious that He is continually pointing out things in His Word that you never saw before when you tried to read it by yourself. And the only thing that can hinder all this is your own will, wanting your own way."

Again Maris was still a long time thinking over the possibilities of such a walk with God.

"And you really think just anybody could have that?—even someone who had—gone—their own way—a long time, and paid no attention to Him?"

"He said so. 'If *any* man hear my voice and open the door I will come in to him and will sup with him, and he with me.' I know that's true," Lane's voice was low and gentle but it rang with glad certainty, "for I've found it so, and there's nothing, not *anything,* that can satisfy your heart like that fellowship with Him."

Just then Maris heard a cautious voice calling, "Maris, Maris." It was Gwyneth sent by Sally to say that dinner was ready.

"Oh, I'm sorry! I'll have to go! I had no idea I had stayed so long. But—I'd like to hear more about this. I'm really interested."

"We'll talk again," said Lane eagerly. "Any time you have a spare minute just give me a call on the phone and I'll meet you here."

"All right, I will!" said Maris happily. "There are a lot of questions I'd like to ask you, things that have come into my mind these last few days. And I do want to know how to understand the Bible."

A great light came into the young man's eyes.

"I'll love to help in any way I can," he said quietly.

Then Maris was gone, and Lane sat there a few minutes in the shadow of the hemlocks thinking, remembering the wistful look in the girl's eyes as he had talked, his heart thrilling that she cared to listen to such things, wondering why he had ever drifted out of touch with a girl like this. Why hadn't he written to her often and kept up their boy and girl friendship? If all that her brother said about her fiancée was true it seemed a terrible thing for a girl like this to be tied for life to a man who was a worldling. Of course it might be that Merrick was prejudiced. But—well—it wasn't his business. Perhaps it was all in God's plan for Maris' life. But oh, he hoped she didn't have to walk a way of sorrow because she had made a wrong choice.

He closed his eyes and could see her sitting there in the opposite chair with the long cool shadows of the branches waving above her softly, and the eagerness in her eyes. He could see the sweet line of cheek and chin, the delicate curving of her lovely lips, the shadows under her tired beautiful eyes, and he wished he could do something to take the weary look from her face.

Then suddenly he flung his hands down from across his eyes and sprang to his feet.

"Look here, Lane Maitland," he said to himself severely, "you'd better snap out of this! This is another man's fiancée you're thinking about! Get busy and think of something else! I wonder what those kids are doing with that paint by this time?" and he turned and hurried away to see.

But the next day, about noon, Gwyneth brought to Maris a little package that she said Lane Maitland had asked her to deliver.

When Maris had time to open it she found it was a beautifully bound Bible, and a note from Lane:

> Dear Maris,
>
> I thought perhaps the notes in this special edition might help with some of your perplexities, and I've jotted down a few references you might look up, in line with what we were saying.
>
> The boys send their love,
>
> As ever,
>
> Lane

Maris touched the soft leather cover happily, fluttered the leaves through with pleasant anticipation, noted the neat sheets of paper here and there slipped in, written over with clear characters, in Lane's handwriting, caught a word or two of explanation, and wished she might have time to sit right down and begin her study. It filled her with comfort to have someone interested in her problems and taking all this trouble to answer her vague questions. She laid the Bible on her bedside table and went about her multitudinous duties of the day heartened for her work, and looking forward to a few moments that she would snatch here and there to pursue this new wonderful study.

It was another busy day, and not until late in the evening did Maris have opportunity to get at her new Bible. Her Bible! For she discovered when she opened it with leisure to look it through that Lane had written her name on the flyleaf.

She had a Bible of course, one that she had had since she was quite a young girl, but this one was most intriguing. It had soft dark blue leather covers, and most interesting and enlightening footnotes, and moreover the little loose leaves in Lane's handwriting put her in touch with many verses that seemed to be written just for her own present needs. She pored over it earnestly, and put it down reluctantly when she happened to glance at her watch and found how late it was.

As she lay down to sleep at last it was with the words of Scripture ringing in her heart:

"When thou passest through the waters, I will be with thee; and through the rivers, they shall not overflow thee: when thou walkest through the fire, thou shalt not be burned; neither shall the flame kindle upon thee."

It was a verse she had learned long ago when she was a child but she had not thought of for years. Now from all the verses Lane had marked it seemed to stand out and comfort her. The Lord was in her, Lane had said, and whatever came to her He would not leave her. She fell asleep with the thought in her mind. She was walking through the waters now, but He was here. He had allowed it all to come to her for some wise reason. And the verse said "When thou passest *through.*" That meant that it would be over sometime. It was a good thought upon which to go to sleep.

FOR the next few days Maris used every leisure moment in studying her new Bible, and following out all the suggestions that Lane had given her in his notes. Now and again questions would come to her mind for which she could not find an answer and she wrote them down in a tiny note book, to ask Lane the next time she saw him.

But there were not many opportunities to talk with Lane, even though he was living just next door. He was much engrossed with his young charges. He had established a private school in the back yard. The two boys were carrying on their studies along the same lines as they would have done in school, only perhaps with a little more individual attention than would have been possible in school. Lane was a fascinating teacher, and the boys adored him. He told them reasons for everything that their young minds questioned, and led them on to wonder over the amazing world in which they lived, giving them now and again a Bible memory verse which clinched the nature study they had been carrying on with birds and squirrels and rabbits and butterflies and flowers as intimate subjects.

Maris, as she heard from time to time a report of their work, realized that her young brothers were enjoying a rare privilege of companionship with this man, the memory of which could not but be of lasting benefit all their lives.

"But how can you spare the time, Lane?" she asked him once in a brief moment when she had speech with him. "Aren't you in some kind of business? I haven't asked Merrick about it, but surely you have interests of your own that must be looked after, and you mustn't let our boys absorb even all your leisure, either."

Lane smiled.

"Don't worry," he said. "They are only helping to fill in an interim. Two positions are open to me in the fall and I'm not sure which I shall decide upon. One will take me to New York. The other is around here. I'll tell you about it sometime when we have more time. But in either case I've got to fix up the house, either to sell, or to live in, and that's going along in fine shape. I have a plumber at work now making alterations, putting in another bathroom or two, a more modern sink, and a new heating plant. I have to more or less supervise those things. And the painters will be here next week to assist the ones who have already started the job on the back kitchen."

He grinned at the boys who were listening wide-eyed, on the other side of the hedge, and they responded with adoring smiles.

"Well, it's just wonderful that you are able to take care of the boys," said their sister gratefully. "I'll never forget it."

"That's nice," said Lane pleasantly. "I like to be remembered." Then he chanted with a merry twinkle in his eye a scrap of the old song:

Thus would we pass from the earth and its toiling,
Only remembered by what we have done.

Maris gave him a quick keen glance as she smiled. Then after an instant, "It will be more than that, Lane," she said gravely.

He looked at her sharply, quizzically, a great wistfulness in his eyes, and then said:

"Now, just what might you mean by that, kind lady?"

"Why," she laughed half embarrassedly, "I don't just know that I can analyze it, but there'll always be more to your memory than just things you have done, no matter how wonderful they were. Why, you're a very dear old friend, you know," she finished lamely, with a glowing color suddenly stealing over her white cheeks.

He looked at her steadily for an instant, considering that, and a gravity began to dawn in his eyes.

"I see," he said, almost formally. "Well, I mustn't keep you any longer." He went away with the little boys trooping after him, and left her standing there watching him with a vague discomfort in her mind. Had she somehow been rude to him? She hadn't meant to be. She had been trying to make him understand how much she appreciated what he was doing for them, how much he meant to them all as a friend. She might have been blundering and awkward in the way she had put it, but she had meant it all right. Had she hurt him? Just what had she meant anyway when she tried to express herself so awkwardly? And also just what had been the significance of that grave withdrawing look in his eyes when he went away?

But she had no time, of course, to consider these questions. The very air seemed bristling with questions anyway for her weary heart, and there was little time to take them to the Bible for satisfaction, even little time for prayer, when she was not almost too weary to keep awake.

Two days later she found a little resting place in the middle of the afternoon. The night nurse had appeared unexpectedly and sent her out to get some air. She wandered over once more toward the hedge and looked across.

She had somehow felt a reluctance to call Lane on the telephone. He might be busy. Someone might hear her and wonder.

But as she looked across the hedge she heard his heavy voice speaking.

"I wondered if you were never coming again, lady."

"Oh," she said, "you're there! I'm glad. There are some things I have so wanted to ask you. Can you wait a minute till I get my Bible?"

"All the afternoon at your service," he said pleasantly. "The boys are doing the back door and steps. They're stationary for a time at least."

Maris ran into the house and was back quickly with her Bible, and she found when she came through the hedge that Lane had his Bible too, the counterpart of hers, only much worn, and with the bloom of hard usage upon its leather cover.

Maris put her hand out and touched it as it lay on the arm of the lawn chair next her own.

"Beautiful with use!" she said wistfully. "I wonder if mine will ever look like that from the same cause. I'm afraid I don't know enough to use mine as much as you have yours."

"You have the same teacher, the Holy Spirit," he said reverently trying not to show his great gladness in his eyes and voice.

"Oh!" she said with a voice full of awe. "That seems too great to be true, that the Holy Spirit would teach me!"

Their eyes met and something sweet and tender flashed in their glances, something that thrilled even to their spirits.

"You don't know how I prize this Bible," said Maris, struggling to free herself from a sense of confusion that she did not understand. "It was so wonderful of you to give it to me. I shall always count it one of my dearest treasures."

Another sudden glad look passed between them, and

then Lane, unaccountably grave again, said in a quiet voice:

"I wasn't sure whether I might presume to give so intimate a gift, but I thought, since you are to be married soon, you would let me call it a wedding present."

A sudden awful silence fell between them like a pall. Something seemed to clutch at Maris' throat and try to strangle her. Her glance went down and a slow color stole up into her cheeks, and then receded quickly leaving them white again as death. After an instant she spoke and her voice seemed constricted, embarrassed. It sounded very little and far away even to herself:

"But you see, I'm not going to be married soon," she faltered.

He looked up quickly, a sort of breathlessness in his voice.

"You're *not?* Oh, you mean you are putting off the day? You are not going to be married on the thirtieth? I thought you would probably postpone it on your mother's account."

"No," said Maris, and suddenly knew that she wanted to tell him, even though nobody else knew yet. "No, I am not going to be married at all. I have broken my engagement!"

"Oh!"

There was a great deal in that simple utterance. Astonishment, question, almost bewildered delight, and quick caution, ending in tender sympathy.

Maris couldn't seem to think of anything else to say and the pause was long. Then Lane said again, in a more studied tone:

"Oh—!" and then added quickly, "I can't say I'm sorry! I didn't know Mr. Thorpe. But of course I know your family are the gainers by this. Is it—? Did you—?" He paused and wished he had not begun that idea. But she was quick to anticipate his meaning.

"I don't know." She gave a vague little laugh. "I haven't got used to it enough to know whether I should count it a calamity or not. In fact there have been so many calamities that I haven't been able to differentiate them yet from each other. And, yes, I suppose I did it because of my family. That is, of course I couldn't go away now. But it didn't *have* to be for that reason. If things had been right—something could have been arranged."

"I understand," he said gravely, and she knew he did.

"I thought you would," she said, although she had had no idea of saying that. The words just came out of her inner consciousness without her knowledge. "That's why I wanted to tell you. The family don't know it yet."

"Thank you," he said, and then after a pause. "The family will be very happy over it."

"Will they?" asked Maris. "I've been wondering."

"They will!" said Lane with emphasis, as if he were very sure.

"It almost seems," said Maris, hesitating, "as if God, perhaps, sent all these things—just to interrupt—!"

"I'm sure He did!" said Lane with a ring of assurance in his voice. "He does things like that sometimes."

The pause was longer this time, and then Maris said with a light little laugh that covered a great deal of feeling very inadequately:

"Well, then, in that case wedding gifts are usually returned. Do you want me to give this Bible back? Because I don't want to do it. I want to keep it always."

His eyes looked at her very tenderly.

"That's what I want you to do, keep it always," he said. Then in a matter-of-fact tone, as he reached for his own Bible:

"Now, shall we get to those questions before you are called away again? By the way, apropos of what we were talking about the other day, here's a bit of a quotation I found last night:

O Lord, my heart is all a prayer,
But it is silent unto Thee;
I am too tired to look for words,
I rest upon Thy sympathy
To understand when I am dumb;
And well I know Thou hearest me.

I know Thou hearest me because
A quiet peace comes down to me,
And fills the places where before
Weak thoughts were wandering wearily;
And deep within me it is calm,
Though waves are tossing outwardly.

She listened as he read and a great longing came into her heart to have an experience like that. To be able to trust and rest and find such a peace. But she couldn't put what she was feeling into words. It seemed to choke her, and the tears were blocking the way.

"Oh!" was all that she could utter.

"Yes," he said smiling, as if he understood. "It's like that."

"You have experienced that!" she challenged in a kind of wonder.

"Sometimes." He wasn't exactly smiling, but there was a sort of radiance in his face as if he were remembering things too wonderful to tell.

"Oh, I would like to have a trust like that!" she said hungrily.

"You can have if you are willing to go all the way with Him," said Lane gently. "Listen to this one:

But all through life I see a Cross
Where souls of men yield up their breath,
There is no life except by death,
There is no vision but by faith,

Nor justice but by taking blame,
Nor glory but by bearing shame,
And that eternal Passion saith,
Be emptied of glory and right and name.

Maris was very still as he finished the words.

"That's very high ground," she said at last. "It makes one's petty outcries and questions seem very small and shaming. I wish I might have had that outlook on life when I was a child, and grown up with it. It certainly would have saved me a lot of mistakes later." She drew a sad little sigh and gazed across the far stretch of lawn with its border of tall trees. "I wasn't brought up to cry for everything I saw, nor to have everything I wanted, but when they came without the asking I guess I was carried away by them, and forgot real values. I guess I can see why the Lord had to send me a lot of hard things all at once."

Lane smiled understandingly.

"Yes. I went through that too. It took a lot of jolts to make me understand. I read something the other day that seemed to fit my case exactly. It said: 'We can't understand why God doesn't want to do nice things for nice people like ourselves! That is because we have never seen ourselves as we are, as He sees us. When we do, we shall be dumb with wonder that He has had anything to do with us, and His infinite gift of Jesus Christ His Son shall be all to us, filling our whole heart and life.' When I came to the place where I saw myself in that way I was bowed with shame. And then when I reached that in spite of my indifference and foolish lack of understanding, He yet wanted me in close relationship to Himself, I was filled with a great overflowing joy. It's wonderful, Maris, when you get to realize that. There's nothing like it!"

Maris looked at him wistfully.

"I'm so glad you're like this," she said suddenly. "I didn't know there were any men, not any *young* men, anyway, that talked this way, that felt as you do. Tell me, how did you get to know God? You weren't interested in such things when you were in school."

"No," he said sorrowfully, "I was going my own way then, just having a good time, the world all before me and everything lovely. I never thought of God. And then when sudden sorrow came, two sharp blows one after the other, I began to think that God was cruel. That He hated me! I almost doubted what I had been taught, that He so loved the world that He gave His only begotten Son to save us. But one day I heard someone say that it is because people live in the things they possess instead of in their relationship to God that God seems at times to be cruel. And then I began to think. I began to reach out to God. For I had pretty well tried out everything else that appealed to me. They all had turned to dust and ashes, and I felt God calling me. And as soon as I was ready to listen I found Him ready to reveal Himself to me. You see I wouldn't listen to Him as long as I was happy and comfortable and had everything I wanted. So He had to send sorrow to bring me to Himself."

"I wonder," said Maris thoughtfully, "if that isn't just what has been happening to me. Oh, you're helping me a lot to get my feet on solid ground. It seemed to me at first when all these things began to happen at our house, that I was utterly dumbfounded. Everything I had believed in or rested upon had failed me. I wondered if there was a God. And yet I had no other refuge. But you are making me begin to get a little glimmer of light."

"Oh, I'm glad!" said Lane, with a lilt in his voice. "But now let's go to His Word. That's better than any explanation of mine. I've been digging deep in this treasure store of late and God has shown me some wonderful things. Turn to the first chapter of Ephesians and let's see what God says about what we are to Him."

So they sat and studied for an hour and a half. Others

might have discussed a trip to Europe, the best modes of travel, the best places to stop, the best side-trips to take, but they were deep in the Word of God, talking about the things of another world.

If Tilford Thorpe could have looked in upon them from behind the hedge that shut away the street he would have been hard put to it to understand what they were doing. With their two heads bent low over their Bibles, fluttering over the leaves, discovering new thoughts, Lane with his Greek Testament casting new light on old familiar words, talking with wonder in their voices of a spiritual world which was as real to them as if they could see it, shyly comparing similar heart experiences in the Lord's dealing with them. It would have been as inexplicable to Tilford as if they had been discoursing in a foreign language concerning some hitherto undiscovered country that they hoped some day to find and dwell within. He would not have understood it at all.

They talked until the little boys finished the door and the steps and came triumphant and clamoring, daubed with paint from their eyebrows down, and demanding that their idol should come and see if it was all right.

Maris suddenly discovered that it was time her patient had her tray and she must leave at once. But the two separated with one quick glad look into each other's eyes. It was only good night they said as they hurried away, but each realized that it was a good night that they had discovered this great bond of interest in the Word of God.

Maris as she crossed her own lawn marveled at the thrill in her heart as she thought on all she had been hearing and reading. It occurred to her to wonder how different things might have been between herself and Tilford if they could have had such sweet converse on the deeper things of life together. But it was scarcely conceivable. Trying to imagine Tilford studying the Bible with her was perhaps the most enlightening vision that had come to her yet, to make plain to her how far apart she and Tilford were concerning everything of real value. They would never have been one, no matter how hard she tried. They had so few points of contact. It would have been herself that would have had to measure to Tilford's standards, for it wasn't thinkable that he would be willing to measure to hers, nor even to try. He was all for this world, and had apparently no interest in another life.

Was it possible that she could have brought him to know the Lord? She stared at the question in her mind, realizing how far she had been from ever trying to get him to think of another world. Perhaps God had meant her to do that when He let her get to know Tilford. Perhaps she had utterly failed Him. Oh, it was all a terrible maze, and there was just one thing she could do now, and that was to take God at His word and go forward, learning to know and trust Him day by day, feeling her way with her hand in God's, believing that He knew the end from the beginning.

As she entered the house it suddenly came to her that tomorrow was to have been her wedding night and she hadn't once remembered it all day! That in itself was startling enough. If someone had told her three weeks ago that that could happen she would have laughed him to scorn. She would not have thought it possible. And now here she was with the whole thing taken out of the picture, and herself fully established in another kind of life, as if that had been a dream.

She had a passing wonder about Tilford. Where was he? What was he doing? Was he hurt and sorrowful? She couldn't imagine it. Only angry, and still stubborn. Why was it that she could see that trait in him now so clearly, and only a short time before she did not see it at all. She had thought him charming and admirable in every way. Why, oh, why did all that have to happen? Why did God let her go through all that experience only to put it away from her forever? Could it be possible that this wasn't the end after all? Was God perhaps going to send Tilford back to her, and give them a new life and new interests in better things together?

But to her amazement she found a shrinking in her heart. Was she, then, just angry with him for the way he had treated her in her trouble? Was she perhaps not being fair to Tilford? Had she ever tried to put herself in his place and realize what his side might be? Or had she taken it all out in finding fault with him? Instead of talking things over with him and giving him a chance to suggest that of course she must stay in her home now when they were in trouble, she had given her ultimatum and handed back his ring. Was that right and fair toward the man a girl had accepted? Could he help it that he had a disagreeable, managing, meddlesome mother who overinfluenced him? Maybe she should have been more gentle with him, and realized that his upbringing had been quite different from hers. Maybe she should have sent for him again and talked it over with him before turning him down so completely.

Of course he had been unsympathetic, and heartless, but there were influences at home back of that. Maybe she was all wrong. Maybe the new life to which she had just been committing herself as she read the Word of God with enlightenment, would require her to ask Tilford's forgiveness, to go on with her marriage possibly, sometime later when conditions at home would allow her to leave. Could that be what God wanted of her?

All these thoughts followed her like a deadly miasma that arose in her path and seemed to smother her, whenever she gave them space.

All the evening as she read to Lexie, who was growing restless as her normal health returned, as she did the hundred and one little tasks that filled the end of the long wearisome day, these thoughts pursued her. As she went to her room at last to prepare for rest, and tried to read her

Bible and recall some of the precious things that had gripped her heart, even as she knelt to pray with that new sense upon her of knowing her Lord as she had never known Him before, she kept thinking of Tilford. A great depression filled her spirit, like a premonition of some looming trial yet before her. She tried again and again to shake it off. She tried to regain the joy that had filled her while she was studying that afternoon with Lane, in that clean healthy happy atmosphere of sacred things, where Heaven was almost as if she could see it with her natural vision.

At last, unable to banish these things, unable to fix her mind upon her prayer, she cried out in great earnestness:

"Oh Lord! Show me definitely if I am right in what I have done. Show me once for all whether Tilford is a man with whom I could walk through life. Don't let me misjudge him, nor be unfair to him. Show me my own heart. Show me if he really loves me, and whether I could love him. I am all bewildered and I want to do what is right. Should I go back to Tilford some time and try to lead him to know You?"

It was a strange prayer, for somehow it seemed to be going against the promptings of her own heart, but she was so tired, and didn't understand herself. At last she arose with a feeling that she had put everything in God's hands, and could trust and rest.

THE sun shone forth gorgeously on June the thirtieth, Maris' wedding morning that was to have been. The fact came to her and challenged her attention the first thing when she woke up. Where was Tilford? Was he feeling dreadfully about it? Ought she to feel sorry for him? Somehow she couldn't summon any sorrow on that score.

There was something however in the atmosphere, or in her own heart, that tinged the day with regret, some pitiful little harking back to the gay things of the world that had occupied so much of her time lately. How she had hoped for a beautiful June day like this for her wedding day! How she had quoted to herself that foolish little saying "Blessings on the bride that the sun shines on!" and hoped it would be hers. Not that she was superstitious, but it was so nice to have all the silly sayings of the world fit in and be propitious.

And now here was the day she had hoped for, a sky without a cloud, a pleasant breeze blowing just a little, the world full of roses and beauty—and no wedding!

A few tears of hurt pride and broken romance stole out to picket the outpost, but were sternly remanded to their own place. Maris meant to have no nonsense today. Not a soul should suspect that she was shaken by the beauty of the day. Indeed she wasn't even sure she was shaken. It was only that it had come to her with such force last night, and again stronger this morning, that perhaps something more was required of her before this matter was buried forever out of sight. And yet what could she do? Her position had been right. She couldn't have a wedding when mother and Lexie were sick. That was settled long ago. Even if they were well by some marvelous miracle, well enough for the wedding to go forward, there was no wedding, for there had been no invitations, and there were therefore no guests!

Over and over these pestering thoughts went rampaging through her mind. She could not understand it. She had been so happy last night out there, turning her thoughts to heavenly things. She had felt that never again would she need to be upset by the things of the world, and now here this morning she was all out of sorts. Not exactly regretting what she had given up, but beset by tormenting thoughts and uncertainties. Tilford would of course have told her that she was worn out nursing her sick sister, and taking unnecessary burdens upon herself. But what would Lane Maitland tell her if he knew? And what would God tell her?

She did not yet know about the besetments of a Christian life, nor realize that Satan immediately attacks the way of any soul who leaves the ranks of his followers. But at last she realized that to trust God fully was all she could do.

As the day grew high the sun rose hotter, and the air was full of bird songs and perfume from flowers, but Maris resolutely put all thoughts of disturbing things out of her mind. The matter was settled. It was in God's hands. It was definitely out of hers. If there was anything wrong with what she had done to Tilford, God would surely show her.

She noticed that her father and Merrick looked at her anxiously when she came down to breakfast. They saw the shadows under her eyes, and wondered if she were sorrowing. They could not help but notice that Tilford had not been there for days.

They were at the table together for a few minutes, and neither Sally nor the nurse were in the room. There was a bit of constraint upon them all, for everybody realized what day this was, and what it was to have meant to them as a family. But it was left to Gwyneth to voice the feeling in all their hearts.

It was just as Sally went out with the empty plate after bringing in more griddle cakes that she mustered courage. That had been Sally's idea of a proper wedding-day breakfast, griddle cakes and sausage. Sally wanted to make the day as pleasant for Maris as possible.

"This would have been an awful pretty day for your wedding, Maris, wouldn't it?" Gwyneth said in a wistful little tone. She had been upstairs the night before trying to find her own maid of honor dress and hadn't been able to locate it.

Maris drew a little quick gasp of a breath and forced a smile.

"Yes, darling, it's a lovely day," she said, trying to pass it off casually.

Merrick looked up with a frown, and kicked his sister Gwyneth under the table.

"Tough luck, Maris!" he said in a tone that tried to sound sympathetic.

Maris looked up with a sudden thrill of pleasure that Merrick who so obviously had disliked Tilford should be offering her sympathy. But before she could answer him her father spoke.

"Maris, I haven't been saying anything. There really wasn't anything to say. But I want you to know that I—that we all—appreciate the beautiful way you have sacrificed yourself, and given up your plans, and gone sweetly about the new order of things without a murmur or a sign that you were terribly disappointed. It is a great grief to me. It will be a great grief to your mother when she gets well enough to realize what has gone on, that you should have had to put off your wedding. It seems as if we could never make it up to you. But I hope and pray that the Lord may somehow in the future years give you good measure of blessing, pressed down and running over, for the hard things you are passing through now."

Her father's eyes were full of love as he looked at her, and suddenly it seemed to Maris that her heart was so full she could not help breaking down and crying. And she mustn't! No, she mustn't. They wouldn't understand. They would think she was suffering terribly about putting off her wedding. And that was not true. It suddenly became plain to her that whatever God was going to show her as her duty for the future, she was not suffering now, except a little in her worldly pride, that she was not marrying Tilford Thorpe today. It was all at once just as plain as day to her that she did not love him. That she never had loved him the way a girl ought to love the man she was to marry.

That might not make any difference with what God would tell her to do in the future. Maybe God would look upon an engagement as too sacred to break, at least at this last minute. But she knew in her heart now that she never should have made it. The thought of marrying Tilford somehow brought a great burden to her.

Oh, if she could go back and do things over again, and walk carefully through her days, waiting on the Lord to send her joy in His own good time, and not go rushing out to seek it!

But she was aware that her father was still speaking to her.

"You know, dear, that just as soon as mother is really

out of danger, and Lexie is well enough to be otherwise looked after, we shall want you to go on with your plans. We realize that this must have been a very unhappy thing for Tilford to put up with, and we shall not want you to feel that you must hold up your plans forever—,"

Maris could stand it no longer.

"Oh, father, dear! Please don't say those things! I ought to have told you all several days ago, only I was so busy, and I sort of wished I could tell mother first. But I am not going to be married at all. I gave Tilford back my ring and broke the engagement several days ago. I wanted you to know it, but somehow there didn't seem to be any right time to tell you."

"But *my dear!"*

The father dropped his knife and fork and looked at her in dismay.

"My dear child! Your mother would not want her illness to have broken up your life, and put a great unhappiness upon you."

"You needn't worry about that, father. I found out I didn't love Tilford the way I ought to if I was going to marry him. I had begun to suspect it before mother was taken sick, but it took her illness to make it really plain to me. So no one need worry about that. I'm not heartbroken nor anything. I'm just glad and thankful I'm here, and can help, and rejoiced that mother's still here too. It would have killed me if I had been married and gone off, and then found mother was sick, and Lexie was sick, and I couldn't get to you!"

There was a dawning joy on the father's face, but he looked at Maris uncertainly.

"But, my dear! Isn't that being very unfair to Tilford? Now at this last minute? What will he say to that? Surely he will not give you up so easily! Does he know yet about your decision?"

Maris lifted her head a little with a proud tilt.

"Tilford has known it for several days. He has had the ring for nearly two weeks, and he hasn't been around here for more than a week. You needn't worry about Tilford. He is angry of course, but I—somehow I don't think Tilford ever really loved me, either, not the way you and mother love each other."

"Oh, my dear!" said Mr. Mayberry, and now his face really glowed with joy. "If that is all true this will be the gladdest house in the universe. You don't know how your mother has worried about you. She felt from the first that Tilford was not the right man for you. But she didn't want to say anything she would have to live down. Oh, my dear! How she will rejoice when she knows it! Oh, I do hope and pray that she may not leave us at least until she knows it."

Suddenly he got up and came around the table, putting his arms gently around his child and stooping down he kissed her softly on the forehead.

"Our little girl!" he said softly. "Our little girl back again. Our *own* again!"

"Great work!" said Merrick huskily getting up and following his father around the table. He stooped over and gave Maris a great bear hug and a resounding smack on her cheek, never knowing that he left a big tear beside the kiss. Merrick was a dear. She never knew before that Merrick cared that much.

"And won't you ever get married, sister? Will you stay with us always?" beamed Gwyneth. "But oh, sister, your *beautiful ring!*"

Suddenly Maris broke down and laughed.

"There are some things better than rings!" she told Gwyneth. "I'd rather be here at home with you all than have all the rings in the universe."

"That isn't the only ring in the world, kid," said Merrick gruffly as he took his cap and prepared to go out to his daily bus route. He alternated, one day early, the next day late. This was his late morning. He wouldn't be home till late in the evening tonight.

Somehow after that talk with her family the doubts and dismay and compunctions of the night before vanished, and Maris was very happy as she got up from the table and kissed her father and brother good bye. Then she stood in the doorway and watched them go away smiling. Father was going down to the office for a few hours. He had been well enough to go every day for the last week.

"Maris," said Gwyneth looking up after they had vanished around the corner, "what I'm worrying about is my maid of honor dress. Do you think I'll have any use for it? It won't stay in fashion long enough till I grow up big enough to wear a long dress, will it? What shall we do with it?"

"Oh, my dear sister. That's nothing to worry about. There are dozens of things to do. We can hem it up and use it for a party dress. It is very simple."

Gwyneth sighed.

"I wouldn't like it to be wasted," she said, "it's so pretty. It's the prettiest dress I ever had!"

"Yes, darling. It is pretty, and you'll wear it and have a lot of enjoyment out of it yet, I'm sure! It's simple enough, hemmed up, to wear to church even." Maris patted her sweet young cheek, and thrilled to think that these dear people all belonged to her. Her precious family!

Then the nurse came downstairs and her eyes seemed to be happier than usual.

"Do you know," she said stepping up to the door and speaking in a jubilant tone, "I believe your mother's pulse is a trifle steadier this morning than it has been at all."

Then all suddenly the morning became brighter than it had seemed before, and Maris' heart grew light as she went upstairs to her duties.

A wedding day! What was a wedding day beside a bit of hope like that. Not a wedding day with Tilford Thorpe, anyway!

The rest of the day went on glad feet. Maris had feared just a little that Tilford might appear on the scene and be disagreeable again, but now it didn't seem to matter. Her dear people were restored to the old-time fellowship that had been broken up ever since she had got to know Tilford Thorpe, and somehow other things grew small beside the joy of the family understanding. If only mother was well enough to know it too! If Tilford came let him come. Somehow that trouble too would dissolve like others.

So the day passed in tender ministrations.

There were duties for the household that she had long put by till a convenient time; they simply could not wait any longer. There were unexpected interruptions of callers, and telephone messages, and the evening came down, without a chance for Maris to go alone and do some Bible study as she had promised herself that morning to do. There was a game to play with Lexie who was allowed to sit up longer now. As she sat there beside the little girl's bed with the bedside table between them holding the Halma board, she could hear the boy's voices over on the Maitland lawn. They were playing ball with Lane! How good he was, caring for those children exactly as if they were his own brothers. Oh, if Tilford had been like that how different things would have been!

The game presently was finished.The boys' voices had trailed off farther, and she knew they were being sent to bed. Lexie would soon be asleep now, and she would have her promised Bible reading. So she sat down at last quietly in her own room, with her new Bible in her hand.

She heard a cab drive down the street and pause somewhere, but she was on the other side of the house from the street, and paid little heed to it. She had given up the thought that Tilford would come. The wedding day was almost over. In a few more hours it would be a thing of the past, a thing that never had been.

The Bible opened to Isaiah, and her eye suddenly fell upon a verse that Lane had marked. She had not seen it before. Such a strange arresting verse, as if it were spoken by the Lord straight to her soul, as if it were a kind of promise for her to take with her into her life:

"No weapon that is formed against thee shall prosper; and every tongue that shall rise against thee in judgment thou shalt condemn. This is the heritage of the servants of the Lord."

She had read so far when the nurse tapped at the door.

"I think there is somebody at the front door," she said, "and I saw Sally go out a few minutes ago. I can't leave your mother just now. Can you go? Your father is asleep."

Maris laid down her Bible and went downstairs, patting her rumpled hair smooth and glancing down at her neat little cotton house dress. Her wedding night and just about the time when she would have been walking down the church aisle to the time of the wedding march!

She went to the door, but at first saw no one, though there was a taxi standing at the curb. Then she discovered a man with a cap drawn low and a rough look about him.

"Are you Maris Mayberry?" he asked in a husky voice that she did not recognize.

"Yes," she answered, her heart beginning to beat excitedly, though she did not exactly know why.

"Well, step out here so your sick folks won't hear. I've got a message from your brother."

Maris with suddenly trembling limbs stepped out.

"Your brother Merrick has been in an accident, and he wants you. Doc MacPherson sent word you were to come with me quick. He may not live but a few minutes. Hurry!"

The man put out a strong hand and seized her wrist as she hurried to the cab.

"Get right in!" he said roughly, pushing her inside as she suddenly drew back and hesitated. "He might die before you get there and he wants to see you quick!"

Maris was pushed off her balance and thrown back into the taxi seat, and before she could get her balance again the man had jumped in beside her and slammed the door shut. She tried to speak, to protest, to ask a question, but the throb of the engine covered her voice and the cab had started on its way. There was a strange acrid smell about, and suddenly a revolting wet cloth was stuffed into her mouth, dripping down her throat in spite of her best efforts not to swallow the liquid. The pungent odor poured over her, filling her nostrils and driving away her senses, till her struggles grew less and less.

"No weapon that is formed against thee shall prosper—" the words floated through her mind like a call as she drifted out of the world she knew. "No weapon . . . this is the heritage of the servants of the Lord—! Oh, God! You are here!"

The light went out and she was away into a dark strange world where there was no longer anything that she could do.

THE little boys had lost their ball as darkness came down, over in the corner of the Maitland lot where the rhododendrons grew, close by the street. The boys had gone to bed, and Lane Maitland was out in the corner hunting among the rhododendrons for the ball. It was foolish of course to look for it when it was getting so dark. Better to wait till morning. But the boys had been distressed lest a neighbor's dog might find it and carry it off, so he had promised to hunt for it at once.

But he couldn't find it, of course. How could a dirty ball show up in the leaves among the rhododendrons? He was just about to go over and get a flashlight from his car which was still standing in the driveway not far away when he heard a car stop in front of the Mayberry house. He paused to look out through the shrubbery and see who it was. Could that be Tilford Thorpe? On Maris' wedding night?

Then he saw a man slink out from the car. No, that shabby sedan was not Tilford Thorpe's shining car, and that thickset, slouchy man with a stealthy gait was not Tilford. But who could it be? Perhaps he had the wrong house. Should he go and enlighten him? No, perhaps it was someone to see Sally. He waited a moment and in the silence of the evening heard the buzzer of the bell next door sound softly. If his ears had not been attuned already to everything that went on in that house he might not have recognized it, it had been muffled so effectively.

The Mayberry front door was standing wide, with only the screen door closed, but the man was not standing in the patch of light on the doorstep, he was in the shadow at the side of the door, where Lane could not see him. He could barely discern an indistinct shadow among the other shadows.

Then he heard someone come to the door. A low muttering from the man. "Maris!" He heard that. Too bad the way everybody bothered Maris, making her come down to the door for every little message. Well, perhaps he would run over himself and speak to her after the man was gone. He could just slip through the hedge and catch her before she went upstairs again. There were some verses he wanted to call her attention to. She might like to have them tonight. So he stood still where he was among the shrubbery.

The street was a quiet one, and there was little traffic at this time of night. The air was not stirring much, even the leaves were quiet, and across the space between his standing place and the Mayberry front door the man's words, though guarded, came in detached fragments. Then he saw Maris come out the door and stand in the shadow near the stranger, who edged along nearer to the street, while Maris followed. They were standing more nearly opposite to his position now, and he could hear that low mutter better. He distinctly heard the word "accident" and caught Merrick's name. And was that "MacPherson" he mentioned? Did the man say "Doctor"? Ah! That word was "dying." His heart missed a beat and he stood in consternation. Surely, surely he was mistaken.

And then to his horror he saw the burly fellow grasp Maris' wrist and draw her toward the sedan which was suddenly beginning to throb rapidly, and before he could stir or even cry out he saw Maris thrust into the car, and heard the door shut.

"Maris!" he called. "Maris, I'll take you!" but the car was already off down the street.

Desperately Lane turned and dashed across the lawn to the driveway where his car stood. He had left it there when he came in in the afternoon thinking perhaps Maris would like to take a short drive in the evening.

He swung into the seat and started his engine almost in one motion. Could he catch that car? Where were they going? Was Merrick really desperately hurt? Or had he not heard aright, and just jumped to conclusions? It was so easy to misunderstand someone at a distance. Who was that man who had come after Maris? One of the other bus drivers? Or just a passerby? Had Doctor MacPherson really sent him? Or was Maris simply on some errand, while he was getting all wrought up over nothing from the few indefinite words he had caught?

These questions danced around him as he drove, and taunted him. He couldn't answer them. He couldn't think it out at all. He couldn't be sure that he was even following the right car now. It was far ahead, and in the darkness he could only see a wink of light. The car that had stood in the street but a minute before might have turned down the pike, though he was almost certain that it had gone straight across. If he could only get a little nearer, enough to recognize it.

Lane stepped on his accelerator making his car shoot forward in great leaps. It was fortunate that there happened to be little traffic on this road just now. He was doing sixty, seventy, seventy-five! But the car ahead was speeding too. Would he make it before they reached the highway where he would be sure to lose them? Blindly he shot ahead, straining his eyes, his hair blowing in the breeze.

They were coming to the highway now. The traffic was thick. The other car was slowing down. The distance between them was less. He could almost read the license. He had made note of that while it stood beside the curb. There! It was dashing through traffic! It was gone! Straight across! He was held up by the light but the instant it changed he dashed across, and on the other side he saw again a speck in the distance, a single car. The road was so shadowed with trees just here that it was hard to discern. If it had not been for the little blinking tail light he would not have been sure whether a car was still there. And sometimes even that light disappeared as if it had been turned off for a minute.

They were coming into the wide country. He knew the general direction. There were no towns for some distance now, and there were wide stretches of fields. Was he going on a fool's errand, following some farmer's car perhaps, much like the sedan he had seen at the Mayberry's curb? Or was this really the car he had started out to follow? Perhaps he was wasting valuable time and ought to go back and report to the police. But just the thought that Maris might be in that car in trouble, and that if he abandoned it and went back now he would be losing the last possible clue, kept him rushing on through the night. Thank God there were telephones. If he got too far away from the city and found he was following the wrong scent he could at least telephone to the police and get action at once. So he kept on. He glanced at his gas. He had plenty. He was glad he had had it filled up just before dinner when he and the boys were out for a drive.

On and on they went, turning now and then an obscure corner into a narrow dirt road, just a country road between fields. But he was still so far behind that he could not read the license plate of the sedan. What could they be going away out here for? It was miles from Merrick's bus line. He couldn't be in an accident away out here! There must be something crooked about this, or else he had not heard aright. Perhaps Maris herself was in some kind of danger! "Oh, Father in Heaven," his heart cried out, "help her! Let me save her."

And now as they turned into a narrow lane he grew cautious. If there were crooks ahead, kidnapers perhaps, and they felt they were being followed there was no telling what they would do to throw him off their trail. So he turned out his lights. There was no danger here of meeting other traffic. They hadn't met a car for miles.

And then suddenly the car ahead turned sharply off the road into a field and went lurching and bumping across the rough ground, slowing down now because it was impossible to speed in such going.

Abruptly Lane stopped his car at the side of the narrow road. He was just emerging from a dense wood which ran on each side and he was well hidden. But the sky was luminous overhead, for the stars were thick and there was the brightness of the soon-approaching moon. The landscape ahead of him stretched far to the horizon, with just at that point no intervening towns or woods to hide the vision. He could discern the lurching car easily now. It showed clearly against the light of the sky. And then suddenly he saw what made his heart stand still with fear. There was a small airplane standing out there in the field, and the car was going straight toward it!

Even as he looked the lights of the plane winked on, and there was the subdued sound of its motor warming up. The car he was following signaled with its headlights. This was all prearranged, that was obvious. He was convinced now that Maris was in that car. He remembered how as he had watched it at the curb it seemed as if she had been forcibly pulled into the car.

What were they going to do with her? Kidnap her? But

why would they kidnap the daughter of a plain business man who was known to have little money?

Ah! But it was known that she was to marry the scion of a millionaire! Perhaps that was it! He ought to have stopped to telephone the police before he came off on this wild chase alone, but how could he? There would have been no clue at all then. Nothing for them to follow even if they knew. It would be just one more kidnaping case with a hopeless wait for contacts from gangsters, and maybe an unknown grave at the end. No, he must do this thing alone! It was almost hopeless, but he must try. He must somehow rescue Maris himself, or at least find out whether she was surely in that car. In a moment more it would be too late perhaps. That plane was revving up. He could not follow it into the sky, that was certain.

If he only had a revolver in his car he might try shooting the air out of those tires and stopping the car before it reached the plane. But he had no gun and likely it would not be wise to try if he had. Criminals would have more guns than he had, and be a thousand times more skilled in their use.

If he started his car again they would know they were being watched and followed and would soon put him out of the running. Perhaps it would be better to try reaching the place on foot. Certainly the other car was making slow progress over the rough ground.

Silently he got out of the car and started into the field, trying to keep as much as possible against the background of the woods so that his moving form would not be visible to the enemy. But he had gone but a few steps before a low sharp whistle reached his ears. They must have sighted him and were signaling one another.

The sedan rushed along over the bumps heedlessly now, and quickly covered the remaining space between it and the plane. He could see a figure detach itself from the plane and run toward the car. Maitland started on a run toward them. The back door of the sedan had swung open and the driver reached in and lifted something, someone perhaps, wrapped in a long dark cloth.

"Maris! Maris!" Maitland's voice rang out, but there came no answering voice, only muttered curses from the men. Another man came from the plane and took one end of the burden, while the thickset one ran back and started his car, lurching wildly away over the field.

"Maris! Maris!" cried Maitland in great gasps as he ran, but the inert burden the men carried gave forth no sound, and an instant later a shot rang out and a bullet spattered by his feet, startling him so that he stumbled and fell, which perhaps saved his life, for the next bullet was aimed a little higher.

But as he dropped he saw the men against the sky lifting their burden into the plane, and almost at once it moved off circling the far end of the field and then rose through the night.

Lane Maitland was on his feet again instantly, but the plane was a mere bird against the night. It carried no light to pick it out among the stars. His heart was heavy with fear.

"Oh God," he cried aloud. "You know where she is! Save her! She is Your child!"

He stumbled blindly back to his car. The other car had disappeared.

He managed to get his car turned, though it was a difficult task in that narrow lane. Then he drove wildly back to town again, trying to think just what he ought to do, trying to order the circumstances in his mind.

Of course there was a possibility that he was all wrong in his first premise. In the darkness he might have mistaken Sally or one of the nurses for Maris, and Maris might be even at that moment safe at home in her bed sleeping.

Although to his sharpened senses this seemed a most remote possibility, he decided that he had better telephone from the nearest station to the Mayberry house and find out before he made any other moves. He had to keep his head and remember that if he had made a mistake it might mean unpleasant publicity and endless embarrassment to the people he loved best in the world.

But if she was not at home where was she?

Was she in that little tramp plane, winging somewhere, through the night? And where? And dead, or alive?

Of course the police would have to know it at once if she was gone. But he would have to contact some of the family first. They might have some answer to it all.

Was Merrick really hurt, dying perhaps, somewhere? Was it conceivable that the call to come to him might have been genuine?

In that case he would have to tell Mr. Mayberry, and how he shrank from bringing more anxiety to that already harassed spirit!

Then next came the wonder who could have done this thing? Just gangsters, for ransom? Had there been a ransom note found yet?

And if not gangsters for ransom, was there any other possibility? Was it conceivable that a quiet girl like that had enemies? Was someone else perhaps in love with her? What was this Tilford Thorpe like anyway? He wished he knew. Of course Merrick's ideas of him must be taken with a grain of salt, for Merrick all too evidently hated him.

Of course Tilford Thorpe would have been the natural person to be informed first, of all that had happened, if he were still engaged to Maris. But Maris had distinctly said that the engagement was broken. Tilford Thorpe then, must be out of the picture, except as he might possibly figure in the gangsters' minds as they laid their plans for ransom.

Just then there loomed the clear red and white lights of a service station off to the left on a macadam road, and he went straight to them and demanded a telephone.

There was only one attendant just then and he was busy outside waiting on a car. He motioned toward the telephone, and Lane hurried into the little office, thankful to have it to himself for the moment.

His voice trembled as he called the familiar number, and he stood there dreading to hear the answer, wondering what the next two or three minutes would reveal. Then he heard the receiver click off at the other end and Merrick's voice, "Yes? Hello!"

"Oh, are you *home?"* he said shakily, weak with relief.

"Sure, I'm home! Where would I be? What's the idea?"

"Well, of course," said Maitland, "but something queer has happened. Is Maris there?" His voice was quivering with anxiety.

"Maris? No. We thought she'd gone out riding with you. The nurse said she heard a car at the door and Maris went out."

Lane Maitland suppressed a groan.

"Oh, then it's true! Listen, Merrick. I'm afraid she's kidnaped. I was out in the yard and a sedan drew up. A man went to your door. I thought I heard him say you'd had an accident and were dying. He said you wanted Maris right away. He said Doctor MacPherson had sent him for her. He took hold of her arm and pushed her in the car and shut the door. I called out but the car started right away. My car was there in the drive so I followed. They went out Lundy's Road, turned into the country, and ended up at a small plane in a field. I was too far away to see much, but I'm sure I saw them carrying someone, rolled in dark cloth, to the plane. It started almost immediately. I called again but the only answer I got was a shot that whizzed by. Merrick, is there anyone who would want to kidnap her, or is it just plain gangsters? We must get busy at once. I have the license number, but that's not much. The plane went north. Should the police know, or what? I'm at a filling station. Sixty-fourth and the pike. Can you give me any suggestion or shall I come straight home?"

"Good night!" said Merrick solemnly. "Are you kidding me, Lane? Haven't you got Maris there?"

"No!" said Lane sadly. "It's all true. Don't waste time. Do you think we ought to tell Thorpe before we report it to the police?"

"No!" said Merrick sharply. "Not that guy. He's no business with our troubles. Not any more. She told us this morning she'd broken the engagement. He hasn't been around for several days. But say! Wait! You don't think maybe—! Lane, I don't know but *he'd* be that mean. I wouldn't put it past him. Maybe he kidnaped her himself!"

"You don't think any man is as low as that, Merrick! Not any man who loved her!"

"Well he'd do anything to get his own way. I have an idea he wanted Maris to go on with the wedding in spite of mother's illness. I know several things they don't know I heard. He's a skunk if there ever was one!"

"Well, don't waste time. This was the wedding day, wasn't it? Would he take her off and hide her or what, do you think?"

"I don't know. Maybe take her on board the ship. Carry her off to Europe! I wouldn't be surprised. They were to sail tonight."

"What ship? What time?" asked Lane sharply.

"The *Emperor*. Midnight. They had a bridal suite or something of the sort. But how could we find out until it was too late, and what could we do if it was so?"

Merrick's voice was full of despair.

"There are always things to do. I'll phone to the ship. You phone to that bird's father and see if you can find out a thing or two. Tell him what's happened. He's likely a decent man even if his son isn't. Better try that before we go calling in the police and getting things in the paper."

"Okay. I'd like a word with that guy's papa!"

"Look out, brother. You must remember you may be talking to enemies. Well, get busy. This number is Fenwick 36498 if you need me. I'll call you as quick as I find out about the ship."

Lane Maitland went to work in a business-like way, and soon got in touch with the ship company. It did not take long. Yes, Mr. Tilford Thorpe had booked passage for himself and wife on their ship, weighing anchor that night at midnight. No, they were not as yet on board, but had sent word that morning that they would arrive early in the evening. Mrs. Thorpe was not well and wanted to have her berth ready. Did the gentleman wish to leave a message for them?

Maitland said no, sharply, and hung up. He put a shaky hand to his lips and tried to still their trembling. So, that was that! It didn't settle the matter fully, but it was at least a clue.

He looked at his watch. There was not too much time. Could he get there before it was too late? And having got there, could he do anything? Would she want him to do anything? Suppose it was only a quarrel between them and Thorpe had made it up?

With perplexities thickening about him he called up the Mayberry house and Merrick answered.

"I couldn't get the old bird," he said gloomily. "He and the mother were out. Nobody knew anything about Tilford."

"Well, they're booked on board, Mr. and *Mrs.* Tilford Thorpe, and expected to arrive soon. They said the lady wasn't so well and wanted to go to bed at once. Now, I think I'd better drive right to New York. I'm thirty miles on the way, and I think I can make it before the ship sails at midnight. I tried to get a plane, but the next one would get me there too late. They couldn't tell me about hiring a special until I got over to the field, and by the time I got there it wouldn't allow much margin. Counting all the time from flying field to dock and so on, I think it's best to drive. Not much traffic this late, and anyhow I might need the car when I get up there. I can always abandon it if it seems best."

"But you ought not to be doing all this,"protested Merrick. "I'm her brother. That's my job."

"Cut that out. You've got to stay by the house. The family have got to be protected from this as long as possible. Nobody will miss me. You tell the boys in the morning, if I'm not there, that I was called away on business and am leaving them to carry on camp and keep up discipline just as if I was there. Tell them there'll be an extra honor stripe on their shoulders if they do."

"Okay," said Merrick solemnly.

"You say your father is asleep?" went on Maitland. "That's good. Perhaps we'll know more before you have to tell him anything. Better tell Nurse Bonner the truth. You can trust her, and she will look after Lexie. My car's filled now, and I'm off. I'll phone you from New York as soon after midnight as I can make a station. So long! Cheer up! God isn't dead!"

"Maybe not," said Merrick drearily. "Oh, I say, Lane, wait a minute. What about those cops? Think I ought to let them know?"

"I guess you ought. In general that's always the first thing to do. If there's one you are sure you can trust to keep it quiet, perhaps it would be well to ask his advice. Of course it isn't necessary to tell the whole family history. Not yet, anyway, but you might say you didn't know but it would turn out just to be a practical joke put on by a friend, or something of that sort, and you will let him know just as soon as you hear from one who has gone to investigate. How would that be?"

"Okay, perhaps. I know the chief up here in our district. He'll keep it under his hat, unless he has an idea it may be gangsters. But I'll hold him off till I hear from you if possible. Would you try the old Thorpe bird again?"

"Perhaps. It might give you some idea whether the family knows about it, in which case keep away from publicity till we know more. Now, keep cool! I wish you knew how to pray!"

"Well, I useta know. I might make a stab at it in a case like this. Take care of yourself, Lane. I don't know what we'd do without you. Good bye. I've got to get busy."

They hung up and Lane jumped into his car and away northward, but poor Merrick, bewildered at the responsibilities thus thrust upon him, gave a dazed look about him and uttered his favorite word when excited:

"Gosh! Can you beat it?"

MARIS came back to consciousness with someone pulling off her slippers and dropping them on the floor.

What floor?

She was instantly aware of disaster, fear, terror that had been about her when she passed out. What had made her pass out? She had never fainted in her life. She had always been proud of that. Ah! Now she knew. She recalled the burly man who had lured her into that awful car, telling her Doctor MacPherson had sent for her, that Merrick had had an accident and was dying and wanted her. It was perfectly clear to her now that there must have been something crooked about the whole thing. Maybe Merrick wasn't even hurt. Maybe it was all a hoax. She had read about people being kidnaped. But why would anyone want to kidnap *her?* All her friends knew that they were not rich people and could not pay a ransom. Surely the criminal world must know that, they were said to be so well informed as to people's private lives.

Stay! They had heard of her engagement to Tilford perhaps. The Thorpes were reputed millionaires. And the underworld scarcely would know yet that the engagement was broken. She had told nobody but Lane and her family. Maybe they had heard it was her wedding night.

Her heart suddenly sank at the prospect. If that was what had happened there would be nobody to come to her rescue. Tilford of course would not be searching for her. Only her dear family would be in anguish. Her poor tired family! Oh, that must not be! Somehow she must get away without their having to suffer. It was entirely up to her.

Yet she was not alone. Almost as if a voice had spoken in her secret heart she heard those words again: "No weapon that is formed against thee shall prosper." Those words she had read in her Bible just before all this awful thing happened. No, she was not alone. Her Lord was with her, living in her!

She did not really think this all out in words, it was just a comforting consciousness that came to her as she lay quite motionless, trying to get her dazed senses back into working order.

The one who was working over her had put on some other shoes that did not belong to her. They were tight and uncomfortable. Now she was fussing about her head, lifting it a little and tucking something underneath, arranging it around her face, pulling out her hair here and there and patting it.

The sudden thought crossed her mind that perhaps they thought she was dead and were preparing her for burial. Almost she cried out, but she held herself in steady control and waited. She must not let it be known that she was conscious. She tried to be utterly relaxed and lie limp, but her heart seemed to beat so wildly that she felt it could almost be heard.

This was a woman working around her. She could hear the rustle of her dress. Once a sleeve brushed across her hand. She was arranging her drapery about her feet. Maris became aware of alien garments upon her, unaccustomed garments, fitted, long, and voluminous. It was as if her inner consciousness went out stealthily spying to convey to her the details of her situation. As if her senses had banded together within her body to feel out and inform her of everything. Her hand that lay quiet at her side came alive suddenly and informed her she was clothed in heavy smooth satin of a soft rich texture. She had a consciousness that her hair had recently been brushed and ordered pleasantly. There was something on her head, a hat or a band or coronet of some sort, and there was a sense of something soft and cloudlike near her cheek and forehead, something light as air, or was that only part of a dream? She lay there trying to think it out. And now she discovered a ring upon her finger twisted slightly, the great stone pressing against the flesh of the next finger. Cautiously she pressed her fingers closer to make sure. A ring, yes. Like her own that she had given back to Tilford. Was this just a dream?

The person who bent above her wore heavy beads about her neck and she could hear them rattle against each other as she leaned over and smoothed the satin on the far side, so of course this must be a woman. She also wore cheap unpleasant perfume that Maris thought had a musty odor. She somehow felt this person was not overly clean. Maris was glad when with a final pat to the draperies the woman walked away. She walked heavily with a quick little nipping tread, as if her shoes were too tight.

What was this place?

Her mind went back to the car in which her consciousness had gone out, and that hateful bitter rag that had been thrust into her mouth. Had this woman been along? Was it she who had sat at the far end of the seat and helped to pull her in? It was all so vague and fraught with awful fear. So now what was this place and how did they get here? She found she had no memory that would suggest it.

The woman seemed to have stepped through a door. It

must be a bathroom for there was a sound of running water. Dared she open her eyes to look around?

Cautiously she lifted her lashes just a tiny bit and then wider, in a quick sharp glance, then shut them again for the woman was returning.

But she had seen enough to show her that she was on board a ship. She had distinctly seen the portholes either side of the dresser and the outline of the room was strangely familiar. It was like the picture of the bridal suite that Tilford had shown her. Had she then been kidnaped by gangsters and were they taking her abroad where her friends could never find her? Panic seized her and she felt the little pulse in her neck begin to throb wildly. But she must not get excited. She had need for every faculty. She must keep calm. She must not appear to be awake. She must think this thing through somehow. Her very life depended on this. The ship did not seem to be in motion. Perhaps there would be a way to escape before it sailed, though that was scarcely likely if her captors were really gangsters. They would have thought out all possibilities of escape and guarded against them. This woman was likely put here as her jailer.

But how did this theory fit with the silken garments she was wearing? Why should they dress her up this way? If she could only get a good glimpse of that woman. Dared she open her eyes and peep at her?

It seemed that she was standing over by the dresser, opening a small handbag, if she could judge by the sound. Cautiously she peered through her lashes. The woman was looking into the mirror and powdering her nose. She studied her an instant before she closed her eyes again. She was a stoutish elderly woman with shingled graying hair. And now, could it be true? She was setting a small youthful hat on her head. Was she perhaps going away? Would there be a chance to escape, or would someone else come?

That terrible man, perhaps, who had pushed her into the car?

The woman was turning her head to get the effect of the hat and as she swung around toward the bed Maris closed her eyes quickly holding herself rigidly quiet, but as she did so she caught a glimpse of the dress she was wearing, and saw that it was white satin, and that that was a wedding veil she had felt about her face, and silver slippers were on her feet!

She was filled with such horror that she could scarcely keep from shuddering and crying out, as she thought of the possibilities that were before her. That awful man—! Oh, what could it all mean? And what could she do? Were they going to try to force her through some horrible marriage ceremony? She could never hope to escape in those garments. She would be marked of every eye.

Then all at once came words ringing back into her heart: "No weapon that is formed against thee shall prosper . . . the heritage of the servant of the Lord," and a quiet self-control came over her. After all, God was here. Nothing could really harm her. Nothing could happen that he could not control.

"Oh, my heavenly Father! Help me!" cried her frightened heart. And then her mind became clearer so that she could think. She hadn't got this thing straight yet. It didn't make sense. People didn't go out and kidnap poor girls and take them on ship board to marry them, or to make sport of them. There was something more to it than that.

The woman was walking about the room now, picking up a few things and putting them into a small overnight bag. She must be going to leave. But who was coming to take her place?

As the woman bent over to fasten the bag, Maris ventured another quick look, and this time she noted a pile of handsome looking baggage over by the bathroom door.

There were initials on some of the pieces. She forced herself to puzzle out the letters. "T.T." Her heart stood still. Those were Tilford's initials! Was it thinkable that Tilford would do a thing like this? Was that his ring on her finger again, and was he "exerting his authority"?

The thought came and looked her in the face as she lay there, struggling to keep her expression from being anything but absolute unconsciousness in sleep. It menaced her with as much horror as when she had thought of that awful kidnaper as a bridegroom. For if Tilford had done this thing to her he was no longer the Tilford whom she had thought she was in love with. He was a despicable tyrant, bound only to conquer and bend her to his will, and she was suddenly filled with a worse fear than before.

"The heritage!" came the words again. "The heritage of the servant of the Lord!"

"Oh, my Heavenly Father! I am Thy servant! The very humblest, the latest perhaps, and surely the very lowest of Thy servants, but still a servant. I claim Thy promise!"

The woman was walking about the room now, placing her suitcase on a chair, putting on a pair of white lacy gloves, tilting her hat a little more to the side, touching her lips with a brighter red. Maris ventured another glimpse and felt sure she was preparing to leave soon. She had glanced at her watch. She wished she knew what time it was, what ship this was. But somehow she must be ready to spring into action if the woman did leave.

But what could she do? She could never rush forth in a white satin dress and a wedding veil. Was there anything about the room that she could wear?

Beneath her lashes once more she explored the side wall next her. There were hooks and a gray tweed coat with a fur collar hanging on one. Whose coat was that? Would the woman take it with her? So she lay and thought out what she would do if she got the opportunity.

And then, all at once she became aware of a throbbing in

the heart of the ship. Was that the engine? There was a ship's bell ringing, a clear sharp sound of warning. Were they weighing anchor already? Was it too late? Oh, her precious mother, and father, and the little sick sister! What would they all think?

But the bell gave another warning resonant ring and it seemed to mean something to the other occupant of the room. She looked at her watch, and picked up her bag, glancing uneasily out the door. Then she closed the door again and came back, as if waiting for something, some signal. Oh, would she think she had to wait till someone came to take her place? Wouldn't there be even a chance to try and get away?

And then there came a voice, clear and ringing: "All ashore that's going ashore! All ashore that's going ashore!"

The woman turned and fairly ran toward the door, glancing casually at Maris there on the bed, so resolutely limp and silent, her eyes not even quivering. As quiet as if she were laid out for burial.

The woman flung open the door and went out shutting it hastily behind her. She had not locked it! The key was still on the inside! Hadn't she meant to lock it? She had not taken the coat with her. Had she forgotten it? Maris dared not stir for a second till she heard the woman's little high heels clicking down the metal edges of the safety treads on the stairs. Even then she opened her eyes most cautiously, with a sinister feeling that somehow Tilford or the other awful man had been spirited in as the woman left. If he were there, if either of them were there, she had planned she would lie utterly limp and still. She would not respond to any effort to bring her to life. It was the only mode of warfare that she could think of for one under a tyrant.

But the next instant she sprang into action. There might be only a moment more and she must do her best.

She flung the costly wedding veil from her head, wiping it from her forehead with its coronet of orange blossoms as if it were abhorrent. She sat up and clutched at the fastenings of her dress. She must get it off if she had to tear it seam from seam. Could it be the dress that Tilford's mother had ordered? How all the chapters of the story were dropping into place!

She struggled out of the dress frantically, then stooped and wrenched at the jeweled buttons of the silver slippers and kicked them from her. She could never walk in them, they were too tight! She bent and groped on the floor for her own little comfortable everyday slippers. Had that woman put them away? She had no time to search. Would she have to go in just silver stockings? Ah! Here they were! She stepped into them gratefully, and then the glitter of the ring caught her eye. Tilford's ring! She tore it from her finger and flung it on the pile of wedding finery on the bed.

Just then a man rushed by the door crying out again, "All ashore that's going ashore! Last call!" and her heart stood still with fear. Now she *had* to go, and she had no dress on, only a little white silken slip!

Wildly she seized the tweed coat from the hook on the wall and caught a whiff of horrid perfume! It was that woman's coat, and she would perhaps return for it! But this was no time to be squeamish. Maris flung it about her, thrust her arms into the sleeves, and drew the fur collar up about her face. Then she cautiously opened the door and looked out.

There was not a soul in sight. The clatter and noise of many tongues rose from a region below somewhere, people saying last things.

There were stairs close at hand, the stairs that woman must have used, but she dared not risk them. She might meet her coming back to get her coat. Wildly she fled along the gallery to another flight and dashed down. Endless stairs, they seemed, wide and low and turning on incessant landings. Would she never get to a place that would lead her off the boat?

Then suddenly as she rounded a turn she saw Tilford Thorpe just below her standing on a lower step talking earnestly with the woman who had just left her; beyond was a glimpse of the outer world, and a gangplank not far away.

Her heart contracted, and her breath came in stifled gasps. She grasped the handrail and reeled back, turning and flying up to the deck above, and back along that to another flight of steps.

Her heart was beating so wildly now that it seemed as if she could not go on, but she took a deep breath and tried to steady herself. At least she knew where they were. But could she ever hope to escape them? Was that gangplank the only path to safety? Would she have to pass under their very gaze? Was there any hope she could do so without being recognized?

"All ashore that's going ashore!" called a voice quite near, and she almost slid down the next stair she came to. A great siren set up a clamor to add to the din, and she found she was trembling in every part of her body. Even her lips were shaking.

These steps she was going down seemed endless. Perhaps she had gone too far, for they landed her amid a lot of bales and boxes and baggage; coils of rope lay in her way, the heat of a furnace came from somewhere on her right. She rushed about trying to find out where she was, and felt like a rat in a trap. A sailor came by.

"You don't belong here, lady. Look alive there! You'll get hurt. Can't you see you're in the way?"

"But isn't this the way to get ashore?" She pointed to a tilting floor that spanned a space over black sullen water.

"No! This is freight. You wantta go up the other end. Better hurry we're just weighing anchor."

Then suddenly he grabbed her and drew her out of the way of a large packing case that was being brought on board by several men.

"Lady, you'll get killed if you don't look out!" He glared at her.

"Oh, I've got to get ashore, and I'm afraid I can't get there in time. Couldn't you put me off here?" she pleaded.

The man looked at her in disgust, then called to one of the men who had just helped with the packing case.

"Here, take this fool woman ashore. She's lost her way, and they're just hauling in the gangplank."

The burly shoreman grinned and swung her up the incline. She had one awful glimpse of the dark water on either side, and then she felt the wharf beneath her feet. She was so relieved that she almost sank down right there.

But suddenly amid the noise and confusion the siren sounded again. She realized that people were all about her, calling farewells to their friends. She looked and the ship was already moving, putting stately distance between it and the dock. There were people crowding all the decks looking down, some smiling, some weeping, confetti hurtling through the air, snarls of paper ribbons like crazy rainbows littering the railings, girls snatching for them and gathering them in like trophies. The ship was gone and she had escaped! She stared for an instant with dazed eyes, unable to take it in, incapable for the moment of further action.

It was just then she saw Tilford, standing on the upper deck by the railing, staring out over the motley company on shore. In a moment more he might see her! Perhaps he could do nothing now. Yet there was no telling. He was still capable of issuing orders. She might find herself under custody! And the woman! She might be somewhere in this crowd perhaps!

Her fear redoubled, Maris turned and stole through the crowd that even in that short time since she had stood there, had milled around her, filling up the way.

Keeping her face away from the ship, she edged between the jostling people. She pushed the fur collar up about her chin, daring not to look up lest she would be looking into the eyes of her erstwhile keeper.

At last she reached the edge of the crowd, and darted away down the long shadowy reach of wharf, her frightened feet fairly flying. There were bales and boxes about in the way. She had to go between them, to weave her way in and out, but she was glad of even so much covering for her flight.

The din on the other end of the wharf seemed farther away now. There were not many people about here, everybody was up at the other end watching the ship's departure. Sudden tears of relief blinded her vision. She was almost at the end of this long wharf now. A dark street loomed ahead, a city street with unknown perils at midnight but that seemed small beside the perils already past. There were lights from an office at the right. She must avoid those, she must keep out of sight as much as possible.

Then, when she was almost minded to rest for an instant she heard footsteps behind her, quick heavy steps, like the woman who had been in her cabin, and fear leaped up in her breast again. The woman had seen the coat perhaps, and was coming after it. She would call the police. There would be another awful time. Oh, she could bear no more. She felt as if she must sink down and rest, she was so tired!

But she started to run with all her might, breathlessly, lightly in her little old slippers, keeping to the shadows as much as possible, not heeding where she went, and then all at once she stumbled on a great coil of rope and went sprawling face downward, her hands outstretched. This was the end. She could go no farther. She would just lie here and let them do what they would. She could not rise and go on!

But those footsteps were coming on now! It was a woman! She peered back fearfully, and just then the woman passed under an arc light and she thought she recognized her. It was, it must be that woman. She was hurrying. She must have seen the coat!

The place where Maris was lying was in the shadow. Yet she dared not risk staying there. Fear stimulated her waning strength, put fight into her soul once more. Her mother and Lexie at home needed her. She must not get into the clutches of kidnapers again, even though Tilford whom she dreaded most was out on that ship sailing away from her. By this time he had likely gone to his cabin, and discovered her flight. There were radios on shipboard, and Tilford's long arm was capable of reaching even to the land. Tilford never gave up a thing he had once started until he had his way.

She struggled to her feet, bruised, and sore, with a long scratch on her arm, and splinters in her hands, but fear was behind her driving her again. Her feet seemed gifted with wings, and she flew on noiselessly toward that spot of light from the windows of the office, toward the darkness of the street ahead. Which should she take? Should she go into that office and claim protection of the people there, summon the police, or should she trust to the darkness of the unknown street? Oh, the street would be safer. She could not trust that woman. She was wearing respectable clothes, she could probably summon friends. And Maris was in a strange array. Nobody would believe her, and she might be hailed to jail charged with stealing a coat!

The thought gave new momentum to her flight. She darted ahead with every ounce of strength that was in her, and not six feet from the street she came into violent collision with a man who was also sprinting, just rounding the corner from the street to the wharf. And suddenly she collapsed in his arms, the breath knocked from her body. This surely was the end!

BACK at the Mayberry home the mother was restless. Perhaps she felt the tenseness in the atmosphere, although Merrick had been very careful. He had called Nurse Bonner from her room just as she was preparing for a good night's rest, and downstairs out of sound from above, he had told her the situation with regard to Maris.

Nurse Bonner was wise. She did not exclaim. She took it calmly with a quick sanity that helped to steady Merrick, who was full of despair over his responsibility.

"Yes," said Nurse Bonner, "it's pretty serious of course, and we'll have to be wise about the invalids. Your father too. Don't waken him unless you have to. Wait at least until you hear from Mr. Maitland. If your father can get a full night's sleep he will be better able to bear whatever comes tomorrow, and really, he can't do any more than is being done tonight. It is imperative of course that not a breath of excitement reaches your mother. She is exceedingly sensitive to noises, even to feelings, in the household. If your father finds out tonight he will be nervous when he sees her in the morning. That must not be. She must think he's gone to his office happily, and that all is well. And we won't say anything to the night nurse yet."

Merrick looked at her gratefully. Her very tones made him feel more like a man, dependable, able to handle this situation in the way it ought to be managed.

"All right," he said. "Sorry to have disturbed you, but I thought somebody ought to understand things."

"Yes," said the nurse, "and don't hesitate to call me in the night the minute you get any news. I'm used to waking at the slightest sound. It doesn't spoil my rest in the least."

"All right!" said Merrick. "I'll call you."

"I'll leave the door open and you can just step in and speak to me. I don't want to disturb any of the others."

"I'll do that," said Merrick, and went back to the telephone with a sense of comfort that somebody else knew what was going on and he wasn't entirely alone.

But in spite of all their caution the situation somehow reached its invisible fingers out and penetrated the sick room. The night nurse came tapping at Nurse Bonner's door a little later.

"I wish you'd come here a minute," she whispered. "My patient is restless and I don't like the way her pulse acts. She keeps calling for Maris. I haven't heard her do that before at all. I went to Miss Maris' door and tapped but she didn't answer. I didn't know whether I ought to waken her or not, she's looked so tired the last few days."

"Maris is out," said Nurse Bonner briskly. "I'll come!"

She threw her kimono around her and was at the bedside almost at once.

"Now see here," she said quietly, as if it were a joke, "what's the matter with this little mother?"

Mrs. Mayberry lifted troubled eyes.

"Maris!" she said piteously. "Maris!"

"Maris has gone out," said Nurse Bonner. "She went for a little ride."

The troubled eyes searched her face.

"Getting—married?" the slow lips formed the words earnestly.

"Oh, no. Nothing like that!" said the nurse.

But the eyes were still troubled, puzzled.

"Her—wedding—day—!" murmured the sick woman.

"Oh, no. Not at all. You've got mixed in your dates. Maris isn't getting married today at all. She wouldn't be married till you were able to be at the wedding. Now be a good little mother and shut your eyes and go to sleep. I'll take care of Maris when she comes and tell her you sent her your love."

She got the sick woman quieted at last and then stole in to see about Lexie, for she had left her door ajar, and now there seemed to be a lot of restless turning over and sighing.

She found the little girl crying.

"I called and called my sister and she's didn't come!" said Lexie with whispered sobs. "I vanted a dwink of vater."

"Well, that's too bad!" said Nurse Bonner. "Your sister had to go out for a little while, but she'll be back pretty soon, I guess. I'll get you the drink of water and then you'll go to sleep like a good little girl, won't you?"

"Wes."

Downstairs Merrick was having troubles of his own. A call had come from the Maitland house. The housekeeper said the little boys had waked up and were demanding Mr. Maitland. So Merrick had to call them to the telephone and give them Lane's message. They responded loyally as Lane had known they would, but their voices sounded most dejected as they said good night. It touched their older brother and he promised to be over the first thing in the morning and let them know how soon Lane would return, and perhaps they could get ready some kind of a celebration to welcome him home. They'd talk it over in the morning.

So at last the little boys went back to their beds, cheered by the thought of a festivity in the offing. They planned to pick strawberries enough for strawberry shortcake for lunch, and then wondered if Lane would object to their decorating with a lot of little flags they had found in the attic.

And Merrick reflected on what a lot of different kinds of troubles there were in this world, all at once, when life had heretofore been such a jolly affair. He decided it was all because of Tilford Thorpe and that blamed wedding.

The ship sailed out on a silver sea, and the New York harbor became a speck in the distance.

Tilford Thorpe turned from watching the shore, and with lips set with determination went to his stateroom. He was expecting to have a bad time for a few minutes with Maris. She would probably be stubborn for a while. But when she found that they were off on their honeymoon actually, and there was no turning back, she would easily come around. Maris had always been so sweet and yielding!

He hoped she would be fully recovered from the sleeping potion that had been given her, and see the immediate necessity of submitting to the marriage service for which he had arranged with the captain, to take place soon after the starting of the ship.

He ascended the steps to his suite with pleasant anticipation. He had Maris now where she couldn't gainsay him. He meant to be very kind and loving to her—after she once came to herself and realized that he had been right—just to make up for taking her away forcibly. Of course she might be a bit upset at that at first, but he would show her such a good time that she would soon forget it. He was glad he had had his mother buy those two evening dresses. They would have a gay time on board and when they got to Paris they could stock up on some really smart clothes for her. Of course she would likely be disappointed not to have her own things that she had prepared for her trousseau, but they wouldn't be much loss. Anything she would have bought would have been far below the standard of what his wife should wear, anyway.

Then he reached his stateroom and opened the door.

There on the bed lay a heap of satin and lace, tossed aside, ripped and torn, as if it had been jerked off in great haste. Half crushed at one side lay the priceless wedding veil, an heirloom in the Thorpe family and yellow with age. It drooped from the coronet of orange blossoms dejectedly, and sparkling out from its ethereal folds there lay the great diamond ring, its prisms flashing gaily with a startled air, as if surprised that it had been rejected.

Tilford stared down on it scarcely believing his senses. She had torn off the wedding dress and gone! She had flung his ring back at him again! But how was this possible? Mrs. Trilby, the woman he had hired to attend her and dress her, had told him just now that she wasn't awake yet. That it would likely be another hour before she was fully free from the sleeping tablet. Had the woman double-crossed him? Sometimes those low-down hirelings did that. Only he had been so sure of this woman. She was to receive another hundred dollars at her home if he found everything all right when he went to his stateroom! And it wasn't conceivable that Maris had bribed her, because Maris would have nothing to bribe with. Maris was penniless.

He stepped forward, incredulous, to lift the ring from the folds of lace, half believing he would yet find Maris beneath the heap of finery, but he stumbled over a little silver shoe, and plunged his arms deep into the lace and satin, the ring evading him and slithering out of sight gaily, as if it enjoyed tantalizing him.

By the time he had found the ring he was thoroughly himself and very angry, trying to plan how he could get revenge on Maris for thus evading him. He could not understand how she had managed to get away. He was sure Mrs. Trilby could not have been down on the deck more than three minutes before the ship sailed. He had himself been standing close at hand when the gangplank was hauled in. Maris had not passed him, he was positive. Besides, how could she get away without any clothes? He had told Mrs. Trilby she might have and take with her the garments Maris was wearing when they took her. She had left the wedding dress behind! She could not have gone without clothes!

He strode to the pile of baggage heaped in the corner. Not one had been disturbed. The expensive outfit that he had made his mother buy was still locked up in those suitcases, and he had the keys in his pocket. He counted everything over. Nothing disturbed. She could not have gone in such a state as that.

He tossed the things on the bed aside. Not even a sheet or blanket was gone! It was inexplainable.

She must be somewhere about, perhaps playing a practical joke on him! Well, in that case he would forgive her, of course, but it was careless of her to fling around expensive clothes and diamonds that way. He would have to teach her to be more careful. Of course she had never been accustomed to such prices as he paid for things and perhaps had not realized.

He strode to the bathroom and looked in, he pulled aside the shower curtain, then peered into a wardrobe. But no Maris appeared. She was not anywhere.

He threw open the door of his stateroom and looked outside but the galleries were alive now with people coming back to their staterooms. There was gay chatter everywhere. People laughing and talking. And he was alone! He had never been so frustrated in his life as he had by Maris Mayberry! Little puritanical hypocrite! Pretending to be so awfully good and then standing him up on his wedding at the very last minute. He would know better than to be fooled by a demure face again. She wasn't his kind of course, but he could have raised her into his class. And she was beautiful, there was no denying that.

He stormed back and forth from bed to portholes, trying to think what he should do. Somehow he meant to get it back on this little girl who had turned him down and scorned his wealth that he had intended lavishing upon her. He would think up a splendid way and take her by surprise. She hadn't heard the last of him yet by any means.

Meantime, he was out on the ocean alone and what was he going to do with himself? Well, there was a famous actress on board. He might amuse himself with her, and manage it that news of his flirtation should get back to some social column in a paper Maris would be likely to see. That would be a good beginning.

He kicked at the rich wedding gown that was trailing off on the floor. The wedding gown that his mother had paid for! It occurred to him that his mother had really made all this trouble, insisting upon that wedding gown. He would tell her so when he wrote. It did his wrathful soul good to blame it on somebody.

It also occurred to him that the captain would be expecting a summons pretty soon for the wedding he was to perform. He had better do something about it at once. So he rang for the steward and sent a note to the captain that the wedding had been called off on account of illness in the family which detained the bride at home.

Having thus disposed of the wedding, he rolled the wedding dress up in a wad along with the veil and orange blossoms and slippers and bestowed them in a suitbox which he ordered the steward to have wrapped and shipped to his home. He was resolved that he would somehow bring it about, sometime in the future, that Maris should yet wear that wedding dress and be married to him. He would take a little time off in Europe on this supposed business trip, and give her mother time to get well, or die, one or the other, and then he would come back and make Maris eat humble pie and have such a wedding as *he* should prescribe. When he once brought her thoroughly to her knees she would do what he said, and like it!

With which resolve he went downstairs to the bar and refreshed himself with several drinks. His wedding night without a bride had to be celebrated in some way. So he drank. Tomorrow he would look up that actress and forget Maris for awhile.

But somehow it was not so easy to forget Maris, and he had to take a good many drinks before the vision of her face in her wedding array faded from his thoughts, and he began to consider other phases of the subject. There for instance was all that money he had paid to the man and woman who carried out his plans. He had had to borrow it from his mother, and he didn't see how he was ever going to pay it back again. Probably dad would find it out and then there would be an awful row! Strange he had so much trouble in his life! Strange he never could have anything he wanted without a fuss.

He, who had been pampered since ever he was born!

He drank so much that he had to be helped up to his stateroom at last, and went to bed dead drunk!

And that was the night that was to have been Maris' wedding night!

MEANWHILE Maris, limp in the arms of an unknown man, dumb with new fear and horror, panted for her breath in the darkness and wished she could die. She was too tired to go on, and too dazed to think a way out of this awful maze of disasters into which she had so innocently walked a few hours ago.

"No weapon . . . shall prosper!" came the words through her despairing mind. Was that then untrue, that promise that had so heartened her? Did God not care?

The man had recovered his balance and was looking down at her. He had been running for that ship that was so noisily sailing away from the dock. Had he missed it after coming so far? And just because some crazy woman had dashed into him and almost upset him?

Even if he dropped her right here and ran on, could he make it? But one couldn't just drop a woman like that who had fallen into his arms, and was apparently almost unconscious, and breathing painfully. She lay like a dead weight in his arms. It was not thinkable that he could lay her down here and dash on, not even for his own important errand!

He held her off a little and looked into her face, and then suddenly he exclaimed and drew her close again, as one draws something precious.

"Maris! Beloved!" he breathed, nor knew what he was saying. "Oh, my dear! Are you hurt?"

He bent over her looking into her face against his shoulder, and suddenly her eyes opened and she looked at him. Then all at once the stark terror within her eyes turned to incredulous wonder, and a great blinding joy. She clung to him, and quivered, hiding her face on his breast. His arms went around her and held her close.

"Oh, Lane!" she whispered. "Oh, Lane!" It was all she could say, and great long shudders of relief shook her slender body.

Then suddenly she remembered and grew tense again.

"Hide me! *Quick!*" she pleaded. "There was somebody after me!"

She turned her head and looked behind her, and then hid her eyes again and shuddered. She was breathless and her voice trailed off.

"There! My darling!" he said gently, patting her head as if she were a little child. "Nobody shall touch you, beloved! I'll take care of you! Come! Are you able to walk? It's only a step to my car!"

With a strong arm supporting her, her hand in his, he set her upon her feet and led her quickly out into the shadows of the street, and across to where he had left his car.

There were people coming away now, a good many of them. She could hear their footsteps, and their voices. She clutched at his arm, but he drew her around the other side of the car out of sight and put her gently in.

"Put your head back and rest," he said. "No one will see you. No one will trouble you any more. I am here to protect you."

She dropped her head back, but her eyes peered out and he saw she was still frightened. It was not until they had driven several blocks away from the wharf and left the crowd entirely behind that she began to relax and be more like herself.

He had his hands full with traffic for a few minutes, but when they reached the Holland tunnel and were speeding down the smooth way he spoke again:

"What are you afraid of, Maris? No one can get you now. They will not recognize you riding along in the car. They cannot see your face enough for that. And what could they do to you now that you are with me and I am here to protect you?"

"Oh," she said, her voice with a little tremble in it was almost between a laugh and a wail, "it's the coat! It is not mine. They might arrest me for stealing. I had to take it. There was nothing else."

He laughed.

"We can pay for the coat, or send it back. Don't worry about that. Just you rest back and shut your eyes. Aren't you too warm in that heavy coat with all that fur about your neck? Don't you want to take it off? We can fling it out of the car window when we get out of the tunnel if you want to."

"Oh, but I can't take it off," she said laughing shakily. "They took my own dress and I had to put on this coat or I never could have got away!"

Lane considered that.

"Well, now see here," he said, "I think we can remedy that. Why don't you put on my coat? I certainly don't need it this warm night. I only happened to have it along because I was hoping to take you riding. It's thin. It's only linen. It surely will be more comfortable than that heavy thing."

"But oughtn't I to send it back to the owner?"

"Do you know who the owner is?"

"No, but there might be a way of finding out. I felt some papers in the pocket when I put it on."

"Well, then we won't throw it out, but you are going to be more comfortable. Here!"

He stopped the car for a moment and slid out of his coat, handing it over to her.

"Now," he said, "take off that coat and hand it out to me. I'm going to get out and open the trunk in the back and get this coat out of your sight. If there are papers in the pocket we must guard them carefully. They might give some clue—"

He got out and Maris hastily changed into the linen coat, and handed the tweed coat through the window. When he got back in again he asked her if that was more comfortable.

"Oh, so much!" she said. "I didn't see how I was going to stand it all the way home."

"Well, now," said Lane, "I don't want to force your confidence, but it's necessary that I telephone Merrick as soon as possible. I wonder—do you want to tell me anything? I don't want you to have to dwell on unpleasant things, but Merrick is liable to have a couple of detectives out scouting right now, and he'll want to know what I've found out!"

"Oh," she said with a quick gasp, "is Merrick all right?"

"Yes, Merrick is quite all right. He's at home safe and well waiting anxiously to hear from me. If it will help you any I'll just tell you what I know. I was out in our yard looking for a ball and heard your friend drive up and tell you that yarn about Merrick. I didn't hear more than a word or two, but it was enough to worry me. I called to you as you were getting in the car that I would take you, but the door was slammed shut and the car shot away, so I followed as fast as I could. What happened next?"

"Not much that I can tell you," said Maris. "They shoved me into the seat and someone caught me in his arms, or her arms, it might have been a woman. They stuffed a bitter wet rag down my throat and I passed out.

That's all I know till I woke up on board that ship with my head going around in circles and some woman taking off my shoes. She lifted my head and fixed something under it, and when I dared open my eyes a little I found I was dressed in a heavy white satin dress, and a veil, and silver slippers. The woman smoothed down my dress and went away, and when I looked again she was powdering her nose and putting on a hat. Then she picked up things around the room and put them in her suitcase. My dress I had worn away was one of them. I think this coat belonged to her. It smells of unpleasant perfume just as she did. She must have forgotten it in her hurry. She got all ready and seemed impatient as if she were waiting for someone. She didn't look my way any more. I was terribly afraid that awful man was coming. But when the second call came to go ashore she just made a dash for the door, and I think she forgot to lock it. I was wondering how I would get out if she locked it. I wondered if the steward would let me out without asking questions if I rang. But she didn't lock it, and as soon as I heard her going down the stairs I jumped up and tore off that dress and veil and those slippers. I found my own shoes, snatched the coat from the hook on the wall and ran. I had an awful time getting off. I couldn't find the way. And once I came on Tilford and the woman talking at the foot of the steps, by the gangplank. I drew back just in time, and then got all mixed up in the freight place. But a sailor put me off there for the other gangplank had been hauled up. I had an awful time getting through the crowd, and I saw Tilford again up on deck. I was sure he would recognize me, so I ducked behind some boxes, and started to run, but I fell over a coil of rope and then I thought I heard the woman coming, so I got up and ran blindly. But when I ran into you I thought the end had come."

Lane's hand went tenderly out and folded over hers, like a blessing, it seemed to Maris.

He was quite still for a minute and then he said:

"Have you any idea who perpetrated this dastardly deed?"

His voice was husky with feeling. He was joyously conscious of that first moment when he had held her in his arms. And he didn't just know where he stood with her.

Maris didn't answer right away. She too was remembering the thrill of his arms about her, and felt a constraint. Her voice was low, almost shamed, when she finally spoke.

"I'm afraid I do," she said sadly. "I'm afraid—no, I mean I'm almost *sure*—it was Tilford Thorpe!"

Her head drooped and her eyes were downcast as if she felt she ought not to tell that, or rather as if it were her own shame she was confessing, not another's.

Lane considered that.

"What makes you think so?" he asked, his voice almost embarrassed.

"Because I saw his initials, 'T. T.,' on the baggage in the stateroom. Because we had had a discussion about a wedding dress his mother wanted me to get, and I'm almost sure it was that dress I was wearing! Because—" she hesitated and again that shamed look crossed her face, "because that woman had put *his ring* on my finger, the ring I had given back to him some days ago! Then, too, I saw him on the ship, you know."

"That's pretty conclusive evidence!" said Lane, his lips setting in a stern line. "It's hard to believe that any man from a respectable family would stoop to a thing like this. But—I won't distress you now by discussing it. The important thing is, Merrick should be told at once that you are found. I'm stopping right here to telephone. Aren't you hungry? I'll bring you a sandwich. Here's my hat. Put it on and pull it down in front if you are afraid anybody might recognize you. I won't be a minute."

Lane dashed out at a bright little wayside restaurant, and

true to his word was back in an unbelievably short time. His message to Merrick had been crisp and brief, but filled with a note of joy that pulsed over the wire to the tired brother and lifted his burden even before he took in all the words.

"Hello, Merrick! Happy ending! It's just as we thought. I've got her safe and sound and we're on our way home! No bloodshed and nobody the wiser yet when we left. Better put the quietus on the cops for the present, at least till we get there."

They were on their way again, thrilling over each other's nearness, and over Maris' swift deliverance. Eating their sandwiches and saying little as they flew along through the night.

At last Maris spoke:

"Where were you going, Lane, when I collided with you? What were you going to do?"

"I don't exactly know," he said gravely. "I was trusting the Lord to guide me. I was expecting Him to open the way as I came to it. I was on my way to catch that ship, even if I had to sail all the way across to find out if you were on it. You see, I had a flat tire on the way up or I'd have been there a full half hour before sailing time, in plenty of time to find your stateroom and go to it, ostensibly to say good bye. That was all the plan I had when I started. If I got as far as that I knew the way would open. I would be shown what to do."

"But I don't understand how you got the idea I would be there. Why did you think I would be on shipboard?"

"Why, you see I followed that car you were in and it took you to a measly little rat of an airplane, and the plane went north, that was all I had to go on. That and the license number of the car. I noticed it while the car stood before your house. But it was Merrick who suggested the ship and gave me the name and time of sailing."

"Why would Merrick think I would be on the ship?"

she asked in a puzzled tone. "*I* would never have thought of Tilford's doing a thing like that. Why, I couldn't believe it myself at first."

"I'm afraid your brother hasn't a very high idea of Mr. Thorpe," said Lane dryly.

"No," said Maris sadly, "I knew he didn't like him, but I thought it was just a prejudice that he would get over when he knew him better. Oh, if I had only realized sooner what he was! But Lane, you have been wonderful. It was marvelous for you to come all this way to find me."

"Wonderful!" said Lane. "*Won*derful?" He gave her a look in the darkness that would have told her volumes if she could have seen the full splendor of it, and then he added in a tone of deep feeling, "Why, Maris, I think I'd have died if I couldn't have gone! You don't know what you mean to me! This is no time to be talking about myself, I know, just when you are finding out the perfidy of the man you thought you were going to marry. Of course you don't want to hear anybody else talk about love now. But, Maris, I guess I've got to tell you that I love you as my very life. I don't want the knowledge of it to be a burden to you. I just want you to understand that I'm one friend who would give his life for you if necessary. Even if in the future you can never care for me, I'll go right on loving you and doing anything I can to care for you. I'll be your brother, or your friend, or just nothing but a servant for times of need if you don't want me to be closer. I want you to know that there is a strong earthly love that carries no obligations, that is yours for the taking, but you don't need to take it if you don't want it."

Lane was silent for a moment, scarcely daring to look toward her, wishing now he had waited until another time to speak. Then Maris spoke in a small voice:

"But I do want it, Lane!"

He brought the car to a sudden stop at the roadside and turned toward her.

"You *do!* Do you mean that, Maris? You're not just saying it because you are grateful for my coming after you?"

"Oh, no!" she said with a great surrender in her voice. "I love you, Lane! I've fought against it almost ever since you came back. It was your coming that made me feel there was something wrong in my feeling for Tilford. At first I was only wishing he might be like you but soon I knew that wasn't enough. I knew that you were taking his place in my heart. I struggled against it with all my might for a few days, but I wasn't able to keep my heart from thrilling every time I saw you coming across the lawn, every time I heard your voice on the telephone, every time I touched that beautiful Bible you gave me! It troubled me very much, because I was going to marry Tilford in a few days, and I knew it wasn't right for me to be thinking of you. I was very unhappy. I wanted him to be *you,* the way you used to be when we were children in school and you used to carry my books home for me and bring me candy—"

Suddenly Lane's arms went out and drew her hungrily to himself, holding her close, his lips against her hair.

"My darling!" he said softly. "My own dear girl!"

She nestled closer to him and felt that suddenly Heaven on earth was open before her.

"Go on!" he breathed. "Tell me the rest."

Her hand slipped up around his neck and she drew his head down. Softly, shyly she laid her lips against his.

"I wish there weren't any of that to tell," she said sadly. "It seems so dreadful that I should have let myself think I was in love with a man like that, when God was preparing this for me!"

"Beloved," he said, his lips against her eyelids, "don't feel that way. Tell me the rest and let's get it over with, and just be thankful God led us back together."

"I know," she said. "I am. I think even this last act was an answer to my prayer. You see Tilford had been very disagreeable about mother's illness, and about my caring for Lexie. He practically insisted I leave them both to nurses and a hired housekeeper, and stay with his mother till the wedding. And when I wouldn't he tried to exert what he called authority over me, by right of his ring that I was wearing. So I gave him back his ring. His actions then did a great deal to open my eyes to his true self, for I had never seen him cross before. He'd always had his own way. But afterward I got to thinking about his disappointment and fearing that perhaps I had not been gentle in my way of saying no. That perhaps I had no right to give back the ring when the wedding was almost at hand. I worried a lot about it, and couldn't sleep. Till at last I just asked the Lord to make it very plain to me whether He wanted me to apologize, and marry him later when mother got well, or give him up. And the answer to that was—" she paused and a shudder went through her, *"this!* This awful thing that happened tonight! It was unmistakable, but it was a terrible lesson for me to have to have."

Lane laid his lips on hers:

"Precious little girl!" he said softly. "Bless the Lord, O my soul, and forget not all His benefits!"

Maris laid her tired head on his broad shoulder, closed her eyes, and let such gladness flow over her as she never had known before. It seemed a healing tide to wipe out all the awfulness of what had gone before.

Presently she asked:

"But did Merrick ask you to come up here after me without even knowing I would be here?"

"Oh, no," said Lane, "he wanted to come himself, but I told him his job was to stick around at home and keep your mother and father from finding out there was anything the matter. But I didn't come up here without knowing there was a possibility of your being here, you know. I telephoned the ship to find out if Mr. Thorpe was booked and they answered yes, that a Mr. and *Mrs.* Tilford Thorpe were booked, and that they were expected to arrive early in the evening."

Maris gasped:

"Oh, did Tilford dare to do that! How *could* he?"

Suddenly Maris dropped her face in her hands and wept, her slender shoulders shaking with great rending sobs.

Lane gathered her into his arms again.

"Don't, beloved, don't feel that way! It is all over. Let's forget it!"

"But oh, to think I almost married a man like that, when there was you waiting for me! How can God forgive me?"

"Dear precious one, say rather how good God was to bring us together in this wonderful way! But now, Maris, I think we have talked enough. You should rest. You are worn out. And besides we should get home as quickly as possible, not only for your sake but for the sake of the family, so that you will be there and have everything normal in the morning. Now, put your head down on my shoulder and go to sleep and we'll be at home in a little while."

So Maris nestled down with her head on Lane's shoulder, and though she was so strangely happy, she fell asleep almost as soon as she closed her eyes.

MR. Mayberry was restless at intervals all night.

When Lane and Maris arrived they came in so quietly that not even a mouse would have been startled by them. Merrick had gone out to meet the car and bring his sister in. They walked on the grass so that their footsteps would not be heard. But in the early dawn of the morning the invalid suddenly asked out of quiet sleep:

"Has—Maris—come yet?"

"Oh, yes," said the night nurse cheerfully. "She's in her room asleep. She'll come in and see you after breakfast."

But Maris was so happy she could not stay asleep. She woke up with the sense of being surrounded by love. The love and the goodness of God in protecting her and bringing her safely home: the love of her dear family for Merrick had given her one of his bear hugs and a genuine loving kiss. She could see he had been terribly frightened. And the great love of Lane Maitland, that seemed too good to be true.

As the morning light sifted through the maple leaves out on the lawn and the birds sang their silver notes in the tops of all the trees around, her heart swelled with thanksgiving and wonder that God had opened up a new world to her, and made her life jubilant with love.

She went into her mother's room in a fresh little pink and white dress with white frills down the front, one of the pretty little frocks she had purchased first for her trousseau. Why shouldn't the pretty things be worn now and gladden the family?

Most unexpectedly her mother's eyes rested upon the dress, and then her glance went to Maris' face, radiant with a quiet smile.

"Are—you—married—yet, Maris?" She asked the question in the slow way she had been speaking ever since she had been taken sick, but there was an anxious breathlessness in the end of the words as if the answer would mean everything to her.

Maris hadn't heard her talk much since her illness. There had been that sweet sad smile the last few days, but nothing more. Now she looked at her mother astonished, but quickly rallied and her eyes lit with a whimsical light as she answered sweetly, "Oh, no, mother dear. Not married. Just Maris yet."

The mother was silent watching her wistfully.

"Tilford kept you out so late—last—night—!" The voice trailed off wearily.

"But I wasn't with Tilford last night, mother," said Maris with a lilt in her voice. "I was with Lane Maitland."

"Oh!" said the mother with relief.

Then a moment later a shadow came into her eyes:

"You—put off—your—wedding—for—me! I'm—sorry!"

"But I'm glad, mother!" She stooped and kissed her mother.

"Dear!" the mother murmured softly. Then, with an effort:

"You—mustn't wait—any longer! Tell Tilford—I'm sorry—delay. Go on—with—wedding!"

Maris smiled tenderly at her mother, and then leaned down and said softly:

"But mother, I'm not marrying Tilford at all. I found I didn't love him enough. Are you sorry?"

A great joy dawned on the mother's anxious face.

"I'm—*glad!*" she smiled. "Now,—I can—go to sleep!"

And she drew a deep breath and closed her eyes.

Maris felt as if she were walking on air as she went downstairs to speak to Lane who stood hungrily at the door signaling her with his eyes.

An hour later the father came downstairs, joy shining from every wrinkle in his kindly face.

"Mother is decidedly better," he said to Maris. "The nurse says she's having the best sleep yet!"

Later in the morning when the doctor came he confirmed the nurse's word that his patient was decidedly better.

Then he went over to see Lexie and said the quarantine could be removed in a couple of days and the little girl would soon be able to go out in the yard in the sunshine.

Gwyneth had gone to her teacher's home and taken her examinations. The little boys were reported as having been exemplary in the matter of maintaining discipline in camp during the rest of the night, and were spending the morning sewing two very crooked yellow stripes to their sleeves. They had cut them from a piece of yellow cambric the housekeeper had hunted up from the attic trunks.

So Maris was very happy as she went about her morning duties. The fear of the night before seemed like a bad dream. Now and again she paused as she passed by the window that looked into the garden. Across on the Maitland lawn Lane was having a game of handball with the boys. Her eyes grew dreamy and sweet as she lifted her heart to Heaven in thanksgiving for her marvelous deliverance, and God's great loving kindness to her who had been so stupid and indifferent to the things that should have been so plain to her.

And her heart went singing:

"Oh, Lane, Lane! How wonderful that he and I are to spend our days together! Why didn't I know that Tilford would never bring me true happiness?"

The little boys finished their game of ball and retired to the garden benches under the hemlocks where Lane had set up a miniature school room. And when they were deep in their studies with enticing promises for the afternoon if they knew their lessons well, Lane betook himself to the garage and looked up those papers in Mrs. Trilby's pocket.

That evening he showed them to Merrick and Maris.

"Here is evidence that will conclusively put a stop to any more interference with Maris," he said as he brought them out of an official looking envelope. "They are two letters written by Tilford Thorpe to this woman, Mrs. Trilby, the first giving her detailed directions about arraying Maris in those wedding things, even to the ring on her finger. The second one deals with the amount of sleeping potion to be administered. They are signed T. Thorpe. Do you know the handwriting, Maris?"

Maris took the papers in trembling hands and read them through, growing very white as she read.

"Yes," she said looking up with quick tears in her eyes, "that's his handwriting!" Then she took out her handkerchief and brushed the tears away.

"Oh, it makes me so ashamed!" she said.

"It's not your shame, sister, it's his!" burst forth Merrick.

Lane gave her a tender smile.

"I wouldn't have troubled you with this," he said, "but I felt you should identify the handwriting. These letters are important. With your permission I am putting them into a safe deposit box in the bank, Maris, in your name, and instructing my lawyer to write a letter to Mr. Thorpe saying that the letters are in safe keeping and will not be used against him as long as he does not trouble you, but if at any time in the future he attempts to annoy you again your family will immediately take steps to let his actions be widely known. That will save you from further worry about the matter, and will at the same time be fair to the young man's family."

"He ought to be strung up!" said Merrick viciously. "He ought to be hanged for kidnaping. But of course I suppose you are right."

"Will father have to know?" asked Maris anxiously.

"No, I shouldn't think so. At least not now," said Lane. "Now, Maris, let's forget it and be happy. God sends sunshine after rain, and rainbows in our clouds. Mother is better, I hear. Let's thank God and sing hallelujah in our hearts!"

"Okay!" said Merrick fervently, and got up and walked away to hide his emotion.

When a few more days had gone by so many happy things were happening that Maris almost forgot that she had been kidnaped and been through frightful tortures of horror before she escaped. Only at night sometimes she would waken with a strange terror possessing her, and think for a minute she was lying on that bed on shipboard. Then all the awful nightmare would return, and she would have to go over every terrible second of the experience and try to think how she might have prevented it all in the first place. And she found that the only way she could dispel the thoughts was to pray.

But the days were too happy now, to allow such nightmares to continue when the morning came. Lane was sure to be over before the sun was very high, to draw her away for a few minutes to the hemlock retreat just across the hedge, where they might have a few words together alone.

And mother was getting well. The doctor jubilantly

admitted it. He said that if she continued to improve she would be able to go off for a few weeks' rest with father, and then she would be as good as new. Of course the nurse must go along to make sure she did not overdo, and to watch her pulse and blood pressure and diet and sleep and a few other minor points.

He said this down at the front door early one evening to the assembled family, Lane included, and Lane watched their expressions of joy and relief as they heard.

But his eyes lingered longest on the father's face. There had come an instant radiance at the news, of course, but then there had succeeded a look of gravity, almost a troubled look, as the proposed trip was mentioned. It was the first time the father had heard of that trip seriously, and Lane knew he couldn't see how it was going to be managed.

After the doctor was gone Lane slipped his arm through Mr. Mayberry's and drew him along the path.

"Come over here to my refuge among the hemlocks a little while. There's something I want to ask you. You come too, Merrick. I want to talk something over with you both."

The father hesitated. He felt he had a great deal to think about just then, ways and means for this trip, which of course had to be if the doctor wanted it.

But he didn't like to refuse Lane. Lane who had been so kind to them all, taking care of the little boys, and helping in countless ways beside, so he allowed himself to be led over to the hemlocks. And Merrick came bringing up the rear, trying to think how he could get a little extra money to help out with.

When they were all comfortably seated with the sweet darkness about them, and the soft slant of moonbeams peeping restfully through the dark lacework of branches, Lane spoke:

"Mr. Mayberry, I'm going to butt in on something that isn't my business. I hope you won't resent it."

"Why, of course not, Lane," said Mr. Mayberry genially. "You've certainly earned the right to talk anything over in this family without feeling you are butting in. I'm sure whatever you suggest will be well worth listening to."

"Thank you, Mr. Mayberry. Well, then, here goes. Hear me through to the end before you jump to conclusions. I heard you tell the doctor just now that you didn't see how you could get away from your business to accompany your wife on this trip the doctor wants her to have—"

"Yes," said the troubled father, passing a thin hand over his furrowed brow, "it's quite impossible just now. I've been away from the office quite a good deal since mother has been sick, and I'm not at all pleased with the way things are going down there. My assistant is well meaning, I guess, but his judgment is not always as good as it should be. It is really imperative that I should be in the office for the next few weeks, unless I am willing to let my business go to the wall."

"Yes, Mr. Mayberry. I was afraid you might feel that way. I've known from one or two things you have said that you were troubled about the business. But you see we all feel that it is also quite imperative for your wife's full recovery that you be with her while she is recuperating. I am sure the doctor feels that the trip without you would not be of the lasting benefit that it would if you were along. It would be better to have even your business go to the wall than to have Mrs. Mayberry do so, wouldn't it?"

"Of course!" said the harassed father with a sigh. "But how am I to finance the trip at all if my business goes to the wall? And how are we to live afterwards?"

"Well, now that's just what I want to talk about. Perhaps I've given more thought to it all than you will feel I had a right to," said Lane pleasantly. "In the first place about that trip. I know a way that that can be accomplished for practically nothing. I've inherited from an old aunt a lovely old place in the mountains of Virginia, where the air is fine, and the neighborhood is so still you can almost hear the clouds go by. It has plenty of big airy rooms, thoroughly furnished, and nobody is there but the housekeeper who used to companion my aunt before she died. She's all alone with the old colored cook who is past master at her trade of tempting appetites. I'm under obligation by the terms of the will to keep the place up as long as Mrs. Morton lives, even if I didn't love it myself. So it's there, and empty, and ready for your occupancy as long as you and Mrs. Mayberry and the nurse want to stay. And you wouldn't need to feel under obligation to me, you know, for you'd only be returning the visit I made at your house when I had that long siege of typhoid fever once. How long was it I stayed with you? Four months I think it was, and I probably wouldn't have been living today if your wife hadn't nursed me, and then fed me afterwards till I was able to go back to work. And you didn't charge me a cent's worth of board either, though I think I ate you out of house and home when I got better."

"But we loved to have you, son! And your father was my best friend for years!"

"Exactly so," said Lane waxing more earnest. "And that's just why I claim the right to step in now and return the hospitality. And it isn't as though it will cost me anything, either, for it won't. Mrs. Morton has a garden with everything needful in it for food, and a cow, and a lot of chickens, and there's an old gardener who attends to it all. It's there anyway, and plenty for a lot more than use it. So much for the trip. And of course I'll take you all down in my car! That goes without saying!"

"Well," said Mr. Mayberry. "That's wonderful! Why, Lane, I can't say thank you enough! Why, of course I'll accept that! It lifts a great burden off my shoulders. You are a dear lad! Your father's own son! But, about my business—"

"Yes, about your business, Mr. Mayberry," said Lane quickly, "I was just coming to that. Maybe you'll think this is preposterous. I don't know, but perhaps when you think it over it won't seem quite so impossible as you think. You see I'm out of a job for the summer, that is when my detention camp is over, of course." He laughed. "You may think I'm very presumptuous, but I was going to propose that you let Merrick and me come in and help you out, at least while you are gone. Merrick tells me that his job ends on Saturday. Of course he hasn't had experience in your office, but he's your son, and would naturally guard your interests, and could be manager, at least in name. And as for me, I've had a good bit of experience right along the lines of your business for the past three years out west. To tell you the truth, while I have two offers for fall, I'm not really satisfied about either of them. I have been waiting till things quieted down so that I could talk business with you. That's really one reason I came back here. You see I've always wanted to be *in* business, not just to be working for somebody else. I've a few thousands to put in, and if you would be willing to try me out there's nothing I'd rather do than be in business with you. I hope you don't think I'm too audacious."

"Audacious! Presumptuous! My dear boy, you are overwhelming! I can't think of anything more ideal than what you have proposed. But I couldn't think of having you put money into my poor little struggling business. It used, of course, to be good and thriving, but the depression has knocked out the foundation from under it. I couldn't think of allowing you to risk money—"

"I don't feel it is any great risk," broke in Lane. "Frankly I've studied over this thing for some time, and I know more about your business than you are aware of. I'm certain that a bit of money just now, and one change in personnel that I have in mind, would put that business on its feet. Don't you feel so yourself?"

"Yes, I do!" said the broken man, his voice shaken with feeling. "Even a *little* money would help. But I couldn't let *you* take the risk—"

"There, now!" said Lane waving his hand, "I don't want to hear any more about that. It wouldn't be you *letting,* it would be me *putting* my money in your concern. And that's what I want to do. You see I don't know anybody in this wide world I'd rather be tied up with than you and Merrick. But even if you don't want me permanently, I figure that in the two weeks before the doctor lets your wife go away, Merrick and I could come down every day to the office and get to know enough about affairs to carry on while you are gone. Could you trust us that much?"

"Trust you?" said Mr. Mayberry. *"Trust* you? Well, I should say! But boy, you don't know how hard pressed I've been. I'm ashamed to tell you just how things stand. There have been three distinct times this last three years that I didn't know from day to day whether I was going to be sold out by the sheriff or not. But please God, He's always seen me through, so far. I'm not entirely down and out yet, but I'm so far near the edge again that I wouldn't dare let anyone else put his money in with me."

"Aw, say, dad, whyn't you make him a full partner and I'll be the office boy, and let old Morgan go work for somebody else? I'll bet he's the one Lane wants to kick out, anyway." He grinned at Lane's look of evident approval. "And you say he's always kicking for a higher salary and threatening to go to Chicago. Let him go! I can learn. I'll bet it won't take me two weeks to get onto enough to keep the old boat afloat while you go off with mother on a second honeymoon."

They talked long, till the moon slipped down toward

the rim of the west, its beams crept away across the lawn, and the world was very still and sweet.

Mr. Mayberry lay back in the big chair, and let himself relax for the first time in months. At last he turned to Lane with a deep sigh of gratitude.

"You don't know what relief you have given me, son!" he said. "To tell the truth I was hard pressed today. I didn't know which way to turn. Morgan got very ugly this morning. He says he has an offer from Chicago at almost twice the salary, and I didn't see just how I was to get along without somebody, yet I could not offer him more salary. But now, it looks to me as if we might weather it. Now I can tell him in the morning that he can accept that Chicago offer and go as soon as he likes." There was eagerness and a new hope in his voice.

"Yes, but dad, you better not let him go till Lane has been over his books. I never did trust that bird! You can't tell what he's pulled off."

"Well, we'll look into that, too! I haven't been so sure myself." Then he laid his hand on Lane's shoulder.

"I shall never forget this night," he said earnestly. "I shall never forget what you have done for me. You are like a real son. Merrick and I both feel so, don't we, boy?"

"Sure do!" said Merrick with a husky choke in his voice.

And as they walked through the shadows back to their respective homes, Lane was thinking in his heart that it wouldn't be long before he was a son indeed. But he wouldn't tell them just yet, not till he and Maris together could tell both mother and father.

IN the morning Mr. Mayberry and Lane went down to the office. Monday Merrick was through his job on the bus and went along. They went joyously, like three boys, and Maris stood in the door with a glad light in her eyes and watched them go. Everything seemed so wonderful! It was sweet to see the three men she loved going off together in that fellowship in a common cause. All eager for the same end.

Lexie was out of quarantine now, and the boys were allowed to come home. They came in shyly, but with a new assured air. They were still cadets and on their honor to keep discipline, which discipline now included silence in or around the house. They walked almost reverently, mindful that God was answering their nightly prayers. The first morning after they had slept at home Maris found them in their rooms, quietly, precisely making their beds.

"Sure! We always do that!" said Alec with a grown-up air. "That's part of our daily routine!"

Gwyneth was very happy. She was out of quarantine in time to attend commencement, and she returned from a visit to her teacher with the joyous news that she had passed in all her studies.

The mother was well enough now to have the children tiptoe in every morning silently and kiss her hand, and watch for her smile.

"Can't I even tell her I've had the measles?" asked Lexie eagerly.

"Not yet, dear. She would just worry over how much we had been through without her, and think we were keeping a lot more things from her."

Maris herself was very happy. Lane was so wonderful! He satisfied her heart so fully! How had she ever imagined Tilford was anything at all to her? Oh, God was so good to her!

Quite swiftly the days went by, till the morning came when Lane was to drive the father and mother down to Virginia.

They kept everything very quiet till the last minute, though it was hard to keep the excitement out of the atmosphere.

It was Merrick who picked his little mother up and carried her down in his strong young arms to the comfortable place that had been prepared for her in the back seat, with the nurse close by her in one of the little middle seats, and her husband in front with Lane who was driving.

The mother gave the children a feeble wave of the hand and a tender smile, as they stood grouped around Maris, with Merrick protectingly just at the side, and then they were gone.

And suddenly Gwyneth's eyes filled with tears.

"Sister, isn't our mother ever coming back again?"

"Why, of course, dear child. We hope she'll come back very soon and be as well and strong as she ever was," said Maris slipping a comforting arm around the little girl's shoulders, and then Lexie came stealing close to her on the other side, and wriggled her hand into Maris'. And suddenly Maris felt how very dear they all were, and how dependent just now upon her, and her heart thrilled with gladness that she was right here with them in their need, and not careering through Europe with a sulky selfish man, spending money for things that were not real and vital to her heart's joy. How good God had been to her!

And her eyes followed down the road, where she could still glimpse the outline of Lane's head and shoulder as he drove the car so steadily, bearing her mother away to rest and refreshment. What a lover, who loved her people also, and would always be one with her in her love for them. One who would never be trying to wean her away from them, nor complain when they needed her. Ah, this was going to be true union of soul!

And all at once she saw that Tilford had only wanted her because he thought she was beautiful, and would grace his home. How much he had harped on her beauty, until she herself had almost believed in it too, though she knew now that mere loveliness of youthful outline and coloring were a poor foundation on which to build the happiness of a lifetime.

"Muvver tumin' back," echoed Lexie with dreamy eyes. "I want muvver to turn wight awound and tum back now. I *wove* muvver."

"Well, muvver can't come right back," said Maris briskly. "We've got quite a lot to do to get mother's room all fixed up pretty and new before she gets back. How would you like to help?"

"Oh, wes, wes!" cried Lexie dancing up and down. "Vat can I do?"

"Well, how would you like to make a lovely motto to pin on the outside of her door for her to see the first thing before she goes into her room? I'll find you a nice big piece of cardboard and you can have your new colored crayons and your stencils and color a letter every day till it's done. Would you like that?"

"Oh, goody, goody," said Lexie. "Wes, I would like dat. What would I say on the motto?"

"Well, you'll have to sit down and think about that. You want to get the very best words of course. You could say 'Welcome,' or 'Welcome Home,' or if you don't get too tired working you might say 'Welcome home, mother dear!' "

"Wes!" said the little girl with shining eyes.

"What about father!" said Gwyneth sharply. "We'll be glad to see father, too. You might make one for father, Alec."

"Aw, naw, that's girl's work!" declared Alec loftily. "Lexie can put father too. 'And father' she can say. I'm going to paint baseboards. I can do that real well, Lane said. You just put sheets of paper down on the floor very close to the wall, and then you hold your brush just so, and paint very carefully. I learned how all right. I can do 'em swell. You want mother's baseboards painted, don't you, Maris?"

"Why of course!" said Maris smiling. "We'll all work at that room. I suppose you could paint the doors, couldn't you, Eric?"

"Oh, sure! I did all the doors of the kitchen over at the other house. You just go over and look at 'em."

"What can I do, sister?" asked Gwyneth in an aggrieved tone.

"Well, there are windows to wash, and new curtains to make. Oh, we'll find a lot for you and me to do."

"Seems as if we ought to manage some new wall paper," said Merrick as he picked up his hat and started toward the door to go to the office, himself the sole proprietor of the business until Lane returned.

"Yes, I was thinking of that. I wasn't sure whether we ought to spend the money just now. Of course, the paper itself won't cost much, it's the putting on. I wish I knew how. I believe I could manage it."

"No! You've got enough to do. I know a fellow who's a paper hanger, and he's out of a job just now. He'll do it cheap. I've still got a little of my bus salary left. I'll stand for the work if you'll get the paper, Maris."

"All right. We'll go down and choose it just as soon as we get the day's work out of the way."

So they scattered to make their beds, with happy voices and smiling eyes, and the first wrench of the departure of father and mother was over. The children plunged gaily into activities. Beds were made as by magic, furniture was dusted and garments picked up and put in place.

"Why couldn't we paint the cellar windows?" demanded the boys. "We can get some paint. I know what kind Lane got. We got some money we earned. I can get Lane's brushes. He won't mind."

So the boys went to work at the cellar windows, and quiet reigned in the yard, save for a gay whistle now and then.

Gwyneth took to washing the first floor windows, with a little help now and then from Sally, and presently the boys finished the cellar windows and began on the first story ones, finishing a whole window before Maris got around to notice and protest. But she found they had really done it well. Lane's coaching had not been altogether in vain, for of course they had had a lot of practice on Lane's house.

When Merrick came home at night he stared at the improvement with wide eyes.

"Say, fellas, that's great work! I might take a hand myself after dinner. Got any paint left? Okay! How about my putting up the old ladder and doing the front gable before dark? Say, we can change the face of the old mansion if we go about it right. Great work! I'm with you, lads!"

Meantime in the house Maris was superintending a

crayon motto by Lexie, and a new bureau scarf that Gwyneth was cross-stitching intermittently with window washing.

The next two or three days went swiftly, and by the time Lane returned there was a distinct difference in the look of the old house, although of course there was still plenty left to be done.

Lane reported that the mother had borne the journey well, and was enjoying the new surroundings, and the nurse felt it was going to make a great change in her in a short time.

Then they all settled down to a regular program, work, interspersed with more work of a different kind.

Lane entered right into everything. He and Merrick were very conscientious about the office, and talked eagerly about their "prospects." He came back in the evening to do his part toward the painting, as interested as the rest in making the old house renew its youth.

After it got too dark to paint the two young men would frequently call up Mr. Mayberry on the telephone and consult him about the business, carefully planning their questions so that they would be calculated to reassure him rather than to worry.

But there was always a few minutes at the end of the evening when Maris and Lane would manage a quiet talk together, sometimes a bit of a walk in the moonlight, sometimes a few minutes sitting among the hemlocks. Though Merrick didn't give them much time alone. It hadn't occurred to him they would want it. He was all full of the business, and talked with Lane constantly, trying to plan ahead for his father.

It was almost as if they had always been together in family interests.

"Good night, Lane," said Merrick one night, "you act just as if you really belonged to the family!" And then suddenly he caught a glance between Maris and Lane, a glance of radiancy.

"Perhaps I do," said Lane dryly.

"Well, you certainly belong a lot more than ever that poor fish of a Tilford did," said Merrick. "I certainly wish you had been around before he ever moved to town."

"Well, I was," grinned Lane, with another sly glance at Maris. "Have you forgotten?"

"No, I haven't forgotten," said Merrick, "but I was just trying to figure out how Maris ever had anything to do with that half-baked jelly-fish after she'd once seen you."

Lane reached over in the soft darkness and caught Maris' hand silently, giving it a gentle squeeze.

"Yes?" said Lane comically. "I've often wondered about that myself. How about it, Maris?"

"You're getting much too personal," said Maris jumping up. "Let's go and take a walk, Lane."

So they walked away into the shadows and left Merrick to wonder, and to speculate, and to wish that Lane were really his brother so that there would be no more need to worry as to what would happen when Tilford got back, and mother got well.

Then the very next day Mr. Thorpe came to call on Maris.

Luckily no one but Maris knew him, so there was no excitement about it. Sally merely announced to her that a gentleman in the parlor wanted to see her. So Maris washed the paint off her nose and one eyebrow and went down stairs. A book agent, she thought it might be. She was well into the living room before she recognized him.

He arose almost shyly, watching her come, and held out an apologetic hand tentatively.

"Perhaps you wish I hadn't come," he said softly. "I wouldn't blame you at all if you did."

Maris in a sudden rebound of pity reached out her hand

and grasped his, giving him a shy, half frightened smile. It wasn't any of it his fault, of course.

"You see I've just found out what Tilford did, and I've come to apologize. Of course I know no apology can ever atone for a thing like that, and I'm not going to try to excuse my son. He did a very terrible thing. He oughtn't to have done it. My only consolation is that it was instigated by his love for you—at least I sincerely hope that was the reason—although my knowledge of his life thus far might make it just as possible that it was done purely to have his own way. I have to be honest and state that that might have had a great deal to do with it. You perhaps do not know, could not realize, that Tilford has always had his own way, and cannot brook being crossed in anything, even if he only *thinks* he wants it. Though I sincerely trust that this time it was because he really wanted you that he dared to do this dreadful thing. But that is no excuse whatever for his having committed a crime, for it was a crime to try and kidnap you and force you to marry him. So I have come to you to make what amends are possible. I scarcely dare ask you to forgive my son. Of course it is his place to ask, not mine, but as his father I must ask you that for my own respite. I have never suffered such anguish as since I knew what my boy dared to do."

Suddenly Maris put out her hand.

"Please don't, Mr. Thorpe," she said gently. "It was not your doing, I am sure of that. And as for forgiving your son, I can forgive of course, and I will. But I must tell you honestly that I can never marry him. You see, even before he attempted to force me to do what he wanted at a time when I did not feel free from home obligations, I discovered that I never had really loved him enough to marry him. And even if he had not hopelessly put himself where I would never dare to trust him again, there was a bigger barrier than that separating us."

"I am not surprised," said the old man with a deep sigh. "Indeed, I must admit that I was absolutely amazed that Tilford had been able to secure the love of such a wonderful girl as you are. I felt that you had great depth of character, great sweetness, and rare culture. I can only grieve that you are not to be a part of our family. But I knew all the time you were too good for my boy, and he would only bring you sorrow. For your sake I am glad you found out in time. You have something almost Heavenly about you, something—God-given, I would call it, and I feel that through my son you have been greatly dishonored by his attempt to carry you away to a foreign land without your consent. So I have come to humbly offer my apologies and beg you to understand that I knew nothing of the plan or I would certainly have made it impossible before the indignity was put upon you. I want you to know that I personally deeply regret the whole matter, and long to have your forgiveness."

"Why, of course, Mr. Thorpe," said Maris earnestly. "I never connected you with it in any way. And I am entirely willing to forgive what has been done, with the understanding that Tilford and I are to be henceforth strangers. God forgives. Why should not I? Perhaps I was to blame in the first place for having let Tilford think I loved him. Perhaps I did not understand my own heart at first."

"You are a very wonderful little girl," said the old man, deeply moved. "You have something that I wish we all had. You have a God that I wish was mine."

"Oh, Mr. Thorpe, I am sure you can have my God. He is glad to accept everyone who comes to Him through His Son Jesus Christ. He loves you. He sent His Son to die for you, and I know He longs to have fellowship with you."

"It may be so!" sighed the old man humbly. "I only wish it might be."

"But it is so!" insisted Maris eagerly. "I know for I have

just been finding out what He has wanted for a long time to be to me, and I was so full of the world I would not let Him. Wait! Let me show you!"

Maris reached over and picked up her New Testament that she had been reading just before dinner.

"Here it is," she said eagerly, handing him the little book. "Won't you take this home with you and study it? It is God's own word to you. You have only to believe it, and trust Him. Here—" she turned down a page, pointing to a marked verse: " 'God so loved the world that He gave His only begotten Son, that whosoever believeth in Him should not perish but have everlasting life.' "

"And here—" she added fluttering the leaves over a little farther to Revelation: " 'Behold I stand at the door and knock: if any man hear my voice, and open the door, I will come in to him and will sup with him, and he with me.' "

She handed him the book.

"Keep it," she said, "I have another. You'll find it is wonderful if you will just give yourself to the study of it."

He looked at her wonderingly, with a kind of worship in his eyes.

"Thank you," he said brokenly. "I only wish God could have granted me the gift of such a daughter as you would have been. I only wish I might have brought up my son to be worthy of you. But, no matter. I don't wish to distress you. I shall always look upon you as one I could have loved deeply as a daughter. But I know you are right in your decision. May God greatly bless you, and may you sometime be able to forget the shameful way in which my son treated you."

He turned to go out the door, and then, fingering the leaves of the Testament, he looked back at her again:

"I shall—always—treasure—this little book. I shall study it because you have given it to me. I hope—I shall some day find your God, and get to know Him. I thank you," he said brokenly.

Then with his head bowed and tears blurring his eyes he went out the door and slowly, sadly down the walk to his car.

Maris stood in the doorway and watched him, tears coming into her eyes. Poor lonely old man! He was the only one of the Thorpe family she could have loved and honored! Would he find the Lord in the little book she had given him? She must pray that the Lord would lead him in His own way to peace and rest in Himself.

"Well, I suppose that old bird came to try and patch things up with you and his precious son, didn't he?"

It was Merrick's voice just behind her that spoke, with a keen dislike in his tone.

Maris turned and Merrick caught the glint of tears in her eyes.

"Yes, and you're just softy enough to be caught by it, too, I'll warrant," he challenged her.

"No, Merrick," she said brushing the tears away from her face. "You're all wrong. He didn't come to patch it up at all. He came to apologize."

"Aw, bologny! That was just his line. He knew he'd get you that way. Good night! I thought you'd had lesson enough. I didn't think you'd fall for that fellow again, the poor weak simp!"

"Stop!" said Maris sharply. "Don't talk that way any more, Merrick. I'm not falling for anybody. I'm just sorry for that father. He's ashamed of his son!"

"Yes, in a pig's eye he is! Whyn't he bring him up right then? Whyn't he teach him a few plain morals I'd like to know? Why does he think you've gotta stand for all his mistakes?"

"Oh, but he doesn't!" said Maris. "I told him plainly I had found out I never really loved his son. I told him I never could trust him again, even if I loved him."

"Aw, *hooey!*" muttered Merrick. "You'll fall again when that guy gets back from Europe. You fell before for a pretty face and a languid air, and I suppose you'll fall again. Mother'll get well and then haveta get sick all over again worryin' about ya. Good night! What's the use of painting the house and fixing things up if you're going through the same performance again? I'm sick of it all!"

Maris glanced up in distress and there stood Lane, looking from one to the other.

"Oh, Lane!" said Maris in relief. "Tell Merrick—about us! Make him understand how silly he is."

Lane stepped over and put a strong arm around Maris.

"What's it all about, sweetheart?" he asked, and then bowed his head over her and kissed her gently.

"Why, you see, Mr. Thorpe, it seems, has just found out about things and he is terribly ashamed and he came to ask my pardon for what his son had done. And Merrick won't believe but what I'm going to run away to Europe and marry Tilford in spite of everything. You'd better tell him the truth."

Lane gathered Maris' free hand into his.

"All right, here goes! Listen, fella, you're making a big mistake. Your sister is not going to marry Tilford Thorpe because she's already fallen for somebody else. It's true Maris is going to be married sometime, as soon as it seems wise taking everything into account,but it's me she's going to marry, and not Tilford Thorpe. So, now, if you've anything to say against that, speak now or forever after hold your peace! We'd have told you some time ago, if we hadn't felt we ought to tell your father and mother first of all. But since you had to get the high-strikes about that poor sorrowful old man perhaps it's just as well to make it all plain right now."

Merrick's face was a study as he listened to Lane. Amazement, incredulity, dawning belief, overwhelming joy succeeding one another quickly.

"Oh, but I say, Lane," he exclaimed huskily, "this is too good to be true! This is the greatest thing ever! Say, I don't deserve this! I'm a chump if there ever was one. I—ask your pardon, Maris! I ought to have known you had more sense than I supposed!"

They had an evening of rejoicing as they worked away together more one in spirit than they had ever seemed to be before.

"Say, I wish dad and mother knew about it!" said Merrick as he put the finishing touches to the door into his mother's room. "Do you know, I believe that would do more than anything else to cure mother. Why don't you and Maris run down and tell them?"

"She might not like it," said Lane with a troubled look.

"*Like* it!" said Merrick. "My eye! What do you think my mother is? Don't you know she's been worried sick lest Maris'll go back to that dud Tilford?"

Maris gave him a quick glance.

"I wish I'd known that, Merrick. It might have opened my eyes sooner," said Maris with a sigh.

"Well, I doubt it," said Merrick. "If you couldn't see how mother felt without anybody telling you, nothing would have done any good. Let's just be glad you've got them open now."

"Well, how about it, Maris? Will you take a run down with me for a day and tell your mother?" asked Lane eagerly.

"I'd love to," said Maris wistfully, "but it would worry her terribly to have me go away and leave the children."

"Nonsense!" said Merrick. "Why can't you get that night nurse to come here for a couple of days till you get back? The kids love her, and she makes them mind like anybody's mother."

And so at last it was settled that if the night nurse could be prevailed upon to look after the children Maris and Lane would drive down early Saturday morning, and stay over Sunday, or part of Sunday, and break the news gently.

Then work went merrily on. The little boys and the two

little girls entered eagerly into the plan of trying to get the house in order for mother, and were terribly pleased to have the night nurse in charge. They felt quite grown up and important to be left behind, and so Maris and Lane got ready for their expedition with great joy in their hearts, and such a light in their faces that Gwyneth told her sister, "Why, Maris, you look as if you had morning in your eyes!"

But it was not until their visit was completed, when with the blessing of the happy parents upon them both they started back home, that they fully realized the great joy of belonging to one another. If Tilford could have caught a glimpse of their faces during that Sunday afternoon that they took their homeward way, he would have known instantly that the idle dream of finally marrying Maris after all, which he still cherished now and again between his various flirtations would never be realized. For there was something gorgeous and glorious, something really eternal in quality, in the joy of their glances, that was almost blinding to an observer.

"Now," said Maris Monday morning after breakfast, "we've got to get to work and finish this house at once, for mother declares she is in a great hurry to get home, and the nurse said she was sure she would soon be able to return."

So the happy children scurried through their breakfast and got to work, finding no task too hard for their eager fingers. And the two young men hurried down town to the office to try and bring business up to the promises Lane had made.

THE wedding was early in October.

Maris hadn't been willing to let her mother have so much excitement sooner, although she had come back home three weeks before with a flush of health on her cheeks, and a joy in her eyes that made it seem almost absurd to be treating her like an invalid. But both Maris and Lane felt that everything should be quiet and calm, and that the mother should have first consideration.

But this was to be no hectic wedding, and best of all there was no heartbreak behind it.

Invitations?

Maris only laughed when Gwyneth reproached her for having burned up the other ones.

"They cost so much, Maris," said the little girl. "You know you said they did! You could just have changed the date on them," she suggested frugally.

"Yes, but you forget that there is one other item, most important, that would have had to be changed also, little sister," said Maris blithely. "The name of the bridegroom happens to be a different one, you know!"

"Oh, that's so!" said Gwyneth astonished. "Well,

couldn't we have got a rubber stamp and stamped them with the other name?"

"It isn't being done, little sister!" said the bride gaily, and then sat down and laughed till she cried. A rubber stamp over Tilford Thorpe's name! What would Tilford say to that?

There was some talk of having the wedding in the garden, just quietly, "for mother's sake" they said. But after the consideration they all agreed that even if there were but very few invited it would be more or less of an excitement to carry on the whole of a wedding at home, and mother would insist on being into it all.

So Lane and Maris talked it over and brought their decision to the parents for approval.

"We're going to have it in the church," said Maris, "and then stop at the end of the wide aisle by the door and shake hands with any of our friends who come."

"That will be sweet," said the mother with shining eyes. "Well, if that is settled we ought to order the invitations at once and get right to work addressing them. There won't be quite as many as there were before, but it always takes time, and I suppose you want them to be mailed, of course, at exactly the right time."

"We're not going to have invitations!" said Maris calmly.

"Well, but *every*body has invitations!" said Gwyneth in horror.

"No," said Maris brightly, "not everybody. *We* don't."

"But aren't you going to let anybody come? What's the use of me being maid of honor if nobody's there? We might just as well have it here at home, just the family."

"Oh, yes, we're going to let people come, anybody who wants to."

"But how will they know?"

"We're going to have it announced in church!"

"Maris Mayberry! How funny! Nobody does that! And

suppose the people didn't go to that church? Suppose they lived in some other town?" burst out Gwyneth again.

"Oh, if there's anybody we're particular about, like people we know real well, we'll either write them notes, or just call them on the phone, and say: Maris is going to be married Thursday morning, at twelve o'clock in the church and we'll be glad to have you with us if you find it convenient."

"Maris, do you mean it?" Gwyneth's eyes were large with wonder.

"Why, surely, dear. Why do we have to go through all that burden of sending out expensive invitations for people to throw in the waste basket? It's all right, of course, if you have money to burn, or if you are noted public characters, but we're not going to try to put on a big show for people to see, so why should we go to all that formality and trouble?"

"My dear," said the mother with a relieved smile, "how wonderful of you to take an attitude like that. It seems to make the marriage ceremony more sacred, when there is not so much fuss and fashion. You know, dear, that's the way your father and I were married. In the church just informally, with all our dear friends, and then just a little supper for the family."

"Yes," said Maris happily, "and Sally is going to cook that supper! Yes, mother dear, no expensive caterers this time! I want everything as different as can be from the way we planned it before. I talked with Sally about it before you came home and she thinks she can do it. She's got a sister and niece who will help, and a couple of brothers for waiters. We're having creamed chicken in little pattie shells, and Sally's best potato salad. She'll make that the day before, of course. And little hot biscuits with butter in them, piping hot, and that delicious concoction she makes out of grapes and melons. The ice cream will come from Shallups, and be in molds of fruit and flowers, and there will be nuts and candies of course. But the wedding cake is all made. Sally made it while you were away, rich and black with fruit, her old recipe. It's great. She made a tiny one so we could sample it. And it's put away in the big tin box to mellow. Now, doesn't that sound good, mother?"

"Wonderful!" said the mother lying back in her chair with a great sigh of relief. "I see I shan't have to do a single thing except look pretty and act stylish."

"That's it, mother! You've caught the idea exactly," cried Maris jumping up to kiss her mother.

So the quiet preparations for the wedding went steadily forward and did not interfere with so much as a wink of the mother's afternoon naps, or other resting time. Oh, she wrote a few notes to her most intimate friends, but that was all, and smiled and said to her husband, "It's really the way a right-minded wedding should be anyway. You and I never felt badly that we didn't spend all we had on frills and folderols. When you have real love it doesn't matter much what else is lacking."

And her grayhaired lover agreed with her and kissed her tenderly.

So the days went by and the wedding morning came.

Maris hadn't invited a single one of her fashionable friends who were to have had a part in the first-planned wedding. But she had written a sweet reserved little note to Mr. Thorpe, Senior, letting him know that she was to be married.

Merrick and the little boys had driven out to a woods that belonged to the Maitland property, and selected and cut a small wilderness of lovely juniper trees. These had been brought to the church and set up about the altar till they made a lovely background for a myriad of tall wonderful pink and white chrysanthemums that stood in stately grace on either side.

And there was a dear old friend of Mrs. Mayberry's,

whitehaired now, and not in active service, but who could still make marvelous music on the organ. It was she who played tender old melodies, and then the wedding march.

Merrick was best man, tall and good looking in his new dark blue serge. He looked very grown up and attractive beside the handsome bridegroom, standing at the head of the aisle.

Lexie in her pink organdy and Alec in a brief white linen suit marched up the aisle heading the procession, and carrying baskets of pink roses which they were to scatter in front of the bride as she came back down the aisle.

Then came Gwyneth, in her treasured pale blue chiffon, taking careful stately steps and holding her wonderful armful of pink roses and delphiniums. Gwynnie held her head as if this were at least a million-dollar wedding. She was enjoying every step to the last degree.

But the eyes of the church full of dear old friends were upon the bride, as she came up the aisle on the arm of her father.

She was wearing the lovely organdy dress that her mother had made, and she looked so sweet that the bridegroom feasted his soul upon her loveliness, and wondered how it came about that God had thought him worthy of so fair a bride. And back in the corner among the shadows, half hidden by a group of small juniper trees, sat an old tired sorrowful man who had almost been her father-in-law. He was watching her keenly, sadly, as she looked up into her own father's tender face with a gay and gallant smile. He studied her simple lovely attire and wondered what his wife had meant by saying that Maris did not know how to dress, and wanted to wear a dowdy homemade affair to their son's wedding. She seemed to him like his ideal of an angel, with her white roses and lilies of the valley in her arm, and the soft mist of bridal veil about her face.

He marveled at the tender beauty of the service, so unique and cognizant of the presence of God in their midst, and he sadly acknowledged to himself that Tilford would never have fitted a service like this, wherein the Presence and guidance of the Lord Christ was invoked for this new household that was being set up. Yet he was humbly thankful in his heart that this lovely bride that was not his daughter had taken time and thought to speak the words and pass on the eternal burning message in God's Word, so that he too could understand what was here going on.

Half way across the ocean came a great floating palace of a boat, bearing on board the lad who would have been the bridegroom if he had been worthy. And sometimes he went gaily among his kind, trifling with brittle hearts, and sometimes he sat apart and planned how he would go back and lay siege to Maris' heart once more.

But Maris was marching down that flower paved aisle, with her hand resting on her dear bridegroom's arm, and her face alight with a love that Tilford Thorpe had never been able to bring to her eyes.

A happy lovely wedding it was, and when they reached the back of the church they paused there, and grouped the family about them, and received happy wishes and congratulations, many of them from humble plain people who loved them. Maris' heart thrilled with the beauty of it all, and it came to her that that other wedding, even though it might have been held in the same church, with costlier flowers about and richer people filling the pews, could never have brought her half the joy and blessing that she found here among plain, loving, simple people who loved the Lord.

"This is the heritage of the servant of the Lord" kept ringing over and over in her head above the sound of old Aunt Mehitable's tender gay organ melodies.

She spoke of it to Lane after they were back in the car

alone together, Merrick having taken the family home ahead of them and brought the car back. She told Lane how that sentence had rung over and over in her ears the night she was escaping, and how it had come today to finish out the ceremony.

Lane smiled tenderly.

"That's the best heritage any soul could have," he said. "It will hold good throughout the years. I could ask for nothing greater for a dowry for my precious wife. 'No weapon that is formed against thee shall prosper; and every tongue that shall rise against thee in judgment thou shalt condemn. This is the heritage of the servants of the Lord.'"

Said Maris, thoughtfully, as she laid a gentle finger on a fragrant lily of the valley. "One ought to walk very courageously with a heritage like that! We must never, never get careless and forget how wonderfully God worked to bring us together again, and how He has saved us!"

Lane's eyes were full of understanding as he watched her, and he murmured softly:

"God grant that we may never forget what He has done for us!"

And then the car turned into their own street, and Maris looking up suddenly saw the house in its new coat of paint as it were for the first time.

"Oh, look, Lane!" she exclaimed, "isn't it wonderful? The house! It looks so clean and beautiful!"

"Yes," said Lane admiringly, "the dear old house! I think I love it just as much as our own!"

"The dear old houses," echoed Maris softly, "I love them both!"

Lane's fingers curled softly about hers, and then the car drew up at the curb, and, there they all were out in front waiting to welcome them! Hand in hand they got out and went in to their beloved family.

"'This is the heritage—!'" murmured Maris in almost a

whisper as together they mounted the steps and smiled at one another.

" 'Of the servants of the Lord,' " finished Lane. "I'm glad we're that, aren't you?"

About the Author

Grace Livingston Hill is well known as one of the most prolific writers of romantic fiction. Her personal life was fraught with joys and sorrows not unlike those experienced by many of her fictional heroines.

Born in Wellsville, New York, Grace nearly died during the first hours of life. But her loving parents and friends turned to God in prayer. She survived miraculously; thus her thankful father named her Grace.

Grace was always close to her father, a Presbyterian minister, and her mother, a published writer. It was from them that she learned the art of storytelling. When Grace was twelve, a close aunt surprised her with a hardbound, illustrated copy of one of Grace's stories. This was the beginning of Grace's journey into being a published author.

In 1892 Grace married Fred Hill, a young minister, and they soon had two lovely young daughters. Then came 1901, a difficult year for Grace—the year when, within months of each other, both her father and husband died. Suddenly Grace had to find a new place to live (her home was owned by the church where her husband had been pastor). It was a struggle for Grace to raise her young daughters alone, but through everything she kept writing. In 1902 she produced *The Angel of His Presence*, *The Story of a Whim*, and *An Unwilling Guest*. In 1903 her two books *According to the Pattern* and *Because of Stephen* were published.

It wasn't long before Grace was a well-known author, but she wanted to go beyond just entertaining her readers. She soon included the message of God's salvation through Jesus Christ in each of her books. For Grace, the most important thing she did was not write books but share the message of salvation, a message she felt God wanted her to share through the abilities he had given her.

In all, Grace Livingston Hill wrote more than one hundred books, all of which have sold thousands of copies and have touched the lives of readers around the world with their message of "enduring love" and the true way to lasting happiness: a relationship with God through his Son, Jesus Christ.

In an interview shortly before her death, Grace's devotion to her Lord still shone clear. She commented that whatever she had accomplished had been God's doing. She was only his servant, one who had tried to follow his teaching in all her thoughts and writing.